MAGAZINES FOR SCHOOL LIBRARIES

MAGAZINES FOR SCHOOL LIBRARIES

For elementary,
junior high school,
and high school libraries

BILL KATZ

R. R. BOWKER COMPANY
NEW YORK & LONDON, 1987

Published by R. R. Bowker Company,
    a division of Reed Publishing (U.S.A.) Inc.
Copyright © 1987 by William A. Katz
All rights reserved
Printed and bound in the United States of America

International Standard Book Number 0-8352-2316-7
International Standard Serial Number 0000-0957

CONTENTS

PREFACE vii
INTRODUCTION ix
HOW TO USE THIS BOOK xiii
ABBREVIATIONS xv

ABSTRACTS AND INDEXES 1
AFRICA 6
  FOR THE STUDENT
AFRO-AMERICAN 7
  FOR THE STUDENT / FOR THE PROFESSIONAL
AGRICULTURE 11
  FOR THE STUDENT / FOR THE PROFESSIONAL
ALTERNATIVES 13
  FOR THE STUDENT / FOR THE PROFESSIONAL
ANTHROPOLOGY AND ARCHAEOLOGY 16
  FOR THE STUDENT
ART 17
  FOR THE STUDENT: GENERAL; ARCHITECTURE; ART
  MUSEUM PUBLICATIONS / FOR THE PROFESSIONAL
ASIA 20
  FOR THE STUDENT: GENERAL; ASIAN AMERICAN;
  CHINA; JAPAN / FOR THE PROFESSIONAL
ASTROLOGY AND PARAPSYCHOLOGY 23
  FOR THE STUDENT
ASTRONOMY 25
  FOR THE STUDENT
ATMOSPHERIC, EARTH, AND MARINE
  SCIENCES 26
  FOR THE STUDENT
AUTOMOBILES 29
  FOR THE STUDENT
AVIATION AND SPACE SCIENCE 32
  FOR THE STUDENT / FOR THE PROFESSIONAL
BIRDS 34
  FOR THE STUDENT
BOATS AND BOATING 36
  FOR THE STUDENT
BOOKS AND BOOK REVIEWS 37
  FOR THE STUDENT / FOR THE PROFESSIONAL
BUSINESS 43
  FOR THE STUDENT / FOR THE PROFESSIONAL
CANADA 46
  FOR THE STUDENT
CITY AND REGIONAL 48
  FOR THE STUDENT
CIVIL LIBERTIES 55
  FOR THE STUDENT

CLASSICAL STUDIES 58
  FOR THE STUDENT / FOR THE PROFESSIONAL
COMICS 59
  FOR THE STUDENT: ELEMENTARY AND JUNIOR HIGH;
  COSTUMED HEROES; FANTASY, ADVENTURE; MAGA-
  ZINES ABOUT COMICS; WAR; WEIRD
COMMUNICATION AND SPEECH 66
  FOR THE PROFESSIONAL
COMPUTERS 67
  FOR THE STUDENT: GENERAL; SPECIFIC BRANDS OF
  COMPUTERS / FOR THE PROFESSIONAL
CONSUMER EDUCATION 70
  FOR THE STUDENT
CRAFTS AND RECREATIONAL PROJECTS 72
  FOR THE STUDENT / FOR THE PROFESSIONAL
CULTURAL-SOCIAL STUDIES 76
  FOR THE STUDENT
EDUCATION 77
  FOR THE STUDENT / FOR THE PROFESSIONAL
ELECTRONICS 83
  FOR THE STUDENT
ENVIRONMENT, CONSERVATION, AND OUT-
  DOOR RECREATION 84
  FOR THE STUDENT: GENERAL; OUTDOOR
  RECREATION / FOR THE PROFESSIONAL
EUROPE 86
  FOR THE STUDENT / FOR THE PROFESSIONAL
EXCEPTIONAL CHILDREN: GIFTED, DIS-
  ABLED, THOSE WITH SPECIAL NEEDS 89
  FOR THE STUDENT / FOR THE PROFESSIONAL
FICTION 90
  FOR THE STUDENT: GENERAL; SCIENCE FICTION
FILMS 93
  FOR THE STUDENT / FOR THE PROFESSIONAL
FISHING, HUNTING, AND GUNS 96
  FOR THE STUDENT
FOLKLORE 98
  FOR THE STUDENT
FREE MAGAZINES 100
  FOR THE STUDENT / FOR THE PROFESSIONAL
GENERAL INTEREST 103
  FOR THE STUDENT: CHILDREN; TEENAGE / FOR THE
  PROFESSIONAL
GENERAL SCIENCE 113
  FOR THE STUDENT / FOR THE PROFESSIONAL
GEOGRAPHY 118
  FOR THE STUDENT / FOR THE PROFESSIONAL

HEALTH AND MEDICINE 119
    FOR THE STUDENT / FOR THE PROFESSIONAL
HISTORY 124
    FOR THE STUDENT / FOR THE PROFESSIONAL
HOBBIES 128
    FOR THE STUDENT: ANTIQUES AND COLLECTING;
    GAMES; GARDENING; NUMISMATICS; PHILATELY
HOME ECONOMICS 132
    FOR THE STUDENT / FOR THE PROFESSIONAL
HORSES 135
    FOR THE STUDENT
HUMOR 136
    FOR THE STUDENT
INDIANS OF NORTH AMERICA 137
    FOR THE STUDENT
JOURNALISM AND WRITING 138
    FOR THE STUDENT / FOR THE PROFESSIONAL
LATIN AMERICA, LATINO (U.S.) 140
    FOR THE STUDENT: LATIN AMERICA; LATINO (U.S.) /
    FOR THE PROFESSIONAL
LIBRARY PERIODICALS 144
    FOR THE PROFESSIONAL
LINGUISTICS AND LANGUAGE ARTS 148
    FOR THE PROFESSIONAL
LITERATURE 150
    FOR THE STUDENT / FOR THE PROFESSIONAL
MATHEMATICS 156
    FOR THE STUDENT / FOR THE PROFESSIONAL
MEDIA AND AV 157
    FOR THE PROFESSIONAL
MILITARY 158
    FOR THE STUDENT
MODEL MAKING 160
    FOR THE STUDENT: FLYING MODELS; MODEL AUTOS;
    MILITARY MINIATURES; MODEL SHIPS; MODEL RAIL-
    ROADS; STATIC MODELS
MOTORCYCLES AND OFF-ROAD
   VEHICLES 165
    FOR THE STUDENT

MUSIC AND DANCE 166
    FOR THE STUDENT: GENERAL; DANCE; POPULAR; RE-
    VIEWS / FOR THE PROFESSIONAL
NEWS AND OPINION 175
    FOR THE STUDENT
NEWSPAPERS 179
    FOR THE STUDENT: GENERAL; NEWSPAPER INDEXES
OCCUPATIONS AND CAREERS 183
    FOR THE STUDENT / FOR THE PROFESSIONAL
PEACE 185
    FOR THE STUDENT
PETS 187
    FOR THE STUDENT
PHOTOGRAPHY 190
    FOR THE STUDENT
POLITICAL SCIENCE 193
    FOR THE STUDENT / FOR THE PROFESSIONAL
PSYCHOLOGY 195
    FOR THE STUDENT / FOR THE PROFESSIONAL
RELIGION 195
    FOR THE STUDENT / FOR THE PROFESSIONAL
SOCIOLOGY 197
    FOR THE STUDENT
SPORTS 199
    FOR THE STUDENT / FOR THE PROFESSIONAL
TELEVISION, VIDEO, AND RADIO 204
    FOR THE STUDENT / FOR THE PROFESSIONAL
THEATER 206
    FOR THE STUDENT / FOR THE PROFESSIONAL
TRAVEL 208
    FOR THE STUDENT
USSR AND EASTERN EUROPE 209
    FOR THE STUDENT
WOMEN 212
    FOR THE STUDENT / FOR THE PROFESSIONAL

INDEX OF TITLES AND SECTIONS 219
INDEX OF TITLES BY AUDIENCE 229

PREFACE

This first edition of *Magazines for School Libraries* follows the successful pattern established over the course of twenty years by five editions of the standard *Magazines for Libraries*, also an R. R. Bowker publication (5th edition, 1986). *Magazines for Libraries*, with its 6,500 titles selected from a universe close to 70,000, is too comprehensive for school libraries; a need for a selection of titles geared specifically to children, teenagers, and those professionals dealing with these groups is now met by *Magazines for School Libraries*. Here then is a unique reference tool necessary for the selection and acquisition of periodicals in all levels of school libraries (elementary, junior high, and high schools).

Titles are arranged by subject and are indexed by title and by school level. Full bibliographical information is given, as well as additional data, as explained in the Introduction. The subject headings have been modified to fit the special needs of the school audience, but, for the most part, the overall arrangement is the same as that of the larger reference work. With minor editing, annotations are taken directly from the fifth edition of *Magazines for Libraries*. Some additional titles, often new magazines, have been added.

After careful consideration, approximately 1,300 titles were selected from the 6,500 in *Magazines for Libraries*. The 1,300 represent those suitable for students, librarians, teachers, and administrators. They are, in the opinion of the editor, the magazines most suitable to the abilities and interests of school-age readers and the needs of professionals in education. The editor believes that these entries provide a range of choices in each subject category.

The plan is to publish an updated edition of this guide every three to four years. Comments from readers will be useful and very welcome.

Designation of Consultants

The name of the consultant who contributed all or a major share of the reviews to a section is given at the head of that section, along with title and address. In some cases, more than one contributor's work appears in a section, and so other names are given. When a contributor's efforts are concentrated in a subsection (as in the Asia Section), that subsection is identified following the contributor's name.

Where the primary contributor is noted at the head of the section, that person's initials are *not* used within the section. However, sometimes initials *are* used within the section (see list of consultants' initials under Abbreviations) because: (1) in the Abstracts and Indexes Section the initials identify who prepared one or more of the various annotations; (2) where more than one individual contributed to a section, as in Business, the initials indicate the division of labor; and (3) sporadically throughout the book, individuals contributed annotations to otherwise complete sections.

The editor revised some sections and acted as overall evaluator of all the sections and individual titles. Here and there titles were added or dropped and annotations revised as necessary. Annotations were also revised with the specific needs of school librarians, teachers, and students in mind. But the amount of revision of the contributor's work is modest. An effort was made to retain individual contributor style and approach. Although the contributors were requested to follow a basic pattern of selection and of writing annotations, they were urged to give a personal interpretation of editorial content.

The editor takes full responsibility for the selection of the titles and for the annotations.

Acknowledgments

The present guide would not have been possible without the able selection of titles and the annotations written by the subject experts. To one and all, thank you.

INTRODUCTION

Anyone working with young people realizes the importance of magazines. Not all young persons read books, but almost every student at least glances at a magazine. And by now it is a truism that students' papers and talks are based, for the most part, on standard periodical articles. Few subjects of study or planned curricular activities fail to include indexes and magazines as well as newspapers. For entertainment, aesthetic delight, and information of both a general and an esoteric nature, there is nothing like magazines. No one realizes this more than the young individual, either in or out of school.

The librarian, the teacher, and the parent must choose not only the best magazines but those that children and young adults *wish* to read. In the preparation of this work, particular stress has been placed on the latter consideration. At the same time, the proper weight has been given to traditional reasons for magazine selection.

Quality is a main criterion of any selection process. Nevertheless, one has to realize that quality is relative to the audience and subject matter. One may, for example, dismiss a magazine about rock music as being of poor quality when compared to one about opera, but this is to confuse content with questions of excellence. One must compare quality honestly within the context of the intended audience and the subject matter. That has been done here, from magazines about agriculture and automobiles to those concerned with comics and television. The selection represents the editor's view of magazines of quality in a given field. It is hardly the final word, but it provides help to the audience for which this guide was written.

Selection Policy

The editor has followed a well-defined approach to the selection of magazines, newspapers, and indexes. It is the same as that employed in the fifth edition of *Magazines for Libraries,* from which these annotations are taken.

The first consideration is the audience. Here, the primary audience is the student, a reader with many of the same interests, values, and needs as adults. At the same time, due weight is given to differences in age, experience, reading ability, education, and curricular requirements.

An effort is made not to insult the intelligence of either the student or the teacher by listing inferior titles. That does not mean that light reading has been excluded. But such selections are balanced with magazines that suggest new frontiers of thought, new challenges, and new educational experiences.

For librarians, teachers, and administrators, the same criteria are followed. Emphasis is placed on what the professional person needs by way of educational assistance, especially to keep up with the changing aspects of the various disciplines. The basic teaching journals and magazines in the subject areas found in the majority of elementary, junior high, and high schools are listed.

Aside from focusing on the audience and judging the subject matter, there are some objective methods of evaluation, of determining whether or not a magazine is of value to a particular library in a particular community. These same criteria, by the way, may be used by the librarian who is trying to choose between two or more titles of equal value.

1. *What is indexed.* Stress is laid on the entries in the *Readers' Guide to Periodical Literature, General Science Index, Humanities Index,* and *Social Sciences Index.* All, of course, are published by the H. W. Wilson Company. Basic professional magazines for teachers and librarians are also frequently indexed in *Education Index* and *Current Index to Journals in Education.* No librarian, teacher, or, for that matter, parent will buy or not buy a magazine because it is or is not indexed. Nor should they, particularly as newer titles sometimes take several years to find their way into an index. Also, a community may have special interests that may not be reflected in the basic Wilson indexing services. To that end, other indexes are included (and annotated), but again, only those likely to be of most value to the audience to which this guide is addressed.

2. *What is found acceptable by other experts.* Rarely does a month go by in which a list of periodicals, usually for a particular grade or subject interest, is not published in one journal or another. Such listings have been reviewed by the editor and accepted in part, rejected, or used simply to confirm earlier choices. The alert school librarian or media specialist should read a few popular titles, as well as the professional journals, since such listings are also published there from time to time. These are of special value either as reminders of new titles or as notification of magazines that may suddenly become of interest because of a new subject in the curriculum.

3. *What is purchased by school libraries of various sizes.* We are grateful to a number of librarians for assisting us by sharing their basic list of periodicals. A word of caution, however: one must consider the hazards of using the studies and selection policies of other libraries, since their final choices must be individual, reflecting the special needs of the persons being served.

4. *Price.* Price must be considered, particularly when designating the essential titles. Prices have tended to level off a bit during the past two years, but periodicals remain expensive, and where there is a choice between one magazine at $25 a year and another at $50, and both are of the same general quality, the vote should go to the former. The price range of similar periodicals should be checked regularly, and unless there is a substantial difference between them, the nod should go to the one that is more reasonably priced.

5. *The intrinsic quality of the individual title.* This is, of course, a major consideration. Articles, features, and stories should be written by qualified authors, and normally the author should be identified in terms of his or her background. The subject matter should be current, accurate, and biased only insofar as the magazine stresses a particular viewpoint, as does the *National Review.* The writing should be acceptable for the grade level that it is intended to reach; the magazine should never "write down" to its audience. The material must be appropriate for the designated readership. If the magazine is for the average high school student, it should be neither too difficult nor too easy. The type of article published should appeal to the intended reader. If the magazine is billed as a popular one, it should be truly "popular" without being insulting. If it claims to be a learned journal, it should be that in more than name; it should contain truly exploratory and original research.

6. *The relation of the magazine to the subject covered.* First and foremost, an effort has been made to include (a) magazines offering an overview of the topic and (b) magazines concentrating on a particular area of the topic that interests a majority of the audience.

7. *Point of view.* This is a prime consideration, particularly in magazines covering current events and controversial subjects. Within the annotation, an effort is made to indicate the political or other bias of the magazine. This seems especially important when dealing with general magazines, which often disguise, knowingly or not, the philosophical convictions of the editor and most of the writers. Needless to say, every major point of view is represented in this guide.

8. *Format.* While content should be the major consideration, it almost always follows (some little magazines excepted) that the format signals the quality of the content. The cover should be attractive—when appropriate—without being ostentatious. One should quickly be able to locate articles, features, departments, and so forth in a good table of contents. If there are illustrations, they should be appropriate, and they should be of good quality. Aside from picture magazines such as *Life,* there should be a good balance between illustrations and copy. All too often, the popular magazine stresses the picture at the expense of the editorial matter, and there is little of real value in the issue. There should be no more than a few editorial or typographical errors. (It may be unreasonable these days to expect a completely "clean" issue, but at least an effort should be visible.) Finally, the magazine should be of a manageable size, not so small that it will disappear on the magazine rack or so large that it won't fit anywhere. The paper, binding, and the like should be sturdy enough to withstand more than

one reader's use. And one can at least hope that the ink will not come off on one's clothing or hands.

9. *Advertising.* Other than journals that are financed by a grant or an institution, most periodicals have advertising. One should ask whether it is appropriate and not offensive, whether there is too much of it, and, finally, whether it is accurate. When there are more advertisements than copy (often the case in women's fashion magazines), the periodical may be acceptable because the ads are of as much interest to many readers as is the editorial material, but this is the exception rather than the rule. Too much advertising (more than 50 percent in any issue) is a signal to try another title.

10. *The relation between the magazine and the curriculum.* This consideration is kept in mind throughout. Not all the magazines are directly related to course work, but where a choice has had to be made between two equally good titles, we have favored the one more likely to be of value to the subject being studied in school.

11. *Will the magazine be read?* There is no guarantee that even the best magazine, measured by the preceding ten points, will be popular. Here instinct, experience, and luck must play a part. Librarians and teachers who truly know the audience should be able to choose, from the 1,300 titles, the 13, 130, or 260 that will actually be read and not serve merely to decorate the library. But popularity should not be the only guide. There are some magazines, particularly back files, which may not be used heavily but are consistently valuable sources of reference not only for today but for years to come; these must be purchased as well. Still, in ordering for the average school library, a major consideration is the desires and needs of the audience, both potential and actual.

Recommendations about Selection

It seems to the editor that there are several other factors that the teacher or librarian should consider in making selections. Some cautions are negative. (1) Don't select a magazine only because it is indexed. Many magazines that are not indexed, at least in popular Wilson indexes, can still be valuable. (2) Don't buy only for people who use the library now. One reason many people stay out of the library is that they have not found any magazines of interest to them. Add to the collection titles that can increase the usership. (3) Don't purchase a publication simply because it is well known. The magazine may be marvelous, but if an audience for it does not exist in your school, it is a waste of money. (4) Don't buy only what is currently well known. Try a few out-of-the-way, different magazines that view the world from an unusual perspective. As one person put it, a good librarian should follow the dictum "When in Rome, do as the Greeks do." (5) Don't seek to acquire "total balance" in the collection. It will probably end up in a state of inertia. Strike out for magazines that will be of concern to the readers. And while every effort should be made to offer various points of view, there is no law that six horse magazines, for example, must be balanced against six automobile titles, particularly if the library is 3,000 miles from the nearest ranch.

There are also positive considerations. (1) Listen to the requests of people who use the library, whether they be students or teachers or administrators. Encourage them to ask for magazines not in the library. (2) Try to find out why those who don't use the library's magazine collection are reluctant to do so. It may well be that the material is too difficult, that it simply does not include areas of their interest, or that it does not serve the curriculum. (3) Include more than curriculum-oriented materials. In this guide, for example, one finds a section on comics. Of course, not all comic books are appropriate, but some are—particularly for slow or reluctant readers—and enough are cited here to allow an intelligent choice. (4) Check the local newsstands and drugstores to see what magazines are new, which sell well, and which are sold out within a day or two. Conversely, check to see which ones are rarely purchased. (5) Be adventuresome, imaginative, and ambitious for the readers. Go out and buy new magazines that have yet to be indexed, evaluated, or judged. Let the readers determine whether or not they should be added to the collection. (6) Read as much as possible in the literature about magazines and their selection. (See the last part of this introduction for a list of periodicals that review magazines.)

Audience

Grade levels and interest levels are at best only approximations. Certain magazines are obviously for young children or for teachers, but the vast majority defy categorization. Students or adults have as many reading interests at as many reading and intellectual levels as there are individual magazines. This is particularly true in later junior high school through high school. Thus, many magazines ostensibly aimed at adults have received a high school designation because they are accessible to students at that level and present either information relevant to the curriculum or general interest material.

This book indicates the approximate reading and interest levels of the audience with three symbols:

Ejh, for elementary/junior high, includes readers from preschool age through about the ninth grade, or ages 14 to 15. There are not many general-interest magazines for really young children (preschool through fourth or fifth grade), but those that exist will be found in the General Interest Section under "Children." Those titles aimed at readers of these ages but focusing on more specialized content—such as *Ranger Rick* or *Cobblestone*—are listed under the appropriate subject heading.

Hs, for high school, includes readers 14 or 15 to 18 (grades 9 to 12). General-interest magazines for this age group are listed in the "Teenage" part of the General Interest Section. As with special-interest magazines directed at younger students, high school level topical magazines are listed under the relevant topic.

Pr, for professional, signals magazines aimed at librarians, teachers, counselors, administrators, coaches, or other school professionals. Many of these professional titles are listed in three sections: Education, Library Periodicals, and Books and Book Reviews. In addition, one will find journals of particular concern to teachers within many of the subject areas. Where such titles appear, they are always grouped together at the end of the section under the heading "For the Professional."

Samples

Now and then the librarian may wish to examine a magazine before entering a subscription. There are two approaches, one obvious and the other not so obvious. The first is to seek out the title in a larger library nearby or, if it is a new magazine, to look for it on a newsstand. The second is to request a sample copy from the publisher. When it is known that the publisher will supply a sample copy, that information is noted in this guide in the bibliographical data preceding the annotation. Since not all publishers answered that query from the editor, ask the publisher for a sample when in doubt.

The request for a sample copy should be made on school library stationery, with a brief note that the periodical is to be considered for permanent addition to the library's collection. Most publishers will grant the request, although in this day of computers and distribution centers far from the editorial rooms of the magazines, there is no guarantee that a sample will be in the next mail.

Reviews

Ongoing reviews of current magazines, many of which are suitable for the audience of this book, are found in the editor's column in *Library Journal.* Now in its twentieth year, the column is an effort to evaluate six to ten magazines in each issue.

Voya is a well-known source not only of excellent book reviews for young people but also for suggestions about magazines. The annotations are as thoughtful as they are current. The *School Library Journal* frequently runs special feature articles about new magazines, as do *American Libraries* and *Wilson Library Bulletin.* See, too, the quarterly *Serials Review* and *Serials Librarian,* which frequently contain specialized bibliographies of general-interest magazines for adults and young people. Both journals are also useful for keeping up with the latest in everything, from the best vendors to cataloging to methods of storage.

The most consistent coverage is by Liz Austrom in her "Magazines for Young People," a regular feature in *Emergency Librarian.* Although many of the titles reviewed reflect the interests of Canadian readers, some are quite suitable for U.S. libraries.

Selma K. Richardson from time to time offers superior coverage of magazines for both children and young people in *Booklist.* She is the author of two guides, *Magazines for Children* and *Magazines for Young Adults,* both published by the American Library Association, in 1983 and 1984 respectively.

Choice has excellent reviews, but many of the titles are too esoteric in that they are directed to larger academic collections. The column does include some popular material and is most useful for its annotations of journals likely to be of interest to teachers and librarians.

Comprehensive Guides

Current information about price, frequency, and the like may be found in the annual *Ulrich's International Periodicals Directory* (R. R. Bowker). This is not a selective guide. It is a straightforward listing of over 65,000 periodicals from around the world.

Companies that offer microform versions of particular titles are listed in the bibliographic information in this book, at least when applicable. Further information about individual titles, as well as other periodicals offered by the companies, may be had by writing them at the addresses given on page xvii.

Basic Manuals

For librarians seeking information about the organization, storage, and care of periodicals, there are several useful books that contain detailed instructions about such matters as establishing a periodical section in the library, the choice of a vendor, how to handle claims, and so forth. By far the most detailed (in fact, too detailed for the average school library) is the classic by Andrew Osborn, *Serial Publications*, 3rd ed. (Chicago: American Library Association, 1980). More pragmatic are Marcia Tuttle's *Introduction to Serials Management* (Greenwich, CT: JAI Press, 1983) and Nancy Jean Melin's *The Serials Collection* (Ann Arbor, MI: Pierian Press, 1982). For a detailed bibliography and for articles on current aspects of periodicals see the Fall 1985/Winter 1986 issue of *The Serials Librarian*.

HOW TO USE THIS BOOK

> Title. Date Founded. *Frequency. *Price.
> Editor. Publisher and Address. Illustrations,
> Index, Advertising. Circulation. *Sample.
> *Date Volume Ends. *Refereed. *Microform.
> Reprint.
> *Indexed. *Book Reviews. *Audience.

The periodicals in this book are listed alphabetically, by title, under the subjects given in the Contents. All subject classifications used, as well as variations in wording of subject headings and as many additional subject cross-references as the editor expected would be useful, are listed in the index. The reader should refer to the index when a title is not found under the first subject consulted.

The bibliographic form of the entries is shown above, and additional explanation follows for items preceded by an asterisk. For an explanation of how consultants', or contributors', names are handled, see Designation of Consultants in the Preface.

The Abbreviations section lists the general abbreviations found in the bibliographic information and the acronyms used for the microform companies and abstracts and indexes.

Frequency and Price

The frequency is given immediately after the founding date, and the symbols used are explained in the General Abbreviations section. The price quoted is the annual subscription rate given by the publisher, usually as of mid-1986. Prices are relative and, of course, subject to change—probably upward. Furthermore, the fluctuation of the dollar makes the prices of foreign magazines even more relative.

The phrase "Controlled Circ." is found after some titles. This means the magazine has a controlled circulation and is sent free to certain individuals whom the advertisers are trying to reach. The magazine is financed solely by advertisements, and the controlled circulation indicates that the publisher has targeted a certain audience or audiences for the advertisers. "Others" means those who are outside of that select audience and must pay for the title. Often the publisher is willing to send the magazine free to libraries, but in any case an inquiry should be made.

Sample

Publishers were asked whether they would send a free copy of the magazine to a library if requested. Those who replied favorably are indicated by the single word "Sample." The request should be made by the head of the library or by the head of the serials department and written on official stationery. The indication that publishers are willing to send samples to institutions does not mean they are necessarily interested in sending them to individual subscribers.

Date Volume Ends

Several librarians indicated it would be helpful to know when a publisher ends a volume—obviously for purposes of binding. The information provided is from the publisher.

Refereed

This term is used to indicate that manuscripts submitted to a magazine are examined by both the editor and one or more specialists in the individual field before approval is given to publish. The readers (sometimes called an editorial board) apparently assure a better chance that the final product will be a contribution to knowledge.

Microform and Reprint

Companies providing microform runs of magazines are indicated, and information concerning the publisher of some reprints is noted. The librarian should consult *Guide to Microforms in Print* and *Ulrich's International Periodicals Directory* for additional information.

Indexed

Information about where titles are indexed or abstracted is given on the first line under the bibliographic data. Also indicated are major subject indexes in which the periodicals are indexed. "Major" must be emphasized. Not all indexing of each title is included. Indexes and abstracts that are employed are annotated in the Abstracts and Indexes Section, which begins this book. *Ulrich's* will provide additional information on indexing but does not indicate whether the index is available online. For the most part all indexes are available in this fashion, particularly since Wilson now has all of its indexes online.

The term *index* in the bibliographic description indicates that the publisher has an index to the periodical. Examination of the magazine will make clear how the index is organized—annually, with cumulations, and so on.

Book Reviews

Information given refers to the approximate number of reviews that appear in a typical issue of the periodical, the average length, and whether they are signed.

Audience

The entry for each magazine indicates its audience. Periodicals for elementary and junior high school students (Ejh) are not separated because it is often difficult to draw the line between these two age groups. The titles and descriptive annotations leave little doubt about the level of maturity for which the magazine is intended. The high school level (Hs) includes readers in grades 9–12, who are 14 or 15 to 18 years old. Professional (Pr) periodicals are intended for school librarians, teachers, counselors, administrators, and other professionals dealing with young people.

ABBREVIATIONS

GENERAL ABBREVIATIONS

a.	Annual	q.	Quarterly
Aud	Audience	s-a.	Twice annually
bi-m.	Every two months	s-m.	Twice monthly
bi-w.	Every two weeks	s-w.	Twice weekly
Ejh	Elementary and junior high school	3/m.	Three per month
Hs	High school	3/yr.	Three per year
m.	Monthly	w.	Weekly
Pr	Professional		

Controlled Circ. Controlled circulation, i.e., free to certain groups.

ABSTRACTS AND INDEXES

API	Alternative Press Index	FLI	Film Literature Index
ASTI	Applied Science and Technology Index	GSI	General Science Index
AbrRG	Abridged Readers' Guide	HAPI	Hispanic American Periodicals Index
Acs	Access	HumI	Humanities Index
ArtI	Art Index	IFP	Index to Free Periodicals
BibI	Bibliographic Index	IGov	Index to U.S. Government Periodicals
BioAg	Biological and Agricultural Index	INeg	Index to Periodicals by and about
BioI	Biography Index		Blacks
BoRv	Book Review Digest	MRD	Media Review Digest
BoRvI	Book Review Index	MgI	Magazine Index
BusI	Business Periodicals Index	MusicI	Music Index
CIJE	Current Index to Journals in Education	NYTI	New York Times Index
CIPE	Consumer Index to Product Evaluation	PAIS	Public Affairs Information Service
CMG	Children's Magazine Guide	PhysEdInd	Physical Education Index
CanEdI	Canadian Education Index	PopPer	Popular Periodicals Index
CanI	Canadian Periodical Index	RG	Readers' Guide to Periodical Literature
CathI	Catholic Periodical and Literature Index	ResEduc	Resources in Education
ChildDevAb	Child Development Abstracts	SocSc	Social Sciences Index
ChildLitAb	Children's Literature Abstracts	WomAb	Women Studies Abstracts
EdI	Education Index	WorAb	Work Related Abstracts
ExChAb	Exceptional Child Education Resources		

CONSULTANTS, BY INITIALS

(Full names and addresses of consultants are given at the head of each section.)

A.M.	Albert J. Milo (Latin America, Latino [U.S.])	A.W.	Allen Wynne (General Science)
		B.G.	Barbara Grossman (Asia)
A.M.C.	Ana Maria Cobos (Latin America, Latino [U.S.])	B.V.	Barbara Via (Library Periodicals)
		C.M.	Connie Miller (Women)
A.P.	Amy L. Paster (Games)		

C.O'C.	Collette O'Connell (Engineering and Technology)
C.R.	Cristine C. Rôm (Literature)
C.R.S.	Charles R. Smith (Art; General Science)
C.T.C.	Craig T. Canan (Journalism and Writing; News and Opinion)
D.A.	David Adams (Hobbies)
D.D.	Douglas A. DeLong (Geography; Sociology)
D.D.P.	Dawn D. Puglisi (Agriculture)
D.E.	Doug Ernest (Environment, Conservation, and Outdoor Recreation)
D.H.	David Horvath (Photography)
D.L.T.	Deonna L. Taylor (Business)
D.N.	David Needham (Music)
D.R.	Deborah Reilly (Alternatives)
D.T.	Daniel Tsang (Asia)
D.V.	David Van de Streek (Boats and Boating)
D.W.	David Wemple (Asia)
E.B.W.	Ellen B. Wells (Horses)
E.C.	Eleanor M. Clarke (Astrology and Parapsychology)
E.F.S.	Edmund F. Santa Vicca
E.M.	Elizabeth Morrissett (Atmospheric, Earth, and Marine Sciences)
E.Ma.	Eleanor Mathews (Agriculture)
F.B.	Fred Batt (Sports)
F.F.S.	Frances F. Swim (Atmospheric, Earth, and Marine Sciences)
F.P.	Frederick Patten (Comics)
F.S.	Frederick A. Schlipf (Model Making)
G.J.	Gloria Jacobs (USSR and Eastern Europe)
G.J.L.	Gary J. Lenox (Hobbies; Theater)
G.L.	Gretchen Lagana (Alternatives)
H.H.	Halbert W. Hall (Fiction)
H.M.L.	Harold M. Leich (USSR and Eastern Europe)
H.S.	Helman I. Stern (Transportation)
H.Y.	Henry E. York (Political Science)
I.M.L.	Ida M. Lewis (Atmospheric, Earth, and Marine Sciences)
I.R.	Irving Roberts (Labor)
J.B.	Jean Bishop (Home Economics)
J.C.	Joan Carruthers (Canada)
J.C.A.	James C. Anderson (Photography)
J.G.H.	Jeanne G. Howard
J.H.	James L. Hodson (Religion)
J.J.A.	Joseph J. Accardi (Humor; Psychology)
J.K.S.	Jean K. Sheviak (General Science)
J.P.	Joanne Polster (Crafts and Recreational Projects)
J.Pa.	Jyoti Pandit (Linguistics and Language Arts)
J.S.	Janet L. Stanley (Africa)
J.W.	Jacob Welle (Occupations and Careers)
J.W.G.	James W. Geary (Military)
K.A.N.	Kathleen A. Nagy (Asia)
K.C.	Karen Chapman (Business)
K.E.B.	Kathleen E. Bethel (Afro-American)
L.A.	Liese Adams (Television, Video, and Radio)
L.H.	Lynn Heer (Automobiles; Motorcycles and Off-Road Vehicles)
L.K.O.	Lillian K. Orsini (General Interest)
L.K.W.	Libby K. White (General Interest)
L.L.G.	Linda L. Geary (Astronomy)
L.M.N.	Lois M. Nase (Electronics)
L.N.J.	Leslie N. Johnson (Art)
L.R.	Lee Regan (Civil Liberties)
L.R.G.	Lenore R. Greenberg (Exceptional Children: Gifted, Disabled)
L.S.	Laurie E. Stackpole (Atmospheric, Earth, and Marine Sciences)
L.Si.	Linda Simmons (Health and Medicine)
L.T.	Leslie Troutman (Business)
M.A.R.	Mary Augusta Rosenfeld (Music and Dance)
M.D.	Melanie Dodson (Business)
M.G.	Mary Ardeth Gaylord (Business)
M.H.R.	Michael H. Randall (Fiction)
MiNe.	Micki S. Nevett
M.J.C.	Mary J. Cronin (Linguistics and Language Arts)
M.J.M.	Marcia J. Martin (Cultural-Social Studies)
M.L.L.	Mary L. Lawson (Business)
M.McK.	Margaret McKinley (General Interest)
M.N.	Margaret Norden (Hobbies)
M.P.	Mary K. Prokop (Consumer Education)
M.Z.	Mary Zeimetz (Labor)
N.L.S.	Norris L. Stephens (Music and Dance)
N.S.H.	Nancy S. Hewison (Health and Medicine)
O.F.W.	Olive F. Whitehead (Birds; Pets)
P.A.	Peter B. Allison (Sociology)
P.A.B.	Paula A. Baxter (Books and Book Reviews)
P.A.F.	Polly-Alida Farrington (Home Economics)
P.B.	Patricia Brauch (Indians of North America)
P.B.A.	Peter B. Allison (Sociology)
P.F.B.	Phoebe F. Phillips (Environment, Conservation, and Outdoor Recreation)
P.S.B.	Patricia Smith Butcher (Education)
P.S.G.	Polly Swift Grimshaw (Folklore)
R.A.W.	Rhea A. White (Astrology and Parapsychology)
R.B.	Robin Braun (Health and Medicine)
R.E.	Richard Ellis (Little Magazines)
R.G.	Richard Giordano (Computers)
R.H.	Robert Hauptman (Literature)
R.J.F.	Robert J. Fryman (Anthropology and Archaeology)
R.J.K.	Robert J. Kibbee (Classical Studies)
R.P.	Roland Person (Fishing, Hunting, and Guns)
S.B.	Sarojini Balachandran (Aviation and Space Science; Electronics)
S.F.	Stephen M. Fry (Philately)
S.G.	Salvador Güereña (Latin America, Latino [U.S.])
S.L.E.	Susan L. Edmonds (Free Magazines)
S.M.W.	Sandra M. Whiteley (Newspapers)
S.S.	Sharon L. M. Siegler (Energy)
S.T.H.	Samuel T. Huang (Communication and Speech; Media and AV)
S.W.S.	Sharon W. Schwerzel (General Science)
T.W.	Theodore Wiener (Middle East)
V.F.C.	Vicki F. Croft (Pets)

V.M.P.   Vivian M. Pisano (Latin America, Latino [U.S.])
V.P.   Victoria Pifalo (City and Regional)
W.C.M.   Wayne C. Maxson (Religion)

W.F.Y.   William F. Young (History)
W.M.   Willard Moonan (Peace)
W.M.G.   William M. Gargan (Films)

MICROFORM AND REPRINT COMPANIES

B&H   Bell & Howell, Microphoto Division, Old Mansfield Rd., Wooster, OH 44691
CPC   Clearwater Publishing Co., Room 400, 1995 Broadway, New York, NY 10023
IA   Information Access Corp., 404 Sixth Ave., Menlo Park, CA 94025
ISI   Institute for Scientific Information, University Science Center, 3501 Market St., Philadelphia, PA 19104
KTO   Kraus Microform, One Water St., White Plains, NY 10601
Kraus   Kraus Reprint & Periodicals, Route 100, Millwood, NY 10546

MCA   Microfilming Corporation of America, 21 Harristown Rd., Glen Rock, NJ 07452
MIM   Microforms International Marketing Corp., Fairview Park, Elmsford, NY 10523
MML   Micromedia, Ltd., 144 Front St. W., Toronto, Ont. M5J 1G2, Canada
Pub   Publisher
RP   Research Publications, 12 Lunar Dr., Woodbridge, CT 06525
UMI   University Microfilms International, 300 N. Zeeb Rd., Ann Arbor, MI 48106
W   World Microfilms Publications, Ltd., 62 Queen's Grove, London, England

MAGAZINES FOR SCHOOL LIBRARIES

ABSTRACTS AND INDEXES

Basic Abstracts and Indexes

ALL LIBRARIES. *General Science Index, Humanities Index, Readers' Guide to Periodical Literature*, and *Social Sciences Index*; if money allows, *Access, Alternative Press Index, Magazine Index, Popular Periodicals Index*. Beyond that, librarians must select subject indexes. See the "Basic Abstracts and Indexes" at the head of each subject section throughout this book. For a detailed listing of services, including good annotations, see *Abstracting and Indexing Services Directory* (Detroit: Gale Research Co. 3 vols. 1983–85).

Almost every index and abstract included here is available online, including the ubiquitous H. W. Wilson Company entries, which can now be accessed via the company's own Wilsonline. For specific information on the online indexes see any of the vendors' listings, as well as: *Directory of Online Databases* (q. $95. Cuadra Associates, 2001 Wilshire Blvd., Suite 305, Santa Monica, CA 90403). Other directories include: *Computer-Readable Databases* (Chicago: American Library Assn., 1985. 2 vols. $157.50), which is available online as Dialog File 230. Then there is *Data Base Directory* (White Plains, NY: Knowledge Industry, 1984 to date, s-a., plus monthly updates, $215), available online via BRS.

Abridged Readers' Guide to Periodical Literature. 1935. 9/yr. $50. H. W. Wilson Co., 950 University Ave., Bronx, NY 10452.

The junior version of *Readers' Guide to Periodical Literature*, this index includes only 68 titles. Most libraries should take the senior title, which is the best-known author-subject index to general periodicals.

Access: the supplementary index to periodicals. 1975. 3/yr. $89.50. John G. Burke, P.O. Box 1492, Evanston, IL 60204.

Access's stated purpose is to complement existing periodical indexes. National general-interest publications are indexed in *Access* until *Readers' Guide* begins indexing them, at which point *Access* deletes them. *Access* indexes about 150 titles, including regional and city magazines and many popular newsstand periodicals. By comparison, *Popular Periodicals Index* analyzes about 40 titles. The third issue of *Access* each year is an annual hardbound cumulation. *Access*

supplements *Readers' Guide* and is, therefore, a useful tool. (M.McK.)

Alternative Press Index. 1969. q. $100 (Individuals, $25). Alternative Press Center, P.O. Box 7229, Baltimore, MD 21218. Sample.

Close to 200 leftist- to radical-opinion journals from the United States, Canada, and the rest of the English-speaking world are indexed. As a matter of policy, "alternative" means only liberal, as the publisher feels the conservative press is already well represented in existing indexes. In addition to periodicals, the index covers some select newspapers, albeit these are often tabloids that some may see as periodicals. The subject coverage ranges from anarchism to feminism to socialism. The problem with this otherwise good index is one the index has had from the outset—it is from 10 months to more than a year late.

Applied Science and Technology Index (Formerly: *Industrial Arts Index*). 1913. m. Service basis. H. W. Wilson Co., 950 University Ave., Bronx, NY 10452.

This is a cumulative index to approximately 400 English-language periodicals. The emphasis is on U.S. publications, with some British and Canadian periodicals also included. The index's main body consists of subject entries to periodical articles. There is about a four-month lag between publication date and indexing. A special section is included for book reviews. Selected by subscriber vote, those journals inside represent the physical and engineering sciences and popular trade and society publications. *Applied Science and Technology Index* is issued monthly, with quarterly and annual cumulations. It is also available in an online version, Wilsonline, which offers online access to the Wilson indexes. *Applied Science and Technology Index* is suggested for all technical collections. (C.O'C.)

Art Index. 1929. q. Service basis. H. W. Wilson Co., 950 University Ave., Bronx, NY 10452.

About 200 periodicals, including some selected yearbooks and museum bulletins, are indexed. The collection covers archaeology, architecture, city planning, industrial design, motion pictures, museology, photography, and television, as well as the standard art designations. This is a required item for most libraries.

Bibliographic Index: a cumulative bibliography of bibliographies. 1937. 3/yr. Service basis. H. W. Wilson Co., 950 University Ave., Bronx, NY 10452.

This index analyzes bibliographies found in the 2,600 periodicals Wilson analyzes for other indexes. Books and pamphlets are also analyzed. A bibliography must contain at least 50 citations to be included. The index emphasizes titles in the Germanic and Romance languages. Authors and subjects appear in a single alphabetic sequence. There are two semiannual issues, with a bound cumulation published in December. (M.McK.)

Biography Index: a quarterly index to biographical material in books and magazines. 1946. q. $70. H. W. Wilson Co., 950 University Ave., Bronx, NY 10452.

This is a guide to biographical material appearing in 2,600 periodicals analyzed in other Wilson indexes, selected additional periodicals, current books of individual and collected biographies, and incidental biographical material in non-biographical books. Each issue has a list of analyzed books, which includes obituaries, letter collections, diaries, memoirs, and bibliographies. The main section is alphabetically arranged by names of biographees, most of whom are American. There is also a list arranged by profession or occupation, as well as an annual bound cumulation and a triennial cumulation. Other biographical reference works such as *Current Biography* and *Contemporary Authors* are themselves compilations of biographies and are not indexes to biographical sources. (M.McK.)

Biological and Agricultural Index: a subject index to periodicals in the fields of biology and agriculture and related sciences. m. (exc. Aug.) $90 (minimum). Rita Goetz. H. W. Wilson Co., 950 University Ave., Bronx, NY 10452.

As a Wilson index, this is a very familiar-looking and easy-to-work-with tool. It covers only English-language periodicals in such fields as animal husbandry, genetics and cytology, physiology, veterinary medicine, and zoology. The index encompasses over 200 periodical titles, all selected by input from subscribers. Like the other Wilson indexes, the subscription price is based on the number of periodicals held by the subscriber covered by the index. This is a good general index and is one most patrons could handle easily. (D.D.P.)

Book Review Digest. 1905. 10/yr. Service basis. H. W. Wilson Co., 950 University Ave., Bronx, NY 10452.

The unfortunate part about this index is: (1) it covers only 80 periodicals; (2) it insists on four reviews for fiction and two reviews for non-fiction before there is an entry—thus effectively eliminating many first books. The positive side: (1) there are brief excerpts from the reviews that indicate the tone of acceptance or rejection, and give a good idea of content; (2) there is an excellent subject index as well as an author-title index. Should be used along with the much more exhaustive, though in some ways more limited, *Book Review Index*.

Book Review Index. 1965. $135. Gale Research Co., Book Tower, Detroit, MI 48226.

This is an author/title index to all book reviews appearing in some 400 periodicals. Casting a much broader net than *Book Review Digest*, this index does lack excerpts from the reviews as well as a subject index. The reviews cited are in abbreviated form and should be read carefully. The order of the checking is to turn to *Book Review Digest* first. Lacking a citation there, move to *Book Review Index*.

Business Periodicals Index. 1958. m. (q. + a. cumulations). H. W. Wilson Co., 950 University Ave., Bronx, NY 10452.

Subject index to approximately 300 important business periodicals. Subjects covered include accounting, marketing, banking, computer technology, economics, finance, industrial relations, insurance, international business, and transportation, as well as such specific industries as chemicals, drugs and cosmetics, and paper and pulp. Some specific company and trade information is also included. Though not so comprehensive as several newer competitors, this index seems to offer thorough and unique subject access points honed over years of experience. This easy-to-use index remains a basic tool for any school library with a business curriculum. (M.G.)

Canadian Education Index. 1965. 3/yr. + a. cumulation. $165. Maureen Davis. Canadian Education Assn., 252 Bloor St. W., S. 8-200, Toronto, Ont. M5S 1V5, Canada. Sample. Vol. ends: No. 3.

This is an author-and-subject index to a selected list of Canadian educational materials, including periodical articles, books, pamphlets, and reports. The journal coverage is quite extensive—about 200 titles encompassing many provincial publications and association newsletters, in addition to education-oriented articles from such general magazines as *Maclean's*. Each issue contains a checklist of monographs and a list of periodicals scanned and indexed. (J.C.)

Canadian Periodical Index (Formerly: *Canadian Index to Periodicals and Documentary Films*). 1938. m. + a. cumulation. Inquire. Sylvia Morrison. Canadian Library Assn., 151 Sparks St., Ottawa, Ont. K1P 5E3, Canada. Sample. Vol. ends: Dec.

A general index to Canadian periodicals, *CPI* currently indexes some 130 titles, giving a fine balance to both popular and scholarly journals. Titles included are in both English and French, though the subject headings are in English only with French cross-references. A very useful feature is the book review section, which lists books by author or title. If any foreign library needs an index to Canadian titles, this is the one. Every library in Canada, no matter the size, should subscribe. (J.C.)

The Catholic Periodical and Literature Index. 1930. bi-m. + biennial cumulation. Service basis (minimum $50). Natalie A. Logan. Catholic Library Assn., 461 W. Lancaster Ave., Haverford, PA 19041. Circ: 1,780. Sample.

This is one of the oldest and longest-running periodical indexes to religious literature, and the editors say it "provides a broad Christian approach to currently significant subjects." However, inasmuch as it covers only Catholic periodicals—and more recently books by and about Catholics with a selection of Catholic-interest books by other authors—there is a sizable segment of Christian literature not covered. The 146 or so periodical titles indexed are international, not restricted to English, and reflect all levels of readership from the popular to the esoteric. Arrangement is "dictionary," with authors, titles (of books), and subjects arranged in one alphabet. Book reviews are indexed, as well as papal documents. (W.M.)

Child Development Abstracts and Bibliography. 1927. 3/yr. $35. Hoben Thomas. Univ. of Chicago Press, 5801 Ellis Ave., Chicago, IL 60637. Circ: 5,800. Sample.

The official publication of the Society for Research in Child Development. It abstracts both books and periodical articles that consider any aspect of child development and related areas. The list of items analyzed makes this a useful buying guide as well. (Note: Libraries that take the organization's journal, *Child Development*, and subscribe to its monographs have a group price of $140 for the three items.)

Children's Literature Abstracts. 1973. q. $16. C. H. Ray, Tany-capel, Bont Dolgadfan, Llanbrynmair, Powys SY19 7BB, England. Index. Circ: 500.

Published by the Children's Libraries Section of the International Federation of Library Associations, this more than 30-page service includes 20- to 75-word abstracts. Over 400 abstracts give access to articles in British, U.S., Russian, Australian, and other journals. In an issue examined, 38 journals were represented. Entries are arranged under subject headings within the fields of children's fiction and non-fiction, psychological and educational criteria, illustration, book selection, awards and prizes, children's book publication of various countries, and authors and illustrators. Each entry gives appropriate bibliographical references (with addresses of the abstracted journals) and a short descriptive annotation. The March issue each year contains indexes. (L.K.O.)

Children's Magazine Guide (Formerly: *Subject Guide to Children's Magazines*). 1948. m. Aug–Mar.; bi-m. Apr. & May. $25. Patricia K. Sinclair. Children's Magazine Guide, 7 N. Pickney St., Madison, WI 53703. Circ: 10,000. Vol. ends: Aug.

CMG indexes 37 periodicals in the main section, plus titles for teachers and librarians in a "Professional Index." Many titles are directed to those in the seventh grade and up. The announcements at the front of *CMG* are valuable in keeping track of events in the volatile world of youth periodicals. (L.K.W.)

Consumers Index to Product Evaluations and Information Sources. 1973. q. $79.50. C. Edward Wall. Pierian Press, P.O. Box 1808, Ann Arbor, MI 48106.

Provides selective indexing of over 100 journals with primary emphasis on U.S. materials. Entries are arranged by 15 broad subject areas, with a keyword index included at the end of each issue. Articles of general consumer interest are briefly annotated; entries for articles concerned with specific products are coded to indicate the type of evaluative material included. This quarterly is aimed at the general consumer, the business office, and the educational library community. Librarians will find it useful for locating product evaluations unavailable in *Consumer Reports* or *Consumers Research*. (Note: Annual cumulations are available separately.)

Current Index to Journals in Education. 1969. m. (s-a. cumulations). $175. Oryx Press, 2214 N. Central at Encanto, Phoenix, AZ 85004.

One of the three major indexes to education material (the other two are *Education Index* and *Resources in Education*). This title indexes and briefly abstracts articles from over 780 major education and education-related journals, nearly twice the number indexed in *Education Index*. There are three approaches: an author index; a subject index, using the same descriptions as *Resources in Education*; and a journal contents index. Most of the items indexed in the subject section receive a pithy four-to-five-line abstract. Because of the greater number of titles indexed as well as the helpful abstracts, this is preferable to *Education Index* and should be a first choice. (P.S.B.)

Education Index. 1929. m. (a. cumulation). Service basis. Marylouise Hewitt. H. W. Wilson Co., 950 University Ave., Bronx, NY 10452.

Though primarily an index to 350 education periodicals, the collection also includes yearbooks and monographs. It is an author-subject index and also offers an index to book reviews in the field of education. *EI* indexes fewer periodicals than does *Current Index to Journals in Education* and provides no abstracts, but its simple alphabetical arrangement with numerous "see also" references often makes it easier for users. *Current Index to Journals in Education* is definitely the first choice where libraries can only purchase one index to education periodicals, but most libraries should own both. (P.S.B.)

Exceptional Child Education Resources. 1969. q. $75. June B. Jordan. Council for Exceptional Children, 1920 Association Dr., Reston, VA 22091. Circ: 1,200.

An extremely valuable tool for those interested in or involved with educating the handicapped. More than 200 journals in special education and psychology are scanned for material on exceptional children. Also indexed are books, dissertations, reports, and surveys, and the material can be retrieved in three ways: by author, title, or subject indexes. Each item receives a nonevaluative 100- to 200-word abstract. No collection in education should be without this abstract, especially where there is an interest in special education. (P.S.B.)

Film Literature Index. 1973. q. + a. cumulation. $225. Linda Provinzano. Filmdex Part II, SUNYA, 1400 Washington Ave., Albany, NY 12222.

A quarterly author-subject index to international film literature appearing in over 300 periodicals, some of which are indexed selectively. Newer as well as established journals are included. "In addition to author's name and over 1,000 subject headings. . . , articles are indexed under such proper-name entries as screenwriters, performers, directors, cinematographers, professional societies, festivals, and awards." Book reviews appear under that heading in cumulated issues. Recent volumes provide expanded coverage of television. Designed for the general reader as well as the specialist, this is the basic index in the field. (W.M.G.)

General Science Index. 1978. 10/yr. Service basis. H. W. Wilson Co., 950 University Ave., Bronx, NY 10452.

An index to 111 general science periodicals, this is a spinoff of the more thorough *Applied Science and Technology Index* and *Biological and Agricultural Index*. It follows the subject pattern established by Wilson in other indexes, and, as usual, there is an author listing of citations to book reviews in a separate section. All the sciences are included, and the index can be recommended for libraries where the science collection is small-to-medium size and does not require the other two indexes. Larger libraries will find that most titles indexed here are indexed in the two other services.

Hispanic American Periodicals Index (HAPI). 1970. a. $240. Barbara G. Valk. UCLA Latin American Center Publns., 405 Hilgard Ave., Univ. of California, Los Angeles, CA 90024.

A necessary tool for all libraries interested in Latin American research, this index offers wide coverage in the social sciences and humanities. The last issue analyzed indexed nearly 250 periodicals with "only the pure and technical sciences . . . excluded." It originally covered Central and South America, Mexico, and the Caribbean, but the scope has been increased to include information relating to U.S. Hispanic groups. There are separate author and subject sections. "Journals published in Latin America are indexed in full. Articles and reviews appearing in journals from other countries are cited only if they concern Latin America or Latin American groups in the United States." The Committee on Bibliography of the Seminar on the Acquisition of Latin American Library Materials (SALALM) assisted in choosing the titles to be indexed. Newsmagazines and popular periodicals are not included. Articles written in English, Spanish, Portuguese, and other Western European languages are listed. This index is a cooperative venture. A panel of, at present, 36 indexers, "professors and Latin American library specialists" from U.S., Latin America, and European institutions of higher learning, prepared the last edition examined.

Humanities Index. 1974. q. Service basis. H. W. Wilson Co., 950 University Ave., Bronx, NY 10452.

This is a cumulative index to English-language periodicals, analyzing almost 300 titles. Subject fields indexed include archaeology and classical studies, folklore, history, language and literature, literary and political criticism, performing arts, philosophy, religion and theology, and theater and film. The main body of the index consists of interfiled author and subject entries. Citations to book reviews follow the main body of the index. This index belongs in libraries with strong interest in literature, folklore, history, and the performing arts. (M.McK.)

Index to Free Periodicals. 1976. s-a. $25. Pierian Press, P.O. Box 1808, Ann Arbor, MI 48106.

With about 50 periodicals being scanned twice a year, the index is arranged by subject plus some title and author headings. The unique aspect of the index is that every periodical scanned is free, or controlled circulation. At any rate, they come at no charge to libraries and cover a vast variety of topics.

Index to Periodicals by and about Blacks. 1950. a. Price varies. Approx. $80. G. K. Hall & Co., 70 Lincoln St., Boston, MA 02111.

Formerly *Index to Periodicals by and about Negroes*. Since 1960, all U.S. Black periodicals published regularly are considered for inclusion. The index contains entries from over 3,000 articles that appeared in 23 journals; however, the collection is always late. Because of publication delays, it is primarily of historical value and is a definite requirement for large research libraries. The index is compiled by the library staff of Central State University.

Index to U.S. Government Periodicals. 1974. $275. Alla Carpenter. Infordata Intl. Inc., Suite 4062, 175 E. Delaware Pl., Chicago, IL 60611.

Close to 200 periodicals published by the federal government are indexed here by subject and by author. The subject matter is as broad as the number of periodicals and, in effect, makes this quite a general index that may provide a key to everything from information on animals to data on water resources and the federal budget. The full text of the periodicals is available on microfiche at about $1,400 a year.

Magazine Index. 1977. m. $1,990. IAC, 404 Sixth Ave., Menlo Park, CA 94025.

This is an index on microfiche, with the publisher providing an enclosed fiche reader that has a rapid-searching mechanism. The microfiche listing is arranged in a single alphabet with interfiled authors, titles, and subjects. About 400 popular U.S. magazines are indexed, including children's, special interest, newsstand, sports, auto, literary, and some academic journals. The monthly fiches now cumulate for the latest five years. Earlier years are cumulated in a separate index to be read on a separate, manually operated fiche reader. Instructions for using the publisher's fiche reader are on the reader and on the microfiche itself, preceding the index. Supplementary paper indexes, "Hot Topics," and "Product Evaluations" are issued monthly in loose-leaf form and are available from the publisher. *MI* is easy to use and should attract many younger users because of its non-traditional format. Many of its titles, however, are indexed in the less expensive *Readers' Guide to Periodical Literature* and *Access*. (M.McK.)

Media Review Digest. 1970. a. $200. Pierian Press, P.O. Box 1808, Ann Arbor, MI 48106.

The publisher scans a wide variety of periodicals—about 200—for reviews of anything classifiable as "media." Arrangement is by form of medium, and there are numerous indexes that allow one to easily find what is needed. There usually is an indication of whether the review is positive or negative. Here, "review" is interpreted in its broadest sense so that much of the material may be no more than a note about the medium. Nevertheless, this remains the one fixed point for finding such material. Index covers films, filmstrips, videotapes, slides, transparencies, globes, charts, and other non-print media.

Music Index. 1949. m. $840. Information Coordinators, Inc., 1435-37 Randolph St., Detroit, MI 18226. Circ: 500. Sample.

The basic index in the field, this covers 350 periodicals from 34 countries and in 19 languages (entries from non-English periodicals are in the language of the country). Arrangement is by subject and author in one alphabet. This collection includes obituaries, first performances, and music reviews. Note: The price varies, depending on the size of the library, and may be less in some situations. The subscription includes the annual cumulations. Interested librarians should call the publisher for a quote.

New York Times Index. See Newspapers/For the Student: General Section.

PAIS. Public Affairs Information Service. Bulletin. 1915. bi-w. Membership. Lawrence Woods. PAIS, 11 W. 40th St., New York, NY 10018. Sample. Vol. ends: Sept.

Despite the title, this is really a general index in that it covers over 800 periodicals and some 6,000 other publications, including government documents. True, the focus is on political and social issues, but in the process the index tends to cover all disciplines ranging from the humanities to the sciences. Also, it has the advantage of being published every two weeks and is one of the more current printed sources. Note the useful listing of the materials indexed in each issue, a particularly good feature because many of the documents are not that easy to locate. The same publisher issues:

PAIS Foreign Language Index (1972. q. $195), which covers the same types of periodicals and documents, but with the emphasis on those published in Europe. Some 400 periodicals in five languages are indexed, with about 2,000 other types of works covered each year.

Physical Education Index. 1978. q. $125. Ronald E. Kirby. BenOak Publg. Co., P.O. Box 474, Cape Girardeau, MO 63701. Vol. ends: Dec.

This subject index to nearly 200 domestic and foreign periodicals published in English—or containing summaries in English—provides comprehensive coverage of dance, health, physical education, physical therapy, recreation, sports, and sports medicine, as well as additional coverage of administration, biomechanics—kinesiology, coaching, curriculum, facilities, history, measurement-evaluation, motor learning, perception, philosophy, physical fitness, research, sport psychology, sport sociology, teaching methods, training, and all sports-related activities. Not indexed are editorials of local interest, letters to the editor, human-interest

stories, general panel-discussion type articles, association-oriented activities, or abstracts from secondary sources when the original article is indexed. Citations to book reviews are offered in a separate concluding section. This is *the* major physical education index. (F.B.)

Popular Periodicals Index. 1973. s-a. $25. Robert M. Bottorff, P.O. Box 2157, Wayne, NJ 07470.

This index reviews 40 periodicals, with authors, titles, and subjects appearing in each listing. There may be a brief explanation if a title does not adequately identify the subject matter of an article. Titles indexed are those that would not be indexed by *Readers' Guide to Periodical Literature. Popular Periodicals Index* does, however, index 26 titles indexed by *Access.* This is useful for libraries of any size, and sufficiently inexpensive that cost should not prevent any library from acquiring it. (M.McK.)

Readers' Guide to Periodical Literature. 1900. s-m. (m. June, July). $95. H. W. Wilson Co., 950 University Ave., Bronx, NY 10452.

The best-known and most popular United States periodical index, *Readers' Guide* indexes nearly 200 periodicals. It may be the only index to which high school students are introduced and may be the only one with which college students are familiar. This means that periodicals indexed in this guide are much more heavily used than others that are not indexed, contributing to uneven usage of the periodicals collection in many libraries. Many librarians intensify this problem by subscribing only to those periodicals indexed in *Readers' Guide* rather than buying periodicals indexed in *Access, Popular Periodicals Index,* or elsewhere. *Readers' Guide* has quarterly and annual cumulations. It is easy to use, with author and subject citations interfiled in one alphabet. An author index of citations to book reviews follows the main body of the index. This will continue to be a popular and heavily used index. (M.McK.)

Resources in Education. 1966. m. Subs. to: Supt. of Docs., U.S. Govt. Printing Office, Washington, DC 20402. Circ: 5,000.

Each year, this title indexes and abstracts 15,000-plus education-related documents—from doctoral dissertations and federally funded research reports to conference proceedings, curriculum guides, and "how-to-do-it" papers. No periodicals are included, so to gain access to them, the sister publication *Current Index to Journals in Education* must be used. All areas of education are covered from preschool to adult and continuing education. Each issue contains four indexes: subject, author, institution, and publication type. All items are listed with complete bibliographic information as well as a succinct, but useful résumé. All education collections should subscribe to this valuable title. (P.S.B.)

Social Sciences Index. 1974. q. H. W. Wilson Co., 950 University Ave., Bronx, NY 10452.

The contents of 307 English-language periodicals are indexed, with coverage including anthropology, Black studies, economics, environmental sciences, geography, health and medicine, law and criminology, planning and public administration, political science, psychology, sociology, urban studies, and women's studies. One of the three or four basic indexes required for all libraries.

Women Studies Abstracts. 1972. q. $60 (Individuals, $30). Sara Stauffer Whaley. Rush Publg. Co., P.O. Box 1, Rush, NY 14543. Sample. Vol. ends: Winter. Microform: UMI.

The basic indexing and abstracting source for research in the study of women, this includes not only feminist and women's studies periodicals, but selectively covers articles of 1,000 words or more in prominent journals in those fields encompassed by the study of women, including education, psychology, public affairs, law, gender studies, and others. Entries are arranged in about 20 categories (employment, mental and physical health, society and government, family, the women's liberation movement, and so on), with author and subject indexes in each issue. There is also a cumulative annual index. Of 500–700 entries per issue, about one-fifth have abstracts. Extensive listings of book reviews are carried in two to three issues per year.

Work Related Abstracts (Formerly: *Employment Relations Abstracts*). 1950. m. $398.50. Sonja Hempseed. Information Coordinators, Inc., 1435-37 Randolph St., Detroit, MI 48226. Circ: 800. Vol. ends: Dec.

Provides succinct (one- to two-sentence) abstracts of articles from over 250 labor, government, professional, and academic periodicals as well as abstracts of a selected number of books. The material is arranged in some 20 sections according to such categories as labor-management relations, personnel relations, safety and health, government policies and actions, labor unions and employee organizations, and so on. Everything is in a loose-leaf binder, and monthly issues can be easily broken up by category and inserted. To further facilitate use, the monthly subject index is cumulative. Though cross-references for subject headings are not included in the monthly issues of the subject index, they do appear in the annual cumulation. As an assist to people using the monthly index, cross-references for subject headings can be found in the biannual subject heading list. This is an important and useful service for the academic library serving people doing extensive research work in the labor-employment-occupation field. For the average school library, however, the *Business Periodicals Index* together with *PAIS* should be sufficient. (J.W.)

AFRICA

For the Student

See also Afro-American Section.

Janet L. Stanley, Chief Librarian, Natl. Museum of African Art Branch Library, Smithsonian Institution Libraries, Washington, DC 20560

Introduction

What has burst forth recently are newsmagazines on Africa, many of them published by Africans. This is probably ex-

plained by two trends: (1) the higher visibility of Africa in world affairs and on world consciousness, for example, the Ethiopian famine and South Africa's policy of apartheid; and (2) the growing disillusionment of Africans and the Third World generally with the paucity or distortion of news about Africa in the Western media. The proliferation of African newsmagazines in the 1980s—and no doubt more will appear—presages the inevitable shakedown, which will leave only the more hardy survivors.

Basic Periodicals

Hs: *Africa: An International Business, Economic and Political Monthly, Africa Report.*

Basic Abstracts and Indexes

PAIS, Social Sciences Index.

For the Student

Africa: an international business, economic and political monthly. 1971. m. $24. Raph Uwechue. Africa Journal, Ltd., Kirkman House, 54a Tottenham Court Rd., London W1P 0BT, England. Illus., adv. Circ: 90,270. Sample. Microform: UMI. *Indexed:* PAIS. *Bk. rev:* 2–3, 300 words. *Aud:* Hs.

The *Time* magazine of African affairs, providing in-depth coverage of current events in Africa, including cultural features, sports, and interviews with African personalities. Founded and edited by a Nigerian, the publication's editorial tone is generally upbeat, emphasizing developmental issues from the African point of view. This is a wise choice if selecting a single general newsmagazine on Africa. Issued in a French edition: *L'Afrique*—since 1977.

Africa Events. 1984. m. $30. M. Mlamali Adam. Dar es Salaam, Ltd., 55 Banner St., London EC1Y 8PX, England. Illus., adv. *Bk. rev:* 3–5, 200–400 words, signed. *Aud:* Hs.

A comparatively new African magazine, weighing in with a crisp editorial style; catchy, pungent headlines; and a clean look. The publication features multipart cover stories, imitating *Time*, and espouses a generally liberal orientation and an East African focus, including Zanzibari politician and columnist, Babu. Similar in scope and coverage to *Africa, Africa Now,* and *Jeune Afrique.*

Africa Now. 1981. m. $40. Peter Enahoro. Pan-African Publns., Dilke House, Malet St., London WC1E 7JA, England. Illus., adv. *Bk. rev:* 2–3, 300–400 words. *Aud:* Hs.

A comparatively recent but now proven entry into the pool of general African newsmagazines, *Africa Now* projects a distinctly African perspective on current events on the continent. Though published in London, its editorial staff is almost entirely African. Similar to *Africa*, it reports, analyzes, and comments editorially on African politics, economic, commerce, and foreign affairs. It has two or three feature articles per issue, e.g., "Africa's trade union crisis," "Dikko, the untold story," and "100 years of partition," and an Art and Culture section, sports report and business summary. In 1984, a U.S. edition was launched, which contains about two-thirds of the material in the international edition, the remaining third devoted to African-U.S. relations.

Africa Report. 1957. bi-m. $28 (Individuals, $21). Margaret A. Novicki. African Amer. Inst., 833 United Nations Plaza, New York, NY 10017. Illus., index, adv. Circ: 14,000. Vol. ends: Nov/Dec. Microform: B&H, UMI.
Indexed: HumI, PAIS, Rrt. *Bk. rev:* 1–2, 400–600 words, signed. *Aud:* Hs.

Aims at informing the U.S. public about Africa with news coverage focusing on U.S. political and economic interests on the continent. Frequent feature articles, e.g., "Africa and the IMF" and "African Women and the UN Decade for Women"; interviews with African leaders; and the country-by-country news update all make this a good first choice for smaller collections that only need one or two African periodical titles.

African Arts. 1967. q. $20. John Povey. African Studies Center, Univ. of California–Los Angeles, Los Angeles, CA 90024. Illus., index, adv. Circ: 6,500. Vol. ends: Aug. Refereed. Microform: UMI.
Indexed: ArtI. *Bk. rev:* 10–15, length varies, signed. *Aud:* Hs.

This basic periodical on the visual arts of Africa contains both scholarly and popular-interest articles on all aspects of African sculptural, decorative, and graphic arts. Usually six to eight articles appear per issue, often based on the authors' field work on the continent. This is notably well illustrated with many color photographs, plus a calendar and reviews of current exhibitions of African art. Of considerable appeal to a general audience.

Afrique Histoire U.S.: the quarterly magazine of African history. 1982. q. $30 (Individuals, $12). Amadou Koly Niang. P.O. Box 88622, Indianapolis, IN 46208. Illus. Circ: 5,000. Sample.
Bk. rev: 5–7, 100–200 words, signed. *Aud:* Hs.

An English translation of the journal *Afrique Histoire* published in Dakar, Senegal, featuring short, popular articles on aspects of African history (especially in Francophone West Africa). The overall tone is benignly polemical: to bring the glories and richness of the African past to a contemporary audience.

Jeune Afrique. 1960. w. $100. Le Groupe Jeune Afrique, 51 avenue des Ternes, B.P. 250, 75827 Paris, France. Illus., adv. Circ: 110,000. Sample. Microform: UMI.
Aud: Hs.

The major comprehensive French-language weekly newsmagazine on Africa, whose coverage concentrates on Francophone Africa. Each issue has several short feature articles, editorial commentary, summary of the week's news and cultural briefs. A companion fortnightly journal by the same publishing group is *Jeune Afrique Economie*, which is less

"African" and more global in scope. They also issue a semiweekly *Confidential Telex* for up-to-the-minute briefings, and a popular cultural magazine, *JA Magazine*, featuring rock-music stars, food, and fashion with an African beat and bent.

Pace. 1978. m. R7.20. Lucas Molete. Pace, P.O. Box 31869, Braamfontein 2017, South Africa. Illus., adv. Circ: 165,000. *Aud:* Hs.

Resembling *Essence* in format and style, this wholeheartedly popular magazine is "paced" to young, educated, urbanized, affluent Blacks in South Africa. It features people in the limelight, human-interest stories, stars of the stage and sports arena, music, fashion, and food. Though focused on South Africa, it pays considerable attention to international personalities, U.S. movies, reggae and rock-music stars.

Talking Drums: the West African news magazine. 1983. w. $95. Elizabeth Ohene. Talking Drums Publns., Madhav House, 68 Mansfield Rd., London NW3 2HU, England. Illus., adv.
Aud: Hs.

Another in the youngest generation of newsmagazines about Africa, by Africans, *Talking Drums* is in direct competition with its contemporaries *Africa, Africa Events,* and *Africa Now.* In style, coverage and format, they are all virtually identical. There is an unspoken Ghanaian orientation to *Talking Drums* (no discredit).

AFRO-AMERICAN

For the Student/For the Professional

See also Africa Section.

Kathleen E. Bethel, African-American Studies Librarian, Northwestern University Library, Evanston, IL 60201

Introduction

The demise of *Ebony Jr!, Black Heritage, Sepia, Minority Voices, Umoja* and the suspended publication of *Negro History Bulletin* and *The Journal of Negro History* have created quite a void for younger and less literate readers, but there has also been a profusion of Black teen and Black beauty magazines.

There are an impressive number of very good regional publications covering Black life and culture. Many of these should be in high school libraries.

Basic Periodicals

Ejh: *Ebony, Negro History Bulletin;* Hs: *Black American Literature Forum, The Black Collegian, Black Enterprise, Callaloo, Ebony, Jet, Negro History Bulletin.*

Basic Abstracts and Indexes

Index to Periodical Articles by and about Blacks, Social Sciences Index.

For the Student

Afro-Americans in New York Life and History. 1977. s-a. $8. Monroe Fordham. Afro-Amer. Historical Assn. of the Niagara Frontier, Inc., P.O. Box 1663, Hertle Sta., Buffalo, NY 14216. Circ: 700. Sample. Vol. ends: July.

Indexed: INeg. *Bk. rev:* 3–4, signed. *Aud:* Hs.

The Historical Association produces a journal focusing on the Black experience in the Niagara Frontier. There are descriptive, analytical, and historical articles on Afro-Americans in New York State. It is not limited in scope to research on the area, but aims to increase the understanding of the broader experiences of Blacks in the United States. It is a well-written publication and is clearly the resource of note for New Yorkers. This is an excellent addition to Afro-American collections.

Black American Literature Forum. 1967. q. $10 (Individuals, $8). Joe Weixlmann. Indiana State Univ., School of Education, Statesman Towers, Rm. 1005, Terre Haute, IN 47809. Illus., index. Circ: 1,000. Sample. Vol. ends: Dec. Microform: UMI.

Indexed: INeg. *Bk. rev:* 1–5, 500–1,000 words, signed. *Aud:* Hs.

Black American Literature Forum began as a tool for school and university teachers. With its emphasis on the approaches to teaching Black literature and its news items for educators, it is a most useful resource. Today it is the official publication of the Division on Black American Literature and Culture of the Modern Language Association. It has taken a decidedly scholarly approach to the discussions of Afro-American writing. It is an important publication for the study of U.S.-Black literature at all levels of education. Contained in the journal are bibliographies, poetry, fiction, prose, interviews, and critical articles, complemented by the reproductions of original graphic works on Black themes. There are also excellent special issues. This publication should augment any collection supporting literature studies.

Black Collegian: the national magazine of Black college students. 1970. q. $10. James Borders. Black Collegiate Services, Inc., 1240 S. Broad St., New Orleans, LA 70125. Illus., adv. Circ: 205,000. Sample. Vol. ends: Mar/Apr. Microform: B&H, UMI.

Indexed: INeg. *Bk. rev:* 3–6, 250–500 words, signed. *Aud:* Hs.

Addressed to Black college students, but very helpful to college-bound students, this title provides useful information relating to career choices as well as feature articles and reviews of books, films, and plays. Current social problems of youth are addressed in various essays. It gives advice on résumé writing, interviewing, and other job seeking skills. It provides significant advice on procedures for applying to graduate and professional schools, as well as leads on scholarships, fellowships, internships, and financial aid. Profiles of successful Black role models, celebrity interviews, Black history, and Black student activities are featured along with Black perspectives on educational, political, economic, and social issues. The advertising is from major employers of Black graduates. Highly recommended.

Black Enterprise. 1970. m. $15. Earl G. Graves. Earl G. Graves Publg. Co., Inc., 130 Fifth Ave., New York, NY 10011. Illus., adv. Circ: 213,000. Sample. Vol. ends: July. Microform: B&H, UMI.

Indexed: BusI, INeg, PAIS, RG, WorAb. *Bk. rev:* 1–2, 250–500 words, signed. *Aud:* Hs.

This publication is devoted to the financial, career, and business interests of U.S. Blacks. It attempts to give sound advice and encouragement. As a business-oriented magazine its aim is to foster conditions that encourage Black economic development. It emphasizes the necessity for Blacks to commit themselves to doing business with each other. It does not neglect the political and social implications of Black economics. *Black Enterprise* covers political developments by giving insights often ignored by other media. Its annual list of the nation's 100 leading Black businesses, annual survey of its readers' attitudes concerning the current economic situation, and the monthly statistics on facets of Black life provide an excellent pulse on Black economic development. The outstanding members of its Board of Economists frequently analyze the economic outlook. Highly recommended.

Blacfax. 1982. q. $5. R. Edward Lee. 214 W. 138th St., New York, NY 10030. Illus. Circ: 1,500. Vol. ends: Dec. *Aud:* Hs.

A 14-page photo-offset title with simple, dignified illustrations presenting the heritage of Black Americans. Mini-biographies of prominent figures and a bibliography are regular features. Most issues have an essay article, sometimes on a controversial subject. This is a solid publication and would be an excellent resource for Black studies. (L.K.W.)

Callaloo: a tri-annual journal of Afro-American and African arts and letters. 1976. 3/yr. $12. Charles H. Rowell. Dept. of English, Univ. of Kentucky, Lexington, KY 40506. Illus., adv. Circ: 500. Sample. Vol. ends: Fall.

Bk. rev: 2–3, 1–3 pages, signed. *Aud:* Hs.

Devoted to the creative works by and critical studies of Black writers in the Americas and Africa, *Callaloo* began as an outlet for southern Black writers who had difficulty getting their work published. It has evolved into an outstanding journal with excellent articles and literary works. Studies of life and culture in the Black world as well as visual art are published. This includes interviews, bibliographies, plays, short stories, poetry, articles of critical thought, photographs, graphics, and some folklore studies. The magazine boasts an impressive editorial board. There have been special issues on such writers as Ernest Gaines, Gayl Jones, and Larry Neal. It is a fine journal that will complement any literature collection. Recommended.

The Crisis: a record of the darker races. 1910. m. (bi-m. June/July & Aug/Sept.). $6. Fred Beauford. Crisis Publg. Co., 186 Remsen St., Brooklyn, NY 11201. Illus., index, adv. Circ: 277,000. Sample. Vol. ends: Dec. Microform: B&H, Kraus, UMI.

Indexed: CIJE, INeg, SocSc. *Bk. rev:* 1–2, 250–500 words, signed. *Aud:* Hs.

This is the oldest Black magazine in the United States and the official publication of the National Association for the Advancement of Colored People (NAACP). *The Crisis* has been an instrumental tool in the long civil rights struggle of U.S. Blacks. Begun by W.E.B. Du Bois to disseminate information on the struggles of the race, it has continued to enhance the cultural and political awakening of Afro-Americans. Although some of the radicalism of Du Bois' era has waned, *The Crisis* is still a hard-hitting, informative journal. Columns on travel, dance, music, and theater and occasional interviews complement items on the "NAACP Battlefront," legal issues, and news. Highly recommended.

Ebony. 1945. m. $16. John H. Johnson. Johnson Publg. Co., Inc., 820 S. Michigan Ave., Chicago, IL 60605. Illus., adv. Circ: 1,450,000. Sample. Vol. ends: Oct. Microform: B&H, MIM, UMI.
Indexed: AbrRG, INeg, MgI, RG. *Bk. rev:* 3–12, 25–250 words. *Aud:* Ejh, Hs.

Commonly referred to as the Afro-American version of *Life* or *Look* magazines, *Ebony* has thrived while the others have not. *Ebony* reports the success Blacks experience in various aspects of American life. It has recorded, illustrated, and commented on civil rights, desegregation, Black Power, Vietnam, and affirmative action. It covers Black history, entertainment, business, health, personalities, occupations, sports, and fashion. There is a special issue each August that takes an in-depth look at a particular facet of the Black dilemma. It is a must for all libraries.

Freedomways: a quarterly review of the freedom movement. 1961. q. $7.50. Jean Carey Bond & Esther Jackson. Freedomways Assocs., Inc., 799 Broadway, New York, NY 10003. Illus., adv. Circ: 5,250. Sample. Microform: UMI.
Indexed: CIJE, INeg, SocSc. *Bk. rev:* 3–10, 1–3 pages, signed. *Aud:* Hs.

Freedomways set the standard of excellence and quality for this genre of publication. It is a tremendous contribution to the economic, political, social, and cultural battles for equality and social progress. It is international in scope and coverage. The articles are extremely well written; contributing editors include James Baldwin, Angela Davis, and Alice Walker. Special issues focus on some aspect of struggle. A valuable feature for librarians is Ernest Kaiser's "Recent Books" section. It offers the best coverage and annotations of titles of interest to the Black community and to those concerned with the struggle for freedom. Recommended.

The International Review of African and African American Art. See Art/For the Student: General Section.

Jet. 1951. w. $36. John H. Johnson. Johnson Publg. Co., Inc., 820 S. Michigan Ave., Chicago, IL 60605. Illus., adv. Circ: 850,000. Sample. Vol. ends: Oct. Microform: B&H, UMI.
Indexed: INeg, MgI, RG. *Bk. rev:* Notes. *Aud:* Hs.

Jet stands today as the single best chronicle of the Black experience in the second half of the twentieth century. It provides a weekly summary of news for and about Black people. All aspects of the Black experience are covered in brief, timely articles. Special features include Black music charts, "This Week in Black History," "Words of the Week," a television listing of Blacks who will appear during the week, a centerfold Black bathing beauty, and "Celebrity Beat." While its cover stories tend to spotlight entertainment or sports figures, the publication contains features of importance to an informed Black populace. Many hard-to-find current news items are included. Highly recommended for schools with Black students.

Journal of Negro History. 1916. q. $30 (Individuals, $25). Alton Hornsby, Jr. Assn. for the Study of Afro-Amer. Life and History, Inc., 1401 14th St. N.W., Washington, DC 20005. Index, adv. Circ: 4,000. Sample. Vol. ends: Winter. Microform: UMI.
Indexed: EdI, INeg, PAIS. *Bk. rev:* 5–10, 500–1,000 words, signed. *Aud:* Hs.

This journal, after a brief suspension, promises to continue the tradition begun by its founder, Carter G. Woodson. It has always been a highly respected scholarly journal. It publishes three to five major articles, book reviews, Association notes, and some documents on Afro-American history. The biographical articles are excellent. It is the journal of note for the study of Black history.

Living Blues. 1970. bi-m. $18. Jim O'Neal & Amy O'Neal. Univ. of Mississippi, Center for the Study of Southern Culture, University, MS 38677; and Living Blues Publns., 2615 N. Wilton Ave., Chicago, IL 60614. Illus., adv. Circ: 5,500. Sample. Microform: UMI.
Indexed: MusicI. *Bk. rev:* 1, 500 words, signed. *Aud:* Hs.

Living Blues makes no attempt to explain, define, or confine the blues. It is an exploration of the blues as a living tradition. Sponsored, in part, by the Center for the Study of Southern Culture at the University of Mississippi, it is a medium of communication and education about the blues. It illustrates and disseminates news and perceptions about the blues as a part of American culture and the Afro-American struggle. It provides book reviews, obituaries, radio guides, record reviews, interviews, features, and blues news from throughout the world. A must for music libraries and collections supporting Afro-American studies. (Note: For numerous other periodicals in this field see the Music and Dance/Popular Section—*Eds.*)

Negro History Bulletin. 1937. q. $16. Bonnie J. Gillespie. Assn. for the Study of Afro-Amer. Life and History, Inc., 1401 14th St. N.W., Washington, DC 20005. Illus., index, adv. Circ: 6,500. Sample. Vol. ends: Oct/Nov/Dec. Microform: UMI.
Indexed: BioI, BoRvI, INeg, RG. *Bk. rev:* 2–5, 1 page, signed. *Aud:* Ejh, Hs.

This journal, published by the Association for the Study of Afro-American Life and History, experienced a suspension in its publication. It was founded by Carter G. Woodson to provide a more popular approach to Black history. It has been a most effective teaching tool for all educational levels. Through this organ the Association for the Study of Afro-American Life and History implements the goals and themes of Black History Month, begun as Negro History Week in 1926 by Dr. Woodson. The biographical articles are well written and well researched. With the cessation of *Ebony Jr!*, the *Negro History Bulletin* may well be the only Black publication for the elementary school level. Highly recommended for all school libraries.

Obsidian: Black literature in review. 1975. 3/yr. $8.50. Alvin Aubert. Wayne State Univ., Dept. of English, Detroit, MI 48202. Illus., index, adv. Circ: 500. Sample. Vol. ends: Winter. Microform: UMI.

Indexed: AHCI, AmerHu, CurrCont, IAPV. *Bk. rev:* 1–3, 2–3 pages, signed. *Aud:* Hs.

This journal complements the study and cultivation of works in English by Black writers worldwide. There are scholarly critical articles on all aspects of the literature, with book reviews, bibliographies and bibliographical essays, short fiction, poetry, interviews, and very short plays. Recommended.

Sage: a scholarly journal on Black women. 1984. s-a. $25 (Individuals, $15). Patricia Bell-Scott & Beverly Guy-Sheftall. Sage Women's Educational Press, Inc., P.O. Box 42741, Atlanta, GA 30311. Illus. Circ: 2,000. Vol. ends: Fall.

Indexed: WomAb. *Aud:* Hs.

The premiere year of this title shows tremendous promise toward the enhancement of women's studies. Its aim is to "provide an interdisciplinary forum for critical discussion of issues relating to Black women; to promote feminist scholarship; and to disseminate new knowledge about Black women to a broad audience." Toward this aim, *Sage* publishes scholarly articles, interviews, essays, resource listings, announcements, and reviews of books, films, and exhibits. Each issue is devoted to a particular theme in the study of Black women's historiography. Published with the support of Spelman College, *Sage* documents the recent thrust in the study of Black women's lives and culture. The most helpful feature of *Sage* may well be its bibliographies and announcements. A must for any library serving Black students.

Southern Exposure. 1973. bi-m. $20 (Individuals, $16). Ed. bd., P.O. Box 531, Durham, NC 27702. Illus., index, adv. Circ: 8,000. Sample. Vol. ends: Nov/Dec. Microform: UMI.

Indexed: Acs, API. *Bk. rev:* 2–5, 1 page, signed. *Aud:* Hs.

Published by the Institute for Southern Studies, a nonprofit organization working for progressive change in the region, *Southern Exposure* is a readable, well-documented, and useful publication. Its aim is to facilitate the building of grass-roots organizations. It wishes to nourish understanding among the diverse cultural groups in the South. Each issue focuses on a topic important to the social, political, or economic development of the South. A most useful feature is the bibliography of materials on the South. Along with its "Southern News Roundup," "Facing South" and "Resources" columns, the "Voices From the Past" feature

makes this a very lively publication. Recommended for any library interested in area studies or in the South.

For the Professional

The Black Child Advocate. 1971. q. $12.50. Ed. bd. Natl. Black Child Development Inst., 1463 Rhode Island Ave. N. W., Washington, DC 20005. Circ: 1,000. Sample.

Aud: Pr.

The goal of the NBCDI is to "work as an advocate for Black children and their families on a national level in the areas of child development, child welfare, research and public policy." The newsletter monitors all legislation on these issues and keeps readers apprised of current regulations, proposals, and changes. A recent issue critiqued the 1985 Model Child Care Standards Act issued by the U.S. Department of Health and Human Services, alerted readers to the proposed fiscal budget in many social services areas, and provided information about the suspected link between aspirin and Reye's syndrome in children. Upcoming conferences of interest to readers are publicized, as are notes about important research documents. (MiNe.)

The Black Scholar: journal of Black studies and research. 1969. bi-m. $30 (Individuals, $20). Robert Chrisman, P.O. Box 7106, San Francisco, CA 94120. Illus., adv. Circ: 10,000. Sample. Vol. ends: Nov/Dec. Microform: B&H, MIM, UMI.

Indexed: API, INeg, PAIS, SocSc. *Bk. rev:* 3–5, 1 page, signed. *Aud:* Pr.

The Black Scholar is a forum where Black ideologies are examined, debated and evaluated by the Black intellectual. It is an articulate, scholarly, and independent periodical of Black studies and research promoting the Black cultural revolution. Its annual "Black Books Roundup" is an important resource listing of currently published titles relating to Black and Third World experiences. The journal is international in scope, offering Black insights on Third World struggles. Each issue is devoted to a particular topic. Its board of contributors is comprised of 52 luminaries. The "Black Scholar Classified," its job listings, is a valuable asset for job seekers. Highly recommended.

CLA Journal. 1957. q. $30. Cason L. Hill. College Language Assn., Morehouse College, Atlanta, GA 30314. Index., adv. Circ: 5,000. Sample. Vol. ends: June.

Indexed: HumI, INeg. *Bk. rev:* 3–5, 2–4 pages, signed. *Aud:* Pr.

This is the official publication of the College Language Association. It offers six to eight articles on widely mixed literary topics. *CLA Journal* is a medium of scholarly expression for members of the organization and for others with similar scholarly interests. There is an annual bibliography of Afro-American, African, and Caribbean literature, with some annotations. It includes articles on language and literature, literary criticism, and book reviews. The journal offers a listing of available academic positions. Each issue includes "CLA News" and a list of CLA officers and committee members. Recommended.

Journal of Black Studies. 1970. q. $54 (Individuals, $22). Molefi Kete Asante. Sage Publns., Inc., 275 S. Beverly Dr., Beverly Hills, CA 90212. Index, adv. Circ: 1,100. Sample. Vol. ends: June. Microform: UMI.

Indexed: INeg, PAIS. *Bk. rev:* 1, 1–2 pages, signed. *Aud:* Pr.

Each issue contains scholarly articles on a wide range of social science questions. The editor favors articles that demonstrate rigorous and thorough research in an interdisciplinary context. This publication promotes Black ethnic studies as an academic discipline by publishing original research about the culture and concerns of people throughout the Black diaspora. The articles are well written and well worth the expense.

Journal of Negro Education: a quarterly review of issues incident to the education of Black people. 1932. q. $12.50. Faustine C. Jones. Howard Univ., Bureau of Educational Research, 2400 Sixth St. N.W., Washington, DC 20059. Index, adv. Circ: 2,000. Sample. Vol. ends: Fall. Microform: Kraus, MIM, UMI.

Indexed: CIJE, EdI, INeg, PAIS. *Bk. rev:* 2–4, 500–1,000 words, signed. *Aud:* Pr.

The Journal of Negro Education presents discussions involving critical appraisals of the proposals and practices relating to the education of Black people. While its primary focus is on the collection and dissemination of facts about the education of Black people, the journal offers an examination of the total Black experience in the United States. Scholarly articles on history, psychology, politics, sociology, and the development of Third World education are included. The journal sponsors and stimulates investigations of issues in Black education. Its summer issue is devoted to a comprehensive study of some particular aspect of the problems in the education of Blacks. Highly recommended.

Negro Educational Review. 1950. 3/yr. $12. R. Gann Lloyd, P.O. Box 2895, General Mail Center, Jacksonville, FL 32203. Illus., index, adv. Circ: 5,000. Sample. Vol. ends: July–Oct.

Indexed: CIJE, EdI, INeg. *Bk. rev:* 1–4, 1–2 pages, signed. *Aud:* Pr.

This is a forum for the discussion of Afro-American issues. The *Negro Educational Review* is an international journal that seeks to present scholarly articles and research reports, descriptions of current problems, and significant compilations on the broad issues of Blacks in education. It provides published, detailed lists of thesis topics on the education of Black people. It also covers the problems of the profession and prints news about Black educators.

AGRICULTURE

For the Student/For the Professional

Eleanor Mathews, Information Services Librarian, Iowa State University Library, Ames, IA 50011

Dawn D. Puglisi, Director, The Bromfield Learning Resources Center, The Ohio State University at Mansfield/North Central Technical College, Mansfield, OH 44906

Introduction

Journals in agriculture cover a wide range of topics—crops, soils, livestock, veterinary medicine, fruits, vegetables, ornamental plants, trees, plant diseases and pests, machinery and supplies, engineering, food processing and distribution, nutrition, farm management, marketing of products, and farm life. Types of periodicals include popular farm magazines, e.g., *Farm Journal* or *Successful Farming*; those of regional interest, e.g., *Progressive Farmer*; those stressing nontraditional approaches, e.g., *Countryside*; youth-oriented, e.g., *4-H Leader.*

Publications produced by governmental agencies play a very important role in disseminating agricultural information. In addition to publishing periodicals, such as *Agricultural Research* and *Farmline*, the U.S. Department of Agriculture produces many serial publications: Farmer's Bulletins and Home and Garden Bulletins have universal appeal. They may be ordered from the U.S. Government Printing Office. At the state level, the land-grant universities distribute information to the citizens of the state through Cooperative Extension Service publications. A list of current publications, most of which are free, is usually available from the university.

Basic Periodicals

Hs: *Agricultural Research, Crops and Soils Magazine, Farm Journal, 4-H Leader.*

Library and Teaching Aids

Agricultural Education, 4-H Leader.

For the Student

Agricultural Research. 1953. 10/yr. $10. Lloyd E. McLaughlin. U.S. Dept. of Agriculture, Information Staff, Rm. 318, Bldg. 005, Beltsville Agricultural Research Center–West, Beltsville, MD 20705. Subs. to: Supt. of Docs., U.S. Govt. Printing Office, Washington, DC 20402. Illus. Circ: 36,000. Vol. ends: June. Microform: B&H, UMI.

Indexed: IGov. *Aud:* Hs.

Do you want to know about the innovations and trends in agricultural research or how your taxes are being spent? The articles in this journal, published by the Agricultural Research Service of the U.S. Department of Agriculture, describe research projects underway in the department. All aspects of agriculture are reported—crop production; postharvest science and technology; crop protection; soil, water, and air sciences; energy; and livestock and animal science. Several black-and-white photos accompany each article, written in a nontechnical language. Patented inventions of the USDA are regularly featured so that they will become better known to individuals and businesses that might benefit from using them. Although no bibliographies are given, the names and addresses of the USDA scientists involved in the research projects are supplied. *Agricultural Research* is a public relations tool of the USDA and reflects the direction and emphasis of this government agency's research. Junior high and high school students will find topics for speeches and papers. (E.Ma.)

Crops and Soils Magazine (Formerly: *Crops & Soils*). 1948. m. (bi-m. Apr-Sept.). $8. William R. Luellen. Amer. Soc. of Agronomy, 677 S. Segoe Rd., Madison, WI 53711. Illus., index, adv. Circ: 19,475. Vol. ends: Sept.

Aud: Hs.

This attractive periodical contains one or two feature articles, two to four pages in length, that describe practical applications of research results or explain basic agricultural science concepts. Writers are extension agronomists, agronomy specialists working in industry, or professors in agricultural colleges. An interesting feature is a box on the title page giving the botanical names of all plants mentioned in the issue. Vocational agriculture instructors will be interested in the list of slide sets, which can be purchased from the American Society of Agronomy. This farm magazine offers basic, practical information in an easy-to-read style. It serves as a good foil to the commercially published popular farm magazines, *Farm Journal* and *Successful Farming*. (E.Ma.)

DVM Newsmagazine: the newsmagazine of veterinary medicine. 1969. m. $24. Craig Fintor. Harcourt Brace Jovanovich, Inc., 7500 Old Oak Blvd., Cleveland, OH 44130. Subs. to: One E. First St., Duluth, MN 55802. Illus., adv. Circ: 20,000. Vol. ends: Dec. Refereed. Microform: UMI.

Aud: Hs.

This is a very unusual publication. Its format is that of a large magazine, it has no table of contents, it is not indexed, and it is very flashy. The readership of this publication could be middle school and up. There are no articles based on laboratory research, but instead small bits and pieces of information from every aspect of the profession, including humorous stories and articles on practice management and pet cemeteries. Features include editorial roundtable discussions with industry leaders; feature reports on emerging areas of importance; and complete coverage of FDA and USDA activities, analyzed and interpreted by the Washington-based editorial staff. (D.D.P.)

Farm Journal. 1877. 14/yr. $10. Lane Palmer. Farm Journal, 230 W. Washington Sq., Philadelphia, PA 19105. Illus., adv. Circ: 1,000,000. Vol. ends: Dec. Microform: UMI.

Indexed: MgI, RG. *Aud:* Hs.

Boasting the largest circulation of any general farm magazine, and directed to almost every interest of the farmer and the farm family, this is published in numerous crop and livestock editions to appeal to all types of farmers and ranchers in the United States. Many of the features are devoted to business advice on farm production and management, or to topics of current or perennial interest. Others report on activities of farmers or producers or other "ag" people, such as the U.S. Secretary of Agriculture. Each issue includes business forecasts, describes new equipment, and runs late news from Washington. Supplements entitled "Livestock Extra" dealing with meat prices, feeding, marketing, health, and breeding are included. Traditional women's features, such as recipes, dress patterns, or family relationships and problems, are contained in each issue. Either *Farm Journal* or *Successful Farming* is standard reading fare for many farm

families, the choice being based on the personal preferences of the readers. Libraries should subscribe to at least one of these to provide access to past articles listed in indexing and abstracting services. (E.Ma.)

Foreign Agriculture. 1937. m. $16. Edwin N. Moffett. U.S. Dept. of Agriculture, Foreign Agricultural Service, Information Div., Rm. 5074, USDA, Washington, DC 20250. Subs. to: Supt. of Docs., U.S. Govt. Printing Office, Washington, DC 20402. Illus., index. Circ: 1,800. Vol ends: Dec. Microform: UMI.

Indexed: BioAg. *Aud:* Hs.

Examines, in one- to two-page feature articles, U.S. agricultural export trade, overseas markets, and competitive foreign production and trade. Graphs, tables, and photographs enhance the articles, which are often written by U.S. agricultural attachés. Marketing News, Fact File, Country Briefs, and Trade Updates are regularly included. This is a useful reference on world agricultural trade in both developed and developing countries for firms selling U.S. farm products overseas. It can be used effectively in political science and economics classes in high school. (E.Ma.)

4-H Leader: the national magazine for 4-H (Formerly: *National 4-H News*). 1923. 9/yr. $6. Larry L. Krug. Natl. 4-H Council, 7100 Connecticut Ave., Chevy Chase, MD 20815. Index, adv. Circ: 70,000. Vol. ends: Dec.

Aud: Ejh, Hs.

Published for adults and young people who lead 4-H clubs. Youngsters 9–19 from the inner city, suburbia, or farms will have fun learning about all kinds of things, from aerospace and rocketry to photography, the art of clothing to veterinary science, or any of nearly 50 other subjects. Articles of one to five pages tell what is happening in 4-H clubs throughout the country and suggest how leaders anywhere might adapt new ideas to their own programs. Graphic design, including four-color cover, informal page design, and modern typefaces reflect 4-H's expanded youth education programs. (E.Ma.)

The National Future Farmer. 1952. 6/yr. $2.50. Wilson W. Carnes. Future Farmers of America, 5632 Mt. Vernon Highway, Alexandria, VA 22309. Subs. to: P.O. Box 15160, Alexandria, VA 22309. Illus., adv. Circ: 484,013.

Aud: Ejh, Hs.

Although the focus is on FFA chapters, this appealing title has much general information on the world of agriculture, some of which will be an eye-opener for urban and suburban teens. There is also a strong vocational section if readers are future-oriented. (L.K.W.)

New Farm. 1979. 7/yr. $15. George DeVault. Regenerative Agriculture Assn., 222 Main St., Emmaus, PA 18049. Illus., adv. Circ: 55,000. Vol. ends: Dec. Microform: UMI.

Aud: Hs.

An alternative to farm magazine writing about conventional agricultural methods. *New Farm*'s goal is to put "people, profit, and biological permanence back into farming by giving farmers the information they need to take charge of their farms and their futures." Recent topics for the two- to four-page articles have been reduced tillage methods, direct wholesale marketing, long lasting legumes, computer software, and fertilizers and sludge. Regular columns include "Rural Delivery" (letters to the editor), "Organic Matter, Questions," and "FONE" (Farmers' Own Network for Extension). For many years Rodale Press published *Organic Gardening and Farming*, but in 1979 the title was split into *Organic Gardening* (see Alternatives Section) and *New Farm*. Every library subscribing to *Farm Journal* or *Progressive Farmer* should also offer their readers another point of view by subscribing to *New Farm*. (E.Ma.)

Organic Gardening. See Alternatives/For the Student Section.

Progressive Farmer. 1886. 3/m, Feb–July, s-m. Jan & Aug-Nov. $12. C. G. Scruggs. Progressive Farmer Inc., Box C-69, Birmingham, AL 35202. Illus., adv. Circ: 650,000. Vol. ends: Dec. Microform: UMI.
Aud: Hs.

A regional farm magazine, published in 17 regional editions. Articles are diverse in coverage—crop and livestock management, equipment, uses for livestock waste, irrigation, weed and disease control, marketing costs, and on-farm computerization. Recipes, gardening tips, clothing patterns, and house plans are also featured. Special sections on commodities, such as beef, pork, peanuts, tobacco, cotton, and soybeans, are included in various issues if the subscriber indicates that she or he produces these commodities. This magazine has a well-established reputation with readers. (E.Ma.)

Successful Farming: the magazine of farm management. 1902. 13/yr. $10. Richard Krumme. Meredith Corp., 1716 Locust St., Des Moines, IA 50336. Illus., adv. Circ: 750,000. Vol. ends: Dec. Microform: UMI.
Indexed: MgI, RG. *Aud:* Hs.

"For families that make farming their business," *Successful Farming* features Monthly Management reports on marketing, land, machinery, and money. Also included are sections on Livestock (Hog, Dairy, and Beef sections to qualified subscribers), Farm Management, Machinery and Crops, and Special Features. Special annual issues include Weed and Insect Guide, Machinery Management, Planting, and Harvesting. From time to time, supplements are included on current topics. *Successful Farming* undergoes a facelift every few years, but the emphasis is always on providing up-to-date, expert farm management information. The information appeals to the farmer following accepted, traditional agricultural techniques. The articles, in a varied and colorful layout, are succinct and informative, interspersed with extensive advertising spreads. The circulation is controlled by requiring subscription orders to show a farm or ranch connection as either owner or operator, or a farm-related occupation, but subscriptions are also available to libraries. This, along with *Farm Journal*, is one of the most widely read popular farm magazines. (E.Ma.)

Veterinary Economics: the magazine of practice management and finance. 1960. m. $30. Michael D. Sollars. Veterinary Medicine Publg. Co., P.O. Box 13265, Edwardsville, KS 66113. Illus., index, adv. Circ: 33,000. Vol. ends: Dec. Microform: Pub., UMI.
Aud: Hs.

This very readable publication helps in the management of a veterinary practice. It deals with such topics as advertising, supervision, determining the size of a new clinic, tax questions, and working on your own versus working with someone else. This publication will be valuable to anyone starting a practice, maintaining a practice, or working toward enlarging a practice. (D.D.P.)

For the Professional

Agricultural Education. 1929. m. $7. Glenn Anderson. Agricultural Education Magazine, Inc., 1803 Rural Point Rd., Mechanicsville, VA 23111. Index. Circ: 10,000. Vol. ends: June. Microform: UMI.
Indexed: CIJE, EdI. *Bk. rev:* 2–3, 300–400 words, signed. *Aud:* Pr.

Primarily intended for teachers of agriculture, especially for the high school vocational agriculture instructor. Each issue has a theme, e.g., "The Teacher of Vocational Agriculture," "Innovative Student Management Strategies." The 8–12 articles on research, education, and teaching methods and techniques are written by university agriculture faculty and high school agriculture instructors. Some articles are expository; others report results of research products; still others emphasize the "how to" or "how it is done in . . ." aspect. Book reviews and the feature "Stories in Pictures" on the back cover complete each issue. This is the journal read by the agricultural education profession. It belongs in the libraries of high schools where there are vocational agriculture and agricultural education programs. (E.Ma.)

ALTERNATIVES

For the Student/For the Professional

See also Civil Liberties; Literature; and News and Opinion Sections.

Gretchen Lagana, Head, Special Collections Department, and Acting Curator of Jane Addams Hull House, The University of Illinois at Chicago, P.O. Box 8198, Chicago, IL 60680

Introduction

At its best the alternative press fills in what the mainstream press (and non-print media) so often leaves out. It possesses the motivation and commercial freedom to explore issues in depth, to highlight and draw attention to little-known or poorly understood aspects of subjects, and to write about events without fear of angering or offending the reader. It explores just about every conceivable field—childbirth and mothering, folksinging, animal rights, art, film, politics, health, economics, gardening, science, religion, farming, agriculture, business, and librarianship, to name only a few. In addition to the information, the alternative press possesses an ambiance, an identity, that reaches out to the reader in ways the mainstream press cannot. One only has to glance at the editorial page and the letters to the editor section of alternatives to experience this. Indeed, the relationship may be akin to that established between the ethnic reader and the ethnic newspaper during an earlier period of our media history.

The reader has a far harder time of it than the librarian in trying to locate alternatives. Some can be found in their own geographic origin of publication. Big city newsstands and bookstores usually carry a selection of the more popular titles. Health food stores will occasionally stock selected environmental and life-style as well as health and nutrition titles. But for the most part they are hard to find. The alternatives listed below represent only a very few of the many available titles. In general, the Alternatives Section includes titles that are not readily categorized; other alternatives will be found throughout the volume under appropriate subject classifications. (G.L.)

Basic Periodicals

Ejh: *Mother Earth News, Organic Gardening*; Hs: *Green Revolution, Mother Earth News, Northwest Passage, OP: Independent Music, Organic Gardening, Whole Earth Review*.

Basic Abstracts and Indexes

Alternative Press Index.

For the Student

Alternative Media (Formerly: *Alternative Press Review & Alternative Journalism Review*; *Underground Press Review*). 1973. q. $15 (Individuals, $7.50). R.J. Smith. Alternative Press Syndicate, Inc., P.O. Box 1347, Ansonia Station, New York, NY 10023. Illus., adv. Circ: 5,000. Microform: B&H.

Indexed: API. *Bk. rev:* Various number and length. *Aud:* Hs.

Alternative Media is published by the Alternative Press Syndicate (APS), a not-for-profit association of over 200 alternative newspapers and magazines. *Alternative Media* possesses a long and colorful history. It successfully made the transition from underground to alternative periodical, and more recently has emerged from serious financial difficulties. Its goal is an ambitious one: "to critique the major media and to showcase all the rest of it—small press publications, filmmakers working on a shoestring, independent news services, pop musicians and more." Recent articles included coverage of Chile's opposition press, a look at media treatment of South Africa's racial policies, and an interview with Harvey Pekal, comic book publisher of *American Splendor*. Short reviews of APS's newest members provide timely and hard to find information on alternative magazines and press. Highly recommended.

Communities: journal of cooperation (Formerly: *Communities: a journal of cooperative living*). 1972. q. $20 (Individuals, $10). Melissa Wenig. Community Publns. Cooperative, 126 Sun St., Stelle, IL 60919. Illus., index, adv. Circ: 3,000. Sample. Microform: UMI.

Indexed: API. *Bk. rev:* Various number, length. *Aud:* Hs.

An estimated 100,000 "intentional communities" exist throughout the world today. They are "dedicated to the common goals of personal growth and social transformation, and range in size and scope from tiny village to space-age city: from back-to-nature simplicity to centers for technological advancement." Devoted to all aspects of communities and cooperative living, *Communities* treats such topics as community participation, social change, well-being (spiritual, physical, mental), appropriate technology, and networking. A recent issue devoted its lead article to the search for materials to teach cooperation to young people. Accompanying that article was an annotated list of books for preschoolers and juveniles; bibliographies on sex equity; and a resource list of games, including cooperative games, cooperative board games, game manuals, and non-competitive communications games. *Communities* contains a section devoted to cooperative groups seeking new members and a "resource" section covering such areas as computers, systems, futurism, cooperation, learning, spirituality, and networking. A basic title for those interested in the problems and rewards of communal living.

East-West Journal. 1971. m. $18. Mark Mayell. East-West Journal, Inc., 17 Station St., P.O. Box 1200, Brookline, MA 02147. Illus., adv. Circ: 100,000. Vol. ends: Dec. Microform: B&H, MIM, UMI. Reprint: UMI.

Indexed: API. *Bk. rev:* 3, 500–1,000 words, signed. *Aud:* Hs.

East-West Journal deals with issues of importance to a healthy life: holistic health, natural life-styles, whole foods, organic gardening and agriculture, science, spirituality, and the arts. It "explores the unity underlying complementary values: traditional and modern, Oriental and Occidental, visionary and practical." Articles are well written and often illustrated. Each issue has sections on the family, natural healing, whole foods, gardening, cooking (this section includes recipes), and books. An annotated list of books on health and well-being available by mail is included. Directories at the back of each issue offer information both on restaurants and stores throughout the country stocking macrobiotic staples, organic produce, and high-quality natural foods and on health-care professionals and clinics offering natural healing therapies as well as modern medical techniques. Information on classes, workshops, and events is also listed monthly. Recommended.

Green Revolution: a voice for decentralization and balanced living. 1943. q. $6. Mildred Loomis. School of Living Press, P.O. Box 388, RD 7, York, PA 17402. Illus., index, adv. Circ: 2,000. Microform: UMI.

Indexed: API. *Aud:* Hs.

One of the oldest surviving alternative publications, *Green Revolution* is written and published by members of the School for Living, an adult education center that stresses the study of human problems. Articles in the 40-page magazine cover a mix of spiritual uplift, practical projects, and decentralization politics. Special issues dealing with such diverse topics as health and Guatemala are common. The low subscription price for libraries makes this an especially attractive acquisition. (D.R.)

Harrowsmith. See Canada/For the Student Section.

Mother Earth News. 1970. $18. Bruce Woods. Mother Earth News, Inc., P.O. Box 70, 105 Storey Mountain Rd., Hendersonville, NC 28793. Illus., adv. Circ: 1,050,000. Sample.
Indexed: Acs, RG. *Bk. rev:* Various number, length. *Aud:* Ejh, Hs.

This is one of the oldest and most successful of the alternative life-style magazines promoting self-reliance, and although it has inspired many imitations, the original still remains the best. *Mother Earth News* functions to keep the reader abreast of the latest do-it-yourself-for-less news and deals with a wide range of topics, including food, health, housing, energy, and the environment. Articles are well written, and the instructions that accompany workshop projects are clear. There are numerous photographs, charts, diagrams, and references accompanying both articles and projects.

OP: independent music. 1979. bi-m. $24. John Foster. P.O. Box 2391, Olympia, WA 98507. Illus., adv. Circ: 6,000. *Aud:* Hs.

This publication is a well-kept music secret in that it circulates among many music fans, but is in few libraries. The offset 80 or so pages are devoted to record reviews. Approximately half of every issue contains signed, 100- to 150-word descriptive and critical comments. The other half is composed of news and features about "hopelessly obscure" types of music and musicians—those artists who cut small-run recordings, are little known, and make up a vast music underground across the country and the world. The types of music reviewed in past issues include all-girl rock 'n' roll groups, music to wash dishes to, and modern classical. Even those who do not buy the records will find hours of entertainment reading about the people who are cutting the grooves. Absolutely fascinating, particularly as it seems to cater to all tastes and all levels of music interest. Recommended for any music collection, and for adventurous librarians.

Organic Gardening (Formerly: *Organic Gardening and Farming*). 1942. m. $12. Rodale Press, 33 E. Minor St., Emmaus, PA 18049.
Indexed: BioAg, RG. *Aud:* Ejh, Hs.

Of the magazines now published by the Rodale Press empire (*Prevention, The New Farm, New Shelter*), this remains the most lively and interesting. Feature articles contain valuable information for those who eschew the chemical approach to gardening and seek a more self-sufficient way of life. Special features offer the reader information on cooking techniques, recipes, and answers to specific questions on gardening, food, and nutrition. News of organic discoveries and a detailed garden calendar are also provided.

Science for the People. 1969. $24 (Individuals, $15). Terri Goldberg. Science Resource Center, Inc., 897 Main St., Cambridge, MA 02139. Illus. Circ: 4,000. Microform: UMI. *Indexed:* API. *Bk. rev:* 1–3, essays and notes. *Aud:* Hs.

In 1969 a small group of scientists, engineers, concerned teachers, students, and activists banded together to form Scientists and Engineers for Social and Political Action (SESPA). This group functioned to organize protests against the involvement of North American scientists and engineers in the Vietnam war. The mimeographed newsletter originally used to communicate to members had by 1970 grown into a national magazine geared toward critiquing the social and political implications of science and technology. It offers a progressive view of science and technology while covering a broad range of issues and attempting to make scientific results available to everyone using everyday language while encouraging the political analysis of science and technology. Feature articles tend to be analytical in tone; contributors are from academic and non-academic fields; many of the articles are based on personal experience. Accompanying illustrations are carefully selected to enhance the text. Feature columns present brief non-technical summaries of recent developments in science and technology. Theme-oriented special issues have included "Decoding Bio-Technology," "Computing the Future," "Science, Media, and Policy-Making," "Science and Technology in Nicaragua and El Salvador," "Water," "Technology and Repression," and "Women and Science." Especially recommended for readers interested in the political analysis of science and technology and for those who want to read about scientific developments in everyday language.

Utne Reader: the best of the alternative press. 1983. bi-m. $24. Eric Utne, P.O. Box 1974, Marion, OH 43305. Illus., adv. *Bk. rev:* Various number, length. *Aud:* Hs.

Utne means "far out" in Norwegian according to the publisher's statement on this ambitious new alternative. Rather than being far out, this magazine pulls together a combination of articles, in *Reader's Digest* style, from both the mainstream and alternative presses. Each issue contains a variety (10–15) of articles reprinted and excerpted from periodicals such as *The New Statesman, East-West Journal, Village Voice,* and *In These Times.* In addition, it features a theme or cover story, with additional excerpts from books and periodicals. Three recent themes have centered around physical fitness, U.S.-U.S.S.R. relations, and the impact of television on our lives. *Utne* has several departments, one of which features summaries of selected articles and themes that appear in other periodicals—about 30 of these at 200 words per review. Titles covered range from the *New York Review of Books* and *The Progressive* to *New Pages* and *Northeast Sun Magazine.* Order information for each of the magazines listed is included. Another department features short reviews on a given theme by various specialists in the alternative press. Topics have included the radical right, animal rights, watchdogs of the right, anarchism, film, and Canadian magazines. Specialists in the alternative press also review titles for a "recommended reading" section. Some will say that a magazine of this sort discourages the purchase of alternatives for the library collection; others, that it does just the opposite. *Utne* makes available much that would be overlooked by the librarian. Its standards in choosing materials to be excerpted and in selecting reviewers has been excellent. Recommended.

Whole Earth Review (Formerly: *CoEvolutionary Quarterly*, *Whole Earth Software Review*). 1974. bi-m. $18. Kevin Kelly & Art Kleiner. Point Foundation, 27 Gate Five Rd., Sausalita, CA 94965. Illus. Circ: 97,000.
Indexed: Acs, API. *Bk. rev:* Numerous, length varies. *Aud:* Hs.

CoEvolutionary Quarterly, the vehicle for Stewart Brand's school of whole system tecology (technology and ecology), was originally published as a supplement to Brand's *Whole Earth Catalog* series. In 1984 Brand published the *Whole Earth Software Catalog*, a computer catalog patterned after the *Whole Earth Catalog*, which, in turn, bred the *Whole Earth Software Review*. The latter functioned to provide an update to information contained in the *Software Catalog*. Unable to keep up both, Brand merged *CoEvolutionary Quarterly* with *Software Review* and renamed it *Whole Earth Review*. The premier issue was published in January 1985 and entitled "Computers as Poison." For those who feel they have lost a friend with the demise of an unadulterated *CoEvolutionary Quarterly*, take heart. In addition to a 24-page computer section aimed at finding out what is really useful in the field of personal computing, it still functions as a potpourri of articles, short book reviews, fiction, and lists of resources.

For the Professional

New Pages: news & reviews of the progressive book trade. 1979. irreg. $12 for 6 issues. Grant Burns. New Pages Press, 4426 S. Belsay Rd., Grand Blanc, MI 48439. Illus., adv. Circ: 5,000.
Indexed: API. *Bk. rev:* Numerous, length varies. *Aud:* Pr.

New Pages reviews "books, periodicals, resource notes and information access, essays, critiques, and news not usually found in the major trade publications." In addition to exhaustive feature articles, each issue features a 9- to 10-page review section of books and periodicals arranged by subject. Many of these fall into the "alternative" category. The reviews are short, averaging about 50 words, and include complete order information. This is an invaluable tool for any librarian who wants to keep abreast of the publishing world of alternatives and for those who seek alternative sources of information.

ANTHROPOLOGY AND ARCHAEOLOGY

For the Student

Robert J. Fryman, Assistant Professor, East Liverpool Campus, Kent State University, East Liverpool, OH 43920

Introduction

Anthropology represents one of the more holistic fields of inquiry into human culture. Concerned not only with the study of existing cultures but also the examination of culture change, human physical development and place among the primates as well as other aspects of cultural behavior, the field seeks to integrate the results of these investigations into a comprehensive understanding of mankind and culture. Archaeology, as a subdivision of anthropology, seeks to explain human cultural development and the processes of culture change through the examination of the material remains of past cultures. Contemporary archaeological investigations reflect this basic anthropological orientation through the types of studies being conducted and the interdisciplinary approach in the analyses on the recovered remains.

The following compilation makes every attempt to present journals appropriate for high school students in the fields of anthropology and archaeology.

For the Student

Archaeology: a magazine dealing with the antiquity of the world. 1948. bi-m. $18. Phyllis Pollack Katz. Archaeological Inst. of America, 15 Park Row, New York, NY 10007. Illus., index, adv. Circ: 70,000. Sample. Vol. ends: Nov/Dec. Microform: SZ, UMI. Reprint: SZ.
Indexed: ArtI, HumI. *Bk. rev:* 3–7, 300–600 words, signed. *Aud:* Hs.

This publication ranks as one of the best general archaeology journals for the interested layperson. Each issue contains four to five major articles dealing with classical archaeology through historic sites excavations, all written in an easily understood style. In addition, each issue contains notices on archaeological-museum displays and field opportunities, current books and film reviews, and tips on photography and travel abroad. *Archaeology* is a good choice for high school libraries.

Early Man. 1979. q. $15. John B. Carlson. Northwestern Archaeology, P.O. Box 1499, Evanston, IL 60204. Illus. Circ: 6,000. Vol. ends: Winter.
Aud: Hs.

Early Man presents a variety of articles dealing with archaeology on a worldwide basis. While the overall emphasis of the journal is on the prehistory and historic archaeology of North America, there are occasional papers on excavations in the Old World. Each issue is amply illustrated with drawings and color photographs. All of the articles written are for the public audience. This journal would be a good selection for high schools, where it will complement *Archaeology*.

Expedition: the magazine of archaeology/anthropology: 1958. q. $12.50. Bernard Wailes. Univ. Museum of the Univ. of Pennsylvania, 33rd & Spruce St., Philadelphia, PA 19104. Illus., index. Circ: 6,000. Sample. Vol. ends: Summer. Microform: JAI, UMI.
Indexed: ArtI. *Aud:* Hs.

The holistic nature of anthropology and its subdiscipline of archaeology are well demonstrated by this publication. Its attractive format, with numerous color photographs and illustrations, provides the interested layperson as well as the professional with well-written articles on archaeological and anthropological topics. Articles range from contemporary Polynesian society to domestic and ritual objects from ancient Crete and the Near East. *Expedition* is a good choice for high school libraries.

Faces. See General Science/For the Student Section.

Journal of Anthropological Research. 1945. q. $30 (Individuals, $20). Philip K. Bock. Univ. of New Mexico, Dept. of Anthropology, Albuquerque, NM 87131. Illus., index. Circ: 1,721. Vol. ends: Winter. Microform: UMI.
Bk. rev: 1–2, 400–1,000 words, signed. *Aud:* Hs.

A highly readable journal for professional and layperson alike, this journal provides a balanced coverage of all subfields of anthropology. Each issue contains from seven to nine articles, averaging 15 to 30 pages in length. This journal is a good choice for large high school libraries.

Plains Anthropologist. 1954. q. $13. Joseph A. Tiffany. Univ. of Iowa, Iowa City, IA 52242. Illus., index. Circ: 850. Microform: UMI.
Bk. rev: 4–5, 250–750 words, signed. *Aud:* Hs.

One of the most interesting journals in the field, this periodical presents a variety of articles on the cultures, both Native American and Anglo-American, of the Plains area. While written primarily for the academic community, the articles are understandable to the layperson. Each issue is profusely illustrated. Larger high school libraries may want to consider this journal.

ART

For the Student: General; Architecture; Art Museum Publications/For the Professional

See also Education; Library Periodicals Sections.

Leslie N. Johnson, Slide Librarian, Department of Art, Williams College, Williams, MA 01267 (General, Art Museum Publications subsections)

Charles R. Smith, Humanities and Reference Librarian, Texas A&M University Libraries, College Station, TX 77843 (Architecture subsection)

Introduction

Art periodicals are a varied lot. They satisfy readers who range from serious scholars to Sunday painters, as well as dealers, collectors, professional artists, and art world groupies, to name only a few. Not all are appropriate for school audiences; but which are depends very much on the level of interest at a particular institution. We offer here a considerable variety, with enough comment in the annotations to guide librarians in their selection.

In previous editions of *Magazines for Libraries*, journals that appeared to have only a "regional" interest were grouped

together, but this is not the case here. Such a grouping seemed to reinforce the notion that art produced outside a few select centers was automatically of lesser quality or lesser interest, not a notion this editor wants to perpetuate. One useful subgroup included here is for journals published by museums. By and large these are so similar in intent that it seemed most efficient to put them together, rather than annotate them separately.

Basic Periodicals
Hs: *American Artist, ARTnews.*

Basic Abstracts and Indexes
Art Index.

For the Student
GENERAL
African Arts. See Africa/For the Student Section.

American Artist. 1937. m. $18. M. Stephen Doherty. American Artist Magazine, 1515 Broadway, New York, NY 10036. Subs. to: American Artist, One Color Court, Marion, OH 43305. Illus., index., adv. Circ: 120,000. Microform: B&H, UMI.
Indexed: ArtI, RG. *Bk. rev:* 7–15, very short to 1,000 words, signed. *Aud:* Hs.

Meant for artists who work in traditional formats, this magazine is filled with technical advice from artists to artists and with color plates of recent work. The March issue contains an extremely useful list of art schools and workshops in the United States.

Art and Man. 1970. 6/school yr. $9 (Teacher's edition, $19). Janet Soderberg. Scholastic, Inc., 730 Broadway, New York, NY 10003. Subs. to: P.O. Box 644, Lyndhurst, NJ 07071. Illus. Circ: 143,000. Vol. ends: May. Microform: UMI.
Indexed: CMG. *Aud:* Ejh, Hs.

This superb magazine is prepared in cooperation with the National Gallery of Art in Washington, DC. It takes a thematic approach and seeks to show the relationships among art, literature, and culture. Students are introduced to great artists from the Renaissance to the contemporary period, and aspiring artists are frequently featured. *Art and Man* is printed on glossy-coated paper with full-color reproductions. There is even a centerfold—"The Masterpiece of the Month." Although targeted for grades 7 to 12, it also can be adapted for younger students. (L.K.W.)

Art in America. 1913. m. $34.95. Elizabeth C. Baker. Art in America, Inc., 850 Third Ave., New York, NY 10022. Subs. to: 542 Pacific Ave., Marion, OH 43302. Illus., adv. Circ: 50,000. Vol. ends: Dec. Microform: B&H, MIM, UMI.
Indexed: ArtI, RG. *Bk. rev:* 3, 300–400 words, signed. *Aud:* Hs.

A glossy, rather large format magazine that covers contemporary art through exhibition reviews, interviews with artists, and relatively long and thoughtful articles on individual artists and movements. As well, leading art historians publish herein articles of high caliber that come off well because of the lavish number of color plates *Art in America* always provides. Coverage is certainly not limited to American art, nor to art events that take place in America, as the title might seem to imply.

Artes de Mexico. See Latin America, Latino (U.S.)/For the Student: Latin America Section.

Artist's Magazine. 1984. m. $21. Michael Ward. F & W Publns., Inc., 9933 Alliance Rd., Cincinnati, OH 45242. Subs. to: Artist's Magazine, P.O. Box 1999, Marion, OH 43305. Illus., adv. Circ: 121,907.
Bk. rev: 4–6, 200–500 words. *Aud:* Hs.

Basically a "how-to" journal for painters who work in relatively traditional modes, *Artist's Magazine* contains many articles on techniques and materials, plus sections on business problems artists face and on places for artists to sell their works. Cartoonists are also considered. Books reviewed tend to be technical. Of interest largely to students who paint old-fashioned, representational pictures or draw cartoons, but there are a lot of them.

ARTnews. 1902. 10/yr. $25.95. Milton Esterow. ARTnews Assocs., 5 W. 37th St., New York, NY 10018. Subs. to: ARTnews Subscription Service, P.O. Box 969, Farmingdale, NY 11737. Illus., adv. Circ: 75,000. Vol. ends: Dec. Microform: B&H, MIM, UMI. Reprints: UMI.
Indexed: ArtI, RG. *Bk. rev:* 3, 350–500 words, signed. *Aud:* Hs.

If one had to choose the one journal that gives the best coverage of the contemporary art world in a journalistic sense, this would be it. Some of the articles are simply billboard journalism for current gallery shows, but even these tend to be long and interesting. The interviews with artists often produce copy of more than passing interest. New York is the center of this magazine's world, but reports from other centers are also included. *ARTnews* deserves special praise for a long piece of investigative journalism in the December 1984 issue, which proved that the government of Austria had not been exactly assiduous in its efforts to return works of art looted by the Nazis from Austrian Jews. As a result of the article, the policies of the Austrian government are changing. This is a magazine that most libraries will want.

Callaloo: a tri-annual journal of Afro-American and African arts and letters. See Afro-American/For the Student Section.

FMR. 1984. m. $60. Franco Maria Ricci S.p.A., Via Corso del Duca 8, 20122 Milan, Italy. Subs. to: 6969 W. Grand River Ave., Lansing, MI 48906. Illus., adv.
Aud: Hs.

A joy to browse, *FMR* may well live up to its claim to be "the most beautiful magazine in the world." Indeed, its sumptuous color reproductions of works of art almost rival the originals. Set off against black backgrounds, to make their colors glow even more intensely, these reproductions provide insights into the work of art and the quality of the painting technique that one usually has to visit the original in some far-off museum to acquire. If these reproductions do not make a reader enthusiastic about art, nothing will. In comparison, the text sometimes seems a bit lightweight, if always clearly written and easy to understand. Art historical articles range from the Renaissance to the nineteenth century, and also cover tribal arts. Illustrations and art history are supported by other essays that contain historical documents and analyses of historical periods. There are also related literary pieces by the likes of the late Jorge Luis Borges. The editorial board reads like a who's who of writers and art historians.

The International Review of African American Art (Continues *Black Art: an international quarterly*). q. $18. Samella Lewis. The Museum of African Amer. Art, 2617 Lincoln Blvd., No. 207, Santa Monica, CA 90405. Illus., adv. Circ: 7,000. Sample.
Indexed: (as *Black Art*) ArtI, INeg. *Aud:* Hs.

A beautifully illustrated journal that concentrates on contemporary Black artists. Interviews with artists and important biographical information are included. Most articles show the artists at work or photographed with their work. The issues examined concentrated on sculpture, and articles ranged from conventional in content to the most avant-garde and challenging. Some poetry is also included. Care is commendably taken to put the illustrations with the appropriate text. This heavily illustrated magazine, which celebrates the talents and contributions of Black artists to the art of the contemporary world, is an important addition to any library. It is certainly essential for an understanding of contemporary Black culture.

National Stampagraphic. 1982. q. $12. Melody Hope Stein, 1952 Everett St., North Valley Stream, NY 11580. Illus., adv. Circ: 3,500–4,000.
Aud: Hs.

Devoted entirely to stamp art, this is more of a trade journal than a vehicle for criticism, and it would probably be most useful in an art school library. In the context of high school libraries, however, it could provide a lot of fun.

ARCHITECTURE

The changes in architecture are being reflected in the changes in the professional magazines. The importance of illustrations is shown in the number of line drawings and black-and-white and color photographs in almost every title. Many states and major American architectural schools are producing publications that are necessary in regional and architectural collections.

Architectural Record. 1891. m. $35. McGraw-Hill, Inc., 1221 Ave. of the Americas, New York, NY 10020. Illus., index, adv. Circ: 76,000. Microform: UMI.

Indexed: ArtI, RG. *Bk. rev:* 1–6, 200–1,000 words. *Aud:* Hs.

Along with *Progressive Architecture*, one of the architectural magazines found in most American libraries. The *Record* is appropriate for students interested in architecture and engineering. Each issue's major articles deal with a single building type. Also included are industry news and articles on office practice, marketing information, design awards, and new advances in technology and products. About two-thirds of each issue consists of advertisements, but these do not get in the way. There are two additional issues each year—one in mid-April, "Record Houses," and another in mid-September.

Historic Preservation. 1949. bi-m. Membership, $25. Thomas J. Colin. Natl. Trust for Historic Preservation, 1785 Massachusetts Ave. N.W., Washington, DC 20036. Illus., adv. Circ: 125,000. Microform: UMI.

Indexed: ArtI. *Aud:* Hs.

The six well-illustrated articles per issue are of interest to those in architecture and history and cover preservation and restoration of historic landmarks and natural sites. Topics include individual projects of historic districts, structures, monuments, and sites; materials and methods of preservation and restoration; and related fields such as preservation of documents.

Progressive Architecture. 1920. m. $45 (Architects and allied professionals, $28). John Morris Dixon. Reinhold Publg., 600 Summer St., P.O. Box 1361, Stamford, CT 06904. Illus., adv. Circ: 73,000.

Indexed: ArtI. *Bk. rev:* 1, 700–1,000 words, signed. *Aud:* Hs.

As one of the major architectural magazines, this should be considered as one of the first purchases in this field. It encompasses the international scene with emphasis on the United States. It is written for the professionals in architecture and related fields, meaning that articles are at a fairly high level. All aspects are covered with two distinct sections per issue, one of design and one of building technology. Major subjects covered include architectural design, interior design, technical areas, and general news of the profession. The importance of products to architecture is reflected in the amount of advertising in each issue—about half. Recommended.

ART MUSEUM PUBLICATIONS

Most U.S. art museums publish bulletins in which their current special exhibitions and objects in their collections are discussed. These articles are often scholarly and can make important contributions to the field. While the format of the publications may vary, the kinds of subjects covered tend to be quite similar. Most libraries will want to have the bulletins put out by the museums in their areas.

Art Institute of Chicago, Museum Studies. 1966. s-a. $25 (Members, $12). Susan F. Rossen. Univ. of Chicago Press, Journals Div., 5801 S. Ellis Ave., Chicago, IL 60603. Illus., index.

Indexed: ArtI. *Aud:* Hs.

Bulletin of the Museum of Fine Arts, Boston. 1903. a. $3. Museum of Fine Arts, Boston, MA 02115. Illus. Microform: UMI.

Indexed: ArtI. *Aud:* Hs.

Cleveland Museum of Art Bulletin. 1914. m. (Sept.–June). $10 (Members, $8). Merald E. Wrolstad. Cleveland Museum of Art, 11150 East Blvd., Cleveland, OH 44106. Illus., index. Circ: 5,000. Microform: UMI. Reprint: UMI.

Indexed: ArtI. *Aud:* Hs.

Detroit Institute of Arts. Bulletin. 1919. q. $6. June Taboroff. Detroit Inst. of Arts, 5200 Woodward Ave., Detroit, MI 48202. Illus. Circ: 7,000. Microform: UMI.

Indexed: ArtI. *Aud:* Hs.

Metropolitan Museum of Art. Bulletin. 1942. q. $18. Joan Holt. Metropolitan Museum of Art, Fifth Ave. and 82nd St., New York, NY 10028. Illus., index. Circ: 95,000. Microform: UMI. Reprint: UMI.

Indexed: ArtI. *Aud:* Hs.

Philadelphia Museum of Art. Bulletin. 1903. q. $6. Howard Batchelor. Philadelphia Museum of Art, Box 7646, Philadelphia, PA 19101. Illus. Circ: 17,000.

Indexed: ArtI. *Aud:* Hs.

Vanguard. 1972. 9/yr. $15. Russell Kezierte. Vancouver Art Gallery Assn., 750 Hornby St., Vancouver, B.C. V62 2H7, Canada. Illus., adv. Circ: 10,000.

Aud: Hs.

Walters Art Gallery. Bulletin. 1948. bi-m. $4/2 yrs. Carol Strohecker. Walters Art Gallery, 600 N. Charles St., Baltimore, MD 21201. Illus. Circ: 7,000.

Indexed: ArtI. *Aud:* Hs.

For the Professional

American Journal of Art Therapy. 1961. q. $25. Elinor Ulman, P.O. Box 4981, Washington, DC 20008. Illus. Circ: 2,500. Microform: UMI.

Indexed: EdI. *Bk. rev:* 2–3, 1,000 words, signed. *Aud:* Pr.

The title is explanatory of content. Most of the material may be employed by educators at almost any level. The articles stress the practical, emphasizing the actual experience or experiments of the scholarly authors. In addition to the case studies and articles, there is news about different programs, research activities, individuals, new publications, and the like. Anyone concerned with the use of art for therapy, no matter what age group or level, will have this high on the list of required reading. (P.S.B.)

Art & Craft. 1936. m. $40. Scholastic Publns., 141 Drury Lane, London WC2B STG, England. Illus., adv. Circ: 19,000. Microform: UMI.

Bk. rev: Notes, signed. *Aud:* Pr.

Published in England, here is a magazine that is devoted almost completely to various projects that can be mastered by young people in elementary and junior high schools. The instructions are as explicit as the illustrations are clear, and almost all of the ideas may be translated into American craft. Each issue tends to stress a particular theme or topic, usually in relation to the craft or material. This is a useful supplement for the more widely focused *Arts & Activities*. (P.S.B.)

Art Education. 1948. bi-m. Membership (Nonmembers, $50). Daniel Cannon. Natl. Art Education Assn., 1916 Association Dr., Reston, VA 22091. Illus., adv. Circ: 10,500. Vol. ends: Dec. Refereed. Microform: UMI.

Indexed: EdI. *Aud:* Pr.

Here the teaching of art is covered from elementary school through the university. The reader is the professional teacher of art and a member of the sponsoring organization. While the material hardly sparkles, it is at least dead center on the topic, and many consider this a first place to turn to learn about the latest in art education, particularly in terms of policy. The primary benefit, however, is the focus on practical classroom activities that help to make art come alive for the students. (P.S.B.)

Arts & Activities. 1937. m. $15. Leven Leatherbury. Pubs. Development Corp., 591 Camino de la Reina, Suite 200, San Diego, CA 92108. Illus., adv. Circ: 22,000. Microform: B&H, UMI.

Indexed: EdI. *Bk. rev:* 5–7, 100 words, signed. *Aud:* Pr.

One of the major contributions of this well-known art education magazine is its superior effort to orient general, nonart teachers in the subject. It assumes that many readers lack a professional art education, and with that in mind it offers articles, features, and news that keep the new teacher advised of developments in the field. At the same time there are practical tips—from kindergarten through high school—for the experienced and trained art teacher. There are useful, if short, reviews of books, audiovisual materials, and other items that assist in bringing the art class to life. In addition, the format and presentation are as lively as those of any magazine in this area. A first choice. (P.S.B.)

Design for Arts in Education (Formerly: *Design*). 1899. bi-m. $32 (Individuals, $20). Heldref Publns., 4000 Albemarle St. N.W., Washington, DC 20016. Illus., adv. Circ: 3,000. Microform: B&H, UMI.

Indexed: ArtI, RG. *Aud:* Pr.

Edited for those who teach the arts (music to fine arts) in secondary grades, the 45 to 50 pages include 10 to 14 articles, primarily by educators and professors of education. The authors meet the problems of funding, curriculum, training of teachers, justification of programs, innovative methods of bringing the arts to students, and others. From the issues examined, there seems to be a general interest in all arts and aspects of art education. The journal is free of advertisements. (P.S.B.)

Illustrator. 1916. s-a. (4 nos.) $4. Art Instruction Schools, 500 S. Fourth St., Minneapolis, MN 55415. Illus., adv. Circ: 70,000.

Bk. rev: 4–5, 100 words, signed. *Aud:* Pr.

By way of an advertising tabloid for the Art Instruction Schools, this serves a useful purpose for others and is well worth the modest price. There is practical advice on illustrating that can be appreciated and used by high school students and interested adults. Successful illustrators give tips on how it is done. Although a trifle too optimistic and cheery for some, the advice seems solid enough. (P.S.B.)

Museum Magazine. 1980. bi-m. $15. David Patterson. Museum Magazine Assocs., 720 White Plains Rd., Scarsdale, NY 10583. Subs. to: Museum Circulation Services, P.O. Box 1300, Bergenfield, NJ 07621. Illus., adv. Circ: 20,000. Microform: UMI.

Bk. rev: 4–7, 300–500 words, signed. *Aud:* Pr.

Well-illustrated with good color plates, this journal contains articles not just on art museums but also on museums of science, natural history, and glass. It literally ranges from aquaria to zeppelins. Helpful to teachers planning field trips.

School Arts. 1901. m. $15. David Baker. Davis Publns., Inc., 50 Portland St., Worcester, MA 01608. Illus., index, adv. Circ: 23,000. Microform: B&H, UMI.

Indexed: Acs, EdI, MRD. *Bk. rev:* Notes, signed. *Aud:* Pr.

Teachers of art and arts and crafts from elementary through high school turn to this regularly. The focus of the magazine is on ideas that the teacher may use to assist in classroom activity. There is a particular emphasis on art education and less on crafts. Of particular value is the up-to-date information on new techniques, new products, and educational tips. There are sometimes detailed reports on approaches to art education at various levels. Although this has undergone several improvements, it is not quite as lively as *Arts & Activities*. At the same time, where a school library takes one, the other should be included as well. They tend to complement one another, and there is little repetition. (P.S.B.)

ASIA

For the Student: General; Asian American; China; Japan/ For the Professional

Barbara Grossman, Senior Research Analyst, New York State Comptroller's Office, Albany, NY 12222, and free-lance writer on Asian affairs

Daniel Tsang, Co-coordinator, ALA/SRRT Task Force on Alternatives in Print, P.O. Box 29627, Philadelphia, PA 19144 (Asian American subsection)

Kathleen A. Nagy, Documents Dept., Kent State University Libraries, Kent, OH 44242 (China subsection)

Japan subsection with the assistance of David Wemple, free-lance writer and librarian, Albany, NY.

Introduction

Those in the United States who are of European heritage may discount the importance of Asia in the world today. Yet the continent of Asia is the home of half the people in the world, the place of origin of all the major religions, and the region whose economies provide both a vast market and a growing threat to our own economy.

It is both important and an adventure to learn of the histories, languages, political events, foods, and customs of the many and diverse countries and cultures of Asia. Where possible, I have tried to suggest a spectrum of publications that cover many aspects of life in one or more Asian countries. For those who want a general sense of life in Asia, but lack the time to read a number of journals or magazines, *Asiaweek* is the best.

Basic Periodicals

GENERAL. Hs: *Asiaweek.*

ASIAN AMERICAN. Hs: *Bridge.*

CHINA. Hs: *China Pictorial, Vista.*

JAPAN. Hs: *Japan Pictorial.*

Basic Abstracts and Indexes

Public Affairs Information Service.

For the Student

GENERAL

Asian Culture. 1972. q. $12. Taichi Sasaoka. The Asian Cultural Centre for UNESCO, 6 Fukuromachi, Shinjuku-ku, Tokyo 162, Japan. Illus. Circ: 2,000.
Aud: Hs.

Informed, readable treatment of art, literature, food, religion, and other aspects of Oriental life by Asia experts and Asian scholars. Each issue focuses on a single aspect of Asian culture: ancient civilizations, children's games, marriage customs, women in Asian villages, eating habits, agrarian festivals, and so forth. Accompanying drawings, photographs, and rubbings charm and illustrate.

Asian Music. 1968. s-a. $20 (Individuals, $15). Ed. bd. Soc. for Asian Music, Hagop Kevorhian Center, New York Univ., 50 Washington Sq. S., New York, NY 10012. Illus. Circ: 500.
Indexed: CurrCont. *Bk. rev:* 1–2, 500–1,000 words, signed. *Aud:* Hs.

Self-described as a journal of the performing arts of Asia, and its articles do discuss music and some contain musical scores and discographies as well as bibliographies. Beyond that, though, *Asian Music* is in some ways a journal of anthropology, evaluating the interrelationships between music and the history and culture of people—from Japanese immigrants and their music in Brazil to the effects of orientalism on the Beatles. Of interest to a diverse audience.

Asian Theatre Journal. 1984. s-a. $20 (Individuals, $10). James R. Brandon. Asian Theatre Program, Dept. of Drama and Theatre, Univ. of Hawaii, Honolulu, HI 96822. Illus. Circ: 600. Vol. ends: Fall.
Bk. rev: 3–5, 1,000–1,500 words. *Aud:* Hs.

What *Asian Music* is to the music of Asia, *Asian Theatre Journal* is to its dramatic arts—Japanese Nō and Kabuki, revolutionary theater in North Korea, Javanese shadow plays, Chinese opera, and much more—discussing each as an art and evaluating its cultural context. Articles are scholarly, but unusually readable. Many contain striking photographs, some in color. Book reviews span as wide a range of books on Asian theater as the feature articles and reports. Audiovisuals as well as books are reviewed. A truly interesting journal for those interested in the theater and Asia in general.

Asiaweek. 1975. w. $75. Michael O'Neill. Asiaweek, Ltd., Tappan Bldg., 22 Westlands Rd., Quarry Bay, Hong Kong. Illus., adv.
Aud: Hs.

Asiaweek is the *Time* or *Newsweek* of Asia. Each week, the staff of correspondents from most parts of the Orient contribute updates on the news and more in-depth analyses of politics, economics, social trends, and art and entertainment in Asia. Editorials and literary reviews reflect Asian points of view, presented in a way that even general readers should find interesting. Photographs are numerous and of good quality. This magazine is a valuable resource for educational institutions, social scientists, and those interested in a greater knowledge of Eastern culture.

Illustrated Weekly of India. 1880. w. Rs.980. K. C. Khanna. Bennett, Coleman & Co., Ltd., Times of India Bldg., Dr. Dadabhai Naoroji Rd., Bombay 400001, India. Subs. to: India Publns., Ltd., 307 Fifth Ave., New York, NY 10016. Illus., adv. Circ: 100,000. Microform: Pub.
Indexed: GInd. *Aud:* Hs.

An oversized imitation of *Life*, this has some 80 newsprint pages devoted to popular events and personalities in India and Asia. Written for a wide audience, the magazine opens with four or five features on politics, economics, news, and people. There is usually an overview piece on some topic of current interest, followed by the normal range of features: film reviews, book reviews, and various departments. The editorial stance is mildly conservative, although most of the coverage is objective, if sometimes a bit too jolly. The illustrations are primarily in black and white, but some less-than-satisfactory color is used as well. The popular treatment makes this a basic title for any high school library seeking an overview of India and parts of Asia.

Korean Newsreview. 1972. w. $75. Kim Seong-jin. Intl. Cultural Soc. of Korea, 34–5, 3-ga, Namsan-dong, Chung-gu, Seoul, Rep. of Korea. Illus. Circ: 20,000.
Aud: Hs.

The magazine to read to learn the most about day-to-day life in South Korea. *Korean Newsreview* is a compilation of news, editorials, and feature articles from Korean daily newspapers, chiefly *The Korean Herald*, one of the two English-language newspapers published there. Relations with North Korea, nontechnical business and economic news, culture, sports, the latest on the 1988 Olympics, the arts, and even spectacular crimes are covered by the magazine—

virtually everything but domestic politics. As all publications in Korea are subject to government "review," accounts of student demonstrations and labor strikes are one-sided, but this does not detract greatly from the *Newsreview*'s value.

ASIAN AMERICAN

Despite media portrayals of Asian Americans as a "model minority," most of the recent immigrants from Asia have had to confront racism, violence, and discrimination in the United States. With movies like *Year of the Dragon* and *Rambo* perpetuating racist images of Asian Americans, a more accurate and realistic picture of one of America's newest immigrant groups is now more needed than ever. The Asian American press is the only place you will find such a picture. This is where we are able to cut through our invisibility in a majority culture, as we begin to build a new life and develop our own space within this society.

Bridge: Asian American perspectives. 1971. q. $15 (Individuals, $10). Diane Mark. Asian Cine Vision, Inc., 32 E. Broadway, New York, NY 10002. Illus., adv. Circ: 2,500. Microform: UMI.
Aud: Hs.

The only Asian American cultural magazine, *Bridge* was for many years the only national magazine of the Asian American movement. Recent issues have been thematic, focusing on areas not covered anywhere else, such as Asian America on stage and film. Published by Asian Cine Vision, which sponsors the annual Asian American film festival from coast to coast, it is highly recommended.

East Wind: politics and culture of Asians in the U.S. 1982. s-a. $12 (Individuals, $8; students, $6). Ed. bd. Getting Together Publns., Inc., P.O. Box 26229, San Francisco, CA 94126. Illus., adv.
Bk. rev: 2, 1,000 words, signed. *Aud:* Hs.

An exciting, vibrant journal documenting culture and politics in the Asian American movement. Special issues have focused on Asian women and on immigration. The entire spectrum of Asian Americans is represented on these pages. Highly recommended.

CHINA

China has had the longest continuous national identity of any country in the world. It has known eras of great power and times of weakness and chaos. The periodicals selected here have been chosen to represent varied historical, political, and cultural periods and points of view. An attempt was made by the compiler to remain objective in choosing titles that have merit for their content, regardless of the editors' political points of view. In some instances, propaganda material issued by the government represents the best material available.

Beijing Review (Formerly: *Peking Review*). 1958. w. $18. Wang Xi. Beijing Review, 24 Baiwanzhuang Rd., Beijing, People's Rep. of China. Illus., index. Vol. ends: No. 52. Microform: B&H, MIM.
Bk. rev: 2–4, 100 words. *Aud:* Hs.

The most widely circulated official English-language publication of the People's Republic of China. Presenting events in China from the Chinese government's viewpoint makes this periodical a must in any Chinese periodical collection. Full-text translations of many official documents and laws will provide the researcher with valuable information on China's official policy. In addition, discussions of international situations and the official Chinese stance on these foreign affairs will provide a great deal of insight into China's position on world affairs. Excerpts of press editorials and commentaries are frequently featured. This publication should form a part of any core collection.

China Now (Formerly: *SACU News*). 1965. bi-m. £12. Larry Jagan. Soc. for Anglo-Chinese Understanding, 152 Camden High St., London NW1, England. Illus., index, adv. Circ: 3,400.
Bk. rev: 2–4. *Aud:* Hs.

The Society for Anglo-Chinese Understanding was founded in 1965 to "promote understanding and friendship" between the British and Chinese. Its aims are to encourage free discussion on a broad spectrum of topics. Subjects covered include any and all aspects of the life and work of the Chinese people. Sources include firsthand observations, reprints of articles, book reviews, and interviews with people who have recently visited China. Valuable for a general understanding of the people and culture of China.

China Pictorial. 1951. m. $15. China Pictorial, Huayuancun, Beijing 28, People's Rep. of China. Illus., index, adv. Microform: MIM.
Aud: Ejh, Hs.

Noted primarily for its illustrations, this journal consists of large colorful photographs and minimal text. Produced by the government of the People's Republic of China for foreign consumption, it is published in English and 18 other foreign languages. The subjects covered are popular topics of interest for a general audience. Focus is on the scenery of China, the life of the people, and works of art. It will give younger audiences an introduction to China. See also *China Reconstructs*.

China Reconstructs. 1952. m. $10. China Welfare Inst., Wai Wen Bldg., Beijing 37, People's Rep. of China. U.S. dist: China Books and Periodicals, Inc., 2929 24th St., San Francisco, CA 94110. Illus., adv. Microform: MIM.
Aud: Ejh, Hs.

One of the popular genre of magazines issued by the People's Republic of China to show China's progress since the revolution. Lavishly illustrated, its articles have political overtones and tend to be short and simplistic. A wide variety of popular subjects are covered, including culture, art, and sports. Although similar in intent to *China Pictorial*, this publication contains fewer pictures and more written articles. It also includes articles written by non-Chinese.

China Sports. $10. m. Ed. bd. China Sports, 8 Tiyuguan Rd., Beijing, People's Rep. of China. Illus.
Aud: Ejh, Hs.

Issued by the government of the People's Republic of China, it is similar in format to *China Pictorial.* The entire magazine is devoted to sports in China or to Chinese in sports. Subject matter ranges from the Olympic games to international kite-flying meetings in China.

Free China Review. 1951. m. $15. King-Yuh Chang. Kwang Hwa Publg. Co., 3–1, Chung Hsio E. Rd. Sec. 1, Taipei, Taiwan, Rep. of China. U.S. subs. to: Chinese Information Service, 159 Lexington Ave., New York, NY 10016. Illus. Circ: 10,000. Microform: UMI.
Indexed: PAIS. *Aud:* Hs.

Current life in Taiwan is the main theme of this publication. Tourism, television programs, cinema, and industry are some of the many topics touched upon. The antiquities of China, ancient and modern artists, and the rich heritage of China are presented in beautiful color illustrations and interesting articles. Included is a chronology of events for the preceding month with news relating to culture, science, and education in Taiwan. Articles on the People's Republic of China are also included. Although a vehicle for Taiwan anti-Communist propaganda, the majority of the magazine stresses current life in Taiwan and historical life and art from China. Some material of value about both countries can be found here.

Vista. 1964. bi-m. Ed. bd. China Publg. Co., P.O. Box 337, Taipei, Taiwan, Rep. of China. U.S. subs. to: Chinese Information Service, 159 Lexington Ave., New York, NY 10016. Illus., index, adv. Circ: 29,500.
Aud: Ejh, Hs.

This is the Republic of China's counterpart to *China Reconstructs.* It contains short articles publicizing the achievements of Taiwan. The writing style is simple and straightforward, with primary emphasis on the color illustrations.

Women of China. 1956. m. $10. Women of China, 50 Deng Shi kou, Beijing, People's Rep. of China. Illus., adv. Vol. ends: Dec.
Aud: Hs.

As the title indicates, this magazine is for and about women. In addition to typical articles on children and child raising, there are stories on current women's roles in the People's Republic of China and biographical sketches of who played a part in the Revolution. Explanation of laws that have been enacted to aid women and any other events that might be of interest or importance to women are included. Fictional short stories are often printed.

JAPAN

Japan Pictorial. 1978. q. $22. Ed. bd. Japan Graphic, Inc., Palaceside Bldg., 1–1, Hitotsubashi l-chome, Chiyoda-ku, Tokyo 100, Japan. Illus., adv.
Aud: Ejh, Hs.

A decade or so ago, few people in the United States were particularly interested in Japan. Now, that country's importance in world economic affairs and its dominance of high-tech industries has triggered a fascination with Japan that all but eclipses the rest of Asia. *Japan Pictorial* is likely to satisfy those with an interest in Japanese culture since it is unencumbered by articles on economics and business. Although the textual parts are somewhat superficial, the oversized, effusive features on Kabuki and on Japanese food, baseball, television, and cities will please the Nipponophile. A general-interest, rather than academic, approach that is suitable for school libraries. (B.G.)

Japan Quarterly. 1954. q. $20. Yoshio Aoki. Asahi Shimbun Publg. Co., 5-3-2 Tsukiji, Chuo-ku, Tokyo 104, Japan. Illus., index, adv. Microform: UMI.
Indexed: IntPolSc, PAIS. *Bk. rev:* Essays and notes, signed. *Aud:* Hs.

Although a quarterly, this is more of a semipopular effort to keep English-speaking people current with trends in Japanese culture. The tone is one of gentle propaganda (the magazine is published by Japan's largest daily newspaper). It does, however, afford a reasonably accurate picture of noncontroversial Japanese events. There are usually five or six articles on "trends and topics," followed by reports on people in the spotlight and briefer pieces on art and literature. Of particular value to librarians: "Recent Publications on Japan," a subject bibliography of books as well as newspapers and magazine articles. In addition, there may be translations of Japanese literature.

For the Professional

Focus on Asian Studies. 1963. 3/yr. $5. Susan L. Rhodes. The Asia Soc., 725 Park Ave., New York, NY 10021. Illus. Circ: 2,000. Vol. ends: Spring.
Bk. rev: 1–3, 250–1,000 words, signed. *Aud:* Pr.

An excellent publication of the nonprofit Asia Society for grade school teachers, to help them learn more about Asia and impart that knowledge to their students. In addition to regular features—book reviews, teaching aids and a calendar of Asian cultural events in the United States— each issue contains several articles revolving around a single aspect of Asian life, e.g., modern leaders, crafts, literature. Articles are written in language simple enough for junior high and high school students to understand, but are sophisticated enough for their adult teachers and other interested readers.

ASTROLOGY AND PARAPSYCHOLOGY

For the Student

Eleanor M. Clarke, Librarian, Ocean County Library, 101 Washington St., Toms River, NJ 08753

Rhea A. White, Reference Dept., East Meadow Public Library, Front St. & East Meadow Ave., East Meadow, NY 11554

Introduction

Astrology and astronomy share a common origin in human beings' first observations of the sky. There they sought the answer to the regulation of the functions of everyday life as well as the source of the supernatural power they felt around them. The unity of those concerns was lost with the rise of the scientific method, the validity of only verifiable data in the three-dimensional world. This method applied to the skies became astronomy, while astrology developed as an occult and often unacceptable body of knowledge. Now, perhaps, in the new age, these two are once again becoming one as the theory of relativity leads us beyond the third dimension to a sense of the unity of all existing matter, energy, and dimensions. This new framework of the scientific world closely parallels astrology's assumption of the unity of the universe and the close relationship and interaction of all its aspects.

The parapsychological journal literature is extensive, considering the number of active persons in this small field. (The Parapsychological Association, formed in 1958, the international professional society of parapsychology, averages 300 members. There are approximately 200 additional persons worldwide with an active interest in some aspect of parapsychology as evidenced by at least occasional publication in book or journal article form. Some of these persons are members of the psychical research societies, which are usually national in scope, and each one has additional members who are interested in the subject, but not actively involved.) Most journals offer research reports. Listed here is a selection of those appropriate for high school readers.

Basic Periodicals

Hs: *American Astrology.*

For the Student

American Astrology. 1933. m. $17.98. Kenneth Irving & Lee Chapman. Astrology, Inc., 475 Park Ave. S., New York, NY 10016. Illus., adv. Circ: 185,000. Microform: UMI.

Aud: Hs.

Founded in 1933 by Paul G. Clancy, this granddaddy of astrology magazines is straight down the middle of the road. It considers factors that "real" astrologers deem important: time changes, mathematical principles, houses, diurnal motion of the planets, fixed stars, and so on. As a result it is far better than average. However, its monthly advice column is based on solar charts (the sun is placed in the first house), thus placing it firmly in the popular category. The table of contents lists a unit on every conceivable topic usually covered in magazines of this type. The single most valuable element is "Your Daily Hourly Guide," with commentary. A daily ephemeris is missing, however, thus reducing the appeal and usefulness of the publication. On the other hand, the number and scope of the articles make this the best of the popular magazines. (E.C.)

Horoscope. 1935. m. $12.50. Julia A. Wagner. Dell Publg. Co., Inc., One Dag Hammarskjold Plaza, 245 E. 47th St., New York, NY 10017. Illus., adv. Circ: 225,000. Vol. ends: Dec. Microform: UMI.

Bk. rev: Various number, length, signed. *Aud:* Hs.

All the basics are featured here as standard items: nation and world, business trends, weather, comprehensive signed book reviews, "Astro-Word Puzzle," "Safety First," lucky numbers, monthly guidance for each sign, yearly forecast for the birthday folks, and much more along these lines. Best of all, at the back of each issue is a month's ephemeris with planetary latitudes and declinations, followed by an elaborate chart detailing daily aspects, plus an analysis by time zone of culminating aspects. That may sound meaningless to the uninitiated, but it can be very worthwhile. The section "Children of the Zodiac," which analyzes the star patterns in the sky for the specific year and season, may make *Horoscope* popular with pregnant astrology buffs. A unique department is "Metroscope," a sketch of a city or town linked to an analysis of its horoscope. Above-average popular astrology magazine. (E.C.)

Journal of Religion and Psychical Research. 1978. q. $8. Mary Carman Rose. Academy of Religion and Psychical Research, c/o Spiritual Frontiers Fellowship, 10819 Winner Rd., Independence, MO 64052. Index. Circ: 400. Sample. Vol. ends: Oct.

Indexed: PAI. *Bk. rev:* 4, 3 pages, signed. *Aud:* Hs.

The Academy of Religion and Psychical Research is composed of members of the Spiritual Frontiers Fellowship, who are interested in scholarly research into parapsychology and religion. The *Journal of Religion and Psychical Research* is the Academy's journal, which was established as a vehicle and forum for dialogue and exchange of ideas among Academy members and others in regard to the interface between religion and psychical research. Each issue contains an average of five articles approximately eight pages in length, abstracts of research, reports of conferences and symposia, an editorial, news, comments, and correspondence. Many of the articles are of general interest, and the format is scholarly but nontechnical. (R.A.W.)

Parapsychology Review (Formerly: *The Newsletter of the Parapsychology Foundation*). 1970. bi-m. $9. Betty Shapin. Parapsychology Foundation, 228 E. 71st St., New York, NY 10021. Index. Circ: 1,500. Sample. Vol. ends: Nov/Dec.

Indexed: PAI. *Bk. rev:* 2, 3 pages, signed. *Aud:* Hs.

The Parapsychology Foundation is a nonprofit educational organization formed to support impartial scientific inquiry into the total nature and working of the mind and to make available the results of such inquiry. The Foundation provides grants for parapsychological research and education, an activity that puts it in contact with active parapsychologists and parapsychological centers throughout the world. Information on these persons and groups and their activities are reported in *Parapsychology Review.* Each issue also contains two articles, three-to-four pages long, of a general educational nature; two full-length book reviews; and four pages of news items, including information on grants, obituaries, awards, educational opportunities in parapsychology, new journals and organizations, and so on. Some issues contain "Recent Library Acquisitions," an annotated list of books newly acquired by the Eileen J. Garrett Library of the Parapsychology Foundation. *Parapsychology Review* is the best source of current information about the field of parapsychology, and its articles and reviews are substantial yet not overly technical. (R.A.W.)

Theta: the journal of the Psychical Research Foundation. 1963. q. $10. W. G. Roll & Rhea A. White. Psychical Research Foundation, Dept. of Psychology, West Georgia State College, Carrollton, GA 30017. Circ: 550. Sample. Vol. ends: Winter.
Indexed: PAI. *Bk. rev:* 5–6, 500–1,500 words, signed. *Aud:* Hs.

The Psychical Research Foundation, established in 1960, is dedicated to the exploration of the possible continuation of consciousness and personality after death. Emphasis is placed on aspects of the living human personality that may survive, thus PRF research includes studies of expanded states of consciousness, out-of-body and near-death experiences, mediumship, mystical and ecstatic states, meditation, and poltergeist and haunting disturbances. All of these subjects are covered in *Theta*, which not only reports on PRF research but carries theoretical, experimental, historical, biographical articles and reports of case and field studies by scholars in the field. Each issue has two to three articles three to four pages long. Correspondence ("Theta Forum") and news items are occasionally included, as well as reprints of classic articles ("Déjà Vu"). (R.A.W.)

ASTRONOMY

For the Student

See also Atmospheric, Earth, and Marine Sciences; and Aviation and Space Science Sections.

Linda L. Geary, Reference Librarian, Akron City Hospital Library, Akron, OH 44309

Introduction

Since the time of Galileo, few periods have seen astronomers on the verge of so many discoveries as the present. Sophisticated computer applications along with space exploration have put within the astronomer's grasp an understanding of the universe never before possible. One has only to think of Voyager, the space shuttle missions, satellite-based telescopes, or large radio antenna arrays to imagine the wonders of the new frontiers that lie ahead. These technologies enable astronomers to reach greater distances with more clarity than ever before, while computers analyze the new data at ever-faster speeds.

Professionals in the field have been aided by the contributions and patience of numerous amateurs whose interests range from variable stars to telescope making. The science has also gained an armchair following with the airing of Carl Sagan's "Cosmos" and the continuing sagas of *Star Wars* and "Star Trek."

The periodicals contained in this section are among the best in the field and will appeal to a variety of interests.

Basic Periodicals

Ejh: *Griffith Observer;* Hs: *Astronomy, Griffith Observer, Mercury, Sky and Telescope.*

For the Student

Astronomy. 1973. m. $21. Richard Berry. AstroMedia Corp., 625 E. St. Paul Ave., Milwaukee, WI 53202. Illus., adv. Circ: 135,000. Sample. Vol. ends: No. 12. Microform: B&H, UMI. Reprint: UMI.
Indexed: RG. *Bk. rev:* 3, 1,000–1,500 words, signed. *Aud:* Hs.

This title has the largest circulation in the field. It features well-written, popular articles with numerous high-quality photographs and illustrations. Each issue is aesthetically pleasing and educational. In addition to stunning photography and illustrations, the contents include a monthly sky almanac and viewing guide; a two-page "star-dome"; tips on how to buy, build, and use astronomical equipment; and observational and photographic techniques. Included also are critical reviews of computer software, astronomical equipment, and audiovisual materials. Two other Astro-Media publications, *Telescope Making* and *Deep Sky*, offer more detailed material for telescope hobbyists and deep sky observers, respectively.

Deep Sky (Formerly: *Deep Sky Monthly*). 1977. q. $10. David J. Eicher. AstroMedia Corp., 625 E. St. Paul Ave., Milwaukee, WI 53202. Illus. Circ: 5,000. Sample. Vol. ends: No. 4.
Bk. rev: 1–3, 900–1,500 words, signed. *Aud:* Hs.

This magazine is devoted to reporting the techniques and results of observing and photographing deep sky objects. The technical level is for skilled amateurs, but contributors are dedicated to serious observation to aid the professional community. There are three or four articles in each issue, in addition to observational tips, maps, drawings, and astrophotography. Reader input is greatly emphasized. Overall, it is an informative publication for amateurs interested specifically in deep sky objects and astrophotography.

Griffith Observer. 1937. m. $8. E. C. Krupp. Griffith Observatory, 2800 E. Observatory Rd., Los Angeles, CA 90027. Illus., index. Circ: 3,000. Sample. Vol. ends: No. 12.
Bk. rev: Occasional. *Aud:* Ejh, Hs.

Published with the intention of stimulating and maintaining an "enduring interest in the physical sciences," this slim magazine is both educational and entertaining. It regularly features three to four articles contributed by Griffith Observatory personnel or outside specialists whose main theme is some aspect of astronomy or the physical sciences as they relate to astronomy. Almost all of the articles are accompanied by good black-and-white illustrations or photographs. The inside back cover features a simplified monthly sky chart and basic observational information. Contributions are consistently lively and written in an informative style without the detail of *Astronomy, Mercury,* or *Sky and Telescope* (see elsewhere in this section). It is especially suitable for a junior high school library physical sciences collection.

Mercury. 1972. bi-m. $21. Andrew Fraknoi. Astronomical Soc. of the Pacific, 1290 24th Ave., San Francisco, CA 94122. Illus., index, adv. Circ: 7,000. Sample. Vol. ends: No. 6. Refereed. Microform: B&H. Reprint: Pub.
Bk. rev: Annual critical bibliography. *Aud:* Hs.

Styled for the general reader, amateur astronomer, and science educator, this title features nontechnical, authoritative articles on topics of current interest and recent advances in the field. Contents include interviews, biographical sketches, interdisciplinary articles, and organization news. Subscribers also receive the Abrams Planetarium's monthly Sky Calendar and Star Map. Particularly strong is the magazine's attention to astronomy education. It includes teaching tips, reading lists, and an annual annotated bibliography of astronomy books published during the preceding year.

Odyssey. 1979. m. $16. Nancy Mack. AstroMedia Corp., 625 E. St. Paul Ave., Milwaukee, WI 53202. Illus., adv. Circ: 90,000. Sample. Vol. ends: No. 12. Microform: B&H, UMI.
Bk. rev: Occasional, 100–200 words. *Aud:* Ejh.

Brilliantly colored from cover to cover, *Odyssey* is a fun-filled educational children's magazine for the 8–12 age group. Each issue contains five to seven excellently written and illustrated articles and regular sections describing basic concepts of astronomy. Topics covered include how to find a constellation, how to count stars, or how to find directions by the sun; stars, pioneer astronomers, and types of galaxies. In addition, the magazine is jam-packed with word games, puzzles, cutout projects, card games, and a continuous space adventure comic strip.

Reflector. 1956. q. Members, $4. Tom Martinez. Astronomical League, P.O. Box 12921, Tucson, AZ 85732. Illus. Circ: 8,800. Sample. Vol. ends: No. 4.
Bk. rev: 1–2, 200–300 words. *Aud:* Hs.

This newsletter provides readers with a digest of amateur astronomy activities across the United States. Each issue carries reports of outstanding projects and events conducted by member groups, announcements of educational and observational opportunities, and consumer services. The Astronomical League, a national federation of amateur astronomy societies, sponsors the annual national amateur astronomy convention and acts as a central link of communication between the affiliated societies.

Sky and Telescope. 1941. m. $20. Leif J. Robinson. Sky Publishing Corp., 49 Bay State Rd., Cambridge, MA 02238. Illus, index, adv. Circ: 75,000. Sample. Vol. ends: June & Dec. Microform: B&H, UMI.
Indexed: RG. *Bk. rev:* 4–5, 350–1,000 words, signed. *Aud:* Hs.

Enjoying a unique reputation for its wide popularity among amateurs and professionals alike, this long-standing magazine features popular and semitechnical articles on all as-

pects of astronomy. In addition to five or six articles, the regular features include shorter news notes, a celestial calendar, a sky chart, and a stargazer's exchange for buying and selling astronomical equipment. Colorful illustrations and photographs make it aesthetically appealing. Although *Sky and Telescope* may share part of its amateur readership with *Astronomy*, it picks up professional appeal with its more mature style and format.

Sky Calendar. 1976. m. $5. Abrams Planetarium, Michigan State Univ., East Lansing, MI 48824.
Aud: Hs.

This is a single 9- by 11-inch sheet. On one side is a chart of the evening skies for the particular month; on the verso, a sky calendar that "provides day-by-day information on stars, planets, and the moon's progress against the constellations." Carefully explained, the charts allow the layperson to find points of interest. This calendar is suitable for all ages and sections of the country. There is an occasional extra sheet on such topics as the conjunction of Jupiter and Saturn. As a reviewer for the *Scientific American* observed, "These pages are a bargain entry into direct observation of the changing order visible in the heavens."

Telescope Making. 1978. q. $12. Richard Berry. AstroMedia Corp., 625 E. St. Paul Ave., Milwaukee, WI 53202. Illus., index, adv. Circ: 2,500. Sample. Vol. ends: Winter. Reprint: Pub.
Aud: Hs.

Advertised as the magazine "for, by, and about telescope makers," this publication provides a friendly forum for the exchange of ideas, tips, and techniques among advanced amateur telescope enthusiasts on an international level. The eight to ten articles in each issue discuss and illustrate all aspects of home-built astronomical equipment from backyard observatories, telescope design, eyepiece testing, mirrors, and mounts to adjustments and abrasives. In addition, a biographical or historical piece concerning noteworthy people, places, events, or types of equipment is often included. A classified product directory appears in every issue to aid readers in locating commercial suppliers. In its completeness of coverage, no other journal compares to *Telescope Making*.

ATMOSPHERIC, EARTH, AND MARINE SCIENCES

For the Student

Ida M. Lewis, Supervisory Librarian, Information Resources Development Branch, National Oceanic and Atmospheric Administration, 6009 Executive Blvd., Rockville, MD 20852

Elizabeth Morrissett, Head Librarian, Montana College of Mineral Science and Technology, Butte, MT 59701

Laurie E. Stackpole, Acting Chief, Library and Information Services Division, National Oceanic and Atmospheric Administration, 6009 Executive Blvd., Rockville, MD 20852

Frances F. Swim, Acting Chief, Library Services Branch, Library and Information Services Division, National Oceanic and At-

mospheric Administration, 6009 Executive Blvd., Rockville, MD 20852

Introduction

The following list suggests some basic journals and related publications in the field of meteorology and climatology appropriate for high school students. Other periodicals tend to be highly technical. The list is by no means exhaustive. The highly technical journals that might be found in advanced research collections are not listed, nor are those publications that are so specific in focus that their appeal is limited. Only English-language publications are described. Librarians should be aware that, in earth sciences, high prices make it essential to watch for quality and suitableness of material.

Basic Periodicals

Ejh: *Sea Frontiers*; Hs: *Earth Science, Geology Today, Maritimes, NOAA, Oceans, Sea Frontiers, Underwater Naturalist, Weatherwise.*

For the Student

American Weather Observer. 1984. m. $20. Steven D. Steinke, 401 Whitney Blvd., Belvidere, IL 61008. Illus., adv. Vol. ends: Dec.
Aud: Ejh, Hs.

Published as a division of the *Belvidere Daily Republican*, this tabloid-size newspaper serves as a regular publication of the Association of American Weather Observers. It includes weather news, weather data from around the country in a comparative format, brief columns on weather folklore, weather history, articles by and about weather observers and chapter news. Although focusing on the amateur observer, it lives up to its description as "the publication for and about the weather enthusiast." Particularly appropriate for schoolchildren and young adults. (L.S.)

Daily Weather Maps, Weekly Series. 1967. w. $60. Supt. of Docs., U.S. Govt. Printing Office, Washington, DC 20402. Circ: 1,700. Microform: Pub.
Aud: Hs.

Published by the Climate Analysis Center of the National Weather Service, NOAA, the charts in this publication continue the publication *Daily Weather Map*, which was an outgrowth of the *Washington Daily Weather Map* first issued as a tissue chart in 1871. The weekly series includes the "Surface Weather Map" (covering the contiguous United States), the "500-Millibar Height Contours Chart" (covering North America), the "Highest and Lowest Temperatures Chart," and the "Precipitation Areas and Amounts Chart." Charts for each day are arranged on a single page. It is issued weekly, for the period Monday through Sunday. Each issue provides a complete explanation of the symbols used on the charts. (L.S.)

Earth Science. 1946. q. $8. Sharon March. Amer. Geological Inst., 4220 King St., Alexandria, VA 22302. Illus., index. Circ: 7,000. Sample: Microform: B&H, MIM, UMI.

Indexed: RG. *Bk. rev:* 12–16, 100–250 words. *Aud:* Ejh, Hs.

Among all of the titles listed here, this is by and large the most popular and the only one that is indexed in *Readers' Guide.* Edited for the individual with an interest in earth sciences—from junior high through almost any age—there is an effort to present sometimes difficult material in an easy-to-understand fashion. The numerous illustrations help considerably. All aspects of earth science and geology are covered. Articles are competent, covering earthquakes, volcanoes, fossils, geological features of various locally interesting sites, and information on crystals and minerals for collectors, with appeal for amateurs, teachers, and hobbyists. Includes news of books, maps, films, and new mineral finds. (E.M.)

Earthquake Information Bulletin. 1969. bi-m. $15. Henry Spall. U.S. Geological Survey, 904 Natl. Center, Reston, VA 22092. Illus. Circ: 8,500. Vol. ends: Nov/Dec.
Aud: Ejh, Hs.

Information for both general and specialized readers, containing lists of earthquakes and data and pictures of both current and historical seismic activity. Suitable for popular collections. (E.M.)

Geology Today. 1985. bi-m. $60. John H. McD. Whitaker. Blackwell Scientific Publns., P.O. Box 88, Oxford, England. Illus., index, adv. Vol. ends: No. 6.
Aud: Hs.

A new journal with short papers, conference reports, field reports, and feature articles on minerals and fossils intended for a popular audience. It is marketed in all continents and has a worldwide coverage of geology news and issues. As one of the few popular journals in the field, it is worth being considered by high schools. (E.M.)

GEOS: a quarterly concerned with the earth's resources. 1974. q. Free in Canada. Jocelyn Marshall. Canada Dept. of Energy, Mines and Resources, Ottawa, Ont., Canada. Illus. Circ: 8,000.
Aud: Hs.

A popular introduction to the mineral resources of Canada for amateurs and students, with good pictures and lively writing. Appropriate for high school collections. (E.M.)

Maritimes. 1957. q. Free. Mary Matzinger. Univ. of Rhode Island, Kingston, RI 02881. Illus. Vol. ends: No. 4.
Aud: Hs.

A general marine science magazine with short, easy-to-read articles, good for high school students to stimulate thinking about career options. Articles, without bibliographies but usually illustrated, are written by faculty and research associates of the School of Oceanography of the University of Rhode Island. A wide variety of topics is covered in each issue. Useful for high school libraries. (I.M.L., F.F.S.)

Mineralogical Record. 1970. bi-m. $25. Wendell E. Wilson, P.O. Box 35565, Tucson, AZ 85740. Illus., index, adv. Circ: 6,200. Vol. ends: No. 6. Refereed. Microform: UMI.
Bk. rev: 3–4, 400 words, signed. *Aud:* Hs.

Wonderful photography makes this magazine a pleasure to look through. Articles are written by both professional geologists and amateur hobbyists. Good articles on localities for mineral hunting fill an important niche. One of the more popular of the periodicals in mineralogy, this comes close to being a general type of magazine for the average high school reader. The style of writing is within the grasp of the average interested reader. There are regular features on everything from collecting to answering reader questions. On occasion, a special issue is given over to a specific topic or geographical area. A useful periodical for high school libraries—at least where there is an interest in the subject. See also *Rocks and Minerals*. (E.M.)

Monthly & Seasonal Weather Outlook (Formerly: *Average Monthly Weather Outlook*). 1946. s-m. $31. Supt. of Docs., U.S. Govt. Printing Office, Washington, DC 20402. Illus. Vol. ends: Dec.

Aud: Ejh, Hs.

This eight-page publication of the Climate Analysis Center, National Weather Service, NOAA, consists primarily of maps summarizing temperature and precipitation information for the month and season (three-month period) immediately preceding publication, and forecasting the temperature and precipitation probabilities during the upcoming 30 days and season. Information includes monthly observed temperature and precipitation for North America and Europe, seasonal observed or predicted temperature and precipitation for the United States, 30-day predictions of temperature and precipitation probabilities for North America and Eurasia, and the predicted pattern of air flow during the next 30 days for the Northern Hemisphere. Tables of seasonal normals for over 100 U.S. locations and of monthly normals for about 150 North American and 50 Eurasian sites provide the user with data for interpreting the maps, which characterize precipitation as light, moderate, or heavy and temperature as warm, near normal, or cold. This publication should be of interest in collections used by schoolchildren for science fair projects dealing with weather. (L.S.)

Nautica. 1984. bi-m. $18 (12 issues). John B. Kittredge. Spinnaker Press, Inc., Pickering Wharf, Salem, MA 01970. Illus., adv. Sample. Vol. ends: Nov/Dec.

Aud: Ejh, Hs.

Nautica is "the first and only magazine available that offers young people, ages 8 and above, a world of nautical and oceanographic content. It is a nonfiction publication striving to motivate and challenge its readers with high interest material chosen from the vast world of the sea." Each issue includes articles on history, adventure, geography, sea life, sports, navigation, science and technology, book reviews, a cartoon, games, and puzzles. The full-color and black-and-white illustrations and photographs on glossy paper are detailed, accurate, and often stunning. The advertisements are few and for related materials of excellent quality. Adults who find this magazine will enjoy it as much as the young people to whom it is directed. (L.K.O.)

NOAA (Formerly: *ESSA*). 1971. s-a. $7. Charles G. Thomas. Office of Public Affairs, Natl. Oceanic and Atmospheric Admin., Washington, DC 20230. Subs. to: Supt. of Docs., U.S. Govt. Printing Office, Washington, DC 20402. Illus. Vol. ends: No. 2.

Aud: Hs.

A well-written magazine concentrating on articles about NOAA programs. Some areas of concern are oceans, atmospheres, weather, fisheries, ocean surveys, and habitat protection. Articles are written for the nonspecialist, and are well illustrated. A first-class periodical for libraries with collections in the oceans and atmosphere, including high school libraries. (I.M.L., F.F.S.)

Oceans. 1969. bi-m. $18. Ed. bd. Oceanic Soc., Membership Services, P.O. Box 10167, Des Moines, IA 50347. Illus., adv. Vol. ends: No. 6. Microform: UMI.

Indexed: RG. *Bk. rev:* 4–5, 150–200 words, signed. *Aud:* Hs.

Official publication of the Oceanic Society, this journal contains many interesting, well-illustrated articles for nonspecialists. Articles cover all aspects of the oceans, including biology, fisheries, technology, sea lore, and more. Authors include scientists and professional writers. First-rate popular magazine about the oceans. (I.M.L., F.F.S.)

Oceanus. 1952. q. $15. Paul R. Ryan. Woods Hole Oceanographic Institution, Woods Hole, MA 02543. Illus., index. Vol. ends: No. 4. Refereed. Microform: UMI.

Aud: Hs.

An international magazine of marine science published by the Woods Hole Oceanographic Institution for all people interested in the oceans. Most articles have short bibliographies and are written by scientists. Many issues have a central theme, such as oceans and climate, marine mammals, sound in the sea. Should be in high school libraries in coastal areas. (I.M.L., F.F.S.)

Rocks and Minerals. 1926. bi-m. $35. Robert I. Gait. Heldref Publns., 4000 Albemarle St. N.W., Washington, DC 20016. Illus., index, adv. Circ: 3,900. Microform: UMI. Reprint: UMI.

Bk. rev: 4, 300 words signed. *Aud:* Hs.

Popularly written articles by geologists cover many aspects of the earth sciences in a more authoritative, less commercial way than *Mineralogical Record*, including articles about collecting sites, regional geological events, mineral exhibits, and shows. The primary audience remains the amateur, the interested student, and the layperson, but the level of writing is more technical and the focus is more on geology and fossils. The authors are concerned with the activities of museums, serious collecting, and various types of exhibits, and are less involved with the individual collector and the how-to-do-it approach. At the same time the material is easy enough to follow and illustrated. A first choice for high school collections. (E.M.)

Sea Frontiers. 1954. bi-m. $18. F. G. Walton Smith. Intl. Oceanographic Foundation, 3979 Rickenbacker Causeway,

Virginia Key, Miami, FL 33149. Illus., index. Vol. ends: No. 6. Microform: UMI.

Indexed: RG. *Bk. rev:* 9–12, 200 words, signed. *Aud:* Ejh, Hs.

A well-illustrated popular magazine covering all aspects of knowledge of the oceans, written by experts for the general public. The book review section is separated by reading level, and includes a list of new books recently received. Subscription includes *Sea Secrets* (see below). Should be in all marine science libraries and school libraries, especially in coastal areas. (I.M.L., F.F.S.)

Sea Secrets. 1957. bi-m. Free (with subn. to *Sea Frontiers*). Intl. Oceanographic Foundation, 3979 Rickenbacker Causeway, Virginia Key, Miami, FL 33149. Illus. Vol. ends: No. 6. *Aud:* Ejh, Hs.

This educational service of the International Oceanographic Foundation is published in question-and-answer format, with questions coming from the members of IOF. Also gives short notices about upcoming activities and other items of interest to members of IOF. Useful in school libraries, especially those in communities near the oceans. (I.M.L., F.F.S.)

Underwater Naturalist. 1962. q. $15. D. W. Bennett. Amer. Littoral Soc., Sandy Hook, Highlands, NJ 07732. Illus. Vol. ends: No. 4.

Bk. rev: 10–15, 50–200 words. *Aud:* Hs.

The official bulletin of the American Littoral Society, an organization that supports coastal zone conservation and educates its members about the natural history of our coastal waters, marshes, and estuaries. The articles, written by scientists for the layperson, aid the society in its goals and are a good source of information about our coastal zones. Should be in high school libraries in the coastal areas, and marine science and conservation libraries. (I.M.L., F.F.S.)

Weatherwise. 1948. bi-m. $22. Ed. bd. Heldref Publns., 4000 Albermarle St. N.W., Washington, DC 20016. Illus., index, adv. Circ: 9,000. Vol. ends: Dec. Refereed. Microform: B&H, UMI.

Indexed: MgI, RG. *Aud:* Ejh, Hs.

Weatherwise was founded in the 1950s as the "magazine of amateur weathermen." The magazine still uses popularly written articles to present and interpret for its readers the science of meteorology, climatology, and weather. Issues carry both timely and historical material and are nicely illustrated. Regular sections include "Weatherwatch," a review of weather events for preceding months and weather maps for that period, weather queries, and classroom experiments. Highly recommended as a general publication for high school libraries. (L.S.)

AUTOMOBILES

For the Student

See also Motorcycles and Off-Road Vehicles; and Sports Sections.

Lynn Heer, Stac Library Center, University of Florida, 307 West Hall, Gainesville, FL 32611

Introduction

The origins of today's motor vehicles can be traced back thousands of years. Primitive roads existed as far back as 15,000 years ago in the Sudan. Archaeological records show that long overland journeys were being made as early as 4,000 years ago. The wheel made possible overland trade between Europe, China, and Arabia. There was an amazing network of Roman roads from Scotland to the Sahara and from Spain to Asia Minor. For the historian and archaeologist this makes a fascinating study, and the world's literature has many legendary travel tales. The sale of travel guides is still a thriving business.

Today the design, production, sale, and service of motor vehicles is the world's largest industry. Nearly everyone is dependent on the motor vehicle in some form for livelihood, food, clothes, and entertainment (including travel). Many technological developments have contributed to the evolution of the motor vehicle into the tremendous variety and forms available today throughout the world. Most recently the application of electronics and aerodynamics has revitalized the industry and reduced pollution from motor vehicles.

This section reviews a few of the many magazines devoted to informative and entertaining articles, reviews, and photos of all types of cars. Most are published in the United States; however, many provide good coverage of motor vehicles from other countries, especially those available for purchase in the United States.

Basic Periodicals

Hs: *Car and Driver, Car Craft, Hot Rod, Motor Trend, Road & Track.*

Basic Abstracts and Indexes

Magazine Index, Readers' Guide to Periodical Literature.

For the Student

Autoweek. 1958. w. $23. Leon Mandel, 740 Rush St., Chicago, IL 60611. Illus., adv. Circ: 134,000.

Bk. rev: Various number, length. *Aud:* Hs.

A newspaper-format weekly devoted exclusively to auto racing. The lengthy articles focus on the car industry, sports sedans, and performance and sports cars. It is a must for all racing fans because of its extensive coverage of the international Grand Prix Formula One and stock car races. A calendar of events lists the important upcoming races, and a lengthy classified section is included in each issue. Recommended.

Car and Driver. 1955. m. $14.98. David E. Davis, Jr. Ziff-Davis Publg. Co., Consumer Div., One Park Ave., New York, NY 10016. Illus., adv. Circ: 75,000.

Indexed: MgI, RG. *Aud:* Hs.

One of the best of the general-interest auto magazines, covering domestic, foreign, and sports cars. Each issue contains several in-depth "road test" articles describing the car's history, lineage, and performance. Specifications are quite detailed on the engine, drivetrain, dimensions and capacities, interior comfort, suspension type, brakes, steering, wheels, and tires. Test results include acceleration, braking, handling, fuel economy, and interior sound level. Several articles in each issue focus on racing and automotive engineering topics for the auto buff. Highly recommended.

Car Care News. 1983. m. $24. Jay Hagins, 4010 Airline Dr., Houston, TX 77022. Illus., adv. Circ: 40,000.
Aud: Hs.

Written for the mechanically inclined who wish to maintain their own cars, this is suitable for both adults and high school students. There are general and specific articles on repair and maintenance of various makes of cars. The emphasis is on practical methods of getting the most out of the car and keeping it in top shape. There are good articles and features on new products and tools, as well as methods for keeping the car tuned, with some information on light trucks. While specific manuals are needed for detailed mechanical work, this offers the kind of overview that is welcomed by auto buffs.

Car Craft. 1953. m. $11.94. Jon Asher. Petersen Publg. Co., 8490 Sunset Blvd., Los Angeles, CA 90069. Circ: 448,000. Microform: UMI.
Aud: Hs.

This title is similar to *Hot Rod* in scope and format. Feature articles describe how to modify cars to obtain more power and speed and to improve high-speed handling. Also included are articles on new and classic cars. A calendar of events covers the major races and race results. There is excellent photography throughout, and numerous ads.

Cars & Parts Magazine. 1957. m. $18. Robert Stevens. Amos Press, Inc., P.O. Box 482, 911 Vandemark Rd., Sidney, OH 45365. Illus., adv. Circ: 115,000.
Aud: Hs.

Restoration of old cars and everything that implies are covered in each well-illustrated issue. There are articles on specific cars, both about their history and about the problems of bringing them back into active service. Numerous how-to-do-it articles cover various aspects from building a minor part to restoration of a horn or light. There is also a running account of auctions, sales, and avid collectors. Of great interest is a classified section that is a marketplace for those looking for cars or parts. A related title by the same publisher is:
  Cars & Parts Annual (1983. a. $4.95. Circ: 60,000). This is a grand list of parts, cars, clubs, and everything else of interest regarding the collecting and restoring of old automobiles. It can be read by both experts and beginners. If nothing else, it will provide hours of happy dreams.

Four Wheeler. 1962. m. $13.87. Bill Sanders. Four Wheeler Publg. Co., 6728 Eton Ave., Canoga Park, CA 91303. Illus., adv. Circ: 100,000.
Aud: Hs.

This is a first-rate magazine on the highly popular four-wheel drive vehicle. Each issue contains several feature articles covering activities such as hunting and racing. Numerous technical articles and departments in each issue provide the latest information on the mechanical parts of vehicles. The emphasis is on keeping the reader's four-wheeler running well and providing information to improve its performance.

Hot Rod. 1948. m. $13.94. Leonard Emanuelson. Petersen Publg. Co., 8490 Sunset Blvd., Los Angeles, CA 90069. Illus., adv. Circ: 900,000. Microform: UMI.
Indexed: MgI, RG. *Aud:* Hs.

This is the high-performance magazine that spawned legions of imitators. *Hot Rod* is written for readers who want speed, performance, and outstanding appearance in their cars. Articles with lots of photos describe how to modify and build high-performance autos. The writing is a mix of personal "how-to" with technical topics.

Low Rider. See Latin America, Latino (U.S.)/For the Student: Latino (U.S.) Section.

Motor. 1903. m. $12. Ken Zino. Hearst Corp., 555 W. 57th St., New York, NY 10019. Illus., adv. Circ: 126,000. Microform: B&H, UMI.
Aud: Hs.

Primarily for the automotive mechanic, this is the basic title of its kind in the field. Each issue covers the latest in maintenance and repair techniques, not only for automobiles but also for light trucks. The articles are technical, although well within the understanding of a high school student involved with mechanics. Features cover new products, labor, legislation, business, and anything of concern to the mechanic.

Motor Trend. 1949. m. $11.94. Tony Swan. Petersen Publg. Co., 8490 Sunset Blvd., Los Angeles, CA 90069. Illus., adv. Circ: 750,000. Microform: UMI.
Indexed: MgI, RG. *Bk. rev:* Various number, length. *Aud:* Hs.

This is one of the best general-interest auto magazines; it covers all types of automobiles. Feature articles describe the new models and projections about automotive industry trends. Three extensive road tests in each issue offer detailed performance data along with several pictures of each car tested. Owner surveys and long-term tests are found in many issues. This title is also known for its prized "Car of the Year" award. A top-notch auto magazine.

National Dragster. 1960. w. $24. George Phillips. Natl. Hot Rod Assn., 10639 Riverside Dr., North Hollywood, CA 91602. Illus., adv. Circ: 50,000. Sample.
Aud: Hs.

A weekly tabloid, this is the dream of every drag racer come true. Each issue covers regional and national events and personalities. There are illustrated articles on the sport, with more illustration than text for many events, plus news and information about tools, equipment, cars, and high-performance technology. The major focus is on racing and this is the place to turn for statistics, upcoming events, rules, and so on. Coverage is international, although most emphasis is on North America.

New Driver. 1977. 4/school yr. $3.90. Margaret Mucklo. Curriculum Innovations, Inc., 3500 Western Ave., Highland Park, IL 60035. Illus. Vol. ends: Apr/May.

Aud: Hs.

A continuing education magazine that focuses on automobile purchase and maintenance, development of driving skills, energy conservation, and the effects of alcohol on driving. Plain facts in a "non-preaching" format. (L.K.W.)

Petersen's Circle Track. 1982. m. $19.95. Petersen Publg. Co., 8490 Sunset Blvd., Los Angeles, CA 90069. Illus., adv. Circ: 95,000. Sample.

Aud: Hs.

Those who race on the oval track, those who build the cars for such races, and even those who simply like to watch will thoroughly enjoy this magazine. Through careful illustrations and clearly written how-to-do-it articles, the authors demonstrate the necessary steps in preparing for a race. Other articles explain the fine techniques of driving and winning. The most prestigious national and international races are covered in depth, as are the state-of-the-art cars. While a good deal of this is quite technical, there is enough easy material to put it within the grasp of the enthusiast, no matter what age.

Petersen's Pickups & Mini-Trucks. 1972. m. $11.98. Petersen Publg. Co., 8490 Sunset Blvd., Los Angeles, CA 90069. Illus., adv. Circ: 160,000. Sample.

Aud: Hs.

This is for the sports enthusiast who loves to take apart and put back together a light truck. There is emphasis on truck testing—and these tests are some of the best now available—and truck customizing and modification—plans are detailed and easy to follow. Regular articles and features show how to select a used truck. In addition, there are articles on personalities and sporting events.

Popular Hot Rodding. 1962. m. $15. Argus Pubs. Corp., 12301 Wilshire Blvd., Los Angeles, CA 90025. Illus., adv. Circ: 271,000. Sample.

Aud: Hs.

This title differs from *Hot Rod* and *Street Rodder* in that there is more emphasis on racing events. At the same time, it does cover much the same territory, e.g., articles on accessories, parts, new products, repair, styling, and so on. The material is well illustrated and quite easy to understand if one has a moderate background in mechanics. The do-it-yourself articles and features are good to excellent, and quite suitable for high school students.

Road & Track. 1947. m. $15.98. John Dinkel. CBS Publns., 1499 Monrovia Ave., Newport Beach, CA 92663. Illus., adv. Circ: 700,000. Microform: UMI.

Aud: Hs.

This is one of the best general auto magazines. Like *Car and Driver* and *Motor Trend*, it emphasizes the sports/performance automobile. The road tests in each issue give extensive details on the performance and mechanical specifications such as drivetrain, suspension, engine, chassis, and body. Each issue includes a number of feature articles on various sports/performance autos and auto racing. Highly recommended.

Street Rodder. 1972. m. $18. McMullen Publg., Inc., 2145 W. La Palma, Anaheim, CA 92801. Illus., adv. Circ: 100,000.

Bk. rev: Notes. *Aud:* Hs.

A more modest version of *Hot Rod*, this has fewer illustrations, fewer advertisements, and fewer articles. At the same time, there tend to be more technical data on engines and construction of various types of chassis. It will appeal to the person who is deeply involved with the subject. A related magazine by the same publisher is:

Street Rodding Illustrated (1980. bi-m. $11.25. Illus., adv. Circ: 84,000). This title has two distinctive features: It reports on races, auto shows, personalities, and events involved with the sport; and it offers detailed information on products and producers of materials for the hot rod. This latter feature will ensure its success among those who are building cars.

Super Customs & Hot Rods. 1985. bi-m. Inquire. Publns. Intl., Ltd., 3841 W. Oakton St., Skokie, IL 60076. Illus., adv.

Aud: Hs.

This is a beautiful magazine that features a lot of high-quality, full-color photos on glossy stock of customized cars, trucks, and vans. The photos are expertly done and are among the best to be found in any auto magazine. "Car Trek," a calendar of events, features the activities of car clubs and auto enthusiasts such as custom and antique shows, races, and swap meets. The articles cover a wide range of topics: both mild and radical customs, restoration of rare classics into unusual street cars, the history of various marques, and automotive design. This is definitely a magazine that any auto enthusiast would enjoy.

Traffic Safety. 1901. bi-m. $10.50. Robert B. Overend. Natl. Safety Council, 444 N. Michigan Ave., Chicago, IL 60611. Illus., adv. Circ: 20,000.

Aud: Hs.

This magazine is devoted to the prevention of traffic accidents and the promotion of safety. Articles cover legislation at the federal and state levels and driving techniques that improve highway safety. The "Safety Library" column lists books, articles, and government documents dealing with safe driving. Accident and fatality statistics are found in each issue. Recommended for most libraries.

AVIATION AND SPACE SCIENCE

For the Student/For the Professional

Sarojini Balachandran, Head, Science/Engineering Services, Olin Library, Washington University, St. Louis, MO 63130

Introduction

The most noticeable event concerning the periodicals in this area is the creeping inflation that has been pushing up their cost almost beyond the reach of all but the best-funded libraries. Another factor is the highly technical subject matter, which precludes many journals oriented to the general reader, although the successful launching of the U.S. space shuttle may have spiked public interest, as did the Russian Sputnik when it started to orbit the earth a few decades ago. For this reason, the leading popular magazines are included in this section. The section also includes a number of periodicals devoted to aviation as a sport.

Basic Periodicals

Hs: *Air Progress, Spaceflight.*

For the Student

Aero. 1968. m. $18. Dennis Shattuck. Fancy Publications, Inc., 5509 Santa Monica Blvd., Los Angeles, CA 90038. Illus., adv. Circ: 73,000. Sample.
Bk. rev: Notes. *Aud:* Hs.

An airplane owner's magazine, this features articles and columns of interest to those who fly their own airplanes. There usually are appraisals of new aircraft, reports on new equipment, safety tips and the like. The magazine is particularly useful for its trustworthy studies of planes and its evaluations of equipment. Beyond that there are articles about personalities, places, and navigational problems. The material on weather and general flying conditions is quite well written. There are good illustrations as well. This will have appeal even to those who do not own a plane, but fly or long to fly. The one catch: the hidden assumption the reader is rich enough to own an airplane.

Air Progress. 1941. m. $7.50. Michael O'Leary. Challenge Publns., Inc., 7950 Deering Ave., Canoga Park, CA 91304. Illus., adv. Circ: 100,000. Sample. Microform: UMI.
Indexed: Acs. *Aud:* Hs.

Aimed at an informed lay audience, this journal covers aviation in all its facets. It deals with all types of aircraft, supportive facilities, air rallies, fly-ins, collegiate meets, air shows, military innovations, FAA enactments, and federal regulations. Analyses of new designs and trends are also presented. Many of its illustrated articles are about aircraft and avionic equipment, including attention to safety for the pilot. Black-and-white as well as color photographs heighten the effects of well-written pieces.

Ballooning. 1967. bi-m. $24. Brian Lawler. Balloon Federation of America, 2226 Beebee St., San Luis Obispo, CA 93401. Illus., adv. Circ: 5,100.
Aud: Hs.

A favorite among those who fly balloons, this is the basic title for the field. A nice combination of the amateur and expert writer carry the fascinated reader through a dozen or more short articles on individuals and the history of the art. Practical tips such as "Landing Distance Calculator" are woven between articles. There are good illustrations, some in color. Although directed to the activist, this will be of interest to the reader who just likes to watch or read about balloons.

Flying. 1927. m. $18.98. Richard L. Collins. Ziff-Davis Publg. Co., One Park Ave., New York, NY 10016. Illus., index, adv. Circ: 331,267. Sample. Vol. ends: Dec. Microform: B&H, MIM, UMI. Reprint: UMI.
Indexed: AbrRG, RG. *Bk. rev:* Various number, length. *Aud:* Hs.

This popular magazine boasts that it is "the world's most widely read aviation magazine," and, indeed, its publishers have the statistics to prove this claim. With the increasing popularity of sports flying, this magazine has been successfully attempting to cater to the informational needs of an enthusiastic audience. Very attractively illustrated articles cover such varied topics as light aircraft design, construction, performance, and equipment. There are different sections dealing with flight safety instruction, FAA regulations, new products in the field, calendars of sports and other events, and letters and editorial commentary on events and trends likely to have an impact on anyone who likes to fly.

Hang Gliding. 1970. m. Membership, $15. U.S. Hang Gliding Assn., P.O. Box 66306, Los Angeles, CA 90066. Illus., adv. Circ: 9,600.
Aud: Hs.

Until 1976, this magazine was entitled *Ground Skimmer.* Although it seems to go through constant change in size and format, it remains the only periodical devoted to the sport. Sponsored by a national association, it features how-to-do-it consumer tips on types of hang gliders, safety features, federal regulations, and just fun articles on soaring.

Homebuilt Aircraft. 1974. m. $16.95. Steve Werner. Werner & Werner Corp., 16200 Ventura Blvd., Suite 201, Encino, CA 91436. Illus., adv. Circ: 38,000.
Aud: Hs.

Directed to people with the courage and persistence to build their own small airplanes, this has changed from an annual to a monthly publication. Apparently there is increased enthusiasm for this type of publication, both in those who actually build the planes and those who spend the time dreaming of the effort. Each issue includes designs, tips on building, news of products, and pilot reports on home-built aircraft. Of added interest: articles and departments devoted to antique planes.

Plane & Pilot. 1965. m. $15.95. Steve Werner. Werner & Werner Corp., 16200 Ventura Blvd., Suite 201, Encino, CA

91436. Illus., adv. Circ: 70,000. Microform: UMI. Reprint: UMI.

Bk. rev: Notes. *Aud:* Hs.

Articles cover a wide range of material from very practical tips on techniques and safety to bits of history and government legislation. The magazine is particularly useful for reports on new aircraft and equipment. Fair-to-good photographs illustrate the text.

Soaring. 1937. m. Membership. Robert N. Said. Soaring Soc. of America, Inc., P.O. Box 66071, Los Angeles, CA 90066. Illus., adv. Circ: 16,800. Sample. Vol. ends: No. 12.

Bk. rev: Various number, length. *Aud:* Hs.

Oriented toward sports-flying enthusiasts, this popular monthly covers all aspects of motorless flight, with special emphasis on sailplanes, gliders, and ultralights, both factory built and home built. Its audience consists, in general, of persons interested in the activity of soaring and gliding, i.e., building and flying gliders and sailplanes. As one of the news dissemination channels of the Soaring Society of America, it contains information on soaring contests and awards, results of flight tests of sailplanes, and flight instruction programs.

Spaceflight (Supplementary available: *Space Education*). 1956. 10/yr. $65. Andrew Wilson. British Interplanetary Soc., 27–29 South Lambeth Rd., London SW8 1SZ, England. Illus., index, adv. Circ: 4,500. Sample. Vol. ends: Dec. Microform: UMI. Reprint: UMI.

Bk. rev: 1–2, 300 words, signed. *Aud:* Hs.

Spaceflight is devoted to persons who are not specialized but are still well informed about what is happening in the field of manned and unmanned space exploration. Sections are devoted to comments and announcements about the British space industry. There are articles of current and historical interest, such as "A Brief History of the Voyager Project"; "Salyut 6 Mission Report"; and "Opportunity for the Space Shuttle." Other regular features of interest to lay readers include society news about conferences, film shows, lectures, and meetings, and the space report and satellite digest, which keeps them informed of ongoing and upcoming events.

Space World. 1957. 12/yr. $18. Leonard David. Palmer Publns., Inc., 318 Main St., Amherst, WI 54406. Illus., adv. Circ: 15,500. Sample. Vol. ends: No. 10. Microform: UMI, B&H.

Indexed: RG. *Bk. rev:* 2–3, 100–300 words. *Aud:* Hs.

Subtitled the "Magazine of Space News," this journal is a veritable digest of events and trends in the world of space research, technology, and space vehicles. In addition to news and commentary, this nontechnical journal contains articles reprinted from other sources, with abundant color photographs and illustrations. Recent issues, for example, have covered such events as the launching of the space shuttle, space laboratories, giant orbiting telescopes, Voyager and Salyut missions, orbiting satellites, and lunar research. Each issue contains a regular report from the Novosti Press Agency on Russian space developments. One attractive feature is the section entitled "Space World Titles," which is an up-to-date index of all previous articles published in the journal. Highly recommended for high school libraries.

Sport Aviation. 1953. m. $25. Jack Cox. Experimental Aircraft Assn., P.O. Box 2591, Oshkosh, WI 54903. Illus., adv. Circ: 87,000.

Bk. rev: Notes. *Aud:* Hs.

The advantage of this magazine is that it covers almost every facet of sport flying, in almost as many types of planes. Any one issue may feature World War I models as well as tips on gliding or piloting a helicopter. All the material is well illustrated. The articles move from the general to the particular in that some give an overview of the sport, while others give precise details on the construction and refurbishing of a particular type of aircraft. Written for both the experienced and the amateur, this is an ideal introduction to the hobby and to the sport.

For the Professional

Air and Space. 1978. q. Free to educators. Linda S. Dubro. Smithsonian Institution, National Air and Space Museum, Rm. 3569, Washington, DC 20560. Illus. Circ: 15,000. Sample. Vol. ends: No. 4. Microform: UMI. Reprint: ISI.

Aud: Pr.

This self-styled "mini-magazine" is directed at aeronautics and astronautics educators at all levels, as part of an outreach program conducted by NASM. The magazine combines information from many sources to provide a condensed overview of the history, science, technology, and social impact of selected aviation and space topics. It is oriented to an informed general readership inasmuch as it deals with such areas as the Viking conquest of Mars, families of stars, space rocks, early flight, and U.S. women in aviation. In addition, it contains such outreach program information as new educational films, museum news, and announcements of new books and special tours. The magazine is attractively illustrated. The fact that it is free should not be overlooked.

Aviation/Space (Formerly: *The Journal of Aerospace Education*). 1974. bi-m. $25. Wayne R. Matson. Aerospace Education Assn., 1910 Association Dr., Reston, VA 22091. Illus., index, adv. Circ: 10,000. Sample. Vol. ends: No. 6. Microform: UMI. Reprint: UMI.

Aud: Pr.

Subtitled the *Journal of Aerospace Education*, this is the official publication of ASAE, an independent nonprofit professional educational organization founded for the promotion, support, and advancement of aviation and space education. In addition to articles on such popular topics as the solar system, the space shuttle program, and hang gliding, the journal features regular sections on new instructional materials available for classroom use, news of awards and scholarships, latest books and reports, career-awareness features aimed at young people, letters and commentaries, and announcements of meetings and conferences.

BIRDS

For the Student

See also Environment, Conservation, and Outdoor Recreation; and Pets Sections.

Olive F. Whitehead, Retired Librarian, 204 South 42nd St., Philadelphia, PA 19104

Introduction

From the time birds appeared in cave drawings to the present field studies, people have been fascinated by these creatures that can fly freely, sing all day, and survive from the barren Antarctic to the equatorial rain forests. Long ago they were domesticated for man's benefit, trained as falcons to hunt, and carried into mines to warn of poisonous gases. Today, birds are still kept as pets for the owners' companionship and delight while watchers who observe birds in their natural habitats have increased into the millions. To appeal to this diversity of interest in birds, there are magazines for popular reading, for the amateur bird watcher, for the doctoral researcher, and for the admirer of caged birds. One magazine, *Wingtips*, has as its purpose bridging the gap between amateur and professional ornithologists. An important activity that furthers the knowledge of bird behavior is bird banding. Periodicals to assist persons who pursue this work are listed. Many state or regional ornithological associations publish excellent periodicals that include bird censuses and field observations. Several examples of these magazines are reviewed in this section. Articles on birds, bird-watching, and research on birds also appear in magazines on conservation, ecology, natural history, wildlife, and biology.

Basic Periodicals

Ejh: *Chickadee;* Hs: *Audubon, Birding, The Living Bird Quarterly.*

Basic Abstracts and Indexes

Readers' Guide to Periodical Literature.

For the Student

American Birds: a bimonthly journal devoted to the birds of the Americas (Formerly: *Audubon Magazine*, Section 2; *Audubon Field Notes*). 1947. bi-m. $18. John Farrand, Jr. National Audubon Soc., 950 Third Ave., New York, NY 10022. Illus., index, adv. Circ: 14,500. Vol. ends: Nov/Dec. Refereed. Microform: UMI.
Aud: Hs.

Major areas of interest are the changing distribution, population, migration, rare occurrence, ecology and behavior of the birds of North and South America, including Middle America and the West Indies. Articles are solicited on problems in field identification. The journal carries, on a regular basis, contributions to both a Site Guide series, which describes birding locales, and a Centers of Learning series, which profiles institutions concerned with ornithology. Four issues have a long section entitled "Changing Seasons," which

lists bird sightings by geographical regions. As appropriate, these sections are subtitled Autumn Migration, Winter, Spring Migration, and Nesting Season. In the July issue "The Christmas Bird Count" for the preceding December is published. This is an attractively illustrated magazine of importance to dedicated field observers.

Audubon (Formerly: *Bird-Lore*). 1899. bi-m. $16. Les Line. National Audubon Soc., 950 Third Ave., New York, NY 10022. Illus., adv. Circ: 350,000. Vol. ends: Nov. Microform: UMI.
Indexed: RG. *Aud:* Hs.

As the science of ecology and the necessity for conservation have come into prominence, the National Audubon Society and its general membership publication have enlarged in purpose and scope to meet these challenges. There are articles on all the natural sciences: botany, zoology, entomology, herpetology, ornithology, and so on, written for the general public. Conservation of natural resources and preservation of habitat and native species are emphasized. This magazine, well written and richly illustrated, will appeal to many readers in addition to those whose prime interest is bird study and bird-watching.

Birding. 1969. bi-m. $20 (Membership, $18). Ron Naveen. Amer. Birding Assn., Inc., P.O. Box 4335, Austin, TX 78765. Illus., index, adv. Circ: 5,000. Vol. ends: No. 6. Refereed.
Bk. rev: 3–6, 150–300 words, signed, includes recordings. *Aud:* Hs.

The purposes of the American Birding Association are to educate the public in the appreciation of birds and their contribution to the environment, to study birds in their natural habitats, and to contribute to the development of improved methods of population studies of birds. This publication presents information to help the field birder: bird identification, rare occurrences, good birding locations, and observations of behavior. The articles are well written and illustrated with photographs and drawings. Every issue has an insert, perforated for removal and filing, on where to find desirable species, descriptions of choice birding locations, and special pointers to aid in field identification. For the expert field birder this magazine is a "must," but others with a casual interest in bird-watching will find many articles of interest.

Bird Watcher's Digest. 1979. bi-m. $11. Mary Beacom Bowers, P.O. Box 110, Marietta, OH 45750. Illus., index, adv. Circ: 42,000. Vol. ends: July/Aug.
Bk. rev: 5–12, 30–75 words. *Aud:* Ejh, Hs.

This attractive magazine contains articles written for it and excerpts from other publications. Varying in length from half a page to eight pages, these articles cover all aspects of bird-watching. Poetry, humor, and cartoons appear amid items on behavior, identification, rare occurrences, bird songs, and ways to attract birds to your backyard. The style of writing is popular and the facts are accurate. The magazine will appeal to many readers in school libraries.

Chickadee. 1979. 10/yr. $15. Janis Nostbakken. Young Naturalist Foundation, 59 Front St. E., Toronto, Ont. M5E 1B3, Canada. Illus. Circ: 90,000.
Aud: Ejh.

Planned as an introduction to the world for children whose ages are three through nine, *Chickadee* presents puzzles, games, jokes, and an animal story in each issue. There is information on all natural life including birds. Its appeal will be strong to children who can handle the magazine and play he games.

Ducks Unlimited. 1938. bi-m. $10 (Membership). Lee D. Salber. Ducks Unlimited, Inc., One Waterfowl Way, Long Grove, IL 60047. Illus., adv. Circ: 630,000. Vol. ends: Nov/Dec.
Bk. rev: Various number, length. *Aud:* Hs.

As the official organ of a private, nonprofit organization, *Ducks Unlimited* presents information that supports its purpose: the conserving of wetland habitat for waterfowl and other wildlife. To effect this purpose, breeding areas for North American ducks are created, preserved, and managed. Featured articles are on field experiences of hunters and observations of waterfowl. It carries information about conservation and restoration of wetlands and breeding grounds for waterfowl. Many of the illustrations are attractive waterfowl pictures in color. Advertising includes waterfowling items and general consumer products. Written for popular appeal.

The Kingbird. 1950. q. $18. Paul DeBenedictis. The Federation of New York State Bird Clubs, Inc., 4000 West Rd., Cortland, NY 13045. Illus. Vol. ends: Fall.
Aud: Hs.

In keeping with the purpose of the federation—"to further the study of bird life"—each issue presents three to four articles based on observations of birds in New York State. These articles report on serious field studies and further the scope of ornithology. Each issue carries a section on bird counts made during the preceding season in ten regions of New York State. This magazine is useful in all northeastern states for comparison with bird counts and censuses.

The Living Bird Quarterly (Formerly: *Living Bird*). 1962. q. $25 (Membership). Jill Crane. Laboratory of Ornithology at Cornell Univ., 159 Sapsucker Woods Rd., Ithaca, NY 14850. Illus., adv. Circ: 6,000. Vol. ends: Autumn.
Bk. rev: 1–15, 50–300 words. *Aud:* Hs.

This attractive magazine from the Laboratory of Ornithology at Cornell University presents articles on all aspects of bird life in readable style. There are numerous illustrations in color. A regular section briefly reviews current research and activities relating to birds and bird studies. Compared with *Audubon*, the articles are shorter and styled to appeal to the general reader. This magazine should be considered by high school libraries in which there are active bird clubs.

The Loon (Formerly: *The Flicker*). 1929. q. $10. Robert B. Janssen. Minnesota Ornithologists' Union, J. F. Bell Museum of Natural History, 10 Church St. S.E., Univ. of Minnesota, Minneapolis, MN 55455. Illus., index. Circ: 1,200. Vol. ends: Winter. Microform: ISI, UMI.
Bk. rev: 1–3, lengthy, signed. *Aud:* Hs.

With the purpose of fostering the study of birds, this magazine contains articles on bird behavior, records of bird counts, and field observations. Some of the articles are based on funded research; others are contributions from careful bird-watchers. A section of short contributions reports unusual field sightings or bird behavior. Birders throughout the Midwest will find this publication of interest.

Nature Canada. 1972. q. $20 (Membership; schools and libraries, $15). Judy Lord. Canadian Nature Federation, 75 Albert St., Ottawa, Ont. K1P 6G1, Canada. Illus., adv. Circ: 17,900. Sample. Vol. ends: Winter.
Indexed: CanI. *Bk. rev:* 1–3, 1 page, signed. *Aud:* Ejh, Hs.

Once known as *Canadian Audubon*, this is a delightful magazine for both amateur and professional naturalists and conservationists. It contains stories about all aspects of Canadian nature and naturalists. Its readable style and excellent illustrations will appeal to the general reader.

The Passenger Pigeon. 1939. q. $8 (Membership). Charles A. Kemper. The Wisconsin Soc. for Ornithology, Inc., W. 330 N. 8275 W. Shore Dr., Hartland, WI 53029. Illus., index. Circ: 1,200. Vol. ends: Winter.
Aud: Hs.

Both the serious researcher and the dedicated bird-watcher will find this magazine of interest. Field studies, bird counts, and personal accounts of unusual sightings or bird behavior are included. While the ornithological data usually pertain to the state of Wisconsin, most articles would be of interest to residents of the Midwest.

Wingtips. 1984. q. $10. Helen S. Lapham, P.O. Box 226, Lansing, NY 14882. Illus., adv. Sample. Vol. ends: Winter.
Bk. rev: 3, 200–500 words. *Aud:* Hs.

Wingtips is a magazine for people who are interested in birds and want to learn more than identification or keeping a life list. Its purpose is to provide a bridge between amateurs and professionals by publishing information on discoveries in ornithology. Reports on endangered and threatened species appear regularly. A section entitled "Bird Information Wanted" announces bird observations required in ongoing research, opportunities for research in ornithology, and grants and awards available. Meeting dates are announced for numerous events of interest to both professional and amateur students of bird life. Interesting observations of bird behavior are solicited. This publication aims to provide dedicated bird-watchers with an opportunity to add to the science of ornithology.

BOATS AND BOATING

For the Student

See also Fishing, Hunting, and Guns; and Sports Sections.

David Van de Streek, Library Director, Pennsylvania State University Library, York Campus, York, PA 17403

Introduction

Since the boating interests of most library users tend to be local, regional, or national, only those periodicals published in the United States and Canada have been included. Most of these magazines, however, have news sections that include international coverage, and many contain feature articles about cruises, destinations, and significant events worldwide, so that readers wanting information about Australian activities for the America's Cup, for example, are assured of adequate coverage.

Very few boating magazines attempt, or are able, to be all things to all boating interests. Most are either about a type of boat or boating activity or are representative of a specific geographic region.

Basic Periodicals

Hs: *Boating, Motor Boating & Sailing.*

For the Student

Boating. 1956. m. $19.98. Roy Attaway. CBS Magazines, One Park Ave., New York, NY 10016. Illus., index, adv. Circ: 191,934. Vol. ends: June & Dec. Microform: UMI.

Indexed: Acs, MgI. *Aud:* Hs.

Perhaps the most popular of all boating periodicals, if circulation can be used as the yardstick, this magazine is intended for the largest boating interest group, that is, for those who favor popularly priced, high performing runabouts, or sports boats. Published by CBS, the magazine has a highly packaged, almost high tech appearance, using color and graphics extensively. Feature articles are very informative, often technical, and primarily performance-oriented. Most are written in the sort of flashy, jargonistic style that seems endemic to high performance enthusiasts. As in many of the high circulating publications, advertising is abundant; although this can be distracting, advertising can serve as a source of product awareness. Appealing to the largest boating consumer group, this publication can serve an audience of interested high school students.

Canoe. 1973. bi-m. $15. John Viehman. Canoe America Associates, P.O. Box 597, Camden, ME 04843. Illus., index, adv. Circ: 45,370. Sample. Vol. ends: Nov/Dec. Microform: UMI.

Bk. rev: 350–500 words, signed. *Aud:* Hs.

Virtually the only magazine available to canoeists and kayakers, this publication does more than adequate justice to either sport. Addressing an audience from beginner to expert, it touches on all aspects of canoeing and kayaking and provides a large amount of technical and practical information. A particular strength is the large number of trips,

both short and lengthy, that are written up; not only are these trips descriptive, but they also contain very important trip preparation information and suggested further readings. Other special features are directories of paddling schools and outfitters, and an annual buyer's guide. Endorsed by the American Canoe Association, the magazine additionally features fine photography and often finely styled prose.

Motor Boating & Sailing. 1907. m. $15.97. Peter Janssen. Hearst Magazines, 224 W. 57th St., New York, NY 10019. Illus., adv. Circ: 165,000. Sample. Vol. ends: Dec. Microform: UMI.

Indexed: MgI, RG. *Aud:* Hs.

One of the oldest and most widely circulated boating magazines, this publication might be the one to purchase if libraries want only one all-purpose periodical. Produced by the Hearst Corporation, it clearly has the look of a successful publication. Covering both sail and power craft, the appeal can be to the neophyte or casual boater, as well as to the seasoned or avid boating person. The writing is sound and authoritative, with feature articles pertaining to virtually every aspect of boating. The price of success, however, is a magazine that is literally heavy with advertising; with issues commonly numbering from 200 to 300 pages, there are relatively few pages that are untouched by advertisements. Perhaps this may be a good source of consumer information, but to a reader wanting textual material, it can be very distracting. Notwithstanding, this magazine has been chosen by many librarians; like *Boating*, it will appeal to interested students.

Nautical Quarterly. 1977. q. $60. Joseph Gribbins. Nautical Quarterly Co., 373 Park Ave. S., New York, NY 10016. Illus. Circ: 20,000. Sample. Vol. ends: Issues numbered consecutively.

Aud: Hs.

Differing from the rest of the genre both in form and in content, this periodical offers an interesting and unique approach to boats and boating. Feature articles are extensive, perhaps the longest in any boating publication, and are augmented by many quality photographs, some of which span two adjoining pages. The articles generally are either historical or provide historical insight to treatments of boats and personalities. Except for one or two pages, there is no advertising to distract the reader or to invite editorial bias. The presentation and packaging, the strength of the subject material, and the quality of the photography all produce a keepsake publication.

Powerboat. 1968. m. $15. Mark Spencer. Nordco Publg., Inc., 15917 Strathern St., Van Nuys, CA 91406. Illus., adv. Circ: 72,000. Sample. Vol. ends: Dec.

Aud: Hs.

Published by racing veteran Bob Nordskog, this claims to be "the world's leading performance boating magazine," and there appears to be little to dispute that. Focusing strictly on engine-powered, high performance boats, this magazine provides coverage of major racing events and personalities, and features performance reports of new boats and equipment. Thorough evaluations that rate speed and handling characteristics, workmanship, and water skiing capability are a boon for the consumer. Noncomplicated writing styles and almost total reliance on color photography extend the appeal of the magazine to almost any level of high performance enthusiast.

Sail. 1970. m. $21.75. Keith Taylor. Sail Publns., Inc., 34 Commercial Wharf, Boston, MA 02110. Illus., adv. Circ: 173,010. Sample. Vol. ends: Dec. Microform: UMI.
Indexed: MgI. *Bk. rev:* 3–5, 300–600 words, signed. *Aud:* Hs.

One of the highest circulating boating periodicals, this one has all the qualities that establish and maintain popularity with a wide range of readers. Limited to sail craft, but international in scope, *Sail* emphasizes the pleasure aspect of sailing and regularly includes features for beginners, families, and die-hard enthusiasts. Articles are often written in a first-person, narrative style and emphasize the basics without straying too far into technical aspects. Issues are thick, from 200 to 250 pages, much of which is advertising. This advertising is integrated well, however, with the feature parts of the magazine, and tends not to be offensive or distracting as in other publications that contain heavy advertising. This publication should be one of the cornerstones of any boating collection.

Small Boat Journal. 1979. bi-m. $15. Thomas Baker. Small Boat Journal, Inc., P.O. Box 1066, Bennington, VT 05201. Illus., adv. Circ: 53,000. Sample. Vol. ends: Issues numbered consecutively.
Bk. rev: 2,500–750 words, signed. *Aud:* Hs.

Encompassing just about every boat smaller than a yacht, this magazine is intended for those whose tastes, ambitions, or budgets are modest; it covers sail-, motor-, and oar-powered boats, and is literally packed with both interesting and usable information. Consistent with the boats that it champions, the magazine does not have a lot of wasted space, and fills several regular columns with more lines per inch than most periodicals. Color photography is used sparingly, but the talents of a graphic artist are prominently displayed in numerous sketches and line drawings. The publication fills a very useful niche and has appeal for boaters who prefer unpretentiousness both in their boats and in their magazines.

Western Boatman. 1983. b-m. $9. Ralph Poole. Poole Publications, Inc., 16427 S. Avalon Blvd., P.O. Box 2307, Gardena, CA 90248. Illus., adv. Circ: 20,000. Sample. Vol. ends: Nov.
Bk. rev: 1,600 words, signed. *Aud:* Hs.

A recently created publication, this has all the components and qualities associated with longer established and successful boating periodicals. It is a general purpose magazine, covering power-boats and sailboats of most sizes and dimensions, and inland waterways as well as the ocean. Features are well written and lengthy and offer a diversity that can appeal to a very wide audience.

BOOKS AND BOOK REVIEWS

For the Student/For the Professional

See also Library Periodicals Section.

Paula A. Baxter, Associate Librarian, Reference, Museum of Modern Art Library, New York 10019

Introduction

Magazines that provide current information on books, or reviews of their contents, are essential purchases for all libraries. Acquisition decisions about individual reviewing services should be determined by the library and its readers. The titles chosen here are meant to give the librarian a wide range of selection; for this reason, only general, broad-category book reviews are listed. Review magazines covering particular topics can be found in specific subject sections. Some reference book reviews have been included here because of their importance to library service. Only English-language magazines have been chosen, although some of these titles treat important foreign publications on occasion.

The magazines featured in this section represent the majority of the most frequently consulted, useful book reviews in print. A few titles have ceased publication since the last edition or did not respond to repeated requests for information so they could not be included in this current list. The titles that do appear are a subjective—but practically oriented—guide to selection tools.

Basic Periodicals

Hs: *New York Times Book Review*; Pr: *Horn Book*.

Basic Abstracts and Indexes

Book Review Digest, Book Review Index, Children's Book Review Index, Media Review Digest.

Basic Selection Aids

Ejh: *Appraisal, Booklist, Center for Children's Books. Bulletin, Curriculum Review, Interracial Books for Children Bulletin;* Hs: *Booklist, Kliatt Young Adult Paperback Guide.*

For the Student

Appraisal: science books for young people. 1967. 3/yr. $12. Diane Holzheimer. Children's Science Book Review Committee, 605 Commonwealth Ave., Boston, MA 02215. Illus., index. Circ: 2,200. Sample. Vol. ends: Fall.
Bk. rev: 40–50, 150–175 words, signed. *Aud:* Hs.

The premise of this energetic, practical book review service is to guarantee quality science works for young readers. Sponsored in part by Boston University's School of Education, each review has a critical annotation by a children's librarian and a specialist in the field. Their dual evaluations give a sharply defined, enhanced perspective to the educational merits of the book in question. Works are rated according to five assessments from "excellent" to "unsatisfactory." A section at the end of each issue examines "Series" publications—a valuable decision aid for classroom personnel. *Appraisal* focuses on important subject matter for acquisition in school library collections.

The Book Review. w. Inquire. Jack Miles. Los Angeles Times, Times Mirror Sq., Los Angeles, CA 90035. Illus., index, adv. Circ: 1,358,420. Vol. ends: Dec. Microform: UMI.

Bk. rev: 12–25, 600 words, signed. *Aud:* Hs.

This is Los Angeles' answer to the *New York Times Book Review.* The *BR* is shorter than its East Coast counterpart, but employs the same general newspaper review tabloid format and features. Basically, each issue has about 12 one-to-two-page reviews and several small sections containing multiple book notes on a related topic. The focus is on best-sellers and selected scholarly titles, with many reviews rendered in an informal, relaxed prose style. One of *BR*'s best features is its attempt to keep abreast of significant titles from western U.S. publishers. As in previous years, subscription information is disappointingly unclear. Recommended for those western libraries where the *Los Angeles Times* is an essential fixture.

Book World (Variant title: *Washington Post Book World*). 1972. w. $13. Brigette Weeks. The Washington Post, 1150 15th St. N.W., Washington, DC 20071. Illus., adv. Circ: 1,045,673. Sample. Microform: RP.

Bk. rev: 15, 100 words, signed. *Aud:* Hs.

Here is another excellent newspaper book review supplement. *Book World* also resembles the *New York Times Book Review* but contains a more streamlined format. The reviews profile about 15 titles, varying in length from one-half to a full page. Featured titles tend to be nonfiction books, often works in history or biography. Reviewers are experts who treat their topics in a clear, analytical manner— much like the prize-winning style employed in the *Washington Post* itself. Other features, many of them essays on current issues in the arts and letters, are alternated with the reviews through every issue. The well-crafted attention to major publishing ventures, from young adult books to best-selling paperbacks, makes this a valuable acquisition guide.

The New York Review of Books. 1963. 22/yr. $28. Robert B. Silvers & Barbara Epstein. New York Review, Inc., 250 W. 57th St., New York, NY 10107. Illus., index, adv. Vol. ends: Jan. Microform: UMI.

Indexed: API, BoRv. *Bk. rev:* 2,000–3,500 words, signed. *Aud:* Hs.

America's intellectual answer to *The Times Literary Supplement,* this publication does not so much review books as it scrutinizes the ideas they represent. The format usually consists of up to nine fairly lengthy essays, three to five shorter reviews, and a letters column. Leading figures in the arts and sciences contribute one-to-five-page responses to new works in their fields. Few other review tools can summon up such a wide range of authorities—from Milan Kundera to Arthur Schlesinger, Jr. The result brings together variable ideological viewpoints and reactions to new works within each issue. Emphasis is on reviews of the best in recently published fiction, with appraisals often made by other authors, for example, V.S. Pritchett. Critical thrusts are wittily underlined by the award-winning graphics of David Levine. The *NYRB* belongs in all libraries as one of the finest mediums for contemporary book criticism.

The New York Times Book Review. 1890. w. $22. Harvey Shapiro. The New York Times, 229 W. 43rd St., New York, NY 10036. Illus., index, adv. Circ: 1,560,000. Vol. ends: Dec. Microform: Pub.

Indexed: BoRv. *Bk. rev:* 50, 50–1,000 words, signed. *Aud:* Hs.

The New York Times remains one of the most authoritative newspapers in circulation; this influential 50-to-60 page review magazine, published with the Sunday *Times,* appeals to a large audience with an appropriately wide range of interests. As a critical review medium, it truly represents all things to all people. An historically distinguishing feature of the *NYTBR* is its ability to offer expertly written, highly readable commentary on current books. Reviews vary in each issue from lengthy essays on scholarly monographs to brief descriptions of paperback fiction. There are regular departments, for example, "In Short" summaries of new novels and nonfiction, punctuated by small graphics and boxed extracts, and occasional special sections on categories, for example, children's books or sci-tech titles. The magazine also profiles best-sellers through lists that should be considered as reliable guides for public library acquisitions. This is the one newspaper book review that is essential for all libraries.

San Francisco Review of Books. 1975. bi-m. $19. Ronald E. Nowicki. San Francisco Pub. Co., P.O. Box 330090, San Francisco, CA 94133. Illus., index, adv. Circ: 15,000. Sample. Vol. ends: Apr. Microform: UMI.

Indexed: NPI. *Bk. rev:* 8–10, 500–1,000 words, signed. *Aud:* Hs.

Another of the large U.S. city book review/literary magazines, *SFRB* takes seriously its mission as a standard bearer for local art and culture. The magazine has a typical tabloid format, with features on San Francisco publishing and literary figures. Special attention is paid to new poetry. The writers reflect various points of view, but the city's well-known liberal orientation is frequently evident. Reviews often stress regionally published books, both fiction and nonfiction, and works from small presses are noted. *SFRB* also now incorporates *Western Publisher;* this feature alone makes the magazine of definite use to libraries in the western portion of the United States.

The Times Literary Supplement. 1902. w. $70. Times Newspapers Ltd., Priory House, St. John's Lane, London EC1M 4BX, England. Illus., index, adv. Circ: 38,000. Sample. Vol. ends: Dec. Microform: MIM.

Indexed: BoRvI, HumI. *Bk. rev:* 100–1,000 words, signed. *Aud:* Ejh, Hs.

TLS reviews major works of fiction and nonfiction on an international scale, although English-language books are covered most frequently. Reviews are by leading authorities who truly have something to say. In fact the results themselves are often small, impeccable pieces of scholarship, written for the edification of learned audiences. All the disciplines are treated, from children's books to scientific monographs—including many important U.S. publications. Pages contain a scattering of poetry, illustrations, incidental obituary tributes, and ads for forthcoming books. Regular sections feature "Commentary" on current cultural events, for example, art exhibitions, cinema, plays, and television films. An "Information Please" column is devoted to regenerated literary questions, and the often witty and provocative letters to the editor endorse or dispute critical points. Occasional issues have a topical theme, with additional contributions by experts in the field. *TLS*, along with the *New York Review of Books*, belongs in all libraries dedicated to providing their readers with the most substantial book review literature available.

For the Professional

Advocate. 1981. 3/yr. $15 (Individuals, $12). Center for Continuing Education, University of Georgia, Athens, GA 30602. Circ: 1,200. Sample.
Aud: Pr.

Here one finds thoughtful articles on the reading and reading habits of young people from about junior high through high school. Both librarians and educators prepare the short pieces. While the focus is on the interests of teachers, much of the material may be used by parents and by librarians. Of particular value to the latter are short reviews of current books both about and for young people. The style is relaxed and most of the material is free of jargon.

Best Sellers: the monthly book review. 1941. m. $18. Edward Gannon. Univ. of Scranton, Scranton, PA 18510. Index, adv. Circ: 1,500. Sample. Vol. ends: Mar. Microform: B&H, UMI.
Indexed: BoRv, BoRvI, CathI. *Bk. rev:* 150–500 words, signed. *Aud:* Pr.

Many librarians and educators will value the practical, sensible nature of the reviews in this publication. Intended for Catholic readers, the reviews objectively describe new works with some attention to the moral issues raised therein. Categories for reviews are divided between fiction (including science fiction) and general nonfiction sections, with attention to titles for young people. Each issue profiles a large number of books; the reviews themselves average about 300 words. Notable works, for example, the latest novel by John Irving, are given lengthier and more critical treatment. General collections, whether public or academic, will be well served by the descriptive powers of this review service.

Bookbird. 1963. q. $14. Lucia Binder & Knud-Eigil Hauberg-Tychsen. Internationales Institut fur Jugenliteratur und Leseforschung, Mayerhofgasse, 6, A-1040 Vienna, Austria. (Pub: Instituto Nacional del Libro Espanol, Santiago Rusinol, 8, Madrid, Spain.) Illus., index, adv. Circ: 2,000. Sample. Microform: UMI.
Bk. rev: Number varies, ½–1 page, signed. *Aud:* Pr.

This is not really a collection development tool but rather an important service for the professional who works with children and books. A publication of the International Board on Books for Young People (IBBY) and the International Institute for Children's Literature and Reading Research, this English-language journal provides news and literary essays on the most pertinent activities of the 16 countries that contribute to this worldwide effort. Articles, criticism, and occasional brief book reviews survey the best of children's literature. Features examine selected relevant topics; a recent article evaluated the status of children's books in developing countries. IBBY sponsors important publishing events, most notably the biennial Hans Christian Andersen Awards.

Booklist. 1905. bi-m. (exc. July & Aug.) $47. Paul Brawley. American Library Assn., 50 E. Huron St., Chicago, IL. 60611. Index, adv. Circ: 37,000. Sample. Vol. ends: Aug. Microform: UMI.
Indexed: BoRvI. *Bk. rev:* 250, 150 words. *Aud:* Pr.

Booklist's clear organizational format facilitates selective scanning. Only recommended titles are reviewed, allowing the reader a quick, high quality overview of the best in new books. The "Upfront: Advance Reviews" feature presents those adult fiction and nonfiction works expected to be in high demand. Regular sections review new books for young adults and children and survey the latest films, video, classroom filmstrips, and selected, educational microcomputer software. There are also numerous selective bibliographical essay features that appear on a rotational basis. These bibliographies show a real attention to the reading needs of ethnic groups and serve as excellent acquisition lists. An inserted section, "Reference Books Bulletin," appearing in each issue constitutes a separate publication with longer profiles of major reference works and more abbreviated entries on continuations, supplements, and serials. *Booklist* is an essential and increasingly valuable selection tool for school libraries.

Books in Canada. 1971. 9/yr. $16.95. Michael Smith. Canadian Review of Books, Ltd., 366 Adelaide St. E., Suite 432, Toronto, Ont. M5A 3X9, Canada. Illus., index, adv. Circ: 35,000. Vol. ends: Nov. Microform: MMP.
Indexed: CanI. *Bk. rev:* 15–20, 500–1,000 words, signed. *Aud:* Pr.

This magazine is in many ways a state-of-the-art report on books and the publishing industry in Canada. *Books in Canada* has developed an attractive format over the last few years. Features consist of profiles or news stories, many of them recording accomplishments in a country that has had its share of literary setbacks and recoveries. Book reviews predominate, whether brief "Critical Notices" or the longer (ca. 1,000 word) section of essays on notable titles. The magazine covers all types of publications, from popular novels to regional art exhibition catalogs. Librarians looking for significant Canadian materials will appreciate the regular "Received Books" lists, in addition to the substantive reviews. Interested readers will find the specialized information lively and the celebrated CanWit contest challenging.

CBC (Formerly: *Calendar*). 1945. 1–2/yr. Membership, $25. Children's Book Council, Inc., 67 Irving Pl., New York, NY 10003. Illus. Circ: 41,000. Sample.
Aud: Pr.

"News of the children's book world," this is a type of *Publishers Weekly* for children's books although it appears on the average of only once or twice a year. It does several things rather well. There are interviews, news about present and future publishing plans of leaders in the field, historical and think pieces on aspects of children's literature, and a most useful section devoted to free and inexpensive materials. While hardly the best item for keeping up with children's books, it certainly offers a solid overview of the field. Note: The $25 membership fee puts you on the mailing list for the life of the library, or at least well into the next century. It is by way of a best buy.

Center for Children's Books. Bulletin. 1945. m. (exc. Aug.) $22. Zena Sutherland. Univ. of Chicago Press, Journals Div., P.O. Box 37005, Chicago, IL 60637. Index, adv. Circ: 9,500. Sample. Vol. ends: July. Microform: UMI.
Indexed: BoRvI. *Bk. rev:* 70, ca. 50 words. *Aud:* Pr.

As a children's book review service, this practical bulletin ranks along with *Horn Book* and *School Library Journal* for quality coverage. *CCBB* reviews about 70 fiction and non-fiction works in brief and primarily descriptive terms, reserving criticism for the designated rating, which ranges from "recommended" to "unusual appeal." Published for the Graduate Library School at the University of Chicago, the quality of this tool is consistently satisfactory in its choice of titles for both school and leisure reading requirements. The publication gives complete bibliographic and pricing information; every effort seems to have been made to keep its contents current and informative for selection purposes.

Children's Book Review Service Inc. 1972. m. & 2 supplements. $35. Ann L. Kalkhoff. Children's Book Review Service, Inc., 220 Berkeley Pl., Brooklyn, NY 11217. Circ: 300. Sample. Vol. ends: Aug.
Bk. rev: 50–60, 100–150 words, signed. *Aud:* Pr.

A modest loose-leaf reviewing service that deserves a larger circulation, *CBRS* surveys selected, new picture books and works for younger, and older, children. The featured titles are briefly and critically annotated, with emphasis on evaluation over description. Reviews are organized into three categories: (1) new picture books; (2) works for younger children; and (3) works for older children. An author index is provided at the back of each issue. The reviewers themselves are children's librarians and educators whose humorous, objective writing styles reveal their successful judgments of juvenile reading matter. The titles chosen for review in this small magazine neatly supplement coverage provided in the other major children's book reviews.

Choice. 1964. 11/yr. $95. Patricia E. Sabosik, 100 Riverview Center, Middletown, CT 06457. Index, adv. Circ: 5,090. Sample. Vol. ends: July/Aug. Microform: UMI.
Indexed: BoRv, BoRvI. *Bk. rev:* 600, 100 words, signed. *Aud:* Pr.

This publication has become one of the most indispensable book review tools. The approximately 600 titles pro-

filed are mainly scholarly, requisite works for research usage in library collections. Reviews are short and incisive, usually authored by professors or librarians; recently, *Choice* bowed to demands from the field and reversed its long-time policy on unsigned reviews. The magazine would be especially useful to school professionals in its reviews of education journals.

Curriculum Review. 1960. 5/yr. $35. Irene M. Goldman. Curriculum Advisory Service, 517 S. Jefferson St., Chicago, IL 60607. Index, adv. Circ: 1,500. Sample. Vol. ends: Nov. Microform: UMI.
Indexed: BoRvI, CIJE, EdI, MRD. *Bk. rev:* 60–100, 500 words, signed. *Aud:* Pr.

The journal is a hard-to-find reviewing service for elementary and secondary school instructional publications, including both books and nonprint materials. Published by the Curriculum Advisory Service, the publication champions editorial objectivity to the exclusion of advertising and other subtle biases. The result is a fair-minded examination of theoretical and practical application writings about curriculum development. Each issue begins with a set of two to five articles that thematically discuss a "hot" educational topic. Recently, a "Computer Center" section has been added to address the growth of this technology in K–12 instruction. The reviews evaluate publications on the basis of educational veracity, organization, and methodology. These reviews are divided into four subject areas: language arts, mathematics, science, and social studies. The end sections contain ordering information, a review index, and a publisher addresses list. *CR* will be wanted by many educators and is an important tool for school library collections.

Directions: bibliographic selections from Baker & Taylor's approval program. 1975. m. Free. Vicki L. Hanson. Baker & Taylor Co., 6 Kirby Ave., Somerville, NJ 08876. Illus., adv. Circ: 4,000. Sample. Vol. ends: Dec.
Bk. rev: approx. 2,500 titles, some annotated. *Aud:* Pr.

This monthly list from one of America's largest jobbers is a good guide to a wide spectrum of recently published books. Titles are arranged alphabetically within about 125 curriculum-oriented categories; as a backup, each issue also carries a title index. Each book has a fairly complete bibliographic citation and reader level ranking. Works in the "Roundup" sections are given short, concise annotations. The real virtue of this publication is as a checklist, since it presupposes users have a broad subject knowledge. Baker & Taylor also publishes two other monthly magazines: *Forecast* and *Book Alert*.

Horn Book Magazine. 1924. 6/yr. $30. Anita Silvey. Horn Book, Inc., Park Sq. Bldg., 31 St. James Ave., Boston, MA 02116. Illus., index, adv. Circ: 20,000. Sample. Vol. ends: Dec. Microform: B&H, MIM, UMI.
Indexed: BoRv, BoRvI, CIJE, MRD. *Bk. rev:* 70–120, 100–300 words, signed. *Aud:* Pr.

Horn Book is one of the oldest, most reputable review journals for children's literature and educational materials.

Every issue contains highly readable articles, ranging from profiles or interviews with prominent figures in the field to scholarly essays on literary manuscripts. However, the reviews are the "meat" of this magazine, covering new editions and reissues, suggested paperback purchases, books in Spanish, and even occasional recommendations for storytelling or audiovisual purposes. The reviews contain concise, critical commentary, usually favorable in tone. A marvelous "Out of Print—But Look in Your Library" section is a goldmine for educational and collection development ideas. The magazine can be quickly scanned through use of its indexes to advertisers and book reviews (by author-title). *Horn Book* is an authoritative tool for professionals who work with preschool to junior high school readers and belongs in every school library.

Interracial Books for Children Bulletin. 1967. 8/yr. $20 (Individuals, $14). Ruth Charnes. Council on Interracial Books for Children, Inc., 1841 Broadway, New York, NY 10023. Illus. Circ: 7,500. Sample. Microform: UMI.

Indexed: API, EdI. *Aud:* Pr.

Racial and sexual judgments in children's literature are the focus of the council's news bulletin. Special concern is shown over good and bad portrayals of stereotypes, societal biases, and so forth, in educational materials. Every issue features five main articles. The regular departments are especially good: "Bookshelf" contains nine to ten short reviews of current fiction and nonfiction, while "Media Monitor" examines racial or minority imagery/attitudes depicted in the latest Hollywood and classroom films. Books are discussed in terms of their curriculum suitability. The articles also evaluate appropriate teaching practices, for example, "Books to Teach About Work," and often append relevant bibliographic lists of suggested acquisitions. Its stimulating perspective makes this magazine essential for all school libraries.

Junior Bookshelf. 1936. bi-m. $17. D. J. Morrell. Marsh Hall, Thurstonland, Huddersfield, Yorkshire HD4 6XB, England. Illus., index, adv. Circ: 3,000. Sample. Vol. ends: Dec. Microform: UMI.

Bk. rev: 70–100, 100 words, signed. *Aud:* Pr.

This review journal offers excellent evaluations of children's books and the juvenile literature publishing industry in England. The emphasis is on no-nonsense information and plenty of it—from the many ads and the selected profile and awards news sections, to the terse annotations for approximately 100 current fiction and nonfiction publications. A regular feature covers "The New Books," and the reviews appear in categories for picture books, books for children ages under 10, books for 10–14 years, and "For the Intermediate Library." Librarians who want their collections to be comprehensive will appreciate the suggestions and erudition in *Junior Bookshelf.*

Kirkus Reviews. 1933. s-m. $225. Ron de Paulo. Kirkus Service, Inc., 200 Park Ave. S., New York, NY 10003. Index. Circ: 5,000. Vol. ends: Dec. 15. Microform: MCA.

Indexed: BoRvI. *Bk. rev:* 150–300 words. *Aud:* Pr.

Kirkus Reviews has had a durable reputation for quality and convenience. This book reviewing service is fairly well known to the general reader and is regularly consulted in many public libraries. The reviews, which often appear several months before the book's actual publication release, provide concise summaries of content. Reviews conclude with critical, "tell-it-like-it-is" judgments that enable the librarian or bookseller to anticipate public demands more clearly. The format is also useful; with a loose-leaf construction and neat divisions between adult and juvenile literature categories, material can be accessed quickly. The "Pointers" section preceding each review category contains highlighted summaries of the issue's featured titles and their significance as new publications. *Kirkus* is an effective, albeit expensive, acquisition tool that should be in most medium-to-large-size school libraries.

Kliatt Young Adult Paperback Book Guide. 1967. 8/yr. $27. Doris Hiatt & Claire Rosser. Kliatt Paperback Book Guide, 425 Watertown St., Newton, MA 02158. Illus., index, adv. Circ: 1,700. Sample. Vol. ends: Nov. Microform: UMI.

Indexed: BoRvI. *Bk. rev:* 400–500, 100–200 words, signed. *Aud:* Pr.

What library serving young people's reading needs can function without paperback books? *Kliatt* reviews only those titles considered worthy of acquisition for classroom or library purposes. Targeted readers are young adults, ages 12 through 19. Reviews focus on new original, reprinted, or reissued publications, and each review is accompanied by a coded assessment of level and quality. Every issue contains serviceable features, including an "Issues & Comments" essay on topical interests and an easy-to-scan "Alert" listing of widely reviewed, significant new titles. The reviews, arranged into eight broad categories, from fiction to recreation, contain succinct, objective descriptions of the books' contents and viewpoints. *Kliatt* appears as a substantial, bound magazine three times a year, supplemented by five shorter, newsletter-format issues. A most helpful selection aid for high school libraries.

Lector. 1982. bi-m. $20. Vivian Pisano. California Spanish Language Data Base, P.O. Box 4273, Berkeley, CA 94704. Illus., index, adv. Sample. Vol. ends: May/June.

Bk. rev: 100, 150–300 words, signed. *Aud:* Pr.

A significant proportion of the population in the United States is Hispanic; *Lector* is a book review service for Spanish-language and bilingual Hispanic literature. *Lector* is published by a nonprofit organization dedicated to the promotion of literacy for Spanish speakers. The information provided in this magazine is invaluable. Feature articles, variously popular or scholarly in nature, explore minority publishing and bibliographical ventures. The reviews are a balance of adult and juvenile publications, including books and nonprint materials. Emphasis is placed on reviewing fiction and nonfiction titles over textbooks or technical literature. These reviews are divided into *Library Journal*-type subject categories. Recommendation codes at the end of each review designate type of audience, collection, and (uncommon but helpful) binding. A "Briefly Noted" section provides additional, unannotated citations for new works. *Lector* is an excellent magazine with a specialized focus that will be of use to any library interested in acquiring Spanish-language materials, and its contents deserve to appear in the standard indexes to periodical literature.

New Pages: news and reviews of the progressive book trade. See Alternatives/For the Student Section.

New Technical Books. 1915. m. (exc. Aug. & Sept.) $15. Edmond Robinson. New York Public Lib., Science & Technology Research Center, Fifth Ave. & 42nd St., New York, NY 10018. Index. Circ: 1,700. Sample. Vol. ends: Dec. *Bk. rev:* 150, 70–100 words, signed. *Aud:* Pr.

This, along with *ASLIB Book List*, is one of the two best book reviews for recent scientific publications. The most noteworthy titles are selected, with emphasis placed on English-language books. Reviews are arranged according to Dewey Decimal Classification, although helpful author-subject catchword title indexes are also provided. The bibliographically complete entries are tersely annotated, averaging four to eight sentences in length. There is no wasted verbiage in this book review. The full range of pure and applied sciences is considered; new titles for works on mathematics, engineering, and industrial technology appear. Another pertinent section describes books with contents that are interdisciplinarily related. *NTB*'s reviews are appropriate for advanced students.

Publishers Weekly. 1872. w. $78. John F. Baker. R. R. Bowker Co., 245 W. 17th St., New York, NY 10011. Illus., index, adv. Circ: 37,838. Sample. Vol. ends: June & Dec. Microform: UMI.
Indexed: BoRvI, BusI. *Bk. rev:* 70, 150 words. *Aud:* Pr.

PW is *the* trade journal for America's publishing and bookselling industry. Consequently, this is a major source that offers advance news about new titles; critical notes on important publications; and a useful series of forecasts, editorials, author profiles, interviews, and bestseller lists. The many ads help book selectors keep a jump ahead of popular reading demands. Large announcement issues, which appear in the spring and fall, pinpoint current publishing trends. Although *Publishers Weekly* reviews are fairly brief and often directed toward the bookseller, libraries will be missing basic information on acquisition if they do not receive this publication.

Quill & Quire. 1935. m. $38. Ann Vanderhoof. Key Pubs. Co. Ltd., 56 The Esplanade, Toronto, Ont. M5E 1A7, Canada. Illus., adv. Circ: 9,000. Sample. Vol. ends: Dec. Microform: MMP.
Indexed: CanB, CanI. *Bk. rev:* 20–25, 250–1,000 words, signed. *Aud:* Pr.

Quill & Quire is required reading for all librarians, publishers, and booksellers in Canada. It provides something for everyone. There are special issues for both library and publishing conventions, for children's literature, for computer books, and so on. Each issue has a large section of library news for the latest innovations and happenings as well as awards, acquisitions, and new publications. The trade news is the other department, covering publishing news, financial reports, rights, and appointments. The book review section is used extensively for collection building and book-selling. The price is modest, as it includes the supplements of the *Canadian Publishers Directory* and *Forthcoming Books*, a list from the National Library of Canada with Cataloguing in Publication information. (J.C.)

Reference Services Review. 1972. q. $42.50 (Individuals, $22.50). Hannelore B. Rader. Pierian Press, P.O. Box 1808, Ann Arbor, MI 48106. Index, adv. Circ: 2,000. Vol. ends: Dec.
Indexed: BoRvI. *Aud:* Pr.

The journal has changed format and approach several times in its career. *RSR* serves as a forum for issues in reference librarianship; it also offers remarkably incisive reviews for fairly recent, important reference publications. Each issue begins with one or two small feature articles, an opinion column, and some sort of profile. The "Reviews and Recommendations" section has variably annotated entries for reference books, series, and even data bases. Special categories of reference works are spotlighted, for example, genealogy dictionaries, field guides to flora and fauna, anthropology, and archaeology encyclopedias. Articles about library practices and research appear in the "Management and Services" section. The very up-to-date "Books Received" listing will assist collection development personnel. A recommended review tool for medium-to-large libraries in which decisions about major reference purchases require the backup of pertinent, specialized reviews.

Revue des Livres pour Enfants. See Europe/For the Professional Section.

Science Books and Films (Variant title: *AAAS Science Books and Films*). 1965. 5/yr. $20. Kathleen S. Johnston. Amer. Assn. for the Advancement of Science, 1776 Massachusetts Ave. N.W., Washington, DC 20036. Index, adv. Circ: 6,500. Sample. Vol. ends: May. Microform: UMI.
Indexed: BoRvI. *Bk. rev:* 300, 200 words, signed. *Aud:* Pr.

This review service assists in the selection of scientific and technical books and nonprint media. Titles are reviewed for designated readers in elementary school through college and for general audiences. Trade books, textbooks (except those for grades K through 12), 16mm films, video programs, and educational filmstrips are covered. The reviews are arranged by Dewey Decimal Classification and are rated by four evaluation definitions, from "highly recommended" to "not recommended." Levels of difficulty are also noted. Reviewers' comments are no-nonsense, highlighted appraisals of content and quality. Materials deficient in technical accuracy are soundly criticized. *Science Books and Films* readily serves curriculum and collection development needs for classrooms and school libraries. Since this journal most often reviews materials meant for the informed layperson, *New Technical Books* might also be a practical supplement.

The Web. 1980. q. $6. Ohio State University, 29 W. Woodruff St., 200 Ramseyer Hall, Columbus, OH 43210. Index. Sample.

Aud: Pr.

Combining the best features of such magazines as the *Horn Book* and *Signal*, this is a highly individualized effort by Charlotte Huck and Janet Hickman, well known people in the field of children's literature. The quarterly is outstanding for two reasons. First and foremost, the book reviews are excellent. Here is not only the opinion of the reviewer, but more often than not comments by students who read the works. Second, each issue is tied to a theme, or a web, which suggests books suitable for the theme and for related curriculum. Normally the focus is on a topical item, from the weather to national holidays. All of this is offered in a modest, yet attractive package.

Women's Review of Books. 1983. m. $25 (Individuals, $14). Linda Gardiner. Wellesley College Center for Research on Women, Wellesley, MA 02181. Illus., adv. Circ: 9,000. Sample. Vol. ends: Sept. Microform: UMI.

Indexed: API. *Bk. rev:* 15, 700–1,500 words, signed. *Aud:* Pr.

Published as a monthly tabloid, this is a feminist book reviewing service. Issues have increased in the last two years, offering lengthier reviews that are critical and descriptive in nature. Reviewers are noted scholars and writers, who provide thoughtful commentary on new publications by and about women. *WRB's* academic focus is often evident since nonfiction and biographies appear frequently. The literary reviews in this journal are stimulating explications in their own right; librarians and other readers interested in women's studies will find relevant works treated here which are frequently bypassed in the mainstream review literature.

BUSINESS

For the Student/For the Professional

Karen Chapman, Assistant Commerce Librarian, University of Illinois at Urbana-Champaign, 101 Library, 1408 W. Gregory Drive, Urbana, IL 61801

Melanie Dodson, Assistant Head, Social Science Center, Bobst Library, New York University, New York, NY 10012

Mary Ardeth Gaylord, Reference Librarian, Kent State University Library, Kent, OH 44242

Mary L. Lawson, Department Head, Business and Economics Department, Minneapolis Public Library and Information Center, 300 Nicollet Mall, Minneapolis, MN 55401. Contributors from the staff of the Business and Economics Department include Irving Robbins (I.R.) and Mary Zeimetz (M.Z.)

Deonna L. Taylor, Librarian, Graduate School of Business Library, New York University, 19 Rector St., New York, NY 10006

Leslie Troutman, Research Assistant, Commerce Library, University of Illinois at Urbana-Champaign, 101 Library, 1408 W. Gregory Drive, Urbana, IL 61801

Introduction

Whether or not its influence is acknowledged, the business world affects virtually every aspect of our lives. Therefore, it is important for libraries to have good business periodical collections, to provide information on trends and changes and events that will ultimately affect consumers. The following is not an exhaustive list of all business periodicals, but it should prove useful as a guide or a starting point. Besides covering general business periodicals, it includes important journals on accounting, marketing, and other business functions.

Economics periodicals are, for the most part, scholarly and technical. Those listed here are appropriate for high-school age readers or offer support to teachers.

Basic Periodicals

Hs: *Business Week.*

Basic Abstracts and Indexes

Business Periodicals Index.

For the Student

Advertising Age. 1930. s-w. $55. Rance E. Crain. Crain Communications, Inc., 740 Rush St., Chicago, IL 60611. Illus., adv. Circ: 79,350. Sample. Vol. ends: Dec. Microform: B&H, UMI.

Indexed: BusI. *Bk. rev:* Notes. *Aud:* Hs.

One of the most durable advertising trade journals, this twice weekly magazine is must reading for anyone involved in the advertising, marketing, or media industries. Concise, well-written articles cover all that is new and noteworthy in ad campaigns, agency maneuverings, products, and broadcast media. Several special issues throughout the year feature detailed rankings and statistical analyses. An excellent choice for libraries with any interest in advertising and communications. (M.D.)

AFL-CIO News. 1955. w. $10. Saul Miller & John M. Barry. AFL-CIO, 815 16th St. N.W., Washington, DC 20006. Illus. Circ: 80,000. Sample. Vol. ends: No. 51. Microform: UMI. Reprint: Pub.

Indexed: BI, WorAb. *Bk. rev:* Occasional. *Aud:* Hs.

This weekly publication is the official newspaper of the AFL-CIO, offering labor's view on current industrial relations issues such as equal pay, tax reform, and unemployment. Frequently, positions and opinions are expressed on government policy or proposals. Legislative update information; biographical notes on AFL-CIO members; editorials; and special reports on key issues, both current and historical, are also included. The *AFL-CIO American Federationist* is no longer separate but appears as an occasional supplement to this publication. Libraries of all sizes could make use of this inexpensive publication. Useful for current awareness and industrial relations research. (M.L.L.)

Barron's: national business and financial weekly. 1921. w. $77. Alan Abelson. Dow Jones & Co., Inc., 22 Cortlandt St., New York, NY 10007. Subs. to: 200 Burnett Rd., Chicopee, MA 01021. Illus., adv. Circ: 300,000. Vol. ends: Dec. Microform: B&H, MIM.

Indexed: BusI. *Bk. rev:* 2–3, 400–600 words, signed. *Aud:* Hs.

This popular newspaper reports on events and trends that affect the value of stocks and other investments. Articles may discuss particular companies, industries, or investment plans, or may describe general trends of the market. Many articles provide recommendations or predictions. The second half of the newspaper provides a wealth of business statistics, from stock prices and dividends declared to treasury bill rates and mutual fund indicators. (K.C., L.T.)

Black Enterprise. See Afro-American/For the Student Section.

Business Week. 1929. w. $39.95. Stephen B. Shepard. McGraw-Hill, Inc., 1221 Ave. of the Americas, New York, NY 10020. Illus., index, adv. Circ: 763,000. Vol. ends: Numbered consecutively. Microform: UMI. Reprint: UMI.
Indexed: BusI, PAIS, RG. *Bk. rev:* 1–2, 400–1,000 words, signed. *Aud:* Hs.

Business Week is the leading weekly newsmagazine for the business community. It provides international coverage of events and people that affect U.S. business, and it reports current news about corporations, business leaders, and business trends. The layout is interesting, and color is used effectively. With its excellent reputation, *Business Week* deserves a place in virtually every library. (K.C., L.T.)

Challenge: the magazine of economic affairs. 1952. bi-m. $33 (Individuals, $28). Myron E. Sharpe. M. E. Sharpe, Inc., 80 Business Park Dr., Armonk, NY 10504. Illus., adv. Circ: 5,500. Vol. ends: Jan/Feb. Refereed. Microform: UMI.
Indexed: BI, PAIS. *Bk. rev:* 1–2, several pp., signed. *Aud:* Hs.

Although written for the layperson, the magazine's contributors tend to be scholars or economists from industry and government. The writing is clear, nontechnical, and objective. Topic coverage is broad, with articles usually discussing high-impact, current issues such as developing countries, tax reform, inflation, debt crisis, foreign trade, and government policies and regulations. Diversity of viewpoints is encouraged. Each issue contains five or six articles, interviews with nationally known figures, and in-depth book reviews. A unique feature is a listing of further readings on each topic. Recommended for high school libraries. (D.L.T.)

Dun's Business Month. 1893. m. $30. Arlene Hershman. Dun & Bradstreet, Inc., Circulation Dept., 875 Third Ave., New York, NY 10022. Illus., index, adv. Circ: 284,448. Vol. ends: June & Dec. Microform: B&H, MIM, UMI. Reprint: UMI.
Indexed: BusI. *Aud:* Hs.

Dun's Business Month is an entertaining business newsmagazine published by Dun & Bradstreet. News items report on events in categories such as Washington, money and markets, environment, labor, and accounting. Feature articles use the same categories to report in-depth on topics such as foreign plant investment, artificial intelligence, and management styles. (K.C., L.T.)

Economic Outlook USA. 1974. q. $27. Univ. of Michigan, Inst. for Social Research, P.O. Box 1248, Ann Arbor, MI 48106. Illus. Microform: UMI.
Indexed: SocSc. *Aud:* Hs.

Looking into the economic crystal ball, the well-known University of Michigan Research Center guesses about coming trends and developments. This is done in a number of ways. First, there is an annual "forecast issue," consisting of articles, charts, and diagrams that plot the coming year's economic and business activities. The other issues correct the forecast and consider new developments, usually through three to five articles. The center has a reputation of being more often right than wrong, and the report is often quoted in the newspapers. The articles are not only timely and well documented but also well written. Much of the material will be of benefit to students. Note, too, that "economics" takes in the whole of life, and issues may move from marriage to recession to buying habits. (D.L.T.)

The Economist. 1843. w. $85. Andrew Knight. Economist Newspaper, Ltd., 25 St. James's St., London SW1A 1HG, England. Subs. to: P.O. Box 904, Farmingdale, NY 11737. Illus., index, adv. Circ: 169,598. Vol. ends: March, June, Sept. & Dec. Microform: UMI. Reprint: UMI.
Indexed: BusI, PAIS. *Bk. rev:* 4–6, 200–400 words. *Aud:* Hs.

The Economist is a newsmagazine of British origin, which reports on economic conditions, current events, and politics around the world. Readers will find articles on such diverse subjects as spying in Spain, elections in Zimbabwe, Japanese airports, and U.S. unemployment. The approach is brisk, with a great deal of information packed into relatively short articles. The tone is conservative, and the headlines and captions of the illustrations are often irreverent. (K.C., L.T.)

Forbes. 1917. w. $42. James W. Michaels. Forbes, Inc., 60 Fifth Ave., New York, NY 10011. Illus., index, adv. Circ: 720,000. Vol. ends: June & Dec. Microform: B&H, MIM, UMI. Reprint: UMI.
Indexed: BusI, RG. *Bk. rev:* 2–3, 50–75 words. *Aud:* Hs.

Forbes is another of the leading business newsmagazines. Malcolm Forbes, editor-in-chief, proudly proclaims his love of the free enterprise system in his "Fact and Comment" column. News stories report on companies, industries, the economy, technology, careers, and so on. Regular columns give advice on mutual funds, capital markets, stock trends, and various aspects of personal investing. Recommended for most libraries. (K.C., L.T.)

Fortune. 1930. bi-w. $42. Henry Anatole Grunwald. Time, Inc., 1271 Ave. of the Americas, New York, NY 10020. Subs. to: 541 N. Fairbanks Court, Chicago, IL 60611. Illus., index, adv. Circ: 661,000. Vol. ends: June & Dec. Microform: B&H, MIM, UMI. Reprint: UMI.
Indexed: BusI, PAIS, RG. *Bk. rev:* 1, 1,000–1,200 words, signed. *Aud:* Hs.

Fortune ranks with *Forbes* and *Business Week* as one of the top business newsmagazines. Articles on corporate performance, selling, technology, money and markets, and so forth, provide current information for managers and investors. Each issue also contains economic forecasts and a column on personal investing. *Fortune* publishes several lists of rankings each year, the most notable being the Fortune 500, a ranking of the 500 largest industrial American companies. Other lists are the International 500, the largest industrial corporations outside the United States, and the Service 500, the largest banks, life insurance companies, utilities, and so on. Recommended for most school libraries. (K.C., L.T.)

ILO Information. 1973. 5/yr. Free. Jan Vitek. Intl. Labour Office, Washington Branch, 1750 New York Ave. N.W., Washington, DC 20006. Illus. Circ: 9,000 (U.S.) Sample. Vol. ends: No. 5.
Indexed: WorAb. *Aud:* Hs.

With the admission of the Solomon Islands in 1984, the ILO accepted its 151st member. This title is published in 15 languages and has a (distributed) circulation of 40,000. The editor named above is the editor-in-chief; the U.S. editor is Claude Choin. This attractive eight-page news sheet is not an "official" record, and opinions expressed in signed articles are those of the authors. Issues consist of 12 to 20 brief articles reporting the activities and concerns of the ILO and summarizing various ILO research studies. Recent articles have covered such subjects as Third World teenage unemployment, the changing role of Chinese women, clandestine migration, the Polish trade union situation, apartheid and black unemployment, and the health syndrome of underemployment. Issues cover an aspect of labor activities not found in other news journals. This useful little magazine is appropriate for large senior high school libraries. (M.Z.)

Money. 1972. m. $29.95. Marshall Loeb. Time, Inc. 10880 Wilshire Blvd., Los Angeles, CA 90024. Subs. to: P.O. Box 14429, Boulder, CO 80322. Illus., index, adv. Circ: 1,500,000. Vol. ends: Dec. Microform: B&H, UMI.
Indexed: BioI, BoRvI, BusI, RG. *Bk. rev:* 1, 700–1,000 words, signed. *Aud:* Hs.

Money is published for those with enough money to worry about how to spend it wisely but not enough to hire money managers. Every issue has a special report—consisting of four or five feature articles—on some aspect of consumer spending or finances. There are six to ten additional pieces on various aspects of spending and investments for the middle-income American. *Money* is written in a popular style for the reader with little technical knowledge of economics, investments, or consumer behavior. Advice and commentary are relatively conservative. Like *Time*, trends and events are brought down to a personal level by interviews with ordinary folks who are in the mainstream of these trends. Issues of *Money* always seem to be among the most worn and tattered of the current periodicals in any library. Recommended for high school libraries. (M.McK.)

Monthly Labor Review. 1915. m. $24. Henry Lowenstern. Bureau of Labor Statistics, 2029 GAO Bldg., 441 G. St. N.W., Washington, DC 20212. Dist. by: U.S. Govt. Printing Office, Supt. of Docs., Washington, DC 20402. Illus., index. Circ: 13,000. Sample. Vol. ends: Dec. Reprint: Pub.
Indexed: BusI, PAIS, WorAb. *Aud:* Hs.

This title provides current information on labor activity in the United States. The section labeled "Current Labor Statistics" includes employment and unemployment figures, hours and earnings, consumer and producer price indexes, wages and productivity, and work stoppages. At least one signed book review and a bibliography are included each month. An important list is "Major agreements expiring next month." Special articles are included each month on subjects such as labor mobility, price trends, and employment costs. (I.R.)

Nation's Business. 1912. m. $22. Robert T. Gray. Chamber of Commerce of the U.S., 1615 H St. N.W., Washington, DC 20062. Illus., index, adv. Circ: 1,100,000. Vol. ends: Dec. Microform: B&H, UMI. Reprint: UMI.
Indexed: BusI, RG. *Aud:* Hs.

Nation's Business publishes information about current events in business. Articles profile companies and managers, describe trends in management practices, discuss the U.S. economy or international trade, and report news from Washington that has consequences for business. Articles are easy to read and understand. (K.C., L.T.)

Women at Work. 1977. s-a. F20. Krishna Ahooja-Patel. ILO Publns., Intl. Labour Office, CH-1211, Geneva 22, Switzerland. Sample.
Aud: Hs.

This journal is devoted exclusively to issues of economic and social concern for women in the labor market throughout the world. Coverage includes reports; news, including legislative action and current events; and generous bibliographic references to information from all countries cooperating with the ILO. One recent issue offered a global survey on maternal protection from 1964–1984, including country-by-country summaries of current laws and regulations governing this area. Worldwide trends and progress for improving the status and conditions of working women are reported. An excellent source for policymakers, students, and other concerned individuals. (M.L.L.)

For the Professional

Accounting Review. 1926. q. $50. Gary L. Sundem. Amer. Accounting Assn., 5717 Bessie Dr., Sarasota, FL 33583. Index, adv. Circ: 18,000. Vol. ends: Oct. Refereed. Microform: MIM, UMI.
Indexed: BusI. *Bk. rev:* 15–36, 400–1,000 words, signed. *Aud:* Pr.

This publication of the American Accounting Association contains scholarly articles, comments, and notes, departments on education research and financial reporting, and book reviews. Articles address such topics as audit planning, accounting practices, and tax rules. The extensive book reviews should be particularly useful to librarians with developed or developing accounting collections. (K.C., L.T.)

Journal of Economic Education. 1969. q. $30 (Individuals, $15). Donald W. Paden. Joint Council on Economic Education. Subs. to: Heldref Publns., 4000 Albemarle St. N.W., Washington, DC 20016. Illus., index, adv. Circ: 1,150. Sample. Vol. ends: Fall. Refereed. Microform: UMI.
Indexed: CIJE. *Bk. rev:* 1–5, 250–750 words, signed. *Aud:* Pr.

This journal presents articles, studies, and research findings in the area of economic education. Coverage includes issues that may influence or be incorporated into the teaching of economics, evaluation of teaching methods, student performance, and new materials and innovations in economic instruction. Although articles concentrate on college-level instruction, coverage is also given to the teaching of economics on the elementary and secondary school levels. A "Professional Information" section provides a variety of notes, reports, revised results, and announcements of meetings, institutes, and symposia. The book reviews appraise new textbooks, writings on economics education, reference materials, and journals. Unique in its field, this journal is recommended for all high school libraries. (P.S.B.)

CANADA

For the Student

Joan Carruthers, Head, Reference Department, Scott Library, York University, 4700 Keele St., North York, Ontario M3J 2R2, Canada

Introduction

Canadians have always been fiercely proud of their periodicals, even though they are as quick to abandon them as they are to start a new title. The deaths of publications are numerous, and there are always stories of near escapes from bankruptcy. Fortunately, public funding by the Canada Council, the Ontario Arts Council, and arts organizations in other provinces has saved and sustained serious journals. Even so, it is sometimes hard to find Canadian journals to buy at newsstands, and one must seek out the good bookshops or periodical specialty stores in order to locate a particular title. Still, the relatively small population does support a good selection of periodicals on every conceivable subject. This section includes general editorial titles. Canadian periodicals in other subject areas are found in those subject sections.

Basic Periodicals

Hs: *Canadian Dimension, Canadian Forum, Maclean's.*

Basic Abstracts and Indexes

Canadian Periodical Index.

For the Student

Ahoy: a children's magazine. 1976. q. $11.95 (Canada). Junior League of Halifax. Ste 209B, 2021 Brunswick St., Halifax, NS. B3K 2Y5, Canada. Illus. Circ: 11,500. Sample.
Bk. rev: notes. *Aud:* Ejh.

A Canadian children's magazine for ages 7 to 12, this has undergone several changes since its founding some 10 years ago. It is now more lively and has more illustrations than previously, and within the last few years seems to stress Canadian interests. Be that as it may, it is among the more imaginative of the group, and is particularly noteworthy for contributions from its own readers. There are the usual puzzles, games and features, but all of them have an added flair in that they not only entertain—they challenge. The poetry and prose are adequate, but the illustrations often are outstanding. Thanks to its excellent editorial work, it is a magazine for all children, in all countries, not just Canada. Incidentally, the circulation has more than tripled in the past few years, which is at least some gauge of its worth.

Beaver. 1920. q. $24. Christopher Dafoe. Hudson's Bay Co., Hudson's Bay House, 77 Main St., Winnipeg, Man. R3C 2R1, Canada. Illus., adv. Circ: 29,000. Sample. Vol. ends: Spring.
Indexed: CanI. *Bk. rev:* 3, 600–700 words, signed. *Aud:* Ejh, Hs.

Published by the Hudson's Bay Company, this magazine is about the North—that wilderness with which the Company has been or is now associated. Good writing and excellent photography combine to produce an attractive package that offers history, biography, articles on wildlife, archaeology, folklore and the native people that live in the area, to name but a few subjects. There is a natural bias toward the history of the Company and its employees, which only adds to the value of the material. Each issue has reviews of northern books. For every high school library with even the slightest interest in the North.

Behind the Headlines. 1940. 6/yr. $7.50. Canadian Inst. of International Affairs, 15 King's College Circle, Toronto, Ont. M5S 2V9, Canada. Circ: 3,000. Sample. Vol. ends: No. 6. Microform: UMI.
Aud: Hs.

This series of booklets is published by one of Canada's most respected institutes and focuses on international affairs as well as the broad perspective of the economic, political, social, diplomatic, and defense interests of Canada. The pamphlets are on one topic, about 25 pages long, written by experts and complemented by good up-to-date bibliographies. Although the emphasis is on Canada, many of the subjects covered are international, such as Egypt under Mubarak or Spanish foreign policy since Franco. For the very modest price, this title is a good investment. Most high school libraries would find it very useful.

Books in Canada. See Books and Book Reviews/For the Professional Section.

Canada and the World (Formerly: *World Affairs*). 1935. 9/yr. $12. Rupert J. Taylor. Maclean-Hunter, Ltd., Business Pubn. Div., 777 Bay St., Toronto, Ont. M5W 1A7, Canada. Illus., index. Circ: 28,000. Sample. Vol. ends: May. Microform: MML.
Indexed: CanI. *Aud:* Hs.

Designed as a teaching aid for high schools, this title is composed of short articles that focus on Canada and its relationship to contemporary happenings around the world. All issues have themes such as the constitution, the land, the Middle East, and so on. The Middle East issue featured articles not only on the modern countries of the area but also on broader topics covering history, from the Sumerians to the Suez canal. Most of the longer articles include suggested activities for projects or student essays. A quiz or crossword puzzle sums up the issue. Well illustrated with photographs and maps, this magazine should appeal not only to students but also to libraries interested in providing easily read and digested, up-to-date information on Canada and foreign relations.

Canada Today/d'Aujourd'hui. See Free Magazines/For the Professional Section.

Canada Weekly. See Free Magazines/For the Student Section.

Canadian Children's Literature. See Literature/For the Professional Section.

Canadian Dimension. 1964. bi-m. $20. Ed. bd. 801–44 Princess St., Winnipeg, Man. R3B 1K2, Canada. Illus., adv. Circ: 4,000. Sample. Vol. ends: Dec/Jan. Microform: IA, MML.
Indexed: API, CanI. *Bk. rev:* 0–1, 1,000 words, signed. *Aud:* Hs.

Although the masthead states that this journal is not "affiliated to any political party or organization," the tone of the editorial production collective is definitely socialist. This is good, for it gives the reader an insight into another facet of Canadian life. Canadian and international news items are treated fairly and accurately by a staff of writers with many outside contributors. This is the place to find out about the labor movement in Canada and elsewhere. A recent issue had a story on the Eaton's strike in Toronto beside another story on the British miners' defeat. Other interests are the peace movement, women, and minority rights. Should be considered by any library that subscribes to *Maclean's*. Every Canadian library should have this magazine on its shelves.

Canadian Fiction Magazine. See Fiction/For the Student: General Section.

The Canadian Forum. 1920. 10/yr. $35. John Hutcheson. Survival Foundation, 70 The Esplanade, 3rd Floor, Toronto, Ont. M5E 1R2, Canada. Illus., adv. Circ: 6,068. Vol. ends: Dec. Microform: MML.
Indexed: CanI, SocSc. *Bk. rev:* 6, 500–2,500 words, signed. *Aud:* Hs.

If any magazine can be said to offer a real flavor of Canada, *The Canadian Forum* is surely the one. Since 1920, it has been dispensing an eclectic mix of poetry, fiction, and public affairs articles, always adjusting slightly to reflect the changes in the country. Now there are articles about immigrants or stress instead of bread lines or the League of Nations, but the feeling of being at the center is the same.

The rights of minorities and the lobbying for change have always been the mandate of *The Canadian Forum*. There are still very expert theater, film, and book reviews. Although it may not seem to have changed, *The Canadian Forum* is always shifting to high gear. Surely there is not a library in Canada that does not subscribe. Libraries in the United States should buy it as well because the perspective is keen and the vision clear.

Canadian Geographic. See Geography/For the Student Section.

Canadian Heritage (Formerly: *Heritage Canada*). 1974. 5/yr. $35 (Individuals, $17). Tom Pawlick. Heritage Canada Foundation, 70 Bond St., Ground Floor, Toronto, Ont. M5B 2J3, Canada. Illus., index, adv. Circ: 30,000. Sample. Vol. ends: No. 5.
Indexed: CanI. *Bk. rev:* 1–3, 250 words, signed. *Aud:* Hs.

This magazine, produced by Heritage Canada, a charitable foundation, covers the conservation, restoration, and preservation of not only architecture but also natural resources such as parks. Features range all the way from the effects of acid rain on Canada's buildings to articles about towns of historical interest, shopping malls, hydroelectric power stations and anything else that is in need of preservation. A recent theme issue covered Canada's national and historic parks, the problems of conservation, and examples of conservation success stories. The departments in each issue include preservation news and a conservation notebook with hints for restoration "how-to" technical advice. For all its general appeal, the magazine is also a good source of travel material, especially for those with an interest in history.

Canadian Library Journal. See Library Periodicals/For the Professional Section.

Canadian Literature: a quarterly of criticism and review. See Literature/For the Professional Section.

Canadian Musician. See Music and Dance/For the Student: General Section.

Canadian Stamp News. See Hobbies/For the Student: Philately Section.

Cape Breton's Magazine. 1972. q. $9. Ronald Caplan. Wreck Cove, Cape Breton, N.S. B0C 1H0, Canada. Illus., adv. Circ: 9,000.
Aud: Hs.

This is a delightful magazine, even if you have never heard of Cape Breton, Nova Scotia. As the subtitle states, it is "devoted to the history, natural history and future of Cape Breton Island." The format is well designed, the magazine is printed on newsprint, with a clean black-and-white cover. Many of the articles are interviews with old-time residents of the region, and the feeling of oral history is so strong that you can hear the cadence of the voices. There is much history of the coal and steel industry, of the fishing industry, and of labor itself, as in an interview with women who worked in the steel plants during World War II. Essays on and interviews with young people who are poets or artists add to the value of the journal, as do articles of interest to tourists such as a survey of wildflowers. In a recent issue the magazine received a Parks Canada Award of Merit for its "contribution to heritage preservation and awareness." For all Canadian and any U.S. libraries interested in Atlantic Canada.

Dance in Canada. See Music and Dance/For the Student: Dance Section.

Essays on Canadian Writing. See Literature/For the Professional Section.

Harrowsmith. 1976. bi-m. $15. James M. Lawrence. Camden House Publg., Ltd., 7 Queen Victoria Rd., Camden East, Ont. K0K 1J0, Canada. Illus., adv. Circ: 160,000. Sample. Vol. ends: No. 6. Microform: MML.
Indexed: CanI. *Bk. rev:* 1, 1 page, signed. *Aud:* Hs.

One of the great success stories of Canadian publishing, which makes alternative living seem like the only way. Articles can be about almost anything from new architecture to wildlife revival to landscaping for energy efficiency, from windmills to weaving. Each issue is a surprise, and most readers can hardly wait for the next bimonthly. Organic gardening is a strong theme timed well to the year, and lists of seed suppliers are included so that your garden can look almost as sumptuous as the photos. Recipes for organic produce are a monthly feature, as are useful departments such as queries and quandaries, questions and answers from the mail and the gazette, and a chronicle of alternative news and thought. Many of the best articles are periodically collected into best-selling books such as the *Harrowsmith Reader* or the *Harrowsmith Northern Gardener.*

Maclean's. 1905. w. $54. Kevin Doyle. Maclean-Hunter, Ltd., Magazine Div., 777 Bay St., Toronto, Ont. M5W 1A7, Canada. Illus., index, adv. Sample. Microform: MML.
Indexed: CanI. *Bk. rev:* 2, 500 words, signed. *Aud:* Hs.

Once a staid monthly devoted to Canadian affairs, the metamorphosis of *Maclean's* has produced a weekly newsmagazine that, although international in scope, is seen in Canadian terms. A recent article on the soccer massacre in Brussels presents the story, but the eyewitness is a Canadian. The "People" section is crowded with celebrities that have made it at home or, more likely, abroad. There are other differences—for example, the writers do not seem to follow a style. One differs from the next. Many of the cover stories are written by a single author, not the group effort seen often in other weekly newsmagazines. Contrary to the doom and gloom that were predicted when the format changed, the magazine has prospered and increased its share of the market. For a magazine that has been around since 1905, it shows no signs of fatigue. If any library of any size would like to know not only what is happening in Canada but how Canadians think and are reacting to world affairs, subscribe. For all Canadian libraries and practically everyone else.

Nature Canada. See Birds/For the Student Section.

Quill & Quire. See Books and Book Reviews/For the Professional Section.

Saturday Night. 1887. m. $28. Robert Fulford. Saturday Night Publg., 500–70 Bond St., Toronto, Ont. M5B 2J3, Canada. Illus., adv. Circ: 140,000. Sample. Vol. ends: Dec. Microform: MML.
Indexed: CanI. *Bk. rev:* 1–2, 2,500 words, signed. *Aud:* Hs.

Canada's own middle highbrow magazine. It looks a little like *The Atlantic,* but its feet are definitely north of the border. The main articles will tackle anything and everything, especially the controversial. The good thing about *Saturday Night* is that, because of its excellent writers and through their keen eyes, the reader will come to understand the country and its problems by just digesting such topics in articles as how the Conservative Party is governing, the life of a manic depressive, racism in Canada, or a hate literature case. Robert Fulford's editorials are erudition with a punch, and the theater and book reviews are a wonder. You know who reads *Saturday Night* because the letters to the editor are the best in the country. For absolutely anyone with even the faintest interest in Canada.

This Magazine (Formerly: *This Magazine Is About Schools*). 1966. bi-m. $15. Ed. bd. Red Maple Foundation, 70 The Esplanade, 3rd Floor, Toronto, Ont. M5E 1R2, Canada. Illus., adv. Circ: 6,500. Sample. Vol. ends: No. 6. Microform: MML, UMI.
Indexed: API, CanEdI, CanI. *Aud:* Hs.

Although the title used to be *This Magazine Is About Schools,* this publication has gone a long way past that now and has become an irreverent newsmagazine that tackles just about any topic so long as it is controversial. Short stories and poetry sit alongside such pungent topics as the Bloody Sunday Massacre in Northern Ireland and the United States in Grenada. The feature columns give opinions on the latest from radio, television, and so on—"Media-Tedia"; the United States—"Letter from Babylon"; and anything that moves on the Canadian culture scene—"Culture Vulture." Canada is certainly not forgotten with articles such as women workers vs. Bell Canada and the slow demise of the Canadian Broadcasting Corporation. For any library seeking a different slant at news reporting.

CITY AND REGIONAL

For the Student

See also Travel Section.

Victoria Pifalo, Circuit Librarian, Robert Packer Hospital, Sayre, PA 18840

Introduction

With there seeming to be no end to city and regional magazines, this section is intended as a guidepost for the genre. These periodicals are valuable for documenting ethnic and geographic differences and fostering current awareness and a sense of history. They also have recreational appeal for armchair travelers. Their modest, if not bargain, prices are another selling point. Generally speaking, the regionals are noncommercial and use the pictorial essay format. The city magazines are commercial with a general interest content.

As in other categories, there are titles that defy neat categorization or strike out into new territory.

Basic Periodicals

There is no basic list. Imagination will dictate preferences beyond the obvious geographic choice.

Basic Abstracts and Indexes

Access, Magazine Index, Popular Periodicals Index.

For the Student

Alaska: the magazine of life on the last frontier (Formerly: *Alaska Sportsman*). 1935. m. $21. Tom Gresham. Alaska Northwest Publg. Co., P.O. Box 4-EEE, Anchorage, AK 99509. Illus., index, adv. Circ: 166,031. Vol. ends: Dec. *Indexed:* Acs. *Aud:* Hs.

Alaska is unique by virtue of its subject matter. The beauty, vastness, potential, and problems of this remote land are explored by various contributors and staff writers. Abundant photographs, often in color, complement stories about the land, wildlife, and Native American culture. While promoting the outdoors and its attendant sports, the editors remain committed to the responsible use of the state's natural resources. Alaska Northwest Publishing Company also publishes the quarterly *Alaska Geographic*, an annual travel guide entitled *Milepost* and a host of other northern-living books.

Alaska Geographic. 1973. q. $30. Alaska Geographic Society, P.O. Box 4-EEE, Anchorage, AK 99509. Illus. Circ: 20,000. Sample. Vol. ends: Dec. *Bk. rev:* 3–6, 250 words, signed. *Aud:* Hs.

This is an outstanding regional publication. Specializing in Alaska and the Northwest Territories of Canada, each issue is devoted to one topic. Photographs are used to excellent advantage. While some issues are mostly pictures, other issues combine photographs, including period pictures for historical topics, with well-written text. Individual issues are available and are sold under the topic title. For all collections in the area, and other school libraries with an interest in the region. (D.D.)

Arizona Highways. 1925. m. $15. Don Dedera. Arizona Dept. of Transportation, 2039 W. Lewis Ave., Phoenix, AZ 85009. Illus. Circ: 700,000. Vol. ends: Dec. *Indexed:* Acs. *Bk. rev:* 3, 250 words, signed. *Aud:* Hs.

Certainly the model for the noncommercial regionals, *Arizona Highways* combines abundant and lavish illustrations with artful writing. The articles in a single issue revolve around a theme with universal appeal and a timeless quality. This is a magazine that provides pleasure for popular audiences on the first and subsequent readings.

Atlanta. 1961. m. $15. Neil Shister. Communication Channels, Inc., 6255 Barfield Rd., Atlanta, GA 30328. Illus., adv. Circ: 56,000. Vol. ends: Apr. Microform: UMI. *Indexed:* Acs. *Bk. rev:* 2,500 words, signed. *Aud:* Hs.

Atlanta must have readers who never get beyond the extensive restaurant guide and calendar of events in the initial pages. For stay-at-home types, the rest of the magazine informs and entertains. Past topics included Atlanta as a vacationland, winter vacation trips elsewhere, political profiles, critical reporting on juvenile delinquency and the correction system, the revival of the downtown shopping district and neighborhoods, nuclear medicine, and music boxes and their tunes. The magazine has a noticeable commitment to fiction, which is unusual for this genre. The tone is upbeat and in keeping with the reputation of the city.

Back Home in Kentucky. 1977. bi-m. $10. Paula S. Cockrel. Cockrel Communications, Inc., P.O. Box 267, Mt. Morris, IL 61054. Illus., adv. Circ: 12,000. Vol. ends: Nov/Dec. *Aud:* Hs.

Back Home in Kentucky is steeped in the traditions and rich heritage of the Bluegrass State. And while this is contrary to its stated editorial objective to promote the virtues of *contemporary* Kentucky, the old-time style is the secret of its success. Articles are kept short and simple, although several are combined to focus on an area of special interest to readers. Catchy titles for the regular departments, a commitment to publishing contributed poetry, and a column on quilting are distinguishing characteristics.

Baltimore Magazine. 1967. m. $12. Metropolitan Baltimore Chamber of Commerce, 26 S. Calvert St., Suite 800, Baltimore, MD 21202. Illus., adv. Circ: 52,000. Sample. *Aud:* Hs.

How can one enjoy living in Baltimore? The answer is found in the articles, features and illustrations in this magazine. Both the history and the future are dutifully reported. There is the usual listing of upcoming events, as well as sometimes excellent historical pieces about the city. In most respects, it is a general magazine—touching all bases from travel to sports and money—with, of course, a Baltimore bias.

Beautiful British Columbia. 1959. q. $7.95. Bryan McGill, 929 Ellery St., Victoria, B.C. V9A 7B4, Canada. Illus. Circ: 350,000. Vol. ends: Spring. *Aud:* Hs.

The splendor of the province deserves nothing less than the excellent photography and fine writing found in this magazine. The articles reveal the land and its history and culture. A helpful and popular feature is the story location map which pinpoints the issue's attractions. This is a stunning photo-essay regional and well worth the modest price.

Blair & Ketchum's Country Journal. 1974. m. $16.95. Tyler Resch. Historical Times, Inc., P.O. Box 8200, Harrisburg, PA 17105. Subs. to: P.O. Box 392, Mt. Morris, IL 61054. Illus., adv. Circ: 275,000. Vol. ends: Dec. Microform: UMI. *Indexed:* RG. *Aud:* Hs.

Few regionals have earned a national readership, but this is one of them. It is imbued with the New England spirit and carries practical information for rural living. Line drawings and color photographs are scattered throughout to illustrate articles on house building, woodstoves, soil erosion, camping equipment, gardening, food, plumbing, weather, wildlife, and so forth. *Country Journal* is an earthy regional celebrating the rural tradition with great success.

Boston Magazine. 1971. m. $15. Metrocorp, 1050 Park Square Bldg., Boston, MA 02116. Illus., adv. Circ: 120,000. Sample.

Indexed: Acs. *Bk. rev:* Notes. *Aud:* Hs.

One of the more substantial, long-lived and better-known city magazines, here one finds a much-above-average level of editorial work. The illustrations, and even the advertisements, reflect the interests of Bostonians. These vary from theater and film to rock concerts and shopping. Current events, personalities and the like are found in each issue, and there is usually a historical piece. The most fascinating thing about the magazine is the concern with local political and social problems. Unlike many city magazines, this one takes a firm stand and is often involved in investigative types of reporting. It can be read by anyone who lives in or near Boston, or who is likely to be visiting.

Charlotte Magazine. 1968. m. $12. Ellen Grissett. Fortune Media, Inc., P.O. Box 221269, Charlotte, NC 28222. Illus., adv. Circ: 15,000. Sample.

Aud: Hs.

The magazine covers not only the main city but also the surrounding areas. Consequently, here is a good regional title, worthy of consideration by anyone living in North Carolina. The usual types of features are found here, including reviews of music, food, and fashions. The articles are not so usual. These are particularly well written and cover not only current topics of interest, but often those of historical import. The editor, too, considers controversial social, political, and economic issues. Also, there are quite good travel pieces.

Chicago (Formerly: *Chicago Guide, WFMT Guide*). 1952. m. $18. John Fink. WFMT, Inc., 3 Illinois Center, 303 E. Wacker Dr., Chicago, IL 60601. Illus., adv. Circ: 221,728. Vol. ends: Dec. Microform: UMI, B&H.

Indexed: Acs, PopPer. *Bk. rev:* 5, 800 words, signed. *Aud:* Hs.

What began as the WFMT radio guide has blossomed into a 300-page glossy. The program guide has been joined by a number of other guides: events, TV Channel 11, local service organizations, and dining. Nestled between the guides and ads are articles on politics and social issues, interviews, portfolios of art and photography, fiction, and reviews. This literate and snappy magazine is virtually indispensable to anyone in Chicago or within striking distance of it.

Cincinnati. 1967. m. $10. Laura Pulfer. Greater Cincinnati Chamber of Commerce, 120 W. Fifth St., Cincinnati, OH 45202. Illus., adv. Circ: 30,000. Vol. ends: Sept.

Aud: Hs.

This ambitious magazine is published by the Greater Cincinnati Chamber of Commerce with obvious skill. It is heavily illustrated and tastefully arranged and has diversity in subject matter and a sense of purpose. Many of the articles are from free-lance writers who are instructed to submit critical pieces exploring problems and suggesting solutions. The results are features on sex education, telecommunica-

tions technology in the twenty-first century, and Huntington's disease.

Cleveland Magazine. 1972. m. $14. Michael Roberts. City Magazines, Inc., 1621 Euclid Ave., Cleveland, OH 44115. Illus., adv. Circ: 41,000. Sample. Microform: UMI.

Indexed: Acs. *Bk. rev:* 4–5, 200 words, signed. *Aud:* Hs.

Contemporary social and political problems interest the editor and writers in this superior city magazine. The pieces sometimes can become controversial, but they tend to look objectively at the city and its people. In addition, one finds features that keep the reader up to date on current events and personalities. Then there are the regular columns and articles that report on everything from films to restaurants. There is good business news, too.

Connecticut. 1971. m. $15. Albert E. Labouchere. Communications Intl., 636 Kings Hwy., Fairfield, CT 06430. Subs. to: P.O. Box 317, Martinsville, NJ 08836. Illus., adv. Circ: 68,000. Vol. ends: Dec.

Indexed: Acs, PopPer. *Aud:* Hs.

The editors have struck a perfect balance between the stories about and the guides to Connecticut. The provocative reporting is tempered by purely human interest accounts. Local attractions are highlighted in the form of a monthly calendar of events, a regular restaurant review column, and occasional seasonal guides. The concise writing style and orderly layout make for easy reading.

Country Magazine. 1980. m. $18. Walter Nicklin. Country Sun, Inc., Suite 205, The Atrium, 277 S. Washington St., Alexandria, VA 22314. Subs. to: P.O. Box 963, Farmingdale, NY 11737. Illus., adv. Circ: 100,000. Sample. Vol. ends: Dec.

Aud: Hs.

Although based in Virginia, *Country Magazine* celebrates the history and beauty of the whole Mid-Atlantic region. With such a territory, its pages are easily filled with descriptions and color pictures of interesting spots to visit. There is a deep appreciation of nature throughout the magazine. A nice touch is the inclusion of serialized fiction. In only five years, *Country Magazine* has captured a large audience and may be recommended to libraries in the states which it covers: New Jersey, Pennsylvania, Delaware, Maryland, District of Columbia, West Virginia, Virginia, and North Carolina.

Dallas. 1922. m. $14. D. Ann Slayton Shiffler. Dallas Chamber of Commerce, 1507 Pacific Ave., Dallas, TX 75201. Illus., adv. Circ: 30,000. Sample. Vol. ends: Dec. Microform: UMI.

Aud: Hs.

Dallas is a no-nonsense business magazine. And as such, there are reports on companies, interviews with prominent people, management tips, news, and community and economic analyses. Its classy format and useful information make this an obvious choice.

Delaware Today. 1962. m. $14. Peter Mucha. Gazette Press, P.O. Box 4440, Wilmington, DE 19807. Illus., adv. Circ: 16,000. Vol. ends: Dec.

Aud: Hs.

Rather than the usual hodgepodge of features and departments, *Delaware Today* unites much of an issue around a theme. In this way, the standard elements of a regional are put to clever use in developing the chosen topic from different angles. Even though there is this scheme, a few feature articles and departments are allowed to depart from the central theme. Residents of the "First State" are well served by this imaginative publication.

Down East. 1954. m. $18.95. Davis Thomas. Down East Enterprise, Inc., P.O. Box 679, Camden, ME 04843. Illus., index, adv. Circ: 75,000. Vol. ends: July.

Indexed: Acs. *Bk. rev:* 1, 500 words, signed. *Aud:* Hs.

Down East—"The Magazine of Maine"—is an unpretentious regional for residents and tourists alike. Abundant illustrations accompany the articles on nature and local attractions. The magazine is rich in Maine humor, and there are extensive real estate listings.

Honolulu (Formerly: *Paradise of the Pacific*). 1888. m. Hawaii residents, $15 (Others, $21). Brian Nicol, 36 Merchant St., Honolulu, HI 96813. Subs. to: P.O. Box 80, Honolulu, HI 96810. Illus., adv. Circ: 34,931. Vol. ends: June.

Indexed: Acs. *Bk. rev:* 1, 1,000 words, signed. *Aud:* Hs.

All the usual ingredients of a city magazine are here. There are features, departments, interviews, news briefs, and guides. There is diversity with coverage of politics, art, economic development, vacation ideas, people, sports, music, and dining. The writing is pithy, and the stories are timely and sometimes controversial. Some originality is shown, as in the perforated fold-out calendar of events, but what really distinguishes *Honolulu* from all the others is the Hawaiian culture that naturally finds its way into the content and influences the style.

Indianapolis Magazine. 1963. m. $11.95. Nancy L. Comiskey. Capitol Communications Corp., 32 E. Washington St., Indianapolis, IN 46204. Illus., adv. Circ: 21,000. Sample. Vol. ends: Dec.

Aud: Hs.

Readers will find a central article dividing the string of departments. A good mix of subjects is offered so that there is something for everybody. An orderly arrangement is created with every article presented in its entirety on successive pages and framed neatly with a black border. The modest graphics are laid out with a nice touch to make things visually interesting.

The Iowan. 1952. q. $15. Charles W. Roberts. Mid-America Publg. Corp., 214 Ninth St., Des Moines, IA 50309. Subs. to: P.O. Box 130, Shenandoah, IA 51601. Illus., adv. Circ: 22,000. Vol. ends: Summer. Microform: UMI.

Aud: Hs.

With its thoughtful, sensitive content and beautiful appearance, *The Iowan* comes across as an oversized *National Geographic*. The articles satisfy science, arts, history, and nature interests and are written by Iowan free-lancers. The color photographs are magnificent, the paper is crisp, and the print size is comfortable. The editors know their business and make this sound publication easy to recommend.

Kansas! 1945. q. $6. Andrea Glenn. Kansas Dept. of Economic Development, 503 Kansas Ave., 6th Floor, Topeka, KS 66603. Illus. Circ: 42,000. Vol. ends: Dec.

Aud: Hs.

The promotional intentions of this state-sponsored regional are couched in beautiful pictorial essays. Few words are necessary when there is page after page of enchanting color photographs. The editors excel at their craft and *Kansas!* merits every bit of the enthusiasm and praise found in the letters to the editor and deserves that exclamation point.

The Little Balkans Review. 1980. q. $10. Gene DeGruson. Little Balkans Press, Inc., 601 Grandview Heights Terrace, Pittsburgh, KS 66762. Illus., index. Circ: 1,200. Vol. ends: Summer.

Aud: Hs.

Here is a regional that strays from the usual pattern. *The Little Balkans Review* is subtitled "A Southeast Kansas Literary and Graphics Quarterly" and the editorial policy assures a mix of fiction, poetry, nonfiction, and graphics somehow related to the area. There are special issues, such as the one designed as a "Birthday Festschrift for James Tate," and other issues have an underlying theme, such as the one on the Civil War. Information on local history and customs and the arts is divulged while often introducing new talent. Each issue is an 8½- by 5½-inch black-and-white booklet numbering approximately 100 pages. The emphasis on scholarly and creative writing distinguishes *The Little Balkans Review* from the pictorial, *Kansas!* This refreshing and entertaining publication is worthy of a larger audience.

Los Angeles. 1960. m. $19. Geoff Miller, 1888 Century Park E., Los Angeles, CA 90067. Illus., adv. Circ: 160,000. Vol. ends: Dec. Microform: UMI.

Indexed: Acs, PopPer. *Aud:* Hs.

With over 250 pages, *Los Angeles* can just about cover it all—entertainment in listings, calendars, and columns; vacation hints and packages; annual guides to summer camps or homes and condominiums; extensive advertising; and several full-length articles. The features tend toward the sensational in subject matter—crime, Hollywood, politics, sex— but are seriously researched and written and masterfully developed. Several satellite columns will accompany a single story to elaborate on different aspects, a most successful attention-getting and attention-retaining device. Humor and quips find a place as well. A marked enthusiasm for the upper-class interests in the Southern California region may limit its appeal, although it certainly has not hurt its circulation.

Louisiana Life. 1981. bi-m. $17. Thomas C. & Nancy K. Marshall. Louisiana Life, Ltd., 4200 S. I-10 Service Rd., Suite 220, Metairie, LA 70001. Illus., adv. Circ: 48,685. Vol. ends: Jan/Feb.

Indexed: Acs. *Bk. rev:* 5, 300 words, signed. *Aud:* Hs.

It is fitting that the state that is the site of Mardi Gras should have such a festive regional. The generous splashes of color photography and the well-chosen and well-constructed human interest features are captivating even for the most casual of readers. The regular departments serve as vehicles to highlight every part of the state. With its statewide focus and fresh approach, this is clearly the first choice of the Louisiana regionals.

Maryland Magazine (Formerly: *Maryland*). 1968. q. $8.50. Bonnie Joe Ayers. Maryland Dept. of Economic & Community Development, 45 Calvert St., Annapolis, MD 21401. Subs. to: P.O. Box 1589, Annapolis, MD 21404. Illus., index, adv. Circ: 40,000. Vol. ends: Summer.

Indexed: Acs. *Bk. rev:* 9, 50 words. *Aud:* Hs.

Being the official magazine of the state of Maryland, the gentle praise and pride in its pages will come as no surprise. The economic health of the state is presented in well-illustrated and well-written stories about local industries, successful people, and up-and-coming communities. A few cultural and historical pieces are included for balance. The ads are few and are relegated to the front and back pages, so as not to detract from the attractive appearance of the magazine.

Miami/South Florida Magazine (Formerly: *Miami: the magazine of South Florida* and *Miami Pictorial*). 1921. m. $12. Erica M. Rauzin. Miami Magazine, Inc., 75 S. W. 15th Rd., Miami, FL 33129. Illus., adv. Circ: 29,500. Vol. ends: Oct.

Indexed: Acs. *Aud:* Hs.

As might be expected, *Miami/South Florida Magazine* is a hefty issue of over 100 pages with substantial, thought-provoking articles as well as lots of advertising. The timely topics are well developed and there is a level of detail that is found in the more sophisticated regionals. All in all, this is a solid, thorough and well-executed publication.

Milwaukee Magazine. 1976. m. $14. Charles Sykes. Milwaukee Magazine, Inc., 312 E. Buffalo St., Milwaukee, WI 53202. Illus., adv. Circ: 39,000. Vol. ends: Dec.

Aud: Hs.

The editors pack a lot in each colorful issue of this award-winning magazine. There are probing features about community affairs and searching profiles of prominent citizens. These tend to be controversial or sensational in nature as witnessed in the letters to the editor. More variety and a little less intensity is found in the regular departments and columns. Not only is there a monthly calendar of events but also a special pull-out leisure guide with a seasonal focus. *Milwaukee Magazine* promises high quality and excitement in each issue.

Mississippi: a view of the Magnolia State. 1982. bi-m. $12. Allyn C. Boone. Downhome Publns., Inc., Suite 254, High-land Village, Jackson, MS 39211. Illus., adv. Circ: 25,000. Vol. ends: July/Aug.

Indexed: Acs. *Bk. rev:* 2, 700 words, signed. *Aud:* Hs.

It may be only three years old and still growing, but *Mississippi* has already established itself as a fine-looking magazine. The outstanding photography and attractive layout and print style are striking. The mix of articles is good with something for everyone: history, vacation ideas, homes, gardens, business, profiles, the arts, sports, food and unique departments on religion and "Being Southern." This is an exciting newcomer to watch.

Missouri Life. 1973. bi-m. $16. Debra McAlear Gluck. Missouri Life Publg. Co., 710 N. Tucker St., St. Louis, MO 63101. Illus., adv. Circ: 30,000. Vol. ends: Mar/Apr.

Indexed: Acs. *Aud:* Hs.

The contributing editors and the free-lance writers and photographers give readers a feel for Missouri by depicting its people. In this way, a wide range of topics can be explored using the appeal of the human interest story. Articles are illustrated, and advertising is minimal, which makes for an attractive magazine and an uncluttered reading experience.

Monthly Detroit. 1978. m. $14. Keith Crain. Crain Communications, Inc., 1400 Woodbridge, Detroit, MI 48207. Illus., adv. Circ: 40,000. Sample.

Indexed: Acs. *Aud:* Hs.

This has an added dimension because of its automobile interests and the emphasis on economics, labor, and business. Much can be learned here by the person who follows the industry and its related activities. At the same time, there are the usual stories on the community and its pursuit of culture. The writing style and the illustrations are much above average, and this is one of the few city magazines that has a broader potential audience than the name indicates.

Mpls. St. Paul Magazine. 1978. m. $14. Brian Anderson. MSP Publns., 12 S. Sixth St., Suite 1030, Minneapolis, MN 55402. Illus., adv. Circ: 47,000. Vol. ends: Dec.

Indexed: Acs. *Aud:* Hs.

This has got what the other city magazines have in terms of bulk and bustle, only it does it in a fun-loving and familiar manner. The editors convey a real sense of belonging to the community and their enthusiasm is contagious. They demonstrate diligence and imagination in announcing the upcoming events around the area, which results in more than one creatively designed guide per issue. Special attention is paid to the arts, not only in the guides but in the features and departments. It would take the most sedentary of readers to defy *Mpls. St. Paul Magazine*'s call to partake of the pleasures of the Twin Cities.

Nashville! 1973. m. $12. Amy Lynch. Advantage Publg., Inc., The Advantage Bldg., 1719 West End Ave., Nashville, TN 37203. Illus., adv. Circ: 25,000. Sample. Vol. ends: Mar. Microform: UMI.

Aud: Hs.

Surprisingly enough, this places considerable emphasis on business—economic outlook, new technology, management tips and local firms. One issue examined also contained a special report on senior citzens. Local personalities, surveys of the community and other noteworthy news are likewise reported. Lighter reading can be found in home and living columns. A basic black-and-white production that adequately puts across the information.

Nevada Magazine. 1964. bi-m. $8.95. C. J. Hadley, Capitol Complex, Carson City, NV 88710. Illus., adv. Circ: 61,000. Sample.

Aud: Hs.

Actually, most of the material here is closer to a typical history magazine than an average regional title. The editor puts great emphasis on articles that have historical interest, and most of these are well illustrated. In addition, there are good pieces on travel, sports, recreation, and, particularly, on the ghost towns of the area. As might be expected, there are personality sketches and pieces about gambling—but this tends to be a minor part of most issues.

New England Business. 1952. bi-w. $18. Kenneth Hooker. Yankee Publg., Inc., 33 Union St., Boston, MA 02108. Illus., adv. Circ: 50,000. Sample.

Indexed: PAIS. *Bk. rev:* Notes. *Aud:* Hs.

Every two weeks there is an illustrated article in this magazine on some individual, business, or potential development in New England. While directed to the business-industrial community, much of the average issues will be of interest to laypeople who are concerned about New England's future. Covering the whole region, it tends to concentrate more on the larger urban centers and manufacturing sections. The material is current, well written, and can be trusted to be an accurate report of matters at that moment. Note: Much of the circulation is controlled, i.e., free; and librarians might ask for a free subscription.

New England Monthly. 1984. $18. Daniel Okrent. New England Monthly, Inc., P.O. Box 446, Haydenville, MA 01039. Illus., adv. Circ: 46,000. Sample.

Aud: Hs.

The idea is to cover activities in all of the six New England states. For the most part the publication succeeds, and there are quite entertaining and informative articles on a wide variety of subjects. Of particular interest are the articles and features on local crafts and craft workers. Most of the material is well illustrated. For those who move about, there is a good listing of restaurants and photographic essays on personalities and events.

New Jersey Monthly. 1976. m. $18. Colleen Katz. Aylesworth Communications Corp., 7 Dumont Pl., Morristown, NJ 07960. Subs. to: P.O. Box 806, Martinsville Center, NJ 08836. Illus., adv. Circ: 95,000.

Indexed: Acs, PopPer. *Aud:* Hs.

This award-winning magazine seems bent on promoting the image of New Jersey. The editorial policy has taken a decided shift from controversial and investigative reporting to optimistic and less meaty articles. Residents who share the good life in New Jersey will find this view of the state's finer points encouraging and entertaining and the guides to local attractions helpful.

Ohio. 1978. m. Ohio residents, $12 (Others, $14). Robert B. Smith. Ohio Magazine, 40 S. Third St., Columbus, OH 43215. Illus., adv. Circ: 100,000. Vol. ends: Mar. Microform: B&H.

Indexed: Acs. *Aud:* Hs.

This elegant magazine has a writing style that commands a close reading and a format that makes doing so a pleasure. The expected stories about people and events transcend the geographic place on the strength of their being so well told. And these articles are given prominence and individuality in the layout. Most are presented in their entirety on successive pages and the column size is varied from two inches to the width of a whole page. Artistic photos and graphics are in harmony with the written material. The ads are unobtrusive. Highly recommended.

Oklahoma Today. 1956. bi-m. $10. Sue Carter. Oklahoma Tourism and Recreation Dept., P.O. Box 53384, Oklahoma City, OK 73152. Illus. Circ: 32,000. Vol. ends: Nov/Dec.

Bk. rev: 2, 250 words. *Aud:* Hs.

Since the early 1980s, *Oklahoma Today* has increased its frequency of publication and its audience. And what accounts for this success? Easy-to-read articles accompanied by numerous and extremely fine color photographs. Content, layout, paper and color quality, and type size are meticulously handled by the editors. This state-sponsored view of the Sooner State is impressive and comes highly recommended.

Oregon. 1975. m. $20. Lydia Lipman. New Oregon Pubs., Inc., 208 S.W. Stark, Suite 500, Portland, OR 97204. Subs. to: P.O. Box 40028, Portland, OR 97240. Illus., adv. Vol. ends: Dec.

Indexed: Acs. *Aud:* Hs.

Oregon is a hybrid combining the focus of a regional with the spunk of a city magazine. The entire state is covered in a couple of well-developed articles on timely topics—sometimes of a controversial nature—and in the reviews, calendars, and guides. The layout helps to generate excitement with splashes of color photography and a bold printing style. *Oregon* may not be the best, but it is catchy.

Pacific Northwest. 1966. 10/yr. $15. Peter Potterfield. Pacific Search Publns., 222 Dexter Ave. N., Seattle, WA 98109. Illus., adv. Circ: 56,000. Sample.

Aud: Hs.

Despite the title, most of the material is concerned not with the whole area, but with Seattle. What is of interest to Seattle residents seems to be the main rule of entry. Articles and photographs, of course, can be appreciated by others. Here are pieces on everything from local politicians to gardening. There are features that consider travel, sports, and recreation. In a word: a general magazine that should have wide appeal for people living in and outside of Seattle.

Pennsylvania Magazine. 1981. q. $8. Albert E. Holliday. Pennsylvania Magazine, P.O. Box 576, Camp Hill, PA 17011. Illus., adv. Circ: 21,000. Vol. ends: Winter.

Bk. rev: 5, 200 words, signed. *Aud:* Hs.

This ambitious newcomer is slowly building its reputation as a modest, but nonetheless engaging, magazine. Naturally, a calendar of events, travel tips, and regional claims to fame can be found. In a conscientious effort to cover all angles of a large and diverse state, the editors lift little-known stories about Pennsylvania from obscurity. In fact, a Pennsylvania Trivia Contest has become a new feature, complete with prizes for the winning entries. The predominantly black-and-white photographs add a nostalgic touch. Readers will painlessly improve their knowledge of the natural resources, history, and culture of the Keystone State. For this reason, educators may find it a good resource in the Pennsylvania classroom.

Philadelphia (Formerly: *Greater Philadelphia*). 1908. m. $15. Ron Javers. MetroCorp., 1500 Walnut St., Philadelphia, PA 19102. Illus., adv. Circ: 141,973. Vol. ends: Dec. Microform: UMI.

Indexed: Acs, PopPer. *Aud:* Hs.

The magazine reflects the hustle and bustle of a city in its packed pages of articles, leisure guides, and ads. Readers from Center City to the outlying areas have a generous collection of features and departments from which to choose. In keeping with the times, investigative reports probing social problems are less prominent than articles to enhance lifestyle. Likewise, film reviews and personal computer reviews have replaced the more traditional book reviews.

Phoenix. 1966. m. $16. Phoenix Publg., Inc., 4707 N. 12th St., Phoenix, AZ 85014. Illus., adv. Circ: 32,000. Sample.

Indexed: Acs. *Aud:* Hs.

Both residents and visitors can enjoy this bright and lively city magazine. The illustrations and articles point out the joys of living in Phoenix and Arizona. There are good-to-excellent reports on local activities, personalities, and economic and social events. Most of it is well illustrated. The way of life here is a bit unique, and anyone wondering what it might be like to live in an area of this type should turn here first for guidance.

Pittsburgh. 1970. m. $17. Martin Schultz. Metropolitan Pittsburgh Public Broadcasting, Inc., 4802 Fifth Ave., Pittsburgh, PA 15213. Illus., adv. Circ: 57,000. Sample.

Aud: Hs.

Best known for its lively writing, good photographs, and general coverage of the entire Pittsburgh area, this is one of the better city/regional magazines. It has fine articles on business, social, and political events. There are good personality sketches and scores of features to keep the reader advised of the latest in the arts, recreation and other events in and around the city. In fact, much of the magazine is addressed to people who live outside the immediate metropolitan area. Be that as it may, the title is a good one for almost any Pennsylvania library.

Portland Magazine (Formerly: *Portland Commerce*). 1894. m. $20. Rolv Harlow Schillios. Portland Chamber of Commerce, 221 N.W. Second Ave., Portland, OR 97209. Illus., adv. Circ: 10,000. Vol. ends: Dec.

Aud: Hs.

"The Magazine of Oregon Life and Business" has a pronounced emphasis on the latter aspect. In annual report fashion, articles highlight Oregon industries and economic trends. A substantial portion of space is given over to news briefs about developments in companies, achievements of businesspeople and seminars. The style and content definitely limit its appeal, but those it does serve are served well.

St. Louis (Formerly: *St. Louisan*). 1969. m. $15. Dawn Hudson. Blest Co., 7110 Oakland Ave., St. Louis, MO 63117. Illus., adv. Circ: 30,000. Sample. Vol. ends: Dec. Microform: UMI.

Indexed: Acs. *Aud:* Hs.

There's no missing the "big city" flavor of this magazine. It is timely, flashy, catchy, stimulating, and provoking. The calendars and guides are extensive, and the articles are well developed. *St. Louis* has chosen content and style with the local urban audience in mind and certainly has value for such readers.

San Antonio Magazine. 1967. m. $12. Sandy Brown. Greater San Antonio Chamber of Commerce, P.O. Box 1628, San Antonio, TX 78296. Illus., adv. Circ: 30,000. Sample. Vol. ends: Dec.

Aud: Hs.

Although information about and for the business community is the main ingredient, *San Antonio Magazine* avoids being too exclusive by carrying articles on business topics with popular appeal and by using a writing style that is inviting and sustains reader interest. In addition, there is recreational information in the events listings, the program guide for the local public television station, and the "Weekend Getaway" department. The Chamber of Commerce has reached beyond its membership with this balanced and tasteful publication.

San Francisco. 1963. m. $18. Ron Hagen. Hagen Group, 950 Battery, San Francisco, CA 98111. Illus., adv. Circ: 31,000. Sample.

Indexed: Acs. *Aud:* Hs.

The arts are a primary concern here, and there are many articles, features and sketches of people involved in some aspect of the performing arts. Other illustrated pieces consider a wide variety of topics from business and travel to politics and matters of concern to consumers. The tone is one of relative ease and luxury, and the whole gives a good overview of the Bay Area and its many interests. A related title:

San Francisco Focus. 1968. m. $1.50. KQED, 500 Eighth St., San Francisco, CA 94103. Illus., adv. Circ: 170,000. Here the emphasis is on arts and entertainment, with primary focus on a calendar of events, restaurants, films and so forth.

The Santa Fean Magazine. 1972. 11/yr. $16.75. Betty Bauer & Marian F. Love. Santa Fean Magazine, P.O. Box 1424, Santa Fe, NM 87501. Illus., adv. Sample. Vol. ends: Dec.

Indexed: Acs. *Aud:* Hs.

The arts figure prominently in well-written stories, the calendar of events, and even in the advertising, most of which is for galleries. The features are most often portraits of local artists with an occasional piece on local history or contemporary life in Santa Fe. Needless to say, the magazine is tastefully compiled with fine color reproduction and elegant print style on heavyweight paper. This is a cultured version of the city magazine, which will find readers in residents and tourists alike.

Southern Exposure. See Afro-American/For the Student Section.

Texas Monthly. 1973. m. $18. Gregory Curtis. Texas Monthly, Inc., P.O. Box 1569, Austin, TX 78767. Illus., adv. Circ: 280,000. Vol. ends: Jan. Microform: UMI.

Indexed: Acs, PopPer. *Bk. rev:* 1–2, 200–500 words, signed. *Aud:* Hs.

The editors have taken on a formidable task considering the mere size, not to mention the diversity, of the state. And they are successful in delivering the news (and making it) in this imposing and exciting publication. Investigative, and sometimes quite daring, the reporting makes for lively reading. Excerpts from recent books, photo-essays, short newsy and witty bits, and arts reviews can also be found in its 200-plus pages. A monthly guide to events covers the major Texas cities and regional centers. Camping guides and the like are worked up into special sections. The monthly puzzle is not a crossword type but will confound the best. The writers enjoy national prominence, which is apparent in the quality of the magazine. A professional publication that adequately covers the state and even reaches beyond its borders.

Vermont Life. 1946. q. $7.50. Thomas K. Slayton, 61 Elm St., Montpelier, VT 05602. Illus., index. Circ: 128,000. Vol. ends: Summer. Microform: UMI.

Indexed: Acs. *Aud:* Hs.

Vermont's natural and human resources are paid tribute to in poetic and pictorial essays. The layout, the abundance of artistic color photographs, and the absence of cluttering ads and listings of events create a visual delight. This and the universal appeal of the articles may explain the magazine's longevity and success. State sponsorship accounts for the uncompromising quality of the publication at an affordable price.

The Washingtonian. 1965. m. Maryland, Virginia, & District of Columbia, $15 (Others, $18). John A. Limpert, 1828 L St. N.W., Suite 200, Washington, DC 20036. Subs. to: P.O. Box 936, Farmingdale, NY 11737. Illus., adv. Circ: 135,927. Vol. ends: Sept. Microform: B&H, UMI.

Indexed: Acs. *Aud:* Hs.

You might expect the *Washingtonian* to be cosmopolitan, and it is. With its strategic location, it is able to monitor the federal government scene closely so that political news and analysis are well covered. The rest of the content is devoted to stories and columns for an educated and prosperous audience: education, personalities, personal finances, real estate, health, events, dining, and even reviews of classy cars. Frankness and wit are among its characteristics.

Wisconsin Trails (Formerly: *Wisconsin Tales and Trails*). 1960. bi-m. $17. Howard W. Mead. Wisconsin Tales and Trails, Inc., P.O. Box 5650, Madison, WI 53705. Illus., index. Circ: 36,000. Sample. Vol. ends: Winter.

Indexed: Acs. *Aud:* Hs.

This 9- by 12-inch glossy magazine is striking for its abundant illustrations and optimistic articles. Brief but pithy stories foster understanding and pride in Wisconsin people, places, and the past. There are seasonal recreational features, stories about unique industries, and local history. The pictorial essay and "Scrapbook" sections reveal little known as well as popular aspects of Wisconsin heritage and life. The publishers publish a separate monthly guide for practical and dated information, which allows *Wisconsin Trails* to function as the showpiece.

Yankee. 1935. m. $15. Judson D. Hale, Sr. Yankee Publg., Inc., Dublin, NH 03444. Illus., adv. Circ: 850,000. Vol. ends: Dec. Microform: UMI.

Indexed: Acs, PopPer. *Bk. rev:* 1–2, 150 words, signed. *Aud:* Hs.

A long-lived general magazine that resembles an almanac in size and offers fiction, poetry, advice for home and garden, people profiles, historical bits, recipes, nature information, a calendar of events, and quaint advertising. Illustrations are plentiful, including a monthly color centerfold of a typical New England scene. *Yankee* fosters a sense of community among New Englanders and those interested in sharing that spirit.

CIVIL LIBERTIES

For the Student

See also Alternatives; News and Opinion; Political Science; and Women Sections.

Lee Regan, Exchange and Gift Unit, U.S. Geological Survey Library, National Center-MS 950, Reston, VA 22092.

Introduction

One of the challenges in searching periodical literature for civil liberties subjects is the extremely diverse range of specific topics under which relevant material can be found, since rights and freedoms can be claimed for all aspects and qualities of living. A selective list of subject cross-references serves as a useful reminder: academic freedom, censorship, children's rights, detention of persons, due process, equality before the law, freedom of (association, information, movement, the press, speech), habeas corpus, human rights, liberty, prisoners' rights, privacy, race discrimination, right to petition, right of property, sex discrimination, voting rights, and workers' rights.

Besides the selections below, a few prerequisite general magazine titles (specifically *Nation* and *Progressive*) are not included on the assumption that they should not need description. A qualifying statement on the selection is that a primary consideration was made to include titles with a national scope, a few titles of international focus excepted. Titles with more regional and local focus, such as *Southern Changes* and *Southern Exposure*, and many titles dealing with specific ethnic groups have not been included. Responsibility for adequate coverage of specific cultural groups and specific rights and support for regional and local publications belongs to each individual librarian.

Basic Periodicals

Hs: *Center Magazine, Social Policy.*

Basic Abstracts and Indexes

Alternative Press Index.

For the Student

Amnesty Action. 1966. m. Membership, $25. Emilie Trautman. Amnesty International U.S.A., 304 W. 58th St., New York, NY 10019. Illus. Circ: 25,000. Sample.
Aud: Hs.

This tabloid provides information about Amnesty International activities and issues of concern, including torture and physical abuse of political prisoners, fair trials for dissidents, prison conditions, and opposition to the death penalty. Features include alerts on individual human-rights cases, international country reports, and synopses of Amnesty International reports, their primary documentary publications.

Center Magazine. 1963. bi-m. Membership, $25. Donald McDonald. Center for the Study of Democratic Institutions, P.O. Box 4068, Santa Barbara, CA 93103. Illus., index. Circ: 15,000. Vol. ends: Nov/Dec. Microform: B&H, UMI.
Indexed: MgI, RG. *Bk. rev:* 4–5, 400–600 words. *Aud:* Hs.

A founder's motto is quoted to describe "the Center's prejudice [as] democracy; its operating procedure, the dialogue." As such, its magazine contains transcribed remarks of panel discussions on a single topic or up to five topics, as well as short articles. The result provides analysis and commentary on public policy issues, with an attempt "to present in each issue the broadest diversity of perspectives in a responsible and tasteful manner." The focus is primarily on domestic affairs and U.S. foreign policy, including such topics as national security and civil liberties; public information, government and the media; arms control; human rights; government ethics; and elitism in Israel.

Civil Liberties. 1949. q. $20. Ari Korpivaara. Amer. Civil Liberties Union, 132 W. 43rd St., New York, NY 10036. Illus.
Aud: Hs.

The ACLU is probably the preeminent national civil liberties organization, often cited in passing by other news sources. Its activities in defense of the Bill of Rights cover all areas of civil rights, including criminal law, immigration, refugee sanctuary, national security, religious freedom, women's rights, and reproductive rights. This 12-page tabloid presents brief summaries of actions, cases, and issues faced by the ACLU. It also documents ACLU policies. Libraries may also want to receive the more local and specialized newsletters of ACLU chapters and projects, with special consideration for *Civil Liberties Alert*, a legislative newsletter published by the ACLU Washington office.

First Principles: national security and civil liberties. 1975. bi-m. $15. Morton Halperin. Center for Natl. Security Studies, 122 Maryland Ave. N.E., Washington, DC 20002. Vol. ends: July/Aug.
Aud: Hs.

This 12-page newsletter, which takes its title from a quote by Thomas Paine, is also well represented by a quote of James Madison carried on every issue: "Perhaps it is a universal truth that the loss of liberty at home is to be charged to provisions against danger, real or pretended, from abroad." In that light, *First Principles* reports on freedom of information, domestic surveillance, media disinformation, and national security issues with news reports on developments in Congress and the courts. Each issue contains a useful annotated bibliography of recent literature in the field.

Freeman: monthly journal of ideas on liberty. 1950. m. $10. Paul Poirot. Foundation for Economic Education, Irvington-on-Hudson, NY 10533. Index. Microform: UMI.
Bk. rev: 1–2, 300–500 words, signed. *Aud:* Hs.

The Foundation for Economic Education is a nonprofit "champion of private property, the free market, the profit and loss system, and limited government." Six to eight short articles in each issue, written by economists, teachers, and businesspersons, present readable, simplified arguments and demonstrations against centralized planning, economic regulation, and similar restrictions on entrepreneurship, property rights and individualism.

Guardian: independent radical weekly. 1948. w. $27.50. William A. Ryan. Inst. for Independent Social Journalism, 33 W. 17th St., New York, NY 10011. Illus., adv. Microform: UMI.
Indexed: API. *Bk. rev:* 2–3, 200–300 words, signed. *Aud:* Hs.

The *Guardian* is the tabloid that reports all the civil rights news that does not appear in most daily newspapers. It reports current rights-related events of U.S. labor, gays, Blacks, women, prisoners, Native Americans, immigrants and all civil liberties. International human rights and liberation struggles are also covered. Some longer essays of analysis are offered but mostly clear, succinct reporting with minimal political rhetoric and a general tone that is activist, people-oriented and anti-establishment.

Hastings Center Report. 1971. bi-m. Libraries, $45 (Individuals, $33). Carol Levine. Hastings Center, 360 Broadway,

Hastings-on-Hudson, NY 10706. Index. Vol. ends: Dec. Microform: UMI.

Indexed: SocSc. *Bk. rev:* 2 per issue, 500–1,000 words, signed. *Aud:* Hs.

The Hastings Center Institute of Society, Ethics and Life Sciences is devoted to the study of ethical problems of the biomedical, behavioral and social sciences, as well as issues in professional and applied ethics. Topics covered in the magazine include abortion, aging, behavior control, genetic screening and engineering, the mentally retarded, and reproductive issues. Regular features include case studies and news from the National Institutes of Health and state legislatures and a two-page annotated bibliography of recent literature. With development and questions of medical technology casting names like Karen Quinlan and Baby Doe into national headlines, this title will be continually useful and valued for its objective commentary.

Human Rights. 1969. q. $5 (Nonmembers, $17). Ed. bd. Amer. Bar Assn., Section of Individual Rights and Responsibilities, 750 N. Lake Shore Dr., Chicago, IL 60611. Illus., adv.

Indexed: SocSc. *Aud:* Hs.

This magazine presents short notices and articles of commentary on current news items, events, and social issues related to civil and human rights. The primary focus is on debates about domestic affairs, such as children's rights, the "comparable worth" debate, outlawing pornography, and nuclear protests, with occasional topics about such foreign situations as apartheid and the United States intervention in Central America. The format and contents are engaging and easily readable. Highly recommended.

Index on Censorship. 1972. bi-m. $25. George Theiner. Writers & Scholars Intl., London/Fund for Free Expression, 36 W. 44th St., New York, NY 10016. Illus. Vol. ends: Dec.

Indexed: PAIS. *Aud:* Hs.

Comparable to the authenticity with which Amnesty International publications document and urge an end to the international practice of torture, *Index on Censorship* attempts to increase awareness of, and to remove barriers to, a free press, academic freedom, and freedom of creative expression. Each issue contains 10 to 15 reports and articles by and about journalists and banned authors in all countries regardless of ideology, including "censorship—American style." Cartoons, poems, samizdat excerpts, and letters from dissidents create a sense of immediacy to the background situations being reported.

Labor Notes. m. $20 (Individuals, $10). Jim Woodward. Labor Education and Research Project, P.O. Box 20001, Detroit, MI 48220. Illus.

Indexed: API. *Aud:* Hs.

A 12-page newsletter, urging "Let's put the movement back in the labor movement," *Labor Notes* consists mainly of news briefs on national union-related events, including some attention to foreign concerns (such as Canadian postal workers and a labor delegation to Central America). A page of "Resources" provides an annotated list of publications.

Liberty: magazine of religious liberty. 1906. bi-m. $6.25. Review & Herald Publg. Assn., 55 W. Oak Ridge Dr., Hagerstown, MD 21740. Illus.

Aud: Hs.

Five or six short articles present personal perspectives, opinions, and news stories regarding the status of religious faith and practice in society. Such domestic events as teaching creationism, faith-versus-medical treatment, and types of religious culture (e.g., Soviet atheism, India). Considering its economical price and the increasing prevalence of religious issues in public debate, this is probably a useful title.

Migration Today. 1973. bi-m. $17. Lydio F. Tomasi. Center for Migration Studies, 209 Flagg Place, Staten Island, NY 10304. Illus., adv. Microform: UMI.

Indexed: CIJE. *Bk. rev:* 2–3 pages of cited works, 50–100 words. *Aud:* Hs.

Migration Today: current issues and Christian responsibility. 2–3/yr. Free. Andre Jacques & Barbo Ries. World Council of Churches, 150, route de Ferney, 1211 Geneva, Switzerland. Illus.

Bk. rev: 5–6, 50–100 words, unsigned. *Aud:* Hs.

Migration Today, published by the Center for Migration Studies, has a more popular orientation and domestic focus than its scholarly counterpart, *International Migration Review*. It features social-adjustment experiences and services for American immigrant groups, with regular news updates and articles on legal developments related to aliens and U.S. policies affecting migrant and refugee flows. The World Council of Churches title is more rights conscious and activist in tone, setting out "to confront those who 'study (migrants)'; to challenge those who 'help them'; to inform those who 'make decisions on them.' " While the CMS title is especially recommended for a wider U.S. audience, affirming ours as a multicultural society, the WCC title is also recommended for urban school libraries with large immigrant populations.

New Perspectives (Continues: *Perspectives*; formerly: *Civil Rights Digest*). 1984. q. Free. Linda Chavez & Christopher Gersten. U.S. Commission on Civil Rights, G.P.O., Washington, DC 29492. Illus. Microform: UMI.

Indexed: CIJE, SocSc. *Bk. rev:* 2–3, 1,000–1,500 words, signed. *Aud:* Hs.

With the U.S. Civil Rights Commission becoming one of the ideological battlefronts of the Reagan Administration, this magazine reflects shifting attitudes relating to enforcement of equal opportunities and promotion of affirmative action in employment and education for minorities. Articles discuss the need for strategies that do not discriminate (e.g., reverse discrimination) nor engender adverse dependencies on governmental entitlements.

News Media and the Law. 1977. q. $20. Jane E. Kirtley. Reporters' Committee for Freedom of the Press, Rm. 300, 800 18th St. N.W., Washington, DC 20006. Illus. Microform: UMI.

Aud: Hs.

Brief articles report events and summarize court cases from around the country, covering the broad spectrum of issues related to freedom of the press, such as libel and privacy; prior restraint, federal and state FOI legislation; court closure (vs. open access by the media, "gag rules"); reporter confidentiality and shield laws. While the brevity of articles leaves a need for additional materials, school libraries should especially consider this magazine to enlighten students to a more critical view of the media and to elicit interest in First Amendment issues.

Our Right to Know. 1981. q. $10. Fund for Open Information and Accountability, 339 Lafayette St., New York, NY 10012. Illus. Circ: 10,000. Sample. Vol. ends: Spring.

Indexed: API. *Aud:* Hs.

Our Right to Know promotes the importance of the Freedom of Information Act and its relationship to other civil liberties concerns. Each issue has four to five articles of news and commentary to that purpose, plus three to four pages of abstracts of news articles under headings of "Privacy and Secrecy in the News," "FOIA in the Courts," and "FOIA in the News."

Reason. 1968. m. $19.50. Robert Pool. Reason Foundation, 1018 Garden St., Santa Barbara, CA 93101. Illus., adv. Microform: UMI.

Bk. rev: 4–6, 500–1,000 words. *Aud:* Hs.

The banner of this magazine is "free minds and free markets." Against government intervention in private enterprise and individual lives, it is probably the best popularization of libertarian views available. Each issue contains four or five feature articles, several departments, shorter comments, and book reviews. Topics covered include a wide variety of subjects, such as entrepreneurs in space, government spending, Spanish socialism, and examples of historical-political economic theory. While it lacks depth, the style of the format is engaging, and it is an effective representative for its viewpoint.

Rights. 1951. bi-m. Membership, $15. Jeff Kisseloff. Natl. Emergency Civil Liberties Committee, 175 Fifth Ave., New York, NY 10001. Illus.

Indexed: API. *Aud:* Hs.

The NECLC aims to "reestablish the freedoms guaranteed by the Constitution and the Bill of Rights" and pursues test cases to that end, involving freedom of speech, press, religion; the right to assemble; travel freely; and to dissent. *Rights* resembles a narrowly focused *Nation* magazine. Each issue contains five or six short articles and a section of highlights from NECLC court actions. Membership includes an annual supplement, the *Bill of Rights Journal*, consisting of eight to ten articles, underwritten by contributions and advertisements. The focus of a recent annual was "Protecting Our Right to Know."

Social Policy. 1970. q. $15. Frank Riessman. Social Policy Corp., 33 W. 42nd St., New York, NY 10036. Illus., adv. Vol. ends: Spring. Microform: B&H, JAI, UMI.

Indexed: API, CIJE, SocSc. *Bk. rev:* 2–3, 1,000–1,500 words, signed. *Aud:* Hs.

Social Policy carries articles on a wide range of social problems and services, with consistent attention to civil rights/civil liberties issues from a social science perspective. Topics have included government secrecy and censorship, democratic schooling, services for the disabled and mentally retarded, and unemployment. Analyses of existing conditions and proposals for new policies are presented in clear, easily readable discussions and commentary that avoid both extremes of rhetorical ideology and overly formalized academia.

CLASSICAL STUDIES

For the Student/For the Professional

See also Art; History; and Literature Sections.

Robert J. Kibbee, Classics Bibliographer, Cornell University Libraries, Ithaca, NY 14803

Introduction

The periodical literature of classical studies presents some special problems for library selectors. As one might expect, scholarly writing dominates. Still, there are a few magazines specifically aimed at school-age classicists or their teachers. Some of the higher-level journals also may be appropriate for high-school students.

For the Student

Classical Bulletin. 1925. q. $6.00. Michael J. Harstad. Div. of Foreign Languages, Asbury College, Wilmore, KY 40390. Circ: 1,300. Vol. ends: Fall. Microform: UMI.

Indexed: APh, CathI. *Bk. rev:* 5, 300 words, signed. *Aud:* Hs.

This journal features four to five brief, readable, but well-documented articles, for the most part explications of literary texts, although most aspects of classical antiquity are touched upon. More unusual is the poetry section, with translations of classical poetry and original poems on classical themes. A recurrent interest is Late Latin, particularly in colonial and Federalist America. Book reviews are usually of works of general interest rather than technical scholarship.

Classical Calliope. 1981. q. $14. Rosalie F. Baker & Charles F. Baker, III. Cobblestone Publg., Inc., 20 Grove St., Peterborough, NH 03458. Illus., index. Circ: 3,500. Vol. ends: Fall.

Aud: Ejh, Hs.

Now less frequent (it appears four times during the school year), but larger, this well-produced magazine is still aimed at the 12–18-year-old age group. It features easy-to-read articles plus games and puzzles to stimulate interest in classical languages and culture. Recommended for all school libraries supporting classics programs.

Greece and Rome. 1931. s-a. $30. Ian McAuslan & P. Walcot. Classical Assn., Oxford Univ. Press, Walton St., Oxford OX2 6DP, England. Adv. Circ: 1,000. Vol. ends: Oct. Microform: UMI.

Indexed: HumI. *Bk. rev:* 4, 400 words, signed. *Aud:* Hs.

Articles range from brief notes to 15 pages. They are well documented but not overly technical. Most articles are literary critical discussions of classical texts with a scattering of historical articles. In addition to the book reviews, there are excellent bibliographic essays on recent work in particular fields and special sections on "School Books" and "Reprints." The books in these sections are coded for academic level of interest. Could be useful to high schools with strong programs in the classics.

For the Professional

·***Classical Journal.*** 1905. q. $18. W. W. deGrummond. Dept. of Classics, Florida State Univ., Tallahassee, FL 32306. Index, adv. Circ: 3,500. Vol. ends: June. Microform: MIM, UMI.

Indexed: EdI. *Bk. rev:* 8, 600 words, signed. *Aud:* Pr.

The four to five lengthy but readable articles are usually concerned with interpretations of literary texts, but history and philosophy are also discussed. The balance of the journal is directed towards teachers. In particular, "The Forum" features brief articles on the place of classics in the high school and college curriculum, teaching hints and resources, and so on. Like *Classical World*, an excellent source for teachers.

Classical Outlook. 1936. q. $15. Richard LaFleur. Amer. Classical League, Miami Univ., Oxford, OH 45056. Illus., index, adv. Circ: 3,000. Vol. ends: June. Microform: MIM.

Bk. rev: 8, 400 words, signed. *Aud:* Pr.

The five to eight articles, directed at high school Latin teachers, include lists of teaching aids and reviews and directories of teaching materials. Book reviews tend to stress classroom utility. Will be helpful to any Latin teacher.

Classical World. 1907. bi-m. $10. Jerry Clack. Classical Assn. of the Atlantic States, Dept. of Classics, Duquesne Univ., Pittsburgh, PA 15282. Adv. Circ: 3,000. Vol. ends: Aug. Refereed. Microform: MIM, UMI.

Indexed: BoRv, BoRvI. *Bk. rev:* 15–30, 300 words, signed. *Aud:* Pr.

CW contains many departments useful to the high school Latin teacher. In addition to two to three brief, readable articles and briefer "Scholia," there is an annual survey of audiovisual material in the classics, along with bibliographies of textbooks, and notes on current teaching practice. There are frequent bibliographic essays on recent scholarship on a particular area or author, e.g., an entire issue devoted to

"Studies in Greek Athletics." A useful adjunct to the similar, but somewhat more scholarly, *Classical Journal*.

COMICS

For the Student: Elementary and Junior High; Costumed Heroes; Fantasy, Adventure; Magazines about Comics; War; Weird

Frederick Patten, Los Angeles Science Fantasy Society. Home: 11863 W. Jefferson Blvd., Culver City, CA 90230

Introduction

If "the child is father of the man" (Wordsworth), then it is important for libraries to take note of the literature that influences childhood. This certainly includes comic books. Whatever their faults or whatever children may be told to read instead, comic books continue to have a tremendous circulation among children at their most impressionable and formative ages. Many children, especially those in disadvantaged circumstances, may find little else to read. Among children who have the advantages of a wider range of literary resources, comic books are still popular because of their bright, attention-holding images and rapid pacing, which make them a quickly read and relaxing form of pleasure when one has no time to settle down with a richer book that requires more leisurely and thoughtful reading.

Comic books can be worthwhile acquisitions for school libraries, especially for slow learners and those with reading problems, as aids to teach and encourage regular reading. The presence of comics in libraries can lead to a more friendly, informal atmosphere, encouraging a greater use of libraries among children who tend to think of them as dull places of no interest. The comic-book format is being used in some schools to teach English to children of foreign-language backgrounds, and some state government offices have commissioned special public service comics for distribution in schools to promote mental health, dental care, and so on.

The comic book industry underwent a more radical evolution during the first half of the 1980s than at any other time in its 50-year history. Major publishers disappeared, along with titles (such as those featuring the Walt Disney cartoon characters) that had seemed permanently established. The distribution of comic books to traditional public newsstands dwindled to insignificance. Instead they were relocated to a growing number of comics-specialty bookshops throughout the United States. Most of these shops make a practice of carrying every comic book published, which has encouraged the growth of many new small-press publishers. There is a greater number of titles today than at any time in the past. However, many of these titles are ephemeral owing to the usual vagaries of small-press publishing. Also, there is a trend toward discontinuing long-running titles (such as *Wonder Woman*, which was started in the 1940s) and replacing them with "mini-series" or "maxi-series" titles that serialize a single story in six to twelve issues. These are then superseded by newer titles that may feature some of the same characters. The industry thinking is that this will make comics more appealing to young readers who would be discouraged by a title with hundreds of issues that are no longer available. However, it makes purchasing comics by mail more difficult because a desired title may have reached the end of its planned run before a subscription order can be processed.

A recent practice among the two major publishers, DC Comics and Marvel Comics, is the integration of practically all of their titles into a common (for each publisher) background universe, and the introduction of "crossover" plotting. The purpose is to convince the readers of any one comic that they need to read *all* of that publisher's titles. Guest appearances of one comic's heroes in another title have been traditional, but now a serialized adventure may switch from one title to another before it is concluded. Libraries that subscribe to any titles from these two publishers should be aware that the stories may be incomplete by themselves and may contain many cryptic references to events taking place in that publisher's other titles. This may create temporary demands from young readers for these other titles.

Currently, the average comic book from DC and Marvel is a 36-page color magazine on cheap newsprint, consisting of approximately 25 pages of features and 11 pages of advertising, for $.75. However, there is a larger variety than before of higher quality comics, offering combinations of more pages, less or no advertising, and better printing, at various higher prices. The newer small-press publishers offer an even greater variety of formats, quality, and prices. Librarians may find it prudent to visit a comics-specialty bookshop to examine the range of titles available. Many of these shops will provide specialized subscription services to local customers and can offer professional advice on the probable longevity of a given title. For libraries in towns that do not have a local comics-specialty shop, there are several large regional distributors that offer a variety of mail-order subscription services to institutions. One of the oldest and most comprehensive of these is Bud Plant, Inc., P.O. Box 1886, Grass Valley, CA 95945. Plant also publishes frequent thick catalogs, listing not only all new comic books but also fantasy-art books and calendars, posters, fantasy-gaming periodicals, underground comics, popular-media magazines, hobbyist books on such collectibles as baseball cards or paperbacks, and similar publications.

ORDERING INFORMATION. Unless otherwise noted, the following addresses and ordering information will apply to all titles reviewed here issued by their respective publishing companies.

DC Comics, Inc., P.O. Box 1308-F, Fort Lee, NJ 07024. Prices given with reviews. There are occasional group subscription discounts.

Marvel Comics Group, Subscription Dept., 387 Park Ave. S., New York, NY 10016. Prices given with reviews. There are occasional group subscription discounts.

For the Student

ELEMENTARY AND JUNIOR HIGH

Archie. bi-m. $3.90/yr. *Archie and Me.* bi-m. $3.90/yr. *Archie at Riverdale High.* bi-m. $3.90/yr. *Archie's Pals 'n' Gals.* bi-m. $3.90/yr. *Archie's TV Laugh-out.* bi-m. $3.90/yr. *Betty and Me.* bi-m. $3.90/yr. *Betty and Veronica.* bi-m. $3.90/yr.

Betty's Diary. 11/yr. $7.15/yr. *Everything's Archie.* bi-m. $3.90/yr. *Jughead.* bi-m. $3.90/yr. *Laugh.* bi-m. $3.90/yr. *Life with Archie.* bi-m. $3.90/yr. *Little Archie.* 11/yr. $7.15/yr. *Pep.* bi-m. $3.90/yr. Archie Comic Publns., Inc., 325 Fayette Ave., Mamaroneck, NY 10543.

Archie Andrews and his friends at Riverdale High—Betty, Veronica, Jughead, and Reggie—are old enough to be U.S. institutions. Unlike the newspaper comic strip, which features humor about teenagers natural to a high school setting written for the adults who buy newspapers, these comic books feature plots for a more juvenile readership, plus puzzle and game pages. Most of these titles contain three or four stories of a half-dozen pages each, playing up the humorous side of teenagers' lives. Betty worries about how to make Archie pay more attention to her; Jughead tries to escape responsibility and loaf as much as possible; the girls scheme to make the boys spend less time on sports and more on them. *Little Archie* differs in that it is a humorous fantasy-adventure title, featuring stories about Archie when he was only six or seven years old and outwitting comedy-relief mad scientists and monsters. Although the stories in these titles are *about* teenagers, the level of the plotting makes them more suitable for elementary and lower junior high grades, or for slow readers.

Care Bears. bi-m. $7.80/12 issues. Star Comics/Marvel Comics Group.

The Care Bears are the cute and cuddly characters created by the American Greetings Corporation to appeal to the plush-doll age group. The Care Bears are all pastel-colored teddies with names like Tenderheart Bear, Friend Bear, Funshine Bear, and Birthday Bear. There are also the Care Bears Cousins, who are plush lions, elephants, bunnies, and other friendly animals. They live in a cloud-castle in the sky, Care-A-Lot, from which they can observe Earth and help unhappy children. The unhappiness is usually caused by spiteful witches and monsters who want to make people miserable because nobody ever loved them. The Care Bears have more than enough love for all, and the villains are invariably reformed when they learn that it is more satisfying to help than to hurt others—because then you will automatically be loved by everyone. This message of spreading happiness around and helping to cheer up those who are unhappy is aimed at children who are just beginning to enter into social contact at the elementary school level.

Ewoks. bi-m. $7.80/12 issues. Star Comics/Marvel Comics Group.

The Ewoks were introduced in the third *Star Wars* motion picture, *Return of the Jedi.* They are a tribe of small, furry, bear-like forest dwellers on the primitive planet Endor. They have since returned to star in two TV specials and a Saturday morning TV cartoon series. The TV cartoons and comic books focus upon three Ewok children: the boys Wicket and Teebo and the girl Kneesaa (daughter of the Ewok chieftain). Their adventures are roughly of a juvenile *Swiss Family Robinson* or *Tarzan* nature. The three go exploring and find an unknown valley inhabited by dangerous creatures that they must keep from escaping into their forest home;

they discover and warn their tribe against an invasion of a reptilian warrior tribe that likes to eat Ewoks; they must trick greedy visitors from outer space into thinking that their world is too dangerous for a gigantic strip-mining operation. The three children are models of self-reliance who always use their wits to escape from or outsmart physically larger opponents who rely only on their strength.

Katy Keene. bi-m. $3.90/yr. Archie Comic Publns., Inc., 325 Fayette Ave., Mamaroneck, NY 10543.

This is a fashion model comic book for young girls. Katy Keene is a beautiful model who meets handsome designers who invariably pick her to display their latest creations. The plots are virtually nonexistent, but the characters are almost always shown in full figure poses and their costumes change almost from panel to panel. The readers are encouraged to send in clothing designs, and those used are acknowledged. Practically every panel contains a statement, "Katy's lounge outfit by . . .," "skating outfits by . . .," "Gloria's gown & cape by . . ." and so on. In one sample issue that contains a single 20-page story, there are over forty credited women's clothing designs, five men's clothing designs, and eight women's hairstyles. This comic book is for fashion-conscious children.

Peter Porker: the spectacular Spider-Ham. bi-m. $7.80/12 issues. Star Comics/Marvel Comics Group.

This title, for juvenile readers, is Marvel Comics' own pastiche of its popular *Amazing Spider-Man* costumed super-hero. The adventures are in a more humorous vein (the villains are all too silly to be frightening), and the entire cast is drawn as funny animals. Peter Porker, a teenage free-lance photographer for the Daily Beagle newspaper, is in reality the super-hero Spider-Ham (which is how he manages to get such newsworthy photos of himself in action). Objectively, the novelty of seeing the Spider-Man cast drawn as funny animals soon wears off, and all that is left is a bland imitation of the regular *Spider-Man* titles. Sales reports indicate that this is the top seller of all of Marvel's Star Comics for young children, so it seems to be what the kids themselves want to read.

Power Pack. bi-m. $9/12 issues. Marvel Comics Group.

Most costumed super-hero magazines feature teenagers or men and women in their 20s. But, what if superpowers were given to young children who are not mature enough to handle them? This is the theme of *Power Pack*, the story of four brothers and sisters between the ages of five and ten who have mighty abilities thrust upon them by a dying alien. They have gradually learned how to use their talents but are not yet sure what they should do with them. *Power Pack* is a "realistic" super-hero serial, thoroughly integrated into the Marvel Universe, with frequent guest appearances of other Marvel heroes. In one story the four children succeed in helping Spider-Man, and the youngest, Katie, has made friends with the five-year-old son of Reed and Sue Richards of the Fantastic Four. These crossovers have brought criticism that *Power Pack* is primarily designed to steer young readers to the other Marvel titles. Nevertheless, it is the only comic book for young readers who want a "real" comic instead of the titles obviously designed for "babies." Its adventures are filled with serious melodrama but are not as horrific as those in the super-hero comics for teen readers. *Power Pack*'s stories teach that mistakes are a natural part of learning and growing and that personal strengths should be developed rather than hidden for fear of being "different"; however, these talents must be used wisely rather than for showing off or gaining superiority over others.

COSTUMED HEROES

Action Comics. m. $9/yr. *Superman.* m. $9/yr. DC Comics, Inc.

Superman is such a mythical figure today that everyone is aware of this comic book's story concept. Superman (real name: Kal El) is the sole survivor of the planet Krypton, who was sent to Earth as an infant by his scientist father to save his life when his world exploded. He was adopted and raised by a kindly midwestern couple, the Kents, and grew up to use his superior Kryptonian powers to fight crime and injustice. When he is not in his Superman persona, he disguises himself as mild-mannered Clark Kent. *Superman*'s background has been renovated several times since the magazine began in 1939, and the publisher has announced a renovation that will be so extensive that *Superman* will discontinue its present numbering system (currently at over 400 issues) and begin again with Volume 2, Number 1. *Superman* is a good action-drama fantasy with pseudo-scientific trappings, suitable for older preadolescents and young teens. *Action Comics* features two short stories per issue, often portraying Superman in a lighter vein. *Superman* features more melodramatic issue-length adventures.

All-Star Squadron. m. $9/yr. *Justice League of America.* m. $9/yr. *The Legion of Super-Heroes.* m. $18/yr. *The New Teen Titans.* m. $18/yr. *Tales of the Legion of Super-Heroes.* m. $9/yr. *Tales of the Teen Titans.* m. $9/yr. DC Comics, Inc.

DC Comics invented the society-of-heroes concept in 1940 by putting a half-dozen or more of its individually popular costumed heroes together in a new comic book. Marvel Comics refined the concept in the 1960s by establishing personality interplay among the characters. The rationale is that such societies enable the heroes to overcome menaces too great for any one of them to handle alone. This guarantees that their adversaries have to be truly awesome, usually science fiction menaces on a planet-destroying level. These titles sell primarily to readers who want their costumed heroes in quantity. Some society comic books are team-ups of heroes who have their own magazine (*Justice League of America* stars Superman and Batman, among others). *All-Star Squadron* is a "nostalgia" title featuring DC Comics' super-heroes of World War II vintage. *Justice League of America* teams DC Comics' current roster of heroes in modern adventures. *The Legion of Super-Heroes* is set in the thirtieth century and stars a galaxy-wide club of teenage heroes, and is written for readers who enjoy cosmic science fiction settings. This and *The New Teen Titans* are more expensive, deluxe magazines printed on high-quality paper and with less advertising per issue. *The New Teen Titans* is a team consisting partly of some of the older heroes' juvenile sidekicks such as Robin from the *Batman* series and partly of original teen heroes. The story quality of society comic books is usually low because the large cast leaves little room for any depth of motivation or development. The society learns of a new threat, and the rest is all fist-flying action. All that the readers seem to care about is that each hero's (and villain's) costume gets fully displayed in action poses.

Alpha Flight. m. $9/yr. *Avengers*. m. $9/yr. *West Coast Avengers*. m. $9/yr. Marvel Comics Group.

These are Marvel Comics' society-of-heroes titles, which are similar to DC Comics' *All-Star Squadron* and others. Most of the generalizations made about DC Comics' society magazines also apply to these, although Marvel's titles usually offer longer stories that are serialized over many issues. This permits a slightly greater depth in plotting. However, new readers will probably find themselves entering at the middle of an adventure in progress, and it may take several issues for the action and background to become clear. The oldest of these titles, *The Avengers*, features some of the most prestigious super-heroes (currently including Captain America, the Sub-Mariner, and the Greek demigod Hercules), but each of these societies undergoes a soap opera evolution of its cast, with one of its members temporarily or permanently leaving every so often and a new hero joining. Thus, each group is always slowly changing its personnel, but the basic plot is always "slam-bang" action against one or more super-villains. The original *Avengers* operate around New York and the industrialized East Coast; the *West Coast Avengers* are a group of heroes who decided that the Pacific states deserved their own society; and *Alpha Flight* is a Canadian team that consists of both Anglo- and French-Canadian heroes.

Amazing Spider-Man. m. $9/yr. *Marvel Tales*. m. $9/yr. *Peter Parker: The spectacular Spider-Man*. m. $9/yr. *Web of Spider-Man*. m. $9/yr. Marvel Comics Group.

Introverted young Peter Parker was bitten by a radioactive spider and given superpowers, but his life is still a mess. He flunked out of college because his crime fighting did not leave him enough time to study, and he cannot hold a regular job; his acquaintances consider him irresponsible because emergencies force him to miss appointments; and he is feared by the public owing to yellow-journal newspaper articles that portray him as a super-showoff or a psychotic vigilante. In other words, his powers do not solve his growing problems; they magnify them. As a result, high school and college readers can really identify with him. The grotesquely costumed super-villains of this comic book's early years have been replaced with more relevant stories featuring realistic and contemporary dialogue and vocabulary. Plots are laid around current news events. *Amazing Spider-Man*, the oldest of the four titles, features Spider-Man and some of the more popular supporting characters that have been developed over the years. *Marvel Tales* consists of reprints of stories featuring Spider-Man from years-old issues of assorted Marvel titles. *Peter Parker: The Spectacular Spider-Man* emphasizes human-interest stories rather than tradi-

tional hero-villain confrontations. *Web of Spider-Man* focuses upon Parker's new life as a traveling free-lance photographer. This provides an excuse to introduce new locations and characters. But there are so many plot crossovers among the titles that feature new stories that readers who are interested in Spider-Man at all have to read them all.

Amethyst. m. $9/yr. DC Comics, Inc.

A common fantasy among children is that of entering a magic world and becoming a mighty warrior or a noble ruler. That is the theme of this title. "When thirteen-year-old Amy Winston steps through the magical doorway in her bedroom wall, she enters an enchanted dimension where she becomes—*Amethyst, Princess of Gemworld.*" Not only does she become a princess, but owing to a dimensional time differential she becomes an 18-year-old warrior maiden, the leader of the forces of right and good in the Gemworld against the tyranny of Dark Opal and his masters, the evil Lords of Chaos. The Gemworld is divided into many colorful kingdoms and ruling houses named after precious and semi-precious stones such as Emerald, Carnelian, Ruby, and Sardonyx. Amy learns that she is really the child of Lord and Lady Amethyst. She was magically sent to our world by the good sorceress Citrina when Dark Opal killed her parents. She was raised as an average girl, but now she must face her destiny back in the Gemworld. Amy is constantly torn between the two worlds. In New York she has the safe, carefree life of a young teenager whose foster parents love her. In the Gemworld she has beauty, power, and respect, but also heavy responsibilities; and, she is the target of both palace intrigues and supernatural dangers. Further, the body of 18-year-old Amethyst is stirred by romantic emotions toward handsome Lord Topaz, which the mind of 13-year-old Amy is unsure how to handle. *Amethyst* is primarily a comic book for adolescent girls, although there is so much dramatic sword-and-sorcery action that many boys enjoy it as well.

Batman. m. $9/yr. *Detective Comics*. m. $9/yr. m. $1.75 ea. DC Comics, Inc.

Batman is "comicdom's" oldest and still most popular costumed but nonsuper-hero. Young Bruce Wayne saw his parents murdered by a thief, and he has devoted his life to fighting crime. In public he poses as a wealthy industrialist and philanthropist, but in private he has trained himself to become a physical fitness master and criminological expert. His somber bat costume is designed to strike fear into the hearts of evildoers. When Batman first appeared in *Detective Comics* in 1938 he operated as a vigilante, but the publisher quickly turned him into an auxiliary of the police, operating within the law. As in other comic books that have spanned decades, there have been many changes of style. Costumed super-villains and campy humor are both long in the past. Batman's long-time ward, Robin, has grown up and left. Today, Batman battles street gangsters and bosses of organized corruption in hard-boiled dramas similar to the adventures of *The Shadow* in the pulps of the 1930s. *Batman* is popular throughout the teenage range. *Batman* contains solo adventures of the Caped Crusader (although he has adopted a second young ward whom he is grooming as a new Robin); *Detective Comics* pairs Batman with a guest-costumed hero from DC Comics' other titles.

Doctor Strange. bi-m. $9/12 issues. Marvel Comics Group.

Most super-hero comic books are based upon a seemingly scientific rationale. Their heroes and villains presumably get their powers from chemical injections or mechanical inventions or from the superior technology of outer-space civilizations. *Doctor Strange* emphasizes sorcery and supernatural might. Stephen Strange was a U.S. society doctor who discovered that magic, witchcraft and similar arcane forces are real. Evil spirits such as the Lords of Hades are constantly trying to prey upon humanity, and greedy humans often try to use mystical powers for their own enrichment. These evil forces have been held in check for ages by a line of good Sorcerers Supreme. Dr. Strange became the disciple of the then-current Sorcerer Supreme, the Ancient One, and eventually became his successor. Although each adventure is in a weird fantasy vein (rather like a Stephen King horror novel), *Doctor Strange* is designed for the regular super-hero market. Stephen Strange is undeniably a super-hero in an eye-catching costume. He is one of Marvel Comics' oldest heroes and has served as a member of Marvel's super-hero teams from time to time. Characters from Marvel's other comic books, such as the Fantastic Four, regularly make guest appearances in his title. His own villains, whether they are warlocks, demons, witches, or necromancers, all wear colorful costumes. *Doctor Strange* is a good title for teenage comic book readers who also enjoy Dracula and werewolf movies.

Fantastic Four. m. $9/yr. Marvel Comics Group.

This is the oldest and most famous of the "realistic" super-hero comic books. However, after 25 years, it has so many imitators that today it is only a typical super-hero title. The Fantastic Four are a team of heroes who each have unique powers. They also have individual personalities and emotions, and the relationship between them is not always smooth. One of the original team, The Thing, has dropped out (he now has his own solo title). He was replaced by the She-Hulk, which gives the title a more modern sexual balance. The team lives in New York City, not some mythical metropolis, and they suffer all the annoyances of both celebrities and legal authorities. (They are constantly having to prove that they did not use excessive force in capturing criminals.) Although its tone is realistic, the *Fantastic Four* is one of the traditional super-hero comics emphasizing conflicts with would-be world-conquering villains such as Doctor Doom or armies of evil outer-space invaders. This is a good magazine for readers from junior high school up.

Thor. m. $9/yr. Marvel Comics Group.

This is a super-hero comic with the trappings of Norse mythology. The hero is Thor, Storm God and son of Odin. Supporting characters include other genuine deities such as Balder, Heimdall, Loki, and Tyr, along with editorially created warriors such as Hogun the Grim, Fandral the Flashing (an Errol Flynn type), and Beta Ray Bill (a space opera alien who wandered into the mythological setting). Thor spends much of his time fighting against the Trolls, Frost Giants, and other dooms from the Norse legends, but he also ventures on enterprises among the gods of Greek mythology and has even journeyed to Hell to confront Satan. *Thor* is a part of the Marvel Universe, so the Storm God frequently crosses paths with the regular costumed super-heroes, and his wanderings often bring him briefly to Earth to fight traditional comic book villains. However, he usually stays in Asgard Valhalla, which looks like a cross between the Fantasyland sector of Disneyland and Rockefeller Center, where semi-divine and fully divine adversaries can hurl thunderbolts and literally raise armies of the dead in their conflicts with each other. The current teenage interest in adventure fantasy, ranging from Tolkien to role-playing games such as Dungeons and Dragons, makes this a popular title.

FANTASY, ADVENTURE

Albedo. bi-m. $6/3 issues. Steven A. Gallacci. Thoughts & Images, P.O. Box 19419, Seattle, WA 98109.

The main feature of this small-press anthology title is the editor/publisher's own *Erma Felna of the EDF*, a sociopolitical science fiction serial. Felna is a quiet but strongly self-reliant woman who tries to do her job without getting back-benched by her anti-feminist superiors or being turned into a pro-feminist symbol by political activists. She is a space force officer in an interplanetary federation that is slowly crumbling from inept leadership, internal separatist movements, and a sadistic terrorist "nonwar" staged by a rival totalitarian space power. The serial's assets are intelligent plotting, realistic characters, and good dialogue. Its liabilities are its very slow pace and (in the opinion of some reviewers) the undermining of the story's serious nature by the author's insistence on drawing all the characters as animals. In fact, all the stories in *Albedo* are drawn with animal characters, although they are not typical "funny animal" froth. One two-issue story by Stan Sakai was a bloody samurai adventure, perfectly straightforward except that it was drawn in a modern U.S.-cartoon style with an animal cast. The effect of *Albedo* is rather like a modern *Aesop's Fables*, in which readers are challenged to look past the surface fantasy to the serious moral themes. The sophisticated plotting and some graphic violence make *Albedo* an unusual but worthwhile title for high school readers.

Cerebus (Formerly: *Cerebus the Aardvark*). m. $1.70/issue; no subscription information. Dave Sim. Aardvark-Vanaheim, Inc., P.O. Box 1674, Sta. C., Kitchener, Ont. N2G 4R2, Canada.

This magazine began as a college humor type of lampoon of Marvel Comics sword-and-sorcery titles. It features a lone funny animal aardvark swordsman in a world of human warriors and wizards. It has evolved into a comedic adventure series set in an increasingly complex imaginary world. Cerebus has shrunk from a stereotyped invulnerable hero to a highly fallible and rather amoral everyman. He wanders among the kingdoms and city states of the land of Estarcion, trying his hand at everything from generalship to politics to thievery to the priesthood. The strong point of this magazine is the witty dialogue and the sardonic interplay between characters. One of author Dave Sim's favorite ploys is to use obvious pastiches of popular culture heroes (such as Groucho Marx) as his supporting characters, portraying them accurately in considerable depth but casting them in unlikely roles. *Cerebus* is another comic book whose letter columns are dominated by college-age readers. It is popular among fantasy-adventure fans who have a sense of humor. It is apparently especially popular among enthusiasts of fantasy role-playing games such as Dungeons and Dragons.

Journey: the adventures of Wolverine MacAlistaire. m. $9/6 issues; $17/12 issues. William & Nadine Messner-Loebs. Fantagraphics Books, 4359 Cornell Rd., Agoura Hills, CA 91301.

Joshua MacAlistaire is a weatherbeaten, taciturn trapper who wanders through the Northwest Territory just before the War of 1812. (Tecumseh and his American Indian Confederation are background elements.) Although MacAlistaire does win his occasional fights with bears, wolves, or Indians, he is not a hero as much as he is a catalyst who sets off action in those around him. Through him, the reader sees a time and place that is glossed over in modern history books—that is, when "the West" meant the Ohio River valley. Some entire issues have been devoted to MacAlistaire's solitary struggles to survive in the wilderness. There is a steady flow of accurate trivia about harsh frontier life. *Journey* is as intelligently written as a good historical novel. However, its stories are very slowly paced. They emphasize the unromantic drudgery and dirt of living close to nature. There are no continuing characters other than MacAlistaire, who is admirable but too cold to be likeable. This limits its appeal among average comic book readers. *Journey* is an intellectual comic book that is rewarding to older readers who will mentally work a bit at getting into the story.

Ms. Tree. m. $24/yr. Deni Loubert. Renegade Press, 10408 Oxnard St., North Hollywood, CA 91606.

This is the only mystery/detective comic book currently being published. Its writer, Max Allen Collins, is an award-winning mystery novelist and the scripter of the *Dick Tracy* newspaper comic strip since 1977. *Ms. Tree*, which features a female private investigator, is admittedly a tribute to the Mickey Spillane/Mike Hammer school of the hard-boiled private eye. (Today's readers might be more likely to draw comparisons with Clint Eastwood's "Dirty Harry" movies.) Michael Tree, a woman despite her name, inherited her murdered husband's private investigation firm and vowed to keep it going in his memory. The mysteries, which are legitimate and intelligent puzzlers, portray considerable brutality and mayhem. Tree is a strong character with a complex personality. She has been gradually growing more violent, until in recent issues she is beginning to wonder whether she needs psychiatric help. This is being argued even more strongly in a spirited letter-column debate between the readers and Collins, who says pointedly that his goal is to present realistic melodrama and believable characters, not necessarily likeable ones or recommended role models for women.

The magazine also contains short book reviews of new hardcover and paperback mystery novels. The writing (and art, by Terry Beatty) are of a high caliber. Mature themes (abortion, prostitution, and drug addiction, for example), graphic violence, and strong language make *Ms. Tree* a popular title for older teen readers.

Star Trek. m. $9/yr. DC Comics, Inc.

This comic book is a continuation of the highly popular *Star Trek* television and motion picture series, which celebrate their twentieth anniversary in 1986. Admiral James T. Kirk and his starship crew have a mission to explore the galaxy, going where no one has gone before. The emphasis is less on physical action and more on battles of wits, as Admiral Kirk and his crew use logic, intelligence, and teamwork to defeat their adversaries on new planets and in deep space. Most of the stories are original, although some are direct sequels to particular TV episodes.

MAGAZINES ABOUT COMICS

Amazing Heroes. s-m. $39.95/yr. ***Amazing Heroes Preview Special.*** $3.95/issue; no subscriptions. Kim Thompson. Fantagraphics Books, Inc., 707 Camino Manzanas, Thousand Oaks, CA 91360.

This thick semimonthly magazine has replaced the defunct *Comic Reader* as the *TV Guide* of the comic book industry. Each issue contains an exhaustive, illustrated checklist of the half-month's scheduled releases from all comic book publishers. The notes for each magazine include the title, issue number, single sentence plot summary, and author/artist credits. A "Newsflashes" department presents the latest news (press releases) from all the publishers. Other contents include lengthy interviews with comics industry personnel, surveys of publishing companies and animated cartoon studios, in-depth plot histories of selected old titles, reviews of current titles, and a letter column. *Amazing Heroes* is considered indispensable by fans who cannot wait but want advance information on the comic books they are going to buy anyway. *Amazing Heroes Preview Special* is a separate 140-page magazine published in June and December. It presents profiles for the next half-year of every comic book to be published.

Cartoonist Profiles. q. $25 (Individuals, $20). Jud Hurd. Cartoonist Profiles, Inc., P.O. Box 325, Fairfield, CT 06430.

This magazine about cartoonists seems to have the support of the National Cartoonists Society, the Association of American Editorial Cartoonists, and similar professional guilds. It features articles by and about cartoonists in all fields (comic strips, political satire, motion picture animation, sports cartoons), both contemporary and historical. These articles are heavily weighted toward technical details—how the artists work, what kinds of pens and inks they prefer, how they develop and use "morgues" of reference art, and so on. Issues have highlighted new newspaper comic strips and their creators; nostalgic reminiscences of famous cartoonists of the past; press releases from the Museum of Cartoon Art in New York; and interviews with current newspaper syndication editors about what kinds of cartooning they are looking for. A large amount of advertising from art supply manufacturers and from the newspaper syndicates indicates a large readership among the cartoonists and editors themselves. This magazine is of interest to all who enjoy reading about comic strips and is especially invaluable to high school and college graphic arts and journalism classes.

Comics Buyer's Guide. w. $12/6 months; $22/yr; $40/2 yrs. Don & Maggie Thompson. Krause Publns., Inc., 700 E. State St., Iola, WI 54990.

"Serving comics fandom weekly" and "for everyone who reads or collects comics old and new!" are the subheadings on this weekly tabloid newspaper designed for serious readers and collectors of comic books. The editors print whatever is sent in, but they attempt to distinguish between the actual news and the press releases. Some readers feel that the *Buyer's Guide* is valuable as a forum for all the press releases in the comic book industry, down to the smallest small-press publisher. There are numerous columns on such topics as how to preserve or restore valuable old comic books; how to distinguish between fair and exorbitant prices for out-of-print issues; the histories of particular titles; and (by a lawyer) the accuracy of legal technicalities and courtroom proceedings as shown in comic book drama. There are dozens of brief reviews of current comic books and many letters from readers discussing the field of comic book collecting and trading. At least once a month there are calendars of comics fandom conventions and rosters of comics fandom clubs throughout North America. There are always pages upon pages of advertisements for old comic books and for materials such as acid-free polyethylene bags in which to store a collection. The *Buyer's Guide* is a popular newspaper wherever there is more than just casual interest in comic books.

Comics Journal. 9/yr. $17.95/yr. Gary G. Groth. Comics Journal, Inc., 707 Camino Manzanas, Thousand Oaks, CA 91360.

The best of several literary reviews of the comic-art field. An average issue is over 100 pages; some specials have gone up to 338 pages. There are the usual columns of news from the comic book industry, but the magazine's specialties are its numerous lengthy reviews, critiques, and interviews. Some interviews with artists, writers, or editors run over 20 pages. There are also transcriptions of addresses and panels at comic-fan conventions; histories of comic book publishing companies and of particular magazines; psycho-sociological analyses of magazines and the types of reader that they appeal to; and the like. Coverage is very thorough for all types of U.S. comic books (general comics, undergrounds, and small-press titles), and there are frequent overviews of foreign comics. There is also coverage, though in less depth, of comics-related motion pictures, animated cartoons, and television programs. Some of the in-depth critiques are sophomorically pretentious, but many are keen and meaningful. There is a lengthy and often acrimonious letter column in which writers and artists or the fans of unfavorably reviewed titles will heatedly defend them. *Comics Journal* is controversial, but it is one of the most informative sources for historical and current data on the comic book industry.

Nemo: the classic comics library. bi-m. $21/yr. Richard Marschall. Fantagraphics Books, Inc., 4359 Cornell Rd., Agoura Hills, CA 91301.

This 68-page magazine is devoted to the serious study of old-time American newspaper comic strips, as well as popular cartoons and magazine illustrations (such as E. W. Kemble's drawings for the original 1886 printing of Mark Twain's *Huckleberry Finn*) of the late nineteenth and early twentieth centuries. There are many articles on forgotten early comic strips of cartoonists who later became famous; one issue reprints a complete four-month sequence of *Dickie Dare*, the first adventure strip of Milton Caniff (*Terry and the Pirates* and *Steve Canyon*). *Nemo* also presents some translations of foreign scholarly articles about U.S. comic strips and book reviews of reprint collections of newspaper strips and popular magazine art. Many of the comics examined and reprinted in depth are too antiquated to appeal to popular tastes today; but *Nemo* is worthwhile to anyone interested in the history of popular art in the United States.

WAR

Conan the Barbarian. m. $7.80/yr. *Conan the King.* bi-m. $12/12 issues. Marvel Comics Group.

In the early 1930s, pulp magazine author Robert E. Howard (1906–1936) created a new genre of swashbuckling fantasy drama set in a prehistoric world. Barbarian swordsmen were pitted against monsters (which the reader recognized as dinosaurs), and the "science" of sorcery (later lost during the Ice Ages) was refined by black-robed wizards. In 1970, Marvel Comics began adapting Howard's tales into comic book form and creating its own sequels. Their popularity has led to the two recent Conan motion pictures. In *Conan the Barbarian*, the brawny, brooding Conan strides across the map of Earth's first forgotten civilizations, slaying dragons, cheating corrupt noblemen, battling evil sorcerers, and heading toward his destiny as usurper of the throne of Aquilonia. *Conan the King* is set later in Conan's life, after he has won his throne and must fight to keep it. These comics are popular with high school students.

Star Wars. bi-m. $9/12 issues. Marvel Comics Group.

This comic book is based upon the immensely popular motion picture series created by George Lucas. *Star Wars* features interstellar science fiction exploits of the heroes of *Star Wars, The Empire Strikes Back*, and *Return of the Jedi*. The evil Galactic Empire and Darth Vader were destroyed in the third film, but remnants of the Empire have allied with new ruthless space peoples to renew their attacks on the Free Planets. Luke Skywalker, Princess Leia Organa, Han Solo and Chewbacca, and the comical robots C3-PO and R2-D2 must venture forth once more to defeat the cruel would-be tyrants of the universe.

WEIRD

The New Mutants. m. $9/yr. *The Uncanny X-Men.* m. $9/yr. *X-Factor.* m. $9/yr. Marvel Comics Group.

Both the X-Men and the New Mutants are teams of young people of assorted races and nationalities who have individual freakish super-powers. Unlike most super-hero comics whose stars are public heroes, these groups are feared and ostracized by humanity because of their differences. These are currently among the top-selling magazines in "comicdom." Good writing and art certainly help, although it is theorized that there is a built-in empathy between these young heroes and readers in their adolescence, who are also experiencing a physiological "mutation" accompanied by new and sometimes confusing emotional stresses. The teens in these two groups (the New Mutants are a spinoff of the original X-Men) vary in personality and taste. They are united by their need for a refuge from the public and a determination to use their new abilities for worthwhile purposes rather than trying to suppress and deny them. The stories are heavy on the psychological interplay among the characters, and on how each learns to live with and use his or her powers—or fails to do so. (It often seems as though these teen heroes all ponder to an overly morbid degree upon their own mortality.) The cast gradually changes, as some members drop out of the team, are killed in action against supervillains, or are even destroyed by their own powers mutating beyond control. Some readers have objected to this evolution of *The Uncanny X-Men* away from their favorite heroes, so to please everyone Marvel Comics has added *X-Factor*, which presents new adventures of the original members of the X-Men group.

Teenage Mutant Ninja Turtles. q. $1.50, $2.25 postpaid, no subscription information. Kevin Eastman & Peter Laird. Mirage Studios, P.O. Box 1218, Sharon, CT 06069.

This has been cited as a joke that grew out of control, or as proof that comic book readers will buy *anything*. It began as an advertisement by two fans for a single-issue parody comic book that was guaranteed to contain everything that comics fans want: mutants, teenage super-heroes, Oriental martial-arts drama, and funny animals. The actual comic book was not humorous, however; it was a competent but standard super-hero adventure in which the heroes happened to be turtles (with a rat mentor) amidst an otherwise normal human cast. It was incredibly successful, immediately selling out and shooting up to $75 on the collectors' market. (This first issue is currently in its fourth printing.) Its creators quickly turned it into an ongoing series, which is continuing to sell extremely well for a black-and-white comic book with mediocre art and standard stories. Part of its popularity is due to the editor/reader rapport expressed through chatty, "Hey, we're only fans just like you guys" editorial pages. The fan market is also supporting *Teenage Mutant Ninja Turtles* T-shirts and a role-playing game. This title is undeniably popular with teenage readers.

COMMUNICATION AND SPEECH

For the Professional

See also Education; Media and AV; and Television, Video, and Radio Sections.

Samuel T. Huang, Coordinator of Computer Reference Service, Reference Librarian, University Libraries, Northern Illinois University, DeKalb, IL 60115

Basic Periodicals

Hs: *Speaker and Gavel.*

For the Professional

C:JET (Communication: journalism education today). 1967. q. Membership. Molly J. Clemons. Journalism Education Assn., Inc., P.O. Box 99, Blue Springs, MO 64015. Illus., index, adv. Circ: 3,000. Vol. ends: Summer. Microform: UMI.
Aud: Pr.

This official quarterly publication of the Journalism Education Association contains articles written by and for secondary school journalism advisers and journalism teachers. Each issue includes five to ten signed articles and several regular features less than 20 pages in length. Reprints of proceedings of national meetings, certification requirements, membership and organizational lists are included annually. Ambivalent about its own title (sometimes it is abbreviated; sometimes it is written out), this professional journal is required reading for its specialized audience.

Communication Education (Formerly: *Speech Teacher*). 1952. q. $35. John A. Daly. Speech Communication Assn., 5105 Backlick Rd, No. E, Annandale, VA 22003. Index, adv. Circ: 4,731. Vol. ends: Oct. Microform: MIM, UMI.
Indexed: EdI. *Bk. rev:* 7–8, 750 words, signed. *Aud:* Pr.

Articles featured in this journal are written by and for teachers of speech communication. The journal strives to provide teachers with practical, well-conceived ideas and resources to improve the teaching and learning of speech communication. Featured articles provide both the theory and research necessary for the improvement of instruction. The sections on "Instructional Practices" and "Reflection" allow for the sharing of new and proven teaching ideas; "ERIC Report" and "Reviews of Teaching/Learning Resources" provide up-to-date information on resources available to improve instruction. An additional useful feature, added to the current volume, is "Software Reviews." The table of contents in each issue contains an abstract of each feature article. It is a useful publication for English and speech teachers.

Journal of the American Forensic Association. 1964. q. $25. Joseph W. Wenzel. Amer. Forensic Assn., Dept. of Speech Communication, Univ. of Wisconsin-River Falls, River Falls, WI 54022. Adv. Circ: 1,500. Vol. ends: Spring. Microform: UMI.
Bk. rev: 4–8, 750–1,000 words, signed. *Aud:* Pr.

This journal is committed to increasing knowledge in all areas of communication theory and practice that are relevant to forensics in schools and colleges. The journal includes pedagogical, theoretical, and critical studies in argumentation, persuasion, discussion, debate, parliamentary deliberation, and forensic activities. Each issue contains five to six articles on the practice and theory of forensics and its teaching. Information on debate tournaments is also included. Useful for forensic faculty members and for those with an interest in debating.

Speaker and Gavel. 1964. q. $5. Bill Balthrop. Delta Sigma Rho-Tau Kappa Alpha Forensic, c/o Bert Gross, Dept. of Speech Communication, Marshall Univ., Huntington, WV 27501. Circ: 1,200. Vol. ends: Summer. Microform: UMI. *Aud:* Pr.

This is the official publication of Delta Sigma Rho-Tau Kappa Alpha National Honorary Forensic Society. It deals exclusively with forensics and debating. Articles are brief, about three to five pages in length. Book reviews are occasionally included. This publication is not scholarly but is designed to provide information for debate teachers and coaches. Recommended for high school libraries.

COMPUTERS

For the Student: General, Specific Brands of Computers/ For the Professional

Richard Giordano, Systems Analyst, Systems Office, Columbia University Libraries, Columbia University, New York, NY 10027

Introduction

The bulk of the publications in this section deals with almost all aspects of computers: their hardware, software, applications, design, management, history, and impact on society.

Basic Periodicals

Ejh, Hs: *Computers and Education, Teaching and Computers*.

For the Student

GENERAL

Byte: the small systems journal. 1975. m. $21. Chris Morgan. McGraw-Hill, 70 Main St, Peterborough, NH 03458. Subs. to: Byte Subs., P.O. Box 590, Martinsville, NJ 08836. Illus., adv. Circ: 339,000. Vol. ends: Dec. Microform: UMI. *Indexed:* ASTI, RG. *Bk. rev:* 5, 50 words, signed. *Aud:* Hs.

Byte still remains the best of all the publications geared toward the user of personal computers. It features catchy layout, solid articles, and superb graphics, and is primarily intended for the experienced users of microcomputers and those with more than limited software and hardware savvy. In each issue are about 12 to 15 articles, most of which deal with software, new hardware, and applications of small processors. While most articles are geared toward the experienced hobbyist, some are technical and of interest only to highly skilled programmers. Some readers, therefore, gripe that this gives *Byte* something of a schizophrenic quality, yet somehow it is successful at serving both audiences without alienating either. Highly recommended to high school libraries where there is interest in micro and minicomputers.

Datamation. 1957. m. $38 (Individuals, $50). Rebecca Barna. Cahners Publg. Co., 875 Third Ave., New York, NY 10022. Illus., index, adv. Circ: 172,748. Sample. Microform: UMI. *Indexed:* BusI. *Bk. rev:* Occasional, 250–500 words, signed. *Aud:* Hs.

Datamation is one of the oldest journals in the field, and it has been consistently one of the best. It is popular among data processing professionals, yet broad enough in scope to be of interest to nonspecialists and hobbyists. *Datamation* serves as the nucleus of a collection for the general computer user. Each issue of this publication is both intelligent and informative; coverage is thoughtful and exhaustive. Feature articles cover a wide range of topics including the history of computing, mini- and microcomputers, algorithms, and programming languages. News briefs, notes on people, detailed reports on technical meetings, and news of new products make up a good part of every issue. An excellent choice for high school collections supporting a computer science or programming curriculum.

Joystik. 1982. m. $17.50. 3841 W. Oakton St., Skokie, IL 60076. Illus., adv. *Aud:* Ejh, Hs.

Directed to the video game enthusiast, this journal is beautifully illustrated with detailed, color video screen representations. Both the home game and arcade possibilities are considered. The articles concentrate on game winning strategies, reviews and ratings of games, and news of top arcade scorers. There are also pieces on the latest in technology and hardware. Aimed primarily at a teenage audience, this is readable and entertaining, and should be a great success in the library. (H.S.)

Microzine. 1985. bi-m. $149. Scholastic, Inc., 730 Broadway, New York, NY 10003. Subs.: Box 645, Lyndhurst, NJ 07071-9986. *Aud:* Hs.

A magazine with a difference, *Microzine* is actually a bimonthly computer disk along with a newsletter and *Handbook*. Available in Apple II, Atari 800, and IBM PC versions, the issues contain four programs, including a "Twistaplot" story, which invites user participation; a lesson in a programming language; a game or interview; and a program that builds a database. The print materials support the disk well. An expensive subscription, but excellent.

Personal Computing. 1977. m. $18. Fred Abatemarco. Hayden Publg. Co., 10 Mulholland Dr., Hasbrouck Heights, NJ 07604. Illus., adv. Circ: 450,000. Sample. *Indexed:* RG. *Aud:* Hs.

Although edited for the layperson, this 190-page popular magazine does require some knowledge of computers. In fact, about half of the seven to eight feature articles assume the reader is familiar with at least the jargon. Still, there are good features on new equipment and regular columns and departments which keep the reader advised of advances in the field.

Personal Computing Plus. 1976. m. $18. Charles L. Martin. Hayden Publg. Co., 10 Mulholland Dr, Hasbrouck Heights, NJ 07604. Illus., adv. Circ: 600,000. Microform: UMI. *Aud:* Hs.

This journal has been merged with the former *Personal Software* and now includes a good selection of material on hardware and software. Articles, features, and illustrations are directed to the layperson who has a personal computer. There is a focus on recreation and on common uses of the micro, from word processing to use for simple calculations, graphs, computations, and the like.

Today. 1982. m. $18 (Free to CompuServe subscribers). CompuServe, 5000 Arlington Centre Blvd., P.O. Box 20212, Columbus, OH 43220. Illus., adv.

Bk. rev: 2–3, 300 words, signed. *Aud:* Hs.

Is another videotex/computer magazine necessary? Probably not, although this one is unusual in that it is a giveaway to CompuServe customers. (CompuServe is the vendor that offers subscribers everything from online access to games to airline guides to legal information.) It is also different in that it focuses almost totally on networking and its clear, well-written articles are directed to laypersons, not to experts. The issue examined included two articles on the use of the computer in the home. This was followed by equally good pieces on business use and an explanation of "Networking with WordStar." Devoted as it is to a particular aspect of computers, and considering the good writing and the coverage, this can be recommended for most libraries. The information in this journal does not date, and it should prove popular with high school students. Send for a sample.

SPECIFIC BRANDS OF COMPUTERS

Anyone who owns a microcomputer, for either home, business, or professional use, will find a magazine dedicated almost exclusively to that brand. Among the major ones being published, all of which have circulations from 40,000 to 200,000, are the following, listed by brand name of computer. Note that most publishers will send the library a sample copy.

For information on other titles of this type, as well as computer magazines in general, see (1) *ABI/Selects* (1983. irreg. $50. Data Courier, 620 S. Fifth St., Louisville, KY 40202). This is a 576-page guide with annotations for over 500 titles. (2) *Microcomputer Periodicals* (1979. irreg. $17. George Shirinian, 53 Fraserwood Ave., No. 2, Toronto, Canada). This has information on 673 titles devoted solely to micros.

APPLE

A +. 1983. m. $30. Ziff Davis, One Park Ave., New York, NY 10016.

Directed to the user of the Apple microcomputer, this has information for both the beginner and the expert who may use the micro in a professional capacity. The same publisher issues *A + Buyers Guide*, which is issued twice a year and is little more than a catalog of new Apple computer material and software.

inCider. 1983. m. $25. CW Communications, 80 Pine St., Peterborough, NH 03458.

For both the beginner and the near expert, this monthly covers material of interest to those who use the Apple II. Good focus on business and professional use of the hardware.

Nibble. 1980. m. $27. Micro-Sparc, 45 Winthrop St., Concord, MA 01742.

The focus is on the use of Apple computers in small business, albeit some articles and features cast a wider net.

ATARI

Analog Computing. 1982. m. $28. Analog Magazine Corp., 565 Main St., Cherry Valley, MA 01611.

Good material on both hardware and software for the Atari. The tutorials are exceptionally clear.

Antic. 1982. m. $24. Antic, 524 Second St., San Francisco, CA 94107.

Here the primary focus is on the use of the micro for recreation and games. There is good material, too, on education and graphics.

COMMODORE

Ahoy. 1983. m. $25. Haymarket, 45 W. 34th St., New York, NY 10001.

This follows the same general pattern as *A +*, but for the Commodore micro and related hardware. A good emphasis on games and educational activities.

Commodore Microcomputers. 1981. bi-m. $15. Commodore Pubns., 1200 Wilson Dr., West Chester, PA 19380.

This covers the whole family of Commodores, with considerable emphasis on the professional use of the micros. The recreational uses of the computer are stressed in the same publisher's *Commodore Power/Play*.

Compute's Gazette. 1983. m. $24. Compute! Publns., Inc., P.O. Box 5406, Greensboro, NC 27403.

Primarily for beginners and those slightly familiar with the Commodore 64 and VIC-20, this stresses games and education. There is good advice on software.

Run. 1983. m. $25. CW Communications, 80 Pine St., Peterborough, NH 03458.

Another title dedicated to the popular Commodore and VIC-20. The primary focus is on entertainment and education.

MacINTOSH

Macworld. 1984. m. $30. PC World Communications, 555 DeHaro St., San Francisco, CA 94107.

This is for the person with a MacIntosh personal computer. There are useful reviews of products and well-written articles for both the beginner and the expert. Good balance between education and business use.

PC/IBM

PC. 1982. bi-w. $30. PC Communications, One Park Ave., New York, NY 10016.

As might be expected, this is among the most popular of the group because it is directed to IBM PC owners. It also appears more frequently than most of the other publications in the field. Coverage is wide and the magazine has a particularly pleasing format and writing style.

PC Products. 1984. m. $25. Cahners, 221 Columbus Ave., Boston, MA 02116.

Limiting the focus to the business use of IBM PCs and compatible computers, the editors evaluate hardware and software and demonstrate various applications. One of the newest, and one of the best.

PC Tech Journal. 1983. m. $30. Ziff Davis Publg. Co., One Park Ave, New York, NY 10016.

As the title notes, this journal provides technical information about the IBM PC. There is considerable data on how to develop methods for extending the powers of the PC.

PC World. 1982. m. $24. PC World Communications, 555 DeHaro St., San Francisco, CA 94107.

This differs from the other PC journals in that it manages to appeal to both the technician and the layperson. It is excellent for its review articles of the latest PC and related developments. The assumption is that the reader is past the elementary stages of using a PC.

TRS

80 Micro. 1980. m. $25. CW Communications, 80 Pine St., Peterborough, NH 03458.

Here the primary focus is on the TRS-80, although as in many of these publications, much of the material is applicable for use with other types of micros. Good evaluations of new hardware and software.

Portable 100/200/600. 1984. m. $25. Computer Communications, 15 Elm St., Camden, ME 04843.

Here the subject is the TRS-80, and the primary focus is on the portable. Useful material on new software and hardware.

For the Professional

Classroom Computer Learning (Formerly: *Classroom Computer News*). 1980. 8/yr. $22.50. Holly Brady. P.L. Inc., 2451 E. River Rd., Dayton, OH 45439. Illus., adv. Circ: 74,000. Sample. Microform: UMI.

Indexed: CIJE, EdI. *Aud:* Pr.

This journal can be used in any grade from kindergarten through the senior class in high school. There is easy-to-understand material for both the beginning teacher and the one with more experience. Articles cover a wide range of interests (and grade levels), with particular emphasis on how the computer may be used in a practical way to improve the educational process. There is useful advice on new software and hardware, and most of it is quite evaluative as well as descriptive. Little of interest to the individual working with a computer is left out. Recommended for all school libraries.

Compute! 1979. m. $24. G. R. Ingersoll. Compute Pubns., Inc., 324 W. Wendover Ave., Suite 200, Greensboro, NC 27408. Illus., adv. Circ: 400,000. Sample. Microform: UMI. *Aud:* Pr.

One of the more popular of the general computing magazines, this is directed to the individual with a microcomputer who uses it at home. There is some interest, too, in educational application. The articles are clear and informative; some effort is made to eliminate all but the most familiar jargon, and little, if anything, is so technical that it is beyond the grasp of the average layperson. Major types of micros are considered, and there is useful information on new software and hardware. Regular features include an excellent column on the place of the computer in society. There is coverage of recreational uses.

Computers and Education. 1976. q. $140. David E. Rogers & P. R. Smith. Pergamon Press, Inc., Maxwell House, Fairview Park, Elmsford, NY 10523. Illus., index. Circ: 1,100. Sample. Vol. ends: No. 4. Refereed. Microform: MIM.

Bk. rev: Occasional, lengthy. *Aud:* Pr.

This journal is concerned with the use of computers in all levels of education, from graduate and undergraduate use to applications in primary and secondary education. Papers cover a broad range of concerns including educational system development, simulation, computer-assisted design, language instruction, graphics, management methods of educational computer systems, the selection of computer systems, and text processing in educational environments. Included are survey papers on new languages, packages, and hardware. Articles such as "Prioritizing Computer Literary Topics," "Computerized Clinical Simulations," and "Methods of Introducing Computers to Faculty" indicate part of its scope. All articles are of uniformly good quality. Contributions tend to be descriptive rather than evaluative or theoretical and vary in their degree of technicality.

Computers, Reading and Language Arts. 1983. q. $22 (Individuals, $16). Fred Felder. Modern Learning Pub., Inc., 1308 E. 38th St., Oakland, CA 94602. Illus., adv.

Indexed: CIJE. *Bk. rev:* 3–4, 50–100 words, signed. *Aud:* Pr.

This computer title is more specialized than *The Computing Teacher* and *Electronic Learning* (see below in this section). It presents articles that explore the effects of computers and other electronic technologies on the teaching of basic reading and language arts skills. A variety of topics is covered, and recent articles have discussed the reliability of computer-based readability formulas to the use of word processors in the reading center. Often based on firsthand experience, the articles explore problems of computer use as well as application. A good title where there is interest in both computers and language arts. (P.S.B.)

The Computing Teacher. 1979. 9/yr. $21.50. David Moursund. Univ. of Oregon, 1787 Agate St., Eugene, OR 97403. Illus., index, adv. Circ: 17,000. Vol. ends: June.

Indexed: CIJE. *Aud:* Pr.

Produced "for persons interested in the instructional use of computers," this title covers methods of teaching about computers, teacher education and the computer, and the impact of computers on education. The articles are brief and very practical—they range from "Problem solving with data bases" to "Using computers in remedial language arts." The articles present a good blend of theory and practice. For related titles, see *Computers, Reading and Language Arts* and *Electronic Learning* in this section. (P.S.B.)

Electronic Learning. 1981. 8/yr. $19. Andrew Calkins. Scholastic, Inc., 730 Broadway, New York, NY 10003. Illus., index, adv. Circ: 50,000. Vol. ends: May/June.
Indexed: CIJE, EdI. *Bk. rev:* Brief notes. *Aud:* Pr.

If you must subscribe to only one educational computing title, this should be it. It is attractive, highly up to date, and strong on the practical. It covers everything one would want to know about using computers in the schools. Articles are brief but informative, presenting information on new products, teaching uses, staff training, and the like. For related titles see *The Computing Teacher* and *Computers, Reading and Language Arts* above in this section. (P.S.B.)

Teaching and Computers. 1983. 8/yr. $19. Scholastic Inc., 730 Broadway, New York, NY 10003. Illus., adv. Circ: 45,000. Sample.
Bk. rev: 6–10, notes, signed. *Aud:* Pr.

Directed to the elementary/junior high school teacher, this is Scholastic's successful bid to keep a tight grip on the homeroom newspaper-magazine field. A typical 60-page issue starts with features such as "teacher talk," "question corner," and "classroom happenings." This is followed by articles written so that uninformed teachers may gain competency in explaining computers and software to their pupils. One issue examined included an explanation of the mechanics of a computer, instruction in the use of computers, a special section entitled "What's Your Computer IQ?" and sections on computing in language arts and social studies. "The program of the month" is followed by step-by-step instructions on how to help students program. Finally there is news of software, which includes grade levels and evaluations and hardware reports. A last page "bookshelf" summarizes recent useful titles. Thanks to the well-written and organized text and the numerous illustrations, the material should be easy to follow for even the most anticomputer teacher. Librarians will also find its clear explanations valuable.

CONSUMER EDUCATION

For the Student

See also Business; and Health and Medicine Sections.

Mary K. Prokop, Reference Librarian, Chatham-Effingham-Liberty Regional Library, Savannah, GA 31499

Introduction

Consumer information is where one finds it. No single source or publication has a corner on providing reliable advice to buyers. People seek information on products and services from books and magazines, from radio and television experts, and over the back fence from the neighbor who has just bought a new lawn mower. Even though word of mouth

and personal recommendation will never go out of style, consumers have become increasingly sophisticated, expecting to be able to find up-to-date, factual information to aid them in decision making, and to find it without undue struggle. Few libraries can afford to stock every journal, but yearly issues of special subject magazines and low-cost government documents are excellent sources of information, often overlooked in the rush to examine one or two well-known titles.

Consumer magazines serve a variety of purposes. Some provide practical advice directly to the public. Others present hard statistics or research findings of interest to relatively few people. All consumer publications contribute to a common end: providing people with sound information that will enable them to make basic decisions affecting themselves, their families, and their communities. Ideally, libraries should own whatever magazines their users need. When choices have to be made, librarians must select carefully from the available titles, keeping the local consumer uppermost in mind.

Basic Periodicals

Ejh: *Penny Power*; Hs: *Changing Times, Consumer Reports, Current Consumer & Lifestudies.*

Basic Abstracts and Indexes

Consumer Index to Product Evaluations.

For the Student

Changing Times: The Kiplinger Magazine. 1947. m. $15. Margorie White. The Kiplinger Washington Editors, Inc., 1729 H St. N.W., Washington, DC 20006. Illus., index, adv. Circ: 1,500,000. Vol. ends: Dec. Microform: B&H, MIM, UMI.
Indexed: AbrRG, CIPE, PAIS, RG. *Aud:* Hs.

This widely read magazine covers topics of interest to most Americans, especially middle-class and above, with the emphasis on personal and family financial health, leisure time, and new products that appeal to upscale consumers. Articles are in depth without being technical and are attractively presented. One of the most readable consumer magazines, *Changing Times* has enjoyed enormous popularity over the years by concentrating its efforts towards serving its target audience. Few libraries will want to be without it.

Common Cause (Formerly: *Frontline* and *In Common*). 1980. bi-m. $20 (Membership). Florence Graves. 2030 M St. N.W., Washington, DC 20036. Illus. Circ: 250,000. Sample. Vol. ends: Nov/Dec.
Indexed: PAIS. *Aud:* Hs.

Common Cause is a nonprofit, nonpartisan government watchdog organization, which since 1970 has lobbied quite vocally in the consumer arena. This magazine is a lively, well-illustrated account of the group's ongoing efforts. Articles are generally brief, but two or three per issue treat a topic at length. Subjects include consumer products and services, goings-on in Congress and at other high levels of government, and just about any timely, political issue affecting the public. Writers are opinionated, but not sensationalists. As important in covering issues as other publications (*Consumer Reports, Consumers' Research*) are for evaluating products.

Consumer Information Catalog (Formerly: *Consumer Information*). 1971. q. Free. Kathryn K. Brown. Consumer Information Center, P.O. Box 100, Pueblo, CO 81002. Sample.
Aud: Hs.

Each issue lists over 200 free or inexpensive publications on products, nutrition, small business, careers, and other consumer topics. It can be mailed regularly only to libraries that distribute at least 25 copies, but school libraries should have no difficulty routing that many to classrooms. A handy item for any library that maintains a vertical file on a low budget.

Consumer News. m. Free. Marion Q. Ciaccio. U.S. Office of Consumer Affairs, Dept. of Health, Education & Welfare, Rm. 621, Reporters Bldg., Washington, DC 20201. Circ: 7,000. Vol. ends: Dec.
Bk. rev: 2–4, 50–100 words. *Aud:* Hs.

In a nutshell, this four-page newsletter "summarizes the Administration's consumer activities and related areas of interest." There are a few "consumer tips" per issue—when to get a flu shot, how to save energy, the latest from the Food and Drug Administration on cordless telephones—and short descriptions of new consumer publications, generally free or of low cost.

Consumer Reports. 1936. m. $16 (Includes *Annual Buying Guide*). Erwin Landau. Consumers Union of the United States, Inc., 256 Washington St., Mt. Vernon, NY 10553. Illus., index. Circ: 2,500,000. Sample. Vol. ends: Dec. Microform: UMI.
Indexed: AbrRg, CIPE, PAIS, RG. *Aud:* Hs.

This is the war-horse of consumer publications, well-thought of, widely demanded, and authoritative. Name recognition, an annual buying guide and retrospective self indexing make *Consumer Reports* popular and easy to use. However, there is always room for improvement, and *Consumer Reports,* like other magazines specializing in product evaluations, does not always fully meet the demand its reputation and longevity have created. Still, it remains the best and most sought-after product-buying guide and belongs in virtually every school library.

Consumers' Research Magazine (includes *Handbook of Buying* issue). 1927. m. $18. F. J. Schlink. Consumers' Research, Inc., 517 Second St. N.E., Washington, DC 20002. Illus., index. Circ: 80,000. Sample. Vol. ends: Dec. Microform: B&H, UMI.
Indexed: CIPE, RG. *Aud:* Hs.

It may surprise many librarians to learn that this title actually predates the better-known *Consumer Reports* by nine years. In any case, *Consumers' Research Magazine* presents other types of information in a different manner. Broad consumer topics (pollution, home renovation, chronic pain)

are considered in addition to specific product reviews. While this may be a strength in terms of scope, it may also account for this magazine's status as a consumer publication of second choice by buyers most concerned about actual brand-name product ratings. If a decision must be made between the two, public demand for *Consumer Reports* may discourage purchase of *Consumers' Research Magazine*, but if at all possible, both titles should be held.

Consumers Union News Digest. 1976. s-m. $48. Saralyn Ingram. Consumers Union of the United States, Inc., 256 Washington St., Mt. Vernon, NY 10553. Illus., index. Circ: 1,500. Sample. Vol. ends: Dec. Microform: UMI.
Aud: Hs.

Prepared by the library staff of *Consumer Reports*, this publication culls widely from print sources, mostly magazines and newspapers, information on products and services of interest to consumers. Excerpts are attention getting, but not sensational, and each original source is cited. As a browsing item, this magazine has appeal, covering such topics as insurance, cars, medicine, and food. There is apparently a cumulative index, but access would be improved if this title were indexed elsewhere, particularly since many of the publications drawn from are indexed in scattered sources, if at all. A handy item for classroom use.

Current Consumer & Lifestudies: the practical guide to real life issues (Formerly: *Current Consumer* and *Current Lifestudies*). 1976. 9/yr. $9.90. Margaret Mucklo. Curriculum Innovations, Inc., 3500 Western Ave., Highland Park, IL 60035. Illus. Vol. ends: May. Microform: UMI.
Aud: Ejh, Hs.

One of the very few consumer publications specifically aimed at junior high and high school classroom use. Accurately subtitled, this magazine deals with divorce, social skills, money management, and other real world subjects in a way that lends itself to student reports. Sources "For More Information" are listed after each article, often government agencies or professional associations. Ideally, high school social studies and psychology classes should order in quantity (there is a discount for bulk subscriptions). Where this is not possible, school libraries should make the title available to supplement classroom assignments.

Food News for Consumers. 1984. q. $9.50. Greg Coffey. U.S. Dept. of Agriculture, Rm. 1160 S., Washington, DC 20250. Illus. Vol. ends: Spring.
Indexed: IGov. *Aud:* Hs.

Like so many government documents, this is a well-done publication, full of useful information, which deserves a wider audience than it probably has. Although the emphasis is on food safety, nutrition, buying power, and consumer trends are also covered. Contributors are experts, but the articles are written for a lay audience. Informative, and valuable to home economics curricula in high school.

Penny Power. 1980. bi-m. $9.95. Charlotte Baecher. Consumers Union, 256 Washington St., Mount Vernon, NY

10553. Illus. Circ: 120,000. Sample. Vol. ends: June/July. *Aud:* Ejh.

"A Consumer Reports Publication for Young People," which gives information on products and advice on how to spend money wisely. A Penny Power Research Team of 21 classes nationwide, representing 8- to 14-year olds, participates in testing products, in discussing proposed topics, and in letting editors know their likes and dislikes. The colorful pages include an analysis of about five products; discussion of a money issue (such as allowances); Pen Power (letters to the editor); Penny Power Club (serialized cartoon); a puzzle; and a center pullout, which is a poster or game. This is a unique periodical, well conceived and executed. Complimentary teaching guides are included with 10 or more classroom subscriptions. (L.K.O.)

CRAFTS AND RECREATIONAL PROJECTS

For the Student/For the Professional

Joanne Polster, Head, American Craft Council Library, 45 W. 45th St., New York, NY 10036

Introduction

The growing numbers of collectors and researchers of contemporary crafts added to the ranks of existing and emerging craftspeople and professionals in the field have sparked changes in craft and craft-related periodicals. Smart, professional formats, with an increased use of full-color photographs, substantive exhibition and book reviews, and in-depth artist profiles and interviews now distinguish the older magazines and are a given for the new ones.

At present, periodicals are the best source of almost every kind of information about the contemporary craft scene. Most craft magazines offer profiles of craftspeople with illustrations—often in full color—of their work, reviews of significant exhibitions, and relevant news of all sorts, including educational and professional opportunities, publications of interest, grant deadlines, and calendars of forthcoming exhibitions and events. Book reviewers often select limited-interest titles, small editions dealing with specialized subjects, and author-published productions that are easily overlooked by other review media. Their display and classified advertising provide access to galleries, educational facilities, sources of supply for materials, tools, equipment, and other services. Some include technical and instructional—but not how-to or step-by-step—articles for specific techniques, the level and quality dependent on the magazine's editorial vision and the audience addressed. Many others, of course, provide detailed step-by-step instructions, often keyed to useful illustrations, and complete patterns and plans.

While there are a few periodicals devoted solely to an exploration of design ideas, philosophic contents, and historical precedents, most magazines combine discussions of these elements with process and business considerations.

Although articles about craftspeople and critiques of their work are beginning to appear in established art magazines, there will always be a need for the specialized craft periodical. This is partly because of a duality in the nature of the craft itself. On the one hand there is production craft—beautiful, yet predictable, and utilitarian; on the other, studio craft—a unique, one-of-a-kind, artistic statement.

There is, moreover, the question of process and material. It is true, of course, that painters and sculptors are concerned, to a degree, with these basic elements. For the craftsperson, however, an intimate and thorough knowledge of process and material is absolutely essential. The success or failure of a craft work is not only dependent on the dimensions of the artist's vision, but also on his or her understanding of scientific principles, material properties and on the effect of technique and technology upon that understanding.

Craftspeople are unique in the art world for their willingness to share their knowledge and experience with others. Craft periodicals are the channels that give a novice access to the master.

Basic Periodicals

Hs: *Home Mechanix, McCall's Needlework & Crafts, Make It with Leather, Popular Mechanics, Popular Science.*

For the Student

American Craft (Formerly: *Craft Horizons*). 1941. bi-m. Membership, $35. Lois Moran. Amer. Craft Council, 401 Park Ave. S., New York, NY 10016. Illus., index, adv. Circ: 35,000. Vol. ends: Dec/Jan. Microform: B&H, UMI.

Indexed: ArtI, MgI, RG. *Bk. rev:* varied, 150–1,500 words, signed. *Aud:* Hs.

American Craft is the foremost magazine covering all media in contemporary (post-1945) craft. As successor to *Craft Horizons*, it is the oldest craft magazine in continuous publication. Its readership includes the professional craftsperson, teacher, advanced student, collector, dealer, arts administrator, and consumer. It features profiles of major craftspeople, with color photographs of their work, and highlights the work of lesser-known and emerging artists. Major exhibitions are reviewed and fully illustrated in color. Included also are articles on private collections, collectors, and galleries that specialize in craft. Regular features include a calendar of current craft exhibitions listed by state; marketing and exhibition opportunities for craftspeople; and announcements of workshops, symposia, conferences, and other events. "Gallery," an eight-page section of black-and-white photographs, presents representative work from about 50 current or recent exhibitions. A news and information insert called "Craft World" provides information about new shops and galleries and reports on symposia, conferences, grant deadlines, new publications, and other material of interest to its wide-ranging readership. Excellent color reproduction, well-designed layout, and the consistently high caliber of work featured convey the idea of excellence in craft. Highly recommended for high school libraries.

Ceramic Arts & Crafts. 1953. m. $14.90. William Thompson. Scott Publns., 30595 W. 8 Mile Rd., Livonia, MI 48152. Illus., adv. Circ: 50,000.

Bk. rev: Occasional. *Aud:* Hs.

Directed to the hobby ceramist, it provides step-by-step instructions and patterns for executing specific projects. All articles are illustrated in full color. This magazine carries a great deal of advertising for ceramic supplies and equipment. This information is not only helpful for the hobbyist, but may be quite useful to anyone considering going into the retail ceramic hobby or materials-supply business. Other features includes a list of upcoming shows, industry news, new products, and a national directory of ceramics studios.

Chip Chats. 1953. bi-m. $5. Edward F. Gallenstein. Natl. Woodcarvers Assn., 7424 Miami Ave., Cincinnati, OH 45243. Illus., index, adv. Circ: 25,000. Vol. ends: Nov/Dec.
Indexed: RG. *Aud:* Hs.

Directed to teachers and to professional and amateur woodcarvers and whittlers, this is primarily a source of information about the activities of fellow enthusiasts. Although it includes information about techniques, new products, and tools and their use, its emphasis is on reports of events, reviews of exhibitions and shows and announcements. The ads are good sources of supplies for the woodcarver. There are good black-and-white photographs. Of the three magazines in this area, this is perhaps the most professional in its format. Being indexed in *Readers' Guide* is also an advantage.

Crafts 'n Things. 1974. bi-m. $8. Nancy Tosh. Clapper Publg. Co., 14 Main St., Park Ridge, IL 60068. Illus., adv. Circ: 400,000. Vol. ends: July/Aug.
Aud: Ejh, Hs.

Subtitled "Craft Ideas to Brighten Your World," this magazine provides plans, patterns and instructions for quick and easy projects that can be executed by people with little or no skills. These projects call for a minimum of tools, equipment and materials. Soft toys, fashion and home accessories, and decorative objects of questionable taste and value are described and illustrated. The quality of the projects and level of design are quite poor. This seems more a vehicle for advertising than a bona-fide consumer publication. This reviewer has serious reservations about any library spending its increasingly shrinking dollars here.

Creative Crafts & Miniatures (Formerly: *Creative Crafts* and *The Miniature Magazine*). 1967. bi-m. $8. Wendie Blanchard. Carstens Publns., P.O. Box 700, Newton, NJ 07860. Illus., index, adv. Circ: 60,000. Vol. ends: Nov/Dec. Microform: UMI.
Indexed: MgI, RG. *Bk. rev:* 3–4, 120 words, signed. *Aud:* Hs.

This is another general, project-oriented magazine whose regular features include step-by-step instructions in tole painting, quilting and other needlework, dollmaking, decoupage, egg decoration, construction of miniatures, and related activities. Classified ads for supplies, tools, and books are helpful to the hobbyist.

Family Handyman. 1950. m. (exc. July & Aug.). $11.97. Gary Havens. Webb Co., 1999 Shepard Rd., St. Paul, MN

55116. Illus., index, adv. Circ: 1,200,000. Vol. ends: Dec. Microform: UMI.
Indexed: MgI, RG. *Aud:* Hs.

This popular do-it-yourself magazine for homeowners covers practical suggestions for repairing and remodeling homes, fabricating built-in furniture and accessories and hints on gardening and decorating. The regular column "Ask Handyman" is one of the most interesting features of the magazine, which has many advertisements for tools and building materials. Indexes to the magazine, published within the magazine itself twice a year, are a convenience for readers who are looking for a solution to a specific problem. Suitable for schools with shop courses.

Fine Homebuilding. 1981. bi-m. $18. John Lively. The Taunton Press, 63 S. Main St., P.O. Box 355, Newtown, CT 06470. Illus., index, adv. Circ: 210,000.
Aud: Hs.

A handsomely designed magazine, illustrated by photographs, both black and white and full color, and by clearly labeled diagrams and plans of construction details. Its emphasis is on construction, techniques and residential design. In addition to instructional articles on the repair and rebuilding of houses and the construction of additions to existing buildings, *FH* presents informational features on historic houses, furnishing plans and elevation as well as photographs, and accounts of homebuilders' experiences in the process of constructing their uniquely designed homes. Included are articles on the use of tools and equipment, special building materials, and energy-efficient technology. There are a number of regular service columns providing tips and techniques, product news, and answers to readers' inquiries. Custom building, remodeling, renovation, and restoration combined with environmental concerns are the emphasis of this excellent magazine. Highly recommended for all school libraries.

Home Mechanix (Formerly: *Mechanix Illustrated*). 1929. m. $9.94. Joseph R. Provez. CBS Publns., Consumer Magazines Div., 1515 Broadway, New York, NY 10036. Subs. to: P.O. Box 2830, Boulder, CO 80322. Illus., index, adv. Circ: 1,500,000. Vol. ends: Dec. Microform: UMI.
Indexed: MgI, RG. *Aud:* Ejh, Hs.

Written primarily for the amateur home handyman and car mechanic, this magazine features articles of about 2,000 words on the care and maintenance of home and auto. The largest portion of magazine's content is devoted to cars. Other articles are devoted to woodworking, gardening, and other similar recreational activities. The magazine is illustrated with many color and black-and-white photographs, along with helpful diagrams and drawings. It is sometimes difficult to tell the difference between this magazine and *Popular Mechanics*. On the whole the material covered is almost identical, as are the approach and reading level.

Kite Lines (Formerly: *Kite Tales*). 1964. q. $11. Valerie Govig. Aeolus Press, 7106 Campfield Rd., Baltimore, MD 21207. Illus., adv. Vol. ends: Summer.
Bk. rev: 1,350 words, signed. *Aud:* Hs.

This handsome publication, subtitled "The Quarterly Journal of the Worldwide Kite Community," is concerned with the art, history, construction, design, and flying of kites. Well-illustrated articles describe the work of kite designers around the world, past and present. Technical articles on kite design include instructions and plans; the focus is on the unusual, innovative and experimental. International kiting events are reported. The service columns include information about new commercial kites offered for sale and a directory of outlets for kites and kiting supplies. The ads are valuable for the kite enthusiast. This is a serious publication of particular interest because of the increased use of kiting principles and construction for the fabrication of "wind art," "kinetic sculpture" and "aerial sculpture." It is highly recommended for school libraries.

Lapidary Journal. 1947. m. $14.75. Pansy D. Kraus. Lapidary Journal, Inc., P.O. Box 80937, San Diego, CA 92138. Illus., index, adv. Circ: 38,000. Vol. ends: Mar.

Indexed: MgI. *Bk. rev:* 2, 300–500 words. *Aud:* Hs.

For "gem cutters, gem collectors, jewelry craftsmen," and rockhounds, this magazine presents roughly 15 short, illustrated articles about various aspects of gem history and collecting, lapidary techniques, gemstone characteristics, and reports of mine tours and rockhounding experiences. Its chief value, however, lies in the ads for equipment and stones that occupy at least half the magazine's pages. In addition, there are over ten pages devoted to a calendar of gem and mineral society shows and activities throughout the country. It carries an extensive listing of classified ads under such headings as "Cutting Materials," "Cut and Tumbled Gems," "Mountings and Findings," "Supplies," "Indian Relics," "Mineral Specimens," "Fossils," "Rock Shops," and "Equipment." The annual "Rockhound Buyer's Guide" (April issue) lists clubs, gem and mineral dealers, and products. School libraries should find a place for this informative and useful magazine.

McCall's Needlework & Crafts. 1919. bi-m. $11.97. Margaret Gilman. Amer. Broadcasting Co., 825 Seventh Ave., New York, NY 10019. Illus., adv. Circ: 1,250,000. Vol. ends: Nov.

Aud: Hs.

A project-oriented instructional publication that provides detailed instructions with diagrams, illustrations, and full-color photographs of the finished product. Covers needlework of all sorts, knitting, and crochet, as well as other related craft activities. None of these non-needlework projects requires much in the way of tools or equipment. For the person who likes to pursue needlework and crafts as recreational, leisure-time activities. Recommended.

Make It with Leather. 1956. bi-m. $12. Earl F. Warren. Leathercraftsman, Inc., P.O. Box 1386, Fort Worth, TX 76101. Illus., index, adv. Circ: 40,000. Vol. ends: Oct/Nov. Microform: UMI.

Bk. rev: Occasional. *Aud:* Hs.

Directed as much to the teacher of arts and crafts as to the amateur leatherworker, this magazine gives detailed instructional information for making anything in leather from belts to saddles. Included in these instructions are plans and patterns as well as helpful hints. The text is clear and well illustrated. Included also are reports from leather guilds and groups around the country, calendars of events, and fairs and festivals. School libraries will find this publication a useful addition to their collections.

The Mallet. 1969. m. Ed. bd. Natl. Carvers Museum Foundation, P.O. Box 389, 14960 Woodcarver Rd., Monument, CO 80132. Illus., adv. Circ: 10,000. Vol. ends: Dec.

Aud: Hs.

An informal magazine with patterns, diagrams, instructions, and tips for wood carving and whittling projects. Includes information about woods, tools, and techniques. Reports on the activities of fellow carvers. Illustrated with black-and-white photographs. This publication is distributed to active members of the National Carvers Museum. Its contents are derived from photos, letters, articles, and patterns submitted by members and supplemented by additional material from nonmembers. A young adults department would be better served by *Chip Chats* or *National Carvers Review*.

National Carvers Review. 1969. q. $6. Willard Bondhus. National Carvers Review, 7821 S. Reilly, Chicago, IL 60642. Illus., adv.

Bk. rev: 4, 450 words. *Aud:* Hs.

Directed to the beginning as well as advanced wood carver, this publication features projects with step-by-step instruction, helpful hints, patterns, and diagrams. It also provides new product news and product evaluations. Profiles of wood carvers and whittlers also appear. A calendar of forthcoming events and a list of wood carving clubs are also provided. A useful publication for hobbyists, teachers, suppliers and proprietors of craft-supply shops. See also *Chip Chats* and *The Mallet*, above in this section.

Popular Mechanics. 1902. m. $9.97. Joe Oldham. Hearst Corp., 224 W. 57th St., New York, NY 10019. Subs. to: P.O. Box 10064, Des Moines, IA 50350. Illus., index, adv. Circ: 1,600,000. Vol. ends: Dec. Microform: UMI.

Indexed: AbrRG, MgI, RG. *Aud:* Ejh, Hs.

A standard "how-to-do-it" magazine that popularizes science and mechanics for all age levels. Emphasis is on practical application rather than theory. Filled with amply illustrated articles on: automobiles and driving, science and inventions, environment, shop and craft, electronics, radio and TV, home and yard, photography, boating, and outdoor recreation. Contains many easy-to-follow directions for numerous such useful projects as sewing centers, patios, sailboards, and so on. Tips are given on the care of automobiles, driving, and how to build, repair, and use equipment.

Popular Science. 1872. m. $13.94. C. P. Gilmore. Times Mirror Magazines, 380 Madison Ave., New York, NY 10017. Subs. to: Popular Science Subscription Dept., P.O. Box 2871, Boulder, CO 80302. Illus., index, adv. Circ: 1,800,000. Vol. ends: Dec. Microform: UMI.

Indexed: AbrRG, MgI, RG. *Aud:* Ejh, Hs.

Popular Science is primarily concerned with science and technology and the consumer products that science is making possible and industry is making available. Photographs and diagrams show how these new products and inventions work. The magazine covers cars, computers, home-improvement materials, cameras, tools, hi-fi equipment, and energy-saving devices of all kinds. Articles are written in simple language for the weekend mechanic. It is divided into three major sections: science and technology, consumer education, and do-it-yourself information. Possibly there is more emphasis on science than in its two competitors, *Home Mechanix* and *Popular Mechanics*, but the difference is not great. Secondary school libraries will find this publication useful for its graphic descriptions and illustrations of what is essentially rather complicated technology.

Quilter's Newsletter Magazine. 1969. 10/yr. $11.50. Bonnie Leman. Leman Publns., P.O. Box 394-S, Wheatridge, CO 80034. Illus., adv. Circ: 140,000.
Bk. rev: 3, 200 words, signed. *Aud:* Hs.

A good source of information about quilts, quilting techniques, patterns, and designs. From time to time, historical material is informally presented. For the most part, articles are illustrated in full color. Of interest to the quilter are its news of quilting events, exhibitions, activities, trends, trade news, and its suppliers' information. Includes template patterns that can be used to make some of the designs described. In view of the current popularity of quilting and patchwork, this is a good publication for the library.

Rock & Gem. 1971. m. $12. W. R. C. Shedenhelm. Miller Magazines, 2660 E. Main St., Ventura, CA 93003. Illus., adv.
Aud: Hs.

Directed to the amateur lapidarist and mineral collector, it presents feature articles about gold prospecting and gem-hunting field trips and describes sites all over the country. It also includes profiles of gems and minerals. Included also are step-by-step instructions for simple jewelry making, faceting, and lapidary techniques. Its buyer's guide supplies lists of new products, materials, and services. A calendar of events and activities of interest to the rockhound is also provided.

The Workbasket. 1935. 10/yr. $5. Roma Jean Rice. Modern Handcrafts, Inc., 4251 Pennsylvania Ave., Kansas City, MO 64111. Illus., index, adv. Circ: 1,800,000. Microform: UMI.
Indexed: MgI. *Aud:* Hs.

As its title signifies, this magazine contains a hodgepodge of different types of activities, which range from needlework, including tatting, to cooking and gardening, with particular emphasis on crocheting and knitting. It is keyed for the person who is looking for practical help, not advice or suggestions on how to improve skills.

Workbench. 1957. bi-m. $6. John E. Tillotson II. Modern Handcrafts, Inc., 4251 Pennsylvania Ave., Kansas City, MO 64111. Illus., index, adv. Circ: 880,000. Microform: UMI.
Indexed: MgI, RG. *Aud:* Hs.

This is for the do-it-yourself fan who wishes illustrated, explicit instructions on how to build everything from a bird house to an addition to the family mansion. There are numerous tips on home improvement, often tied in with the advertisements. The writing and the illustrations are pleasant, clear, and quite understandable to the high school student interested in crafts and carpentry.

For the Professional

Ceramics Monthly. 1953. m. (exc. July & Aug.) $18. William C. Hunt. Professional Publns., P.O. Box 12448, Columbus, OH 43212. Illus., index, adv. Circ: 40,000. Vol. ends: Dec. Microform: UMI.
Indexed: ArtI, MgI. *Bk. rev:* 2–4, 250 words. *Aud:* Pr.

Ceramics Monthly is the magazine for the teacher. It features technical articles about ceramic procedures and specific techniques, glazing processes, and production methods, generally written by their practitioners. Articles, illustrated by photographs and plans, describe kilns, kiln building, and related subjects. Health hazards are also discussed. There are frequent articles about foreign potters, potteries, and ceramic processes. Its profiles and interviews of working potters usually include technical information about their work. *CM* also addresses the historical side of ceramics, including articles about U.S. potters and potteries of the past. There are reviews of significant exhibitions and commentary on current issues in ceramics. Its service columns, "Suggestions from Our Readers" and "Questions Answered by *CM* Staff," provide a clearinghouse of information for readers. There is a calendar of forthcoming events, exhibitions, fairs, and festivals useful both for the potential exhibitor and spectator/collector, and brief reports on exhibitions—both group and solo—workshops, lectures, symposia, and funding and grant information. Of considerable value is the April issue, containing a directory of summer course offerings in ceramics throughout the country. The ads are invaluable for suppliers' information. This is a basic, serious, professional publication that is highly recommended.

Studio Potter. 1972. s-a. $12. Gerry Williams. P.O. Box 65, Goffstown, NH 03045. Illus. Circ: 8,000.
Indexed: ArtI. *Aud:* Pr.

Although *Studio Potter* should be required reading for the professional potter and teacher of ceramics, it has sections to interest the general reader as well. Highly technical information on all aspects of the ceramic process, production, and design is accompanied by excellent photographs, informative plans and diagrams, and charts and tables. These articles are written by and for professionals. Energy conservation, the reuse of materials, health hazards, studio planning and design, and equipment and material evaluations are also covered. Feature articles are occasionally devoted to little-known or extinct production potteries of the past with wonderful reproductions of old photographs. *Studio Potter's* uniqueness, however, lies in its concern for the ceramist as a person, with his or her life-style, and with the physical and human dimensions of the profession. While you will not find articles on marketing here, you will find an analysis of the physical tension and stress that affect the back, hands, and arms—the potter's occupational hazard—with measures to relieve the problem. The general reader and ceramics collector will be interested in the section of each issue that is devoted to potters living in a specific place or condition, e.g., "Montana's Potters" or "Urban Potters." These sketches present biographical and visual material, including photographs of each ceramist and his or her work and workspace. The individual artists describe their work, design ideas and philosophy. Recent issues have dealt with thematic concerns to the field, e.g., explorations of innovative ceramics, the aesthetics of function, philosophic approaches to function by art historians and prominent potters, and the influence of ancient traditions. Highly recommended for all libraries.

CULTURAL-SOCIAL STUDIES

For the Student

See also History; Linguistics and Language Arts; and Literature Sections.

Marcia J. Martin, Reference Dept., University of South Carolina, Columbia, SC

Introduction

Those titles which embrace several disciplines in the social sciences or humanities are included within this section. The study of a particular relationship between disciplines, of a particular theme or geographic location from the point of view of a variety of disciplines, or of a methodology used in various disciplines distinguishes them as a group. Since these journals are often overlooked by students of a single field of study, librarians have an increased responsibility to be aware of them and to encourage their use by their potential clientele.

Basic Periodicals

Hs: *Futurist, Impact of Science on Society.*

Basic Abstracts and Indexes

Humanities Index, Social Sciences Index.

For the Student

Critical Inquiry. 1974. q. $55 (Individuals, $27.50). W. J. T. Mitchell. Univ. of Chicago Press, 5801 Ellis Ave., Chicago, IL 60637. Illus., adv. Circ: 3,700. Vol. ends: June. Refereed. Microform: UMI.
Aud: Hs.

With well-known critics and celebrities as regular contributors, each issue of *Critical Inquiry* is a must for large school libraries. Essentially, this journal offers interdisciplinary and comparative criticism of all aspects of modern culture, from music and art to literature and photography. Even popular culture is given a place. The writing style is usually as lively as it is scholarly, and as innovative as it is imaginative. The journal is edited for the teacher and the

student but has wide appeal for the better-educated layperson. Highly recommended.

Futurist: a journal of forecasts, trends, and ideas about the future. 1967. bi-m. $25. Edward Cornish. World Future Soc., 4916 St. Elmo Ave., Washington, DC 20014. Illus., index, adv. Circ: 35,000. Vol. ends: Dec. Microform: UMI.
Indexed: RG, SocSc. *Aud:* Hs.

This colorful, easy-to-read, highly illustrated journal is published by a nonprofit, nonpolitical society trying to look at the future and tell its readers what to expect. Each 68-page issue is filled with provocative articles dealing with future prospects in areas ranging from education to economics to religion. In addition to feature articles, every issue includes news notes about world trends and forecasts in health, environment, technology and so forth. Most libraries should subscribe.

Humanities. 1980. bi-m. $14. Judith Chayes Neiman. Natl. Endowment for the Humanities, 1100 Pennsylvania Ave. N.W., Washington, DC 20506. Subs. to: Supt. of Docs., U.S. Govt. Printing Office, Washington, DC 20402. Illus. Circ: 5,000. Sample. Vol. ends: Dec. Microform: UMI.
Indexed: IGov. *Bk. rev:* Various number, length, essays, signed. *Aud:* Hs.

This tabloid is the principal communications vehicle of the National Endowment for the Humanities. A few articles and book reviews are featured, but probably more important are the calendars listing application deadlines for grants and fellowships, and detailed descriptions of projects funded by the Endowment. Brief descriptions of grants and fellowships awarded by the NEH are also included.

Impact of Science on Society. 1950. q. 80f. Jacques G. Richardson. UNESCO, 7 place de Fontenoy. 75700 Paris, France. Subs. to: Unipub/Bernan Assoc., 10033 Martin Luther King Highway, Lanham, MD 20706. Illus., adv. Circ: 4,185. Microform: MIM.
Indexed: PAIS, SocSc. *Aud:* Hs.

Focusing on the effect of science and technology on worldwide society, each issue of this journal opens with an editorial observation or comment followed by five to ten articles. Some issues are devoted to a single subject, such as "Man's Addictions and How to Deal with Them." Articles usually include lists of supplementary references, "To Delve More Deeply," which are particularly useful to students. Because of the wide scope, the effort to make material comprehensible to the layperson, and the importance of the topics, the magazine is recommended for almost all types and sizes of libraries. Published in English, French, Chinese, Russian and Korean.

International Social Science Journal. 1949. q. $37. Ali Kazancigil. UNESCO, 7 place de Fontenoy, 75700 Paris, France. Subs. to: Unipub/Bernan Assoc, 10033 Martin Luther King Highway, Lanham, MD 20706. Illus., index. Circ: 4,500. Sample. Vol. ends: No. 4. Microform: MIM, UMI.
Indexed: PAIS, SocSc. *Aud:* Hs.

A scholarly interdisciplinary journal of the social sciences, this publication is useful to both students and informed adults. The seven to ten articles in each issue all deal with a single topic, such as "Migration" or "Industrial Democracy." Often, the various articles approach the issue at hand from different international settings. A listing of books received, recent UNESCO publications, and national distributors of UNESCO publications completes every issue. The journal is published in English, French, Spanish and Chinese editions.

Journal of Popular Culture. 1967. q. $25. Ray Browne. Dept. of Popular Culture, Bowling Green State Univ., Bowling Green, OH 43403. Illus., adv. Circ: 2,500. Vol. ends: Spring. Refereed. Microform: UMI.

Indexed: HumI. *Bk. rev:* 3–12 (irreg.), length varies, signed. *Aud:* Hs.

Every aspect of popular culture from music videos and TV's *Dallas* to fast food and video games is covered in this journal of middle- to lowbrow culture. Often, an issue is devoted to a specific topic, such as children's literature and culture or Japanese popular culture. Other issues include 10 to 15 articles on a variety of subjects, both general and specific (folklore, sports, science fiction, movies). Contributors are primarily from colleges and universities, but the writing is at a level that can be appreciated by general audiences.

Social Science Quarterly. 1920. q. $36 (Individuals, $20). Charles M. Bonjean. Univ. of Texas Press Journals, P.O. Box 7819, Austin, TX 78712. Illus., index, adv. Circ: 2,300. Vol. ends: Dec. Refereed. Microform: MIM, UMI.

Indexed: PAIS, SocSc. *Bk. rev:* 20–25, 300–600 words, signed. *Aud:* Hs.

Each 200- to 300-page issue of this academic journal contains material dealing with all aspects of the social sciences. Four to five articles in every issue deal with topics "Of General Interest," with another three to five papers devoted to a single topic of timely interest, such as "Research on Race and Ethnicity" or "The Media and Politics." The authors are leading scholars, and they use the most recent quantitative tools of social science scholarship. A "Research Notes" section and excellent book reviews complete each issue. A basic title in the field.

EDUCATION

For the Student/For the Professional

See also Communication and Speech; and Psychology Sections.

Patricia Smith Butcher, Reader's Adviser in Education and Psychology, Trenton State College Library, Trenton, NJ 08625

Introduction

Education periodicals are both plentiful in number and highly specialized in content. More than 750 education and education-related titles are indexed in *Current Index to Journals in Education*, which gives some idea of the difficulties involved in selecting titles for inclusion within this section. In addition to the large number of titles, there is also a wide variety. The education titles listed in this section are a selection; this is by no means an inclusive listing of education journals. Included are research journals, "how to teach it" titles, and general interest education magazines. Most of the titles are U.S. publications indexed in one or more places. Titles giving guidance or information to teachers in specific curriculum areas—e.g., *The Physics Teacher*, *Art and Craft*, or *English Education*—can be found in the appropriate sections of this book.

Basic Abstracts and Indexes

Current Index to Journals in Education, Education Index, Psychological Abstracts.

For the Student

The familiar classroom periodicals issued by Scholastic and Xerox are described in general here rather than listed title by title. Most of the titles are in the category of textbooks. The space in this guide is reserved for diverse types of magazines. They follow a similar, set pattern, differing only in terms of appeal for the grades to which they are directed. Anyone who wishes a complete descriptive list of the titles, along with samples, need only write Scholastic et al.

Curriculum Innovations. 3500 Western Ave., Highland Park, IL 60035.

Another of the classroom magazine educational publishers, Curriculum Innovations offers the usual number of magazines, but they produce the two best, and most often found in schools. The first, *Science Challenge*, is for grades six through high school and is similar in intent and scope to Scholastic's *Science World* and Xerox's *Current Science*. It may be better than the others in one respect—more attention is given to in-depth studies of a particular topic. The material is well illustrated. The other exemplary magazine—*Writing*—is for the same age group and hopes to give the reader interest in two aspects of the subject: authors and their writing habits and the basics of good English. It's a pleasant, sometimes informative combination that will help to arouse interest in students involved in writing themselves. There are useful photographs.

Scholastic Magazines. 730 Broadway, New York, NY 10003.

The best known of several educational publishing firms which concentrate on so-called classroom magazines, Scholastic magazines are now sold in over 50 percent of U.S. classrooms. Many, although not all, contain advertising that has a particular appeal to teenagers.

Formats vary, but all are made to look like newsstand magazines, with striking covers and good illustrations throughout. The magazines are written and edited for specific age groups and for specific needs of the classroom. All are primarily for the U.S.A., and the newsmagazines usually show how well the U.S. system functions, whether at the work or entertainment level.

Thanks to over 60 years of such publishing, the publisher knows what appeals to the various audiences, and the magazines can be quite entertaining and informative. The real question is whether or not they should be found in a library—particularly as they are so closely associated with the classroom. The answer is probably not.

Most of the individual magazines include special teachers' guides which show how the material in the student edition may be used in the classroom.

The various titles may be divided in different ways, but some of the more useful by subject would include:

NEWS TITLES. These are the typical newspapers in that they stress current economic, political and social events. They are all weeklies; there are special features on everything from movies and books to television and fashion. The appropriate audiences are indicated for each. *Scholastic News* appears in six editions, grades 1–6, thus covering elementary school. *Junior Scholastic* is published in one edition and is intended for junior high. *Scholastic Update*, also in one edition, is for high school.

LITERATURE AND LANGUAGE ARTS TITLES. Ranging from 16 to 32 pages, these high-quality, well-illustrated weeklies (or biweeklies) vary in price from $3.95 to $5.25.

Scholastic Sprint: grades 4–6 (for reading motivation and remedial)
Scholastic Action: junior high (for below-level readers)
Scholastic Scope: junior high (for low to average readers)
Scholastic Voice: junior high (for average to above average readers)
Literary Cavalcade: high school (for above average readers)

FOREIGN LANGUAGE TITLES. From 8 to 14 pages, these are well illustrated. Numerous games, features, puzzles and so on help the student to master the language. They vary in price from $2.95 to $3.50 per 6 to 8 issues a year.

French: *Bonjour*; *Ca va*; *Chez Nous*
German: *Das Rad*; *Der Roller*; *Schuss*
Spanish: *Hoy Dia*; *Que tal*; *El Sol*

The interested librarian need only write the publisher for full details about each of the above Scholastic magazines, as well as several other titles, ranging from *Science World* and *Scholastic Dynamath* to *Scholastic Let's Find Out*.

Xerox Education Publications. 245 Long Hill Rd., Middletown, CT 06457.

Best known for its *Weekly Reader* series (which moves from kindergarten through the fifth grade), this is a rival to Scholastic magazines. Here there is more focus on the elementary grades than the teenager, and the publications are not so extensive. Nevertheless, they are quite as good as those issued by Scholastic.

Should the library subscribe? Probably not, although there are two exceptions: *Current Events* and *Current Science*, both annotated elsewhere in this guide.

Other classroom papers move from *Buddy's Weekly Reader* through *Read*, a title which encourages what the title suggests. The publications are issued weekly, i.e., 27 issues a year, and range in price from $1.95 per year to $5.50 per year.

Full information about these and other publications may be obtained by simply writing the publisher.

For the Professional

Adolescence. 1966. q. $40 (Individuals, $30). William Kroll. Libra Publns., Inc., 391 Willets Rd., Roslyn, NY 11577. Illus., index, adv. Circ: 3,000. Sample. Vol. ends: Winter. Microform: UMI.
Bk. rev: 10, 100 words. *Aud:* Pr.

"An international quarterly devoted to the physiological, psychological, psychiatric, sociological, and educational aspects of the second decade of human life," this is a must for all professionals working with adolescents. Approximately 20 articles per issue emphasize this interdisciplinary approach; recent articles pertained to sex-education programs, anorexia nervosa, and drinking and drugs. High schools with large budgets may wish to purchase the journal for their professional collections. (MiNe.)

American Education. 1965. 10/yr. $23. Beverly Powell Blondell. Subs. to: Supt. of Docs., Washington, DC 20402. Illus. Circ: 28,000. Vol. ends: Dec. Microform: MIM, UMI.
Indexed: CIJE, EdI, PAIS, RG. *Aud:* Pr.

Brief, informative articles on policy, practices, and research at all levels of U.S. education. The material ranges from an interview with the "Teacher of the Year" to "A Reprint of the President's Call for Excellence in Education." Outstanding educational programs are highlighted, and special attention is paid to describing federal programs for education. The articles are easy to read, jargon-free, and directed to the interested layperson. This publication of the Office of Education presents topical material on education in a palatable format. It is a good general education title that deserves a place in most libraries.

American Educator: the professional journal of the American Federation of Teachers. 1977. 4/yr. Membership (Nonmembers, $2.50). Liz McPike. Amer. Federation of Teachers, AFL-CIO, 555 New Jersey Ave. N.W., Washington, DC 20001. Illus., adv. Circ: 530,000. Vol. ends: Winter. Microform: UMI.
Indexed: CIJE. *Aud:* Pr.

A highly readable, semipopular collection of six to seven articles per issue on current topics in U.S. education. The material ranges from an update on education for the handicapped to an analysis of TV news coverage of education. It resembles *American Education* (see above in this section) in both style and content. Articles are authored by academics, teachers, and free-lancers, and the union point of view is usually unobtrusive.

American Secondary Education. 1970. q. $15. Bill J. Reynolds. Bowling Green State Univ., Rm. 319, Education Bldg., Bowling Green, OH 43403. Illus., adv. Circ: 2,600. Sample. Microform: UMI.
Indexed: EdI. *Aud:* Pr.

Articles on secondary education, as well as material on the general subject of education, appear in this title. Written by secondary school administrators, as well as faculty from colleges of education, the material runs the spectrum from a discussion of the voucher system to the use of microcomputers in a particular high school. Most of the articles consist of description and opinion on various issues of interest to secondary school teachers. Although not a serious rival to *Phi Delta Kappan* or the *NASSP Bulletin* (see below in this section), this journal would be useful in collections specializing in material on junior and senior high school teaching.

Childhood Education. 1924. 5/yr. $40. Lucy Prete Martin. Assn. for Childhood Education Intl., 11141 Georgia Ave., Suite 200, Wheaton, MD 20902. Illus., index, adv. Circ: 14,000. Vol. ends: Apr/May. Microform: UMI.

Indexed: CIJE, EdI. *Bk. rev:* 20, 150 words, signed. *Aud:* Pr.

This journal is the voice of the Association for Childhood Education International (ACEI). It is written in a popular style understandable by layperson and professional and is suitable for parents and for professionals involved in the education of children and young adults. The articles stress the practical approach to child development. Recent ones included "Educating Young Children About Sexual Abuse" and "Spanking in the Schools." Often an issue will explore a particular theme, such as "The Emerging Adolescent." The goal is to "stimulate thinking rather than advocate fixed practices," and the journal achieves this admirably. Regular departments include book reviews of books for children and professionals, reviews of films and pamphlets, summaries of current research in magazine articles and ERIC documents, software reviews, information from the field, and comments from readers and the editor. It is recommended that this magazine be considered by all libraries for purchase. It is essential for libraries supporting teachers, teachers-in-training, teacher educators, day-care workers, and administrators. (MiNe.)

Children Today (Formerly: *Children*). 1954. bi-m. $14. Judith Reed. Children's Bureau, Administration for Children, Youth & Families, Office of Human Development Services, U.S. Dept. of Health & Human Services, P.O. Box 1182, Washington, DC 20013. Illus. Circ: 18,000. Vol. ends: July/Aug. Microform: MIM, UMI.

Indexed: CIJE, EdI, RG. *Bk. rev:* 2–4, lengthy, signed. *Aud:* Pr.

A well-rounded interdisciplinary journal for the professions serving children. Specialists contribute approximately seven popularly written articles per issue concerned with children, youth, and families as well as articles for the professional. Regular departments include news and reports from the field, book reviews, and a page of U.S. government publications that are related to children. The latter would be extremely useful in ordering free and inexpensive material. (MiNe.)

Clearing House: for the contemporary educator in middle and secondary schools. 1928. m. (Sept–May). $28. Ed. bd. Held-

ref Publns., 4000 Albemarle St. N.W., Washington, DC 20016. Illus., adv. Circ: 5,000. Vol. ends: May. Microform: UMI.

Indexed: EdI. *Aud:* Pr.

This is a title for teachers and administrators of middle schools and high schools. The emphasis is on the practical, and the articles cover all subject areas. Each issue contains 10 to 12 short, usually descriptive, articles. Topics range from teacher burnout to the presentation of a plan to relieve test anxiety. A regular feature is "Innovations in the Classroom," which presents classroom-proven methods of instruction. This is a very readable, useful title for those involved in secondary school teaching.

Curriculum Review. See Books and Book Reviews/For the Professional Section.

Day Care and Early Education. 1973. q. $44 (Individuals, $19). Randa Roen. Human Sciences Press, 72 Fifth Ave., New York, NY 10011. Illus., adv. Circ: 25,000. Vol. ends: Summer. Microform: UMI.

Indexed: CIJE, EdI. *Bk. rev:* 2, 100–150 words, signed. *Aud:* Pr.

A magazine for teachers and administrators in the child-care and early education field. Articles are written in a semi-popular style and present descriptions of programs and teaching techniques, usually written from firsthand experience. All areas from staff administration to curriculum and safety are covered. Regular departments present stories for children, simple learning activities, and arts and crafts ideas. This would be a useful third choice after *Young Children* and *Early Years* (see below in this section).

Early Years. 1971. 9/yr. $16. Allen Raymond. Allen Raymond, Inc., P.O. Box 1266, Darien, CT 06820. Illus., adv. Circ: 160,000. Vol. ends: May. Microform: UMI.

Indexed: EdI. *Bk. rev:* Brief notes. *Aud:* Pr.

A publication written for teachers at the preschool through grade four levels. It resembles *Learning* and *Instructor* in its practical, hands-on format, but differs in that the material is geared for the earlier grades. Written "for teachers and by teachers," the tone is down to earth and practical; each issue contains brief how-to articles, as well as discussions of new trends in early childhood education. Ads abound; regular columns include reviews of software and children's books. Also included is a section called "Your Green Pages," which contains graded teaching activities geared to the month. This is a gold mine for new early childhood teachers. For related titles see also *Day Care and Early Education* and *Young Children* in this section.

Education Daily: the American education's independent daily news service. 1968. d. $399. Cynthia Carter. Capitol Publns., Inc., 1300 N. 17th St., Arlington, VA 22209. Index. Sample. Microform: UMI.

Aud: Pr.

Education Daily is a six-page newsletter that appears five days a week. Its primary focus is on elementary and secondary education. It presents up-to-the-minute information and national, state, and local events. Included is news from

Congress, the Education Department, and the courts. Legislation, conferences, research, and federal budget news also appear. In short, if you need access to the latest information on education, this is a vital title. It is expensive, but large school districts and education libraries needing the most current education information may find it valuable. Capitol Publications is a private firm that publishes a number of newsletters in business, data/telecommunications, human services, and health. It also publishes a number of specialized titles in education, some of which are the following:

Education Computer News. 1984. bi-w. $147. Covers trends, products, legislation, and research on all areas of educational technology.

Education of the Handicapped. 1975. bi-w. $157. Current news and legislation on federal, state, and local efforts to educate the handicapped.

Federal Grants and Contracts Weekly. 1977. w. $191. A ten-page weekly noting new federal grants and contracts. It profiles key agencies and updates new legislation, regulations, and the like.

Higher Education Daily. 1973. d. $413. A daily report on federal, state, and local government activities affecting colleges and universities. Indexed quarterly and annually.

Nation's School Report. 1928. 22/yr. $116. Reports on how school administrators are paring costs and coping with administrative and financial problems.

Report on Education of the Disadvantaged. 1968. bi-w. $141. Washington news on Chapter 1, bilingual education, child nutrition programs, etc.

Report on Education Research. 1969. bi-w. $146. News from the Education Department, the National Institute of Education, and major education labs; centers on research activities, results, and funding.

School Law News. 1973. bi-w. $150. A ten-page newsletter with information on legal decisions, pending court cases, and critical issues that affect schools.

Education Digest. 1935. 9/yr. $15. Lawrence W. Prakken. Prakken Publns., Inc., 416 Longshore Dr., P.O. Box 8623, Ann Arbor, MI 48107. Index, adv. Circ: 38,000. Vol. ends: May. Microform: UMI. Reprint: UMI.
Indexed: EdI. *Bk. rev:* 5, 100–125 words. *Aud:* Pr.

Drawing on what the editors consider to be the best in today's educational writing, this magazine condenses or publishes in full some 15 to 20 articles a month. Articles are drawn from a pool of more than 400 titles, such as *USA Today* and *American Education* and they cover topics from preschool education to trends in college and university teaching. The articles are brief and the style depends on the original source. This is a title for libraries that want education titles but cannot afford a large number of journals.

Elementary School Guidance and Counseling. 1967. q. $16 (Nonmembers, $20). Susan Crabbs & Michael Crabbs. Amer. Assn. for Counseling and Development, 5999 Stevenson Ave., Alexandria, VA 22304. Index, adv. Circ: 18,000. Vol. ends: Apr. Microform: UMI.
Indexed: CIJE, EdI. *Aud:* Pr.

A blend of descriptive articles and research studies on all aspects of guidance and counseling at the elementary and middle school levels. This is a useful compilation of material for those with guidance responsibilities. The authors are elementary school guidance counselors and those who teach it at the college level. The articles are usually well written and topical. For a related title, see the *School Counselor,* below in this section.

Elementary School Journal. 1900. 5/yr. $35 (Individuals, $25). Thomas Good. Univ. of Chicago Press, 5801 Ellis Ave., Chicago, IL 60637. Illus., index, adv. Circ: 7,600. Vol. ends: May. Microform: MIM, UMI.
Indexed: CIJE, EdI. *Aud:* Pr.

Original studies, reviews of research, and conceptual analyses of trends in elementary school teaching and learning. Topics range from "Teacher stress" to "Children's views of spelling." The articles are addressed to the professional educator and administrator and are usually authored by education faculty from colleges and universities. The quality of the writing is scholarly; the subjects timely and well presented. Despite its title, teachers looking for "how-to-teach-it-good" material will be better served using *Instructor* or *Learning* (see below in this section).

The Good Apple Newspaper. 1972. 5/yr. $12. Gary Grimm and Don Mitchell, P.O. Box 299, Carthage, IL 62321. Illus. Sample. Vol ends: June.
Indexed: CMG. *Aud:* Pr.

A highly imaginative newspaper approach to ideas for teachers of grades 2 through 8. The editorial matter covers all subjects, with almost as many innovative approaches. It is designed for the teacher, not for the child. According to the publisher, each issue is crammed with "games, projects, contracts, task cards, posters and ready to use skill building activities." There is no reason to argue. Unlike related types of instructional material published by Scholastic or Xerox, this is far from conventional. It is an ideal paper for the teacher, and, incidentally, for the parent.

High School Journal. 1917. bi-m. $15. Gerald Unks. Subs. to: Univ. of North Carolina Press, P.O. Box 2288, Chapel Hill, NC 27514. Illus., index. Circ: 2,000. Sample. Vol. ends: Apr/May. Microform: UMI.
Indexed: CIJE, EdI. *Aud:* Pr.

This journal presents "research, informed opinion, and—occasionally—successful practices" in the broad field of secondary education. Each issue contains six to eight brief articles dealing with such topics as "The new Christian schools" or "The student's right to privacy." Theme issues such as "Authoritarianism and dogmatism" are common. Articles are authored by professors of education more often than by secondary school teachers. For those with a special interest in high school teaching, policies, and practices, this is a useful title. Collections in search of additional material in this area may wish to consider *American Secondary Education* (see above in this section).

Independent School. 1941. q. $15 (Nonmembers, $17.50). Blair McElroy. Natl. Assn. of Independent Schools, 18 Tremont St., Boston, MA 02108. Illus., index, adv. Circ: 8,750. Sample. Vol. ends: May. Microform: UMI.

Indexed: CIJE, EdI. *Bk. rev:* Essays, signed. *Aud:* Pr.

This is a title for teachers and administrators in elementary and secondary independent schools. Articles are practical and descriptive and are authored by independent school teachers and administrators, as well as by faculty from higher education. Topics range from how to implement a school community service program to a discussion on SAT coaching. The articles present opinions and explore a variety of social, political, and educational issues affecting independent schools. An insert in each issue is the *NAIS Reporter,* a quarterly newsletter presenting association news, publications, conferences, and so on. This is an essential item for every independent school library.

Industrial Education. 1914. 9/yr. $14. Andrew J. Cummins, 1495 Maple Way, Troy, MI 48084. Illus., index, adv. Circ: 45,000. Vol. ends: Dec. Microform: UMI.
Indexed: CIJE, EdI. *Aud:* Pr.

Essential reading for technical and vocational education teachers, this title is replete with practical articles on everything from tool safety to a discussion of robotics programs. The material is written by instructors from colleges and universities as well as high school teachers. Articles are brief, descriptive, and often well illustrated with photos and/or diagrams. Ads are plentiful and there are numerous announcements of new products, media, and upcoming workshops and conferences in the field. For similar titles see *School Shop* and *Technology Teacher,* below in this section.

Instructor. 1891. 10/yr. $20. Leanna Landsmann. Subs. to: P.O. Box 6099, Duluth, MN 55806. Illus., index, adv. Circ: 267,166. Vol. ends: May. Microform: UMI.
Indexed: CIJE, EdI. *Aud:* Pr.

Directed to the elementary school teacher, this magazine is a gold mine of activities, ideas, and resources to make classroom teaching and learning an active, fun experience. The emphasis is on the practical. Brief articles, usually written by experienced grade school teachers, share successful learning activities and ideas for zippy lessons. There is an abundance of illustrations, material on curriculum, trends in education, and arts and crafts suggestions. This title is similar to *Learning* (see below), and both provide excellent sources of ideas for new and experienced teachers. If only one can be selected, *Learning* wins by a very fine hair.

Integrateducation. 1963. 6/yr. $20. Meyer Weinberg. Horace Mann Bond Center for Equal Education, Rm. 2220, University Library, Univ. of Massachusetts, Amherst, MA 01003. Illus., adv. Circ: 1,500. Sample. Microform: MIM, UMI.
Indexed: CIJE, EdI, INeg, PAIS. *Aud:* Pr.

This title assesses the broad implications of the educational integration of minorities, e.g., Blacks, religious groups, American Indians, women. Academics and school administrators are the authors of the usually well-written articles. They report on a wide range of topics: the pros and cons of tax breaks for parents of private school students to the gender of secondary school principals. Topics are both historical and contemporary and cover issues in preschool through higher education. For collections needing material on the education of minority groups, this is a good choice.

Learning: the magazine for creative teaching. 1972. 9/yr. $18. Maryanne Wagner. Subs. to: Learning, P.O. Box 2580, Boulder, CO 80322. Illus., index, adv. Circ: 202,000. Vol. ends: Apr. Microform: UMI.
Indexed: CIJE, EdI. *Bk. rev:* Various number, length. *Aud:* Pr.

Like its competitor, *Instructor* (see above in this section), this magazine is addressed to activity-oriented grade school teachers. Several brief articles discuss such issues in elementary education as misbehavior and standardized math tests and serve to keep the reader professionally alert. However, the strong suit of this title is its emphasis on practical suggestions, games, and activities for involving students in learning, such as "Writing Letters to Learn Math" and "Using the Classics in the Classroom." Pull-out, curriculum-related posters are attractive and useful, software and books are discussed, and holiday activities are suggested. In short, this is a bonanza for teachers in search of ideas. *Learning* is a shade more substantial and attractive than *Instructor,* so if you must select only one of these titles, this should be it.

NASSP Bulletin: the journal for middle level and high school administrators. 1917. 9/yr. $40 (free to members). Natl. Assn. of Secondary School Principals, 1904 Association Dr., Reston, VA 22091. Illus. Circ: 35,000. Vol. ends: May. Microform: UMI.
Indexed: CIJE, EdI. *Bk. rev:* 3–4, 50–75 words, signed. *Aud:* Pr.

Education from an administrator's viewpoint. This journal contains 12 to 15 brief articles, often on a theme such as discipline or curriculum planning. The material is focused, clearly written, and usually concentrates on answering problems rather than philosophically analyzing issues. Writers are professors of education as well as principals and superintendents. This title would be useful in education collections in need of an administrative outlook. The association also puts out *NASSP New Leader* (9/yr. Membership), containing news about secondary education and professional activities and *The Practitioner* (q. Membership), a newsletter for the administrator, focusing on school management.

Negro Educational Review. See Afro-American/For the Professional Section.

Phi Delta Kappan. 1915. 10/yr. $25 (Individuals, $20). Robert W. Cole, Jr. Phi Delta Kappa, Inc., Eighth and Union, P.O. Box 789, Bloomington, IN 47402. Illus., index, adv. Circ: 140,000. Vol. ends: June. Microform: UMI.
Indexed: CIJE, EdI. *Bk. rev:* 3–5, 100–300 words, signed. *Aud:* Pr.

An outstanding general education title, which should appeal to anyone interested in the present state and future of education. The 15 to 20 articles in each issue are clearly written, lively, and topical. A blend of discussions, opinions, and research on all topics in education makes for interesting reading. Controversial topics are well handled by presenting all sides of the issue. Special issues on a single theme such as compensatory education or teacher effectiveness appear three or four times a year, but most issues contain material that ranges widely over a multitude of subjects. If the collection can afford only one journal in education, this is it.

Pre-K Today. 1986. 8/yr. $32. Helen Benham. Scholastic Press Inc., 730 Broadway, New York, NY 10003. Illus., adv. Sample. Vol ends: June.

Aud: Pr.

Directed to teachers of pre-kindergarten age children, this Scholastic publication stakes out a place for itself in the more popular, less scholarly approach to young children. There are not only two to three articles for the professional teacher, but a good 10 pages of "ready to use teaching ideas." An otherwise good magazine has two faults. The price is too high for 50 pages (which include ads), and often the copy is written in such a way that the writer seems to envision the teacher at the same understanding level as the student. Still, for what it does, it does well indeed.

Preschool Perspectives. 1984. 10/yr. $18. Pamela Tuchscherer, P.O. Box 7525, Bend, OR 97708. Illus., index. Sample.

Aud: Pr.

Targeted specifically for educators of young children three-to six-years old, this quality newsletter provides very practical, up-to-date information on child development, teaching strategies, and management in an easy-to-read format. Articles on music, art, helping children to cope with separation, and the shy child have appeared, and new resources are featured. One issue printed a useful list of toy manufacturers that replace lost pieces along with their addresses. It has already won the 1985 Gold Award in the 13th Annual Newsletter Award Competition in the subscription category for "overall excellence, appropriate design, typography and printing quality." Preschool teachers find it invaluable. (MiNe.)

Principal. 1921. 5/yr. $85. Leon Greene. Natl. Assn. of Elementary School Principals, 1920 Association Dr., Reston, VA 22091. Illus., index, adv. Circ: 24,000. Vol. ends: May. Microform: UMI.

Indexed: CIJE, EdI. *Aud:* Pr.

Elementary and middle school principals are the audience for this title. Each issue contains six to eight brief articles on various topics of interest to school administrators: public relations, incompetent teachers, scheduling, and so on. The authors are either education academics or school administrators. The writing is clear, the articles practical and informative. This title stands a bit above most of the standard education titles. It should be essential reading for school principals and merits a place in professional education collections. For a related title, see *NASSP Bulletin*, above.

School Counselor. 1952. 5/yr. $20 (Nonmembers, $25). Claire Cole. Amer. Assn. for Counseling and Development, 5999 Stevenson Ave., Alexandria, VA 22304. Illus., index, adv.

Circ: 18,000. Vol. ends: May. Microform: UMI.

Indexed: CIJE, EdI. *Bk. rev:* 15–18, 200–250 words, signed. *Aud:* Pr.

The target audience here is both elementary and sec-

ondary school guidance counselors, but the format is very similar to that of the association's other title, *Elementary School Guidance and Counseling* (see above in this section). Articles present theory, low-key research, and descriptions of programs and practices and are written by practitioners and educators in the field of guidance and counseling. The writing is clear and the material has practical applications.

School Shop. 1943. 10/yr. $15. Lawrence W. Prakken. Prakken Publns., Inc., 416 Longshore Dr., P.O. Box 8623, Ann Arbor, MI 48107. Illus., index, adv. Circ: 45,000. Vol. ends: May. Microform: UMI.

Indexed: EdI. *Aud:* Pr.

High school, junior high, and vocational school teachers of industrial, vocational-technical education will find this a useful title. Short, practical articles on methods, curriculum, trends, and materials are clearly presented. The emphasis is on keeping the teacher current in the field. Also printed are notices of conferences, product news, and news of federal implications for the teaching of the subject. (See also *Industrial Education* and *Technology Teacher* in this section.)

Social Education. 1937. 7/yr. $43. Charles Rivera. Natl. Council for the Social Studies, 3501 Newark St. N.W., Washington, DC 20016. Illus., adv. Circ: 17,500. Vol. ends: Nov/Dec. Microform: UMI.

Indexed: CIJE, EdI. *Bk. rev:* Occasional. *Aud:* Pr.

As the official journal of the National Council for the Social Studies, this title presents material of interest to all social studies teachers, elementary through college. However, most of the articles seem geared to the teacher at the junior and senior high levels. Articles discuss teaching problems, methods, and social studies curriculum. Material is topical and interesting.

Technology Teacher (Formerly: *Man/Society/Technology*). 1939. 8/yr. $20 (Members, $30). Kendall Starkweather. Amer. Industrial Arts Assn., 1914 Association Dr., Reston, VA 22091. Illus., index, adv. Circ: 7,500. Vol. ends: May/June. Refereed. Microform: UMI.

Indexed: CIJE, EdI. *Bk. rev:* 3–4, 50–75 words, signed. *Aud:* Pr.

This title provides a forum for the exchange of ideas relating to industrial arts/technology education. Its audience consists of teachers at high schools, technical institutes, and colleges. Brief articles report on teaching methods, curriculum/philosophies, job opportunities, and new technology in the field. The writing is clear and very practical. Regular departments note new research, media, conference news, and association notes. This is a basic title in the field and is very similar to *Industrial Education* (see above).

Theory into Practice. 1962. 4/yr. $30 (Individuals, $16). Donald Lux, 174 Arps Hall, 1945 N. High St., Columbus, OH 43210. Illus., index, adv. Circ: 5,000. Vol. ends: Fall. Microform: MIM, UMI.

Indexed: CIJE, EdI. *Aud:* Pr.

Each issue is devoted to a single theme, such as "Classroom Communication," "Early Adolescence," or "Microcomputers." Diverse points of view are presented in the 10 or 12 articles per issue. The articles are stimulating, well written, and authored by academics from the field of education. A useful item for active teachers and administrators.

Today's Catholic Teacher. 1967. 8/yr. $14.95. Ruth Matheny. Peter Li, Inc., 2451 E. River Rd., Dayton, OH 45439. Illus., adv. Circ: 60,000. Sample. Vol. ends: May. Microform: UMI. *Aud:* Pr.

For teachers and administrators of Catholic elementary and secondary schools, this title presents short, practical articles on a variety of issues. Authored by Catholic school teachers, the articles discuss general education issues such as readability formulas and more religious-oriented topics such as the teaching of science and religion, as well as fostering vocational awareness.

Totline. 1979. bi-m. $12. Jean Warren. Warren Publg. House, 1004 Harborview Lane, Everett, WA 98203. Illus., adv. Circ: 8,000. *Aud:* Pr.

Subtitled "The Activity Newsletter for Home or School," this magazine has expanded to over 20 pages full of ideas for projects. Activities are suggested on themes such as holidays, with appropriate stories, songs, poems, craft and snack ideas. Movement exercises, activities to develop the young child's self concept, are all part of the stress on creativity. Libraries with strong preschool programming will find this as useful as preschools and day-care centers and will want to feature it in parenting collections. (MiNe.)

Young Children: the journal of the National Association for the Education of Young Children. 1944. 6/yr. Membership (Nonmembers, $20). Ed. bd. Natl. Assn. for the Education of Young Children, 1834 Connecticut Ave. N.W., Washington, DC 20009. Illus., index, adv. Circ: 42,000. Vol. ends: Sept. Microform: KTO, UMI. *Indexed:* CIJE, EdI. *Bk. rev:* 3–4, 100–150 words, signed. *Aud:* Pr.

For early childhood educators, this title has more depth and substance than *Early Years* (see above in this section). The articles keep readers abreast of the latest developments in early childhood education. Research, theory, and practice are presented in an easy-to-read style. Related titles are *Day Care and Early Education* and *Early Years* (see above in this section), but this should be the first choice because of its higher quality.

ELECTRONICS

For the Student

See also Computers; and Television, Video, and Radio Sections.

Sarojini Balachandran, Head, Science/Engineering Services, Olin Library, Washington University, St. Louis, MO 63130

Lois M. Nase, Assistant Engineering Librarian, Princeton University, Princeton, NJ 08544

Introduction

Electronics is an area where for every scholarly journal there is also a journal oriented to the hobbyist and the weekend enthusiast. This section emphasizes the latter type.

Basic Periodicals

Hs: *QST, Radio-Electronics.*

For the Student

Audio. 1917. m. $17.94. Eugene Pitts III. CBS Magazines, 1515 Broadway, New York, NY 10036. Subs. to: P.O. Box 5316, Boulder, CO 80302. Illus., index, adv. Circ: 125,000. Vol. ends: Dec. Microform: UMI. *Indexed:* MgI. *Aud:* Hs.

A magazine that is perfect for those who want to play the best musical recordings on the best electronic equipment to obtain perfection in sound. The editors offer one to three feature articles each month detailing how to build a particular piece of equipment or how to overcome problems. Five to six equipment profiles are offered in each issue that give a great deal of information and exact specifications about a particular product. Of great value also are the music reviews, which describe new recordings in all styles of music and grade them on sound and performance of the artists. Finally, there is an annual equipment directory in October that supplies the specifications for many types of equipment from disc players to loudspeakers. Highly recommended.

Modern Electronics. 1984. m. $16.97. Art Salsberg. Modern Electronics, Inc., 76 N. Broadway, Hicksville, NY 11801. Illus., adv. *Bk. rev:* 3, 150–300 words. *Aud:* Hs.

A newcomer to the marketplace, but it is a good new source of information. It is similar to *Radio-Electronics* because both titles have articles mainly on how to build or design components. This title has particularly good illustrations and diagrams. There are also articles on programming ideas for microcomputers. A nice feature is the product evaluations section, which gives a description of the component, the details of its operation, and a chart with the specifications. Highly recommended.

QST. 1915. m. $25. Paul L. Rinaldo. Amer. Radio Relay League, 225 Main St., Newington, CT 06111. Illus., index, adv. Circ: 130,000. Vol. ends: Dec. Microform: UMI. *Bk. rev:* 1, 500–700 words, signed. *Aud:* Hs.

A fine magazine devoted to the interests of amateur radio enthusiasts. The beginner is provided with in-depth instructions on constructing or purchasing equipment. Many recent technical articles describe computer applications for designing and running the radio station. New operating rules, dockets under consideration by the FCC, and license requirements are published regularly. Events and conventions sponsored by the American Radio Relay League and other organizations are listed. Lengthy corporate advertisements and classified sections provide information on new and used equipment. Highly recommended.

Radio-Electronics. 1929. m. $15.97. Art Kleiman. Gennsback Pubs., Inc., 200 Park Ave. S., New York, NY 10003. Illus., adv. Circ: 225,000. Vol. ends: Dec. Microform: UMI. *Indexed:* MgI, RG. *Aud:* Hs.

A fine magazine for the electronics hobbyist who is interested in building components and making informed purchases of new products. It is a title with a long history, and it is indexed in many standard sources. Articles cover topics ranging from building integrated circuits to buffers to features on automotive electronics to robotics. There are special sections on new equipment, computers, video components, and radios. A classified section and an advertising index provide nice avenues to find the needed parts or products. Highly recommended for the medium-sized to large library.

ENVIRONMENT, CONSERVATION, AND OUTDOOR RECREATION

For the Student: General; Outdoor Recreation/For the Professional

See also Fishing, Hunting, and Guns; and Sports Sections.

Doug Ernest, Assistant Reference Librarian, Colorado State University, Fort Collins, CO 80523

Phoebe F. Phillips, Head, Monographic Cataloging, Robert Manning Strozier Library, Florida State University, Tallahassee, FL 32306

Introduction

Though environment and conservation seem to be cyclical in the emphasis our country gives them, it is interesting to note that new titles dealing with these topics continue to appear, just as acid rain continues to be a topic of newscasts. It is to be hoped that the concern for clean air and water and the concern for hazardous wastes issues will continue to generate a serious and scholarly approach to solutions.

Basic Periodicals

GENERAL. Hs: *International Wildlife, National Wildlife, Sierra.*

OUTDOOR RECREATION. Hs: *Backpacker,* any suitable regional or state title.

For the Student

GENERAL

American Forests: the magazine of forests, soil, water, wildlife, and outdoor recreation. 1895. m. $15. Bill Rooney. Amer. Forestry Assn., 1319 18th St. N.W., Washington, DC 20036. Illus., adv. Microform: UMI. *Indexed:* Acs, BioAg, BoRvI, GSI. *Bk. rev:* 1–3, 300–500 words, signed. *Aud:* Hs.

The American Forestry Association is a "national citizens' conservation organization—independent and nonpartisan—dedicated to the protection and intelligent use of the nation's forests and related resources." The stated objective is to provide the leadership that will lead to "enlightened public policy" and "management practices" in soil and water conservation. Topics range from urban forestry to air pollution, acid rain, and the AFA's National Registry requirements. The subscription price includes membership in AFA and assumes support of the "stewardship" approach to natural resources. For a wide breadth of subject matter and diverse reading, you can consider this periodical as satisfying general audiences very well.

The Conservationist. 1946. bi-m. $5. John J. DuPont. New York State Dept. of Environmental Conservation, 50 Wolf Rd., Albany, NY 12233. Illus. Circ: 180,000. Sample. Vol. ends: May/June. Microform: B&H, UMI. *Indexed:* CIJE, GSI, RG. *Bk. rev:* 1–3, 500 words, signed. *Aud:* Ejh, Hs.

Excellent color illustrations make this an appealing browsing item for many students. Pieces include a wide range of topics. Beautiful artwork is also in evidence in the issues. An outstanding investment for the money for any school library's holdings. Recommended.

Florida Naturalist. 1917. q. Members, $15. Beo Barton. Florida Audubon Soc., 1101 Audubon Way, Maitland, FL 32751. Illus., index, adv. Circ: 25,000. *Bk. rev:* 3, 50–200 words, signed. *Aud:* Hs.

Though the articles are brief, they are well written. However, the only color photography is the cover photo. Each issue is generally only about 20 pages long and consists of topics on wildlife and ecosystem problems. Geared to the general audience, it also includes information valuable for interested students.

International Wildlife. 1971. bi-m. Membership, $12. John Strohm. Natl. Wildlife Federation, 1412 16th St. N.W., Washington, DC 20036. Illus. Vol. ends: Nov/Dec. Microform: B&H, UMI. *Indexed:* GSI, MgI, RG. *Aud:* Ejh, Hs.

"Dedicated to the wise use of the earth's resources," this publication's 50-plus pages are chock-full of color photographs and interesting tidbits on the aspects of nature that exist all around us but are seldom noticed. As the title indicates, it is international in scope. It has excellent photography, and the text is easy to read and informative. Excellent for browsing; the photography alone makes the magazine worth acquiring.

National Wildlife. 1962. bi-m. Membership, $12. John Strohm. Natl. Wildlife Federation, 1412 16th St. N.W., Washington, DC 20036. Illus., adv. Circ: 766,900. Sample. Vol. ends: Oct/Nov. Microform: B&H, UMI. *Indexed:* AbrRG, GSI, MgI, RG. *Aud:* Ejh, Hs.

The best-known and best general magazine devoted to the protection of the environment. In addition to beautifully illustrated articles on all aspects of nature (soil, forests, minerals, wildlife), there is material on outdoor activities: camping, animal photography, and the like. Articles are generally summarized in the table of contents after each title. "Wildlife Digest," a regular feature, includes topics well beyond what the title would imply, such as "passive smoking" and "nuclear waste warning," which affect the environment.

Not Man Apart. 1970. 10/yr. $15. Friends of the Earth, 1045 Sansome St., San Francisco, CA 94111. Illus., adv. Circ: 32,000. Sample.

Indexed: API. *Bk. rev:* Various number, length. *Aud:* Hs.

Motivated by the same attitudes and insights that have made *Sierra* such a popular title, this is of a similar type. It is not as elaborate and there is more emphasis on the technology of keeping the environment safe and sound. The authors tend to stress alternative sources of energy and alternative approaches to using the environment that are not found that often in the more popular *Sierra.* There are up-to-date reports on legislation and political action, as well as informative book reports. A good title for any library with a concern about the environment.

Sierra: the Sierra Club bulletin. 1893. bi-m. Membership, $29 (Nonmembers, $12). John Keough. Sierra Club, 530 Bush St., San Francisco, CA 94108. Illus., index, adv. Circ: 180,000. Vol. ends: Dec. Microform: B&H, UMI.

Indexed: BioAb, RG. *Bk. rev:* 4, 500–1,000 words, signed. *Aud:* Hs.

Considers impact on the environment of political and social issues, as well as providing information on camping, hiking and more. The magazine takes a definite stand on issues of environmental import. Includes full-page, color photographs of scenic areas in the United States and Canada. *Sierra* sponsors an annual photography contest on subjects ranging from wildlife, outdoor recreation, and "designs in nature" to national parks and monuments. Includes index in November/December issue.

Water Spectrum (Formerly: *Water Spectrum, Issues, Choices, Actions*). 1970. q. $7.50. Joyce Hardyman. U.S. Army Corps of Engineers Water Resources Support Center (WRSC), Fort Belvoir, VA 22060. Subs. to: Supt. of Docs., Govt. Printing Office, Washington, DC 20402. Illus. Circ: 14,000.

Indexed: IGov. *Bk. rev:* 7, 100 words. *Aud:* Hs.

Both black-and-white and color photography make this highly illustrated periodical a good browsing item. Topics range from resource management to river recreation and water quality protection. Contributors range from Wildlife Management Institute vp's to social scientists. Articles are readable and topics appeal to a wide audience.

Wilderness (Formerly: *The Living Wilderness*). 1935. q. Membership, $25 (Libraries, $20). T. H. Watkins. Wilderness Soc., 1400 I St. N.W., Washington, DC 20005. Illus. Circ: 80,000. Sample. Vol. ends: Summer. Microform: B&H, UMI.

Indexed: GSI, MgI, RG. *Aud:* Ejh, Hs.

After *National Wildlife,* this is the best general conservation magazine for teenagers. It supports conservation efforts at all government levels, stimulates public support, and pushes for scientific studies of the wilderness. In addition to conservationist studies and opinions, there are beautiful, full-page, color photos and multicolor maps. "Viewpoint," a regular feature, presents lengthy editorial comment on issues related to the environmental stance of the society.

OUTDOOR RECREATION

Adirondack Life. 1970. bi-m. $12. Laurie Storey. Adirondack Life, 420 E. Genesee St., Syracuse, NY 13202. Illus., adv. Circ: 48,000. Sample.

Bk. rev: Notes. *Aud:* Hs.

A combination regional and out-of-doors sport magazine, this deals with recreation and conservation in northern New York State. The articles, which are usually illustrated, tend to concentrate on the sport of the moment, e.g., skiing in the winter and backpacking in the summer. There are regular features on personalities and the history of the area. A particularly useful addition is the calendar of events and recreational facilities directory.

Backpacker. 1973. bi-m. $18. John A. Delves III. Ziff-Davis Publg. Co., One Park Ave., New York, NY 10016. Illus., adv. Circ: 165,000. Vol. ends: Nov. Microform: B&H.

Indexed: Acs, MgI. *Aud:* Hs.

This magazine has something to offer for many types of outdoor recreationists: hikers, campers, cross-country skiers, and kayakers, among others. Feature articles on outdoor locales usually include not only glossy photographs but also "expedition planners" that give the reader practical advice for planning his or her own trip. The focus is generally on outings in the United States or Canada. Also included are numerous articles on gear for those who wish to keep up with the latest advances or styles in camping chic. (D.E.)

Canoe. See Boats and Boating/For the Student Section.

National Parks: the magazine of the National Parks & Conservation Association (Formerly: *National Parks & Conservation Magazine: the environmental journal*). 1919. bi-m. Membership (Associate members, $18). Michele Strutin. Natl. Parks & Conservation Assn., 1701 18th St. N.W., Washington, DC 20009. Illus., index, adv. Circ: 45,000. Microform: B&H, UMI.

Indexed: RG. *Aud:* Ejh, Hs.

A nonpartisan review dedicated to the protection of the national parks and monuments of the United States. Interests extend, however, to all aspects of environment. Includes illustrated articles on both famous and lesser known parks. Features provide updates on action in legislatures and government agencies, news items, and commentaries on national conservation issues. Annual index is included with the November/December issue. An excellent magazine for most libraries.

Outdoor Canada. 1972. 8/yr. $17.97. Sheila Kaighin. Outdoor Canada Magazine, Ltd., 953A Eglinton Ave. E., Toronto, Ont. M4G 4B5, Canada. Illus., adv. Circ: 140,000. Sample. Vol. ends: Dec/Jan. Microform: MML.

Indexed: CanI. *Aud:* Hs.

An informative magazine for those who fish, hike, or canoe. The well-illustrated articles make even the armchair traveler yearn for a trip to Yoho or the Queen Charlotte Islands. When national parks are discussed, a useful section on how to get there is always appended. How-to sections discuss equipment selection and care. There are good departments on wild animals, birds, fish, outdoor photography, fishing, fly of the month, outdoor health, nutrition and even how to cook what you find in the wild edibles column. Recommended for libraries with an interest in wildlife and conservation or travel. (J.C.)

Outside. 1976. m. $18. John Rasmus. 1165 N. Clark St., Chicago, IL 60610. Illus., adv. Circ: 220,000. Vol. ends: Dec. Microform: B&H.
Indexed: Acs. *Bk. rev:* 1–3, 200–500 words, signed. *Aud:* Hs.

Many outdoor sports—downhill skiing, bicycling, surfing—beyond hiking and climbing make up the contents of this periodical. There are frequent articles on globe-trotting expeditions or gruelling adventures that will appeal to those who like to read about such experiences, as well as to the few who actually participate. Other articles explore areas closer to home. In all, *Outside* is aimed at a general audience rather than the devotees of each sport.

Rand McNally Campground and Trailer Park Directory. 1960. a. $12.95. Rand McNally and Co., P.O. Box 728, 8255 N. Central Park, Skokie, IL 60076. Illus., adv. Circ: 290,000. *Aud:* Hs.

An annual and consequently quite a current guide to parks, both private and public, where one may camp or put a trailer for a night. Complete information is given on everything from facilities to costs, as well as possible recreational activities. There are numerous maps of the states, provinces, and Mexico. Apparently the listings are not influenced by the advertising. Librarians might also wish to look at the following:
   Wheelers RV Resort & Campground Guide. 1971. a. $9.95. Print Media Services, Ltd., 1310 Jarvis Ave., Elk Grove, IL 60007.
   Woodall's Tenting Directory. 1964. a. Price varies. Woodall Publg. Co., 500 Hyacinth Pl., Highland Park, IL 60035.

Walking! Journal: the art, science and sport of walking. 1983. q. $8. Kevin Kelly. Walking Journal, Inc., Box 454, Athens, GA 30603. Illus., adv. Circ: 4,000.
Aud: Hs.

A relatively new magazine not aimed directly at a juvenile audience, but certainly appropriate for teens interested in walking as sport and pastime. The magazine contains practical advice for walkers of all ages and interesting articles on both the physiology and psychology of walking. Interesting features include book and product reviews, a "walking companions wanted" section, and a calendar that lists races and walking events.

Wyoming Wildlife. 1936. m. $8. Chris Madson. Game & Fish Dept., Cheyenne, WY 82002. Illus., index. Circ: 41,000. Sample. Vol. ends: Dec.
Aud: Hs.

This beautiful magazine emphasizes responsible hunting and fishing, environmental issues, and wildlife management. The superb color photographs and illustrations will interest any audience, including very young children. The biologists, planners, and wardens on the staff of the Game and Fish Department offer editorials, travelogues, and articles on hunting safety, history, and law enforcement, as well as a series of features on individual species of wildlife. The annual photo contest issue serves as an eloquent inventory of the state's natural resources. A recent editorial noted that non-Wyoming subscribers outnumber those in-state by three to one, evidence of the magazine's broad appeal. Inexpensive, yet carefully produced, this magazine sets a standard for similar state and commercial publications.

For the Professional

Journal of Environmental Education (Formerly: *Environmental Education*). 1967. 4/yr. $27. Robert S. Cook, Roderick Nash & Robert E. Roth. Helen Dwight Reid Educational Foundation, 4000 Albemarle St. N.W., Washington, DC 20016. Illus. Vol. ends: Summer.
Indexed: CIJE. *Aud:* Pr.

This technical journal provides a unique perspective on the overall impact of environmental issues in education. It goes beyond the teaching of ordinary environmental courses to discuss the impact of attitudes and environmental "experiences" on the classroom. Illustrations are generally black-and-white graphs and tables. Articles tend to be lengthy and heavily documented with abstracts. Provision is made for Spanish and French abstracts of articles. Contributors tend to be faculty members of colleges and universities, and the executive editors are all university professors.

Nature Study (Formerly: *ANSS News*). 1946. q. $10. Helen Ross Russell. Amer. Nature Study Soc., c/o Helen Ross Russell, 44 College Dr., Jersey City, NJ 07305. Illus., index. Circ: 800. Sample. Vol. ends: Dec. Microform: UMI.
Aud: Pr.

The ANSS publishes this journal to "heighten environmental awareness and sensitivity." Teaching about the natural world is the primary emphasis, with articles written by association members on public policy, individual species of wildlife, especially those on the endangered list, classroom tips, and effective field trip planning. News of environmental education centers in the United States, book reviews, and frequent bibliographies are helpful for teachers.

EUROPE

For the Student/For the Professional

See also USSR and Eastern Europe Section.

Introduction

In this section, "Europe" encompasses primarily France, Italy, and Germany. The journals are limited to popular picture and newsmagazines and those representing literature, culture, and politics. Prices are in dollars as of late 1985. These are subject to change, depending upon the fate of the dollar.

Basic Periodicals

Hs: Choose foreign language periodical to suit class.

For the Student

Champs-Elysées. 1984. 7 issues, $52. Dominique Laurent, P.O. Box 158067, Nashville, TN 37215.
Aud: Hs.

Essentially, *Champs-Elysées* is a practical lesson in spoken French but delivered in a sparkling, entertaining fashion. The "magazine" is in two parts. The cassette, or the first part, consists of about 40 minutes of news and notes on travel, cooking, entertainment, current affairs, and sports; most of the items are interlaced with popular French songs that are taken from the average French person's weekly experience. The second part is a printed version of the cassette material. This is in French with a vocabulary of basic words and idiomatic expressions. It is assumed that the listener (audience) has a year of basic French at the high school level. The material is rather easy to follow, and the reader (an announcer with a quite winning voice and manner) gives it a zestful emphasis. As the reports and music are about today's French events, it has a current appeal rarely found in traditional language lessons. While there are seven issues a semester, a full subscription ($100) consists of 14 cassettes sent over the school year. Supervised by experienced U.S. teachers, this is an effort that should have wide appeal.

Epoca. 1950. w. $99. Sandro Mayer. Arnoldo Mondadori Editore, 20090 Segrate, Milan, Italy. Illus., index, adv. Circ: 392,000.
Bk. rev: 2–3, notes. *Aud:* Hs.

One of Europe's best pictorial magazines. The photographs are often in color and are found on almost all of the 100 or more pages. There is some sensational material, but the focus is on the week's political, social, and economic events. The result is a relatively serious, well-written, and carefully edited news-pictorial magazine. Depending upon the issue, the editorial matter can be at least as important as the photographs. There are major in-depth stories in each issue. Recommended for any library where there is an interest in Italian.

Espresso. 1955. w. $78. Livio Zanetti. Editorale l'Espresso, S.p.A., Via Po 12, 11198 Rome, Italy. Illus., adv. Circ: 337,000. Microform: UMI.
Bk. rev: 3–4, 200 words, signed. *Aud:* Hs.

The general news/picture magazine of Italy, *Espresso* follows the usual format—that is, photographs and various departments divided nicely by topic. There are masses of advertisements also, and each 200-or-so-page issue is as much a tribute to Italian economics as it is to its editors. The number opens with news about Italy; moves on to news about the world and the European scene; and then becomes divided into news about society, culture, science, economics, and so on. The reporting is fairly objective and middle-of-the-road. *Espresso* offers both the Italian and the outsider a good overall view of Italy week by week.

L'Express. 1957. w. $70. S.A. Express Union, 78, rue Olivier-de-Serres, 75039 Paris, France. Illus., adv. Circ: 600,000.
Bk. rev: 2–3, 200 words, signed. *Aud:* Hs.

The basic French newsmagazine, similar to *Der Spiegel* in Germany and *Time* and *Newsweek* in the United States. All have a similar format. In the last few years or so, the magazine has taken on a brighter, some would say, more semipopular appearance. There are illustrations, many in color, on every page. A strong effort is made to attract readers with personal notes on leading people in the news. For example, there is a "Portrait" section in almost every issue. The format is standard. Two or three lead stories from the news of the week are followed by commentary on world events, economics, the world of France, and the like. Then there is a turn, as in U.S. newsmagazines, to comments on science, the arts, books, and so on. On a whole, *L'Express* is quite easy to read and well within the grasp of most U.S. students with high school French and an appreciation of the vernacular. The 74- to 80-page magazine should be found in any school library with an interest in France or the French language.

German Tribune. 1962. w. $19. Friedrich Reinecke Verlag GmbH, Schoene Aussicht 23, 2000 Hamburg 76, Fed. Rep. of Germany. Illus. Circ: 24,000. Sample.
Bk. rev: 7, total 16 pages. *Aud:* Hs.

For those who do not know the language very well, this publication offers a splendid way of keeping up with West German activities. Each week the editor offers English translations of newspaper articles that have appeared in the German press. Some are reprinted in full, but many are condensed. The object is to offer all viewpoints, which is done quite well. Most of the material is no more than a week to three weeks old. The selection is excellent and, while not extensive, gives the reader a fair overview. Although West Germany is the focus, there is valuable material about East Germany as well.

Oggi. 1945. w. $78. Rizzoli-Corriere della Sera, Via A. Rizzoli 2, 20132 Milan, Italy. Illus., adv. Circ: 802,000. Microform: UMI.
Aud: Hs.

Similar in format to *Paris Match*, but on a lower grade of paper and with less-appealing photographs, this is the picture magazine of Italy. There are masses of advertisements in the 120–150 pages, and these are laced with the usual type of stories, from news about sports and movie stars to television figures and events (usually sensational) in the news. The appeal is to the mass audience, and it more than succeeds in this endeavor. Quite easy to read and amusing to thumb through, *Oggi* is a basic magazine wherever there is a large Italian audience.

Panorama. 1962. w. $87. Arnoldo Mondadori. Lamberto Seche, 20090 Segrate, Milan, Italy. Illus., adv. Circ: 346,000.
Aud: Hs.

One of the leading weekly newsmagazines in Italy. *Panorama* has a format that has been compared with the U.S.

Time and *Newsweek*. It includes sections on business, sports, and cultural affairs. *Panorama* is bound by all the leading Italian libraries and cited in the halls of parliament. It has attained considerable circulation in most European capitals and among the Italian community in New York.

Point. 1972. w. $100. Claude Imbert. FSEBDO, 140 rue de Rennes, 75006 Paris, France. Illus., adv. Circ: 335,000. *Aud:* Hs.

The French *Time/Newsweek/Der Spiegel*—all rolled into 90 pages of illustrations, news, and advertisements. The point of view is slightly left of center, but for the most part an effort is made to please most of the French. The divisions are standard—for example, the issue opens with news of France, Europe, and the world, and then moves to special sections from economics and cinema to books. One most useful feature is that each number begins with a guide that briefly summarizes activities in France—primarily in Paris, from music and theater to sports. There is also a three- to four-page "lettre confidentielle," of news just off the wire and tinged by a bit of sensationalism. The advertising is impressive, although not as much as in the German version, *Der Spiegel*. A basic title for general reading collections in any school library with an interest in current French news.

Scala International. 1961. m. $12. Frankfurter Societaets-druckerei GmbH., Frankenallee 71-81, 6000 Frankfurt 1, Fed. Rep. of Germany. Illus., adv. Circ: 330,000. *Aud:* Hs.

A picture magazine published not only in German but also in Spanish and English. Although a shadow of the much more sensational and expensive *Stern*, it is more sophisticated; the photographs and other illustrations are similar to the *Stern* type. Free of any ties to large conglomerates, this monthly is more independent than the other illustrated periodicals. A typical rather than a major journal. Note: The English and Spanish editions have the same content and are at the same price.

Scandinavian Review. 1913. q. $15. Patricia McFate. American Scandinavian Foundation, 127 E. 73rd St., New York, NY 10021. Illus., index, adv. Circ: 7,000. Sample. Vol. ends: Dec. Microform: UMI.

Indexed: MLA, PAIS. *Bk. rev:* 5, 450 words, signed, plus notes. *Aud:* Hs.

In 90 pages of illustrations and short features, the authors and editor paint a rosy picture of the Scandinavian countries. This is more like a literary review along the lines of *The Saturday Review*, but with a touch of travel and quite thoughtful pieces on the arts, including architecture. Prominent Scandinavians are usually featured, although the individual is likely to be an author. The publication is written in English, and there is even fiction and poetry. All and all, a quite useful general magazine for most collections.

Der Spiegel. 1947. w. $182. Rudolf Augstein, Postfach 110 Brandstwiete, 19 Ost West Strasse, 2000 Hamburg, Fed.

Rep. of Germany. Illus., adv. Circ: 1,100,000. Sample. Vol. ends: Dec.

Bk. rev: 1–3, 200 words, signed. *Aud:* Hs.

The best-known newsmagazine in Germany, and for that matter in Europe, this is the voice of a relatively liberal group of writers. Looking at an average copy, the first thing that strikes a U.S. reader is its size. An average issue is two to three times the size of *Time* or *Newsweek*, which it resembles. Most of the 250 to 300 pages are given over to advertisements that indicate the Germans are doing quite well. The editorial material is divided in the usual fashion—that is, a section on Germany, another section on Europe and the rest of the world, sports, culture activities, personalities, book reviews, and so on. There are pictures, but fewer than in U.S. newsmagazines. The editorial tone is lively, yet fairly objective; in many ways it has a much better coverage of the news than is found here. There are often quite long and in-depth essays. A must for almost all schools with a German-language program.

Stern Magazin. 1947. w. $151. Gruner & Jahr GmbH and Co., Warburgstrasse 50, 2000 Hamburg 36, Fed. Rep. of Germany. Illus., adv. Circ: 2,000,000. Microform: UMI. *Aud:* Hs.

Germany's primary picture magazine, a combination of *Life* and *Time* or *Newsweek*. Published by the Springer group, it is directed to the German middle classes and reflects their values in its editorial material. Coverage is primarily of the week's past events in Germany, although it does include Europe and the remainder of the world from time to time. With the addition of the word *magazin* to its title in the 1980s, the magazine has made a concerted effort to be something more than an oversized *People*. There is now more editorial matter than in the past, but it remains a highly popular approach to people and activities. Readers in the United States, too, are struck by the nudity, which the Germans treat much as we do violence—that is, they seem to treat it casually and as part of the passing scene. A good title for those with less than a scholarly interest in Germany and for those who enjoy looking at pictures and stumbling through a bit of the prose.

For the Professional

Revue des Livres pour Enfants. 1965. bi-m. $12. Genevieve Brisac. Centre National du Livre pour Enfants, Joie Par les Livres, 8 rue Saint-Bon, 75004 Paris, France. Illus., adv. Circ: 4,000.
Aud: Pr.

A French equivalent of the Center for Children's Books, the French Documentation Center on Children's Literature publishes this useful bimonthly overview of children's books. An effort is made to review new titles consistently, and many issues are covered—for example, themes of interest to children and children's libraries, 200 paperbacks for children, and five illustrators. Each issue has a list of books on a special subject, such as China, the Olympics, or the family in the novel. Once each year, the best books of that year are listed. This is a standard source of French titles for children and, as such, highly recommended.

EXCEPTIONAL CHILDREN: GIFTED, DISABLED, THOSE WITH SPECIAL NEEDS

For the Student/For the Professional

See also Health and Medicine Section.

Lenore R. Greenberg, Librarian, Anchor Savings Bank, 5323 Fifth Ave., Brooklyn, NY 11220

Introduction

For information about magazines "suitable for use by persons who are unable to read or handle conventional print materials," see: *Magazines in Special Media: Subscription Sources* (Washington, DC: The Library of Congress, 1985). This includes brief annotations and full information about braille, cassette, disc, large-type and Moon-type media. Following the list is an index to subject and to various media. The circular is free from the Library of Congress via the Reference Section, National Library Service for the Blind and Physically Handicapped.

Basic Abstracts and Indexes

Current Index to Journals in Education.

For the Student

Chart Your Course! 1980. 8/yr. $20. Fay L. Gold. G/C/T Publg. Co., Inc., P.O. Box 6448, Mobile, AL 36660. Illus. Circ: 10,000. Sample. Vol. ends: May.
Aud: Ejh.

The publisher claims that this is "the world's first magazine by and for gifted, creative and talented children." Of course the content depends on submissions by young contributors, but each issue usually includes articles, prose, poetry, reviews, essays, puzzles, games, art photos, and comics. Regular features are "Write Away, Right Away!" (a list of pen pals) and "Letters to the Editor." This unique magazine is printed on heavy stock paper, and the illustrations are done primarily in one or two colors. The attractive layout offers variety and invites children to look, read, and do. A great forum for budding authors, illustrators, and photographers. (L.K.O.)

Kaleidoscope. 1980. s-a. $5.50. Carson Heiner. United Cerebral Palsy of Akron and Summit County, 318 Water St., Akron, OH 44208. Illus.
Aud: Hs.

Subtitled "National Literary/Art Magazine for Disabled," this magazine welcomes a variety of writing and art produced by the handicapped. According to the editor, the periodical will publish works of successful artists and writers as well as amateurs. Material is carefully selected, and the result is good reading for just about anyone, e.g., the issue examined included work by Larry Eigner, a distinguished

cerebral palsied poet; Clayton Turner, a paralyzed artist of considerable reputation; and a group of lesser-known writers from many parts of the United States. A short biographical sketch is given for each contributor, and there are brief pieces on overcoming disabilities. Highly recommended for any type or size of library, because it reaches not only the disabled but also others who can learn much from the fine material in each issue.

Light Magazine. 1932. a. Free. Margi Stapleton. Braille Inst. of America, Inc., 741 N. Vermont Ave., Los Angeles, CA 90029. Illus. Circ: 80,000. Sample.
Aud: Hs.

The voice of a nonprofit group dedicated to assisting the blind, this magazine reports on the organization's activities, particularly in terms of counseling, education, and job placement. It should be noted that this is free and should be found in most libraries. The information is of invaluable aid to both the blind and those working with the blind.

For the Professional

Education of the Handicapped. See *Education Daily* in Education/For the Professional Section.

Exceptional Children. 1934. 6/yr. $25. James E. Yeseldyke. Council for Exceptional Children, 1920 Association Dr., Reston, VA 22091. Illus., index, adv. Circ: 63,000. Sample. Vol. ends: May. Microform: UMI.
Indexed: CIJE, EdI. *Bk. rev:* 5–7, 300 words, signed. *Aud:* Pr.

This journal, the official journal of the Council for Exceptional Children, is concerned with children who are gifted, have behavior or communication disorders or learning disabilities, are mentally retarded, or are physically or visually handicapped. Specialists in the field contribute fairly technical articles on planning curriculum, current research and developments, and suggestions for the classroom. Departments report on professional conferences and news, upcoming events, book reviews, classified advertisements, and professional opportunities. (MiNe.)

The Exceptional Parent. 1971. 8/yr. $24 (Individuals, $16). Stanley D. Klein. Psy-Ed Corp., 605 Commonwealth Ave., Boston, MA 02215. Illus. Circ: 22,000. Vol. ends: Dec. Microform: UMI.
Bk. rev: 1 or more book excerpts, 2 pages. *Aud:* Pr.

Recommended by Ann Landers, this magazine offers supportive and practical advice in a very readable manner for parents of exceptional or disabled children, as well as professionals. Each issue features a specific topic in addition to monthly columns; recent themes included recreation, employment, and new products. (MiNe.)

G/C/T (Gifted/Creative/Talented Children). 1978. bi-m. $19.50 Marvin Gold. G/C/T Publg. Co., P.O. Box 66654, Mobile, AL 36606. Illus., adv. Circ: 12,000. Sample. Volume ends: Nov/Dec. Microform: UMI.
Bk. rev: 15–20, 300 words, signed. *Aud:* Pr.

This 60-page publication targets parents and teachers of gifted youth as its audience. About 14 feature articles are full of practical suggestions and supportive advice for the frustrating-yet-rewarding job of working with the gifted. Glossy pages, plentiful illustrations and photos, and a humorous touch make this an attractive and highly accessible periodical. (MiNe.)

Gifted Children Monthly (Formerly: *Gifted Children Newsletter*). 1980. 11/yr. $24. James Alvino. Gifted & Talented Publns., Inc., P.O. Box 7200, Bergenfield, NJ 08621. Illus., adv. Circ: 45,000.
Aud: Pr.

"For the parents of children with great promise," this useful journal has recently expanded from 8 to 25 pages. Articles promote recognizing and inspiring creativity in children, with practical suggestions on expanding their horizons in science, music, art, and other areas of enrichment. Departments include idea exchange from other readers, recommended books for children selected by Barbara Elleman of *Booklist,* an "Ask the Experts" column, and a new section on software and computer books. The March issue includes a summer camp directory. An excellent feature is the pull-out section called "Spin-Off" for gifted children, with puzzles, projects, contests, and information; a parent's guide is also included. (MiNe.)

Journal of Learning Disabilities. 1968. 10/yr. $45 (Individuals, $36). Gerald Senf. Subs. to: 5615 W. Cermak Rd., Cicero, IL 60650. Illus., index, adv. Circ: 16,000. Vol. ends: Dec. Refereed. Microform: UMI.
Indexed: CIJE, EdI. *Bk. rev:* Occasional. *Aud:* Pr.

Research reports, case studies, opinion papers, and discussions on the multidisciplinary topic of learning disabilities. Each issue contains eight to ten articles written by special educators, usually from higher education. The articles are well written and practical and would appeal to both special education teachers and regular classroom teachers who teach the learning disabled. This title should be in education collections needing special education titles. (P.S.B.)

The Musical Mainstream. See Music and Dance Section/For the Professional.

Remedial and Special Education. 1964. 6/yr. $37 (Individuals, $28). James Kauffman. PRO-ED, 5341 Industrial Oaks Blvd., Austin, TX 78735. Illus., adv. Sample. Vol. ends: Nov/Dec. Microform: UMI.
Indexed: CIJE, EdI. *Aud:* Pr.

"Interpretation of research literature and recommendations for the practice of remedial and special education" are the stated aims of this title. Most of the material focuses on special education at the elementary school level, and many of the articles report the results of experimental studies. Articles cover the gifted but learning disabled as well as the mentally handicapped. (P.S.B.)

Talking Book Topics. 1935. bi-m. Free. Publn. and Media Section, Natl. Library Service for the Blind and Physically Handicapped, Library of Congress, Washington, DC 20542. Circ: 190,000. Vol. ends: Nov/Dec.
Aud: Pr.

The current availability of talking book records, cassettes, and other forms is routinely listed and annotated. Full bibliographic information is given for each entry. Division is by adult and children, fiction and nonfiction. The publication is issued in large type for those with limited sight. From time to time there are special features, news, letters from readers and so on. There is a section, too, on magazines. A must for all libraries serving the blind. *Note:* The publication is available free to individuals, and the librarian should make this subscription policy known.

Teaching Exceptional Children. 1968. q. $15. June B. Jordan. Council for Exceptional Children, 1920 Association Dr., Reston, VA 22091. Index, adv. Circ: 52,000. Vol. ends: Summer.
Indexed: CIJE, ChildDevAb, EdI. *Aud:* Pr.

Teachers involved with disabled, gifted, or handicapped children will find this a useful journal. Each issue presents eight articles that are quite readable, even though they are geared for the specialist. Information about the professional organization is included, and a column provides for the exchange of information, questions, and answers. (MiNe.)

FICTION

For the Student: General; Science Fiction

Halbert W. Hall, Head, Special Formats Division, Sterling C. Evans Library, Texas A&M University, College Station, TX 77843 (Science Fiction subsection)

Michael H. Randall, Assistant Head, Serials Department, University Research Library, University of California, Los Angeles, CA 90024 (General subsection)

Basic Periodicals

GENERAL. Ejh: *Short Story International: Seedling Series*; Hs: *Short Story International: Student Series*.

SCIENCE FICTION. Hs: *Analog, Locus*.

For the Student

GENERAL

The titles in this section include the best established general fiction magazines, as well as some promising newcomers. Representative specialized fiction magazines are also included. As a rule, poetry and drama are not included in titles listed here. Some of the titles in this section do, however, include other forms of material, such as reviews, essays, and interviews, in addition to fiction selections. (M.H.R.)

Canadian Fiction Magazine. 1971. q. $30. Geoffrey Hancock, P.O. Box 946, Sta. F, Toronto, Ont. M4Y 2N9, Canada. Illus., adv. Circ: 1,800. Microform: UMI.
Indexed: CanI. *Bk. rev:* 1–3, 900–1,000 words, signed. *Aud:* Hs.

Each issue of this publication features up to 20 works of contemporary fiction by writers in Canada and Canadians in other countries. Also included are interviews with Canadian authors, essays, photographs, and graphics. Some issues provide in-depth treatment by covering single authors or special themes such as fiction translated from the unofficial languages of Canada. High editorial standards and a commitment to a Canadian literary identity form a strong and winning combination in *Canadian Fiction Magazine.*

Fiction. 1972. irreg. $20/3 issues. Mark Jay Mirsky. Dept. of English, City College of New York, New York, NY 10031. Illus. Circ: 5,000. Microform: UMI.

Aud: Hs.

Fiction is an outstanding medium for the publication of writing by highly talented authors. New short fiction by contemporary U.S. writers comprises the bulk of most issues, but previously published stories, book excerpts and translations may also be present. The 15 to 20 writers whose work appears in each issue of *Fiction* include famous bestselling novelists as well as lesser known but first-rate authors. Highly recommended.

Merlyn's Pen. 1985. q. $9.95. Merlyn's Pen, Box 1058, E. Greenwich, RI 02818. Illus. adv. Circ: 15,000. Sample. Vol. ends: April/May.

Bk. rev: 2–3, notes, signed. *Aud:* Ejh, Hs.

Filled with contributions from student writers in grades seven to ten, this magazine offers quality juvenile writing and art in a variety of genres—short stories, poems, plays, essays, drawings, photos, cartoons and word games. Material is selected by a board of teachers and professional writers and edited only lightly. That the editors take contributions seriously is evident not only in the quality that they publish but also in the response policy: students are promised a personal response to submissions within six to eight weeks. Teachers receive a four-page Teacher's Guide that gives hints on how to use the issue's material to teach literary techniques. An excellent entry.

Scholastic Voice. 18/yr. $3.95. Scholastic, Inc. Subs. to: 902 Sylvan Ave., Englewood Cliffs, NJ 07632. Illus.

Aud: Hs.

What is language, and how is it used properly? To answer that question the editors of this typical Scholastic classroom magazine draw upon examples from modern and classical literature, from various channels of communication (including television) and from material the average ninth to twelfth grader is likely to read. Excerpts and full entries are included for consideration. While hardly the kind of title the average teenager is likely to read on his or her own, it can be used nicely to supplement more rigorous language arts courses.

Short Story International: seedling series. 1981. q. $14 (Students, $3.95). Sylvia Tankel. SSI, P.O. Box 405, Great Neck, NY 11022. Illus. Circ: 14,000. Sample. Vol. ends: Dec.

Aud: Ejh.

This journal in paperback format reprints about eight stories, primarily from books and magazines, in each issue.

SSI seeks to give an international flavor to the reading of children in grades 4–7. The "Contents Page" notes the country from which the stories come and in which they are set. In the issue examined, Canada, England, India, Israel, the United States, and Vietnam were represented. For each story there is at least one drawing done in black and white by staff artists. Probably most useful in classroom libraries, *SSI* should attract the reluctant reader and whet the appetite of the avid reader. (L.K.O.)

Short Story International: student series. 1981. q. $16 (Individuals, $14). Sylvia Tankel. Intl. Cultural Exchange, P.O. Box 405, Great Neck, NY 11022. Illus. Circ: 14,000. Vol. ends: Dec.

Aud: Hs.

This spinoff of *SSI, Short Story International* is aimed at students in grades 8 through 12. Each issue contains seven to ten contemporary short stories from authors throughout the world. This periodical not only can be used in connection with teaching programs in writing, language and literature but serves as well to further an understanding of other societies and cultures.

SSI, Short Story International. 1977. bi-m. $22 (Individuals, $20). Sylvia Tankel. Intl. Cultural Exchange, P.O. Box 405, Great Neck, NY 11022. Illus. Circ: 71,000. Vol. ends: Dec.

Aud: Hs.

This periodical reprints previously published short stories by contemporary authors from around the world. Other than translation into English if necessary, the stories are not abridged or revised. Entertaining and well written, the stories help to further the publisher's goal of encouraging better understanding among peoples. Set in varying locales, the stories impart a flavor of different countries and cultures, yet show a human universality of experience and character. *SSI* introduces to English-language readers works from societies that they would otherwise not have encountered. *SSI* received a United Nations medal for its contribution to international understanding through literature.

SCIENCE FICTION

The science fiction magazine scene continues to change rapidly. Many titles have recently ceased to publish, and new titles continue to appear each year, so the net availability of science fiction magazines has not changed significantly. Several titles have been announced in recent months, the major one being *L. Ron Hubbard's To the Stars,* edited by Fred Harris, but no issues are available for review as yet. Libraries seeking science fiction and fantasy titles should seek an evaluation copy before making selection decisions. *The Last Wave,* edited by Scott Edelman, is another title that merits consideration, but no issues were available for annotation for this volume because the publisher moved.

Access to science fiction remains essentially the same, provided by Donald B. Day's *Index to the Science Fiction Magazines 1926–1950* (Portland, OR: Perri Press, 1952; reprinted, Boston: G. K. Hall, 1982); Norman Metcalf's *Index to the Science Fiction Magazines 1951–1965* (El Cerrito, CA: Metcalf, 1968); Erwin Strauss's *Index to the SF Magazines*

1951–1965 (Cambridge, MA: MIT SF Society, 1966); the New England Science Fiction Association's series of indexes, *Index to the Science Fiction Magazines 1966–1970;* and *The NESFA Index: Science Fiction Magazines and Original Anthologies* (1971–   ). New titles include the *Index to the Science Fiction Magazines* (1977–   ) and the *Index to the Semi-Professional Fantasy Magazines* (1982–   ), both edited by Jerry Boyajian and Kenneth R. Johnson and published by the Twaci Press in Cambridge.

Mike Ashley's *Complete Index to Astounding/Analog* (Oak Forest, IL: Weinberg, 1981) remains the definitive index to that magazine and the best existing model for science fiction magazine indexing. Another new access tool is *Monthly Terrors: An Index to the Weird Fantasy Magazines Published in the United States and Great Britain,* by Frank H. Parnell and Mike Ashley (Westport, CT: Greenwood, 1985. 602 pp.). This title performs a significant service in providing minimal access; librarians will regret the lack of citations to page numbers for the stories, however. Finally, the history of the science fiction magazines is being definitively covered by *Science Fiction, Fantasy and Weird Fiction Magazines,* edited by Marshall Tymn and Mike Ashley.

Access to the book reviews in Science Fiction continues to be provided by *Science Fiction Book Review Index 1923–1973* (Detroit: Gale Research, 1975), *Science Fiction Book Review Index 1974–1979* (Detroit: Gale Research, 1981), *Science Fiction and Fantasy Book Review Index 1980–1984* (Detroit: Gale Research, 1985), and *SFFBRI: Science Fiction and Fantasy Book Review Index, 1985–   * (SFFBRI, 3608 Meadow Oaks Lane, Bryan TX 77802).

The annotated listings in this section include the existing commercial science fiction magazines, the major critical journals, and a selection of fan publications (fanzines) judged to be supplemental to the other magazines and representative of the fanzine publishing phenomenon. (H.H.)

Amazing Science Fiction Stories. 1926. bi-m. $9. George H. Scithers. TSR, Inc., P.O. Box 110, Lake Geneva, WI 53147. Illus., adv. Circ: 12,000. Vol. ends: Mar.
Bk. rev: 15–20, 50–500 words, signed. *Aud:* Hs.

Each issue of *Amazing* features six to ten stories, plus interviews, essays on SF topics, book reviews, movie reviews, editorials, and letters. *Amazing* appears regularly and includes fiction by both established writers and newcomers, some of which is nominated for science fiction awards. The nonfiction materials are interesting and provocative, while the book and movie reviews offer reasonable guidance for the reader. *Amazing* is a good support title for active SF collections.

Analog: science fiction science fact. 1930. 13/yr. $19.50. Stanley Schmidt. Davis Publns., 830 Lexington Ave., New York, NY 10017. Subs. to: Analog, P.O. Box 1936, Marion, OH 43306. Illus., adv. Circ: 125,000. Vol. ends: Dec. Microform: MCI, UMI.
Indexed: Acs, BoRvI, MgI. *Bk. rev:* 8–12, 200–500 words, signed. *Aud:* Hs.

Analog remains a mainstay in the magazine science fiction field, presenting literate, thoughtful SF, somewhat more technologically oriented than the offerings of other SF magazines. In addition to the usual five to six fiction offerings, it generally features one or two nonfiction pieces, of varying quality, but almost always interesting, and pointed, thought-provoking editorials. The book review column contains sound evaluations of current offerings. *Analog* remains one of the core titles for any SF collection.

Fantasy Review (Formerly: *Fantasy Newsletter*). 1978. m. $20. Robert A. Collins, 500 N.W. 20th St., Boca Raton, FL 33431. Illus., adv. Circ: 2,600. Vol. ends: Dec.
Indexed: BoRvI. *Bk. rev:* 25–80, 100–400 words, signed. *Aud:* Hs.

Fantasy Review has a new scope, achieved primarily through the merger of *Science Fiction and Fantasy Book Review* into *Fantasy Review.* Since that merger, *Fantasy Review* has continued to offer both quality coverage of the fantasy and science fiction fields and what is perhaps the most comprehensive and consistent reviewing source available today. Issues feature articles on various topics in the field, interviews with notable personalities, coverage of the specialty and fan presses, and news notes. For any SF research collection or any library supporting an active SF clientele, this should be a core title.

Isaac Asimov's Science Fiction Magazine. 1977. 13/yr. $19.50. Gardner Dozois. Davis Publns., 380 Lexington Ave., New York, NY 10017. Subs. to: P.O. Box 1933, Marion, OH 43305. Illus., adv. Circ: 125,000. Microform: UMI.
Bk. rev: 6–15, 50–100 words, signed. *Aud:* Hs.

Asimov's continues to maintain its position as one of the top SF magazines, ranking with *Analog* and *The Magazine of Fantasy and Science Fiction* in quality. Each digest-sized issue features five to seven fiction pieces, an editorial by Asimov, columns on books and gaming, nonfiction essays, a convention listing, and a letter column. The editorial reins have just passed from Shawna McCarthy to Gardner Dozois, but highly significant changes in editorial direction are not expected. Desirable for any library with an active cadre of SF readers.

Locus: the newspaper of the science fiction field. 1968. m. $24. Charles N. Brown. Locus Publns., P.O. Box 13305, Oakland, CA 94661. Illus., adv. Circ: 7,500. Microform: UMI.
Bk. rev: 5–15, 100–500 words, signed. *Aud:* Hs.

Locus is the premier source of news available for the SF and fantasy fields. In the course of a year, it provides an amazing array of information, including feature articles, news stories, photographs, obituaries, surveys, awards (including the "Locus Awards"), market reports, book announcements, convention listings, convention reports, lists of books published, classified and display advertising, media notes, book reviews, and other information. *Locus* offers comprehensive coverage of the field and remains a core title for most libraries supporting even moderate interest in science fiction.

The Magazine of Fantasy and Science Fiction. 1949. m. $17.50. Edward L. Ferman. Mercury Press, P.O. Box 56, Cornwall, CT 06753. Illus., adv. Circ: 60,000. Microform: MCI, UMI.

Indexed: BoRvI, MgI. *Bk. rev:* 2–10, 200–1,000 words, signed. *Aud:* Hs.

The Magazine of Fantasy and Science Fiction continues to maintain its reputation as one of the highest quality fiction magazines in the field. Each issue offers six to ten quality stories, a review column, a film column, and Isaac Asimov's monthly science column. Asimov's column continues to explore an amazing breadth of scientific material in interesting, readable and accurate articles. *F&SF* is a core journal for any library with an active SF clientele.

Starlog. 1976. m. $27.49. David McDonnell. O'Quinn Studios, 475 Park Ave. S., New York, NY 10016. Illus., adv. Circ: 160,000.

Aud: Hs.

Each 70- to 76-page issue features articles and interviews on the SF movie and television scene and includes news notes, TV episode guides, and articles on special effects in the media. *Starlog* should appeal to the younger SF/motion picture viewers, but it also contains a surprising amount of detail and fact in its coverage.

FILMS

For the Student/For the Professional

See also Communication and Speech; and Television, Video, and Radio Sections.

William M. Gargan, The Harry D. Gideonse Library, Brooklyn College, CUNY, Brooklyn, NY 11210

Introduction

Film has enjoyed a remarkable growth in the years since the making of *The Great Train Robbery* in 1903. It has developed in a number of different directions and has exerted, and will probably continue to exert, a profound influence on a large segment of the world's population. In an effort to portray, describe, explain, historicize, and otherwise capitalize on the rapid developments in filmmaking and film viewing, numerous magazines and journals have sprung up. Recently, however, a number of bibliographies and handbooks have begun to appear. In addition to the list that follows, the following may prove useful: *Factfile: Film and Television Periodicals in English* (Washington, DC: American Film Institute, 1979) and the *International Film Guide* (London: Tantivy Press, 1985). The newly published *Union List of Film Periodicals: Holdings of Selected American Collections* (Westport, CT: Greenwood Press, 1984) should prove a real aid in providing access to the titles covered in this section.

Basic Periodicals

Hs: *American Film, Film Comment, Film Quarterly, Young Viewers.*

Library and Teaching Aids

Film and Video News, Landers Film Reviews, Sightlines, Young Viewers.

For the Student

American Film (Formerly: *AFI News*). 1975. 10/yr. Membership, $20. Peter Biskind. Amer. Film Inst., John F. Kennedy Center for the Performing Arts, Washington, DC 20566. Illus. Circ: 125,000. Sample. Vol. ends: Sept. Microform: UMI. Reprint: UMI.

Bk. rev: 1–3, 1,200 words, signed. *Aud:* Hs.

This publication of the American Film Institute presents clear, interesting articles on U.S. film and television with an eye toward Hollywood. Although it has always provided excellent coverage of current films and popular film personalities, recent issues appear to be devoting more and more space to television. "Dialog on Film," a regular feature, presents, in an interview or seminar format, a lively discussion on various aspects of film with well-known critics or filmmakers. Additional departments provide news, editorial matter, and columns on TV and video. Numerous photos and illustrations are included. This is a basic title for most libraries. Highly recommended.

Cineaste. 1967. q. $13 (Individuals, $10). Gary Crowdus. Cineaste Magazine, 200 Park Ave. S., New York, NY 10003. Illus., index, adv. Circ: 6,500. Sample. Vol. ends: Fall. Microform: UMI.

Indexed: API. *Bk. rev:* 6, 500–1,000 words, signed. *Aud:* Hs.

Subtitled "America's Leading Magazine of the Arts and Politics of the Cinema," this journal delivers what it promises. Its 50 to 60 pages are packed with politically oriented material on both U.S. and foreign films. On the whole, the articles are clear, straightforward, and rational. The emphasis is intellectual rather than emotional. Each issue contains three or more interviews with noted individuals in the film world as well as five to ten full-length film reviews. In addition, capsule reviews of 16mm films and brief mentions of recent releases appear regularly in its "Film Guide."

Cinemacabre. irreg. $8/3 issues. George Stover, P.O. Box 1005, Baltimore, MD 21204. Illus., adv. Circ: 3,000.

Aud: Hs.

Subtitled "An Appreciation of the Fantastic," this 5½- by 8½-inch glossy magazine embraces all aspects of the genre. Each 64-page issue is crammed full of well-written articles about fantastic film, video, and television. Articles are informational and analytical rather than prescriptive. In this respect, they display a marked contrast to the "how-to" articles presented in *Cinemagic.* Interviews with the directors and actors are regularly included, as well as several detailed film reviews. Reviews are signed, three to four pages in length, and fairly timely. Numerous photos, a few in color, accompany most articles. Written in a straightforward, easily accessible style, this title should prove a popular acquisition for most libraries.

Cinemagic: the guide to fantastic filmmaking. 1972. q. $13.99. David Hutchison. Starlog Press, Inc., 475 Park Ave. S., New York, NY 10016. Illus., adv. Circ: 25,000.

Bk. rev: 2, 500–1,000 words, signed. *Aud:* Hs.

An interesting magazine devoted to the creation of special effects and the production of fantastic films. Each 68-page issue provides four or five step-by-step articles detailing methods that can be used to create makeup, visual effects, and sound effects. There are also articles on animated classics and interviews with contemporary artists on the current state of animation. Topics covered in recent issues included careers in special effects, the use of cable controls, and the choreography of fight scenes. Specific, clearly written instructions and helpful illustrations make even fairly technical material readily accessible to amateur as well as semiprofessional filmmakers. Reviews of new equipment, lenses, and optical gadgets are regularly featured; there are also two noteworthy departments, "Producer's Bulletin Board" and "Filmmakers' Forum." The Bulletin Board lists film projects in current production or near completion, along with a short summary, the running time, and the address of the distributor; the Forum provides a place for readers to exchange ideas on experimental techniques. This is a useful title for both the novice and the experienced filmmaker. With the demise of *Moving Image*, it becomes the major source of information on special effects for 8mm and 16mm film.

Film Comment. 1962. bi-m. $12. Richard Corliss. Film Soc. of Lincoln Center, 140 W. 56th St., New York, NY 10023. Illus., index, adv. Circ: 35,000. Sample. Vol. ends: Nov/Dec. Microform: UMI. Reprint: ISI, UMI.
Indexed: HumI, RG. *Bk. rev:* 2–3, 1,500 words, signed. *Aud:* Hs.

An excellent general interest film magazine containing original, well-written articles by such prominent critics and columnists as Andrew Sarris and Molly Haskell. Features in issues examined included an article on the Hollywood novel, an interview with Jack Nicholson, and a tribute to Francoise Truffaut. Although the emphasis is on U.S. movies, foreign films also receive good coverage. Separate sections dealing with television and independents appear in most numbers. The unique style of this magazine, enhanced by numerous photos and pleasing layouts, lends it appeal for popular as well as academic audiences; interested students should find it quite accessible. The articles are informative and serious without being "scholarly" or pedantic. A basic acquisition for any library interested in film.

Film Culture. 1955. irreg. $12/4 issues. Jonas Mekas, G.P.O. Box 1499, New York, NY 10001. Illus., index, adv. Circ: 5,500. Sample. Microform: UMI. Reprint: UMI.
Indexed: ArtI. *Aud:* Hs.

This 150- to 300-page journal is one of the few publications to give serious consideration to experimental and avant-garde films. It has been said that it is for the United States today what *Cahier du Cinema* was for France in the 1950s. Articles include lectures, interviews with filmmakers, and news of film festivals, as well as insightful essays and critiques. Although there are no book reviews per se, there is a substantial list of "books received." Publication is very irregular; double and even triple issues often appear as part of the four-issue subscription price. There is, as editor Jonas Mekas points out, "no regular financial backing." A new issue is published only after enough money is collected to pay the printer for the previous issue. Yet issue after issue does eventually appear and they are well worth the wait. Any library with a serious interest in film will want this magazine.

Film Quarterly. 1945. q. $19 (Individuals, $11). Ernest Callenbach. Univ. of California Press, Berkeley, CA 94720. Illus., index, adv. Circ: 8,500. Sample. Vol. ends: Summer. Microform: UMI. Reprint: UMI.
Indexed: ArtI, HumI. *Bk. rev:* Various number, length, signed. *Aud:* Hs.

Begun in 1945 as the *Hollywood Quarterly*, this journal focused on the social and cultural aspects of film and radio. In 1958, after a series of changes, it assumed its current title. Since then, it has become more international in scope and has grown in reputation. Each issue contains five or six features on various aspects of film. Articles in issues examined ranged from a look at computer characters in films to an analysis of misogynistic violence in Hitchcock. The writing is authoritative and scholarly, yet free of jargon or specialized language. This approach makes it of interest to general audiences. The detailed film reviews in each issue are more informative than most, although they will be more useful as critical studies than as viewing guides, since they are seldom timely. The book reviews are equally comprehensive and should prove a boon for the film bibliographer. The editor promises greater coverage of documentary and experimental film in future volumes.

Media Sight. 1983. q. $7.95. Geoffrey Schutt, P.O. Box 2630, Athens, OH 45701. Illus., adv.
Aud: Hs.

According to the editor, the 60 pages of this magazine are an invitation to a "trip back into yesteryear; the world of the Saturday afternoon matinee and the dime comic book." The emphasis is on pulps and popular culture, with articles focusing on such topics as science fiction, the Three Stooges, Buster Crabbe, and everyone and everything so terrible as to be amazingly good. Copy and numerous illustrations, all on newsprint, vibrate with the excitement of the dedicated midnight to six o'clock in the morning television viewer and the student who reads *Mad* at the newsstand. For these aficionados, this title is highly recommended. It covers the field as well as anything currently available. Incidentally, the publisher and writers nicely sidestep horrors and the sexually suggestive.

Monthly Film Bulletin. 1934. m. $20. Richard Combs. British Film Inst., 81 Dean St., London W1V 6AA, England. Index. Circ: 10,000. Sample. Vol. ends: Dec. Microform: W.
Aud: Hs.

Published by the British Film Institute, the *Bulletin* provides timely coverage of recent films. The average 15-page issue carries about 15, 500- to 1,000-word reviews on newly released features, as well as a few reviews of short subjects. Especially interesting are the retrospective reviews that appear in each issue. All reviews are signed and provide clear-cut summaries and critiques. Detailed information appears prior to each review, including such facts as the director, the film's length, its distributor, and a list of credits. Similar to its defunct U.S. counterpart *Film Facts* but more international in scope, this periodical will be useful in most libraries.

Photoplay: movies and video (Formerly: *Photoplay Movie and Video Monthly; Photoplay Film and TV Scene*). 1950. m. $22.50. Lisa Dewson. Infonet, Ltd., Times House, 179. The Marlowes, Hemel Hempstead, Hertfordshire HP1 1BB, England. Illus., adv. Circ: 51,771.
Bk. rev: 2–3, 500 words. *Aud:* Hs.

This publication, which absorbed the more scholarly *Films Illustrated*, falls somewhere between being a film journal and a fanzine. The typical 62-page issue contains several feature articles, news and editorial matter, and 300- to 500-word reviews of current films. The emphasis is on Hollywood and on commercially successful films. Articles tend to focus on popular screen personalities such as Tom Selleck, Eddie Murphy, Ali McGraw, and Diane Keaton, although essays on the making of particular films such as *The Falcon and the Snowman* and *A View to a Kill* are also featured. Similar coverage is provided for video and television. Each issue contains numerous black-and-white and some color illustrations. The eye-catching covers might be especially effective on a browsing rack.

For the Professional

Film and Video News: international review (Formerly: *Film Video News; Film News: the international review of AV materials and equipment*). 1984. q. $12. John Grandits. Gorez Goe Publishing Co. (Subsidiary of Carus Corp.), 1016 Church St., Peru, IL 61354. Illus., adv. Circ: 2,000. Microform: UMI. Reprint: UMI.
Bk. rev: 2–10, signed. *Aud:* Pr.

This publication has undergone several alterations in recent years, including two title changes. It suspended publication in 1981 but returned in 1984 with a somewhat altered scope and format. The articles and reviews are now organized more closely along curriculum lines. Regular departments, only some of which appear in any one issue, include sports, anthropology, language arts, medicine, sociology, business, history, biography, environment, fine arts, women's studies, and nuclear issues. It continues to be an excellent source of information on educational media and equipment. Especially useful for elementary and secondary school libraries.

Film Library Quarterly. See Library Periodicals/For the Professional Section.

Journal of Film and Video (Formerly: *University Film Association. Journal; University Film Producers Association. Journal*). 1947. q. $7.50. Patricia Erens. Dept. of Communication Arts and Sciences, Rosary College, 7900 W. Division St., River Forest, IL 60305. Illus., index. Circ: 1,300. Sample. Vol. ends: Fall. Refereed. Microform: UMI. Reprint: UMI.
Bk. rev: 1–3, 1,500 words, signed. *Aud:* Pr.

"Focuses on the problems and substance in teaching the fields of film production, history, theory, criticism, and aesthetics." The emphasis here is holistic, with a special interest in "articles which break down the traditional boundaries between film production and film study, between film and photography, between film and video." A typical issue contains about five articles devoted to various aspects of filmmaking. Reports on various conferences, a couple of detailed book reviews, and lists of books received are also included. Author indexes are provided in number 4 (Fall) of each volume. Volume 31, number 4 (Fall 1979), contains a cumulative subject/author index for 1947–1979. Highly recommended for high school libraries supporting programs in film.

Landers Film Reviews: the information guide to 16mm films. 1956. q. $45. Bertha Landers. Landers Associates, P.O. Box 27309, Escondido, CA 92027. Index. Circ: 3,600. Sample. Vol. ends: Summer.
Aud: Pr.

An excellent guide to 16mm film. The average issue contains about 125 brief reviews describing the contents of each film. Technical qualities are commented on to a lesser extent. The film's subject, purpose, and intended audience are clearly stated. A "Source Directory" in the front of each issue lists addresses of distributors. The cumulative annual index has been discontinued with volume 29, but each issue retains its own title and subject indexes. This is an especially important title for elementary and secondary schools.

Sightlines. 1967. q. $18. Nadine Covert. Educational Film Library Assn., Inc., 45 John St., Suite 301, New York, NY 10038. Illus., index, adv. Circ: 3,000. Sample. Vol. ends: Summer. Microform: UMI. Reprint: UMI.
Bk. rev: Various number, length. *Aud:* Pr.

Formed by the merger of the *EFLA Bulletin, Filmlist,* and *Film Review Digest*, this publication is directed toward libraries, schools, colleges, and community organizations that utilize 16mm films. Articles on film and video production, reports on festivals and awards, and EFLA news are featured in most issues. Supplements listing the availability of feature films on 8mm and 16mm and video are regularly included. Recommended for libraries involved in the collecting, lending, and programming of 16mm informational and educational films.

Young Viewers. 1979. q. $20. Robert Braun. Media Center for Children, 3 W. 29th St., New York, NY 10001. Illus. Sample.
Aud: Pr.

Originally part of *Sightlines*, this title became a separate publication in the fall of 1979. Each 15-page issue addressed itself to various aspects of children's viewing, with a strong emphasis on programming. Beginning in 1984, the format shifted to that of a review/newsletter containing detailed reviews of child-tested films, reviews of books on children's media, requests for proposals or scripts, and news of developments in the field of children's media. A brief "Previews" section, providing short descriptive as well as critical annotations for eight to ten titles, has also been added. A directory of distributors follows the reviews. Interviews with the makers and users of films are sometimes featured. This is a basic acquisition for school libraries providing film programs for children. Highly recommended.

FISHING, HUNTING, AND GUNS

For the Student

See also Environment, Conservation, and Outdoor Recreation; and Sports Sections.

Roland Person, Assistant Undergraduate Librarian, Southern Illinois University, Carbondale, IL 62901

Introduction

Fishing, hunting, and shooting are enjoyed by millions of Americans of both sexes and nearly all ages. The appeal and interest range from the child with a worm and a pole to the adult professional in any of these three areas. As a result, school libraries, both urban and rural, should have a good selection of these titles.

Besides being of use in these subject areas, many of these titles provide valuable information in other areas. The thorny issue of gun control and firearms regulation, both state and national, is a major concern that occupies a great deal of attention here, in factual as well as subjective presentations not found in more readily available library titles. In addition, there is much of value about conservation and outdoor recreation. People interested in sports have played a major historical role in the development of wildlife legislation, conservation laws, and the establishment of state and federal parks and refuges. Their continual concern, emotional, intellectual, and financial, is reflected in the pages of magazines.

In spite of the lack of indexing, libraries should seriously consider adding more of these titles to their collections. The readers' interest is clear and the value is evident.

Basic Periodicals

Ejh: *Field & Stream, Outdoor Life;* Hs: *Field & Stream, Outdoor Life, Petersen's Hunting, Sports Afield.*

For the Student

American Hunter. 1973. m. $15. Tom Fulgham. Natl. Rifle Assn., 1600 Rhode Island Ave., N.W., Washington, DC 20036. Illus., adv. Circ: 1,465,000. Vol. ends: Dec.
Aud: Hs.

Members of the National Rifle Association of the United States may receive this title in place of or in addition to the basic journal *American Rifleman.* Many of the editorial staff appear in both magazines. It is primarily for those more interested in hunting than in the technical aspects of guns. There are articles about wildlife management and biology, hunting dogs, wilderness travel, camping, and, of course, hunting around the world. Well illustrated and profession-

ally written, this is an excellent magazine. The "Official NRA Journal" is published in each issue as it is in *American Rifleman.* The choice of a hunting magazine is between this title and *Petersen's Hunting;* the latter is bigger and better and has greater variety.

American Rifleman. 1885. m. $15. William F. Parkerson III. Natl. Rifle Assn. of America, 1600 Rhode Island Ave. N.W., Washington, DC 20036. Illus., adv. Circ: 1,400,000. Vol. ends: Dec. Microform: UMI.
Indexed: MgI. *Bk. rev:* 3, 50 words. *Aud:* Hs.

This official journal of the National Rifle Association (NRA) contains a variety of articles and departments on firearms, shooting, handloading, and related topics in addition to NRA news and activities. Given the NRA's prominence in firearms issues and its political activism, this is useful for school libraries interested in its reference value.

Arkansas Game and Fish. 1968. bi-m. Free. Jane E. Rice. Arkansas State Game & Fish Commission, 2 Natural Resources Dr., Little Rock, AR 72205. Illus. Circ: 78,500. Sample. Vol. ends: Nov/Dec.
Bk. rev: 1, 250 words, signed. *Aud:* Ejh, Hs.

This colorful magazine is an excellent example of what state conservation agencies can accomplish. The photos and artwork are of high quality; the articles are well written and even display an unexpected sense of humor. Feature subjects include hunting ethics, law enforcement, conservation, woodcraft, and personalities. "Wildlife Lines: Current Events" is a regular column consisting of short news notes and inspirational quotes. Another regular column is "Kids' Activity Page." Worth paying for, but it's free!

The Black Powder Report. 1972. m. $18. David M. Baird. Buckskin Press, 220 McLeod St., P.O. Box 789, Big Timber, MT 59011. Illus., adv. Circ: 8,000. Sample. Vol. ends: Sept.
Bk. rev: Varied number, length, signed. *Aud:* Hs.

The Black Powder Report is aimed at "those black powder enthusiasts who look upon their black powder firearms as being a direct link with their forefathers." This folksy magazine features articles on history, weapons, personalities, rendezvous, poetry and songs, frontier life (women's, too, not just men's) and a great deal of attention to Native American history and lore. There is lots of camaraderie evident in the letters section, and some international news items.

Bowhunter. 1971. bi-m. $14. M. R. James. Blue-J, Inc., 3808 South St., Fort Wayne, IN 46807. Illus., adv. Circ: 150,000. Vol. ends: Aug/Sept.
Aud: Hs.

Subtitled "The Magazine for the Hunting Archer," this is a big, well-illustrated magazine with many articles, most written in the first person. Topics include hunting all kinds of North American big game, personalities in the field, notes on equipment, and Professional Bowhunters Society news. Competition archery is not covered. A good choice for libraries when students are more interested in hunting than in competition or technical information.

Deer & Deer Hunting. 1977. bi-m. $18. Al Hofacker & Rob Wegner. The Stump Sitters, Inc., 114 W. Glendale Ave., P.O. Box 1117, Appleton, WI 54912. Illus., adv. Circ: 80,000. Sample. Vol. ends: July/Aug.

Aud: Ejh, Hs.

This title is concerned with more than trophies. One issue, for example, had articles on deer camps, phenomenal scent, chemical communication, hunting accidents, and part of a series on taxidermy. Lots of color photos, clear illustrations, and a nontechnical style make this a good choice for wildlife collections in school libraries.

Field & Stream. 1895. m. $13.94. Duncan Barnes. CBS Magazines, 3807 Wilshire Blvd., Suite 1204, Los Angeles, CA 90010. Illus., adv. Circ: 2,003,000. Sample. Vol. ends: Apr. Microform: B&H, MIM, UMI.

Indexed: AbrRG, Mgl, RG. *Aud:* Ejh, Hs.

For many years the premier hunting and fishing magazine and the largest in circulation (the two closest are *Outdoor Life* and *Sports Afield*), this excellent publication belongs in every library, and backfiles have great historical value. The July 1985 ninetieth anniversary issue displays some of that history: Zane Grey's *Riders of the Purple Sage* was serialized here; authors ranging from Robert Ruark to Jean Shepherd have appeared; A. J. McClane, Corey Ford, and Ed Zern are synonymous with the title. In addition to broad coverage of hunting, fishing, and related outdoor activities, this magazine continues to have a strong voice on conservation, outdoor education, and legislation affecting outdoor sports. Quality fiction and humor also mark this magazine. There are now five regional editions with special coverage of hot spots by area and regional news items. Unlike most titles in this section, it has long been indexed—a big plus for library use.

Fly Fisherman. 1969. bi-m. $16.97. John Randolph. Historical Times, Inc., 2245 Kohn Rd., P.O. Box 8200, Harrisburg, PA 17105. Illus., adv. Circ: 137,000. Sample. Vol. ends: Sept. Microform: B&H, UMI.

Bk. rev: 1, 1,000 words, signed. *Aud:* Hs.

"Each truly great fisher is a lover of the stream he fishes," says a university administrator and author in a recent issue. That pleasure, and intellectual as well as practical interest in all aspects of fishing, is conveyed in the well-written articles. Besides the act, or art, of fishing, there are articles on insects, equipment, fish, places to go, even fiction. Well done and an excellent choice.

Fur-Fish-Game—Harding's Magazine. 1925. m. $9. Ken Dunwoody. A. R. Harding Publg. Co., 2878 E. Main St., Columbus, OH 43209. Illus., adv. Circ: 180,000. Sample. Vol. ends: Dec.

Aud: Hs.

"Down to earth" its readers call it, and that is an apt description. Articles have a strong appeal for outdoors people without the snobbishness of some magazines. In addition to a wide range of hunting and fishing articles, there is a strong conservation stress, and, unlike other general mag-azines, there is considerable coverage of trapping. The appeal is to practitioners, novices as well as veterans, some of whom may fish, hunt, or trap for a living, rather than the trophy hunter. The inexpensive price, the outdoor ethic, and appeal to the "ordinary outdoors person" make this a good choice for many libraries, particularly in rural areas.

The In-Fisherman. 1975. bi-m. $15. David Csanda. Al Lindner's Outdoors, Inc., P.O. Box 999, Rte. 8, Brainerd, MN 56401. Illus., adv. Circ: 250,000. Sample.

Indexed: Acs. *Aud:* Hs.

Subtitled "A Journal of Fresh Water Fishing," this was begun by Ron and Al Lindner as a series of study reports, with no advertising, and modeled after scientific journals. This publication has expanded into the largest fishing magazine (in pages per issue devoted to fishing). Lavishly illustrated, well-written articles. One issue had articles ranging from plastic worm presentation to European angling methods to float fishing the Great Lakes to the importance of color in lures. Fly-fishing is a recently added subject, as is emphasis on international angling methods and equipment. The magazine sponsors television specials and nationwide radio programs, and even a camp for children. Fine all-fishing coverage; an excellent choice for wide appeal.

Muzzle Blasts. 1932. m. Membership, $16. Maxine Moss. Natl. Muzzle Loading Rifle Assn., P.O. Box 67, Friendship, IN 47021. Illus., adv. Circ: 27,000. Sample. Vol. ends: Aug.

Bk. rev: 1,400–500 words, signed. *Aud:* Hs.

The official publication of the National Muzzle Loading Rifle Association, this is the oldest among a growing number of journals aimed at black powder shooters and those interested in all that goes with buckskinning. Besides articles on muzzleloaders and related equipment, there are historical pieces, articles on rendezvous, biographies of historical figures, new products, legislative reports, and association news. Unlike many other gun magazines, there is considerable attention to the role of women plus frequent appearances of women authors. A good choice to appeal to a growing audience interested in authentic recreation of the past two centuries.

Outdoor Life. 1898. m. $13.94. Clare Conley. Times Mirror Magazines, Inc., 380 Madison Ave., New York, NY 10017. Illus., adv. Circ: 1,512,000. Sample. Vol. ends: Dec. Microform: B&H, UMI.

Indexed: AbrRG, MgI, RG. *Aud:* Ejh, Hs.

Holding second place in circulation among the world's outdoor magazines, *Outdoor Life* emphasizes hunting and fishing with articles about personal experiences in the field. Other articles and columns are concerned with conservation, boating, dogs, new products, bowhunting, guns, shooting, and cooking. As one of the few magazines in this section to have been indexed very long (see also *Field & Stream* above in this section), it has to be a first choice for most libraries. This magazine has always been a favorite of outdoorsmen and the circulation figure shows it. This journal is more likely to have the "true-life adventure" story than most other titles.

There now are regional editions for local interest, and in 1984 it began including some fiction.

Pennsylvania Game News. 1929. m. $6. Robert S. Bell. Pennsylvania Game Commission, 8000 Derry St., Harrisburg, PA 17105. Illus. Circ: 180,000. Sample. Vol. ends: Dec. Microform: UMI.

Indexed: BioAb. *Bk. rev:* 3–9, 100–150 words. *Aud:* Hs.

Many state game commissions, or the equivalent agency, publish magazines and this is a fine example of how good they can be—and of the number of subscribers. Besides the expected news and features from around the state, there are stories and personal accounts ranging from songbirds to woodchucks, from trapping to dogs. Columns include archery, guns, a young artists' page, and one called "Outdoor Wildlife Learning." Conservation and outdoor education are major emphases in state wildlife magazines, making them especially useful for school and public libraries. With prices like this, more than one such publication might find a niche in any library. See also *Wisconsin Sportsman*, below in this section.

Petersen's Hunting. 1973. m. $2. Craig Boddington. Petersen Publg. Co., 8490 Sunset Blvd., Los Angeles, CA 90069. Illus., adv. Circ: 275,000. Sample. Vol. ends: Dec. Microform: UMI.

Aud: Hs.

Widely ranging in subjects categorized as big game, small game, upland game, waterfowl, exotic (e.g., safaris), and general, this fine magazine also offers ranges in audience level from beginner to expert. Departments include black powder, bowhunting, gun dogs, handloading, even vehicles for hunting. All this, plus historical articles and conservation emphasis, makes this title a good choice for any library. Bigger and more varied than *American Hunter*, with which it has much in common.

Sports Afield. 1887. m. $13.97. Tom Paugh. Hearst Corp., 959 Eighth Ave., New York, NY 10019. Illus., adv. Circ: 518,000. Sample. Vol. ends: Dec. Microform: B&H, UMI.

Indexed: Acs, MgI. *Aud:* Ejh, Hs.

The oldest of the big three general outdoor magazines (with *Field & Stream* and *Outdoor Life*), it has only more recently been indexed, which may account for its relatively rare appearance in libraries. However, its quality and range of coverage and the illustrations equal or surpass those of the other two and it would be a fine choice for any library. Columns and features go beyond hunting and fishing to include camping, nature, boating, vehicles, African game, and many others. Recently the editors have stressed the entire outdoors experience with articles on art, Indians, cooking, weather and wildlife organizations; this sets it somewhat apart from most hunting and fishing magazines. A big classy publication.

Wisconsin Sportsman. 1972. 7/yr. $9.95. Tom Petrie. Great Lakes Sportsman Group, P.O. Box 2266, Oshkosh, WI 54903. Illus., adv. Circ: 72,000. Sample. Vol. ends: Dec.

Aud: Ejh, Hs.

The Great Lakes Sportsman Group publishes four regional outdoor magazines (the others are *Michigan Sportsman*, est. 1976; *Minnesota Sportsman*, est. 1977; and *Pennsylvania Outdoors*, est. 1982). General articles may run in two to four of these magazines, only a few articles are peculiar to each state. Topics cover fishing, hunting, conservation, how-to-do-it articles, natural history, and some fiction. The color photography is excellently reproduced and the whole magazine is very professionally done. Squirrel and rabbit hunting are not covered. Any of these four titles would be a good, inexpensive choice for pleasurable, attractive reading, but none has the depth of the big three general outdoor magazines (*Field & Stream, Outdoor Life, Sports Afield*).

FOLKLORE

For the Student

Polly Swift Grimshaw, Curator, Folklore Collection, Indiana University, Bloomington, IN 47405

Introduction

The subject of folklore is especially important in a democratic society, for it is the discipline that concentrates on the life-styles and traditional behavior of the nonelite. Attempts are made to learn about the ideas, attitudes, fantasies, aspirations, prejudices, and motivations of the common man, woman, and child, of minority cultures, of grass-roots American society, through folklore. There has been a considerable upsurge of interest in folklore by the government and public sectors. In January 1976, by act of Congress, an American Folklife Center was established in the Library of Congress. At about the same time, the Smithsonian Institution created a Folklife Unit in its organization. Television and the popular press have provided the impetus for the public to search for their roots. The study of folklore is being introduced to students in elementary and high schools to encourage this interest and familiarize them with their nation's cultural development. Folklore journals are also beginning to report on the study of the interaction among technology, culture, and contemporary folk groups, and those listed here are representative of the types of publications that are available to nurture and pursue these interests.

For the Student

Foxfire. See General Interest/For the Student: Teenage Section.

Journal of American Culture. 1978. q. $25. Popular Culture Assn., Bowling Green State Univ., Bowling Green, OH 43403. Illus.

Bk. rev: 5–10, 500–800 words, signed. *Aud:* Hs.

One of several journals published by the Popular Culture Association, this publication is devoted entirely to the folk and popular culture of North America. Many of the articles focus on the effects of technology on the U.S. public, i.e., fast foods, automobiles, advertising, the press, and the introduction of prestige symbols (e.g., parlor organ). Research develops into other interesting areas, such as how play, humor, sport, stereotypes, myth, and art reflect change in values and ideals. Since all the articles are well documented, they are very useful for further research.

Journal of American Folklore. 1888. q. Membership, $35. American Folklore Soc., 1703 New Hampshire Ave. N.W., Washington, DC 20009. Index, adv. Vol. ends: Dec. Refereed. Microform: UMI. Reprint: Kraus.

Indexed: HumI. *Bk. rev:* 12–20, 500–1,200 words, signed. *Aud:* Hs.

As the official publication of the American Folklore Society, the journal publishes scholarly articles focusing on all the genres of the discipline and is geographically international in scope. Here also can be found articles dealing with new theories and techniques of the field and their subsequent debates in following issues. This breadth of coverage in each issue (unless devoted to a particular subject) recommends this journal for all audiences. Each issue also has sections dealing with notes from the field, society announcements, critical book reviews followed by brief discussions of a larger number of new titles, reprints and so forth, and a separate "Record and Film Review" section. These latter sections are especially helpful for secondary school teachers. The annual "Folklore Bibliography" section has been dropped.

Journal of Regional Cultures. 1981. s-a. $12.50. Ray B. Browne. Popular Culture Center, Bowling Green State Univ., Bowling Green, OH 43403. Illus. Vol. ends: No. 2. Refereed.

Aud: Hs.

Articles in this journal focus on differences that make a region unique and their influence on other areas of the country. Subjects can include agricultural practices, vernacular architecture, "art, circuses, fashions, foodways, folk culture, frontier and prairie concerns, games, history, humor, language and literature, psychology, religions, street customs, fairs, and women."

Material Culture (Formerly: *Pioneer America*). 1984. 3/yr. $15. Allen G. Noble. Dept. of Geography, Univ. of Akron, Akron, OH 44325. Illus. Vol. ends: No. 3. Refereed. Microform: UMI.

Bk. rev: 700–800 words. *Aud:* Hs.

This journal will be very helpful for those who are interested in a folkloristic approach to pioneer material culture. This can include regional variations of vernacular architecture (e.g., log and sod houses, barns and mills, to 20th-century bungalows). Detailed drawings are sometimes given to illustrate these variations. There are also informative articles describing the relationship of technology to changes in the use of tools and other implements. The new editors will focus more on "interdisciplinary artifactual studies on history and folklife, psychology and anthropology, trades and industry, geography and sociology, food and clothing and creativity and play."

Mid America Folklore (Formerly: *Mid-South Folklore*). 1973. 3/yr. $10. George Lankford. Arkansas College, Batesville, AR 72501. Vol. ends: Winter.

Bk. rev: 8–9, 500–700 words, signed. *Aud:* Hs.

This regional journal has articles covering the culture of the south-central United States—Arkansas, Kentucky, Louisiana, Mississippi, Missouri, Oklahoma, Tennessee, and Texas. The editors strive to provide a forum for the discussion of regional approaches in current U.S. folklore scholarship.

New York Folklore (Formerly: *New York Folklore Quarterly*). 1975. s-a. $15/4 mos. Paula T. Jennings, 116 Pinehurst Ave., New York, NY 10033. Illus., index. Refereed.

Bk. rev: 4–5, 400–500 words, signed. *Aud:* Hs.

Although this is primarily a journal devoted to folklore of New York State, a number of issues contain material from other areas of the United States. All the genres of the discipline are covered, i.e., folk song, ethnic and urban folklore, myths and legends, humor, children's lore, oral narratives, folklife studies, folk art, and lore pertaining to current timely events (e.g., gasoline lore, garage sale lore, family oral narratives). These scholarly articles present as much raw data and controversial information as possible and can be very useful to students writing papers.

Pennsylvania Folklife. 1949. q. $8. Wm. T. Parsons, P.O. Box 92, Collegeville, PA 19426. Illus.

Aud: Hs.

This journal is published for the popular audience, with very good pictures, diagrams, maps and so forth, on the Pennsylvania Dutch. The majority of the material presented is concerned with all areas of folk life—vernacular architecture (including barns), cooking, costume, symbolic aspects of folk art, medicine, gravestones, and other folk customs. Other articles focus on all sorts of handwork (by both sexes) and the ever popular auction. The articles are generally well documented and should help the novice get off to a good start.

Western Folklore (Formerly: *California Folklore*). 1947. q. $25. California Folklore Soc., P.O. Box 4552, Glendale, CA 91202. Index. Microform: UMI.

Indexed: MusicI. *Bk. rev:* 10–13, 500–800 words, signed. *Aud:* Hs.

One of the better regional journals, this publication has a wide appeal to all types of readers. Although many of the earlier volumes were limited to articles on the Pacific slope area, issues within the past ten years have also been concerned with other areas of the world and provide for the reader variant texts of tales, songs, proverbs and so on. Interesting articles concerning material culture, superstitions, and current popular phenomena are also given. The book reviews offer critical evaluations of recent publications, and a limited, but good, film and record review section is also included. The annual index is more than helpful. In addition to the author/title/subject listing, the editors offer a tale type and motif number index for easy retrieval. This is a much appreciated feature for most researchers.

FREE MAGAZINES

For the Student/For the Professional

Susan L. Edmonds, Reference Librarian, Somerville Public Library, Somerville, MA 02143

Introduction

This is a sampling of "house magazines" and other publications that are available to libraries on a complimentary basis.

House magazines are publications produced by companies, associations, and other organizations for use by employees, stockholders, and prospective customers. Companies and other organizations use house magazines to educate and inform large audiences about new products, current research, and staff news. Some house organs, known as controlled magazines, contain specialized information that would not interest nonprofessional readers. These publications are sent to select groups who publishers feel would benefit from receiving such periodicals.

Librarians' opinions are varied concerning the usefulness of free materials when the time and effort required to obtain them are considered. Those on limited budgets are inclined to cull every likely source to supplement standard resources.

Included here are representatives of this vast field. Variety is shown not only in the industries and interests represented but also in format, quality, and level of presentation.

Magazines with *controlled circulation* are those distributed free to a particular type of audience. Sometimes the publisher is reluctant to send these to libraries. In that case, if the magazine is wanted, ask a reader (whether student or teacher) to request a subscription and then pass it on to the library. Devious, perhaps, but so is the policy of the magazine that won't support libraries.

Note: A word of special thanks to Adeline M. Smith, who from the first through the fourth editions of *Magazines for Libraries* edited the section on free periodicals. Some of her annotations, slightly modified, are included here because she was (and is) the last word on such matters. For those seeking additional free titles, Ms. Smith's book is highly recommended. This is *Free Magazines for Libraries* (Jefferson, N.C.: McFarland & Co., 2nd ed. 1985). The annotated guide classifies and describes 452 free publications.

Basic Periodicals

Ejh: *Horizons;* Hs: *Adventure Road, Ford Times, Horizons.*

For the Student

Adventure Road. 1964. q. Free (Individuals, $2). Amoco Enterprises, Inc., 200 E. Randolph, Chicago, IL 60601. Illus., adv. Circ: 1,800,000. Vol. ends: Winter.
Aud: Hs.

The "adventure" refers to the travel and recreation focus of this well-illustrated magazine. Edited for adults and suitable for teenagers, the well-written articles cover a wide variety of topics ranging from nature to participant sports and camping. The sponsor is the country's largest single motor club, and much is made of driving safety and the historical and natural sights one may enjoy on a trip of any length. There are fine color illustrations on nearly every page. The free-lance and staff-written pieces are quite objective, and if sometimes a bit pedestrian, still they are free of advertising.

Agenda. 1968. m. Free. Edward Caplan. Office of Public Affairs, AID, Rm. 4953, State Dept. Bldg., Washington, DC 20523. Illus., index. Circ: 15,000. Vol. ends: Dec.
Aud: Hs.

A government publication, this is the voice of the Agency for International Development. The focus is on developing countries, and, more specifically, their problems and how those problems are met by the AID. The editorial content varies from administration to administration. Under the Reagan Administration, the articles are more conservative than in the past, as might be expected, and there is not quite the free-swinging debate that often took place in the past. Still, the magazine draws on outside experts for articles, and the 30 or so pages are well edited and illustrated. The magazine is useful for every high school library.

Aramco World. 1949. bi-m. Free. Paul F. Hoye. Arabian Amer. Oil Co., 340 Shoreham Bldg., 15th and H Sts. N.W., Washington, DC 20005. Illus. Circ: 150,000. Vol. ends: Nov/Dec.
Aud: Hs.

Although the primary purpose of this—like most house organs—is to show the positive points about the international oil company, the fact remains that the 50 or so pages contain excellent signed articles and equally fine color photographs. Experts are sought to write the material, and from time to time it even seems at odds with the best interests of the sponsoring company. Still, the primary focus is on the noncontroversial piece ranging from easy-to-understand discussions of archaeology and exploration to architecture and the customs of people in the Arab and Islamic worlds covered by the Arabian American Oil Company. A useful source of material for both adults and teenagers on the Middle East and its background, if not on its serious economic and political problems.

Canada Weekly. 1945. w. Free. Carole Stelmack. External Information Program Div., Dept. of External Affairs, 125 Sussex Dr., Ottawa, Ont. K1A 0G2, Canada. Illus. Circ: 16,000 English; 7,000 French; 1,625 Spanish; 1,500 Portuguese (not distributed in Canada). Sample. Vol. ends: Dec. 31.
Aud: Hs.

Essentially, this is a running account of the political, social, and economic life of Canada. The eight- to ten-page newsletter reports on activities of the government over the previous week. The news is obviously partisan and rarely does one find criticism. The photos are few, but adequate. Note that the newsletter is published in a number of languages besides English.

Carnegie Quarterly. 1953. q. Free. Avery Russell. Carnegie Corp. of New York, 437 Madison Ave., New York, NY 10022. Illus. Circ: 36,000. Vol. ends: Winter.
Aud: Hs.

An eight-page newsletter which reports on projects sponsored by the Carnegie Corporation. The goal of the philanthropic foundation is to promote the advancement and diffusion of knowledge and understanding in the United States. Each issue focuses on a certain project and what the corporation is doing to increase awareness. Recent issues have covered the state of public education in the United States and how scholars can help stop nuclear war. Articles are signed, and contributors have done work on the projects. Information on approved grants and staff news are also included.

Changing Challenge. 1974. irreg. (3 to 4/yr). Free. Hugh Wells. General Motors Corp., G.M. Bldg. 11-269, 3044 W. Grand Blvd., Detroit, MI 48202. Illus. Circ: 45,000. Vol. ends: No. 3 or No. 4.
Aud: Hs.

The focus is on transportation, but beyond that the magazine makes no effort to advertise or otherwise feature its own products. Experts, usually from outside the company, may write on all aspects of past, present, and future modes of transport, and not only automobiles and trucks. The format, illustrations, and editing are outstanding. A magazine suitable for almost every collection.

Conoco. 1970. q. Free. Maury Bates. Conoco, Inc., 1007 Market St., Wilmington, DE 19898. Illus. Circ: 42,000. Vol. ends: No. 4.
Aud: Hs.

The oil industry puts its best foot forward here. The well-illustrated articles cover the obvious (the economics and politics of oil production) and the not so obvious (adventure stories about the discovery of new sources of energy). The writing is fair to good, albeit the editorial matter is not all that objective and not up to what is found in *Aramco World* (see above in this section). Still, this is a most attractive and useful title for high school libraries.

Enthusiast. 1916. 3/yr. Free (to libraries and factory-registered owners of Harley-Davidson vehicles on request). Buzz Buzzelli. Harley-Davidson Motor Co., Inc., P.O. Box 653, 3700 W. Juneau Ave., Milwaukee, WI 53201. Illus. Circ: 156,000. Vol. ends: Winter.
Aud: Hs.

Designed for the motorcycling public, this publication has been reduced from 20 to 15 pages, but still provides good coverage of the sport and its machines. Articles feature information on touring, engineering, and Harley-Davidson products. Full-color photographs of the company's latest models are displayed throughout the magazine. Most readers tend to be young males. Recommended for high school libraries.

Exxon USA. 1945. q. Free. Downs Matthews. Exxon Co.,

U.S.A., P.O. Box 2180, Houston, TX 77001. Illus. Circ: 250,000. Sample. Vol. ends: Winter.
Indexed: PAIS. *Aud:* Hs.

A high-quality offering of another of the major oil companies achieves a wide variety of subject matter with and without direct connection to the company's operations. Six substantial articles per issue choose such topics as oil exploration and ancillary material on the land and water areas affected. Signed articles are credited to well-qualified authors and staff writers, with authors' backgrounds often noted. It has excellent overall design, fine quality illustrations consisting of professional color photos, and original artwork by competent illustrators.

Ford Times. 1908. m. Free. Arnold S. Hirsch. Ford Motor Co., Dearborn, MI 48121. Subs through local Ford dealers only. Illus., adv. Circ: 1,044,045. Vol. ends: Dec.
Aud: Hs.

Librarians are instructed to make requests through their local Ford dealers. Although published by an auto company, this publication contains no more automotive-related articles than most magazines targeted for the general audience. Each issue features 10 to 12 well-written pieces on travel, automobiles, outdoor recreation, food, and regional interest. Several articles give background history on parts of the United States or assist the reader in making plans for a vacation trip. A regular feature gives recipes for favorite dishes from restaurants across the nation. The writing style is simple and should interest both the student and general reader. Illustrated, with minimal advertising.

Horizons. q. Free. Bernard Kovit. Grumman Corp., Bethpage, NY 11714. Illus. Circ: 54,000.
Aud: Ejh, Hs.

Written for a general audience, this publication focuses on the Grumman Corporation's work in the field of aeronautics. Articles concentrate on the company's interest in military aircraft and the space program. Several articles are devoted to the history of military planes and offer some interesting data on the technological advances that have occurred. Diagrams accompany the articles and provide detailed drawings of the older models. Excellent color photographs of jetfighters, bombers, and space stations will appeal to young readers. There is also a centerfold of the latest-released Grumman jetfighter. Technical data is minimal, but enough to hold the attention of military plane enthusiasts. Recommended for school libraries.

Marathon World. 1964. q. Free. Norman V. Richards. Marathon Oil Co., 539 S. Main St., Findlay, OH 45840. Illus. Circ: 70,000. Sample. Vol. ends: No. 4.
Aud: Hs.

Another of the oil magazines, this is similar to *Conoco, Exxon USA,* and so forth. There are the usual good illustrations, the easy-to-follow articles, and the subtle material emphasizing the wholesome quality of the oil company. *Marathon* covers most of the eastern and southern United States, and there are pieces on the history, economics, and social issues of these regions. Extremely well done, the magazine ranks right up there among the best of its type.

The Orange Disc. 1933. q. Free. Robert Cairns. Gulf Oil Corp., P.O. Box 1166, Pittsburgh, PA 15230. Illus. Circ: 325,000. Sample. Vol. ends: Spring, every 3rd yr.
Aud: Hs.

This primarily is a house organ for Gulf Oil. The material on travel, refineries, and historical background makes it suitable for high school libraries. The photographs are excellent.

Profile. (High School News Service). 1956. 6/yr. (Nov.-Apr.). Captain Clark M. Gammell, USN, Bldg. X-18, Naval Sta., Norfolk, VA 23511. Illus. Circ: 30,000. Vol. ends: Apr.
Aud: Hs.

Regular issues consist of articles on job skills, training, life-styles, and programs in which members of the uniformed services participate. A special information number is published in January, which discusses basic facts about service life. This is a valuable presentation of information on all aspects of every branch of the service, ranging from enlistments and commissioning programs to pay and other benefits. An appeal is made to women and minorities to join by showing them engaging in various activities. This publication is distributed to high school, college, and public libraries, but those not on the subscription list will want to provide it for their patrons. Requests must be made on school letterhead and signed by the requesting official.

The Royal Bank Letter. 1943. bi-m. Free. Robert Stewart. Royal Bank of Canada, P.O. Box 6001, Montreal, P.Q. H3C 3A9, Canada. Circ: 375,000. Sample. Vol. ends: Nov/Dec.
Indexed: PAIS. *Aud:* Hs.

Despite the title, this is not an economic newsletter. On the contrary, the four-pager is devoted to a single topic of interest to high school students. The 2,500 to 3,500 words concern everything from popular psychology and the social sciences to the humanities. Subject matter may concentrate on writing, art, health, and such. A useful, easy-to-read publication which can be nicely inserted into the vertical file.

Science Dimension. 1969. 6/yr. Free. Wayne Campbell. Natl. Research Council of Canada, Public Relations and Information Services, M-58, Ottawa, Ont. K1A 0R6, Canada. Illus. Circ: 130,000 (French—57,000, English—73,000). Vol. ends: No. 6.
Aud: Hs.

Serving as the official publication for the National Research Council of Canada and reporting on current research being conducted in the universities and research institutions across Canada, this magazine provides excellent exposure for the work being done by Canadian scientists. Every 15-page issue contains interviews, articles, and essays by two resident columnists. The interviews are with scientists, who discuss their work and how they became involved with their particular subject. The articles are written for the nonspecialist, but occasionally the vocabulary is technical. Vocabulary definitions are included to assist readers in understanding the material. Columnists give interesting perspectives on the role of science, especially in Canada. Full-color photographs and graphs are scattered throughout the magazine to illustrate the work being done. The entire publication is enjoyable to read and should appeal to students.

Sun Magazine. 1923. q. Free. Peter E. Brakeman. Sun Co., Inc., 100 Matsonford Rd., Radnor, PA 19087. Illus. Circ: 135,000. Vol. ends: Winter.
Aud: Hs.

The Sun Company is a major resources firm with coal and petroleum operations in the United States and Canada. The company uses its magazine to show the general public what it is doing about the problem of exploitation of natural resources and the demands of an energy-hungry world. A typical issue is 26 to 30 pages long and consists of four to five well-written articles. Recent issues have discussed oil decontrol, energy conservation, and the laying of pipeline through wildlife areas. The publication also features stories on Sun employees and the organizations supported by the company. Color photographs are used to illustrate the various activities undertaken by Sun and its employees. Articles about people and their occupations in a big oil company may appeal to many students.

Venezuela Up-to-Date. 1949. q. Free. José Egidio Rodriguez. Embassy of Venezuela, Information Service, 2437 California St. N.W., Washington, DC 20008. Illus. Circ: 34,000. Sample. Vol. ends: Winter.
Indexed: PAIS. *Aud:* Hs.

Many embassies issue free periodicals which hail the glories of their country; Venezuela is no exception. In this, however, the style is fairly objective and the writing is as good as the black-and-white photographs.

For the Professional

Canada Today/d'Aujourd'hui. 1970. irreg. (7/yr.). Free. Judith C. Webster. Canadian Embassy, 1771 N St. N.W., Rm. 300, Washington, DC 20036. Illus. Circ: 100,000. Vol. ends: Dec.
Aud: Pr.

Distributed free in the United States, this government-sponsored magazine is intended primarily for people in the fields of government, education, business, and the media. Each issue is devoted to a particular aspect of Canadian culture, and topics selected tend to be noncontroversial and appealing to a U.S. audience. Recent issues have included articles on Canadian television, current sports stars, elections and trade relations. Issues consist of 12 to 16 pages, with short articles intermingled among color photos and graphs. Since the pieces are brief, the graphs are important in interpreting the material. Reproduced in eye-catching colors, the graphs contain a great deal of pertinent statistical information. A valuable resource on Canada for the general reader.

GENERAL INTEREST

For the Student: Children; Teenage/For the Professional

Margaret McKinley, Head, Serials Dept., University Research Library, University of California, Los Angeles, CA 90024

Lillian K. Orsini, Former Faculty Member, School of Library & Information Science, SUNY at Albany, Albany, NY 12222 (Children subsection)

Libby K. White, Schenectady County Public Library, Liberty and Clinton Sts., Schenectady, NY 12305

Basic Periodicals

Ejh: *Cricket, Electric Company Magazine, Highlights for Children, Sesame Street Magazine;* Hs: *Courier, Horizon, Life, National Geographic Magazine, Scholastic Update, Seventeen, Teen, World Press Review.*

Basic Abstracts and Indexes

Children's Magazine Guide (Formerly: *Subject Guide to Children's Magazines*), *Readers' Guide to Periodical Literature.*

For the Student

CHILDREN

The magazines reviewed in this section are general interest magazines specifically intended for use by or with children ages 3–14. The availability of magazines in a format suitable for the visually impaired child is indicated in the entry. Magazines for this age group that focus on specific topics can be found listed under that topic elsewhere in this book. An indispensable tool for access to children's magazines is the *Children's Magazine Guide,* which indexes approximately 50 periodicals and is published with semiannual accumulations. It is available from: Children's Magazine Guide, 7 N. Pinckney St., Madison, WI 53703.

Adventure. 1962. m. $7.50. Sue C. Jones. Southern Baptist Convention, Sunday School Bd., 127 Ninth Ave. N., Nashville, TN 37234. Illus. Sample. Vol. ends: Sept.
Aud: Ejh.

A leisure-reading magazine. Issues include short stories, articles, poetry, and activities that are related to the Southern Baptist Sunday School curriculum for children ages 8–11.

Ahoy: a children's magazine. See Canada/For the Student Section.

Barbie. 1983. q. $5. Karen Harrison. Telepictures Pubns., Inc., 300 Madison Ave., New York, NY 10017. Illus., adv. Circ: 750,000. Sample. Vol. ends: Nov.
Aud: Ejh.

Barbie is a fashion and life-style magazine for girls ages 6–12. It is published with the cooperation of Mattel Toys, and the magazine features the doll on the cover and on its editorial pages. Features include clothing fashions and beauty tips, an article on a young female celebrity, and seasonal crafts. Regular departments are: "Your Page" (letters from readers), "What's Happening" (brief notes on new movies, TV shows, records, and books), and "Tricks and Teasers" (puzzles and jokes). The magazine is illustrated in striking, full color and printed on glossy paper. Truly a "pop" culture magazine for less sophisticated pre-teeners.

Chart Your Course! See Exceptional Children: Gifted, Disabled, Those with Special Needs/For the Student Section.

Chickadee. 1979. 10/yr. $10.95. Janis Nostbakken. Young Naturalist Foundation, P.O. Box 1700, Buffalo, NY 14271. Illus., index. Circ: 100,000. Sample. Vol. ends: Dec.
Indexed: CMG. *Aud:* Ejh.

Depending heavily on the excellent pictorial material, this companion to *Owl* is intended for children under age 9. Its aim is to interest children "in their environment and the world around them." Nature is the subject treated most often in brief articles and a read-to-me story or poem. The activities, games, and puzzles invite children to fill in or cut out. Best for parents to share with children at home.

Cricket. 1973. m. $18.50. Marianne Carus. Open Court Publg. Co., P.O. Box 100, La Salle, IL 61301. Subs. to: P.O. Box 2672, Boulder, CO 80321. Illus., adv. Circ: 150,000. Vol. ends: Aug.
Indexed: CMG. *Aud:* Ejh.

Cricket is the only truly literary magazine for children ages 6–12. The editorial board includes Isaac Singer, Lloyd Alexander, Eleanor Cameron, Virginia Haviland, and others. Internationally known authors and artists are contributors of never-before-published stories, poems, and articles, which make up the major portion of each issue. Also included are excerpts from published materials; a page each of jokes, puzzles, craft projects; and a section devoted to contributions from young readers. The excellent format is complemented by predominantly black-and white illustrations (cover is in full color). Highly recommended also to storytellers as a source for new and exciting literature to share with children.

Dollstars Magazine. 1986. q. $7.97. Dollstars Magazine, P.O. Box 412, Mt. Morris, IL 61054. Illus. Circ: 200,000.
Aud: Ejh.

This glossy title capitalizes on the burgeoning sales of dolls, stuffed animals, and plastic figures by offering news, features, "interviews," and articles on such licensed characters as Cabbage Patch Kids, Pound Puppies, Garfield, Transformers, and others, including, of course, Barbie. Features include the "Dollywood Reporter," giving news of new books, records, movies, or products featuring name dolls; a pin-up poster; a pen-pal exchange; and jokes from Shari Lewis's Lamb Chop. Lewis, listed as Executive Editor, contributes at least one article per issue, along with Peggy and Alan Bialosky, who have made it big with bears.

The Electric Company Magazine. 1974. 10/yr. $9.95. Susan Dias-Karnovsky. Children's Television Workshop, 200 Watt St., P.O. Box 2924, Boulder, CO 80322. Illus. Circ: 375,000. Sample. Vol. ends: Dec/Jan.
Indexed: CMG. *Aud:* Ejh.

Intended for graduates of "Sesame Street" and prepared in conjunction with the television program, the magazine emphasizes the visual and the animated. A typical issue includes jokes, puzzles, comics, short articles, stories, and things to make and do. Although the material is typical of that found in other magazines, it is noteworthy for its imaginative and colorful approach to helping children improve their reading, math and thinking skills. Should be especially useful with beginning and reluctant readers, ages 6–10.

Highlights for Children. 1946. 11/yr. $17.95. Walter B. Barbe. Highlights for Children, Inc., 2300 W. Fifth Ave., P.O. Box 269, Columbus, OH 43216. Index. Circ: 1,850,000. Sample. Vol. ends: Dec.

Indexed: CMG. *Aud:* Ejh.

Highlights states that its purpose is "to help children grow in basic skills and knowledge, in creativeness, in ability to think and reason, in sensitivity to others, in high ideals and worthy ways of living." This purpose is emphasized by the "Guide for Parents and Teachers," which indicates reading levels of materials and how a particular item may be beneficial to the child. Contents include stories, poems, and signed, informative articles on a variety of subjects. Games, puzzles, word fun, craft ideas, and several cartoon features complete each issue. Off-white paper, appropriate typeface, and the sometimes excellent black-and-white and full-color illustrations make up the format for this general interest magazine, which provides "wholesome fun," and is worth buying.

Hot Dog! 1979. 9/yr. $9.95. Grace Maccarone. Scholastic, Inc., 730 Broadway, New York, NY 10003. Illus. Sample. Vol. ends: Dec.

Aud: Ejh.

Seven- and eight-year olds should be delighted with *Hot Dog!* Articles on a variety of topics and well-known personalities, brevity, color, comical characters, tipped-in baseball cards, stickers, and a pullout poster will appeal to even the most reluctant reader. A recent issue carried one story with sustained text—a chapter from *Charlie and the Chocolate Factory*, preceded by an article titled "Hot Dog Visits a Chocolate Store." Jokes, puzzles, a "Garfield" cartoon, "Lucky Book Club" selections and a contest are regular features.

JAM (Just About Me). 1983. 6/yr. $14. Ulla Colgrass, 56 The Esplanade, Suite 202, Toronto, Ont. M5E 1A7, Canada. Illus. Sample. Vol. ends: Dec.

Bk. rev: 8, 140–150 words, signed. *Aud:* Ejh.

This Canadian magazine is intended for children ages 10–15. It entertains and informs youngsters about their own society and future. Feature articles deal with sports, education, science, medicine, health, and the environment. Regular features include book and movie reviews, a word game, "Jamscope" (horoscope), and an advice column. Black-and-white photographs and illustrations on glossy paper complement the colorful and easy-to-read writing.

Jack and Jill. 1938. 8/yr. $11.95. Christine French Clark. Benjamin Franklin Literary and Medical Soc., Inc., P.O. Box 567, Indianapolis, IN 46206. Subs. to: P.O. Box 10681, Des Moines, IA 50381. Illus. Circ: 500,000. Sample. Vol. ends: Dec.

Aud: Ejh.

Presents a variety of materials to suit the interests of children ages 6–8. Each issue contains a few stories; "Herbie's Health Pages," which emphasizes nutrition and physical fitness; poems; puzzles; jokes; games; easy recipes; a featured cartoon; and contributions of stories, poems, and pictures in the "From Our Readers" section. The two- and four-color illustrations and black-and-white photographs are generally good and well placed. A good choice to encourage independent reading among the upper age group, otherwise to be placed on the "Parents as Reading Partners" list.

National Geographic World. 1975. m. $9.95. Pat Robbins. Natl. Geographic Soc., 17th and M Sts. N.W., Washington, DC 20036. Illus., index. Circ: 1,500,000. Sample. Vol. ends: Dec.

Indexed: CMG. *Aud:* Ejh.

Winner of the EDPRESS Golden Lamp award for excellence in educational journalism, *World* is intended for children ages 8–13 and is produced with the same concern for accuracy and quality as its parent magazine. The emphasis is on the pictorial—splendid full-color photographs in an 8½- by 10¾-inch format printed on glossy paper. It contains articles and features on a variety of subjects and about other children, games, projects, a supersized pullout poster, and contributions from readers. There is no advertising, and the subscription price is unusually low. A must for all libraries.

Owl. 1976. 10/yr. $10.95. Sylvia Furston. Young Naturalist Foundation, P.O. Box 1700, Buffalo, NY 14271. Illus., index. Circ: 100,000. Sample. Vol. ends: Dec.

Indexed: CMG. *Aud:* Ejh.

Corresponding with the launch of "Owl/TV" on the Public Broadcasting Service in November, 1985, Canada's largest children's publication was made available through a U.S. distributor at a lower price. The primary aim of the periodical is "to expand children's knowledge of the world around them and to challenge them to think about the effect people have on their surroundings." Intended for children ages 7–14, it includes a wide range of material, mostly nonfiction. Articles are about animals, science, technology, natural phenomena, experiments, and people. The activities, puzzles, games, and a cartoon story are creative and challenging. The layout is varied and aesthetically pleasing. Printed on glossy paper and with stunning color photographs, including an animal centerfold each month, the magazine reflects high editorial and artistic standards.

Sesame Street Magazine. 1970. 10/yr. $10.95. Children's Television Workshop. Subs. to: P.O. Box 5200, Boulder, CO 80321. Illus.

Indexed: CMG. *Aud:* Ejh.

Intended for ages 2–6, the magazine has the same educational goals as the *Sesame Street* television program, and the same familiar characters. Each issue includes arithmetic games, easy-to-read stories, pre-reading exercise, a color or draw page, and things to cut out. The illustrations and graphics are in color, and one often finds the text in Spanish and English. A "Parent's Page" tells adults how to help youngsters learn from and enjoy using the material.

Stickers. 1982. q. $10. Ira Friedman, 10 Columbus Circle, Suite 1300, New York, NY 10019. Illus.
Aud: Ejh, Hs.

The title tells all. The features, stories, illustrations and departments are for one thing and one thing only—the collection and the use of stickers. There is everything here from how they are manufactured to where they may be purchased. The magazine should get an A plus for imagination, although the subject matter may leave some adults far from excited. But then it's for the kids, not their parents.

Turtle. 1979. 8/yr. $11.95. Beth Wood Thomas. Children's Better Health Inst., P.O. Box 567, Indianapolis, IN 46206. Illus. Circ: 425,000. Sample. Vol. ends: Dec.
Aud: Ejh.

Intended for preschoolers, ages 2–5, who, with adult help, can learn the alphabet, numbers, shapes, and word skills. The stories, poems, rebus rhymes, puzzles, hidden pictures, and dot-to-dots will, not doubt, amuse and occupy children, although the magazine does not get high marks for the poor poetry and the inaccurately portrayed (squirrel with a striped tail) and colored (brown pea pods) objects in the illustrations. Special emphasis is placed on good health habits throughout the magazine.

TEENAGE

Teens, young adults, adolescents—what's in a label? Who exactly comprises the audience for titles in this section? Shall we say grades 8–12, ages 13–18? In real life, the grade and age ranges are elastic, with stretch on both ends and marked individual differences at every level and turn. A Public Library Association Task Force sees the teen as one who no longer feels herself or himself a child but is not considered an adult by others. A philosophic approach idealizes the teen as the "everyperson" of the shifting physical, emotional, and interest states of our post-modern world. Working with teens in libraries is a puzzlement and the fulfillment of that old cliché—"Let it be a challenge to you!" The culture of teenhood is eclectic, contradictory, and encompassing; thus, in collection development, consideration must be given to the titles annotated in this section as well as to the cross-references. The culture of teenhood is on the cutting edge of our shared future. Ideas and information in all size units and formats are keys to that future. To the teen, the magazine is a user-friendly guide encouraging participation in learning.

The magazines included in this section are about equally divided between teen-directed titles (e.g., *Boys' Life* and *Seventeen*) and such general interest adult titles as *The Atlantic* or *People Weekly* that are appropriate for a high-school student. Included in this latter group are more academic titles such as *American Scholar* and *Daedalus* that students may find useful for research papers.

American Scholar. 1932. q. $15. Joseph Epstein. United Chapters of Phi Beta Kappa, 1811 Q St. N.W., Washington, DC 20009. Illus., index, adv. Circ: 28,500. Vol. ends: Autumn. Microform: B&H, UMI.
Indexed: BioI, HumI, PAIS, RG. *Bk. rev:* 5–9 essays, signed. *Aud:* Hs.

Having celebrated U.S. intellectual and artistic life for over half a century, *American Scholar* continues to thrive with a robust circulation. It publishes the most distinguished U.S. writers and academicians and features contemporary U.S. poetry. Aristides' (actually Editor Epstein) column, "Life and Letters," brings sociological observation and literature together with flawless grace. An afternoon spent with an issue of *American Scholar* is like a trip through time to the lost age of elegant literary salons. It should be required reading for people in hot pursuit of the future, read and reread slowly and leisurely. (M.McK.)

Americana. 1973. bi-m. $12. Michael Durham. Americana, 29 W. 38th St., New York, NY 10018. Illus., adv. Circ: 361,000. Microform: B&H
Indexed: RG. *Bk. rev:* Various number, length. *Aud:* Hs.

Articles, illustrations, and features herald the importance of America's past as it pertains to collecting, crafts, and related areas ranging from art to architecture. The combination of historical and how-to-do-it material is balanced by pieces on travel—particularly to historical places in the United States. There is considerable space given to restoration, cooking, decorating, and even gardening. The only prerequisite is that it have something to do with America's past. The material is elementary. It is useful for information on the basic holidays from Thanksgiving to Christmas, and at this level may be employed in school libraries. (M.McK.)

The Atlantic. 1857. m. $9.95. William Whitworth. Atlantic Monthly Co., 8 Arlington St., Boston, MA 02116. Subs. to: Atlantic Subn. Processing Center, P.O. Box 2547, Boulder, CO 80322. Illus., adv. Circ: 325,000. Vol. ends: June & Dec. Microform: B&H, UMI.
Indexed: AbrRg, BioI, BoRv, BoRvI, RG. *Bk. rev:* 2–3 essays, 7–9 notes, signed. *Aud:* Hs.

Tackling the most complex of today's controversial issues, *The Atlantic*'s authors are proficient at transforming the incomprehensible into the intelligible. Each issue includes four to six extended analyses of various aspects of U.S. society or foreign affairs. Poetry, humor, and fiction appear in each issue, with leisure activities, art, and fashion explored in a number of columns. There is sure to be something in *The Atlantic* which will appeal to virtually every thoughtful reader. Highly recommended. (M.McK.)

Boys' Life. 1911. m. $10.80. Robert E. Hood. Boy Scouts of America, 1325 Walnut Hill La., Irving TX 75038. Illus., adv. Circ: 1,600,000. Vol. ends: Dec.
Indexed: Acs, CMG, MgI. *Bk. rev:* 1, 400 words, signed. *Aud:* Ejh, Hs.

From Cubs to Eagles, this is the official magazine of boy scouting. *Boys' Life* consists of six informative and well-written general interest articles. This title stresses active interests with a very broad definition. Strongest sections are on sports, outdoor adventure and recreation, science, hobbies, and crafts. Profiles tend to be on sports figures. There is at least one piece of fiction per issue. A regular department, "Comics," includes Bible stories. This magazine is suggested for "all boys 8–18." Articles about cars, bicycles, and electronics are geared to the upper age range, but *Boys' Life* remains predominantly a magazine for younger teenage boys. (L.K.O.)

Bulletin of the Atomic Scientists. 1945. 11/yr. $25 (Individuals, $22.50). Harrison Brown. Educational Foundation for Nuclear Science, 5801 S. Kenwood, Chicago, IL 60637. Illus., index, adv. Circ: 22,300. Vol. ends: Dec. Microform: B&H, UMI.
Indexed: BioI, BoRv, RG. *Bk. rev:* 4–8, 300–2,500 words, signed. *Aud:* Hs.

In spite of its forbidding title, this is a magazine for the informed and inquiring general reader. Though the dominant theme of many issues is the control of nuclear power, many articles comment on other technological, scientific, or political matters of international concern. Contributors are experts in their fields, but their writing is clear and free of undefined, esoteric terms and scientific jargon. The editors are vitally concerned with the roles and responsibilities of scientists as informed citizens of the modern world. This is an influential and often-quoted publication, and highly recommended. (M.McK.)

California (Formerly: *New West: the magazine of California*). 1976. bi-w. $12. Harold Hayes. New West Communications Corp., 11601 Wilshire Blvd., Los Angeles, CA 90025. Subs. to: P.O. Box 2585, Boulder, CO 80302. Illus., adv. Circ: 320,000. Vol. ends: Dec. Microform: UMI.
Indexed: PopPer. *Bk. rev:* 1–2 essays, signed; 2–9 notes. *Aud:* Hs.

California was, in the late 1970s, a transplanted easterner, an offshoot of *New York*. Now, with a new title, it has completed its transformation into a Californian. The topics of its feature articles are Californian, but are far from provincial or pedestrian. Pieces are sophisticated, thoroughly researched, and tightly written. *California*'s photography captures the reader's attention and the feature articles hold it. In monthly columns, California's arts, events, and consumer opportunities are reported. (M.McK.)

The Center Magazine. 1967. bi-m. Membership, $25. Donald McDonald. Robert Maynard Hutchins Center for the Study of Democratic Insts., P.O. Box 4068, Santa Barbara, CA 93102. Illus. Circ: 18,000. Vol. ends: Dec. Microform: UMI.
Indexed: Biol, PAIS, RG, SocSc. *Aud:* Hs.

The Center Magazine probes the inner workings of contemporary society, addressing specific aspects in some detail. Reports of the sponsoring center's projects may be serialized in consecutive issues and frequently include seminar proceedings as well as articles. "Public Affairs, the Media, and the Democratic Process" was one such project. The publication presents a broad spectrum of viewpoints in pursuing the stated purpose of the center to examine "basic issues confronting democratic societies." Contributors are opinion makers with national and international reputations. Carefully edited and highly readable, *The Center Magazine* deserves a place in any library with a readership concerned with the problems of the modern world and prospects for a better future. (M.McK.)

Courier (Formerly: *UNESCO Courier*). 1948. m. $11. Edouard Glissant. UNESCO, Place de Fontenoy, 75700 Paris, France. Illus., adv. Circ: 40,000. Vol. ends: Dec. Microform: B&H, UMI.
Indexed: RG. *Aud:* Hs.

Courier presents cross-cultural views of education, art, living conditions, natural resources, history, and politics, frequently emphasizing Third World nations. Many issues have themes such as archaeology, food, women, or ricelands. Articles are accurate, well-researched, and written in an uncomplicated, direct fashion. This is an especially useful periodical for junior high school and high school students. The periodical provides a valuable service in making its audience aware of the immensity of our earth and the diversity of its peoples and their cultures. Published in 31 languages. (M.McK.)

Current Biography. 1940. m. $35 (Cumulation, $35). H. W. Wilson Co., 950 University Ave., Bronx, NY 10452.
Aud: Hs.

Though this is generally thought of as a reference work, in recent years it has become a relatively popular magazine as well. It can be read cover to cover for the dozen or more biographical pieces on today's leading national and international figures. The colorful cover, which features a personality, gives it a dimension not often considered with basic reference works. At any rate, the 2,000- to 2,500-word entries are about as objective as those found anywhere—some might say, bland—and the information is well presented and accurate. (M.McK.)

Daedalus. 1955. q. $16. Stephen R. Graubard. Norton's Woods, 136 Irving St., Cambridge, MA 02138. Subs. to: P.O. Box 515, Canton, MA 02021. Index. Circ: 20,000. Vol. ends: Fall. Microform: UMI.
Indexed: BoRvI, HumI, PAIS. *Aud:* Hs.

Among the top handful of significant academic journals published in the United States today, *Daedalus* is the offical publication of the American Academy of Arts and Sciences. Each issue has a theme relevant to contemporary U.S. society. The authors published here are senior academicians or leading intellects of the day. Well edited and well written, *Daedalus*' intended audience consists of perceptive, educated readers. (M.McK.)

Encounter. 1953. 10/yr. $39. Melvin J. Lasky & Anthony Thwaite. Encounter, 59 St. Martins Lane, London WC2N 4JS, England. Subs. to: Expediters of the Printed Word,

Ltd., 515 Madison Ave., New York, NY 10022. Illus., index, adv. Circ: 17,000. Vol. ends: June & Dec.

Indexed: BoRv, HumI. *Bk. rev:* 18 essays, signed. *Aud:* Hs.

Encounter resembles *American Scholar* in its breadth of interests and *Daedalus* in its concerns with political affairs and social problems. The publication features interviews with internationally known statespeople, politicians, and philosophers. There are analyses of literature, the arts, philosophy and language. Writers assume that their readers will have had an extended formal education, and the editors assume that readers will have time to ponder long, carefully constructed and quite detailed articles. There are a number of short notes and comments that amuse and instruct, and major contemporary poets are also published. In 1985, *Encounter* took on a new, glossy look that is pleasing to the eye. (M.McK.)

Esquire. 1933. m. $17.94. Lee Eisenberg. Esquire, 2 Park Ave., New York, NY 10016. Subs. to: P.O. Box 2590, Boulder, CO 80321. Illus., adv. Vol. ends: June & Dec. Microform: B&H, UMI.

Indexed: RG. *Bk. rev:* 1 essay, signed. *Aud:* Hs.

Esquire is one of the few U.S. magazines published today that may still be described as a general-interest periodical, though there is a gentlemanly masculine editorial perspective about it. Each issue carries information about contemporary living, life-styles, sports, finances, and entertainment. Some issues may have such themes as "Under Forty Achievers" and "The Soul of America." Every issue is superbly written and edited, and any general collection of periodicals should certainly include it. (M.McK.)

Exploring. 1971. q. $1.50. Robert E. Hood. Boy Scouts of America, 1325 Walnut Hill La., Irving, TX 75038. Illus. Circ: 375,000. Vol. ends: Sept.

Aud: Ejh, Hs.

News of the Explorers, the senior division of the Boy Scouts. The U.S. Explorers' organization is open to boys and girls who are 14 and graduates of grade 8. This magazine is far more than a service to its sponsoring membership. Among the subjects it has addressed in its 24 pages are mountain men, teen suicide, the Culinary Institute of America (in the career section), white river rafting, and teen refugees from Southeast Asia. A good general title. (L.K.W.)

Foxfire. 1967. q. $9. Eliot Wigginton. Foxfire Fund, Inc., Rabun Gap, GA 30458. Illus. Circ: 6,000. Vol. ends: Winter.

Indexed: Acs. *Aud:* Hs.

Foxfire is a lichen that glows in the dark. The contents of this magazine are drawn from the almost forgotten indigenous Appalachian culture. The idea of preserving the culture of the mountain people in print was conceived by an English teacher in rural Georgia, but the researchers and writers are area high school students. The young people record oral history and document, step by step, traditional craft-making. Subjects of *Foxfire* include personal histories,

musical compositions, home remedies, and log cabin building. Articles from this magazine have appeared in mass-circulation magazines and collected in best-selling anthologies. This title remains the prototype and inspiration for similar magazines and projects everywhere. (L.K.W.)

Harper's Magazine. 1850. m. $18. Lewis H. Lapham. Harper's Magazine Foundation, 2 Park Ave., New York, NY 10016. Subs. to: P.O. Box 1937, Marion, OH 43305. Illus., index, adv. Circ: 150,000. Vol. ends: June & Dec. Microform: B&H, UMI.

Indexed: BioI, BoRv, BoRvI, RG. *Aud:* Hs.

Harper's lively commentary on contemporary politics, culture, and society is written with verve and great style. Lewis Lapham's monthly column, "The Easy Chair," cajoles readers into bending their minds in untried ways to view U.S. politics and life-style. A major portion of each issue is now devoted to "Readings," which are excerpts from books, periodicals, newspapers, speeches, and press releases. They enlighten and amuse. For the excellence of its writers and the keenness of their insights, *Harper's* deserves a place in all high school libraries. Recommended as a basic title. (M.McK.)

Horizon. 1958. 10/yr. $21.95. Gray D. Boone. Horizon Pubs., 570 Seventh Ave., New York, NY 10018. Subs. to: P.O. Drawer 30, Tuscaloosa, AL 35402. Illus., index, adv. Circ: 65,000. Vol. ends: Dec. Microform: B&H, UMI.

Indexed: RG. *Bk. rev:* 1 essay, signed. *Aud:* Hs.

Horizon is a splendid magazine, delighting the eye and mind with excellent photography and writing. Each issue has five to seven feature articles on art, filmmaking, writing, theater, dance, museums, or other aspects of life well lived in the United States. There are frequent reports of arts activities in specific U.S. cities, plus armchair arts tours of foreign countries and cities. *Horizon* would be a worthwhile addition to high school collections. (M.McK.)

Info AAU. 1929. m. $4. Mike Bowyer. Amateur Athletic Union, 3400 W. 86th St., Indianapolis, IN 46268. Illus. Circ: 7,000. Vol. ends: Dec.

Aud: Hs.

An eight page, fold-over newsletter. This is the official magazine of the organization that oversees the competition in 20 sports. *Info AAU* also reports on activities for teens, such as the Junior Olympics and physical fitness programs. Very complete. (L.K.W.)

Jet. See Afro-American/For the Student Section.

Junior Scholastic. 1937. 18/school yr. $6 (Teacher's edition, $15). Lee Baier. Scholastic, Inc., 730 Broadway, New York, NY 10003. Subs. to: P.O. Box 644, Lyndhurst, NJ 07071. Illus., adv. Circ: 830,000. Vol. ends: May. Microform: UMI.

Indexed: CMG. *Aud:* Ejh.

For younger teens, this is an excellent magazine with an eye-catching format. *Junior Scholastic* emphasizes human interest topics. For example, an analysis of Chile looks at the life of a Chilean boy with ambitions to be a rodeo champion. An issue is divided into "World," "Current News," "U.S. History," and "Skills" sections. Helpful maps often accompany articles. The amount of information in and the range of this 16-page publication are truly amazing—for example, pieces entitled "The Golden 20's," "High Tech Medicine," and "Farmers in Crisis," are all written in clear, understandable language. See Education/For the Student Section for the student issue. (L.K.W.)

Keynoter. 1950. 7/yr. $4. J. P. "Pete" Tinsley. Key Club Intl., 3636 Woodview Trace, Indianapolis, IN 46268. Illus. Circ: 90,000.
Aud: Hs.

A 16-page newsletter that promotes the objectives of Key Club, a Kiwanis affiliate. *Keynoter* reports on the activities and projects of Key Clubs organized in high schools, and on their annual convention. Key Clubbers see themselves as forward-looking contributors to their communities. The tone is positive and upbeat. (L.K.W.)

Knowledge. 1977. q. $20. O. A. Battista. 3863 SW Loop 820, Suite 100, Fort Worth, TX 76133. Illus. Circ: 2,500. Vol. ends: Winter.
Bk. rev: 7–12, notes. *Aud:* Hs.

Knowledge features short, concise articles on a wide variety of topics, primarily in the pure and applied sciences, health and medicine, and world peace. Intended for the general reader without a scientific or technical background, *Knowledge* resembles *Sunshine Magazine* and *Ideals* in its editorial policies and perspective. The information provided is accurate and presented in a simple, readable style. High school librarians should consider acquiring *Knowledge* for readers with an aversion to the watered-down science notes in many general-interest periodicals. (M.McK.)

Life. 1978. m. $27. Henry Anatole Grunwald. Time, Inc., 10880 Wilshire Blvd., Los Angeles, CA 90024. Illus., adv. Circ: 1,500,000. Vol. ends: Dec. Microform: UMI.
Indexed: Acs. *Aud:* Hs.

Life is a born-again periodical. Its emphasis on photography accompanied by brief texts is similar to the old *Life*, but the newer version is full of rainbow colors. In addition, the new *Life* features some articles in which the emphasis is on the text, with the photographs that accompany them supplementing the written word. Some feature pieces are designed to amuse and others to educate or instruct. *Life*'s writing is excellent, and the photographs range from outstanding to spectacular. It is unquestionably superior to the plebeian *People*. Teachers will find many of the photographs appropriate for clipping files or classroom display. *Life* will be a decorative and worthwhile addition to collections in libraries. Recommended. (M.McK.)

Mother Jones. 1976. 10/yr. $18. Deidre English. Foundation for Natl. Progress, 1663 Mission St., San Francisco, CA

94103. Subs. to: 1886 Haymarket Sq., Marion, OH 43302. Illus., adv. Circ: 220,000. Microform: UMI.
Indexed: Acs, PAIS, PopPer, WomAb. *Bk. rev:* 1 essay plus notes, signed. *Aud:* Hs.

Mother Jones takes its name from Mary Harris Jones, a socialist and union organizer who was one of the great orators of her day. The editors of *Mother Jones* follow in her footsteps, being advocates of social and political reform. They pride themselves on their investigative reporting, and many of the feature articles are staff-written. Each issue includes three feature articles, a potpourri of short news items, and occasional fiction. Several column editors comment on various aspects of U.S. life and culture. *Mother Jones* is written in a popular, readable style, and its photography, while not meeting *Life*'s standards, is adequate. (M.McK.)

National Geographic Magazine. 1888. m. $15. Wilbur E. Garratt. Natl. Geographic Soc., 17th & M Sts. N.W., Washington, DC 20036. Illus., index, adv. Circ: 10,500,000. Vol. ends: June & Dec. Microform: UMI.
Indexed: BioI, RG. *Aud:* Ejh, Hs.

The monthly arrival of the yellow-bordered *National Geographic Magazine* has, for over a century, signalled library users and home subscribers to prepare for several hours of unparalleled armchair travel and adventure. *Geographic* authors—experts in their fields—present novel views into industrial, primitive, and scientific corners of the world as well as documenting everyday life in the United States. They offer glimpses of the distant past and the remote future. Articles that stress the need for conservation of natural resources appear frequently, their arguments strengthened by the *Geographic*'s outstanding photography. This photography provides a benchmark against which other periodicals may measure the quality and impact of their own photos. Separate maps are frequently inserted in issues. *Geographic* entertains and informs in equal parts. There is something for every reader, from the third grader struggling with the spelling of the names of foreign cities to the natural scientist struggling with a rapidly changing world. All libraries should subscribe. (M.McK.)

New York Magazine. 1968. 50/yr. $33. Edward Kosner. News Group Publns., Inc., 755 Second Ave., New York, NY 10017. Subs. to: P.O. Box 2979, Boulder, CO 80322. Illus., adv. Circ: 430,841. Vol. ends: Dec. Microform: B&H, UMI.
Indexed: BioI, RG. *Aud:* Hs.

New York Magazine is now only one of many periodicals bearing the names of large cities in the United States. It is, however, unique in its emphasis on editorial content rather than advertising. Some of its articles are aimed at a local audience, but many of them have much broader appeal. The writing is graceful and witty. The illustrations and photographs are excellent. The *New York Magazine* Competition is a favorite of those who love the twists and turns that the English language can take. "Cue New York" is an entertainment guide for New York City and surrounding areas, and includes movie, theater, music, dance, art, and restaurant listings as well as radio and television guides. (M.McK.)

The New Yorker. 1925. w. $32. William Shawn. The New Yorker, 25 W. 43rd St., New York, NY 10036. Illus., index, adv. Circ: 478,000. Microform: B&H, UMI.

Indexed: BioI, BoRv, BoRvI, RG. *Bk. rev:* 1–2 essays plus notes, signed. *Aud:* Hs.

Volumes have been written about *The New Yorker* and its editors. Each issue includes fiction, poetry, commentaries on current political events, and reports on significant social concerns. "Goings On About Town" lists and reviews, in one or two succinct sentences, visual- and performing-arts events and exhibitions at museums and libraries. In addition, there are extended theater, music, film, dance, and record reviews, with occasional commentaries on sports or fashions. The *New Yorker*'s reputation has been built on its incomparable prose and poetry and not on its graphics. Its three-column layout has not varied for many years, which is comforting for devoted readers, who always know what to expect. The weekly does represent the finest in American periodical publishing, and it publishes the best American writers. (M.McK.)

Omni. 1978. m. $24. Bob Guccione. Omni Publns., 1965 Broadway, New York, NY 10023. Illus., adv. Circ: 1,000,000. Vol. ends: Sept. Microform: B&H, UMI.

Indexed: Acs. *Aud:* Hs.

Omni offers a slick, highly visual approach to popularized science and technology, with a bow or two to the "arts." A broad variety of material is offered, both in content and presentation. Each issue contains editorials on topics of current interest, articles on new developments in science and technology, profiles of individuals, interviews, and a "Continuum" section consisting of capsule reports on topics of interest. Issues are rounded out by regular columns on books, movies, computers, humor, and other topics and by occasional photo essays. Almost all of the items are illustrated with quality photographs or artwork. *Omni* is best suited to a popular readership. (H.H.)

Parabola: the magazine of myth and tradition. 1976. q. $18. Lorraine Kisly. Parabola, 150 Fifth Ave, New York, NY 10011. Illus., adv. Circ: 16,000. Vol. ends: Fall.

Indexed: BoRvI. *Bk. rev:* 6–8, 1,000 words, signed. *Aud:* Hs.

Each issue of *Parabola* has a single theme—wholeness, exile, theft, or food—and brings together myth, folklore and religion in ancient and contemporary cultures. There are myths told by surviving natives of ancient cultures, with poetry, interviews, and fiction also included. Black-and-white photography or artwork is skillfully used to complement the text of every article. The periodical's sensitive and thoughtful attention to the study of myth and culture in ancient and modern religions makes it an important title for larger general collections. (M.McK.)

People Weekly. 1974. w. $51.50. Henry Anatole Grunwald. Time, Inc., 10880 Wilshire Blvd., Los Angeles, CA 90024. Subs. to: Time & Life Bldg., 541 N. Fairbanks Court, Chicago, IL 60611. Circ: 2,800,000. Vol. ends: June & Dec. Microform: B&H, UMI.

Indexed: BioI, RG. *Bk. rev:* 5–6 notes, signed. *Aud:* Hs.

As the title suggests, articles and photographs of well-known personalities, performers, artists, writers, politicians, and others with broad popular appeal dominate each issue of *People Weekly*. There are also profiles of ordinary people. The periodical emphasizes the positive aspects of its subjects' life-styles and practices responsible journalism. With rare exceptions, it avoids social, political, and religious controversies. *People Weekly* will be heavily used in any library that houses it, and readers will demand it. (M.McK.)

The Reader's Digest. 1922. m. $13.97. Kenneth O. Gilmore. Reader's Digest Assn., Pleasantville, NY 10570. Illus., index, adv. Circ: 18,000,000. Vol. ends: June & Dec. Microform: B&H, UMI.

Indexed: AbrRG, BioI, RG. *Aud:* Hs.

Reader's Digest is published in 16 languages in addition to large-type, braille, and talking records. Junior editions are popular in elementary and secondary schools. What other American magazine approaches this diversity in language and format? The pint-sized periodical also has a gallon-size masthead. *Reader's Digest* markets middle-American conservatism quite successfully. In its book condensations, the art, grace, and style of the originals are heavily veiled, but the abridgments are widely read. This is the only magazine that many people will read, and it will be demanded by users in libraries. Librarians should be prepared to supply the publication. (M.McK.)

Right On! 1971. m. $11.95. DS Magazines, Box 150, Burbank, CA 91503. Illus., adv. Circ: 300,000. Sample. *Aud:* Hs.

Fanzine of black stars in the television, film, record, and sports industries; the same publisher produces *Tiger Beat*. This magazine is broader in its coverage and more sophisticated in its tone than its white counterpart and emphasis falls on all entertainment leaders rather than teen idols. The excellent photographs, some color on the glossy inserts to the newsprint format, add to the reading appeal. Articles and interviews, news briefs, and fact sheets predominate; still, the grooming and beauty articles go beyond the usual fanzine limits. Little is available on black entertainment figures for any age level, and this magazine is a worthwhile addition.

Saturday Evening Post. 1971. 9/yr. $12.97. Cory SerVaas. Benjamin Franklin Literary and Medical Soc., Inc., 1100 Waterway Blvd., Indianapolis, IN 46202. Subs. to: P.O. Box 10675, Des Moines, IA 50380. Illus., adv. Circ: 757,000. Vol. ends: Dec. Microform: B&H, UMI.

Indexed: BioI, BoRvI, RG. *Aud:* Hs.

In contradiction to standard bibliographic sources which cite a beginning date of 1821, the *Post* announces on its masthead that it was founded in 1728. The revived *Post* started in 1971. Presently, it favors conservative, high-fiber life-styles, profiles Americans with spotless reputations, and includes traditional fiction. The *Post* promotes healthful living through instruction and examples. Humor and whimsy abound in the publication's fiction, cartoons, and feature articles. The magazine will appeal to those readers who hold traditional family values in high esteem. It does have a loyal readership and for that reason, ought to have a place. (M.McK.)

Saturday Review. 1924. bi-m. $16. Frank Gannon. Saturday Review, Suite 460, 214 Massachusetts Ave. N.E., Washington, DC 20002. Subs. to: P.O. Box 10010, Des Moines, IA 50340. Illus., adv. Circ: 250,000. Microform: B&H, UMI.
Indexed: AbrRG, BioI, BoRv, BoRvI, RG. *Bk. rev:* 2–5 essays; 8–18, 100–300 words, signed. *Aud:* Hs.

Since the 1960s, *Saturday Review* has undergone a number of well-publicized changes in format and editorial content. Under Norman Cousins's editorship there was more involvement with international politics and societal concerns. Now it is a general arts review. Commentaries on art, letters, music, theater, film, and television are lively and will entertain the educated reader. Providing a showcase for contemporary U.S. artists and writers, the periodical informs and educates while it amuses. In its current *persona, Saturday Review* is sophisticated, witty, and well turned out. It should be considered for any library with an interest in contemporary U.S. writing and art. (M.McK.)

Scholastic Update (Formerly: *Senior Scholastic*). 1920. bi-w/ school yr. $7.50 (Teacher's edition, $19). Eric Oatman. Scholastic, Inc., 730 Broadway, New York, NY 10003. Subs. to: P.O. Box 644, Lyndhurst, NJ 07071. Illus., adv. Circ: 211,000. Vol. ends: May. Microform: UMI.
Indexed: AbrRG, BioI, CMG, FLI, MgI, RG. *Aud:* Hs.

A perennial that continues to challenge the average and above-average student to read and think critically. Recently, single public affairs topics have been the focus of individual issues. Topics have included "Conflict and Change in Latin America," "The Free Press," and "The Drug Trade." A worthy supplement to social studies courses. (L.K.W.)

Seventeen. 1944. m. $13.95. Midge Turk Richardson. Triangle Communications, Inc., 850 Third Ave., New York, NY 10022. Subs. to: P.O. Box 100, Radnor, PA 19088. Illus., adv. Circ: 1,517,697. Vol. ends: Dec. Microform: UMI.
Indexed: AbrRG, BioI, FLI, RG. *Aud:* Ejh, Hs.

Seventeen remains the best friend of the United States' high school girls. A fresh-faced, well-behaved image—there is no sleaze here! The magazine is highly pictorial, a whirl of color. Content and ads intermingle, as do various types of presentation. Fashion and beauty are the abiding interests; recently, health, family problems and getting ready for college have been getting more attention. There is usually a short story and occasionally a nod to literature (for example, "17 Super Summer Reads"). Regular departments are "Sex and Your Body" and "In the Spotlight," an entertainment guide with interviews of stars and brief film reviews. Some of the contributions are by teens. A copy runs up to 200 pages; however the September "Back to School" issue can hit 300 pages plus. A best-selling item. (L.K.W.)

16. 1957. m. $15. Randi Reisfeld & Hedy End. Sixteen Magazine, Inc., 157 W. 57th St., New York, NY 10019. Illus., adv. Circ: 400,000. Vol. ends: Dec.
Aud: Ejh, Hs.

A fan magazine for girls aged 10 to 17, replete with pinup boys in "red-hot centerfold posters in living color." (Not that hot—and respectably clothed!) The worlds of rock and film are represented by up-and-coming stars such as Rob Lowe, Julian Lennon, and Matt Dillon. There also seems to be an effort to include Hispanic entertainers. Articles give advice on how to break into show business. Regular departments include contests and prizes, fan club lists, and movie reviews. (L.K.W.)

Smithsonian. 1970. m. $18. Don Moser. Smithsonian Assocs., 900 Jefferson Dr., Washington, DC 20560. Subs. to: P.O. Box 2953, Boulder, CO 80321. Illus., index, adv. Circ: 2,000,000. Vol. ends: Mar. Microform: UMI.
Indexed: RG. *Bk. rev:* 3–4, 600–1,000 words, signed. *Aud:* Hs.

Smithsonian is interested in everything that would interest the Smithsonian Institution itself, which consists of a mind-boggling array of subjects. Virtually any topic imaginable has a chance of appearing in *Smithsonian*, including, in recent issues, pumas, tower cranes, truckers, itinerant Indian performers, and fleas. There are eight to ten substantial articles in each issue, written for nonspecialists and containing a wealth of information. In addition, suggestions for additional reading are provided in a single section. The quality of the illustrative material is excellent. High school students should have no trouble reading and understanding most of the articles, which cover a wide variety of curriculum areas. Consequently, *Smithsonian* would be a valuable addition to high school libraries. (M.McK.)

Southern Living. 1966. m. $18. 820 Shades Creek Pkwy., Birmingham, AL 35209. Illus., adv. Circ: 2,260,000. Sample. Microform: UMI.
Indexed: RG. *Aud:* Hs.

Considering the circulation of this regional magazine, it really is closer to a general title and in the same league as, for example, *New York Magazine.* Each issue features both specific and general articles on some aspect of living in the southern states. This may range from an illustrated piece on a historical home to an overview of a current political situation. Much of the focus is on the good life, i.e., articles and features on gardening, cooking, the home, and travel. The format is as attractive as the writing is professional. If a bit bland, at least it has vast appeal, not only for those in the south, but for every part of the country. (M.McK.)

Sunset: the magazine for western living. 1898. m. $14. William Marken. Lane Publg. Co., 95 Willow Rd., Menlo Park, CA 94025. Illus., index, adv. Circ: 1,500,000. Microform: B&H, UMI.
Indexed: MgI, RG. *Aud:* Hs.

This is probably the most popular general title in the west. In advertisements, the publisher claims, and rightfully, that *Sunset* is "a travel guide, a gardener's friend, a cookbook, a handyman's helper, an arts and crafts idea source, and a practical guidebook on better living." Distributed to 13 western states (including Hawaii and Alaska), with four regional editions, this publication is tailored to the needs of readers in particular areas. The unique formula makes it possible to give sound gardening advice or news notes on building which do not jar with climate or financial conditions in a given city or community. There is a vast amount of illustrations and advertising, but it is all well balanced with sound, though usually brief, editorial material. A required item in the west, and of some interest to others who are home or travel-centered. (M.McK.)

Sunshine Magazine. 1924. m. $9. Larry Henrichs. House of Sunshine, E. Route 16, Litchfield, IL 62056. Illus. Circ: 90,000. Sample. Vol. ends: Dec.
Aud: Ejh.

The cover of each issue of *Sunshine Magazine* proclaims that it is "easy to read" and "for the whole family." The very young and the traditionally oriented elderly will, however, find it most appealing. Every issue includes fiction, poetry, personal reminiscences and children's pages. The magazine resembles *Ideals* in its cheerful portrayal of conventional life. It would be a useful addition to libraries with teenagers struggling with basic reading skills. (M.McK.)

SuperTeen. 1977. m. $12. Sterling's Magazines, Inc., 355 Lexington Ave., New York, NY 10017. Illus., adv.
Aud: Hs.

This teen fanzine has changed dramatically over the last few years and, as a result, is now one of the four top favorites (*Right On!, Tiger Beat,* and *Sixteen* are the others). Where formerly each issue focused upon one teen idol for the entire 80 pages, now there is a much broader base: Young stars from the television, film, and pop rock fields are all covered (although TV holds the majority) in pin-ups, articles, and news briefs. The newsprint format now has glossy inserts for its color photographs. More females appear here than in similar fanzines, and there is also much more self-help advice for the young teenage girl in both the media articles (Olivia Newton-John gives tips for making new friends) and in three or four separate fashion/beauty articles or columns.

Teen. 1957. m. $12.95. Roxie Cameron. Petersen Publg. Co., 8490 Sunset Blvd., Los Angeles, CA 90069. Illus., adv. Circ: 1,000,000. Vol. ends: Dec. Microform: UMI.
Indexed: Acs, RG. *Aud:* Ejh, Hs.

Right up there in popularity with the best of them, *Teen* smartly touches bases with just about all the interests of girls aged 13–18, with an occasional nod to the male population. Fashion and beauty receive the traditional treatment. Along with detailed "looking-good" instructions, readers can expect reports on the magazine's "Great Model Search" and on the "Miss Teenage America" contest. As in similar titles, every season brings a big fashion spread. Here, too, the trend is toward health-related articles. A "Celebrities" section follows the comings and goings of film, TV and rock luminaries. Features tend to be serious—for example, "Premature Parenthood," "Compulsive Eating" and "Mood

Swings." Every issue includes short fiction and poetry by teens. Regular departments offer advice on medical and personal problems and analyze horoscopes. (L.K.W.)

TeenAge. 9/yr. $12. Highwire Associates, P.O. Box 948, Lowell, MA 01853. Illus., adv. Circ: 216,000.
Aud: Hs.

Written primarily for young women from ages 14 to 18, this offers a straightforward view of teenage life. The articles, features, numerous illustrations and advertisements add up to a sensible, middle-class viewpoint. Questions covered vary from sex and beauty to cooking and careers, although there is a particular emphasis on the young woman in the professions. It is assumed most of the readers will be going on to higher education. A unique twist: a good deal of the material is written by teenagers. There are excellent interviews, although often with less than brilliant celebrities. Still, the individual comes through the publicity, and the lesson is obvious.

Teen Bag. 1977. m. $9. Lillian Smith. Lopez Publns., Inc., 21 W. 26th St., New York, NY 10010. Illus., adv.
Aud: Ejh, Hs.

Several glossy pages of color photographs interspersed with newsprint pages place the format a step above that of an all-newsprint fanzine; the targeted audience is the middle teens. There is emphasis on television idols, with a few representatives from other entertainment fields. Speculations, gossip, interviews, news items, and contests appear in a series of undistinguished articles. Far from a good magazine, but *Teen Bag* has an attractive format and an older clientele than *Tiger Beat*. Buy it if you must.

Teen Generation. 1940. bi-m. $7 (Canada). Quadrelle Publications, Inc., 621B Mt. Pleasant Rd., Toronto, Ontario M4S 2M5. Illus. Circ: 165,000. Sample.
Aud: Ejh, Hs.

Another basic Canadian magazine for young people, although not up to the quality of *Ahoy*. Perhaps "quality" is not the right descriptor in that this entry is geared for a different audience, one more bent on following current teen trends in fashion, sports, and entertainment. The *Ahoy* audience, too, tends to be a bit younger. Be that as it may, this particular title can be recommended for its good coverage of teen interests, not only in Canada, but in other parts of the globe. Particularly valuable for the solid career information and the down-to-earth advice on problems likely to bother the readers.

Teen Times. 1945. q. $4. Deb Olcott. Future Homemakers of America, 1910 Assn. Dr., Reston, VA 22091. Illus. Circ: 90,000. Vol. ends: June/July.
Aud: Hs.

Prepared for FHA/HERO (Home Economics Related Occupation) chapters in secondary schools. These chapters, incidentally, have both male and female members, and the magazine reflects this fact. Articles on project ideas, outstanding youth leaders, family life, vocational preparation and so on, discuss opinions and observations about issues affecting teens in general. (L.K.W.)

T.G. (Formerly: *Today's Generation*). 1940. 6/yr. $7.50. Donna Douglas & Stoney McCart. 621 B Mt. Pleasant Rd., Toronto, Ont. M4S2 M5, Canada. Illus., adv. Circ: 163,000. Vol. ends: Nov/Dec.

Aud: Hs.

This title for English-speaking Canadian high schoolers is a cross between a classroom magazine and a fan magazine. Despite its generous coverage of beauty and fashion, *T.G.* is not entirely female-oriented. Guided by an advisory board of students and teachers, the magazine tackles a vast array of adolescent concerns in its 40 pages: pop and rock, cars, nuclear war, friendship, and suicide. Articles are well written with an "up-front" style. The young adult career section in which entire industries are surveyed (computers, health, transportation, construction) is exemplary. (L.K.W.)

Tiger Beat. 1967. m. $9.95. DS Magazines Inc., Box 150, Burbank, CA 91503. Illus., adv. Circ: 360,000.

Aud: Ejh, Hs.

Directed to the young teenager, this covers the worlds of movies, television, music and just about anything else of interest to the reader. There are numerous color photographs, as well as black-and-white illustrations of the stars. As might be expected, the interviews and articles tend to be more fictional than real, but they sound inspirational and there is nothing anyone can object to in a dream. Of particular interest is the focus on the teen star.

Town and Country. 1846. m. $24. Frank Zachary. The Hearst Corp., 959 Eighth Ave., New York, NY 10019. Subs. to: P.O. Box 10082, Des Moines, IA 50340. Illus., adv. Circ: 284,000. Microform: B&H, UMI.

Indexed: Acs. *Aud:* Hs.

Town and Country caters to the conspicuously rich, reports on their social and business activities, and suggests better and faster ways to spend money. Its essays are lengthy and informative and its photography is splendid. Upwardly mobile readers would be served as well by *Vanity Fair.* (M.McK.)

Treasure. 1970. m. $18. Jim Williams, Jess Publg. Co., Inc., 6280 Adobe Rd., Twentynine Palms, CA 92277. Illus., adv. Circ: 36,000. Sample.

Aud: Hs.

Anyone of any age or background looking for treasure will find information here to brighten the day and the prospects of actually locating something. Most of the illustrated articles are held within the scope and financial resources of an individual, usually with a metal detector or with prospecting abilities. There are more ambitious, but for the most part historical, pieces on deep-sea treasure hunting. At the other extreme is advice on how to value a bottle one may find in an abandoned dump. In addition to all the how-to-do-it data, there is information on activities of individual treasure hunters. The same publisher issues a related title:

Treasure Search. 1973. bi-m. $9.50. Circ: 22,000. This provides maps of where treasure may be found. The hints are based on past experience, history, and information from readers. Also, there are fine equipment reviews. (M.McK.)

Tú. See Latin America, Latino (U.S.)/For the Student: Latin America Section.

Vanity Fair. 1983. m. $12. Tina Brown. Condé Nast Publns., 350 Madison Ave., New York, NY 10017. Subs. to: P.O. Box 5229, Boulder, CO 80322. Illus., adv. Circ: 259,753. Vol. ends: Dec.

Bk. rev: 1–3, 800–1,200 words, signed. *Aud:* Hs.

The new *Vanity Fair* assumes the title and volume numbering of an earlier title. Splendidly written, the reincarnated monthly is a pleasure to read and reread. But then, with writers like Styron, Updike, and Didion, it ought to be. The photography is equally impressive. Feature articles may cover publishing, writers, travel, personalities, food, fashion, and other aspects of an expensive, sophisticated life-style. The East Coast Liberal Establishment will be most pleased with *Vanity Fair*'s editorial viewpoint, but its serious articles are genuinely thoughtful and its playful ones, amusing and sometimes outrageous. Brief commentaries on the contemporary social, fashion, or political scene are interspersed with posed or candid snapshots of celebrities in an umbrella feature called "Vanities." Film, theater, television, book, and other arts reviews appear in "Arts Fair." (M.McK.)

The Village Voice. 1955. w. $32.76. David Schneiderman. 842 Broadway, New York, NY 10003. Subs. to: P.O. Box 1905, Marion, OH 43302. Illus., adv. Circ: 150,000. Microform: UMI.

Indexed: Acs, BoRvI. *Bk. rev:* 5–8, essays, signed. *Aud:* Hs.

The Village Voice, a newsprint tabloid, exposes scandals in all aspects of U.S. society and reports on controversial issues. Its feature articles are long and carefully constructed, with in-depth coverage of the visual and performing arts in New York City. There are reviews of serious and popular music, books, and art. The writing in *The Village Voice* is excellent, including some sizzling reviews. Libraries with large general collections should acquire the newspaper as should libraries with collections in the arts and humanities. (M.McK.)

World Press Review: news and views from the foreign press (Formerly: *Atlas: world press review*). 1961. m. $19.95. Alfred Balk. World Press Review, 230 Park Ave., New York, NY 10169. Subs. to: P.O. Box 915, Farmingdale, NY 11737. Illus., index, adv. Circ: 100,000. Vol. ends: Dec. Microform: UMI.

Indexed: BioI, PAIS, SocSc. *Aud:* Hs.

World Press Review reprints or excerpts feature stories from foreign newspapers and magazines, many of which are English-language publications. News from Europe, Latin America, Asia/Pacific, the Middle East, and Moscow appears in several columns according to topic. Foreign opinions of U.S. political events or major political figures are regularly featured. "Letters to the Editor," cultural events, cartoons, and the usual columns one would expect to find in a general editorial magazine are excerpted from the foreign press. This is a useful publication for high schools since it covers current events in foreign countries, reporting that is not readily available in other sources. It also presents foreign perspectives on U.S. events. (M.McK.)

YM (Formerly: *Young Miss*). 1953. 10/yr. $14. Phyllis Schneider. Gruner & Jahr U.S.A. Publg., 685 Third Ave., New York, NY 10017. Subs. to: P.O. Box 3060, Harlan, IA 51593. Illus., adv. Circ: 700,000. Vol. ends: Dec. Microform: UMI.
Indexed: CMG. *Aud:* Ejh, Hs.

YM aims to attract an older crowd of teenage girls than its predecessor. Nifty in appearance, it is full of the latest ideas in beauty, fashion, food, and entertainment. *YM* asks to be taken seriously. Each issue contains major articles such as "Waiting for a Chance to Live," about a 19-year-old who needs a heart transplant, and "Children of Alcoholics." With a concentration on literary pursuits, a fiction and poetry section showcases the talent of teens. Regular departments and numerous contests invite reader participation. A bright addition to the field. (L.K.W.)

For the Professional

Ideals. 1944. 8/yr. $15.95. Kathleen S. Pohl. Ideals, 11315 Watertown Plank Rd., Milwaukee, WI 53226. Illus. Circ: 274,000. Vol. ends: Nov. Microform: UMI.
Aud: Pr.

Each issue of *Ideals* is filled with poetry, photography, artwork, recipes, and inspirational articles related to a single theme, such as U.S. independence, Mother's Day, or Christmas. Traditional values are celebrated, and readers will find *Ideals* reminiscent of an earlier time in U.S. culture and life. Teachers in elementary schools will be able to use its poetry and photographs to supplement textbooks and to create bulletin board displays. (M.McK.)

GENERAL SCIENCE

For the Student/For the Professional

Sharon W. Schwerzel, Science-Technology Librarian, Strozier Library, Florida State University, Tallahassee, FL 32306

Jean K. Sheviak, Serials Librarian, Rensselaer Polytechnic Institute, Troy, NY 12180

Charles R. Smith, Humanities and Reference Librarian, Texas A&M University Libraries, College Station, TX 77843

Allen Wynne, Librarian, Mathematics-Physics Branch, University Libraries, Campus Box 184, University of Colorado, Boulder, CO 80309

Introduction

The publications in this section generally encompass more than one branch of science. The journals range from popular titles to those magazines offering material to science teachers. Highly technical periodicals have been omitted.

Basic Periodicals

Ejh: *Discover, Ranger Rick, Science World*; Hs: *Discover, Natural History, Physics Today*; Pr: *American Biology Teacher, American Journal of Physics, Physics Teacher.*

Basic Abstracts and Indexes

General Science Index.

For the Student

Animal Kingdom. 1898. bi-m. $10. Eugene Walter, Jr. New York Zoological Soc., Bronx, NY 10460. Illus., adv. Circ: 130,000. Sample. Microform: B&H.
Bk. rev: Various number, length. *Aud:* Hs.

A popular approach to animals by the experts at the New York Zoological Society, this publication covers everything from common zoo animals to not so common fish. The well-illustrated articles are written for the layperson. An effort is made to make them as lively as they are easy to understand. In a year the authors will have moved from reports on animal behavior to articles on conservation and anthropology. (C.R.S.)

Appraisal: science books for young people. See Books and Book Reviews/For the Student Section.

Biology Digest. 1974. m. (Sept.-May). $89. Mary Suzanne Hogan. Plexus Publg., Inc., 143 Old Marlton Pike, Medford, NJ 08055. Illus., index. Vol. ends: May. Microform: B&H.
Bk. rev: 3, 300–500 words. *Aud:* Hs.

Biology Digest selectively abstracts articles from about 200 periodicals, many of them technical, ranging from *Journal of Immunopharmacology* through *Psychology Today* to *Illinois Wildlife*. Articles chosen present "significant new information relevant to the biological sciences" and are appropriate for students and educators at the secondary and undergraduate levels. About 400 abstracts of up to 325 words appear in each issue, and these are organized into several sections: "Viruses, Microflora, and Plants," "Animal Kingdom," "The Human Organism," "Infectious Diseases," "Population and Health," "Cell Biology and Biogenesis," "Environmental Quality," and "General Topics." Also included is a feature article on some area of biological research, several book reviews, and author and key word indexes. A cumulative index is published for each volume and must be ordered separately ($19.50). *Biology Digest* will supply copies of most of the articles abstracted for a small fee. This is a good tool for keeping abreast of the biological literature. It is well done and an excellent choice for high school libraries. (J.K.S.)

Contemporary Physics: a review of physics and associated technologies. 1959. bi-m. $184. J. S. Dugdale. Taylor & Francis, 4 John St., London WC1N 2ET, England. Illus., index, adv. Sample. Vol. ends: Dec. Refereed.
Bk. rev: 16–20, 200–300 words, signed. *Aud:* Hs.

This journal is for both nonspecialists and students (advanced senior high). The periodical supplies interpretive survey-type articles contributed by known authorities, broadly encompassing not only the major fields of physics but also new technologies utilizing physical principles. Its scope passes far beyond the traditional limits of the discipline. Language is kept relatively unsophisticated to best serve the intended audience, but some technical knowledge is necessary. About three or four articles appear in each issue. Some issues also carry essay-type book reviews, which further act as tutorials in specific fields. Other, shorter reviews of books are included in each issue, plus notices of other books received. (A.W.)

Current Science. 1927. bi-w. 18/yr. $9.90 (10 or more, $4.95). Vincent Marteka. Xerox Education Publns., 4343 Equity Dr., Columbus, OH 43228. Illus., index. Circ: 406,236. Sample. Vol. ends: May.

Aud: Ejh.

Intended for grades 6–10, this biweekly covers most of the latest advances in science and technology. Each issue includes articles covering subjects in the life, health, physical and earth sciences. The lead article is an attention-getting, believe-it-or-not-type article, such as "Spider Eats Bird." Regular departments include "Science News Briefs," and such activities as Science Trivia games and quizzes on particular articles. Illustrations and photos in black and white and color supplement the lucidly written, informative text. The teacher's edition offers questions for discussion, pages that can be reproduced, and exercises for developing skills in critical thinking. This magazine is available in braille. (L.K.O.)

Discover. 1980. m. $24. Henry A. Grunwald. Time, Inc., Time-Life Bldg., 541 N. Fairbanks Court, Chicago, IL 60672. Illus., adv. Circ: 850,000. Vol. ends: Dec. Microform: B&H, MCR, UMI.

Indexed: GSI, RG. *Aud:* Ejh, Hs.

This popular science journal is readable by the junior high and high school student as well as by the general public. Aimed at the nonscientific community and interested layperson, the format follows other Time-Life magazines and is highly recommended for all collections. Available in braille from Talking Book Record. (S.W.S.)

Dolphin Log. 1982. q. $10. Pamela Stacey. The Cousteau Soc., Inc., 8430 Santa Monica Blvd., Los Angeles, CA 90069. Illus. Sample. Vol. ends: Dec.

Aud: Ejh, Hs.

Science and nature activities and articles relating to the sea and its creatures are highlighted in this authoritative magazine. Full-color illustrations and photographs, printed on glossy paper, supplement the informative articles. Regular departments are: "News from Calypso," "Creature Feature," and current "Nature News." Also available with a family membership contribution to the Cousteau Society. (L.K.O.)

Endeavour. 1942. (n.s., 1977). q. $40. Trevor I. Williams. Pergamon Press, Inc., Maxwell House, Fairview Park, Elmsford, NY 10523. Illus., index, adv. Circ: 10,000. Vol. ends: No. 4. Microform: MIM, UMI.

Bk. rev: 20–25, 200–300 words, signed. *Aud:* Hs.

Published by Imperial Chemical Industries from its beginnings until Pergamon Press took over publishing responsibility in 1977. Most articles are commissioned to be a "review of the progress of science and technology in the service of mankind." Well-illustrated short articles cover every science and are paced to a wide audience in terms of interest and level of sophistication. A good balance between different disciplines is maintained in each issue. Recommended for high school libraries. (C.R.S.)

Faces. 1983. 10/yr. $16.50. Cobblestone Publishing Inc., 20 Grove St., Peterborough, NH 03458. Illus.

Indexed: CMG. *Aud:* Ejh, Hs.

The publishers of *Cobblestone* join forces with the American Museum of Natural History in New York to introduce young people to the fascination of natural history and anthropology. There are some 8 to 10 articles in each well-illustrated number. Some issues concentrate on a particular subject, but the majority are content to examine the ways of people in all ages, places and conditions. Numerous projects for children are scattered throughout the magazine. It's the type of title which may be enjoyed almost as much by adults as by younger people.

Impact of Science on Society. See Cultural-Social Studies/For the Student Section.

Mosaic (Washington). 1970. bi-m. $16. Warren Kornberg. Natl. Science Foundation, 1800 G St. N.W., Washington, DC 20550. Illus. Circ: 13,000. Vol. ends: No. 6. Microform: MCA, UMI.

Indexed: IGov. *Aud:* Hs.

The National Science Foundation source for informing the general public and the scientific and educational communities. The clear, nontechnical language and the explanatory illustrations will allow lay persons as well as scientists in unrelated fields to keep abreast of the frontiers of research in a wide range of scientific disciplines. (C.R.S.)

Natural History. 1900. m. $18. Alan Ternes. Amer. Museum of Natural History, Central Park W. at 79th St., New York, NY 10024. Illus., index, adv. Circ: 450,000. Vol. ends: Dec. Microform: MIM, UMI.

Indexed: RG. *Bk. rev:* 1, 1,000 words, signed. *Aud:* Hs.

Extremely good photographs and popular writing style and format make *Natural History* a useful addition to collections of conservation, anthropology, geography, and astronomy—almost anything of interest to the nature lover. The articles are authoritative and are written by experts who have conducted the fieldwork and research projects. Recommended. (C.R.S.)

Orion: nature quarterly. 1982. q. $10. M. Gilliam & George Russell. Myrin Inst., 136 E. 64th St., New York, NY 10021. Illus.

Bk. rev: 15–20, 250 words, signed. *Aud:* Hs.

What does one expect to find in yet another general nature magazine? *Orion* offers about three to four articles (for example, one on moral theory and treatment of animals, a second on urban violence, and a third by Laurens van der Post from a 1976 talk). In addition, there are 15 to 20 well-written book reviews. The writing style is clear, the black-and-white illustrations good, and the 60 or so pages quite suitable for teenagers. The idea of this magazine, according to the editor, is to stress how nature enriches and renews our lives. The authors and reviewers stick to the editorial command. The subscription price is reasonable. If you want another natural history magazine, this is a good bet. It might pay, though, to see how it develops; in any case, ask for a sample copy. (C.R.S.)

Physics Today. 1948. m. $56. Gloria B. Lubkin. Amer. Inst. of Physics, 335 E. 45th St., New York, NY 10017. Illus., index, adv. Circ: 71,453. Sample. Vol. ends: Dec. Refereed. Microform: Pub, UMI. Reprint: Pub.

Bk. rev: 3–5, 300–500 words, signed. *Aud:* Hs.

Informative, interpretive, and authoritative, this periodical is, probably, the best single choice for a generalized treatment of physics at this level. Well-written articles by specialists review physics research; its applications to other fields; its philosophy and history; trends in education, government, industry; and problems of the profession. Features may be scholarly and technical or informal and nontechnical, depending on the given subject matter. Regularly featured sections serve as a news medium for physicists—detailed reports of technical meetings, activities of the American Physical Society, personalia, and calendars. A section offering good book reviews and a checklist of new books received provides a fertile area for librarians selecting physics titles. Highly recommended for any high school library that would like to acquire more than a general science periodical. (A.W.)

Ranger Rick. 1967. m. $12. Trudy Farrand. Natl. Wildlife Federation, 1412 16th St. N.W., Washington, DC 20036. Illus. Circ: 710,000. Sample. Vol. ends: Dec.

Aud: Ejh.

This magazine comes with membership in the Ranger Rick Nature Club. It is designed to give children ages 6–12 a program of activities and information that will help them learn about wildlife and about the environment. More than half of the pages is given to pictorial matter. Stunning full-color photographs and illustrations of fish, fowl, insects, and mammals on high-gloss stock supplement the lucidly written material—stories about other children, science features, and projects; and clever word games, jokes, mazes, and puzzles. Special issues, once or twice a year, concentrate on a part of the world (e.g., tropical islands). Highly recommended. (L.K.O.)

Science Books and Films. See Books and Book Reviews/For the Professional Section.

Science Challenge. See under *Curriculum Innovations* in Education/For the Student Section.

Science Dimensions. See Free Magazine/For the Student Section.

Science for the People. See Alternatives/For the Student Section.

Scienceland. 1977. 8/yr. $11.95 (Student ed.); $24 (Deluxe ed.). A. H. Matano. Scienceland, Inc., 501 Fifth Ave., Suite 2102, New York, NY 10017. Illus. Sample. Vol. ends: May. *Aud:* Ejh.

Intended for children in the kindergarten and primary grades, the intent of *Scienceland* is "to nurture scientific thinking." The 8½- by 11¾-inch glossy pages are filled with excellently detailed full-color illustrations on a given theme, such as "Let's Compare" (animal sizes and shapes). Each issue includes a one-page vocabulary, providing definitions and pronunciations, and a one-page pictorial quiz on the contents. Thought-provoking questions to the reader are interspersed with the easy-to-read factual information. (L.K.O.)

Science News. 1921. w. $29.50. Joel Greenberg. Science Service, Inc. Subs. to: 231 W. Center St., Marion, OH 43305. Illus., index, adv. Circ: 165,000. Sample. Vol. ends: Dec. Microform: B&H, MIM, UMI.

Indexed: GSI, RG. *Aud:* Ejh, Hs.

This publication has offered popularizations of scientific developments since its original introduction as *Science News Letter*. Currently, the periodical concentrates on short announcements and interpretations of scientific developments for the week, as gleaned from research journals, symposia, interviews, and so forth. All fields of science are covered. Contributions are written mostly by staff editors. Facts are well documented, and the prose is readable and appropriately illustrated. Two indexes per year facilitate fact finding. Recommended for any type of library seeking quick, popularized and international news coverage in science and technology. (C.R.S.)

Science World. 18/yr. $8. Scholastic, Inc., 730 Broadway, New York, NY 10003. Illus., adv. Sample.

Indexed: CMG. *Aud:* Ejh.

Primarily for students in grades 4 to 6, but some of the material is suitable for older children. Each 20 or so page issue includes good photographs and coverage of events over the past two weeks. The writing style is as lively as the format, and an effort is made not only to discuss current issues, but to give good background material on basic scientific laws and experiments. It is a second choice to its rival *Current Science* for one reason only—it usually carries advertising, which is out-of-place.

Scientific American. 1845. m. $24. Jonathan Piel. Scientific Amer., Inc., 415 Madison Ave., New York, NY 10017. Illus., index, adv. Circ: 635,131. Sample. Vol. ends: Dec. Refereed. Microform: B&H, MIM, UMI.

Bk. rev: 4, 1,000 words, signed. *Aud:* Hs.

Needing little introduction to the library world, the magazine has been interpreting scientific and technological advances and theories to lay people for well over 125 years. It is by far the best general science publication available. Articles vary in sophistication, and experts have stated that some of the more cogent reviews in their own fields have been published here. The general reader, however, will be able to find material written at his or her level and directed toward his or her interests, ranging from research in prehistory to the latest developments in energy. The quality is high, and the contributors are distinguished specialists from both academia and industry. Each issue contains a carefully balanced selection from the physical, life, and behavioral sciences; many articles are beautifully illustrated. Special departments such as mathematical games and home-style experiments invite reader participation. Also, a review section briefly reports on research developments gleaned from the more specialized journals. (C.R.S.)

3-2-1 Contact. 1979. 10/yr. $10.95. Jonathan Rosenbloom. Children's Television Workshop, One Lincoln Pl., New York, NY 10023. Illus. Circ: 300,000. Sample. Vol. ends: Dec. *Aud:* Ejh.

Contact specializes in science and technology and is intended for the 8–14 age group. Printed on glossy paper, issues are filled with informative articles, puzzles, projects, experiments, questions and answers, and a serialized science mystery starring "The Bloodhound Gang." The feature articles cover a variety of subjects from animal training to kidney transplants. The layout is inviting and the many excellent full-color illustrations and photographs supplement a thoughtfully conceived magazine. (L.K.O.)

Your Big Backyard. 1980. m. $8.50. Sallie A. Luther. Natl. Wildlife Federation, 1412 16th St. N.W., Washington, DC 20036. Illus. Circ: 200,000. Sample. Vol. ends: Dec. *Aud:* Ejh.

Developed to help preschool children ages 3–5 to learn about the world of nature, the pages are highlighted by splendid color photographs of animals and wildlife, superb in detail. Each issue is designed "to help children start . . . toward beginning reading." The text is printed in large type and carefully placed on each page. The "Read to Me" story, the poems, puzzles, games, and projects can easily be completed with help from adults. A letter to parents, included in each issue, offers ideas and suggestions on how to fully utilize the magazine with children. Highly recommended. (L.K.O.)

For the Professional

American Biology Teacher. 1938. 8/yr. $35. John R. Jungck. Natl. Assn. of Biology Teachers, 11250 Roger Bacon Dr., Reston, VA 22090. Illus., adv. Circ: 11,300. Vol. ends: Dec. Refereed. Microform: UMI.
Indexed: CIJE, EdI, GSI. *Bk. rev:* 7–11, 300–800 words, signed. *Aud:* Pr.

This publication of the National Association of Biology Teachers is aimed at biology teachers of middle school, high school, and beginning undergraduate students. Articles are written by scientists and teachers, and those in each issue's "How-to-do-it" section give suggestions on teaching methods and tools. Others describe natural history phenomena or current research. Book reviews are accompanied by five or six signed reviews of audiovisual materials appropriate for classroom use. Useful articles from other journals are

discussed in the "Research Reviews" section. Each issue also includes one article on computer applications. Basic for junior and high school libraries. (J.K.S.)

American Journal of Physics (Formerly: *American Physics Teacher*). 1933. m. $104. John S. Rigden. Amer. Inst. of Physics, 335 E. 45th St., New York, NY 10017. Illus., index. Circ: 9,660. Sample. Vol. ends: Dec. Refereed. Microform: Pub, UMI. Reprint: Pub.
Bk. rev: 3–4, 600–800 words, signed. *Aud:* Pr.

The primary readers of this journal are those persons teaching physics at the secondary school level. As an official publication of the American Association of Physics Teachers, it is "devoted to the instructional and cultural aspects of physical science." The journal encourages "expository style contributions on any physics-related topic which will significantly aid the process of understanding or learning physics." Papers treating historical/philosophical and cultural subjects of interest to the physics community or having "novel instructional methods in the classroom or laboratory" are welcomed. The level of writing is aimed at the generalist, omitting highly mathematical or specialized presentations, making most papers appropriate reading for students. The book reviews, which appear in each issue, are lengthy, informative, and well written. Audiovisual materials are also reviewed. This journal is so closely geared to undergraduate teaching needs that it is highly recommended for any academic library. (For another excellent publication by the American Association of Physics Teachers, see *Physics Teacher*, below in this section.)

BioScience (Formerly: *AIBS Bulletin*). 1950. m. $52. Ellen W. Chu. Amer. Inst. of Biological Sciences, 1401 Wilson Blvd., Arlington, VA 22209. Illus., index, adv. Circ: 18,000. Vol. ends: Dec. Refereed. Microform: UMI.
Indexed: BioAg, CIJE, MgI, RG. *Bk. rev:* 9–10, 450–800 words, signed. *Aud:* Pr.

The official publication of the American Institute of Biological Sciences, *BioScience* covers the entire range of current topics in biology and is suitable for both specialists and general audiences. Included are several articles averaging four to eight pages (up to 5,000 words), features and news, and editorials. "The Biologist's Toolbox" report includes equipment and computer software descriptions and reviews, and a special book issue is published once a year. *BioScience* is an important source for job announcements. For researchers, students, and many teachers wanting to keep up with developments in biology. (J.K.S.)

Education in Chemistry. 1963. bi-m. $87. Michael Withers. The Royal Soc. of Chemistry, Burlington House, London W1V 0BN, England. Illus., index, adv. Circ: 6,000. Vol. ends: Dec. Microform: UMI.
Indexed: ChemAb. *Bk. rev:* 5–6, 300–500 words, signed. *Aud:* Pr.

Short articles written by practicing teachers in high school and college on practical chemistry, experiments, biographies, and designing software. News on recent awards, interviews, a section on new products, and meeting notices are also included in each issue. On a par with the *Journal of Chemical Education*, the journal is important for high school collections. (S.W.S.)

Journal of Chemical Education. 1924. m. $40. J. J. Lagowski. Amer. Chemical Soc., Div. of Chemical Education, 1155 16th St. N.W., Washington, DC 20036. Illus., index, adv. Circ: 25,000. Sample. Vol. ends: Dec. Refereed. Microform: UMI.
Indexed: BioAb, ChemAb, CurrCont, EdI, GSI, SCI. *Bk. rev:* 5, 300–400 words, signed. *Aud:* Pr.

Written for teachers and high school students, the articles cover all aspects of chemistry. Included are laboratory experiments, demonstrations, methodology, problems in teaching, history, and safety tips. Software, new instruments and products, and chemicals are reviewed. For all high school libraries. (S.W.S.)

Mosaic (Washington). 1970. bi-m. $16. Warren Kornberg. Natl. Science Foundation, 1800 G St. N.W., Washington, DC 20550. Illus. Circ: 13,000. Vol. ends: No. 6. Microform: MCA, UMI.
Indexed: IGov. *Aud:* Pr.

The National Science Foundation source for informing the general public and the scientific and educational communities. The clear, nontechnical language and the explanatory illustrations will allow lay persons to keep abreast of the frontiers of research in a wide range of scientific disciplines. For libraries interested in NSF works and an overview of U.S. research efforts.

Naturescope. 1984. 10/yr. $18. Judy Braus. Natl. Wildlife Federation, 1412 16th St. N.W., Washington, DC 20036. Illus. Sample. Vol. ends: June.
Aud: Pr.

This magazine is a unique activity series for teachers, parents, nature centers, and youth leaders of children ages 3–13. Each issue features a nature subject, such as astronomy, birds, volcanoes, or dinosaurs, and is divided into sections beginning with preschool activities and ending with advanced activities. The objectives, materials, age levels, and subjects are highlighted in the left-hand margin for each reference. Included are fascinating facts and fun activities: games, puzzles, pictures, stories, songs, crafts and a complete minicourse on the subject, plus questions and answers to reinforce learning and a glossary of terms. The "Copycat Pages," which may be reproduced, contain games, puzzles, worksheets, and mazes. Clear, detailed illustrations in black and white with one other color are printed on heavy stock paper. Issues may be preserved to start or reinforce a nature and science library. Highly recommended. (L.K.O.)

Physics Education. 1966. 6/yr. $70. E. Deeson. Inst. of Physics, 47 Belgrave Sq., London SW1X 8QX, England. Subs. to: Amer. Inst. of Physics, 335 E. 45th St., New York, NY 10017. Illus., index, adv. Circ: 3,200. Sample. Vol. ends: Dec. Refereed. Microform: Pub.
Bk. rev: 15–20, 100–500 words, signed. *Aud:* Pr.

Stressing pedagogy and education at the high school and undergraduate levels, the publication is in part the British counterpart to the *American Journal of Physics* (see above in this section). Fifteen to 20 articles per issue touch on new advances in physics, teaching techniques, laboratory demonstrations, notes on experiments, small pieces on physics apparatus, reports of technical conferences, and a variety of news bits. The information sections and conference news relate to education in the United Kingdom, yet the tutorials and teaching principles are universal in application. The title is recommended for any high school library seeking another publication with a focus on education. (A.W.)

Physics Teacher. 1963. 9/yr. $52. Donald Kirwan. Amer. Assn. of Physics Teachers, Dept. of Physics and Astronomy, Univ. of Maryland, College Park, MD 20740. Illus., index, adv. Circ: 8,675. Vol. ends: Dec. Refereed. Microform: Pub, UMI. Reprints: Pub.
Indexed: EdI. *Bk. rev:* 9, 150–300 words, signed. *Aud:* Pr.

This journal is another respected publication of the American Association of Physics Teachers (see also the *American Journal of Physics*, above in this section). The *Physics Teacher* is "dedicated to the strengthening of the teaching of introductory physics at all levels." Although particularly commendable for those instructing at the high school level, it is also useful in junior colleges and undergraduate university curricula. Three to four features in each issue blend authoritative essays on current topics in physics and interviews with scientists on current trends in science education, evaluation of curricula, and other problems of the educator. Brief communications on classroom techniques, laboratory demonstrations, new equipment and tips on improving apparatus are regularly published. The book review section includes evaluation of films and other audiovisual materials. This periodical is highly recommended for any library supporting physics instruction at a beginning level. (A.W.)

School Science and Mathematics. 1901. 8/yr. $22 (Members, $19). Gary G. Bitter. Subs. to: Executive Office, 126 Life Science Bldg., Bowling Green State Univ., Bowling Green, OH 43403. Illus., index, adv. Circ: 4,000. Vol. ends: May. Microform: UMI.
Indexed: CIJE, EdI. *Bk. rev:* 5–6, 75–100 words, signed. *Aud:* Pr.

Articles on the teaching of math and science at both the elementary and secondary school levels are presented in this official journal of the School Science and Mathematics Association. Although short research-study articles do appear, the main thrust of the journal is the presentation of practical methods for teaching, and even the research studies have direct classroom applications. Other regular features include a software review section and a "problem department," where readers can exchange interesting mathematical problems and their solutions. Most of the articles are written by higher education faculty in the sciences and math. This is a good title for math and science teachers looking for creative, thought-provoking teaching material. (P.S.B.)

Science Activities. 1969. q. $30. David P. Butts. Helen Dwight Reid Educational Foundation. Heldref Publns., 4000 Albemarle St. N.W., Washington, DC 20016. Illus., index, adv. Circ: 1,100. Vol. ends: No. 4. Refereed. Microform: Pub, UMI.

Indexed: CIJE, EdI, MRD. *Bk. rev:* 4–5, 200–500 words, signed. *Aud:* Pr.

Written for the science teacher, articles are a source of experiments, explorations, and projects for all levels of students. Includes a news column and a classroom aids department, which covers computer hardware and software, classroom aids, and audiovisual materials. A good source of new ideas for the classroom teacher. (S.W.S.)

Science and Children. 1963. 8/yr. $42 (Individuals, $32). Phyllis R. Marcuccio. Natl. Science Teachers Assn., 1742 Connecticut Ave. N.W., Washington, DC 20009. Illus., index, adv. Sample. Vol. ends: May. Microform: UMI.

Indexed: CIJE, EdI. *Bk. rev:* 8–12, 50–100 words, signed. *Aud:* Pr.

A carefully edited, well-illustrated magazine for use by the science teacher in the elementary grades, including junior high school. Articles, usually by teachers, cover various methods of making science a living subject for students. Considerable emphasis in the 8 to 12 articles is on practical and tested methods. Concentration is on astronomy, biology, chemistry, earth sciences, and physics. Other items consider reports from the supporting organization, notes and articles on education, and so forth. The regular features include reviews not only of new books but also of audiovisual materials and scientific kits. This is the basic magazine of its type, and it should be found in all teacher collections in elementary and junior high school libraries. (C.R.S.)

The Science Teacher. 1934. 9/yr. $42. Juliana Texley. Natl. Science Teachers Assn., 1742 Connecticut Ave. N.W., Washington, DC 20009. Illus., index, adv. Circ: 22,000. Vol. ends: May. Microform: UMI.

Indexed: CIJE, EdI. *Bk. rev:* 8–10, 50–100 words, signed. *Aud:* Pr.

Articles are on methods of teaching science in high school and for the most part are written by high school teachers. Other columns and features concentrate on the activities of individuals and the association. Reviews of software, audiovisual materials, and teaching aids are an important feature. (S.W.S.)

Technology Review. 1899. 8/yr. $27. John J. Mattill. Massachusetts Inst. of Technology. Subs. to: Massachusetts Inst. of Technology, Rm. 10–140, Cambridge, MA 02139. Illus., index, adv. Circ: 75,000. Sample. Vol. ends: Nov/Dec. Microform: UMI.

Indexed: PAIS. *Bk. rev:* 3–4, 500–800 words, signed. *Aud:* Pr.

Although published by the Alumni Association of the Massachusetts Institute of Technology, with special editions for its students, this publication will find wide appeal to professionals and the interested general public. The magazine reports changes in technology (science, engineering, architecture, planning, and the related social sciences) and its impact on our culture. Feature articles are written on a layperson's level and are by distinguished contributors. The interesting content of high quality and the good format recommend *Technology Review* for medium to large libraries. (C.R.S.)

GEOGRAPHY

For the Student/For the Professional

Douglas A. DeLong, Acquisitions Librarian, Milner Library, Illinois State University, Normal, IL 61761

Introduction

Geography is a multifaceted discipline that concerns itself with humankind's place in the environment (human geography) as well as with the environment itself (physical geography). The results of geographical investigations can be found in many of the magazines included here. Both popular magazines and scholarly journals have been reviewed. Additional titles can be found in the fourth edition, 1980, of the *Annotated World List of Selected Current Geographical Serials*, by Chauncy D. Harris (available for $8 from the Department of Geography, University of Chicago).

Basic Periodicals

Ejh: *National Geographic World;* Hs: *Canadian Geographic, Focus, Geographical Magazine.*

For the Student

Canadian Geographic (Formerly: *Canadian Geographical Journal*). 1930. bi-m. Membership, $22. Ross W. Smith. Royal Canadian Geographical Soc., 488 Wilbrod St., Ottawa, Ont. K1N 6M8, Canada. Illus., adv. Vol. ends: Dec/Jan.

Indexed: CanI, SocSc. *Bk. rev:* 4–6, 400–600 words, signed. *Aud:* Hs.

With the desire of "making Canada better known to Canadians and to the world," this magazine beautifully covers the geography of Canada. Fully illustrated articles and photo-essays explore all aspects of Canadian physical geography. While the emphasis is on the current scene, historical subjects—like the recent centennial of Canadian national parks—are also explored. Most issues also have at least one article on Canada's renewable resources, such as Canada's fishing industry. For all Canadian libraries and U.S. libraries along the border, plus other libraries with an interest in geography or Canadian studies.

Focus. 1950. q. $10. Janet Crane. American Geographical Soc., 156 Fifth Ave., Suite 600, New York, NY 10010. Illus. Circ: 3,500. Vol. ends: Oct. Microform: UMI.

Indexed: RG. *Aud:* Ejh, Hs.

This publication, formerly devoted to popular but thorough analyses of one country, region or area, underwent a drastic change in 1985. It is now a mainly color quarterly, with four articles in each issue. Those articles, each with several large pictures and maps, are an attempt to "put the knowledge and experience of geographers, and those with affinities to geography, in a readily available format." There is a natural tendency to compare *Focus* with *The National Geographic Magazine*. Articles are shorter and are written by professional geographers, but are more specific and more objective. A good source of geographical information written by professional geographers, but for the general public.

Geographical Magazine. 1935. m. $35. Ian Bain. Magnum Dist. Ltd., Watling St., Milton Keynes MK2 2BW, England. Illus., adv. Circ: 62,800. Vol. ends: Dec. Microform: W.
Indexed: SocSc. *Bk. rev:* 4–6, 300–350 words, signed. *Aud:* Hs.

A popular British geographical magazine, with articles of interest to the general reader. While the emphasis is on Britain and the Commonwealth areas, other regions are not slighted. This monthly includes two sections of interest: a "Travel Guide," with news notes from throughout the world; and "Geographer's World," dealing more with geographical news. The advertisements should not be ignored; interesting tours are often described. Should be considered by any library wanting a popular geographical magazine with a different orientation.

National Geographic Research. 1985. q. $40. Harm J. deBlij. National Geographic Soc., 1145 17th St. N.W., Washington, DC 20036. Illus.
Aud: Hs.

Directed to the *Scientific American* type of reader, here are eight to ten well-illustrated articles, which represent original research not to be edited and popularized for *National Geographic*. Articles "reflect the range and diversity of the research the Society supports . . . archaeology, entomology, geology, herpetology . . . historical geography, biogeography, botany and primatology." While essentially for the scientific community, the work offers the interested layperson an exceptionally well-edited general science magazine. One is given a tour of "late Permian and Triassic Tetrapods of Southern Brazil," complete with numerous charts and line drawings. Right behind, often with full color photographs, is a study of a Bronze Age cemetery, a report on the 1983 season at the Neolithic site of Ain Ghazal, and an explanation of how the Atlantic walrus communicates. Shorter features consider landslides, a little known predator, and ants. There's much more, and a good deal of it is technical, sometimes downright difficult to follow. Still the journey is worth the effort. It's absolutely required.

For the Professional

Journal of Geography. 1902. 7/yr. $34. Anthony R. deSouza. Natl. Council for Geographic Education, Western Illinois Univ., Macomb, IL 61455. Index, adv. Circ: 4,000. Vol. ends: Dec. Microform: UMI.
Indexed: CIJE, EdI, SOCI. *Bk. rev:* 3–4, 300–800 words, signed. *Aud:* Pr.

The official organ of the National Council for Geographic Education is directed at teachers of geography. It empha-

sizes methods of teaching geography, suggesting techniques and audiovisual aids, but also contains some professional articles. Written by teachers in the field, the well-illustrated articles include footnotes and occasionally a bibliography. Sections are regularly found on remote sensing, classroom projects, and a preview of films available for teaching geography. Microcomputer software is reviewed in some issues. For larger school libraries, all school education collections, and comprehensive collections supporting large geography departments.

HEALTH AND MEDICINE

For the Student/For the Professional

Robin Braun, Director of the Medical Library at St. Elizabeth's Hospital, 736 Cambridge St., Brighton, MA 02135
Linda Simmons, Medical Librarian, Kaiser Sunnyside Medical Center, 10200 S.E. Sunnyside Rd., Clackamas, OR 97015

Introduction

The health field is currently undergoing rapid change. Concerns with the rising costs of health care and new technologies and methods in health care delivery have focused attention on the health care system. The public has shown growing interest in the health care system and an increasing desire to participate in it. At the same time, the fitness movement and a heightened consciousness of nutrition and behavioral and environmental influences on health have created a school curriculum reaching back to the early grades that focuses on wellness—the individual developing healthful living patterns.

We have tried to take these trends and perspectives into account in offering this selection, while at the same time selecting carefully, from the more than 2,600 journals available, those appropriate to school audiences, whether students or teachers.

Basic Periodicals

Ejh: *Child Life, Children's Digest, Children's Playmate, Humpty Dumpty's Magazine*; Hs: *FDA Consumer, Health*.

For the Student

Alcoholism: the national magazine. 1980. 5/yr. $18.75. Christina Johnston. Alcom, Inc., P.O. Box 19519, Seattle, WA 98109. Ilus., adv. Circ: 30,000. Sample. Vol. ends: June/July.
Bk. rev: 1,250 words. *Aud:* Hs.

Addiction, treatment, and recovery are the broad subject areas in this potpourri of materials for alcoholics and those who live or work with them. A few featured articles appear in each issue. A recent issue focused on children of alcoholics, discussing fetal alcohol syndrome, teenage addiction, and child abuse. Most of the magazine is devoted to short departments, e.g., "D.C. Diary," "Counselors Casebook," and "Media Watch." There is an extensive calendar of events, workshops, and other activities. (L.Si.)

American Health: fitness of body and mind. 1982. 10/yr. $14.95. T. George Harris. Amer. Health Partners, 80 Fifth Ave., New York, NY 10011. Illus., adv. Circ: 550,000. Vol. ends: Dec.

Aud: Hs.

Providing an upbeat approach to the health magazine market, *American Health* focuses on medicine, mind and body, nutrition (with recipes), fitness, teeth, skin, hair, and consumer concerns. Representative article titles reflect a currency and relevance of scope: "Fast Medicine: Doc-in-the-Box"; "PMS, Insomnia . . . or Thyroid?"; "Does Your Office Have Bad Habits?" A list of medical advisers is provided; many articles are written by physicians and other experts. Most items are short and easy to read; longer feature articles often include suggestions for further reading. Many foods and drugs are advertised. Photographs and illustrations are used effectively. This is an attractive, accurate, all-purpose health magazine. (L.Si.)

Bestways: your health, diet and nutrition magazine. 1973. m. $18. Barbara Bassett. Bestways Magazine, Inc., 1501 S. Sutro Terrace, P.O. Box 2028, Carson City, NV 89702. Illus., index, adv. Circ: 300,000. Sample. Vol. ends: Dec.

Aud: Hs.

A magazine focusing on health as a function of nutrition with a few articles on nonfood topics like relaxation, exercise, and beauty. Frequently sold in health food stores, *Bestways* is similar to *Prevention*, both in articles and advertisements. "Fish Oils & a Healthy Heart"; "Basil: The King of Herbs," and "Dietary Fiber—Your Passport to Health" reflect this content. However, *Prevention* displays better research methods and writing style. (L.Si.)

Child Life. 1921. 8/yr. $11.95. Steve Charles. Children's Better Health Inst., P.O. Box 567, Indianapolis, IN 46206. Illus. Circ: 100,000. Sample. Vol. ends: Dec.

Aud: Ejh.

One of eight magazines from the same publisher, this health magazine (6½ by 9⅛ inches in size) is directed to children ages 7–9. Each issue carries stories, articles, poems, puzzles, activities, reader contributions, and a page addressed to parents and teachers. The short, easy-to-read stories, the light approach to factual articles, and the great variety of activities should attract even the most reluctant reader. The title has been around since 1921, but the magazine has changed from a general interest magazine to a mystery and science-fiction magazine, and now, to a health magazine. (L.K.O.)

Children's Digest. 1950. 8/yr. $11.95. Kathleen B. Mosher. Children's Better Health Inst., P.O. Box 567, Indianapolis, IN 46206. Illus. Circ: 200,000. Sample. Vol. ends: Dec.

Aud: Ejh.

This magazine, intended for children ages 8–10, is now a health-oriented publication. Fiction, nonfiction, poetry, games, puzzles, recipes, and activities are all concerned with safety, nutrition, and exercise. Readers' original stories and poetry are featured regularly. It is printed on off-white paper, and the illustrative material, usually in two colors, is ordinary but adequate. Libraries should purchase only if additional material on this subject is needed. (L.K.O.)

Children's Playmate. 1929. 8/yr. $11.95. Kathleen B. Mosher. Children's Better Health Inst., P.O. Box 567, Indianapolis, IN 46206. Illus. Circ: 254,000. Sample. Vol. ends: March.

Aud: Ejh.

The illustrated stories, poems, articles, and activities for children ages 5–7 stress good health habits, nutrition, exercise, and safety rules. Regular features include a cartoon, "Woof-Woof and Flip Plea," easy recipes, simple science articles, a page addressed to parents and teachers, and reader contributions. A few full-color, but mostly one-color, adequate illustrations complement the content. Consider for library purchase as supplementary material for the beginning reader. (L.K.O.)

Current Health. 1977. 9/yr. $4.95 (Minimum 15 subs. to one address). Laura Ruekberg. Curriculum Innovations, Inc., 3500 Western Ave., Highland Park, IL 60035. Illus., index. Sample. Vol. ends: May.

Aud: Ejh.

Intended primarily for use by students in grades 4 through 7, this "one-of-a-kind" periodical provides health education with current health information. The major areas covered in each issue are: nutrition, disease, drugs, first aid and safety, your healthy environment, fitness and exercise, your personal health, and psychology. The first article is a feature that is introduced on the full-color cover. On the lighter side, there are riddles, word games, and puzzles. The writing style is simple and lively, and two-color illustrations supplement the text. Each issue includes a free teacher's guide. (L.K.O.)

Expecting. 1967. q. Free. Evelyn A. Podsiadlo. Gruner & Jahr USA Publg., 685 Third Ave., New York, NY 10017. Illus., adv. Circ: 1,150,000. Sample. Microform: B&H, UMI.

Bk. rev: 1, 150 words. *Aud:* Hs.

An excellent choice for a high school library. Distributed on request and through obstetricians, family physicians, nurse-midwives, and childbirth educators, this journal reflects the same broad, popular interests to be found in the publisher's other journal, *Parents.* It is carefully written and well illustrated. Articles cover every aspect of pregnancy: hygiene, maternity fashion, husband-wife relations, prenatal development, budgeting, nursery planning, diet and so forth. Medical articles are written by doctors, registered nurses, and nurse-midwives. There is no fiction. (R.B.)

FDA Consumer. 1967. 10/yr. $17. William M. Rados. Supt. of Docs., U.S. Govt. Printing Office, Washington, DC 20402. Illus. Circ: 13,000. Sample. Vol. ends: Dec/Jan. Microform: B&H, IA, MIM, UMI.

Indexed: CIPE, IGov, RG. *Aud:* Hs.

Produced and written primarily by the staff of the Food and Drug Administration, this 40- to 50-page document informs consumers about health-related products and services. A half-dozen feature articles such as "Feeding Animals Wonder Drugs and Creating Super Bugs," "Safety Tips for the Outdoor Chef," and "Asthma Is All in the Head and Chest" reflect current FDA positions and often focus on the agency's activities—e.g., "Ad Campaign Will Warn about Health Fraud." Regular departments are "Updates," including recent warnings on products; "The Notebook," a potpourri of news releases from the FDA and the Federal Register; "Investigators Reports," from FDA officials; and "Summaries of Court Actions," including seizure actions, labeling violations, and so forth. Provides a reliable source for current government positions on health care issues. (L.Si.)

Health (Incorporating: *Family Health* and *Today's Health*). 1969. m. $22. Hank Herman, P.O. Box 6030, Palm Coast, FL 32037. Illus., adv. Circ: 1,000,000. Vol. ends: Dec. Microform: B&H, UMI.

Indexed: RG. *Aud:* Hs.

Recent covers of this magazine featured the familiar faces of Mary Decker, Geraldine Ferraro, Cheryl Tiegs, and Joan Lunden. This women's magazine attempts to give the most up-to-date and scientifically sound information about preventive medicine, fitness, proper nutrition, and better health care. Articles on infertility, relaxation, diets for stress, and prenatal influences delineate the target audience. Advertisements for food and drugs abound. Writing is popular and easy to understand. (L.Si.)

Health Letter. 1973. bi-w. $19.50. Lawrence E. Lamb. News America Syndicate, P.O. Box 19622, Irvine, CA 92713. Index. Circ: 10,000. Vol. ends: June & Dec.

Aud: Hs.

Dr. Lawrence E. Lamb, medical columnist for News America Syndicate, writes this four-page newsletter. Each bi-weekly issue contains four to eight topics drawn from current medical journals. Journal articles are cited, summarized, and interpreted. Recent titles include "The Coffee Cholesterol Connection," "Beer Drinkers and Gout," "Fainting from Fitness," and "Estrogens Don't Cause Breast Cancer." Special single-topic issues appear occasionally. Each volume's table of contents, published on a semi-annual basis, serves as an index to that volume. Emphasis is added to major points with underlining. (L.Si.)

Human Life Review. 1975. q. $15. J. P. McFadden. Human Life Foundation, Inc., 150 E. 35th St., New York, NY 10016. Index. Circ: 15,000. Sample. Vol. ends: Fall. Microform: B&H, UMI.

Aud: Hs.

The *Human Life Review* furnishes a well-researched and thoughtful presentation of the right-to-life faction in the abortion debate. Abortion is the major subject considered, but capital punishment, embattled fatherhood, and Orwell's *1984* are typical of other topics covered. Authors are well

respected, with literary and legal figures predominating. This is a fine choice for libraries wanting a lucid right-to-life journal to balance their collections. (R.B.)

Humpty Dumpty's Magazine. 1952. 8/yr. $11.95. Christine French Clark. Children's Better Health Inst., P.O. Box 10681, Des Moines, IA 50381. Illus. Circ: 600,000. Sample. Vol. ends: Dec.

Aud: Ejh.

The transfer from Parents Magazine Enterprises has changed the character of *Humpty Dumpty*. It is now a health-oriented magazine for ages 4–6. Although the contents are divided into two sections: "Herbie's Health Pages" and "More Fun," there is little difference between the material—nutrition, safety and exercise are emphasized throughout the magazine. Included are several easy-to-read stories, a play, poems, and a variety of games, puzzles, and things to make and do. One or two pages are informational pieces addressed to parents and teachers. The two-color illustrations are adequate but unexciting. Best for home-library purchase. (L.K.O.)

Journal of Drug Issues. 1971. q. $35. Richard L. Rachin, P.O. Box 4021, Tallahassee, FL 32303. Illus., index, adv. Circ: 850. Vol. ends: Fall. Microform: UMI.

Bk. rev: 1–2, essay, signed. *Aud:* Hs.

This journal discusses drug policy issues, focusing on their social, legal, political, economic, historical, and medical aspects. Recent article titles include "Communist Ideology and the Substance Abuser," "Targeting of Magazine Alcohol Beverage Advertisements," "The Cannabis-Cocaine Connection: A Comparative Study of Use and Users," and "Sin or Solace? Religious Views on Alcohol and Alcoholism." Occasional issues are devoted to a single theme, e.g., social thought on alcoholism. Articles are well written, readable, and thought provoking. The context of drug use and the institutional forces shaping drug policy are emphasized. Anyone seeking insights into this area will find the *Journal of Drug Issues* an excellent resource. (L.Si.)

Medical Detective. 1981. q. $11.95. Steve Charles. Children's Better Health Inst., P.O. Box 567, Indianapolis, IN 46206. Illus. Circ: 600. Sample. Vol. ends: Summer.

Aud: Ejh.

This quarterly introduces children ages 10–12 to the world of medical investigation. Approximately eight signed articles and stories about people or occurrences present the hows and whys of disease and treatment. Cartoons and several activities, such as mazes and puzzles are included. Black-and-white illustrations adequately complement the text. Probably most useful in school libraries as supplementary material for health classes. (L.K.O.)

Medical Self Care: access to medical tools. 1976. bi-m. $15. Tom Ferguson & Michael Castleman. Medical Self-Care Magazine, Inc., P.O. Box 1000, Point Reyes, CA 94956. Illus., adv. Circ: 30,000. Sample. Microform: UMI.

Bk. rev: 10–15, 200–500 words, signed. *Aud:* Hs.

An important alternative source of medical information for the layperson, founded by Tom Ferguson, a graduate of Yale Medical School. Articles are down-to-earth—e.g., "The Joy of Homebirth," "Self-medication," "Enjoying Menopause"—and most provide additional resources and lists of references. Women's health receives a large share of the coverage (three special issues in a four-year period) but the regular column "Men's Health" indicates a balanced concern for both sexes. The aim of the magazine is to encourage the individual's participation in his or her own health care through sharing information. *Medical Self Care* offers libraries seeking less conventional approaches to medical care an important option. (L.Si.)

Medical Update: a monthly newsletter. 1978. m. $12. Timothy Ehrgott, P.O. Box 10683, Des Moines, IA 50381. Illus., index. Circ: 55,000. Sample. Vol. ends: June.

Aud: Hs.

The Medical Education and Research Foundation, a division of the nonprofit Benjamin Franklin Literary & Medical Society, publishes this six-page newsletter covering a variety of subjects. Unsigned articles discuss research studies, summarize material from medical journals, announce new technologies, and update current medical thought. "Strokes," "Aborigines and Diabetes," and "Calcium and High Blood Pressure Update" are examples of recent articles. Two pages are devoted to "Cancer Prevention Monthly." This is an easy-to-read publication useful for quick, newsy items, but *Medical World News* would be a better choice for students (see below). (L.Si.)

Medical World News: the newsmagazine of medicine. 1960. s-m. $35. Annette Oestreicher. HEI Publg., Inc., 7676 Woodway, Suite 112, Houston, TX 77063. Illus., adv. Circ: 120,000. Sample. Vol. ends: Dec. Microform:UMI.

Aud: Hs.

Subtitled "The Newsmagazine of Medicine," this publication is packed with short, newsy items broadly classed under two headings: clinical medicine and political-social. A lengthy, in-depth cover story tackles larger problems, e.g., "Abortion," "Malpractice Costs: The Pressure for Relief Mounts," and "Pharmacogenetics: A Key to Drug Response." Written for the health care professional, this is also an excellent source for consumers and for students seeking information on health care economics, court cases, government regulation, new drug therapies, technological innovations, and controversial aspects of medicine. A medical *Time* or *Newsweek* in its style and coverage. (L.Si.)

Monthly Vital Statistics Report. 1952. m. Free. U.S. Natl. Center for Health Statistics, 3700 East-West Hwy., Hyattsville, MD 20782. Illus., index. Vol. ends: Apr.

Aud: Ejh, Hs.

A monthly presentation of birth, death, marriage, and divorce information for the United States. The information is compiled in a variety of tables and analyzed by a variety of categories: U.S. total, national region, state, sex, age,

month, cause of death, and so forth. A good source of authoritative, timely, basic demographic information to supplement almanac and census information. Some comparison between past and present data is given. Number 13 of each volume is an annual summary. Occasional supplements focus on a particular subject, e.g., induced terminations of pregnancy. A journal of wide potential appeal. (R.B.)

Population Reports. 197?. bi-m. Free. Ward Rinehart. Population Information Program, Johns Hopkins Univ., 624 N. Broadway, Baltimore, MD 21205. Illus. Vol. ends: Nov. Refereed.

Aud: Hs.

This journal, supported by the U.S. Agency for International Development, is designed to "provide an accurate and authoritative overview of important developments in the population field." There are 13 series in *Population Reports:* oral contraceptives; intrauterine devices; sterilization, female; sterilization, male; law and policy; pregnancy termination; prostaglandins; barrier methods; periodic abstinence; family planning programs; injectables and implants; world health; and special topics. Each issue is a 30- to 40-page article devoted to a specific topic, e.g., impact of family planning programs on fertility or minilaparotomy and laparoscopy. There are extensive bibliographies for these well-written articles. One of the best choices for international family planning. High school libraries will find it useful. (R.B.)

Prevention. 1950. m. $13.97. Robert Rodale. Rodale Press, Inc., 33 E. Minor St., Emmaus, PA 18049. Illus., index, adv. Circ: 2,821,501. Vol. ends: Dec. Microform: B&H, UMI.

Indexed: MgI, RG. *Aud:* Hs.

A popular health magazine focusing on nutrition as the key to good health. "Eating for One," "Best & Worst Diet Ideas," "Give Yourself the Iron Test," "The Good Meats," "Boost Your Brainpower," and "The World of Healthy Foods" all appeared in one issue along with a regular department on nutrition. Advertisements also favor foods and vitamin and mineral supplements. Although nutrition dominates content, many articles propose other natural preventives for health problems, e.g., exercise. Environmental health and government legislation are reported in the department "Health Front." A veterinarian contributes regularly in "Your Healthy Pet." The editor, Robert Rodale, has become a leading figure in the area of consumer health issues. His monthly editorial often reflects this position. (L.Si.)

Public Health Reports. 1878. bi-m. $21. Marian Priest Tebben. Supt. of Docs., U.S. Govt. Printing Office, Washington, DC 20402. Illus., index. Circ: 8,000. Sample. Vol. ends: Dec. Refereed.

Indexed: PAIS. *Aud:* Hs.

The official journal of the U.S. Public Health Service, *Public Health Reports* categorizes its articles as prevention, policy, or general, with an occasional special section. Examples are work site health promotion, nutrition monitoring, and research in the Department of Health and Human Services; unreported dog bites in children; and public health aspects of physical activity and exercise. A broad range of health prevention and control, public health research, and federal health policies is covered. Articles are well written and well documented, and provide statistical information useful to high school and college students, as well as practitioners. (R.B).

Shape. 1981. m. $20. Christine MacIntyre, 21100 Erwin St., Woodland Hills, CA 91367. Illus., adv. Circ: 550,000. Sample. Vol. ends: Aug.
Aud: Hs.

Shape is devoted to physical fitness in women. Features regularly appearing are "Fitness/Sports Medicine," "Psychological Fitness," "Nutrition/Weight Control," and "Beauty/Travel/Fashion." The editorial board of medical and health care professionals is listed in the front of the magazine. Noteworthy departments written by experts in their fields include "Inside Exercise," with clear explanations of how the body works during exercise; "Do It Right," with pointers on correct technique to avoid strains and injuries; and "Womancare," devoted to women's unique health aspects. Colorful photographs and illustrations supplement the text. This is a specialized addition to the health care field. (L.Si.)

Studies in Family Planning. 1963. bi-m. Free. Valeda Slade. Population Council, One Dag Hammarskjold Plaza, New York, NY 10017. Illus., index. Circ: 8,600. Sample. Vol. ends: Dec. Refereed. Microform: KTO.
Aud: Hs.

This international journal addresses family planning and related health issues with special emphasis on developing countries. Recent articles covered Peruvian community characteristics and fertility, breastfeeding in developing countries, and family planning in India. Authors are specialists in family planning, sociology, public health, and related disciplines. Well-documented articles would be suitable for use in area studies and sociology programs. Each issue has seven to ten abstracts of books, articles, reports, and occasional papers reviewed by the editorial committee. (R.B.)

Vibrant Life: a Christian guide for total health (Formerly: *Your Life and Health* and *Life and Health*). 1904. bi-m. $12. Ralph Blodgett. Review and Herald Publg. Assn., 55 W. Oak Ridge Dr., Hagerstown, MD 21740. Illus., adv. Circ: 45,000. Sample. Vol. ends: Dec.
Aud: Hs.

Owned by the General Conference of Seventh Day Adventists, *Vibrant Life* is specifically aimed at Christian families with readers between the ages of 25 and 50. Articles are accepted that promote a happier home, better health, and a more fulfilled life. Recent typical titles included "Guidelines for Better Nutrition," "Common Drugs Can Be Abused Too," and "Can Exercise Improve Mental Func-

tion?" Articles are well written and sometimes include a religious viewpoint, e.g., "Does God Answer?" There is a vegetarian theme throughout the nutrition pieces and recipes for which the Adventists are noted. (L.Si.)

World Health. 1958. 10/yr. $12.50. John Bland. World Health Organization, 525 23rd St. N.W., Washington, DC 20037. Illus., index. Circ: 160,000. Sample. Vol. ends: Dec.
Aud: Hs.

The official magazine of the World Health Organization, *World Health* is an international journal aimed at the general public. It is available in English, French, German, Portuguese, Russian, and Spanish; also in Arabic and Persian, four times a year. The journal is semipopular and well illustrated. The authors are international and have widely varied backgrounds. Topics include nutrition, primary health care in many nations, and programs for the control of specific diseases such as malaria. WHO goals, programs, and progress are reported. This is an attractive publication that high school students would find interesting. For those needing more detailed or technical information on international health, *WHO Chronicle* is preferred. (R.B.)

For the Professional

American Journal of Public Health. 1911. m. $50. Alfred Yankauer. Amer. Public Health Assn., 1015 15th St. N.W., Washington, DC 20005. Illus., index, adv. Circ: 35,000. Vol. ends: Dec. Microform: B&H, MIM, UMI.
Bk. rev: Occasional, length varies. *Aud:* Pr.

Official journal of the American Public Health Association. Public health, as covered in this publication, includes personal and environmental issues. Recent articles addressed comparative risks and costs of male and female sterilization, government regulation of occupational safety, and asbestos disease. Articles dealing with school health programs appear frequently. While the major focus is public health in the United States, other countries receive some attention. Physicians and research scientists are the main authors and intended audience but many articles are appropriate for informed members of the general public. A monthly newspaper, *Nation's Health*, is available from the same source for $8. Its focus on legislation and regulatory activity and trends makes it a good choice for a current awareness/digesting service for public health topics. (R.B.)

Physician and Sportsmedicine. 1973. m. $39. Allan J. Ryan. McGraw-Hill, Inc., 4530 W. 77th St., Minneapolis, MN 55435. Illus., index, adv. Circ: 113,000. Vol. ends: Dec. Refereed. Microform: UMI.
Indexed: CIJE, GSI. *Bk. rev:* 3–4, 50–200 words, signed. *Aud:* Pr.

This journal serves the physician's professional and personal interest in the medical aspects of recreation, physical exercise and sports. In fact, any reader with an interest in sports, whether as participant, parent, physical educator, or physician, will find something of interest. Articles are brief and readable. Color sports photographs accompany many articles. Most articles focus on the prevention and treatment of sports injuries, athletic training and conditioning, and physical fitness programs. Recent article titles include "The Effects of Aerobic Dance on Cardiovascular Fitness," "Injuries in Youth Football," and "Allergic Reactions to Exercise." Unlike the more technical *Medicine and Science in Sports and Exercise* or *American Journal of Sports Medicine*, this journal will appeal to both amateur and professional athletes with or without an M.D. (L.Si.)

RN. 1937. m. $24. James A. Reynolds. Medical Economics Co., Inc., Oradell, NJ 07649. Illus., index, adv. Circ: 375,000. Vol. ends: Dec. Microform: UMI.
Aud: Pr.

RN is full of topics of interest to the layperson as well as the nurse or nursing student. Sample titles are "Don't Just Tell Your Patients—Teach Them," "Pulverizing Kidney Stones: What You Should Know about Lithotripsy," and "Therapeutic Touch: Maybe There's Something to It After All." Departments like "Patient's Advocate," with titles like "When to Tell a Patient the Doctor is Wrong," will interest the layperson. A wide variety of subjects including diseases, emergency care, and wounds and injuries appear in each issue. (L.Si.)

HISTORY

For the Student/For the Professional

See also Cultural-Social Studies; Political Science; and Sociology Sections.

William F. Young, Coordinator of Reference Services, State University of New York, Albany, NY 12222

Introduction

History's continuing and complex relationship with both the humanities and the social sciences is uniquely reflected in the following selection of journals. Like literature, history is concerned with understanding and interpreting human motivation and behavior and the consequences of that behavior. The number of popular historical magazines and the support for a wide variety of local history publications illustrate that narrative history and biography continue to find favor among the general reading public. Traditionally allied with the humanities, the discipline has also always shared much with the social sciences. Historical scholarship is noted for its use of critical methods to determine the authenticity of historical evidence. Detailed, analytical, and highly specialized research, intended for a limited academic audience, has for quite some time been characteristic of history as a profession. Much of this research is reported in specialized journals dedicated to specific countries, chronological periods, or precise subject fields.

In the last 20 years, many historians have turned to interdisciplinary and complex quantitative techniques as a way of recreating past societies and learning how ordinary people lived. The activities of many historians have indeed become inseparable from those of political scientists, anthropologists, and sociologists.

The gap between scholar and public has perhaps never been greater. Too much, however, may be made of this distinction. Students will find well-written, interesting, and lively studies within the most esoteric of journals, and whole new scholarly areas, such as psychohistory and oral history, enjoy a significant degree of general appeal. At the same time, even popular narrative history is ultimately dependent on the findings of the specialized researcher. What is clear is that historical writing flourishes, attesting to people's fascination with all aspects of the past through an extraordinary variety of publications.

Basic Periodicals

Ejh: *American Heritage, American History Illustrated*; Hs: *American Heritage, American History Illustrated, American West, Early American Life, History Today*.

For the Student

Americana. 1973. $13.90. Michael Durham. 29 W. 38th St., New York, NY 10018. Illus., adv. Circ: 400,000. Vol. ends: Jan. Microform: UMI.
Indexed: RG. *Bk. rev:* 5–7, 350 words, signed. *Aud:* Ejh, Hs.

A popular magazine with numerous black-and-white and four-color illustrations and with a decided emphasis on U.S. arts and crafts. Other articles are concerned with general matters of history, culture and social trends. The writing style is such that it can be appreciated by almost any age group, although the greatest appeal is to young people and adults. Particularly good for the how-to-do-it articles. While not purely a history magazine, and really more appropriate for the general collection, it is found in the history section of many libraries.

American Heritage: the magazine of history. 1954. bi-m. $24. Byron Dobell. Amer. Heritage Subscription Office, P.O. Box 977, Farmingdale, NY 11737. Illus., index, adv. Circ: 142,000. Vol. ends: Oct./Nov. Microform: B&H, MCA, UMI.
Indexed: AbrRG, RG. *Aud:* Ejh, Hs.

This popular and successful magazine focuses on all aspects of the U.S. experience, whether monumental or trivial. Recent issues, for example, included a short history of AT&T, a discussion of why poison gas was not used in World War II, and a look at those who made the music for silent screen films. The very readable articles are of varying length. The numerous photographs and other illustrations result in a very handsome effect. Both the quality of this publication and its broad appeal make it a standard selection for most school libraries.

American History Illustrated. 1966. 10/yr. $18. Ed Holm. Historical Times, Inc., 2245 Kohn Rd., P.O. Box 8200, Harrisburg, PA 17105. Illus., index, adv. Circ: 120,000. Microform: UMI.

Indexed: RG. *Bk. rev:* 2–9, 200–300 words, unsigned. *Aud:* Ejh, Hs.

The origin of this successful and entertaining publication is the belief of its founder that "this country needed a magazine devoted to the popularization of American history." This is achieved through short, well-written articles dealing with all phases of the U.S. experience, each colorfully illustrated. A recent special issue focused on the last year of World War II. Articles on gangster Bonnie Parker, naturalist John Audubon, and writer L. Frank Baum of "Oz" fame illustrate the eclectic nature of this interesting publication. A magazine that appeals to youthful readers.

American West. 1964. bi-m. $15. Thomas W. Pew, Jr. Amer. West Publg. Co., P.O. Box 1960, Marion, OH 43305. Illus., adv. Circ: 150,000. Vol. ends: Nov. Microform: UMI.

Bk. rev: 10–21, brief book notes. *Aud:* Hs.

A glossy and colorful publication crammed with photographs, illustrations, and, incidentally, an abundance of advertisements. This popular magazine is dedicated to the history and culture of the far western states. Several years ago the editors promised to deal with "live history" since "the people and places [the West is] made of are still there to be seen and listened to today." Interesting articles on "Those Pants That Levi Gave Us" and "Abandoned Grain Elevators" are typical examples of this direction. In addition to the six articles per issue, special features include "Gourmet and Grub," "Hidden Inns and Lost Trails," and "Western Snapshots," consisting of photographs that portray today's West as well as "bygone days" sent in by readers. Recommended for its appeal to a wide range of audiences.

Arizona and the West: a quarterly journal of history. 1959. q. $15. Harwood P. Hinton. Library C327, Univ. of Arizona, Tucson, AZ 85721. Illus., index. Circ: 1,200. Vol. ends: Winter. Microform: UMI. Reprint: Kraus.

Bk. rev: 9–15, 500 words, signed. *Aud:* Hs.

In a recent issue the editor provided a short history of this journal and concluded that it has become a "showpiece" for scholarship in Western history. He noted that surveys by historians regularly single out this quarterly "as one of the best journals in its field." The editor's kudos are justified. This journal "strives to present in a readable, attractive manner the most authoritative writing on the Trans-Mississippi West today." Such writing is mostly done by academics and, while indeed readable, the tone is nevertheless scholarly. Photographs and other illustrations add to the overall appeal of this well-edited publication. As few as one or as many as four articles may appear in a given issue. All aspects of Western history are covered, including biographical studies. The book reviews, together with an annotated listing of other books, comprise a useful bibliographical source for the study of this region. Of interest for school libraries in Western states.

British Heritage (Formerly: *British History Illustrated*). 1981. bi-m. $20. Gail Huganir. Historical Times, Inc., 2245 Kohn Rd., P.O. Box 8200, Harrisburg, PA 17105. Illus., index, adv. Circ: 62,000. Microform: UMI. Reprint: UMI.

Bk. rev: 3–4, 200–400 words. *Aud:* Hs.

Britain's past is the subject of this entertaining and appealing magazine. People, places, and events from all ages of this island's colorful past are featured in heavily illustrated and readable articles. Recent issues included studies on "Lawrence of Arabia," "The History of English Pudding," and "The Royal Pavilion at Brighton." The tone is decidedly popular, with suggestions for further reading appended to each main feature. A regular and interesting feature is "News from London."

Civil War Times Illustrated. 1959. 10/yr. $18. John E. Stanchak. Historical Times, Inc., 2245 Kohn Rd., P.O. Box 8200, Harrisburg, PA 17105. Illus., index, adv. Circ: 120,000.

Bk. rev: 250–300 words, signed. *Aud:* Hs.

The apt subtitle to this semipopular periodical is "A Magazine for Persons Interested in American History Particularly in the Civil War Period." It examines all phases of the War Between the States, with some emphasis on military events and biography. The articles are skillfully written, but the numerous photographs and other illustrations are the key to this magazine's popular appeal. A selection particularly suited to the layperson.

Cobblestone. 1980. m. $18.50. Carolyn P. Yoder. Cobblestone Publg., Inc., 20 Grove St., Peterborough, NH 03458. Illus., index. Circ: 45,000. Sample. Vol. ends: Dec. *Aud:* Ejh.

Subtitled "The History Magazine for Young People," each issue explores a single theme, drawing from the political, business, scientific, artistic, and literary areas of life in the period covered. It presents U.S. history in a fresh, new way: through firsthand accounts, biographies, stories, maps, poems, games, puzzles, songs, recipes, and book and film sources for further study. Clear black-and-white illustrations and photographs, many from museums and historical societies, add another dimension to this excellent periodical. Also available are back issues and a teacher's activity guide. (L.K.O.)

Early American Life. 1970. bi-m. $15. Frances Carnahan. Historical Times, Inc., P.O. Box 8200, Harrisburg, PA 17105. Illus., adv. Circ: 360,000. Microform: UMI. Reprint: UMI.

Indexed: Acs, MgI. *Bk. rev:* number and length vary. *Aud:* Hs.

This handsome and colorful magazine would be an excellent and popular choice particularly for high school and public libraries. *Early American Life* means a focus on the colonial period and up to approximately the mid-nineteenth century. The articles are readable and interesting, and deal with such matters as crafts, antiques, and historic sites as well as historic events. The particular interest here is in the daily lives of people of the period and the restoration of homes, the latter which are displayed in attractive photographs. Regular features include information about antiques and listings of forthcoming craft and antique exhibits. Highly recommended.

Frontier Times. 1953. bi-m. $14. John Joerschke. Western Publns., P.O. Box 2107, Stillwater, OK 74076. Illus., index, adv. Circ: 100,000. Sample. Vol. ends: Nov.

Bk. rev: 5, 350 words, signed. *Aud:* Hs.

As indicated by the publisher, *Frontier Times* and *True West* (see below in this section) are essentially the same magazine, published under different titles in alternating months. Both attempt to provide "a taste and feel of the Wild West then and now," by covering western history and culture from pre-Civil War days to the present. Easy reading, with good authentic photographs and illustrations, the magazines include factual accounts; reviews of nonfiction books; columns on western films and travel, family history, cooking, miscellany; and a separate section of queries asking readers to share information. With its topical variety, it is likely to be of interest to high school readers. (E.F.S.)

History Today. 1951. m. $39. Juliet Gardiner. 83-84 Berwick St., London WIV 3PJ, England. Illus., index, adv. Circ: 32,000. Vol. ends: Dec. Microform: UMI.

Indexed: RG. *Bk. rev:* 8–18, various lengths, signed. *Aud:* Hs.

A readable and handsomely illustrated magazine featuring articles written by historians but aimed at the intelligent layperson. The major emphasis is on Britain, but articles may be found on all places and time periods in the seven features that normally appear in each issue. Some of the contents may be somewhat too esoteric for the general reader interested in reading history. Nevertheless, intelligent suggestions for further reading and well-written book reviews are other aspects that make this monthly journal a good choice.

Illinois Historical Journal (Formerly: *Journal of the Illinois State Historical Society*). 1899. q. $15 (Individuals, $12.50). Mary Ellen McElligott. Illinois State Historical Soc., Old State Capitol, Springfield, IL 62706. Illus., index. Circ: 2,900. Microform: UMI.

Bk. rev: 3–13, 600 words, signed. *Aud:* Hs.

Numerous photographs and drawings which illustrate the contents of this journal result in a pleasing typographical effect. The contributors are mostly academics, and the subject focus centers not only on the state but the entire Midwest. A significant number of the articles deal with the city of Chicago. An occasional feature is "Lincolniana," highlighting materials related to Abraham Lincoln owned by the Historical Society. The society also publishes *Illinois History: a magazine for young people*, which is free to all schools in Illinois and available for $3 a year out of state.

International Journal of Oral History. 1980. 3/yr. $40. Charles E. Morrissey Pubs., 11 Ferry Lane W., Westport, CT 06880.

Bk. rev: vary in number in length. *Aud:* Hs.

Considering the rapid development of this field, this journal fills a genuine need. The articles include not only the results of oral history projects but also focus on techniques and examinations of methodology. For example, one issue featured a look at the oral histories of western American women and relationship to similar quantitative studies. In addition to articles, this publication also regularly includes news of local history projects and evaluations of materials "used in the various processes of recording, transcribing, indexing, cataloging and housing of oral histories."

Journal of Negro History. See Afro-American/For the Student Section.

Journal of the West. 1962. q. $30 (Individuals, $25). Dean Coughenour, P.O. Box 1009, 1531 Yuma, Manhattan, KS 66502. Illus., adv. Circ: 4,500.

Indexed: HumI. *Bk. rev:* 20–30, 250–500 words, signed. *Aud:* Hs.

"Devoted to the history, culture and other facets of the development of the West," here are some 100 pages with numerous black-and-white illustrations to support the dozen or so articles. Written as much for the layperson as for the historian, the articles are well documented and, what is rare, equally well written. A wide range of subject matter is considered, and from time to time a special issue is given over to a single subject such as "Western films." Of particular interest to librarians is the extensive book review section. Most of the books, again, are for both laypersons and historians, with emphasis on the former. Anyone who enjoys riding off into the sunset will be delighted with this journal, which should find a place in the general reading section.

Military History. See Military/For the Student Section.

Montana: the magazine of western history. 1951. q. $15. William L. Lang. Historical Soc., 225 N. Roberts St., Helena, MT 59601. Illus., index, adv. Circ: 10,000. Vol. ends: Autumn. Microform: UMI. Reprint: UMI.

Bk. rev: 10–20, 500–1,000 words, signed. *Aud:* Hs.

The five well-written and well-documented articles that appear quarterly are presented in an attractive format augmented by numerous photographs and other illustrations. The chief focus is, naturally, on Montana and the Far West in general. The primary chronological interest appears to center on the late nineteenth and early twentieth centuries. Many of the articles are biographical in nature. This is an entertaining and handsome magazine, possessing both academic and popular appeal. Recommended for libraries in the West.

Negro History Bulletin. See Afro-American/For the Student Section.

Prologue: the journal of the National Archives. 1969. q. $12. Timothy Walch. National Archives and Records Service, Trust Fund Board, Eighth St. and Pennsylvania Ave. N.W., Washington, DC 20408. Illus., adv. Circ: 7,500. Microform: UMI.

Indexed: IGov. *Aud:* Hs.

The stated aim of this periodical is to bring public attention to "the resources and programs of the National Archives, the regional archives and the presidential libraries." It achieves this, at least in part, by publishing studies on all aspects of American history based on the large and eclectic holdings of these institutions. The articles are furthermore illustrated with photographs and other materials from the archives. This handsome publication also serves as a newsletter, providing the public with news about accessions, declassified records, and other archival information. The contents, particularly the articles, will appeal to a wide audience.

Old West. 1964. q. $8. John Joerschke. Western Publns., P.O. Box 2107, Stillwater, OK 74076. Illus., index, adv. Circ: 100,000. Sample. Vol. ends: Summer.
Bk. rev: 5, 350 words, signed. *Aud:* Hs.

Similar in format to its sister magazines *True West* and *Frontier Times, Old West* is narrower in scope, with a distinct concentration on frontier history in the United States from 1830–1910. In addition to regular stories presenting original research on the history of the American West, *Old West* includes monthly columns on genealogy and western cooking and travel; book reviews; and notes on western events. Illustrations highlight most stories. Recommended as a solid addition to a high school library collection. (E.F.S.)

Roots. (Formerly: *Gopher Historian*). 1972. 3/yr. $5. Mary Nord. Minnesota Historical Society, 240 Summit Ave., St. Paul, MN 55102. Circ: 4,500. Sample.
Aud: Ejh.

This is quite typical of several local historical society publications for children—this one ideal for ages 10 to 14. The scope is limited to Minnesota historical events and regional and national personalities who had an influence on Minnesota history. There are excellent illustrations, and the short articles are written for the young person with an interest in the subject. Material is factual, and never cute. While of limited interest to those outside of the state, it serves here as an example of what may be available. Librarians should consult with their city, county, and state historical societies for information on such magazines, not to mention brochures, exhibits, and other pertinent activities.

Timeline. 1984. bi-m. $18. Christopher Duckworth. Ohio Historical Soc., 1985 Velma Ave., Columbus, OH 43211. Illus.
Aud: Hs.

There are now a number of state historical journals that attract both laypersons and historians, which strike a balance between scholarship and lively discussion. *Timeline* joins those ranks. The issue examined (October 1984) includes about a dozen articles. These move from Lincoln and his friend Stanton, to a portfolio of Currier and Ives prints, to a consideration of railroad depots. Almost all of the text and the superb reproductions will attract the attention of anyone remotely concerned with this country's past. While

Ohio is the focus, most of the material has a wider interest. It is a general historical magazine for just about everybody's taste.

True West. 1953. bi-m. $14. John Joerschke. Western Publns., P.O. Box 2107, Stillwater, OK 74076. Illus., index, adv. Circ: 100,000. Sample. Vol. ends: Dec.
Bk. rev: 5, 350 words, signed. *Aud:* Hs.

See *Frontier Times* earlier in this section.

The Western Historical Quarterly. 1970. q. $18 (Individuals, $14). Charles S. Peterson. Utah State Univ. of Agriculture and Applied Science, Logan, UT 84322. Illus., index, adv. Circ: 3,000. Vol. ends: Oct.
Indexed: HumI. *Bk. rev:* 30, 370 words, signed. *Aud:* Hs.

This is the publication of the Western Historical Association, the stated purpose of which is to promote "the study of the American West in all of its varied aspects." This quarterly plays a large role in meeting this purpose. The contents concentrate on "the western movement in the United States, Canada, and Mexico," with special attention to "the frontiers of occupation and settlement from the Atlantic seaboard to the Pacific and the political, economic, social, cultural and intellectual history of the west." Among the regular features is a classified list of recent articles and, in the July issue, a list of dissertations relevant to the field. One additional benefit is that members of the association (dues, $25) also receive a subscription to *American West* magazine. *WHQ* will appeal to many general readers.

For the Professional

History: review of new books. 1972. 8/yr. $40. Cornelius W. Vahle, Jr. Heldref Publns., 4000 Albemarle St. N.W., Washington, DC 20016. Circ: 1,000. Microform: UMI.
Indexed: BoRvI. *Aud:* Pr.

A helpful and authoritative selection aid for any library acquiring historical works. *History* provides reasonably current evaluations of books one to five months after publication. The reviews, written and signed by specialists, discuss content, strengths and weaknesses, authors' credentials, and audience addressed. Complete bibliographic information is also given. The reviews average approximately 400 words each and cover all geographical and chronological areas. There is an author index plus a lengthy "feature review" in each issue.

The History Teacher. 1967. q. $22 (Individuals, $15). William F. Sater. Soc. for History Education, Dept. of History, California State Univ., 1250 Bellflower Blvd., Long Beach, CA 90840. Index, adv. Circ: 4,000. Vol. ends: Aug. Microform: UMI.
Indexed: CIJE. *Bk. rev:* 28–30, 350 words. *Aud:* Pr.

A very useful publication for the historian as teacher at the high school level. Articles appear on both teaching technique and trends in historical scholarship. More precisely, the contents deal with such topics as curricula and programs, methods of evaluation in teaching, historiography, and historical interpretation. Over the last few years, for example, several articles have appeared dealing with the use and impact of computer technology within the discipline. Textbooks and current media relevant to history and education are reviewed, as well as a small selection of books. Twice a year, subscribers also receive *Network News Exchange*, containing short items and announcements about conferences or workshops. This publication is highly recommended for history teachers concerned with teaching effectiveness and current trends.

HOBBIES

For the Student: Antiques and Collecting; Games; Gardening; Numismatics; Philately

David Adams, Assistant Librarian, The Cloisters, Metropolitan Museum of Art, Fort Tryon Park, New York, NY 10040 (Gardening subsection)

Stephen M. Fry, Music Librarian, The University of California, Schoenbey Hall, Los Angeles, CA 90024 (Philately subsection)

Gary J. Lenox, Librarian, University of Wisconsin Center-Rock County, 2909 Kellogg Ave., Janesville, WI 53545 (Antiques subsection)

Margaret Norden, Reference Librarian, Falk Library of the Health Sciences, University of Pittsburgh, Pittsburgh, PA 15261 (Numismatics subsection)

Amy L. Paster, Assistant Librarian, Pennsylvania State University, University Park, PA 16802 (Games subsection)

Introduction

Periodicals on the subjects of antiques, gardening, numismatics, and philately are grouped here under the main heading of Hobbies. The magazines offer the novice and the seasoned collector invaluable information on their hobby of choice. School libraries will certainly want to collect many of these periodicals to satisfy the tastes of student hobbyists and to open the door for collecting by new enthusiasts.

Basic Periodicals

Ejh: *Dragon, Electronic Games*; Hs: *Games, Flower and Garden, American Philatelist.*

For the Student

ANTIQUES AND COLLECTING

Antique Automobile. 1937. bi-m. $12. William E. Bomgardner. Antique Automobile Club of America, 501 W. Governor Rd., Hershey, PA 17033. Illus., index, adv. Circ: 40,000. Vol. ends: Nov/Dec. Microform: UMI.

Bk. rev: 3–5, 300–400 words. *Aud:* Hs.

A useful guide for buffs seeking to learn the history of automobile models. Included in this publication are articles featuring specific cars or manufacturers, club activity news, automobile meet lists, and advertisements for sale and exchange of cars and parts. It is a beautifully produced house organ, nostalgically celebrating a bygone era of elegance, luxury, and innocence.

Collectors News and the Antique Reporter. 1960. m. $11.50. Linda Kruger. Spokesman Press, P.O. Box 156, Grundy

Center, IA 50638. Illus., adv. Circ: 30,000. Vol. ends: Apr.

Bk. rev: 10–15, 100–200 words. *Aud:* Hs.

People apparently collect as wide a variety of objects as can be imagined—doorknobs, cigar bands, comic books, license plates, calendars, Coca Cola curios, railroad tickets, duck decoys, fruit jars, postcards, electric meters, Naziana, Hopalong Cassidy memorabilia, and, of course, bottles. Classified advertisements, short articles on various collectibles, some display advertisements, and numerous book advertisements make up each monthly issue. A section of advertisements for antique sales and auctions is also included.

Collector's Showcase. 1981. bi-m. $20. Donna Kaonis. Collector's Showcase, P.O. Box 6929, San Diego, CA 92106. Illus., adv. Circ: 12,233.

Bk. rev: 4, 100–150 words. *Aud:* Hs.

One of the most attractive magazines for collectors, it includes features on everything (mostly old) that people collect, from children's sand pails to robots to superman comics to sheet music. Emphasis is on toys and advertised items (beer, ketchup). A sheer delight, it should be considered for popular culture collections.

GAMES

Chess Life (Formerly: *Chess Life and Review*). 1933. m. $25. Larry Parr. U.S. Chess Federation, 186 Rte. 9W, New Windsor, NY 12550. Illus. Circ: 55,000. Sample. Vol. ends: Dec. Microform: UMI.

Bk. rev: 2, 500 words, signed. *Aud:* Hs.

The basic chess magazine in the field, primarily because it is the official publication of the U.S. Chess Federation. The publication's primary mission is to provide news of international, national, and local significance to members. Its secondary mission is to print articles, notes, and features on how to improve the game. Particularly useful for the close analyses of master games and the excellent interviews.

Computer Gaming World. 1981. bi-m. $13.50. Russell Sipe. Golden Empire Publns., Inc., 1337 N. Merona St., Anaheim, CA 92803. Illus., index (annual index), adv. Circ: 15,000.

Aud: Hs.

This publication is for the computer gaming enthusiast who desires a detailed review of the latest games. It includes sections on the newest games, with ratings by the readers; reviews of games (including name, type, system, number of players, author, price, publisher); and game strategies. An annual index is included. Back issues are available.

With the growing popularity of the home computer there has been an increase in the number of publications dealing with home computer games. Some of the titles libraries may wish to include:

Computer Games. 1984. bi-m. $15. Carnegie Publns. Corp., 888 Seventh Ave., New York, NY 10106. Illus., adv.

Electronic Fun. m. $2.50. Viare Publg. Co., 350 E. 81st St., New York, NY 10028.

Video Games. 1982. m. $2.95. Pumpkin Inc., 350 Fifth Ave., New York, NY 10118. Adv.

Dragon. 1976. m. $24. Kim Mohan. Dragon Publg., P.O. Box 110, Lake Geneva, WI 53147. Illus., adv. Circ: 120,000. Sample.

Aud: Ejh, Hs.

The sole purpose of this illustrated magazine is to show the reader different approaches to Dungeons and Dragons, a game which seems to be understood by most young people, but few adults. Various strategies of play are suggested. There are interviews with winners, and numerous features which point out new equipment and new approaches to the contest. While some of this is suitable for elementary grades, the primary interest is at the high school level.

Electronic Games. 1981. m. $28. Joyce Worley. Reese Communications, Inc., 460 W. 34th St., New York, NY 10001. Illus., adv. Circ: 200,000. Sample.

Aud: Ejh, Hs.

Divided about evenly between computer games and those found in coin-operated business centers, this provides a welcome challenge for the reader. There are numerous articles on how the player—who may range from a youngster to an adult—may improve his or her game. Still, the primary point of the illustrated magazine is to offer information on new games. Most of this is descriptive, though a bit of it can be critical. A good source for librarians looking for current material on new video/computer games.

Frisbee Disc World. 1976. q. $5. Dan Roddick. Intl. Frisbee Disc Assn., P.O. Box 970, San Gabriel, CA 91778. Illus. Circ: 12,000.

Aud: Hs.

Though frisbee in the 1980s is not as popular as it was in the 1970s, it is still very much around, and this magazine is a good one for fans. The periodical has the usual features, articles, and interviews with frisbee buffs. There is some coverage of local events, and each issue has a listing of regional and local chapters of the sponsoring agency.

Games. 1977. m. $15.97. Jerry Calabrese. Playboy Enterprises, Inc., 919 N. Michigan Ave., Chicago, IL 60611. Illus., adv. Circ: 700,000.

Aud: Hs.

With a circulation larger than that of many general magazines, this is the basic title in the area, and one that should be found in most general collections. The publisher has hired expert writers to put together monthly issues on every aspect of games. Here, one finds articles and short pieces on television games, chess, gambling, cards, intellectual puzzles and so on. There are also a number of original games and such things as photo identification problems. Much of the material is to be worked out in the magazine itself—a drawback of some proportion for libraries attempting to keep "clean" copies. Highly recommended nevertheless.

News in Chess. 1984. $39.50. Elsevier. Subs. to: A. Henderson, P.O. Box 2423, Noble Sta., Bridgeport, CT 06608. Illus. Sample. Vol. ends: No. 4, Apr.

Aud: Hs.

The "new" sets this apart from the other standard chess magazines in that it is one of the latest and, more important, one of the most international. Over 5,000 selected games per year are included, with all major players and tournaments reported in algebraic notations which are understood by chess players. Both good and bad moves are noted. The same publisher issues a yearbook and a keybook with more than 3,000 opening variations.

Northwest Chess Magazine. 1947. m. $8. Washington Chess Federation. Northwest Chess, 4715 Ninth N.E., Seattle, WA 98105. Illus.

Bk. rev: 1–2, 500 words, signed, notes. *Aud:* Hs.

This may be the most readable chess magazine in the United States. It is in no way provincial and will be of interest to any chess fan. The offset, 40-page newsprint journal is filled with chess materials, including fiction, artwork, and interviews. This is the official publication of the Washington Chess Federation and other federations in the region.

GARDENING

Family Food Garden. 1973. bi-m. $12. Robert Fibkins. FFG, Inc., 464 Commonwealth Ave., Boston, MA 02215. Illus., adv. Circ: 350,000. Sample.

Aud: Hs.

Edited for the dedicated amateur home food farmer, this periodical gives directions on how to raise a wide variety of produce. The assumption is that energy, not the size of the garden, is the primary factor. The how-to-do-it methods outlined in the articles are practical and easy to follow as are the illustrations. In addition to instructions on how to grow food, there are handy tips on cooking, preserving, and otherwise presenting the crops on the dining room table. Both vegetables and fruits are covered.

Flower and Garden. 1957. bi-m. $6. Rachel Snyder. Modern Handcraft, Inc., 4251 Pennsylvania Ave., Kansas City, MO 64111. Illus., index. Circ: 600,000. Sample. Vol. ends: Dec. Microform: UMI.

Indexed: RG. *Bk. rev:* 3–4, 100–300 words. *Aud:* Hs.

The only gardening magazine indexed in *Readers' Guide* and the one enjoying the largest circulation of any in the United States, this is by far the most popular of the group abstracted in this section. It well deserves its half-million-plus readers. The articles, illustrations, and features are not only timely but geared for a vast range of interests as well as growing conditions. Primarily for beginners, it has a great deal of advertisements, which suggest the joys of the garden. During winter, a good deal of the focus is on indoor plants. With the first touch of spring, though, the editor moves outdoors to lawns, flowerbeds, and trees. Some attention is given to vegetables as well as flower arranging and life in a greenhouse. Actually, it is difficult to think of any aspect of gardening which is not examined in one issue or another.

Garden. 1976. bi-m. $12. Ann Botshon. The Garden Soc., New York Botanical Garden, Bronx, NY 10458. Illus. Circ: 30,000. Vol. ends: Dec. Microform: UMI.

Bk. rev: 4–5, 200–400 words, signed. *Aud:* Hs.

Though this section does not include the publications of many botanical gardens, this is one that deserves mention and is of interest to any gardener. The focus is on plants, horticulture, botany, forestry—in fact, almost every aspect of the outdoors involving some aspect of gardening. The illustrated articles are exceptionally well written, and rarely technical. There are excellent features, including a lucid book section. Throughout the year, the authors consider outstanding and different types of plants and growth as well as the world's great gardens. The how-to-do-it pieces will be of value to both beginner and expert, particularly when the concern is with growing plants indoors. Both the marvelous illustrations and the clearly written articles make this an outstanding title for almost any library.

NUMISMATICS

Bank Note Reporter. 1973. m. $12.50. Robert Lemke. Krause Publns., Inc., 700 E. State St., Iola, WI 54900. Circ: 5,000. Sample. Vol. ends: Dec.

Aud: Hs.

This newspaper surveys paper money and bank notes throughout the world. It regularly reports on the activities of the U.S. Bureau of Engraving and Printing, the U.S. paper money market, foreign bank note prices, and exchange rates. Announcements of new issues and miscellaneous news, as well as offers of sale, fill the remaining pages. Several of these columns are contributed by authorities on numismatics. A 12-year index was included in the January 1985 issue; hereafter an annual index will be published. The illustrations and photos are poor in quality.

Coin Prices. 1967. bi-m. $8.50. Bob Wilhite. Krause Publns., Inc., 700 E. State St., Iola, WI 54900. Illus., adv. Circ: 100,000. Sample. Vol. ends: Nov. Microform: PMC.

Aud: Hs.

The "standard guide to all U.S. coin values" concentrates on the various aspects of buying and selling coins, including grading, analyzing the coin market, and minting errors. Detailed charts indicate the current prices of coins in several grades of condition, as well as the prices of commemoratives, paper money, and auction sales. There are many coin illustrations, albeit on paper of poor quality.

Coins. 1962. m. $14.50. Arlyn G. Sieber. Krause Publns., Inc., 700 E. State St., Iola, WI 54900. Illus., adv. Circ: 124,500. Sample. Vol. ends: Dec. Microform: MIM, UMI.

Aud: Hs.

Subtitled "The Complete Guide to U.S. Coin Values," this magazine emphasizes U.S. numismatics; however, it covers foreign coinage, scrip, and tokens, as well. Each issue features several high-quality, signed articles on such topics as history, values, and the coinage of a particular nation. Regular columns include historical vignettes, U.S. and world news items, a calendar of conventions and shows, tips on collecting and coin values, and an editor's letter. The commercial and classified advertisements and offers of sales,

which are omnipresent in this field, fill the remaining pages. Most of *Coins* is printed on unsubstantial newsprint.

PHILATELY

American Philatelist. 1886. m. $24. Amer. Philatelic Soc., Inc., P.O. Box 8000, State College, PA 16801. Illus., adv. Circ: 54,000. Vol. ends: Dec.

Bk. rev: 10–12, 300 words. *Aud:* Hs.

The official organ of the nation's oldest and largest philatelic society, this journal is recognized for its high quality and superior technical production. Traditional philatelic research and postal history articles comprise the bulk of the journal, and advertisements from carefully screened APS member-dealers share space with news items about current and forthcoming events. Many regular feature columns cover specific popular areas of interest. A calendar of upcoming shows, a large book-review section, and an interesting question-and-answer column are important features. A separate APS section includes information on the many specialist affiliate societies of the APS, details on the annual APS conventions, recent society news, and APS-related information. Recommended for all libraries.

Canadian Stamp News. 1976. bi-w. Can. $18. John Denner. McLaren Pubs., Ltd., P.O. Box 10,000, Bracebridge, Ont. P0B 1CD Canada. Illus., adv. Circ: 20,213.

Bk. rev: Occasional. *Aud:* Hs.

A popular tabloid stamp newspaper of Canada, this bi-weekly publication concentrates on news and material of current interest in the stamp world, particularly Canadian. Announced stamp issues of all countries are listed (often the subject of background articles), stamp-issuing series and programs are described, awards and honors are cited, and forthcoming newsworthy events are detailed. Important auction realizations are cited, and news releases from the various philatelic organizations are published. For general collections.

Gibbon's Stamp Monthly (Formerly: *Stamp Monthly*). 1927. m. £17.90. John Holman. Stanley Gibbons Publns., Ltd., S. Parkside, Ringwood, Hants, BH24, 3SH, England. Illus., index, adv. Circ: 30,000. Vol. ends: May.

Bk. rev: 6–10, 50 words. *Aud:* Hs.

House organ of Stanley Gibbons, publishers of the foremost British stamp catalogs, this journal is an unusual blend of the popular and the more specialized. One of the most fascinating features, which has been running for more than 60 years, is "Through the Magnifying Glass," which details minor varieties of common stamps from all countries and all periods; this is a happy hunting ground for the collector, especially of Commonwealth issues. The articles are well researched and include much useful information on modern issues, postal history, and background data on stamps and their use. The *Gibbons Catalogue Supplements* keep the catalog up to date. A *British Stamps* supplement caters to specialist collectors of British stamps and postal history. Recommended for all collections.

Linn's Stamp News. 1928. w. $22.95. Michael M. Laurence. Amos Press, Inc., P.O. Box 29, Sidney, OH 45365. Illus. Circ: 75,000.

Bk. rev: Occasional. *Aud:* Hs.

Largest and most widely circulated stamp weekly in the world. News of philately around the globe is extensively covered in a weekly average of 96 tabloid pages. Comprehensive articles on U.S. and foreign news issues, news happenings in philately, tips for beginners, forthcoming stamp shows, auction coverage, and trends of U.S. and foreign stamp prices appear weekly. The first issue of each month features Linn's U.S. Stamp Market Index—the Dow Jones Industrial Average of the stamp market—tracking the price movements of rare U.S. stamps. Articles on postal history, traditional philately, and investments appear regularly. Such weekly features as the "Question Corner and Collectors' Forum" give readers an opportunity to correspond with other collectors. Most popular areas of the hobby are treated in columns, which are staggered throughout the month. More mail order advertising is found in this than in any other U.S. publication; therefore, the newspaper is a good way to keep up with the current state of the philatelic marketplace.

National Stampagraphic. See Art/For the Student: General Section.

Mekeel's Weekly Stamp News. 1891. w. $8. George F. Stilphen. Severn-Wylie-Jewett Co., P.O. Box 1660, Portland, ME 04104. Illus., index, adv. Circ: 16,000.

Bk. rev: Occasional, brief. *Aud:* Hs.

Oldest of the tabloid-size weeklies, this newspaper contains data on current events, announcements of forthcoming shows and exhibitions, society news, and other current-awareness information. New issues are covered by interesting background articles, and some space is usually given to the most popular aspects of the hobby. Its small size and limited advertising space are somewhat balanced by its very economical cost when compared to the other major weeklies. For comprehensive collections and general collections, especially where economy is a deciding factor.

Minkus Stamp and Coin Journal (Formerly: *Minkus Stamp Journal*). 1966. q. $6. Belmont Faries. Minkus Publns., Inc., 41 W. 25th St., New York, NY 10010. Illus., adv. Circ: 22,000. Vol. ends: Dec. Microform: UMI.

Bk. rev: Occasional. *Aud:* Hs.

Formerly *Minkus Stamp Journal*, this is the house organ of the publishers of the popular Minkus catalog. A few years ago it began providing numismatic articles as well as philatelic information. Attractively produced with many color illustrations, the journal is slanted toward the general and novice collector. Articles are usually well written and informative with some emphasis on topical collecting. The quarterly supplement to the *Minkus Worldwide Catalogue* is perhaps the journal's most useful feature. For youthful and general collections.

Scott Stamp Monthly (Formerly: *Scott's Monthly Stamp Journal; Scott's Monthly Journal*). 1920. m. $18. Wayne Lawrence. Scott Publg. Co., 3 E. 57th St., New York, NY 10022. Illus., adv. Circ: 28,500.

Bk. rev: 2–4, 300 words. *Aud:* Hs.

This is the house journal of the Scott Publishing Company, publishers of the Scott catalogs. The journal usually contains several good feature articles of general interest. The regular monthly updates of the *Scott Standard Postage Stamp Catalogue* and the *U.S. Specialized Catalogue* keep the reader up to date on new varieties and catalog changes. A nice touch is the topical index of new issues, listing the stamps by depicted subjects, a practical aid for the thematic collector. U.S., Canadian, and UN new issues and future programs are also outlined chronologically. The editorial column includes a variety of information on newly discovered varieties and other useful matters. The excellent long book reviews are another noteworthy feature.

Stamp Collector Newspaper (Formerly: *Stamp Collector; Western Stamp Collector*). 1931. w. $16.95. Michael Green. Van Dahl Publns., Inc., 520 E. First St., Albany, OR 97321. Illus., adv. Circ: 27,695.

Bk. rev: Occasional. *Aud:* Hs.

Formerly called *Stamp Collector* and *Western Stamp Collector*, this tabloid provides good coverage of news and current events in philately, especially for the United States and Canada. New issues of both countries receive comprehensive attention, and the information given for foreign new issues, although somewhat less detailed, is nevertheless adequate for the general collector. Exhibitions, stamp shows, events sponsored by major societies, awards received, and other such occasions are given broad coverage. New publications are the subject of occasional review articles, and some postal history and philatelic articles are also published. U.S. and Canadian philatelic subjects are given good coverage, and the listing of forthcoming special cancellations to be used throughout the United States is particularly valuable. Philatelic investments and the stamp market are the topics of regular features, and the large amount of advertising serves to keep the collector up to date on the state of the marketplace.

Stamp World. 1981. m. $12. Wayne Lawrence. Amos Press, P.O. Box 29, Sidney, OH 45365. Illus., adv. Circ: 28,651. Vol. ends: Dec.

Bk. rev: 1–5, 200–300 words. *Aud:* Hs.

Most recent of the nationally distributed general philatelic periodicals, this journal is an attempt to reach the general public not usually in touch with the standard philatelic journals and newspapers. Wide national distribution has served to popularize philately, and this is a fine introduction to the collector who is a stranger to philatelic publications. Very attractively produced, with many color illustrations, the articles concentrate on the most popular aspects of the hobby. Articles tend to be short and informative, written in an informal style. A good magazine for youth and beginners. Recommended for all libraries.

Stamps. 1932. w. $16.50. August Perse. H. L. Lindquist Publns., 153 Waverly Pl., New York, NY 10014. Illus., index, adv. Circ: 28,000. Microform: UMI.

Bk. rev: Occasional. *Aud:* Hs.

A popular stamp journal of long standing, emphasizing news and current events in the hobby, this magazine also contains much detailed information, particularly on U.S. and Canadian issues. Market updates, reports on current periodical literature, new issue information, stamp club news, recent discoveries, postal history notes, announcements of upcoming stamp exhibitions, auction reports, and similar items make up about half the journal. The rest is given over to advertising, which provides a good resource for the collector seeking new material.

HOME ECONOMICS

For the Student/For the Professional

See also Consumer Education; Sociology; and Women Sections.

Jean Bishop, Head of Public Services, Montana College of Mineral Sciences and Technology Library, Butte, MT 59701

Polly-Alida Farrington, Librarian, Rensselaer Polytechnic Institute, Troy, NY 12180

Introduction

Is the American family disappearing, or is it in a transition that is evolving into a stronger life-style? From the Home Economics literature now being published, the family is thriving. However, the focus is shifting from the traditional structure to the awareness and acceptance of various social units. Families are searching for more enriching relationships, and the home is still viewed as the miniature building unit of society.

Two other areas that form part of the home economics curriculum are found in this section: food and nutrition and the home.

Selected titles in this section emphasize useful publications for leaders and educators in the field of home economics. They will be of interest to professionals who are endeavoring to interpret scientific and researched information into practical concepts that may be useful to the individual member of our population.

Basic Periodicals

Ejh: *Choices*; Hs: *Better Homes & Gardens, Choices.*

Basic Abstracts and Indexes

Current Index to Journals in Education, Education Index.

For the Student

AHEA Action. 1974. 4/yr. $7.50 (or membership). Anne Swearingen. Amer. Home Economics Assn., 2010 Massa-chusetts Ave. N.W., Washington, DC 20036. Illus., index. Sample. Microform: UMI.

Aud: Hs.

Published by American Home Economics Association to keep members updated on current home economics activities. Printed in tabloid format, the publication covers meetings, legislation, grants, and includes classified advertising. Longer, scholarly articles are reported in the AHEA's *Journal of Home Economics* and *Home Economics Research Journal*. (J.B.)

Better Homes & Gardens. 1922. m. $12.97. David Jordan. Meredith Corp., Locust at 17th, Des Moines, IA 50336. Illus., index, adv. Circ: 8,000,000. Microform: B&H, UMI.

Indexed: RG. *Aud:* Hs.

By and large one of America's most popular magazines for ideas about the home, this is a mainstay in almost all public and many high school libraries. Its success is based upon easy-to-understand articles, which move from hints on furnishings and decoration to cooking and yardwork. These are augmented by black-and-white and colored photographs and illustrations. Throughout there is a mass of advertising, which many readers find almost as appealing as the editorial materials. Beyond that, the editor takes in the interests of any middle-class family. Each issue, for example, will have something about health, travel, money, and loads and loads of data on new products and shopping hints. There is little controversy here, unless it be the choice of a wallpaper, but at the same time there is much to challenge the family member whose home is the center of the universe. See, too, the numerous other publications under the *Better Homes & Gardens* banner listed below:

All Time Favorite Recipes. 1977. a. $3.95. Many of these are from the mainline magazine, but others come in from readers and other sources. Practical, easy to follow.

Better Homes & Gardens Country Home. 1979. bi-m. $2.95. Much like the mainline magazine. But, as the title suggests, the slant is toward the upper middle-class family living in the country or the suburbs. Particularly impressive for hints on cooking and remodelling.

Black Family. 1980. bi-m. Carolyn Shadd, 360 N. Michigan Ave., Chicago, IL 60601. Illus., adv. Circ: 200,000. Sample.

Aud: Hs.

A type of *Better Homes & Gardens*, this publication differs in that there is more interest in general family matters than simply on how to improve the home. Still, there are numerous articles on the concerns of a home owner. Beyond that, one finds short pieces on a wide variety of topics, from finance and health to travel. The illustrations are adequate, and the style of writing easy enough to follow.

Bon Appetit. 1956. m. $15. Paige Rense. Bon Appetit, P.O. Box 10776, Des Moines, IA 50340. Illus., index, adv. Circ: 1,300,000.

Aud: Hs.

A basic magazine for all cooks. Most articles emphasize recipes, but there is also coverage of travel, food trends, cooking equipment, and wines. "Cooking Class" and "The Basics" are particularly helpful to novice cooks and good refreshers for old pros. Many recipes come from readers. "R.S.V.P.," "The Cook's Exchange," and "Too Busy to Cook" are all regular columns that feature readers' recipes. Recipes emphasize simple but interesting preparations. A popular and fun cooking magazine for libraries. (P.A.F.)

Capper's Weekly. 1879. bi-w. $13.50. Dorothy Harvey. Stauffer Communications, Inc., 616 Jefferson St., Topeka, KS 66607. Illus., adv. Circ: 400,000. Sample.
Aud: Hs.

Now over 100 years old, and well known in the Midwest, *Capper's* comes out every two weeks—not once a week as the title suggests. It offers the small-town resident and farmer sensible advice on a wide variety of topics, from gardening and cooking to a down-home women's section. Much of the material is donated or otherwise sent to the paper by the faithful readers. One has a sense that almost each and every one of the 400,000 readers is a member of a large family. This spirit is carried throughout the paper, even to news about the world at large. Still, the primary interest is in the home, particularly in the traditional role of the woman looking after children. In its way, it is as lively as it is fascinating. This is the type of publication that deserves a wide readership in larger communities.

Choices (Formerly: *Co-ed*). 1956. 8/yr. $6. Kathy Gogick. Scholastic Magazines, Inc., 730 Broadway, New York, NY 10003. Illus., index, adv. Circ: 900,000. Sample.
Aud: Ejh, Hs.

Designed for home economics classroom use for both male and female students. *Choices* contains popular interest articles dealing with family relationships, child care, home improvement, and personal health. It is colorful and written in an easy-to-read style. The teacher's edition, *Forecast for Home Economics*, gives supplemental, researched information. Recommended for elementary, junior high, and high school libraries. (J.B.)

The Cook's Magazine. bi-m. $18. Judith Hill. Pennington Pubs., 2710 North Ave., Bridgeport, CT 06604. Illus., index, adv. Circ: 180,000.
Bk. rev: 2–3, 300–500 words, signed. *Aud:* Hs.

Described as "The Magazine of Cooking in America" and "The Magazine for Serious Cooks," this is the magazine for the cook who wants more than just a recipe. Articles emphasize skills and knowledge that help the cook understand how a process works and the history and uses of ingredients. (P.A.F.)

Family Economics Review. 1943. q. $12. Marilyn Doss Ruffin. Family Economics Research Group, USDA/ARS, Federal Bldg., Rm. 442A, Hyattsville, MD 20782. Illus. Circ: 11,000. Sample. Microform: UMI.
Indexed: IFP, IGov. *Aud:* Hs.

Published by the Family Economics Research Group under the Agricultural Research Service to inform citizens of transactions of public business required by the law for this department. Well-documented articles are written by professionals in economics, nutrition, clothing, and sociology. Abstracts of new government publications in family economics are included, along with some regular features covering new U.S. Drug Administration publications, costs, and consumer prices. Tables are included on "Cost of Food at Home" and "Consumer Prices." *Family Economics Review* is prepared in a concise style primarily for home economics agents and home economics specialists of the Cooperative Extension Service. (J.B.)

Gourmet. 1941. m. $18. Jane Montant. Condé Nast, Ltd., 560 Lexington Ave., New York, NY 10022. Illus., index, adv. Circ: 656,000. Sample. Microform: UMI.
Indexed: MgI, RG. *Aud:* Hs.

Although recently taken over by Condé Nast, Ltd., the high level of writing has been maintained. Each issue contains many lengthy and interesting articles that give a personal view of travel, food, and wine. *Gourmet* has more pages than it used to and has a bit broader scope. Giving in to modern life-styles, recipes that can be completed in 45 minutes or less are now highlighted. Regular features cover restaurants around the world and wine. "*Gastronomie Sans Argent*" emphasizes a single inexpensive ingredient and a variety of recipes using that ingredient. "Cooking with Jacques Pépin" is a new feature—a step-by-step cooking lesson in each issue. Recipes can be a challenge for novices (and sometimes for experts!). But since *Gourmet* includes so much more than just recipes—the best of food, wine and travel, enhanced by elegant photography—it should be considered. (P.A.F.)

Home Economics Association of Australia. Journal. 1969. 3/yr. $15. Edith M. Cox. The Home Economics Assn. of Australia, P.O. Box 303, Broadway, NSW, 2007, Australia. Illus., adv. Circ: 1,300. Sample.
Bk. rev: 1–2, 250–300 words, signed. *Aud:* Hs.

Official publication of the Home Economics Association of Australia. Short, factual, two-to-four paged features by a wide range of professionals cover education, family, nutrition, and marketing. Pieces are written mainly by Australian authors, with extensive bibliographies using international references. News is included from the National Health and Medical Research Council. Metric measurements are commonly used. Good for objective family life comparisons dealing with worldwide problems. (J.B.)

The Homemaker. 1979. bi-m. $11. National Extension Homemakers Council. Subs. to: The Homemaker Magazine, Inc., 7375 E. Peakview Ave., Englewood, CO 80111. Illus., adv. Circ: 250,000. Sample. Microform: B&H.
Bk. rev: 4–6, 50–2,000 words. *Aud:* Hs.

Editorial content focuses on ways to enhance homemaking as a lifestyle. Includes articles on regional recipes, beauty, health, nutrition, crafts, consumer values and money-saving tips, sewing and stitchery, interesting homemaker personalities and experiences, humor, travel, family relationships and family finances, home care, gardening, and other homemaker interests. Special departments include "Information Worth Writing For," "The Best of Extension," "The Up-to-Anything Cook," and "The Home Library." One of the better informative publications with popular interest, this publication is highly recommended for a school library collection. (J.B.)

Nutrition Action. 1974. 10/yr. $20. Greg Moyer. Center for Science in the Public Interest, 1501 16th St. N.W., Washington, DC 20036. Illus. Circ: 36,000.

Indexed: API. *Aud:* Hs.

A good consumer-oriented 16-page newsletter full of useful information on nutrition, diet, and health. Each issue contains a three- to five-page feature article. Recent issues have covered stress pills and meat in America. "In the Public Interest" contains short watchdog-type items informing the public on consumer issues including bills before Congress (e.g., ban of sulfites) and movements to force greater honesty in advertising. "Eater's Digest" contains a wide range of features. Answers to readers' questions, "Truth in Advertising," "Buyer Beware," "Healthy Cook" (recipes), "Informed Consumer," and "Interviews" are some of the features of the newsletter. All of these are a page or two in length and not all features appear in all issues. Each provides basic information aimed at educating consumers and giving them a practical knowledge of nutrition. (P.A.F.)

Vegetarian Times. 1974. m. $19.95. Paul Obis. Vegetarian Times, 41 E. 42nd St., Suite 921, New York, NY 10017. Illus., adv. Circ: 105,000. Sample. Microform: UMI.

Indexed: NPI. *Bk. rev:* 2–3, 500 words. *Aud:* Hs.

Feature articles cover a wide range of topics related to health, nutrition and living a "natural life." Recent articles dealt with natural soaps, Japanese noodles, spring greens, exercise, recipes from the international Culinary Olympics, and a test of your nutritional knowledge. This is an informative magazine sure to be of interest and value to readers. (P.A.F.)

What's New in Home Economics. 1936. 9/yr. Millie Riley. WNHE, 655 15th St. N.W., Suite 310, Washington, DC 20005. Illus., index, adv. Circ: 17,000. Sample. Microform: B&H, UMI.

Aud: Hs.

Short, concise articles covering all current interest subjects written by professionals in the field. Editors make selections and decisions upon considering the needs and interests of home economics teachers and other home economics professionals. Special departments report regularly on "freebies," buyer's guide, upcoming events, new technology, media centers, management, parenting, foods, fashion, and personal development. (J.B.)

For the Professional

Executive Housekeeping Today. 1980. m. $18. 929 Harrison Ave., Suite 305, Columbus, OH 43215. Illus., adv. Circ: 8,000. Sample.

Aud: Pr.

Good resource for vocational training. This management magazine is published by the National Executive Housekeepers Association for personnel involved in institutional housekeeping for hospitals, hotels, and motels, colleges and universities, government installations, and similar activities. Features focus on products and services, industry and association news, and problem-solving approaches to management. Deals with such subjects as dust control, laundry operations, floor care, pest control, grounds maintenance, and safety. (J.B.)

Forecast for Home Economics. 1952. 8/yr. $10. Kathy Gogick. Scholastic, Inc. 730 Broadway, New York, NY 10003. Subs to: P.O. Box 644, Lyndhurst, NJ 07071. Illus., index, adv. Sample. Vol. ends: May/June. Microform: B&H, UMI.

Indexed: CIJE, EdI, MgI. *Aud:* Pr.

A professional magazine for home economics educators. Articles emphasize teaching techniques, current topics of interest and sources of teaching aids. Lesson plans and visuals are included, and feature articles are written to supply the educator with researched background information. Covering any subject of interest to young men and women enrolled in home economics classes, this is published as a teacher supplement to the student edition, *Choices.* (J.B.)

Journal of Home Economics. 1909. q. $20. Constance Burr. Amer. Home Economics Assn., 2010 Massachusetts Ave. N.W., Washington, DC 20036. Illus., index, adv. Sample. Refereed. Microform: UMI.

Indexed: CIJE, EdI, MRD, PAIS. *Bk. rev:* 2–6, 250–300 words, signed. *Aud:* Pr.

Official publication of the AHEA written to improve the quality and standards of the individual and family life. Articles are written by secondary and college educators, and analyze current and future trends in home economics with teaching methods suggested. Regular features include new publications and visuals, new products and services, and a forum discussion on a current topic. Basic and important to the professional, this journal is recommended for high school libraries. (J.B.)

Tips and Topics. 1960. q. $4. Linda R. Glosson. College of Home Economics, Texas Tech Univ., P.O. Box 4067, Lubbock, TX 79409. Illus. Circ: 5,000. Sample. Refereed.

Aud: Pr.

A newsletter that contains well-researched reports of timely topics focusing on a central subject. Many teaching techniques and lesson plans are suggested and are "designed for in-service and pre-service education of persons involved in any phase of home economics education." Some book reviews are included. Special sections include resources that are available. Highly recommended. (J.B.)

Vista. 2/yr. $20. Sask. Home Economics Teacher's Assn., 2317 Arlington Ave., Saskatoon, Sask., S7K 3N3, Canada. Illus. Sample.

Indexed: CanEdI. *Bk. rev:* 1–2, 100 words, signed. *Aud:* Pr.

Includes a variety of discussions and lesson plans to aid the home economics teacher. *Vista* endeavors to provide students with the experience and knowledge necessary for making sound decisions and for managing available resources as individuals, family members, and as part of society. Articles cover the study of foods, clothing, finance, housing, and family life. The official publication of the Saskatchewan Home Economics Teacher's Association, the publication includes a special section on "News and Views." Although the diagrams and illustrations are of inferior quality, the print is clear and easily read. (J.B.)

HORSES

For the Student

Ellen B. Wells, Chief, Special Collections Branch, Smithsonian Institution Libraries, Washington, DC 20560

Introduction

Magazines catering to the horse industry continue to proliferate. Many specialize in breeds or activities, with growing emphasis on the business aspects of horse breeding, training, and competition. Some editors, because of controversies in breed promotion groups, now publish disclaimers of favoritism. Most breed magazines emphasize versatility and youth activities. Those with massive advertising include indexes to advertisers, and some include glossaries of equestrian terminology.

Basic Periodicals

Ejh, Hs: *Horseman.*

For the Student

American Saddlebred. 1983. bi-m. $35 (Membership). Linda A. Albery. Amer. Saddlebred Horse Assn., Inc., 929 S. Fourth St., Louisville, KY 40203. Illus., adv. Circ: 6,200. *Aud:* Hs.

New journal devoted to the American Saddlebred horse, used almost exclusively for riding and driving in horse shows. The publication emphasizes breeding, show reports, association news, and tips on the business and management aspects of raising, training, and selling horses. Promotion of junior riders and of versatility programs is gaining in importance. Each issue features a glossary of terminology, useful to neophytes. Occasionally, there are historical articles on the breed and early personalities.

Appaloosa News. 1946. m. $15. Don Walker. Appaloosa Horse Club, Inc., 309 S. Ann Arbor, Suite 100, Oklahoma City, OK 73128. Illus., adv. Circ: 21,000. *Aud:* Hs.

Typical breed magazine, with standard format. Emphasis is on people who are raising and showing Appaloosa horses, and the Appaloosas themselves. Articles on shows, personalities, and racing predominate. There are occasional articles of general interest on health care, training, and riding. Special issues include racing, performance, youth, and stallion. Features include show results, sales reports, and classifieds.

Arabian Horse World. 1960. m. $36. Jan Schuler, 2650 E. Bay Shore Rd., Palo Alto, CA 94303. Illus., index, adv. Circ: 25,000. *Aud:* Hs.

Catering to the growing interest and investments in Arabian horses, this magazine is known for its lavish color illustrations both in the articles and in the heavy advertising. Arabians from all over the world are reported on, and articles appear on breeding, sales, bloodlines, show results, and history. Occasionally, there are general articles on health care, training, and riding. Special annual issues include pieces on stallions, mares, and Egyptian and Polish Arabian horses.

Chronicle of the Horse. 1937. w. $35. Peter Winants, P.O. Box 46, Middleburg, VA 22117. Illus., index, adv. Circ: 20,000. *Aud:* Hs.

One of the best general magazines reporting on equestrian activities, with some emphasis on the sport horse. Much space is devoted to show results, with features on major thoroughbred races on the flat and over fences, and polo. Some foreign competitions are also reported on. Book reviews are somewhat uncritical. An important source for late-breaking news, this is the official publication of at least seven equestrian organizations. Should be in every library with an interest in the horse world.

Horse & Horseman. 1972. m. $12. Jack Lewis. Gallant/Charter Publns., P.O. Box HH, Capistrano Beach, CA 92624. Illus., adv. Circ: 90,000. *Aud:* Hs.

Appeals to young competitors in English and Western style shows, and some rodeo events. How-to articles discuss problems in riding style, training horses, and showing. Features include problem horse/problem rider columns, veterinary and health care, new products, and apparel.

Horse Illustrated. 1977. m. $15.97. Jill-Marie Jones. Fancy Publns., Inc., P.O. Box 2430, Boulder, CO 80321. Illus., adv. Circ: 40,000. *Aud:* Hs.

Aimed particularly at the young adult, this heavily illustrated magazine emphasizes how-to articles on training and riding, breed profiles, and news of horse shows and other equestrian events. Features include reports on new books, veterinary commentary, horse behavior, product news, and young rider pages.

Horseman. 1956. m. $18. Linda Blake, P.O. Box 1990, Marion, OH 43306. Illus., adv. Circ: 200,000.

Aud: Ejh, Hs.

Long-lasting magazine for Western- and English-style riders, with sound basic articles as well as personality and news features. Some emphasis on safety and self-analysis of riding problems. Features include new products.

Morgan Horse (Formerly: *Morgan Horse Magazine).* 1941. m. $22.50. C. Edward Perkins. Amer. Morgan Horse Assn., P.O. Box 1, Westmoreland, NY 13490. Illus., adv. Circ: 10,000.

Aud: Hs.

Heavily illustrated, with much in color, this solid breed magazine emphasizes the Morgan as an English-style show horse. Special issues highlight stallions, mares, and the Grand National Morgan horse championship shows. Substantive articles appear regularly on breed history, horse care, conditioning, grooming, training horses, and riders. Recent stress has been given to versatility of the Morgan, particularly in driving and in western-style riding, as well as in saddle-seat showing.

Paint Horse Journal. 1966. m. $15. Bill Shepard. Amer. Paint Horse Assn., P.O. Box 18519, Fort Worth, TX 76118. Illus., adv.

Aud: Hs.

Devoted to horses marked by large spots of bay or black color on a white field. Reports on showing and racing predominate, with some useful general articles on practical aspects of horsemanship. Well illustrated and produced, special issues include racing, performance, recreational, stallions, and several major show issues.

Performance Horseman. 1982. m. $18. Pamela Goold. Gum Tree Store Press, Inc., Gum Tree Corner, Unionville, PA 19375. Illus., adv. Circ: 30,000.

Aud: Hs.

Described as a "how-to-do-it publication . . . for the serious Western-style rider with a commitment to competition and/or breeding show horses." There is a pleasant mix of articles on Western-riding concerns (reining, pleasure riding, trail horse competition), with articles on basic horse care and handling. Health, nutrition, and breeding have prominent space in this journal. Some features and departments are also published concurrently in *Practical Horseman.*

Practical Horseman (Formerly: *Pennsylvania Horseman).* 1973. m. $18. Pamela Goold. Gum Tree Store Press, Inc., Gum Tree Corner, Unionville, PA 19375. Illus., adv. Circ: 52,600.

Aud: Hs.

Described as a how-to-do-it publication for the serious English rider interested in breeding, training, conditioning horses for hunting, jumping, dressage, and combined training. Articles provide well-illustrated information on stable management, training skills, nutrition and health, and economics of the horse business. Pictorial clinics are special and well-known features of *Practical Horseman.*

Western Horseman. 1936. m. $15. Chan Bergen. Western Horseman, Inc., P.O. Box 27780, San Diego, CA 92127. Illus., adv. Circ: 155,000. Microform: UMI.

Aud: Hs.

One of the best general horse magazines, this publication emphasizes the stock horse in the western part of the country, its uses, its breeds, and its history. Often featuring cowboy art, *Western Horseman* reports regularly on rodeo events, trail riding, personalities, and ranches. Features include new merchandise and reports on new books. Special issues include the October breed issue, vacations, and training.

HUMOR

For the Student

Joseph J. Acardi, Director, Janesville Public Library, 316 S. Main St., Janesville, WI 53545

Introduction

There is a shortage of good humor magazines in this country. Although the *Standard Periodical Directory* lists 29 titles under "Humor and Satire," up to half of them no longer exist by the time the list goes to press. That leaves few choices for the librarian who is looking to round out a magazine collection with something on the lighter side. The following titles represent a variety of types of humor magazines. There is surely at least one title in this list that can fill the humorless void found in most periodical collections. Be adventurous. You and your patrons will be glad you did.

Basic Periodicals

Ejh: *Muppet Magazine;* Hs: *Mad, National Lampoon.*

For the Student

Journal of Irreproducible Results. 1955. 4/yr. $3.90. Alexander Kohn. Journal of Irreproducible Results, Inc., P.O. Box 234, Chicago Heights, IL 60411. Illus., adv. Circ: 42,000. Vol. ends: No. 4.

Aud: Hs.

The official organ of the Society for Basic Irreproducible Research, this satirical journal has experienced not only an upsurge in circulation over the past few years (understandable, in light of its extremely modest subscription price), but has also found its way into a couple of prominent indexes. Dedicated to the proposition that "neither science nor man can survive the rigors of our age without a sense of humor," the 20 or so articles featured in *JIR*'s 32 pages cover such topics as "The Physical Dimensions and Value of Swearing" and "Moral, Nutritional and Gustatory Aspects of Cannibalism." For the price, it is a genuine bargain.

Mad. 1952. 8/yr. $10.75. Albert B. Feldstein. E. C. Publns., Inc., 485 Madison Ave., New York, NY 10022. Illus. Circ: 2,000,000. Vol. ends: "Never."
Aud: Hs.

There have been no major editorial changes in *Mad* since the July 1955 issue, when the publication changed from what was essentially a comic book to a magazine. Since then, the "usual gang of idiots" has continued to keep *Mad* at the top of the humor heap by poking liberal fun at the issues, fads, and politics of our time. Its great success lies in the fact that it strives to attract a normal, middle-class audience. The familiar face of Alfred E. Neuman has come to be regarded as the ultimate symbol of *Mad*ness throughout the world, and that face becomes even more prominent every four years at election time. One of these times he may even capture the popular vote. A "must" for nearly every library's collection.

Muppet Magazine. 1982. q. $6.00. Katy Dobbs. Telepictures Pubns., Inc., 300 Madison Ave., New York, NY 10017. Illus., adv. Circ: 525,000. Sample. Vol. ends: Nov.
Aud: Ejh.

This is "a children's humor magazine based on the zany humor and character delivery of the Muppet show Muppets. . .strictly an entertainment magazine skewed for 7- to 14-year olds who are media hip." Regular features in this popculture magazine are: "Editorial" (by Kermit), "Muppet Mailbag," "Muppet Roundups" (record notes), "Ask Mr. Honeydew," and "Miss Piggy's Advice Page." The rest of the issue includes articles on sports and show business personalities, a film spoof, things to make and do, and sometimes a pullout poster. The format is inviting and eyecatching with its full-color illustrations and photographs on glossy paper. There are many ads for products of interest to the intended audience. (L.K.O.)

National Lampoon: the humor magazine for adults. 1970. m. $9.95. P. J. O'Rourke. National Lampoon, Inc., 635 Madison Ave., New York, NY 10022. Illus., adv. Circ: 650,000. Microform: B&H.
Aud: Hs.

Over the years, *National Lampoon* has produced not only a successful magazine of devastating satire, but also a Broadway revue, several hit movies, and a number of books and record albums. The leading purveyor of "outrageous" humor, it has also been accused of being sick, gross, victimizing, and in poor taste at various times. *Lampoon* continues to hurl most of its barbs at politicians, women, homosexuals, and ethnic groups. In more recent issues the humor has become less cerebral, unless you consider a bash on the head

cerebral. Despite its sometimes questionable taste, *National Lampoon* is still the leading example of an adult humor magazine in this country.

INDIANS OF NORTH AMERICA

For the Student

Patricia Brauch, Head of Reference, Brooklyn College Library, City University of New York, Brooklyn, NY 11210

Introduction

The reasons for the high casualty rate among North American Indian periodicals are the lack of financial strength due to the drying up of federal funds, the lack of advertising, and the shortage of trained personnel. Indian periodicals, for the most part, are not published punctually or regularly. Sometimes they merge or die. *Wassaja* was our most serious loss. Sometimes they reappear, or new ones spring up when funding has been restored or a new source has been found.

The titles I have listed are for, by, and about North American Indians. No archaeological publications are included. We see the Indians' deep interest in sports, concern about the environment, and great sense of humor. The world can be seen from a North American Indian vantage point.

Basic Periodicals

Ehj: *Quinault Natural Resources*; Hs: *Akwesasne Notes*.

Basic Abstracts and Indexes

Alternative Press Index; Current Index to Journals in Education.

For the Student

Akwesasne Notes. 1969. 6/yr. $8. Peter Blue Cloud. Mohawk Nation Council, Rooseveltown, NY 13683. Illus. Circ: 20,000. Vol. ends: Dec. Microform: B&H, KTO, MCA, UMI.
Indexed: API. *Bk. rev:* Occasional. *Aud:* Hs.

This newspaper, the official publication of the Mohawk Nation at Akwesasne, is concerned not only with native affairs but also attempts to call the attention of all peoples, native or otherwise, to their common problems and to look at some of the possible answers together. News reports and articles cover such topics as ecocide, the arms race, religious and political freedom, and health. Other features are a poetry page, film reviews and advertisements for their book store. International in scope, it should appeal to a wide audience. Highly recommended.

Indian Artifact Magazine. 1982. q. $15. Gary L. Fogelman, R.D. 1, P.O. Box 240, Turbotville, PA 17772. Illus., index, adv. Circ: 10,000. Sample.
Bk. rev: 1–2, 5–600 words, signed. *Aud:* Ejh, Hs.

A glossy magazine for the amateur and collector of Indian artifacts. Contains short popular articles and good quality black-and-white photographs. Typical articles are on Indian artifacts and crafts, exciting finds and excavations, and Indian life and customs. Professional and amateur collectors are encouraged to contribute articles on any subject connected with the hobby. Recommended for school libraries.

Quinault Natural Resources. 1978. q. Free. Jacqueline Storm. Quinault Dept. of Natural Resources and Economic Development, P.O. Box 189, Tahola, WA 98587. Illus.
Aud: Ejh, Hs.

This shiny, attractive magazine with beautiful black-and-white photos is published, free, by the Quinault Department of Natural Resources as an "educational service to stimulate community interest and participation in QDNR, its programs and the Quinault Indian Reservation's natural resources." It covers environment, ecology, forestry, fishing, industry, and community development. Some issues have a special supplement, for example, one on the Quinault fisheries. There are items on the return of the Potlatch, interviews, and poetry. Regular features are a resources puzzle page and the retelling of an Indian legend. Its appeal is wider than the Quinault Indians. One letter to the editor came from Switzerland.

Rencontre. 1979. q. Free. Diane Bilodeau. SAGMAI, 875 Grand-Allée Est, P.Q., G1R 4Y8, Canada. Illus.
Bk. rev: 2–4, 65–75 words. *Aud:* Ejh, Hs.

A colorful magazine (in English) for Quebec's Amerindian and Inuit population. It brings information on the government of Quebec, programs available, and organizations that may be of use to Native Québecois. Areas covered are economics, politics, education, and culture. A regular feature is a children's corner of puzzles and games. The Christmas issue had a charmingly illustrated children's story. There is a section on new books and publications. For schools and libraries wanting information on the North American Indian.

Tsa' Aszi (The Yucca). 1973. q. $9. Jean Dunnington. Ramah Navajo School Board. CPO Box 12, Pine Hill, NM 87321. Illus. Circ: 1,200. Microform: CPC.
Aud: Ejh, Hs.

The "Yucca" began as a cultural journalism project for Navajo high school students. In 1982, federal funds were withdrawn and a last issue was published with a grant from the National Endowment for the Humanities. Now, after a two-year gap, it has begun publishing again. Although smaller in size, it still has the same fine quality. There are stories, poetry, personal anecdotes, interviews, and folklore. All are beautifully illustrated by photographs and line drawings. For school libraries serving North American Indians.

Turtle Quarterly. 1979. q. $3. Tim Johnson. Native American Center for the Living Arts, 25 Rainbow Mall, Niagara Falls, NY 14303. Illus. Circ: 3,000. Sample.
Bk. rev: Occasional. *Aud:* Hs.

In spite of funding difficulties, *Turtle* is still with us. Its 16 pages of newsprint and artistic photographs are concerned with the arts and social issues of Native Americans, primarily those in New York State. There are excellent articles on museum collections, performing arts, and exceptional people. There are reports on exhibitions, conferences, and special events. There is a pull-out section for children. Other features include a calendar of events and a directory. Recommended for schools with an interest in Native American arts.

Whispering Wind, the American Indian Past and Present. 1967. bi-m. $11. Jack B. Heriard. Louisiana Indian Heritage Association, 8009 Wales St., New Orleans, LA 70126. Illus., adv. Circ: 4,000. Vol. ends: Winter. Microform: MCA.
Aud: Hs.

This attractive, popular periodical is published by the Louisiana Heritage Association, whose purpose is "to study the customs, traditions, dances and crafts of the American Indian and to establish high standards." There are articles on crafts and clothing, often with how-to instructions. There are recipes, short stories, and poetry. One fine article was on humor among the different tribes. All are beautifully illustrated by line drawings and photographs. Regular features are news highlights and coming events such as powwows and exhibitions. There were no book reviews in the last six issues. Recommended for high schools.

JOURNALISM AND WRITING

For the Student/For the Professional

See also Literature; and Television, Video, and Radio Sections.

Craig T. Canan, free-lance journalist, P.O Box 120574, Nashville, TN 37212

Introduction

Journalism is a basic field that concerns anyone who reads a newspaper or views TV. The journalism reviews still play a positive role, and subscribing to at least one basic journalism review is at least as important for libraries of any size or type as carrying the more specialized periodicals in the field. With a growing demand by consumers for impartial reporting, librarians should consider carrying more periodicals that explain precisely in what news areas bias exists, how to recognize it, and therefore how to neutralize advertiser and other outside influence by reading between the lines.

A steady, more popular trend in magazines devoted to journalism is a greater share of attention to the electronic media. With the increasing popularity of audio media such as cable television, both specialized and reviewing journalism periodicals have featured more articles in this field. Even older journals like *Writer's Digest* have increased their coverage of the electronic media. Such coverage is one more reason why this periodical should be in most libraries.

Basic Periodicals

Ejh: *School Press Review*; Hs: *Quill & Scroll, The Writer*.

For the Student

Access. 1976. m. $36 (Individuals, $24). Samuel A. Simon. Natl. Citizens Committee for Broadcasting, P.O. Box 12038, Washington, DC 20005. Circ: 2,000. Sample.
Aud: Hs.

Finally there is a periodical available that specializes in offering criticism of broadcasting. *Access* was initiated by Ralph Nader to critique and democratize all aspects of the broadcast industry, including television and radio. This small tabloid features stories on such subjects as the debate over advertiser boycotts, legislation, conflicts of interest, and "talking back to your TV set." Its analysis of a Pennsylvania public television station was carried by national wire services and major newspapers, gaining national acclaim. Journalism reviewing is combined with Nader-style ideas for action in a way that should interest all consumers—that is, everyone. It should be a first choice for all libraries.

Columbia Journalism Review. 1962. bi-m. $16. Spencer Klaw. Graduate School of Journalism, Columbia Univ., New York, NY 10027. Illus., index, adv. Circ: 34,000. Microform: B&H, UMI.
Indexed: HumI, PAIS. *Bk. rev:* 5–6, length varies, signed.
Aud: Hs.

The best known, the most prestigious of all of the journalism reviews, this publication is basic. The reporters objectively cover all aspects of the media from television and radio to newspapers and magazines. The typical issue opens up with short reports on legal cases, individuals, bloopers, censorship, and just about anything else that makes the daily activities of journalism. The four or five primary articles tend to be investigative, and may be concerned with one type of publication or a particular publisher. The editor claims the journal is an effort to "assess the performance of journalists and help define—or redefine—standards of honest, responsible service." In a bright, easy-to-understand style the magazine does just that, and it is indispensable for most libraries.

Mediafile. 1980. m. $15. Bernard Chanian. Media Alliance, Bldg. D, Fort Mason, San Francisco, CA 94123. Illus., adv. Vol. ends: Dec.
Indexed: API. *Bk. rev:* 2–3. *Aud:* Hs.

This media review concentrates on national journalism with occasional articles on California media affairs as well. A typical issue may offer articles ranging from journalists being jailed in El Salvador to the Freedom of Information Act, and to the presentation and media reaction to the nuclear television show *The Day After.* Most of the copy in this tabloid newspaper is written by professional journalists, with the balance coming from educated lay persons. The *Columbia Journalism Review* remains the first choice among journalism reviews, but this one can nicely supplement the Columbia University product. Recommended.

Quill: a magazine for journalists. 1912. m. $18. Ron Dorfman. The Society of Professional Journalists, 840 N. Lakeshore Dr., Suite 801, Chicago, IL 60611. Illus., adv. Circ:

30,000. Sample. Vol. ends: Dec. Microform: UMI.
Aud: Hs.

This magazine now offers more general news of appeal to those outside the Society. Its six to eight features cover all aspects of the world of journalism, including ethics and promotions, and it periodically contains book reviews. It also has wide interest because of frequent articles on media personalities, advertising, censorship, and other specific aspects of print and audio media. At least two of the eleven yearly issues are special numbers covering subjects like journalism awards. The emphasis is on journalism as a profession, not only a trade.

Quill & Scroll. 1926. q. $9. Richard P. Johns. School of Journalism and Mass Communication, The Univ. of Iowa, Iowa City, IA 52242. Illus., adv. Circ: 20,002. Vol. ends: May. Microform: UMI.
Indexed: CIJE. *Bk. rev:* 6–8, 130–200 words, signed.
Aud: Ejh, Hs.

The official magazine of the International Honorary Society for High School Journalists. All phases of high school publishing, information on journalism careers, and other developments are presented from a professional point of view. Articles have covered sports-writing, investigative reporting, yearbook staffing, computers in school publishing, journalism ethics, and the role of the teacher/adviser. A good source for workshops, courses, higher education programs, and scholarships. *Quill & Scroll* News Media Evaluation sponsors the distinguished George H. Gallup Award for junior and senior high newspapers and news magazines. The magazine also holds annual writing, photo, and current events quiz contests. A regular column, "The Newest Books in Journalism," is not to be missed by anyone with an interest in the field. (L.K.W.)

Scholastic Editor's Trends in Publications (Formerly: *Scholastic Editor*). 1921. 7/yr. $16. Tom Rolnicki. Univ. of Minnesota, 620 Rarig Center, 330 21st Ave. S., Minneapolis, MN 55455. Illus., adv. Circ: 2,500. Sample. Vol. ends: May.
Indexed: CIJE. *Bk. rev:* 150–200 words, signed. *Aud:* Ejh, Hs.

Much like *Quill & Scroll,* this is a how-to magazine for editors and teachers involved with school publications. Articles, usually derived from personal experience, explain how to put together newspapers, yearbooks, and magazines and give tips on how to succeed as a journalist or editor, methods of writing, markets, and the like. While there is some information at the college level, the primary emphasis is on the high school student effort. One of the best for journalism classes.

School Press Review. 1925. 9/yr. $12. Laura Lisabeth. Columbia Scholastic Press Advisors Assn., P.O. Box 11, Central Mail Rm., Columbia Univ., New York, NY 10027. Illus., adv. Circ: 2,800. Sample. Vol. ends: Mar. Microform: UMI.
Indexed: CIJE. *Aud:* Ejh, Hs.

The *School Press Review* specializes in covering student writing in elementary, junior high, and some high school newspapers and magazines. Examples are presented of effective student writing taken directly from the publications in which the writing originally appeared. A special section reviews news of the student press since the last issue. Other departments include letters and a guest editorial section. Some news of the association is also included. Librarians will probably wish to request a sample before ordering.

The Writer. 1887. m. $17. Sylvia K. Burack. The Writer, Inc., 120 Boylston St., Boston, MA 02116. Adv. Circ: 55,000. Vol. ends: Dec. Microform: UMI.

Indexed: RG. *Aud:* Hs.

One of the two main how-to writers' periodicals in the United States, this magazine's articles mainly involve fiction, with an emphasis on book writing. A key purpose is to inspire and encourage the would-be writer. Features like "The Six Most Asked Questions about Writing," "What Makes Us Write," and "Why Editors Use Form Rejection Slips" are examples of how the magazine explains writing in an elementary fashion. If one examines issues over a several year period, it is noticed that article ideas seem to be recycled—almost as if rewritten under new titles. Each 48-page issue includes a unique "Quotes for Writers" column that could possibly inspire beginning writers and also includes market information similar to but less complete than that in the *Writer's Digest.*

Writer's Digest. 1920. m. $21. William Brohaugh. Writer's Digest, 9933 Alliance Rd., Cincinnati, OH 45242. Illus., index, adv. Circ: 170,000. Sample. Vol. ends: Dec. Microform: MIM, UMI.

Indexed: Acs, PopPer. *Aud:* Hs.

Like *The Writer*, this 60-to-70-page monthly explains the basis of writing. However, it is much more popular and progresses beyond that limited point by explaining precisely how to tailor an article to the specific needs of various markets. Articles cover techniques of fiction and nonfiction as well as photojournalism, playwriting, cartooning, and writing for radio and television. The market coverage is superior to *The Writer* in quantity and depth. Each issue provides one to three full-length articles on specific markets in addition to the general market information supplied in the other magazine. *Writer's Digest* is an essential tool for the successful professional writer as well as the beginner. Because of its scope, it is a first choice for advanced high school libraries.

Writing. See under *Curriculum Innovations* in Education/ For the Student Section.

For the Professional

Columbia Scholastic Press Advisors Association Bulletin. 1941. q. $6. James F. Paschel. CSPAA, P.O. Box 11, Central Mail Rm., Columbia Univ., New York, NY 10027. Illus. Circ: 1,800. Vol. ends: Winter. Microform: UMI.

Indexed: CIJE. *Bk. rev:* 5–6, short. *Aud:* Pr.

The *Bulletin* serves as the organ of the CSPAA as well as being published to help secondary school teachers who teach journalism and advise students on the publishing of their school newspapers, magazines, and yearbooks. Arti-

cles discuss ethics, teaching methods, and school publication writing and production. This is a basic teaching aid that is appropriate in libraries of all secondary schools producing any type of publication.

The Writing Instructor. 1981. q. $12. Rhonda Schuller. Freshman Writing Program, Univ. of Southern California, Los Angeles, CA 90089. Circ: 1,000. Vol. ends: Dec.

Aud: Pr.

Aimed at writing teachers in secondary schools and colleges and universities, this is an effort to "combine theory with pedagogy in a non-technical, useful way." The seven to ten articles, by students and teachers, may move from the writing conference and the composing process to role playing to see the writer's role. There is considerable emphasis on practical application of theory. The editors succeed in their purpose of "maintaining high standards without being stuffy." A required item for many teachers.

LATIN AMERICA, LATINO (U.S.)

For the Student: Latin America; Latino (U.S.)/For the Professional

Ana Maria Cobos, Manager, Borderline Project, Latin American Center, University of California, Los Angeles, CA 90024

Salvador Güereña, Chicano Studies Librarian, Colección Tloque Nahuaque (Chicano Studies Collection), University Library, University of California, Santa Barbara, CA 93106

Albert J. Milo, Assistant Director, Commerce Public Library, Commerce, CA 90040

Vivian M. Pisano, San Francisco Public Library, San Francisco, CA 94102

Introduction

Libraries in the United States have faced major challenges in filling the informational and recreational reading needs that exist within the Latino community. The large and growing Latino population in this country already comprises the seventh largest Spanish-speaking nation in the world. But what is most important to note here is the diversity that exists within this community. Latinos are varied in their backgrounds and interests and are just as varied in their language preference, encompassing the spectrum from monolingual English to bilingual to monolingual Spanish. It is precisely for this reason that libraries need to be informed about the availability of periodicals from which to choose. These cover Latin America, Spain, and Luso-phone countries, as well as the interests of U.S. Latinos, which are now receiving much more attention. Periodicals are available in English, Spanish, and in bilingual format. They also reflect the range of interests from popular recreational reading to very scholarly approaches.

The excitement regarding this increased pool of available periodicals is tempered by several notable problems of particular concern to libraries. These involve the relatively poor bibliographical control and indexing of these titles, particularly those of popular interest, which are largely absent from the standard periodical reference sources. Another problem for libraries has been the high rate of cessation of

Latino periodicals. Libraries should recognize this situation and not be dissuaded from subscribing to new periodicals that may appear if these would be of interest to their Latino constituencies. (S.G.)

Note: Reviews prepared by V.M.P. and A.J.M., which have given credit to *Revistas,* have been excerpted with the permission of *Revistas: An Annotated Bibliography of Spanish Language Periodicals for Public Libraries,* 1983, compiled by Bibliotecas Para La Gente, Periodical Committee.

Basic Periodicals

Ejh: *Chispa, Geomundo*; Hs: *Américas, Geomundo, Notitas Musicales, Tú.*

For the Student

LATIN AMERICA

Américas. 1949. m. Spanish edition. $12. Jack Lowe. Organization of Amer. States, 17th & Constitution Aves., N.W., Washington, DC 20006. Illus., index. Circ: 100,000. Microform: UMI.

Indexed: AbrRG, HumI, RG. *Aud:* Hs.

Latin American topics are the main focus of most articles, which have included indigenous tribes, folk art, archaeological discoveries, textiles, and cooking. This is a beautifully illustrated magazine that will appeal to a broad audience. (V.M.P./*Revistas*)

Artes de México. 1957. q. $35. José Losada Tomé. Artes de México y del Mundo S.A., Amores 262, Mexico 12, D.F., Mexico. Illus., index, adv. Circ: 20,000.

Aud: Hs.

An exceptional periodical, *Artes de México* is bright and colorful, devoting each issue to one aspect of Mexico's arts, broadly defined. Hence, its subjects have included anything from the art of the charros, or Mexican cowboys, to the history of Franciscan architecture in Mexico or Mexican costumes and textiles. Each number sports numerous black-and-white photographs as well as color plates. The commentary is in Spanish, being fully translated into English, and occasionally French, which will be found at the rear of each issue. This feature enhances the value of the magazine for libraries in this country. Each issue is physically substantial, appearing in an 8¾- by 12¾-inch format, and averaging between 100 and 140 pages in length; occasionally the numbers are hardbound. (S.G.)

Automundo Deportivo. 1949. m. $60. Jesús González Díaz. Editorial Mex-Ameris, S.A., Av. Morelos No. 16, 4 Piso, Mexico 1, D.F., Mexico. Illus., adv.

Aud: Hs.

This is a sports magazine written entirely in Spanish. It covers a broad selection of sports, such as tennis, football, and auto racing. Although it is published in Mexico, it includes coverage of sports in both the United States and Mexico. In fact, the coverage for certain recent issues was heavily weighted in favor of U.S. sports, in particular NFL

football. All cover stories were on teams and players in the NFL football league! On the other hand, conspicuously absent are stories on "futbol," or soccer, a sport extremely popular among Latino men. Includes many colored photographs and is similar to *Sports Illustrated* in format and size. Suitable for high school libraries. (A.J.M.)

Balón: futbol mundial. 1963. w. $34.84. Antonio Elizarras Corona. Periodismo Especializado, Presidentes 187, Col. Portales, Mexico 13, D.F., Mexico. Illus.

Aud: Hs.

One of the most complete magazines on international soccer, *Balón: futbol mundial* includes detailed information on clubs, scores, players and other topics of interest to aficionados. Many photographs and drawings are included. (V.M.P./*Revistas*)

Burbújas. 1975. $1.25/issue. Mexico: Provenemex, dist. by EDINSA, P.O. Box 2145, San Ysidro, CA 92073. Illus.

Aud: Ejh.

A spinoff from the popular Mexican children's television series of the same name, *Burbújas* appeals to a wide audience. Preschoolers enjoy the cartoons, while older children appreciate the stories. The magazine's focus is popular rather than literary. (V.M.P./*Revistas*)

Caribbean Review. 1971. q. $12. Barry B. Levine, Florida Intl. Univ., Miami, FL 33199. Illus., index, adv. Circ: 5,000. Microform: UMI.

Indexed: PAIS. *Bk. rev:* 10–12, 250–350 words, signed. *Aud:* Hs.

This glossy, well-illustrated title is "dedicated to the Caribbean, Latin America, and their emigrant groups," with an emphasis on the social sciences. Its wide range of topics have included "Politics, Caribbean Style"; "Varieties of Labor Organization: The Caribbean and Central America Compared"; and "Collages, Carvings and Quilts: The Visual Arts of St. Vincent." In addition to its concise book reviews, a four-page "Recent Books" section is a valuable update on publications dealing with the region and its peoples, arranged into seven general subject areas, including one on reference books. Materials published about the Chicano/Latino experience in the United States are cited as well. This handsome quarterly will have broad appeal and is recommended for libraries that have an interest in the Caribbean area. (S.G.)

Chispa. 1979. m. $28.20. Inovación y Comunicaciones, México, D.F., Mexico. Subs. to: Donars Spanish Books, P.O. Box 24, Loveland, Colorado, & EBSCO, P.O. Box 4069, Burlingame, CA 94010. Illus.

Aud: Ejh.

An educational magazine children enjoy. Each issue features experiments, crossword puzzles, and questions-and-answers on various subjects. A regular section, *Achicate,* is translated from the Canadian *OWL Magazine* published by The Young Naturalist Foundation. The color and black-and-white illustrations are attractive. Contributors have expertise in education and the sciences. (V.M.P./*Revistas*)

Claudia. 1965. m. $24. Hilda O'Farrill de Kelly. Editorial Mex-Ameris S.A., Av. Morelos No. 16, 4 Piso, Mexico 1, D.F., Mexico. Illus., adv. Circ: 102,577.

Aud: Hs.

This fashion-and-beauty magazine has numerous articles intended for women. Topics include family health, gardening, and interior decorating. Also included are brief news clips about the film industry, TV world, book reviews, recipes, horoscopes, short stories, and strange and unusual facts. (V.M.P./*Revistas*)

Contenido. m. $22. Armando Ayala Anguiano. Editorial Contenido, Calle Darwin No. 101, 11590 Mexico, D.F., Mexico. Illus., adv.

Bk. rev: Irreg. *Aud:* Hs.

This current-events magazine is published in the format and size of *Reader's Digest*. However, unlike *Selecciones del Reader's Digest*, which takes its articles from other books and magazines, *Contenido*'s articles are originals. The articles tend to be six to eight pages in length and cover such topics as interviews, world events and health issues. Occasionally condensations or excerpts from books are included. A recent issue included a condensed version of a Mario Vargas Llosa work. Moreover, *Contenido* tends to carry more articles on Latin America written by Latin Americans in contrast to *Selecciones*, which simply takes works written in English by U.S. writers and translates them into Spanish. (A.J.M.)

Cuadernos Americanos: la revista del nuevo mundo. 1942. bi-m. $35. Jesús Silva Herzog. Coyoacán 1035, Colonia del Valle. Delegación Benito Juárez, 03100 Mexico, D.F., Mexico. Illus., index, adv. Circ: 1,750.

Aud: Hs.

One of the oldest and most highly regarded journals published in Latin America. Whether the topic is sociopolitical or literary, whether it be a contemporary issue or of historical interest, the reader will discover a wide range of first-rate scholarship. While primarily dealing with Latin America, there are occasional articles that are related to Iberian interests, international relations, or that examine U.S. current affairs. Literary criticism is largely Hispanic but does not exclude other literatures. Published in Spanish, the journal issues its own annual index. It is recommended for Latin American collections. (S.G.)

Fem. 1976. bi-m. $24. Nueva Cultura Feminista A.C., Av. México No. 76-1, Col. Progreso Tizapán, Mexico 20, D.F., Mexico.

Bk. rev: 1–2, 500–1,000 words, signed. *Aud:* Hs.

Fem is an unusual feminist magazine, which advances progressive issues in Mexico on behalf of the Mexican woman. This includes such social and political concerns as the opposition to forced sterilization and the promotion of women's interests within national institutions and international forums. It is also a veritable fountain of creative and artistic expression, providing women's perspectives on art and the cinema. Included are short stories and poetry selections.

"En Pocas Palabras" is a regular feature, which gives brief news and notes that deal with women: groups and issues and events in Mexico, Latin America, and abroad. Thematic special issues have been devoted to the elderly, to young women, and even Chicanos. This is a very readable and copiously illustrated, thought-provoking periodical, which merits inclusion in library collections serving the interests of Latinos. (S.G.)

Geomundo. 1977. m. $32. Pedro J. Romanach. De Armas Publications, 605 Third Ave., Suite 1620, New York, NY 10016. Illus., index, adv. Circ: 7,189.

Aud: Ejh, Hs.

Similar to *National Geographic*, this periodical contains beautiful photographs to illustrate articles that feature animals, world cultures, and the natural sciences. *Geomundo* is a favorite for basic popular collections because of its attractive cover, layout, and Latin American focus. (V.M.P./*Revistas*)

Hola. w. $105. Madrid: Hola, dist. by EBSCO, P.O. Box 4069, Burlingame, CA 94010. Illus.

Aud: Hs.

This very expensive, very popular large-format general pictorial magazine from Madrid is a cross between *Life* and a tabloid. It is full of gossipy articles on the jet set and international celebrities from the entertainment world. The publication is profusely illustrated with photographs in color and black and white. Special sections include fashion, beauty, recipes, and recordings. (V.M.P./*Revistas*)

Hombre del Mundo. 1975. m. $27. Pedro Romanach. Editorial América, S.A, Vanidades Continental Bldg., 6355 NW 36th St., Virginia Gardens, FL 33166.

Aud: Hs.

The title suggests that this magazine might solely appeal to men. It does not. Its 8½- by 11-inch format resembles that of *Time* or *Newsweek*. Recent cover stories have appeared on such diverse people as Dr. William de Vries, the Pope, and Ronald Reagan. There is a little bit of everything in this magazine—something for everybody. Other recent issues examined contained articles on heart transplants, Steven Spielberg, men's fashions, India, golf, the Uruguayan president, Poland, and stress. Does a library need more than one generalist magazine in Spanish? Emphatically yes! Why should the Spanish speaker be restricted to choosing from one magazine for his or her news, while the English speaker can choose from *Time, Life, Reader's Digest*, and so forth. Therefore, *Hombre del Mundo* is recommended for high school libraries. (A.J.M.)

Impacto. w. $83.20. Mario Sojo Acosta. Publicaciones Llergo, S.A., c/o Pressmag, Inc., 219 W. Calton Rd., Laredo, TX 78041.

Aud: Hs.

This magazine resembles *Life Magazine*. The resemblance is also in the area of size: *Impacto* is 9½ by 13 inches in size. It is richly illustrated with both black-and-white as well as color photographs. It carries such features as articles on world events, Ronald Reagan, China, art, culture, Japanese gardens, and Nicaragua. The fact that it is published in Mexico is noticeable in local news stories, as for example the State of Queretaro and the Miss Mexico Beauty Pageant. Articles are very brief. They are usually accompanied by numerous photographs and rarely exceed more than one page in length. Strongly recommended for high school libraries. (A.J.M.)

Mecánica Popular. m. $30. Santiago J. Villazón. Editorial América, S.A., Subscription Service Dept., P.O. Box 230, Patterson, NY 12563. Illus., adv.

Aud: Hs.

This Hearst Corporation publication is the Spanish counterpart to the English version of *Popular Mechanics.* However, the magazine is not an exact translation of the English issues. It is also smaller in size than its English counterpart; the average number of pages is 100, while the English edition averages 250 pages per issue. In terms of content, the topics covered are very similar. Regular sections are devoted to the categories of automobiles, photography, electronics, sports/aviation, and carpentry. There are easy-to-read assembly diagrams and handy tips on "how to" construct or repair items. It will appeal primarily to men who like the concept of "doing it yourself." The automobile reviews will appeal to a wider audience. It is unfortunate that this magazine is not indexed to increase its usefulness. Highly recommended. (A.J.M.)

Notitas Musicales. m. $15.60. Notitas Musicales, S.A., Calle Olivo No. 4, Desp. 203, Mexico 20, D.F., Mexico. Illus., adv.

Aud: Ejh, Hs.

This magazine is aimed primarily at the young adult. A recent issue examined contained articles on both the singing industry, as well as the movie industry of the United States and Mexico. There was also a featured article on Michael Jackson. Two regular features that are popular include a listing of the Top 10 in Mexico as well as the lyrics to actual recorded songs. The magazine is primarily written in Spanish, but song lyrics that were originally recorded in English are printed in English. Recommended for junior high school and high school libraries. (A.J.M.)

Tú. m. $16.00. Irene Carol. Editorial America, S.A., Subn. Services Dept., P.O. Box 230, Patterson, NY 12563. Illus., adv.

Aud: Hs.

This woman's magazine written totally in Spanish is aimed at a teenage audience. It regularly includes articles on rock stars (e.g., U2 and the Rolling Stones) and movie stars (e.g., Matt Dillon, Rob Lowe, and Tom Cruise). Other common topics include fashions (e.g., sweaters), exercises, beauty tips (e.g., fingernail care), and worldwide list of pen pals. A recent issue contained a librarian's nightmare, a cutout for a sunvisor. Much to the surprise of the reviewer, not only had the sun visor cutout been left intact by patrons,

so, too, had all the photograph pinups! Recommended for high school libraries. (A.J.M.)

LATINO (U.S.)

Aztlán: international journal of Chicano studies research. 1970. s-a. $20 (Individuals, $15). Chicano Studies Research Center, Univ. of California, Los Angeles, 405 Hilgard Ave., Los Angeles, CA 90024. Circ: 1,500. Microform: UMI.

Indexed: SocSc. *Bk. rev:* 3–7, 350–1,100 words, signed. *Aud:* Hs.

The outstanding scholarly journal of Chicano studies, *Aztlán,* serves as a forum for research and essays in the social sciences and the arts. According to the editors, "The Journal's focus is on critical analysis, research, theory, and methodology as they relate to Mexicans as a group, in the United States, and in Mexico." Rigorous standards of academic research are upheld. While they are scholarly, the articles are also very readable and cover a variety of topics including history, art, sociology, linguistics, politics, economics, law, education, and literature. Most issues also include research notes on such topics as "Hispano-Mexican Pioneers of the San Francisco Bay Region" or "Mexican Women in Los Angeles Industry in 1928." *Aztlán* should be an indispensable part of all collections concerned with the Chicano and Mexican experience. It also has broader application beyond these areas and may be useful to serve the interests of other Hispanic communities in the United States as well. (S.G.)

Caminos. 1980. m. $12. Katharine A. Díaz. Caminos Corp., P.O. Box 54307, Los Angeles, CA 90054. Illus., adv. Circ: 45,000. Sample.

Bk. rev: 2–3, 25–50 words. *Aud:* Hs.

This five-year old general magazine is going through a transitional phase. Some of the changes recently noted have been a change in editor, a diminution in issue length, and an abandonment of having all articles fully translated into English and Spanish. Except for advertisements, all articles are now written exclusively in English. The magazine's perspective is definitely Southern California, especially Los Angeles, although occasionally national issues, such as immigration legislation and East Coast stories, do appear. Back issues may be purchased at $2.50 each. The magazine often devotes its issues to such themes as immigration, careers, media, movie industry, and artists. It holds an annual Hispanic of the Year Award contest, which recognizes significant contributions by Hispanics in various fields. As part of one's subscription a separate Annual National Hispanic Conventioneer issue is received that announces the conferences and conventions of Hispanic organizations. Despite its Los Angeleño orientation, *Caminos* is recommended for high-school libraries because of its general coverage, the importance of Los Angeles in its Latino population, and the fact that it is one of the few such magazines that is indexed. (A.J.M.)

Casino Discos. m. $12. Miami: Casino Publg. Division, dist. by Luis Tigera, 1225 W. 18th St., Chicago, IL 60608; Natl.

Distributors Magazines, 3750 N.W. 28th St., Rm. 201, Miami, FL 33142; and EDINSA, P.O. Box 2145, San Ysidro, CA 92073.

Aud: Ejh, Hs.

This attractive entertainment magazine appeals to fans of radio, television, film and the international recording industry. It lists the hit records in Miami, New York, Madrid, and Mexico. (V.M.P./*Revistas*)

Coqueta. m. $42. Vanidades Continental, dist. by EBSCO, P.O Box 4069, Burlingame, CA 94010. Illus.

Aud: Ejh, Hs.

Similar to *Seventeen* in style, this teen fashion magazine has articles on grooming, clothes, advice columns, pen-pal exchange, and interviews with popular teen stars. (V.M.P./*Revistas*)

Lector. See Books and Book Reviews/For the Professional Section.

Low Rider. 1977. m. $15. Sonny Madrid. Aztlán Communications, 1915 Hartog Dr., San Jose, CA 95131. Illus., adv. Circ: 90,000.

Bk. rev: Irreg. *Aud:* Ejh, Hs.

"Low Riders" are proud owners of carefully modified, classy automobiles that can be raised or lowered instantly a foot or more at the flick of a switch, through the use of hydraulics. These cars are driven low, slow, mean, and clean. Easy-riding aficionados would not be caught without the magazine, which is usually snapped up from store racks the day it arrives. This is definitely a hot item for Latino youth, whether the locale is El Paso, Tucson, or Los Angeles. But this glossy car magazine offers more than attractive young ladies modeling crafted cars. It is more than an advertising outlet for hydraulics and Zoot Suit clothing. Issues may also include news features of concern to the Chicano community, interviews with Latino celebrities, historical essays, or articles on current issues. For the lovelorn, "Escucha La Tia Chucha" is a popular advice column that regularly dispenses practical wisdom on girl/guy relationships. *Low Rider* is published in English, albeit flavored occasionally with slang expressions. This is an important Chicano magazine which fills a need, enjoys a loyal following, and should therefore find a place in libraries. (S.G.)

Nuestro. 1977. m. $22. Betty South. Americana Communications Corp., Nuestro, P.O. Box 40874, Washington, DC 20016. Illus., adv. Circ: 198,000.

Bk. rev: 1, 3 pages, signed. *Aud:* Hs.

Although it has been published only since 1977, *Nuestro* is one of the oldest popular magazines published in the United States for Hispanics. When it was first published, it was questionable whether or not there was a suitable market to keep it going. There was a controversy over whether *Nuestro* should be printed in English or Spanish or both. It chose to print its articles in English, although for some strange reason it chose a Spanish word for its name (*Nuestro* means "ours") and printed the captions to photographs in Spanish. It has since discontinued printing its captions in Spanish. Because it has offices in Los Angeles and in New York, it

gives a fairly balanced coverage of all Latino groups, especially Chicano, Puerto Rican, and Cuban. It emphasizes news coverage in the United States. It has a broad coverage of topics, such as sports, health, music, cooking recipes, and personalities. A recent issue even contained original poetry. It is highly recommended for libraries with English-speaking Hispanics. (A.J.M.)

For the Professional

Yelmo: la revista del professor de español. 1971. 3/yr. $20. Manuel Criado de Val, Apdo. 877, Madrid, Spain. Circ: 3,000. Sample. Microform: UMI.

Bk. rev: 1,500–2,500 words, signed. *Aud:* Pr.

Aimed at teachers of Spanish, *Yelmo* deals with the theory and methodology of instruction and provides an outlet for articles that deal with linguistics and its specialized aspects, such as sociolinguistics or the problems of translation. An interesting recent contribution was a two-part glossary of new sociopolitical terminology that appeared in several issues. Literary topics and bibliographies are included. A separate section regularly reprints newspaper and magazine articles that deal with themes and problems involving the Spanish language. The publication appears entirely in Spanish. (S.G.)

LIBRARY PERIODICALS

For the Professional

See also Books and Book Reviews Section.

Barbara Via, Reference Librarian, Graduate Library for Public Affairs and Policy, University Libraries, SUNY at Albany, Albany, NY 12222

Introduction

With tight library budgets and new library periodicals appearing yearly, it is difficult for library professionals to keep up with their literature. The periodicals listed in this section represent a selection of titles covering virtually every facet of the field. The titles included run the gamut from standard periodicals, suitable for most any professional collection, to titles intended specifically for school librarians. Local and regional publications have, for the most part, been excluded. The rationale for this is that librarians are usually familiar with the publications originating in their regions.

Basic Periodicals

Pr: *American Librarian, Emergency Librarian, SLJ/School Library Journal, School Library Media Quarterly, Top of the News, VOYA: voice of youth advocates, Wilson Library Bulletin.*

For the Professional

American Libraries. 1907. m. (exc. bi-m. July/August). Membership (Nonmembers, $30). Arthur Plotnik. Amer. Library Assn., 50 E. Huron St., Chicago, IL 60611. Illus., index, adv. Circ: 41,500. Vol. ends: Dec. Microform: B&H, MIM.

Indexed: MgI. *Aud:* Pr.

The official bulletin of the American Library Association, this is a colorful, very readable magazine that does an excellent job of keeping the reader apprised of the U.S. library scene. Although the feature articles are not in-depth research pieces, they are well written and thought-provoking. The regular features include a readers' action exchange, news items, the "Source" (a selection of current-awareness resources) and ALA news. A particularly useful feature is the "Bulletin Board," a checklist of announcements. An essential purchase for all libraries.

Bookbird. See Literature/For the Professional Section.

The Book Report: the journal for junior and senior high librarians. 1982. 5/yr. $30. Carolyn Hamilton. Linworth Publg. Co., 2950 N. High St., P.O. Box 14466, Columbus, OH 43214. Illus., index, adv. Circ: 10,000. Vol. ends: Mar.
Indexed: BoRvI. *Bk. rev:* 90–120, 110–130 words, signed.
Aud: Pr.

A colorful, and, yes, entertaining magazine. This publication contains a fount of information beyond its stated interest—the theory and operation of secondary school libraries. The main topic may be "Public Relations" or "Teaching Library Skills." The workshop types of articles provide insights and innovative ideas. The book review is awesome in the breadth of its coverage and standard of criticism; reviewers, who are practicing librarians, grade the titles. There are sections on nonbook media, software, and library supplies. A hands-on magazine for all who work with teens. (L.K.W.)

Canadian Children's Literature. See Literature/For the Professional Section.

Canadian Library Journal. 1944. bi-m. Membership (Nonmembers, Can. $30). Sheila Nelson. Subscription Manager, Canadian Library Assn., 151 Sparks St., Ottawa, Ontario K1P 5E3, Canada. Illus., adv. Circ: 6,000. Vol. ends: Dec.
Indexed: CanI. *Bk. rev:* 10–15, 300–800 words, signed.
Aud: Pr.

The official journal of the Canadian Library Association is more akin to the *Library Journal* than to ALA's *American Libraries*. Each issue contains several lengthy nontechnical, but well-researched and well-written articles. Issues covered tend to include the "hot topics" of the day, such as online public access catalogs, microcomputer library applications, and the information age. The October issue covers the annual conference in depth. This is a must for all Canadian Libraries. U.S. library schools should have this—other collections should consider it for its Canadian perspective on universal library issues. The Association's newsletter, *Feliciter,* is also a must for both Canadian and U.S. library school collections.

Catholic Library World. 1929. 10/yr. Membership (Nonmembers, $30). John T. Corrigan. Catholic Library Assn., 461 W. Lancaster Ave., Haverford, PA 19041. Illus., index, adv. Circ: 3,000. Vol. ends: June. Microform: UMI.
Aud: Pr.

The official publication of the Catholic Library Association, this is one of the better association publications. It has a pleasing format, and its coverage is broader than its title implies. It does offer a solid amount of practical information and collection-building resources for Catholic libraries, but it also includes many articles of interest especially to school libraries, public as well as private.

Collection Building. 1978. q. $55. Arthur Curley. Neal-Shuman Pubs., 23 Cornelia St., New York, NY 10014. Vol. ends: Winter.
Aud: Pr.

This journal would be of interest to anyone with collection development responsibilities in any kind of library. Recent issues have covered such topics as collection development, policymaking, and information on resources for grants. Each issue includes four or five lengthy articles plus regular columns by distinguished librarian authors. Sandy Berman's column, "Alternatives," offers particularly interesting reading on some pretty eclectic topics. He has dealt with "Alternative Comix" as well as "Men's Music" (the work of gay and feminist men). Another column of note is the "Library-Publishing Connection." This journal covers an essential aspect of any library's work in a lively, highly readable style and should be considered.

Emergency Librarian. 1973. 5/yr. $30. Ken Haycock & Carol-Ann Haycock. EL Circulation Dept., 70 Bond St., Ground Floor, Toronto, Ont. M5B 2J3, Canada. Illus., adv. Circ: 3,500. Vol. ends: May/June. Microform: UMI.
Indexed: CanEdI. *Aud:* Pr.

A Canadian publication aimed at teachers and librarians working with children and young adults in public and school libraries. Each issue includes four or five articles, as well as reviews of professional reading, children's recordings, magazines for young people and paperbacks for children and young adults. Started in the early 1970s as an alternative, feminist, mimeographed journal, in recent volumes *EL* has switched gears and become a slick journal for children's librarians. It continues to provide creative concepts and stimulating articles. The writing is imaginative, and the coverage of children's and young adult librarianship broad enough that librarians anywhere will find this worthwhile.

Film Library Quarterly. 1967. q. $15. William Sloan. Film Library Information Council, P.O. Box 348, Radio City Sta., New York, NY 10101. Illus., adv. Circ: 1,300. Microform: UMI.
Aud: Pr.

The official organ of the Film Library Information Council, this journal includes articles on film makers, the history of film, documentary films and so on. Each issue includes book reviews, as well as video and film reviews. The coverage of diverse film-related topics is very good. Recent issues have had articles on film subject headings, film programming at a public library, and video production.

Lector. See Books and Book Reviews/For the Professional Section.

Library Hi Tech. 1983. q. $39.50 (Individuals, $19.50). C. Edward Wall. Pierian Press, P.O. Box 1808, Ann Arbor, MI 48106. Illus., adv.

Indexed: CIJE. *Bk. rev:* 5–10, 300–500 words, signed. *Aud:* Pr.

For coverage of new and forthcoming technologies for libraries, this journal is a real find. Each quarterly issue of approximately 120 pages is packed with articles on every aspect of library technology imaginable. Although coverage is geared to U.S. libraries, there are a few articles on international library technology. The issues are well organized. The contents pages also include a subject index for the issue. This journal is particularly valuable for readers trying to keep up with the latest advances. The articles are readable and do not require an advanced degree in computer science on the part of the reader. A scattering of humorous pieces is a welcome touch. Recommended for all library collections with an interest in technology.

Library Journal. 1876. s-m. (m. Jan., July, Aug., Dec.). $55. John M. Berry. R. R. Bowker Co., Magazine Div., 245 W. 17th St., New York, NY 10011. Illus., index, adv. Circ: 26,634. Vol. ends: Dec. Microform: UMI.

Indexed: EdI, MgI. *Bk. rev:* 200-300, 100–300 words, signed. *Aud:* Pr.

The venerable *Library Journal* should be in every library professional collection. It offers a combination of news items, an events calendar, regular departments, which include people news, reviews of new magazines, and a checklist of free or inexpensive materials to write for, as well as lengthy, well-written, and often critical, feature articles on library issues. Special issues include: the Annual Buying Guide, which is a comprehensive product and service directory; new fall books and new spring books issues; science and technology books guide; and religious books guide. The regular book reviews are abundant, concise, and useful. No other library science periodical comes close to matching *Library Journal* for coverage of topics and book selection guidance. A necessary purchase for all library collections.

Library Technology Reports. 1965. bi-m. $145. Howard S. White. Amer. Library Assn., 50 E. Huron St., Chicago, IL 60611. Illus., index. Vol. ends: Dec.

Aud: Pr.

Library Technology Reports provides up-to-date, conveniently packaged information on library systems, equipment, and supplies for library administrators. An authority on the topic under consideration in each issue writes a thorough, state-of-the-art guide complete with detailed, brand-name information. Recent issues have focused on photocopiers, microform-reader printers, electronic spreadsheet systems, and automated options for serials control. These reports are authoritative and very timely. They provide an excellent source for information that would otherwise be very difficult to track down. As a sort of consumer's guide for library equipment and systems, almost any library will find this journal worthwhile. Individual issues can be purchased separately.

Newsletter on Intellectual Freedom. 1952. bi-m. $15. Judith Krug. Subscription Dept., Amer. Library Assn., 50 E. Huron St., Chicago, IL 60611. Illus. Circ: 3,200. Vol ends: Nov. Microform: UMI.

Bk. rev: 1–3, 500–800 words, signed. *Aud:* Pr.

Published by ALA's Intellectual Freedom Committee, the newsletter reports on challenges to intellectual freedom across the United States. Also provided are details on court rulings affecting intellectual freedom, book reviews and Intellectual Freedom Committee reports. A particularly noteworthy feature is the continuing bibliography of journal articles on intellectual freedom. This newsletter is a basic source for this crucial information and should be in every library collection.

Online: the magazine of online information systems. 1977. q. $78. Jeffery K. Pemberton. Online, Inc., 11 Tannery Lane, Weston, CT 06883. Illus., index, adv. Circ: 3,600. Vol. ends: Nov. Microform: UMI.

Bk. rev: 5–8, 300–500 words, signed. *Aud:* Pr.

Online places most emphasis on practical articles relating to database searching. Recent issues have included articles on total library integrated automation and strategies for training managers to use an IBM Personal Computer effectively in their work. The articles are often well illustrated with diagrams and charts. Coverage of online news is good and includes fairly extensive notes on European activities.

The Reference Librarian. 1981. q. (2 vols/yr.). $53/vol. (Individuals, $32/vol.). Bill Katz & Ruth A. Fraley. Haworth Press, Inc., 28 E. 22nd Street, New York, NY 10010. Refereed.

Indexed: CIJE. *Aud:* Pr.

Each issue of this monographic series is devoted to a single theme; articles are solicited from qualified authors. Some topics that have been treated include: reference services for children and young adults, evaluating reference collections, and new technology and reference services. The 25 or so articles in each issue provide coverage of the theme. The editors do not hesitate to include articles representing "alternative" opinions on the theme. Thus, the reading is often lively and the articles thought-provoking. Each issue serves as a nice overview of a particular area of reference librarianship.

RQ. 1960. q. Membership (Nonmembers, $20). Kathleen M. Heim. RASD, Amer. Library Assn., 50 East Huron St., Chicago, IL 60611. Illus., index, adv. Circ: 6,000. Vol. ends: Summer. Refereed. Microform: UMI.

Indexed: CIJE. *Bk. rev:* 30–40, 200–500 words, signed. *Aud:* Pr.

An attractive publication of the Reference and Adult Services Division of ALA (RASD), *RQ* continues to grow into a more substantial journal with each volume. The regular columns include: "The Exchange," in which readers engage in helping each other with difficult reference queries, a government information column, and one on adult services. All of the column editors regularly explore problems that public service librarians are faced with. The feature articles cover the gamut of issues from user satisfaction with online reference services to reference service and map librarianship. The writing level continues to improve, and the articles are generally well documented. The "Sources" section, which provides reviews of databases, reference books and professional reading, is an invaluable part of this journal. The materials reviewed are well chosen and the reviews are truly evaluative. *RQ* is a basic journal for librarians.

Rural Libraries. 1980. 2/yr. $6. Center for the Study of Rural Librarianship, College of Library Science, Clarion Univ. of Pennsylvania, Clarion, PA 16214.

Aud: Pr.

Given the huge numbers of libraries serving rural populations in the United States, this journal was long overdue. It is a very good effort, with informative articles written not only by librarians but also by sociologists, marketing professors, and the like. In the issue examined an extensive article on marketing the rural library was particularly interesting. The format of this journal is plain and simple, but its contents make this a must purchase for the thousands of libraries situated away from metropolitan centers.

SLJ/School Library Journal. 1954. m. (exc. June & July). $47. Lillian N. Gerhardt. R. R. Bowker Co., 245 W. 17th St., New York, NY 10011. Illus., adv. Circ: 44,000. Vol. ends: Aug. Microform: UMI.

Indexed: EdI, CIJE. *Bk. rev:* 150–200, 200–300 words, signed. *Aud:* Pr.

Without a doubt the best library journal published for children's, young adult, and school librarians. *School Library Journal* has three or four excellent articles in each issue. They are lengthy and provide a wealth of information and ideas. For example, a recent issue included a super guide to audiovisual programs for computer know-how. The regular columns are great. "Up for Discussion" provides a forum for library problems; a professional reading column provides detailed reviews of books for children's and young adult librarians. The reviews sections are invaluable: computer software, audiovisuals, and books are reviewed concisely and in large numbers. This is a must for all libraries serving children and young adults.

School Library Media Quarterly (Formerly: *School Media Quarterly*). 1952. q. $10 (Nonmembers, $20). Jack R. Luskay. Amer. Assn. of School Librarians, 50 E. Huron St., Chicago, IL 60611. Illus., index, adv. Circ: 7,400. Vol. ends: Summer. Microform: UMI.

Indexed: CIJE, EdI. *Bk. rev:* 8–10, 500–1,000 words, signed. *Aud:* Pr.

Published by the American Association of School Librarians, a division of ALA, this is an attractive and well-edited publication. Each issue of 75 or more pages includes five or six articles as well as numerous regular departments including news and notes on people and publications, readers' queries, an idea exchange, reviews of professional books, and software reviews. The articles are well written and range from the practical (weeding the school media collection) to theoretical (the future of school libraries). Although not as comprehensive as *School Library Journal* in news coverage and reviews, this journal, along with *Top of the News*, is an essential for school library collections.

Signal. See Literature Section.

Top of the News. 1942. q. Membership (Nonmembers, $25). Marilyn Kaye. Subn. Services, Amer. Library Assn., 50 E. Huron St., Chicago, IL 60611. Illus., index, adv. Circ: 9,500. Vol. ends: Summer. Microform: UMI.

Bk. rev: 2–5, 150–200 words, signed. *Aud:* Pr.

As a source for ideas and critical thinking on issues of concern to librarians serving children and young adults, this journal is excellent. Jointly published by the Association for Library Service to Children and the Young Adult Services Division for ALA, *TON* provides news of both divisions' activities, as well as other news of interest to the intended audience. The eight to twelve articles are often thoughtfully critical and provide well-rounded coverage of both children's and young adult library services. The articles are written for the most part by practicing librarians and reflect the reality of library work with young people. This, along with *School Library Journal*, is a basic source for any library serving children and/or young adults.

The Unabashed Librarian. 1971. q. $20. Marvin H. Scilken. The Unabashed Librarian, G.P.O. 2631, New York, NY 10116. Illus.

Aud: Pr.

Subtitled the "How I Run My Library Good" letter, this newsletter aims for practical rather than theoretical approaches to library problems. A typical issue of 32 pages includes brief contributions from practicing librarians on such topics as outreach services, public library guidelines for video and copyright, and fund-raising by direct mail. The articles are detailed and provide enough information so that other libraries could easily adapt the ideas presented. The good humored slant of *The Unabashed Librarian*, plus its practical information, makes it a title worth considering.

VOYA: voice of youth advocates. 1978. bi-m. $20. Dorothy M. Broderick & Mary K. Chelton. VOYA, 3936 W. Colonial Pkwy., Virginia Beach, VA 23452. Illus., index, adv. Circ: 3,000. Vol. ends: Feb. Microform: UMI.

Bk. rev: 200–300, 100–200 words, signed. *Aud:* Pr.

Aimed at the librarian responsible for young adult services, VOYA is a well-edited journal of reviews, feature articles, and news. Over half of each issue is devoted to reviews of books, audiovisuals, recordings, games, and other materials for young adults. The reviews are concise and helpful. The feature articles are refreshingly open-minded and occasionally controversial. The overall quality of this journal is high. It publishes more reviews of young adult materials than any other source. Highly recommended for school libraries.

Wilson Library Bulletin. 1914. m. (exc. July/Aug.). $30. Milo Nelson. H. W. Wilson Co., 950 University Ave., Bronx, NY 10452. Illus., index, adv. Circ: 24,450. Vol. ends: June. Microform: UMI.

Indexed: EdI, PopPer. *Aud:* Pr.

The only privately published general-interest library periodical other than *Library Journal, Wilson Library Bulletin* is a polished monthly that provides an excellent view of the current U.S. library scene. Articles frequently focus on user services and new technology. Regular columns cover the publishing industry, school library technology, dateline Washington, and Will Manley's wonderful column, "Facing the Public," in which he writes on every manner of library patron interaction. Reviews—of children's picture books, young adult books, murder mysteries, films, records, professional reading, library software, reference books and general book reviews—are selective and well written. This is a basic purchase for most professional collections.

Y-A Hotline: an alert to matters concerning young adults. 1977. irreg. $3.50/6 issues. L. J. Amey, School of Library Services, Dalhousie Univ., Halifax, N.S. B3H 4H8, Canada.
Aud: Pr.

Produced by students in the Young Adult Literature and Media Interests course at Dalhousie University, this is a lively, information-packed newsletter. Reviews of young adult-oriented materials are well written and refreshingly honest. The articles focus on various services for young adults as well as topics of interest to young adults themselves. An inexpensive resource for any library serving young people.

LINGUISTICS AND LANGUAGE ARTS

For the Professional

Mary J. Cronin, Director of University Libraries, Loyola University of Chicago, 6525 N. Sheridan Rd., Chicago, IL 60626

Jyoti Pandit, Government Documents/Reference Librarian, Main Library, Reference Dept., SUNY at Stony Brook, Stony Brook, NY 11794

Introduction

During the last decade, linguistics has progressed considerably from basic anthropological concepts of learning language through phonology, morphology, and syntax to transformational grammar and other areas. It is difficult to assemble a group of journals that reflect completely the wide range of interests. An attempt has been made to introduce titles concerned with basic linguistic content, with the relationship between linguistics and other disciplines, and with second language learning and teaching.

This section also includes titles aimed at teachers of language arts, both of English and other languages. For foreign language teachers, a basic resource for any individual language is the official publications of the Teachers Association in the field, since these will include current information and calendar sections, as well as articles on literature and pedagogy. Equally important are the titles covering foreign language teaching from a linguistic or methodological point of view. These journals will be of interest to teachers from all areas of language specialization.

Basic Periodicals

For general foreign languages: *Foreign Language Annals, Language Learning, Modern Language Journal.*

For the Professional

British Journal of Language Teaching. 1962. 3/yr. $25. A.P. Dyson. British Assn. for Language Teaching, Oxford Univ. Language Teaching Centre, 41 Wellington Sq., Oxford OX1 2JF, England. Index, adv. Circ: 2,000.
Bk. rev: 10–15, 500 words. *Aud:* Pr.

Most of the articles are brief and practical, with a strong orientation to classroom teaching of various languages. There are frequent examples of different teaching and study approaches, with comparative discussions of the methodologies used in other countries. Although some of the material covered is geared to the British teaching profession, most of the articles are of general interest.

English Education. 1969. q. $12. Allen Berger. Natl. Council of Teachers of English, 1111 Kenyon Rd., Urbana, IL 61801. Illus., index, adv. Circ: 1,683. Vol. ends: Dec. Microform: UMI.
Indexed: CIJE, EdI. *Aud:* Pr.

Pithy, informative articles presenting practical ideas and research studies on the teaching of English from the elementary school level through higher education. The material is written for and by those who teach the teaching of English/language arts to future teachers. Topics cover curriculum, methodology, and certification. Although not an essential item, this title would be useful to those in English education. (P.S.B.)

First Language. 1980. 3/yr. $40 (Individuals, $27). Kevin Durkin. Science History Publns., Ltd., Alpha Academic, Halfpenny Furze, Mill Lane, Chalfont St. Giles, Buckinghamshire HP8 4NR, England. Adv. Vol. ends: Oct.
Bk. rev: 3–7, 5–10 pages, signed. *Aud:* Pr.

This title fills the gap between researchers and practitioners by publishing current findings and current problems in all areas of first language development. The brief research overviews describe the goals of new products. Information regarding conferences, meetings, and publications is covered. Forthcoming current topics are noted in previous issues to alert the researchers and the readers. Most of the examples and issues in the articles are about children acquiring the English language as their first language. Such topics as "Abstracts of the 1982 Child Language Seminar" and other specialized subjects are discussed in special issues of the journal. (J.Pa.)

Foreign Language Annals. 1967. 6/yr. $40 (Individuals, $35). Vicki B. Galloway. Amer. Council of the Teaching of Foreign Languages, 579 Broadway, Hastings-on-Hudson, NY 10706. Index, adv. Circ: 9,000. Microform: MIM, UMI.
Aud: Pr.

This journal seeks to serve teachers, administrators, and researchers teaching at any level of language. It is "dedicated to advancing all phases of the profession of foreign language teaching." Among the areas regularly covered are reports of educational research, descriptions of innovative and successful teaching methods, classroom experiments, and surveys of teacher concerns. There are also sections featuring programs of interest and a calendar of events. Highly recommended for both high school and academic libraries.

Language Arts. 1924. 8/yr. $35 (Individual members, $30). David Dillon. Natl. Council of Teachers of English, 1111 Kenyon Rd., Urbana, IL 61801. Illus., index, adv. Circ: 6,208. Vol. ends: Dec. Microform: UMI.

Indexed: CIJE, EdI. *Bk. rev:* 10–15, children's, 50 words, signed. *Aud:* Pr.

For language arts teachers in the preschool through middle school, this is a basic and extremely useful title. It is a potpourri of articles, debates, interviews, poetry, letters, program descriptions, and position papers. The material is well written, topical, and very practical. Often articles present views from other disciplines such as psychology and linguistics that have implications for language arts teaching. An extremely well put together title, this should be required reading for all involved in teaching the language arts. (P.S.B.)

Language Learning: journal of applied linguistics. 1948. q. $35 (Individuals, $20). Alexander Z. Guiora. Dept. of Linguistics, Univ. of Michigan, Ann Arbor, MI 48109. Circ: 3,000. Microform: UMI.

Indexed: EdI. *Bk. rev:* 4–8, 800–1,500 words, signed. *Aud:* Pr.

Scholarly articles on the process of language acquisition for children, the theories of second language learning, and the linguistic aspects of foreign languages. A number of topics in each issue would be of direct interest to foreign language teachers, including the role of student attitudes and motivation in learning, predicting oral proficiency, and factors influencing the maintenance of a second language.

The Modern Language Journal. 1916. q. $30 (Individuals, $13). David P. Benseler. Univ. of Wisconsin Press, Journals Div., 114 N. Murray St., Madison, WI 53715. Index, adv. Circ: 6,000. Vol. ends: Dec. Microform: MIM, PMC, UMI.

Indexed: CIJE, EdI, HumI. *Bk. rev:* 42–50, 700–1,000 words, signed. *Aud:* Pr.

This journal is published by the National Federation of Modern Language Teachers Association. It is basically "devoted to pedagogical research and topics of professional interest to all language teachers" from elementary school to graduate level. The articles cover language-teaching methods, process, and effects. Language learning by audiovisual aids is emphasized. Experimental research in teaching foreign languages is often discussed. Articles with linguistic analysis and literary interests also appear in this publication. The reviews are categorized according to subject or language, such as pedagogy, French, German, linguistics, and so on. This basic journal should be extremely helpful to teachers of foreign languages. (J.Pa.)

Reading in a Foreign Language. 1983. s-a. $13. Ray Williams & Alexander Urquhart. The Language Studies Unit, Univ. of Aston in Birmingham, Gosta Green, Birmingham B47ET, England. Illus., index, adv. Sample. Vol. ends: Sept.

Bk. rev: 5–6, 1–2 pages, signed. *Aud:* Pr.

This periodical is devoted to practical and theoretical aspects of learning and teaching the reading of a foreign language or a second language. The book reviews feature classroom textbooks, books of professional concern, and reports of conferences. All the articles are written in English. The main objective is to improve standards of reading foreign languages. Articles often discuss and analyze the sound patterns of the second language to facilitate correct pronunciation while reading. This title is useful to readers of foreign languages and foreign language learners. (J.Pa.)

The Reading Teacher. 1947. 9/yr. $30 (Members). Janet Ramage Binkley. Intl. Reading Assn., P.O. Box 8139, Newark, DE 19714. Illus., index, adv. Circ: 56,000. Vol. ends: May. Refereed. Microform: UMI.

Indexed: CIJE, EdI. *Bk. rev:* 5–6, 250 words, signed. *Aud:* Pr.

The basic journal for teachers of elementary and middle school reading. Reading in high school and beyond is covered in the same association's *Journal of Reading* (see above in this section). Articles cover current theory, research, and practices and discuss issues from "Current Reading Methods in China" to "Sexism in Children's Literature." Articles are brief, topical, and usually clearly written. This is a clearinghouse for all kinds of reading information—from software evaluations to conference and association news to a brief section where teachers can present good teaching ideas and activities. This title should be scanned by every reading teacher and deserves a place in any medium-to-large education collection. (P.S.B.)

Research in the Teaching of English. 1967. 4/yr. $20 (Individuals, $15). Judith Langer & Arthur Applebee. Natl. Council of Teachers of English, 1111 Kenyon Rd., Urbana, IL 61801. Illus., index, adv. Circ: 3,300. Vol. ends: Dec. Microform: UMI.

Indexed: CIJE, EdI. *Aud:* Pr.

Although this title can be used by teachers of English at all levels, it would be of special interest to those in the elementary and secondary schools. Each issue contains four to six research-based articles, usually authored by professors of education. The tone is scholarly and the articles require some knowledge of research design and terminology. Teachers interested in actual methods of teaching would be better served by *Language Arts* (see above in this section). This title is of more use to schools of education and serious researchers in the field of the teaching of English. (R.S.B.)

Verbatim: the language quarterly. 1974. q. $10. Laurence Urdang, P.O. Box 157, Essex, CT 06426. Circ: 12,000.

Bk. rev: 3–5, 250 words, signed. *Aud:* Pr.

A 12- to 16-page newsletter that is particularly witty, extremely entertaining, and always useful for the person who takes some pride in language. Short articles, letters, and notes trace the history and development of words, ruminate about the language, discuss philology, consider dictionaries and citations, and cover just about everything of interest to the linguistics lover. And all of this is done in a nonacademic, non-jargonistic way that makes each issue a delight to read. The book reviews—which move from novels concerned with linguistics to dictionaries—are excellent. *Verbatim* is recommended for libraries where there are readers interested in language but not in the technicalities of the average linguistic study.

Yelmo: la revista del profesor de español. See Latin America, Latino (U.S.)/For the Professional Section.

LITERATURE

For the Student/For the Professional

See also Alternatives; Fiction; and Women Sections.

Robert Hauptman, Assistant Professor, Learning Resources Services, St. Cloud State University, St. Cloud, MN 56301

Cristine C. Rom, Library Director, Cleveland Institute of Art Library, 11141 East Blvd., Cleveland, OH 44106

Introduction

The magazines in this section are drawn from three different sections in *Magazines for Libraries*—Literature, Literary Reviews, and Little Magazines. All three types of periodicals are concerned with literature, whether the writing or evaluation of it. Magazines entered under "Literature" specialize in critical evaluation and are frequently aimed at the specialist. "Literary reviews" also contain fiction, poetry, drama, interviews, and graphics, and may extend their boundaries beyond pure literature to the arts, social commentary, politics, history, and other areas. They also are more likely to appeal to the general reader.

The little magazines, born with Harriet Monroe's *Poetry* in 1912, also contain a broader subject matter. They differ from literary reviews in scope and aesthetics, offering new talent and experimental writing and art to a select audience.

Basic Periodicals

Ejh: *Stone Soup*; Hs: *Literary Cavalcade, Paris Review, Poetry*.

Basic Abstracts and Indexes

Humanities Index.

For the Student

American Poetry Review. 1972. bi-m. $9.50. Ed. bd. World Poetry, Inc., 1616 Walnut St., Rm. 405, Philadelphia, PA 19103. Illus., adv. Circ: 24,000. Sample. Vol. ends: Nov/Dec. Microform: UMI.

Aud: Hs.

This folded, 50-page tabloid presents, in a nonvarying format, a wide selection of previously published and, in many cases, well-known writers (such as James Dickey, Robert Penn Warren, Gunter Grass, and Tess Gallagher) along with newer writers. Each poet is usually represented by several pieces and often a photo. Special features, such as on contemporary Serbian poets, and interviews enliven issues. This is a basic selection for general literature collections. (C.R.)

Antaeus. 1970. s-a. $20/4 issues. Daniel Halpen. Ecco Press, 18 W. 30th St., New York, NY 10001. Illus., index, adv. Circ: 6,000.

Aud: Hs.

Antaeus is an extremely handsome literary review that consistently publishes outstanding contemporary authors. A recent special issue concentrated on art and contained 16 pieces—virtually all by well-known writers. Consider just a few of these: Italo Calvino's "Birds of Paolo Uccello," John Pope-Hennessy's "Leonardo: Landscape Painter," Sartre on Tintoretto, Baudelaire on Delacroix, and Charles Wright on Giorgio Morandi. The colorful Uccello reproduction on the cover is stunning. Associated with *Antaeus* are Paul Bowles, Donald Hall, John Hawkes, W. S. Merwin, and Edouard Roditi. A superb review, highly recommended.

Black American Literature Forum. See Afro-American/For the Student Section.

Cricket. See General Interest/For the Student: Children Section.

Gargoyle. 1976. s-a. $12 (Individuals, $10). Richard Peabody, Jr. & Gretchen Johnsen, P.O. Box 3567, Washington, DC 20007. Illus., index, adv. Circ: 2,500. Sample. Microform: UMI.

Bk. rev: Various number, length, signed. *Aud:* Hs.

This is a first-rate magazine. It publishes poetry and prose by well-known (e.g., Richard Kostelanetz, Lynn Ward, Hugh Fox) and not-so-well-known writers. The editors consider themselves "Anglophiles" and past issues have featured many British writers; East Coast writers tend to dominate the U.S. representatives. Most issues print original art and literature, in-depth interviews, and, frequently, signed book reviews (100–1,500 words). The magazine's layout is clean, and the graphics pleasing. The format and length vary, and recently the editors have dedicated one issue yearly to new fiction. *Gargoyle* is, further, a useful guide to East Coast little magazine and small press activity; editor Peabody is not only a participant but also an inveterate small press observer and commentator. Nice packaging, good editing, knowledgeable reviews, an inexpensive price, and a gold mine of information on alternative publishing all argue for *Gargoyle*. (C.R.)

The Georgia Review. 1947. q. $9. Stanley W. Lindberg. Univ. of Georgia, Athens, GA 30602. Illus., index, adv. Circ: 4,100. Vol. ends: Winter.

Indexed: HumI. *Bk. rev:* 1–4, grouped, 5–12 pages, signed, plus 8–10 brief notices. *Aud:* Hs.

Still one of the top four or five literary reviews in the United States. Each generous volume (four issues) contains close to 1,000 pages of first-class fiction (Leslie Epstein), poetry (Bin Ramke, Brendan Galvin, and Louis Simpson), essays (Northrop Frye and Borges), graphics (colorful covers and diverse portfolios), and reviews, often by such well-known authors as Jared Carter and Peter Stitt. At $9.00, *The Georgia Review* remains one of the best bargains in American publishing. Highly recommended.

Grand Street. 1981. q. $24 (Individuals, $20). Ben Sonnenberg, 50 Riverside Dr., New York, NY 10024. Illus., adv. Circ: 1,500. Sample. Vol. ends: Summer.

Aud: Hs.

Grand Street is probably the finest new literary review to appear during the 1980s. Many of the best contemporary creative writers and critics have been published here since 1981: Narayan and Gass (fiction); Carver, Hacker, and Merrill (poetry); John Hess's astonishing exposé of the *New York Times*, Irving Howe on sects, Northrop Frye on the Bible, Leon Edel on Blackmur, and Ted Hughes on Plath's journals (essays); and graphic portfolios. Not only are these 200 pages attractive, enticing, and influential, but the editor also cares about his contributors and pays them handsomely. This is a must for all literature collections. Highly recommended.

The Hudson Review: a magazine of literature and the arts. 1948. q. $18. Paula Deitz & Frederick Morgan. Hudson Review, Inc., 684 Park Ave., New York, NY 10021. Index, adv. Circ: 2,600. Vol. ends: Winter. Microform: UMI. Reprint: AMS.
Indexed: HumI. *Bk. rev:* 2–7, grouped, 3–9 pages, signed. *Aud:* Hs.

Some time ago, *The Hudson Review* celebrated its thirty-fifth anniversary. This prestigious review gathered together 250 pages of outstanding criticism, fiction, and poetry. Louis Simpson, A.R. Ammons, the venerable Marvin Mudrick, and Richmond Lattimore are among those represented. Recent issues are equally impressive. The lengthy "Chronicles" (in addition to the reviews) on art, theater, poetry, fiction, dance, and film are still the best places to go in order to keep up with contemporary culture. Recommended.

The Kenyon Review. 1979. q. $18 (Individuals, $15). Philip D. Church & Galbraith M. Crump. Kenyon College. Subs. to: P.O. Box 1308L, Fort Lee, NJ 07024. Illus., index, adv. Circ: 13,000. Vol. ends: Fall. Microform: UMI.
Bk. rev: 3, some grouped, 4–5 pages, signed. *Aud:* Hs.

The influential, but defunct, *Kenyon Review* was resuscitated in 1979, and it certainly presented an impressive array of writers—Nabokov, Cortázar, Steiner, and Beckett. Then in 1983, a change in editors brought with it a change in editorial direction (perhaps not blatantly obvious to readers, but there nonetheless). No longer is the "ideology of literature" stressed. Now "the aesthetic integrity" of the literary, artistic, or musical work is what is important, and thus there is a strong connection between the current *KR* and the old series edited by John Crowe Ransom. A recent number, for example, contains fiction (Gina Berriault), poetry (Dave Smith), essays (Robert Pack), and reviews. A good choice for all literature collections.

Literary Cavalcade. 1948. 8/school yr. $9 (Teacher's edition, $19). Michael Spring. Scholastic, Inc., 730 Broadway, New York, NY 10003, Subs. to: P.O. Box 644, Lyndhurst, NJ 07071. Illus., adv. Circ: 310,000. Vol. ends: May. Microform: UMI.
Aud: Hs.

A contemporary literature magazine with high standards. It contains interviews, "how-to" articles, short stories, poetry, and plays. Famous authors such as Truman Capote, Saul Bellow, George Orwell, and John Steinbeck have been represented, along with student writers. Every issue lists the favorite books of a famous personality. The final issue of the year publishes the work of Scholastic award winners. (L.K.W.)

The Massachusetts Review: a quarterly of literature, the arts, and public affairs. 1959. q. $12. John Hicks. Memorial Hall, Univ. of Massachusetts, Amherst, MA 01003. Illus., index, adv. Circ: 2,000. Vol. ends: Winter.
Indexed: HumI. *Aud:* Hs.

Here is general culture material including poetry (Dabney Stuart and Willis Barnstone), fiction, essays, and graphics. *MR* is fond of intercalating attractive chapbooks, or sections, and a recent number contains Benjamin Rush's *Plan of a Peace Office for the United States*, illustrated by Leonard Baskin (most unusual). Special issues have been devoted to women and comedy. A consistently excellent journal and a good choice for all collections. Recommended.

Obsidian: Black Literature in Review. See Afro-American/For the Student Section.

The Ohio Review (Formerly: *The Ohio University Review*). 1957. 3/yr. $12. Wayne Dodd. English Dept., Ohio Univ., Ellis Hall, Athens, OH 45701. Index, adv.
Bk. rev: 2–4, some grouped, 4–11 pages, signed. *Aud:* Hs.

This is an attractive journal that concentrates on poetry (Anna Akhmatova and David Citino), fiction (Robert Taylor, Jr.), and interviews (Reg Saner), but also publishes some criticism. There are two nice features here. The first is the intercalated chapbook, a substantial middle section given over to a body of work by a single poet, e.g., John Addiego. The second is the lengthy review. Over the years, *OR* has published Robert Bly, W. S. Merwin, James Wright, Donald Hall, and a host of other outstanding contemporary writers. Recommended.

Paris Review. 1953. q. $16. George A. Plimpton et al. The Paris Review, 45-39 171st Place, Flushing, NY 11358. Illus., index, adv. Circ: 8,000. Sample. Vol. ends: Winter.
Indexed: HumI. *Aud:* Hs.

The thirtieth anniversary of Plimpton's *Paris Review* has passed, and the celebration was awesome—almost 300 packed pages. There were three of the famous interviews (with Cortázar, Ionesco, and Philip Roth), fiction (T. C. Boyle), art, and a plethora of poetry (Joseph Brodsky, Raymond Carver, and Anne Waldman). Another recent number is equally impressive with an especially fine collection of Warhol photographs (of Capote, Ginsberg, Vidal, Baldwin, and others). For almost 100 issues the *Paris Review* has published the outstanding writers of the twentieth century. It is a superb journal. Highly recommended.

Ploughshares. 1971. q. $14. Ed. bd., P.O. Box 529, Cambridge, MA 02139. Illus., index, adv. Circ: 4,000. Microform: UMI.
Bk. rev: Various number, length, signed. *Aud:* Hs.

Ploughshares is a sophisticated magazine dedicated to publishing new writers and rediscovering the neglected and publishing them with an impressive line-up of big names: Robert Bly, Robert Creeley, Anne Waldman, Ted Berrigan, and so on. Special issues (such as the 1984 issue entitled "Biography, Fiction, and Autobiography") and a policy of rotating coordinating editorship provide different insights and directions in *Ploughshares* issues. Original poetry and prose, interviews, art, book reviews, and criticism are the magazine's mainstay. This is a solid magazine suitable for any literature collection. (C.R.)

Poetry. 1912. m. $22. Joseph Parisi. Modern Poetry Assn., 601 S. Morgan St., P.O. Box 4348, Chicago, IL 60680. Index, adv. Circ: 6,500. Vol. ends: Mar. & Sept. Microform: B&H, UMI.
Indexed: BoRv, BoRvI. *Bk. rev:* 5–10, length varies, signed. *Aud:* Hs.

Poetry, begun by Harriet Monroe in response to what she saw as distressing contemporary disinterest in serious verse, is considered by most to be the first U.S. little magazine. It has, under a succession of editors, continued to serve up serious poetry, often being the first place of publication for many of the century's writers. While the magazine still prints new talent, more recently, many of *Poetry's* contributors are big league—John Ashberry, Joan Colby, Dannie Abse, Maxine Kumin, and Michael Blumenthal, for example. In addition to poetry, the magazine offers occasional articles, criticism, and news notes on establishment prizes and big-name poets. This historically important magazine still offers a rich fare of poetry by establishment writers and some new talent and is recommended for all academic libraries. (C.R.)

Raritan: a quarterly review. 1981. q. $16 (Individuals, $12). Richard Poirier, Rutgers Univ., 165 College Ave., New Brunswick, NJ 08903. Adv. Circ: 3,000. Vol. ends: Spring.
Bk. rev: 2–3, 8–13 pages, signed. *Aud:* Hs.

Partisan Review moved on from Rutgers University, and *Raritan* has come along to take its place, but it is not merely a substitute. *Raritan* is an excellent journal, which emphasizes critical and cultural commentary of an enticing order. James Guetti writes on Wittgenstein and literary theory, and Edward Said on Foucault. There is also poetry (Kenneth Koch), fiction (Deirdre Levinson), and lengthy reviews. The editor goes out of his way to accommodate the brightest critical lights, and since 1981 Kenneth Burke, Robert Coles, Lincoln Kirstein, Harold Bloom, Elaine Showalter, and many other equally distinguished writers have graced these pages. Recommended for all libraries.

Salmagundi: a quarterly of the humanities and social sciences. 1965. q. $16. (Individuals, $9). Robert Boyers. Skidmore College, Saratoga Springs, NY 12866. Index, adv.
Aud: Hs.

Salmagundi concentrates on issues in the humanities and social sciences. Contributors of creative work and especially critical commentary are frequently outstanding. Here is William H. Gass on "The Death of the Author"; Raymond Aron on "Democratic States and Totalitarian States," followed by a discussion with Aron, Jacques Maritain, et al.;

Christopher Lasch on "1984: Are We There?" plus Calvino and Snodgrass—all in one regular issue. Another double number contains Charles Newman's 200-page "Post-modern Aura: The Act of Fiction in an Age of Inflation," plus work by Ben Belitt, René Girard, and Rudolf Arnheim. Staggering! *Salmagundi* is one of our premier quarterlies, and it belongs in all collections. Highly recommended.

Scholastic Scope. 1964. 24/school year. $7 (Teacher's edition, $19). Katherine Robinson. Scholastic, Inc., 730 Broadway, New York, NY 10003. Subs. to: P.O. Box 644, Lyndhurst, NJ 07071. Illus., adv. Circ: 1,046,000. Vol. ends: May. Microform: UMI.
Aud: Hs.

A high-lo language arts magazine, this publication offers a balanced program of reading for pleasure and improvement in vocabulary and comprehension. Competency test help is given on a regular basis. Published in newsprint and in a large typeface, with a glossy-coated cover, many features have film or TV tie-ins. (L.K.W.)

The Sewanee Review. 1892. q. $18 (Individuals, $12). George Core. Univ. of the South, Sewanee, TN 37375. Index, adv. Vol. ends: Fall. Microform: KTO. Reprint: KTO.
Indexed: HumI. *Bk. rev:* 7, 600–1,200 words, signed, plus 4, grouped, 5–9 pages, signed. *Aud:* Hs.

The Sewanee Review, like its sister journal *The Southern Review,* remains one of the more important cultural forums in the United States. Fiction (Robley Wilson, Jr.), poetry (William Logan, Vassar Miller, and Hayden Carruth), essays (Calvin Bedient), brief reviews, and review essays are included in every issue. The lengthy grouped reviews can present as many as eight related titles. There can be no better way to survey recent work in a particular area than through these comments. Recommended.

Shakespeare Quarterly. 1950. q. $40 (Individuals, $35). John F. Andrews. Folger Shakespeare Library, 201 E. Capitol St. S.E., Washington, DC 20003. Illus., index, adv. Circ: 2,700. Vol. ends: Winter. Microform: UMI. Reprint: AMS.
Indexed: HumI. *Bk. rev:* 7–10, some grouped, 400–2,600 words, signed. *Aud:* Hs.

Nicely illustrated and eclectic, *SQ* contains five essays on any aspect of Shakespeare and his world. Additionally, there are brief notes, announcements, countless theater reviews from around the world, and book reviews. Each volume also contains the supplementary "World Shakespeare Bibliography." Another special supplement covers "Teaching Shakespeare." Despite its cost, *SQ* belongs in virtually all collections. Recommended.

Sing Heavenly Muse: women's poetry and prose. 1977. 2/yr. $11 (Individuals, $9). Sue Ann Martinson, P.O. Box 14059, Minneapolis, MN 55414. Illus., adv. Circ: 2,000.
Aud: Hs.

"Feminist in an open, generous sense [in order to encourage] women to range freely, honestly and imaginatively over all subjects, philosophies, and styles," *Sing Heavenly*

Muse exists to foster the work of women poets, fiction writers, and artists. In spite of this dedicated existence, men's writing is not uncommon; at one point, an entire issue featured "Men's Writing About Women." Local and beginning writers are especially encouraged—the journal held a poetry contest for previously unpublished poets—but better known authors (for example, Meridel LeSueur) also appear. Carol Bly guest-edited a special fiction issue, submissions for which participated in a fiction contest. *Sing Heavenly Muse* is high quality in content and appearance and offers a good, representative selection of the creative writing women are doing. (C.M.)

Sipapu. 1970. s-a. $8. Noel Peattie, Rte. 1, P.O. Box 216, Winters, CA 95694. Illus., index. Circ: 400. Sample.
Bk. rev: Various number, length. *Aud:* Hs.

Sipapu is a "newsletter for librarians, collectors, and others interested in the alternative press," which, for Peattie, includes small, underground, Third World, dissent, peace, feminist, and anarchist presses. For over a decade, the magazine has published the front-line literature of these movements; the editor's latest concern is peace in a nuclear weapons world. Peattie's broader concerns, on the other hand, have not changed: informing and educating readers about movements and publications outside the mainstream and challenging librarians, in particular, to expand their intellectual horizons. The bulk of each issue is devoted to an interview with an alternative pressperson, publication announcements, and reviews; also found here are numerous news notes. *Sipapu* does contain useful information on specific little magazines but is included here for the wider context it provides and its intelligent consideration of all forms of alternative publishing. (C.R.)

Small Press Review. 1967. m. $22 (Individuals, $16). Len Fulton & Ellen Ferber. Dustbooks, P.O. Box 100, Paradise, CA 95969. Adv. Circ: 2,500. Sample. Vol. ends: Dec.
Bk. rev: 5–10, 150–500 words, signed. *Aud:* Hs.

For almost 20 years, *Small Press Review* has reliably and knowledgeably kept track of small press and little-magazine publishing. The number and length of reviews have decreased over the years, and feature articles are less frequent. Much of the magazine's pages are now devoted to keeping track of other magazines and presses (through its "Feedback" and "News and Notes" sections) and updating the annual *International Directory of Little Magazines and Small Presses* (in "New Listings"). Writers will appreciate notices of calls for manuscripts, upcoming contests and grant deadlines, and workshop and poetry readings. A comparatively large part of each magazine is given over to letters to the editor—always lively reading—which give some indication of the concerns, questions, and squabbles found among small publishers. *Small Press Review* and the *International Directory of Little Magazines and Small Presses* are the best resources for keeping track of English-language independent publishing and should be in every library. (C.R.)

The Southern Review. 1965 (Original series, 1935–1942). q. $9. James Olney & Lewis P. Simpson. Louisiana State Univ.,

43 Allen Hall, Baton Rouge, LA 70803. Index, adv. Circ: 2,800. Vol. ends: October. Microform: K.T.O., UMI. Reprint: Kraus.
Bk. rev: 2–6, some grouped, 3–20 pages, signed. *Aud:* Hs.

The original *Southern Review* was founded by Robert Penn Warren; after a lapse of many years the new series was instituted, and in its current form it is a general cultural review, with no noticeable Southern bias. There is always an abundance of poetry (William Stafford and Daniel Helpern) and fiction here, and the cultural essays are outstanding. A recent number contains an interview with, an essay and poetry by, and an article on Robert Duncan, plus Harold Bloom on James Dickey and M. L. Rosenthal on Laura Riding. There is also an interview with Czeslaw Milosz. This is a staggering quantity of first-rate material for a single issue. Each volume contains four equally potent numbers—1,000 pages in all. A superb, reasonably priced journal, which is highly recommended for all collections. (See also *The Sewanee Review* above in this section.)

The Spirit That Moves Us. 1975. s-a. Inquire. Morty Sklar, P.O. Box 1585-ML, Iowa City, IA 52244. Illus. Circ: 1,800. Sample. Vol. ends: Fall/Winter.
Aud: Hs.

The Spirit That Moves Us is among the brightest of the nation's little magazines. Sklar is a brilliant editor who never shies away from trying something new, and his magazine has taste, clarity, and good looks. Sklar prints unsolicited materials from big names (e.g. Marge Piercy, Charles Bukowski, and W. P. Kinsella) as well as the never-before-published. Issues include poetry, prose, and art; special theme issues are frequent, such as *Nuke-Rebuke*, Nobel prize-winner Jaroslav Seifert's *The Casting of Bells*, and *The Actualist Anthology*. Morty Sklar never rests on the success of past issues but continues to produce challenging new ones. This excellent magazine is a cornerstone to any little magazine collection and a recommended addition to literature collections as well. (C.R.)

Stand. 1952. q. $12. Ed. bd. Stand Magazine, Ltd., 179 Wingrove Rd., Newcastle-upon-Tyne NE4 9DA, England. Illus., index, adv. Circ: 5,000. Sample.
Bk. rev: 10–15, 250 words, signed. *Aud:* Hs.

Now over 30 years old, this is a perfect example of the little magazine that by now is a well-established member of the larger literary scene. Note, too, the extraordinary circulation. The magazine has gained attention and fame because of its concentration on new poets, and particularly those from the northern part of England. At the same time the established older voices are printed regularly. The book reviews are excellent and offer U.S. readers a quick way to keep up with the best of poetry from England. A basic title for libraries outside of England (as well, of course, as in England). (C.R.)

Stone Soup. 1973. 5/yr. $17.50. Gerry Mandel & William Rubel. Children's Art Foundation, P.O. Box 83, Santa Cruz, CA 95063. Illus. Circ: 9,000. Vol. ends: May.
Aud: Ejh.

Stone Soup is the only literary magazine devoted exclusively to children's writing and art. Its purpose is "to encourage children to think about the world around them and to express themselves in meaningful stories and beautiful pictures." Editors select only the very best from material submitted by children from all over the world. Each issue includes stories, poems, book reviews, and black-and-white drawings done by children ages 6–12. The no-nonsense format is conservative and aesthetically pleasing. An "Activity Guide" is bound into each issue and details a variety of projects specifically geared to the material in each issue. This magazine offers quality work in a quality format and is highly recommended for school libraries. (L.K.O.)

TriQuarterly. 1964. 3/yr. $22 (Individuals, $16). Reginald Gibbons. Northwestern Univ., 1735 Benson Ave., Evanston, IL 60201. Illus., index, adv. Circ: 3,500. Microform: UMI. Reprint: Kraus.

Indexed: HumI. *Bk. rev:* Occasional, 4, 1–7 pages, signed. *Aud:* Hs.

Reginald Gibbons, the new editor of *TriQuarterly*, has shifted the emphasis here; now there is still lots of fiction—by Abe, Oates, and Ward Just (pieces can run to 35 pages)—but there is also more poetry (Buzzati, Keeley, Carruth, Pastan, Enzensberger, and Guillén), and commentary by Alberti. Additionally, there have been some recent imaginative specials on John Cage, Poland, Spain, and the outstanding Chicago number with contributions from Bellow, Hansberry, K. Shapiro, Petrakis, G. Brooks, and countless others. These solid 200- to 250-page issues ("Chicago" runs 450 oversize pages) are invariably handsome and contain stunning graphics. Studs Terkel calls *TriQuarterly* "one of the most exciting literary magazines in the country." This reviewer calls it the premier literary review currently being published. No library should be without it. Highly recommended.

World Literature Today. (Formerly: *Books Abroad*). 1927. q. $35 (Individuals, $23). Ivar Ivask. Univ. of Oklahoma Press, 1005 Asp Ave., Norman, OK 73019. Illus., index, adv. Circ: 1,900. Vol. ends: Autumn. Reprint: Kraus.

Indexed: HumI. *Bk. rev:* See below. *Aud:* Hs.

This publication's 150–200 pages are divided into two sections. The first contains some ten essays or interviews with contemporary writers, as well as commentaries and a generous number of illustrations. Issues are either general or are devoted to a specific topic or writer, such as the Czeslaw Milosz and Odysseus Elytis numbers, both of which influenced the Swedish Academy in its decisions to present these authors with Nobel Prizes, or the lovely Paavo Haavikko issue, devoted to the eighth winner of the prestigious Neustadt Prize. The heart of the journal lies in its second section, "World Literature in Review." These 100 or so pages are divided first linguistically, e.g., French, Italian, other Romance languages, Russian, other Slavic languages, and Greek. The linguistic categories are in turn subdivided by genre: fiction, verse, criticism, memoirs, anthologies, and

so on. The countless reviews are usually brief and constitute an excellent survey of the current state of world literature. The authors of both the essays and the reviews are top-notch: Czeslaw Milosz, Milan Kundera, M. Byron Raizis, George Economou, Theodore Ziolkowski, and so on. *WLT* is one of the finest literary journals published and highly recommended.

For the Professional

American Literature: a journal of literary history, criticism, and bibliography. 1929. q. $18 (Individuals, $14). Edwin H. Cady. Duke Univ. Press, East Campus, Durham, NC 27708. Index, adv. Circ: 4,200. Vol. ends: Dec.

Indexed: HumI. *Bk. rev:* 19–26, 400–1,300 words, signed. *Aud:* Pr.

Sponsored by MLA's American Literature Section, *AL* contains six substantive essays on all aspects of American literature. Melville's *Omoo* turns up, as does Dickinson, Wallace Stevens, Hawthorne, and Whitman. Each issue contains briefer notes, many book reviews, and the valuable "Select, Annotated List of Current Articles on American Literature." An important journal, recommended for all literature collections.

Bookbird. 1962. q. $14. Lucia Binder. Knud-Eigil Hauberg-Tychsen, Mayerhofgasse 6, A-1040 Vienna, Austria. Illus. *Aud:* Pr.

This journal is issued by I.B.B.Y. (International Board on Books for Young People), an organization whose purpose is to promote greater understanding among the children of the world through children's literature. Approximately 45 countries contribute material to the journal through the associate editor named from each country. Each issue includes two major articles and several shorter pieces on some facet of children's literature: reviews of children's books of international interest from a number of countries, reviews of professional literature, news from I.B.B.Y. national sections, and a calendar of events. The text is written in English, but a summation of the major articles is done in Spanish. It is a fascinating and unique publication, which should be of interest to anyone interested in children's literature. (L.K.O.)

Canadian Children's Literature. 1975. q. $14 (Outside Canada, $16.60). Mary Rubio & Elizabeth Waterston. C C Press, P.O. Box 335, Guelph, Ont. N1H 6K5, Canada. Illus., adv. Circ: 2,000. Sample.

Indexed: CanI. *Aud:* Pr.

The editorial policy states that this quarterly is devoted "to the literary analysis, criticism and review of books written for Canadian children." Each issue, thematic in approach, is an interesting, often scholarly, blend of literary analysis and book reviewing. A few articles are written in French, or in French and English, but the text is predominantly English. Black-and-white illustrations from material discussed and photographs appear occasionally. Contributors are authors, librarians, teachers of children's literature, and university professors. This is an impressive journal, which will be of interest to book selectors, students, teachers, and researchers. (L.K.O.)

Canadian Literature: a quarterly of criticism and review. 1959. q. $30 (Individuals, $25). W. H. New. Univ. of British Columbia, 2029 W. Mall, Vancouver, B.C. V6T 1W5, Canada. Index, adv. Circ: 2,000. Microform: UMI. Reprint: Kraus. *Indexed:* CanI, HumI. *Bk. rev:* 39–44, some grouped, 500–2,100 words, signed. *Aud:* Pr.

We have now passed the twenty-fifth anniversary of *CL*, perhaps Canada's premier literary critical journal. Solid 200-page, topical issues cover "The Moral Novel," "Science and Literature," "Documenting the Landscape," and specific Canadian geographical areas or authors. "Personal Experience and the Creative Writer," for example, contains pieces by Irving Layton, Clark Blaise ("Mentors"), and others. There is also an opinions and notes section, and poems are scattered throughout. The book reviews, which take up fully half of each issue, cover Canadian materials, but U.S. volumes do turn up. English usually and French occasionally are the languages used. Belongs in Canadian libraries and all but the smallest U.S. collections.

Children's Literature in Education. 1969. q. $22.50 (Individuals, $13.50). Anita Moss. Agathon Press, Inc., 49 Sheridan Ave., Albany, NY 12210. Illus. Sample. *Indexed:* EdI. *Aud:* Pr.

International in scope, this journal is the cooperative effort of children's literature experts from the United Kingdom and the United States. An average issue moves from articles on facets of children's literature to opinion pieces to annotated subject bibliographies. There is an occasional black-and-white reproduction of an illustration. While there seems to be an emphasis on the scholarly, the editors do not ignore material that will be of practical value to teachers and librarians working with elementary and junior school students. Should also be of interest to teachers and students of children's literature. (L.K.O.)

Essays on Canadian Writing. 1974. q. $36. Jack David & Robert Lecker, 307 Coxwell Ave., Toronto, Ont. M4L 3B5, Canada. Illus., adv. Circ: 1,200. Sample. Refereed. Microform: MML. *Indexed:* CanI. *Bk. rev:* 8, 5 pages, signed. *Aud:* Pr.

Publishing long critical essays about Canadian literature in general as well as about specific authors of fiction, drama and poetry, this journal moves over the whole canvas from Anna Jameson to Alice Munro, from Thomas Chandler Haliburton to Robertson Davies. Each issue runs to about 200 pages or more and offers solid scholarship combined with great readability. The editors, Jack David and Robert Lecker, do themselves proud and deliver a journal for a very modest price. Should be in any library interested in Canadian literature. (J.C.)

Journal of Modern Literature. 1970. q. $16 (Individuals, $12). Maurice Beebe. Temple Univ., 921 Humanities Bldg., Philadelphia, PA 19122. Illus. Vol. ends: Nov. Microform: UMI. *Aud:* Pr.

Scholarly periodicals are often boring, pedantic, and indistinguishable from each other. Along with *Boundary 2* and *World Literature Today*, the *Journal of Modern Literature* is a magnificent exception. The frequently lengthy critical articles focus "on the modernist period from about 1885 to 1950," can be handsomely illustrated, and are generally extremely interesting, e.g., "Courting Bluebeard with Bartók, Atwood, and Fowles" or the uneasy friendship of W. C. Williams and Wallace Stevens. There are occasional special issues. One double number per volume, running 200 pages, is devoted entirely to a bibliographical review of the year's critical publications in English. It is aptly divided into general subjects and individual writers; the former category is subdivided into ten parts including reference, literary history, and criticism of poetry. Many of the entries within each section are annotated, sometimes extensively. Its advantages are obvious: the annotations are well developed, the comments are timely, and the price is reasonable. This is an exceptional journal that is highly recommended. (R.H.)

The Lion and the Unicorn. 1977. a. $7.50 (Individuals, $4). Geraldine De Luca & Roni Natov. Dept. of English, Brooklyn College, Brooklyn, NY 11210. Illus. Circ: 1,000. *Aud:* Pr.

Subtitled "A Critical Journal of Children's Literature," each issue explores one theme or genre or one aspect of the field of children's literature. Back issues have focused on comedy, fantasy, social issues, biography, and informational books, to list a few, and they include book reviews, critical pieces, and interviews. The articles are concise, analytical, and often critical and should appeal to students and professionals interested in this subject. (L.K.O.)

Signal: approaches to children's books. 1970. 3/yr. $14.50. Nancy Chambers. Thimble Press, Lockwood Sta. Rd., South Woodchester, Stroud, Glos. GL5 5EQ, England. Illus. Vol. ends: Sept. *Aud:* Pr.

Signal's aim is "to reflect the children's book world from many points of view, offering its contributors as much article space as they need to present their ideas fully." This British journal includes a collection of articles dealing with such subject areas as: history of children's books, critical theory and practice, and educational practice and research as it relates to literature and reading, among others. As of January 1985, "The Signal Selection" of notable new books is published and sold separately as an annual publication. Approaches in articles range from the practical to the scholarly, and most of the contributors are British authors, publishers, teachers, and other professionals concerned with children's literature. (L.K.O.)

MATHEMATICS

For the Student/For the Professional

Basic Periodicals

Hs: *Journal of Recreational Mathematics, Mathematics Magazine.*

For the Student

Fibonacci Quarterly. 1963. q. $25. Gerald E. Bergum. The Fibonacci Soc., Univ. of Santa Clara, Santa Clara, CA 95053. Index. Circ: 900. Sample. Vol. ends: No. 4. Refereed. *Aud:* Hs.

Devoted to the "study of integers with special properties." Various levels of difficulty, from problems requiring only high school-level proficiency to sections suited to senior undergraduate and graduate studies. Contributions are solicited from students and teachers, with problems provided for class work. Each issue has some 10 to 15 articles, with a number of problems and proofs submitted by readers.

Journal of Recreational Mathematics. 1968. q. $25. Joseph Madachy. Baywood Publg. Co., 120 Marine St., P.O. Box D, Farmingdale, NY 11735. Illus., index. Sample. Vol. ends: No. 4. Refereed.
Bk. rev: 3, 300 words, signed. *Aud:* Hs.

As the title indicates, this is an effort to make mathematics fun, and therefore one of the few journals in this section that can be recommended for the general collection. It serves all levels, all interests. At the same time, the problems, articles, and discussions make the point that math is applicable to almost every kind of activity—from winning a chess game to putting up a skyscraper. The material is as accurate as it is lively, and the magazine appeals not only to mathematicians but to those who might be afraid of the subject. A good choice for almost any collection.

Mathematical Log. 1957. q. $2. Mu Alpha Theta, Univ. of Oklahoma, Dept. of Mathematics, Norman, OK 73019. Illus. Microform: Pub.
Aud: Hs.

Mu Alpha Theta, the National High School and Junior College Mathematics Club, supplies a good bit of educational and diversional material in its slim news organ. In addition to notes on meetings and chapters, it publishes short essays and problems contributed by educators and members, as well as occasional reprints from other publications. Includes discussions on educational and employment opportunities for students. (Free copies are circulated to chapters of the society.)

The Mathematical Scientist. 1976. s-a. $13. B. C. Rennie. CSIRO/Australian Mathematical Soc., Dept. of Mathematics, Univ. of Queensland, St. Lucia, Queensland 4067, Australia. Index. Circ: 1,000. Vol. ends: July. Refereed. *Aud:* Hs.

This publication commenced in 1976 and beginning in 1985 will share publication with CSIRO, Division of Maths and Statistics, and the Australian Mathematical Society. It is principally a journal of general mathematics/statistics. Although based in Australia, the publication is international in scope, with a number of U.S. authors represented in each issue. It is recommended as a general-interest math periodical that will appeal to a wide readership. (J.G.H.)

Mathematics and Computer Education (Formerly: *The MATYC Journal*). 1967. 3/yr. $35. George M. Miller, P.O. Box 158, Old Bethpage, NY 11804. Illus., adv. Circ: 3,500. Refereed. Microform: UMI.
Indexed: CIJE. *Bk. rev:* 200–300 words, signed. *Aud:* Hs.

Devoted to development of materials for the improvement of classroom effectiveness in high schools, two-year colleges, and the first years of college and university in the teaching of mathematics and computer science. The computer articles and software reviews are written by computer teachers. The mathematics articles are in two categories: regular articles, and classroom notes that allow useful minor points to be brought to the readers. The Problem Department presents five new problems, as well as solutions to previous problems, in each issue.

Mathematics Magazine. 1926. bi-m. (Sept.-June). $28. Doris Schattschneider. Mathematical Assn. of America, 1529 18th St. N.W., Washington, DC 20036. Index. Circ: 8,000. Vol. ends: No. 5. Refereed. Microform: UMI.
Bk. rev: 2–3, 300–500 words, signed. *Aud:* Hs.

This is one of the few mathematics titles that can be read for enjoyment by laypersons and young students (the aforementioned *Journal of Recreational Mathematics* is another). The papers, by teachers and professors, vary in length and difficulty, but all offer the interested reader insight into either new research or methods of approaching teaching. There is an interest, too, in historical aspects of the subject, and these pieces tend to be particularly well written. Even the nonmathematician should find things of interest here, but the journal is particularly directed to the student and teacher from the secondary level through the academic ranks. Recommended for most collections.

Scholastic Dynamath. See under *Scholastic Magazines* in Education/For the Student Section.

For the Professional

Arithmetic Teacher. 1954. m. (Sept.–May). $35. Harry B. Tunis. Natl. Council of Teachers of Mathematics, 1906 Association Dr., Reston, VA 22091. Illus., index, adv. Circ: 32,000. Vol. ends: May. Refereed. Microform: UMI.
Indexed: CIJE, EdI. *Bk. rev:* 3, 250–500 words, signed. *Aud:* Pr.

The basic periodical for the teaching of mathematics in an elementary school, this offers specific ideas about how to improve teaching methods. The emphasis is on new approaches to pedagogical techniques. There are contributors from both teachers and those who teach the teachers, and from professional mathematicians. Reports on research are included. A useful feature offers reviews not only of books, but of related materials, including computer software. There are regular suggestions for puzzles, games, and other devices to make mathematics more interesting to young students. A basic title for elementary school collections.

Journal for Research in Mathematics Education. 1970. 5/yr. $17. Jeremy Kilpatrick. Natl. Council of Teachers of Mathematics, 1906 Association Dr., Reston, VA 22091. Illus., index. Circ: 4,423. Vol. ends: No. 5. Refereed. Microform: UMI.

Aud: Pr.

Concerned with mathematical research into educational problems, this is directed to teachers, primarily those teaching the elementary and secondary grades. In this respect it is similar to *Arithmetic Teacher.* There are numerous reports of studies, detailed articles covering the current findings about teaching methods, and just about anything concerned with ways of making the subject more lively and useful for students.

Mathematical Gazette. 1894. 4/yr. £10. V. W. Bryant, Dept. of Pure Mathematics, Univ. of Sheffield, Sheffield S3 7RH, England. Index, adv. Vol. ends: No. 4. Refereed. Microform: UMI.

Bk. rev: 50, 200–500 words, signed. *Aud:* Pr.

Although primarily concerned with mathematics education and teaching in the English classroom, the publication should not be overlooked by U.S. libraries. The variety of expository papers, ranging from elementary to more advanced mathematics, the creative approaches described in teaching methods and the interesting general articles make the journal a splendid choice for mathematics collections. A large and comprehensive book review section provides a good checklist of foreign publications.

The Mathematics Teacher. 1908. m. (Sept.–May). $40. Ed. bd. Natl. Council of Teachers of Mathematics, 1906 Association Dr., Reston, VA 22091. Illus., index. Circ: 39,000. Refereed. Microform: UMI.

Indexed: EdI. *Bk. rev:* 4–10, 350–800 words, signed. *Aud:* Pr.

Unlike its rivals (*Arithmetic Teacher* and *Journal for Research in Mathematics Education*), this is directed only at secondary schools and two-year colleges. The signed articles are concerned primarily with the teaching of math, but there is some interest in the role of mathematics in society. The magazine now contains material on computers, software, and related areas, with a good section on new products, programs, and instructional materials. The book reviews are coded for different grade levels. A first choice for high school libraries.

MEDIA AND AV

For the Professional

See also Communication and Speech; Television, Video, and Radio Sections.

Samuel T. Huang, Coordinator of Computer Reference Service, Reference Librarian, University Libraries, Northern Illinois University, De Kalb, IL 60115

Basic Periodicals

Ejh, Hs: *Media & Methods.*

For the Professional

Audio-Visual Communications. 1961. m. Controlled circ. (Others, $13.50). Mike Yuhas. Media Horizons, Inc., 475 Park Ave. S., New York, NY 10016. Illus., adv. Circ: 36,000. Microform: UMI.

Aud: Pr.

Anyone involved with AV (in business or at the academic level) will turn to this publication for news about new equipment. If nothing else, the numerous advertisements alert the reader to developments in the field. New techniques and technologies of communication are discussed in the articles and features. There are helpful updates, too, of such things as videotex and teletex. The magazine is filled with ideas for better uses of AV in instruction, public relations, sales, and so forth.

ECTJ: educational communication and technology journal (Formerly: *AV Communication Review*). 1953. q. $24. William Winn. Assn. for Educational Communications and Technology, 1126 16th St. N.W., Washington, DC 20036. Index, adv. Circ: 5,000. Vol. ends: Winter. Refereed.

Indexed: CIJE, EdI. *Bk. rev:* 2–4, length varies, signed. *Aud:* Pr.

This official publication of the Association for Educational Communications and Technology is a scholarly journal of theory, research, and development in the fields of educational media, learning systems, educational television, computerized instruction, and other aspects of the teaching-learning process related to technology and communication. Research-oriented articles are contributed by professors in these fields. Each issue focuses on a single theme, such as "social aspects of educational communication and technology"—the theme of a recent issue. A regular issue contains four lengthy, critical book reviews and eight to ten abstracts of recent research. It is an important journal for students in the field of media and educational communication.

Education Technology: the magazine for managers of change in education. 1961. m. $69. Lawrence Lipsitz. Educational Technology Publns., Inc., 720 Palisade Ave., Englewood Cliffs, NJ 07632. Illus., index, adv. Circ: 5,000. Vol. ends: Dec. Microform: UMI.

Indexed: CIJE, EdI, ExChAb. *Bk. rev:* 3–5, 250 words, signed. *Aud:* Pr.

This publication covers all phases of educational media and technology from the elementary grades through higher education. Articles are research-oriented and are contributed by college faculty and media specialists. These articles are short, practical, and well written for general readership. Each issue contains information on the newest developments and materials in the field, such as computers, microcomputers, videodiscs, pocket calculators, and so forth. Information about adapting and utilizing this equipment in schools is also provided. Each issue includes not only educational professional literature reviews but also educational technology product reviews and film reviews. A useful publication for teachers and academic libraries.

EITV (Formerly: *Educational and Industrial Television; Educational Television*). 1968. m. $15. Charles S. Tepfer. C. S. Tepfer Publg. Co., Inc., 51 Sugar Hollow Rd., Danbury, CT 06810. Illus., index. Vol. ends: Dec. Refereed.
Bk. rev: 3–4, 2 pages. *Aud:* Pr.

This quality publication, colorfully presented, serves both educators and media industry professionals. It provides current information about the best ways to use media in industry and the latest in new equipment. It also features informative articles on such subjects as public access media, interactive videodiscs, telecommunication and satellite technology, and videoconferencing and closed-circuit television conventions. Occasionally, book and film reviews as well as product reviews are included. This is a well-written publication.

Media & Methods (Formerly: *Educator's Guide to Media and Methods*). 1965. 6/yr. $27. Michele Sokoloff. Amer. Soc. of Educators, 1511 Walnut St., Philadelphia, PA 19102. Illus., adv. Circ: 45,000. Vol. ends: Dec. Microform: B&H.
Indexed: CIJE, EdI. *Bk. rev:* 4–6, 500 words, signed. *Aud:* Pr.

This journal on teaching technologies contains articles, news items, and reviews of educational films, television, hardware and software, and other audiovisual materials and their applications. The journal aims to link media resources with classroom needs. In a recent issue, a typical article, "Linking the New Technologies with Special Education," calls attention to the multitude of technological opportunities promoting increased independence for students in special education classes. This is a basic journal for the school expert or teacher who is involved with any form of audiovisual materials. Each issue includes book reviews, media reviews, software reviews and previews, and product premieres. A regular issue contains four articles written in an informal style, often from an innovative—even radical—educational viewpoint. Highly recommended for all types of libraries.

Media Spectrum. 1974. q. $10. Margaret Grazier & Marilyn Matecon. Michigan Assn. for Media in Education, 3338 School of Education Bldg., Ann Arbor, MI 48109. Illus., index, adv. Circ: 1,000. Sample. Vol. ends: No. 4.
Indexed: LibLit. *Aud:* Pr.

This journal is primarily for media specialists, librarians, and media instructional developers in Michigan high schools.

Each issue focuses on a single topic—e.g., "High Technology in Education" or "Creating a Nation of Readers." The articles are well written and practical. Each issue contains brief reports on state activities, one or two articles on problem solving of a how-to-do-it nature, letters, and chatty comments on events and personalities. The cover of each issue is designed by a graphic artist from Michigan schools. The emphasis on Michigan schools limits its value elsewhere.

Tech Trend (Formerly: *Instructional Innovator*). 1956. 8/yr. $24. Dan Levin. Assn. for Educational Communications and Technology, 1126 16th St. N.W., Washington, DC 20036. Illus., index, adv. Circ: 14,000. Vol. ends: Dec. Refereed. Microform: UMI.
Indexed: CIJE, EdI, MRD. *Aud:* Pr.

This leading journal, directed at teachers involved in the adaptation of technological resources to the fields of learning, focuses on special topics in the "new kind of literacy." Its aim is to keep the reader up to date on such things as the use of instructional media in schools; the uses of microcomputers with very young children; the use of some form of electronic text in higher education in the future; ways for starting filmmaking classes; and the fundamentals of animation. Complementing these articles are features on new books, recently introduced products and research notes. A special feature, "Instructional Resources," covers "ideas and techniques for improving and mediating the curriculum, particularly at the K-12 level." This publication differs from others in the field in that it has a broader audience, which includes not only the K-12 instructors, but also those at the college and university level as well as people affiliated with special libraries involved with audiovisuals. This journal, with its solid format and compelling writing style, is an essential title in most instructional libraries.

MILITARY

For the Student

James W. Geary, Associate Professor, Library Administration, Kent State University Libraries, Kent, OH 44242

Introduction

Since time immemorial, there has been concern for defending one's hearth and home against intruders. Depending on the society and historical setting, the influence of a military establishment has varied. Its presence nevertheless remains constant, particularly in the minds of young adults who face the possibility of having to don a uniform. Regardless of one's point of view toward the military, it is an integral component of modern society and, to a greater or lesser degree, affects all citizens. Insofar as possible, people should have at least some understanding of an institution that affects their daily lives.

If the large number of military periodicals is any indication, interest in the U.S. military and pertinent international developments continues to be widespread. The titles also encompass many and diverse areas of inquiry. Except for those magazines and journals that have a strict historical focus, the principal editorial emphasis in the majority of the periodicals identified in this section is on present-day concerns. The past is not necessarily ignored, because many of these same titles include one or two historical articles per issue. Among the subjects discussed are those on assessing, meeting, and reacting to actions that originate in the Soviet Union. Other topics of current interest include strategy, tactics, technology, and personnel-related matters.

Basic Periodicals

Hs: *Military History, Military Images.*

For the Student

Air Force Magazine (Formerly: *Air Force and Space Digest*). 1918. m. $15. John T. Correll, 1501 Lee Hwy., Arlington, VA 22209. Illus., adv. Circ: 212,000. Sample. Vol. ends: Dec. Microform: UMI.

Bk. rev: 6–8, 150–1,000 words, signed. *Aud:* Hs.

Contains, as regular features, an excellent book review section in which two to three titles are critically examined while other books are described in brief. Each issue also has 8 to 11 articles. These pieces are neither documented nor overly technical and should appeal to a general readership. Although one article usually tells the combat exploits of an earlier Air Force hero, the primary emphasis is clearly on the latest developments and applications in aerospace technology, international and national defense policies, and general operations. This title has other attractions for librarians and interested laypeople: There is a yearly almanac, usually appearing in the May issue, that presents a veritable gold mine of facts and figures concerning the Air Force. The location of bases, types of aircraft and missile systems in use today, lists of Air Force "Aces," and current military pay scales are but a few of the numerous categories included. Other issues contain special sections of interest and value— for example, "Soviet Aerospace Almanac," usually in the March issue, and, in December, an annual survey called "Military Balance." The tables and charts that accompany some of the articles within these special issues have reference value.

Air Reservist. 1949. q. (Free to members of the Air National Guard and select members of the Air Force Reserve). Tom Wright. Bolling Air Force Base, Washington, DC 20332. Illus. Vol. ends: Sept. Microform: UMI.

Aud: Hs.

Comparable in some respects to *Army Reserve Magazine* and *National Guard* (see below in this section). *Air Reservist* appeals primarily to individuals who are members of active air reserve units. The articles concern general operations and reserve activities. There are also other timely pieces, for example, "Tax Guide for Air Guard and Reserve." In order to better serve older students who are seeking part-time jobs or the spirit of adventure, high school librarians who have an air reserve unit in the vicinity may want to try to acquire this magazine.

Army Reserve Magazine. 1955. q. Free. Capt. Robert H. Pratt. Office of the Chief—Army Reserve, DAAR-PA, Washington, DC 20310. Illus. Circ: 480,000. Sample. Vol. ends: Fall. Microform: UMI.

Aud: Hs.

Similar in orientation to *Air Reservist* and *National Guard* (see elsewhere in this section). With a purpose of providing timely information to current and prospective members, *Army Reserve* understandably aims at a select group. Articles average six to seven per issue and discuss topics such as mobilization, field exercises and maneuvers, and staying in shape. High school librarians, particularly those who have a nearby army reserve unit, should obtain a copy of this title for the potential part-time soldiers in their midst. The brief essays on physical fitness have wide appeal.

Leatherneck: Marines magazine. 1916. m. $10. Ronald D. Lyons. Marine Corps Assn., P.O. Box 1775, Quantico, VA 22134. Illus., index, adv. Circ: 80,000. Sample. Vol. ends: Dec. Microform: UMI.

Bk. rev: 2, 300–750 words, signed. *Aud:* Hs.

Except for the inclusion of advertising and book reviews, *Leatherneck* follows a format similar to titles published by other branches of the U.S. military. All are intended primarily for active-duty personnel, especially those in the lower enlisted ranks. They inform readers about pertinent developments and benefits. They are also designed to inspire pride in the service, with *Leatherneck* being the best example. The articles, averaging nine per issue, are amply illustrated but not documented. Each issue usually contains at least one essay with a historical emphasis on subjects such as Marine aviators in World War I and World War II. Present-day interests are not ignored, especially in pieces on select military installations or naval ships. Special features include cartoons, "Gyrene Gyngles," and rosters of retiring Marines.

Leatherneck and other service magazines have a useful purpose beyond serving active-duty personnel. They provide the public, especially young people who are considering military service, with an insider's view of the armed forces. Depending on the interests of the user population, high school libraries may wish to acquire *Leatherneck* in addition to any of the three titles noted below:

Airman: official magazine of the U.S. Air Force. 1955. m. $37. Lt. Col. Gene E. Townsend. Air Force Service Information and News Center, Kelly Air Force Base, TX 78241. Illus. Circ: 800,000. Sample. Vol. ends: Dec. Microform: UMI.

Aud: Hs.

All Hands: magazine of the United States Navy. 1923. m. $20. JOC Barbara A. Cornfeld, Hoffman No. 2, 200 Stovall St., Alexandria, VA 22332. Illus., index. Sample. Vol. ends: Dec. Microform: UMI.

Aud: Hs.

Soldiers: the official United States Army magazine (Formerly: *Army Digest*). 1946. m. $21. Lt. Col. Charles G. Cavanaugh, Jr., Cameron Sta., Alexandria, VA 22304. Illus., index. Circ: 225,000. Vol. ends: Dec. Microform: UMI.

Aud: Hs.

Military Affairs: the journal of military history, including theory and technology. 1937. q. $30 (Individuals, $20). Robin Higham. Amer. Military Inst., Eisenhower Hall, Kansas State Univ., Manhattan, KS 66506. Illus., index, adv. Circ: 2,680. Sample. Vol. ends: Oct. Refereed. Microform: KTO.

Bk. rev: 19, 175–750 words, signed. *Aud:* Hs.

Sponsored by the American Military Institute, this journal is international in scope and encompasses a broad chronological period, but with a distinct emphasis on pre-1945. The articles, usually six per issue, are detailed, scholarly, and well written. Appropriate illustrations often accompany them. There are also occasional historiographical essays. Regular features include book reviews, news notes on the American Military Institute, and lists of pertinent journal articles. Compilations of recent doctoral dissertations in the field of military studies appear less frequently. A basic title. See also *Military History*.

Military History. 1984. bi-m. $10. C. Brian Kelly. Empire Press, P.O. Box 2309, Reston, VA 22090. Illus., adv. Circ: 130,000. Sample. Vol. ends: May/June.

Bk. rev: 2–5, 200–1,100 words, signed. *Aud:* Hs.

Each issue of this relatively recent title contains six sections, including one on weaponry and another on book reviews. There are also three major articles. In addition, there is usually one interview of a participant in an event—for example, the observations of Major General Harry W. O. Kinnard, who led American forces in the Battle of the Ia Drang in November 1965. The basic articles cover battles ranging from "Night of the Assegais," which concerns an 1879 British military action at Rorke's Drift in Southeast Africa, to "Their Shots Quit Coming," another story of George Armstrong Custer's last stand at the Little Big Horn. None of the pieces are documented, but they are readable and amply illustrated. Photographs or reproductions of paintings accompany each article. In some respects, *Military History* is a popularized version of *Military Affairs* (see above in this section). It should be considered for inclusion in the collections of many high school libraries.

Military Images. 1979. bi-m. $16. Harry Roach, 918 Liberty St., Allentown, PA 18102. Illus., index, adv. Circ: 3,000. Sample. Vol. ends: May/June. Microform: UMI.

Bk. rev: 100–450 words, signed. *Aud:* Ejh, Hs.

This richly illustrated 32-page magazine has a popular orientation and should appeal to a broad audience ranging from teenagers to senior citizens. It is of special interest to collectors, photographers, and military historians. In each issue there are two to seven distinct sets of photographs pertaining to aspects of the U.S. military in the pre-1939 period—especially the Civil War and World War I. Well-written narratives accompany most of these. Some issues also contain "Stragglers" a section of miscellaneous, partially identified photographs. A cumulative index of the articles published appears every five years.

National Guard (Formerly: *The Guardsman*). 1947. m. $4. Major Reid Beveridge, One Massachusetts Ave., Washington, DC 20001. Illus., adv. Circ: 67,000. Sample. Vol. ends: Dec.

Aud: Hs.

Similar in purpose to the *Air Reservist* and *Army Reserve Magazine* (see above in this section) except that this periodical includes material of interest to members of both the air and army guard forces. Each issue contains news items along with four articles, which usually focus on current activities although occasional historical articles appear. This magazine should prove of interest to young men and women who are contemplating service in a local guard unit, and therefore should be considered for high school library collections.

MODEL MAKING

For the Student: Flying Models; Model Autos; Military Miniatures; Model Ships; Model Railroads; Static Models

Frederick A. Schlipf, Executive Director, The Urbana Free Library, 201 South Race St., Urbana, IL 61801; Adjunct Professor, Graduate School of Library and Information Science, University of Illinois, Urbana, IL 61801.

Introduction

The magazines in this section are concerned with building, operating, and collecting models of railroads, airplanes, automobiles, ships, military armor and soldiers, and other types of machinery, buildings, and figures.

A large number of people are actively involved as hobbyists in these areas. Nobody knows how many of them are really out there, but the evidence from magazine subscriptions, association memberships, and hobby sales suggests that there are probably between one and two million adults and young adults in the United States who are serious model builders, operators, or collectors.

Model magazines often presuppose a fairly extensive knowledge on the part of the reader—not a high level of general education, but familiarity with the field and with its technical vocabulary. This approach is obviously essential in any specialty publishing area, but some people are surprised to discover it in an area for which no formal training exists, and newcomers to the hobby may become frustrated with the magazines when they first encounter them. Hobby magazine publishers deal with this problem in two ways. First, many of them publish general books designed to introduce people to the basics of the hobbies. Second, most try to provide a little introductory material each month, often in the form of regular columns or special articles on the fundamentals of modeling.

Basic Periodicals

Ejh, Hs: *Model Airplane News, R/C Modeler, Model Railroader.*

For the Student

FLYING MODELS

Flying Models. 1929. m. $17. Robin W. Hunt. Carstens Publns., P.O. Box 700, Newton, NJ 07860. Illus., adv. Circ: 35,000. Sample. Vol. ends: Dec.

Aud: Hs.

Flying Models is the oldest of all U.S. flying model magazines and one of the oldest model-making magazines in the world. Although it is not as thick as some of the other flying model magazines, it has more editorial material each month than some of them do. Contents include the usual columns, construction articles, product reviews, and meeting reports, but there is a substantial number of more general articles as well. *Flying Models* is the only flying model magazine that devotes a major section each month to articles on model boats, and as a result it is widely read by modelers interested in r/c boats and boat racing.

Model Airplane News. 1929. m. $25. Dan Santich. Air Age, Inc., 837 Post Rd., Darien, CT 06820. Illus., adv. Circ: 95,000. Sample. Vol. ends: June & Dec. Microform: UMI. *Aud:* Ejh, Hs.

Model Airplane News is the second oldest U.S. flying model magazine and is second only to *R/C Modeler* in popularity. Of all the flying model magazines it has by far the most attractive physical format and frequently the best photography, with a fair amount of color work. As in the other magazines in this area, much of the editorial content consists of regular monthly features on various specialties (including a regular column for beginners), construction articles, and product reviews. *Model Airplane News* includes more material on prototype airplanes than the other magazines do, and it seems to pay more attention to scale models. It runs a monthly column on r/c boats and has occasional coverage of r/c cars.

Model Aviation. 1975. m. $13.50 (Individuals, $18; schools, $9). Carl R. Wheeley. The Academy of Model Aeronautics, 1810 Samuel Morse Dr., Reston, VA 22090. Illus., adv. Circ: 80,000. Vol. ends: Dec.

Aud: Hs.

Model Aviation is the official organ of the Academy of Model Aeronautics (AMA). With 100,000 members, AMA is probably the largest association of model builders in the nation—although its huge membership is due in part to provision of liability insurance to its members. *Model Aviation* is even more structured than the other flying model magazines, with a large number of monthly columns on the various specialized areas of flying models. It also includes monthly reports from national and regional officers and a calendar of forthcoming events that runs to ten or more pages. It provides extensive coverage on contests and competitions, which is appropriate for an organization that establishes rules for and sponsors contests in over 100 categories. Although *Model Aviation* is clearly an organizational publication, it has a large amount of solid, general material and is highly regarded in the field. Unlike the other flying model magazines, however, it covers only airplanes and provides no material on r/c boats or cars. Its subscription rates for schools are particularly reasonable.

Model Builder. 1971. m. $25. William C. Northrop, Jr. RCMB, Inc., 621 W. 19th St., P.O. Box 10335, Costa Mesa, CA 92627. Illus., adv. Circ: 67,000. Sample. Vol. ends: Dec. *Aud:* Hs, Pr.

Model Builder covers a somewhat wider range of models than the other major magazines, which usually limit themselves to high-tech propulsion and control systems. One of its unusual features, for example, is a monthly plan for a rubber-band-powered airplane in "peanut scale," small enough for the plan to be printed on the center spread of the magazine. Another unusual feature is the monthly column "For Teachers Only," with material designed for teaching model aeronautics to students in grades 4–6. The rest of the magazine has the usual mix of columns, construction articles, product reviews, reports on meetings and contests, and occasional general articles.

R/C Modeler. 1963. m. $24. Patricia Crews. Donald W. Dewey, 144 W. Sierra Madre Blvd., Sierra Madre, CA 91024. Illus., adv. Circ: 110,000. Sample. Vol. ends: Dec.

Aud: Ejh, Hs.

With a circulation of 110,000, *R/C Modeler* is the most popular of all flying model magazines and second only to *Model Railroader* among all model-making magazines. It is also about 50 percent thicker than any other flying model magazine because of the huge volume of advertising it carries. This advertising has made *R/C Modeler* the standard hobby source for commercial information. The general belief is that many hobbyists buy it specifically for its advertisements from manufacturers and its multipage sales lists from mail-order houses. The editorial contents of *R/C Modeler* are fairly typical. About a dozen columns or standard features appear each month; the rest of the magazine consists primarily of construction articles, in-depth kit reviews, reports on events, and a few general articles. Radio control boats and cars are covered briefly, and there are occasional book review articles.

MODEL AUTOS

Model Auto Review. 1982. bi-m. £14.70. Rod Ward, 120 Gledhow Valley Rd., Leeds LS17 6LX, England. Illus., index, adv. Circ: 6,000. Sample. Issues numbered continuously.

Bk. rev: 5, 100–300 words, signed. *Aud:* Hs.

Model Auto Review is generally regarded as the best and most authoritative magazine specializing in diecast model cars, but it has a format that may put off the unenthusiastic. The magazine covers the usual range of topics in static model cars, including articles on conversions, kit reviews, prototype articles, and so forth, but the majority of attention is devoted to diecast models as collectible objects, and most of the advertising is aimed at collectors. The articles approach the subject in a variety of ways. Many survey new production, usually covering the work of a certain manufacturer or the manufacturers of a specific country. Others deal with the history of the various companies or with models of specific sorts of prototypes, such as Volkswagen beetles or Mobil Oil trucks. The editorial contents are literate, fun to read, and bluntly judgmental. The thing that sets *Model Auto Review* apart from most other model magazines is its amazingly compact format. The text is reproduced from typescript, reduced to about 6 point size and crammed onto each page along with a welter of little black-and-white pictures (about a dozen per page) of informational rather than artistic value. Not a square inch is wasted on white space, and articles ramble in and about each other, separated by heavy rulings that zigzag across the pages. Another hundred or so models are illustrated in color inside and outside the covers of each issue.

Scale Auto Enthusiast. 1979. bi-m. $15. Gary Schmidt. Highland Productions, 1413 N. 60th St., Milwaukee, WI 53208. Illus., index, adv. Circ: 35,000. Sample. Vol. ends: Mar/Apr.

Aud: Hs.

Scale Auto Enthusiast is the leading publication devoted exclusively to the construction of static models of automobiles. Most of its articles are concerned with scale modeling and include kit reviews and articles on kit construction, super detailing, modification, and so forth. Most of the concern is with injection-molded styrene kits, but articles also deal with low-volume production in metal, resin, and so on. Other articles deal with prototype information, general construction methods, and contest results. A small amount of space is devoted to diecast models. The magazine's classified ad section is large, with many listings from modelers seeking specific kits or kit parts. The quality of photographs, editing, and layout is generally high, but the technical drawings can be disappointing. For some reason, perhaps because so many new products are introduced each year, model car publications tend to run long articles listing new products in more or less mishmash form, and *Scale Auto Enthusiast* does this too; it may be typical of the field, but it makes the magazine harder to read.

MILITARY MINIATURES

Military Modelling. 1970. m. $23. Kenneth M. Jones. Model and Allied Publns., Argus Specialist Publns., Ltd., P.O. Box 35, Wolsey House, Wolsey Rd., Hemel Hempstead, Hertfordshire HP2 4SS, England. Illus., index, adv. Sample. Vol. ends: Dec.

Bk. rev: 4–12, 100–500 words, signed. *Aud:* Hs.

Military Modelling is published by Model and Allied Publications, a British specialty firm that publishes about ten model-building magazines. This title covers the entire field, but places particular emphasis on prototype information on historical military uniforms, with excellent color paintings and extremely detailed text. It also includes articles on military history, military armor and vehicles, outstanding figures and dioramas by hobbyists, model techniques, new commercial products, and hobby shows, contests, and other activities. Brief attention is paid to toy soldiers and to wargaming, but the central thrust of the magazine is prototype military costume and its reproduction in high-quality scale miniatures. Although the emphasis is on British uniforms, coverage is definitely worldwide. *Military Modelling* is well written and printed, with excellent color and black-and-white photographs, and is the most satisfactory general magazine devoted to its subject.

Old Toy Soldier Newsletter. 1977. bi-m. $15. Jo Sommers & Steve Sommers, 209 N. Lombard, Oak Park, IL 60302. Illus., adv. Circ: 2,000. Sample. Vol. ends: Dec.

Bk. rev: 0-2, 100–200 words. *Aud:* Hs.

Despite the word "newsletter" in its title, *Old Toy Soldier Newsletter* is actually an attractively produced specialty magazine. Like *Toy Soldier Review,* the other major U.S. publication devoted to antique toy soldiers, it is concerned with collecting what were originally low-cost, mass-produced toys rather than expensive scale models. Most of the articles in *Old Toy Soldier Newsletter* are fairly scholarly, examining in detail various aspects of the history and production of the major toy firms of Europe and the United States. It also includes calendars of forthcoming collectors' events and a wide variety of advertisements for old soldiers and for modern production in a similar style. The magazine is simply but cleanly printed, with most of the text reproduced from typescript. Photographs are generally very good, although none are in color, and the quality of writing is generally excellent. Compared with *Toy Soldier Review, Old Toy Soldier Newsletter* is concerned more specifically with toy soldiers (as opposed to related toys); it has a more research-oriented flavor and less nostalgic material, and is substantially shorter.

Toy Soldier Review. 1984. q. $12. Bill Lango. Vintage Castings, Inc., 127 74th St., North Bergen, NJ 07047. Illus., adv. Circ: 1,300. Sample.

Aud: Hs.

Toy Soldier Review is aimed specifically at collectors of old toy soldiers and related toys. Articles cover a range of topics. Most are historical articles on various types of figures, manufacturers, toy military vehicles, and other collectible objects of a similar nature, such as military theme toy trains, bubble gum cards, and cereal premiums. Other topics covered include collectors and their collections, shows and sales, general nostalgia for old toy soldiers, and modern toy soldiers made to resemble the classic toys of days gone by. Quite a lot of emphasis is placed on U.S. collectibles—such as dime store soldiers—that were originally extremely inexpensive. Unlike some other collectors' magazines, such as *Train Collectors Quarterly, Toy Soldier Review* includes information on values, sales prices, and general rarity. Technically the magazine is quite good. Despite its small circulation it is typeset and cleanly pasted up. It has no color illustrations, and the quality of black-and-white photographs varies from excellent to rather poor. The writing is generally very good, although some articles slip through in considerable need of editing. Compared with *Old Toy Soldier Newsletter* it is less scholarly in its approach and concerned with a much greater variety of toys.

MODEL SHIPS

Model Ship Builder. 1979. bi-m. $18. Jeffrey A. Phillips. Phoenix Publns., P.O. Box 128, Cedarburg, WI 53012. Illus., adv. Circ: 12,000. Sample. Vol. ends: Sept/Oct.

Bk. rev: 1–4, 100–2,500 words, signed. *Aud:* Hs.

Model Ship Builder, like all the magazines in this section, is concerned primarily with the construction of large, accurate scale models of historic ships. Although coverage ranges from plastic kits to completely scratch-built models, emphasis is on scratch-building wooden ships and on building and improving wooden ship kits. Each issue contains seven or eight major articles and a variety of news notes. Article topics range from scratch-building specific models (which may require a long string of articles in subsequent issues), to extremely detailed kit reviews (with information necessary to correct the manufacturers' errors), to historical articles (sometimes recommending appropriate kits), to ship plans. It also includes articles on building techniques, although many techniques can be picked up from the construction articles. *Model Ship Builder* is generally nicely put together, but it is obviously a smaller budget operation than are the model train or plane magazines. One of the most useful sections is "Ship Builder's Shop," which lists and briefly annotates over 200 books from various publishers, which *Model Ship Builder* offers for sale; libraries should find this a useful source of titles for collection development.

Ships in Scale. 1983. bi-m. $18. Scottie Dayton. Model Expo Publns., 12 Just Rd., Fairfield, NJ 07007. Illus., index, adv. Circ: 17,000. Sample. Vol. ends: July/Aug.
Bk. rev: 0–5, 150–600 words, signed. *Aud:* Hs.

Ships in Scale is similar to *Model Ship Builder.* It is concerned with the construction of large, historically accurate models of both sailing and of steam-powered ships. It covers both kit assembly and scratch-building, and places the heaviest emphasis on sailing ships. Articles include kit reviews, scratch-building projects, maritime history, shop techniques, methods of modeling special details, and so forth. Like other ship-building magazines, it tends to have long articles that continue for many issues, often for more than a year. Comparing *Ships in Scale* with *Model Ship Builder* is difficult, since they have similar contents and are aimed at a similar market. *Ships in Scale* tends to have slightly more editorial material, broken up into more but shorter articles. It concentrates somewhat less on sailing ships, and pays a little more attention to radio control. *Model Ship Builder* is more likely to include full sets of plans. *Ships in Scale* devotes relatively more attention to the assembly and improvement of difficult kits as opposed to straight scratch-building; this is perhaps less elegant, but it may reflect the needs of the majority of modelers. *Ships in Scale* is well printed. Because of its concentration on the history and detail of ships it will appeal not only to modelers but also to people who simply like ships.

MODEL RAILROADS

Continental Modeller. 1979. bi-m. £7.10. David Lloyd. Peco Publns. and Publicity, Ltd., Beer, Seaton, Devon EX12 3NA, England. Illus., index, adv. Vol. ends: Dec.
Bk. and video rev: 0–6, 100–200 words. *Aud:* Hs.

Aimed at British model railroaders interested in equipment from throughout the world, *Continental Modeller* covers not only Continental equipment, but also U.S., Austra-

lian, Oriental, and so forth. It is published by Peco, which also publishes *Railway Modeller,* and has basically the same format and staff.

Model Railroader. 1934. m. $22.50. Russell G. Larson. Kalmbach Publg. Co., 1027 N. Seventh St., Milwaukee, WI 53233. Illus., index, adv. Circ: 182,850. Sample. Vol. ends: Dec.
Bk. rev: 0–10, 50–350 words, signed. *Video rev:* 0–5, 150–600 words, signed. *Aud:* Ejh, Hs.

Model Railroader is the dominant magazine in model railroading, with a circulation nearly twice that of any other model magazine—railroad or otherwise. It covers virtually the entire spectrum of model railroad activities, including the construction of model locomotives, cars, and buildings; layout design, construction, and wiring; prototype information; and features on contests, meetings, outstanding individual models and layouts, and leading personalities and companies in the field. It also includes extensive schedules of forthcoming events, and its classified ad section is by far the largest in the model railroad field. Coverage in such areas as live steam, European model trains, and antique toy trains, however, is limited to very occasional features. Although some material aimed at beginners is included, most of *Model Railroader*'s articles tend to be of the state-of-the-art variety, and this sometimes puts off people who are looking for simple projects. The magazine's production standards are high. Photographs are finely printed—many in color. Most articles are illustrated with excellent artwork by staff draftsmen, and editing and composition are consistently professional. For the library subscribing to only one model railroad magazine, *Model Railroader* is clearly the choice. The problem is that so many libraries subscribe to *Model Railroader* and nothing else that access to other fine publications on model trains is far too limited.

Railroad Model Craftsman (Formerly: *Model Craftsman*). 1933. m. $18. William C. Schaumburg. Carstens Publns., P.O. Box 700, Newton, NJ 07860. Illus., index, adv. Circ: 90,000. Sample. Vol. ends: May.
Bk. rev: 0–4, 200–1,000 words, signed. *Aud:* Hs.

Railroad Model Craftsman is *Model Railroader*'s major competitor and an excellent magazine. It stands strongly in second place among the U.S. general-purpose model railroad magazines. Like *Model Railroader,* it covers virtually all aspects of model railroading, including construction of model locomotives, railroad cars, and suitable trackside buildings; design, construction, and wiring of layouts; prototype detail; product and book reviews; and conventions, contests, and other hobby activities. Because of their very similar scope and intentions, it is hard to draw firm comparisons between the two magazines. *Craftsman*'s articles are sometimes a little more down-to-earth and suited to the skills of the ordinary modeler, and it has more "quickie" one-evening projects. It devotes a little less space to electronics. Its book reviews tend to be a little longer and more thorough, and it pays more attention to old toy trains (although its coverage is sometimes inaccurate). All in all, however, these are minor differences. Both magazines are trying to reach the same audience and are looking for the same kind of material. *Model Railroader* has twice the circulation and therefore more money to spend. In turn it has its own staff of professional photographers and artists—which *Craftsman* does not—and this is apparent in published artwork and photographs. *Railroad Model Craftsman* is a strong magazine pitted against the most popular of all model-building magazines and does very well.

Railway Modeller. 1949. m. £18.20. John Brewer. Peco Publns. and Publicity, Ltd., Beer, Seaton, Devon EX12 3NA, England. Illus., adv. Circ: 95,500. Vol. ends: Dec.

Bk. rev: 0–5, 100–200 words, signed. *Aud:* Hs.

Railway Modeller has the widest circulation of any model railroad magazine published in England and is probably second only to *Model Railroader* worldwide. It is published by Peco, which is also a manufacturer of model railroad products, particularly track. Like *Model Railroader* and *Railroad Model Craftsman* in the United States, *Railway Modeller* covers a general range of model railroad subjects, but it places relatively less emphasis on operation and electrical systems and more on finished layouts. In large part this reflects the British tradition of model railroading, which tends to be one of uncluttered layouts with careful attention to accurate historical detail and large numbers of scratch-built structures. By contrast, Continental layouts tend to look like spaghetti bowls of trackage. *Railway Modeller* advertises itself as "for the average enthusiast modelling British railway practice." By "average enthusiast," Peco means a modeler without an elaborate home workshop or semi-professional technical skills. Like many British magazines, *Railway Modeller* has articles written in a chatty, personal style quite unlike much U.S. writing. This is a good choice for a library that wants a magazine on British model railroading, but it is necessary to remember that more U.S. hobbyists use Continental equipment than British equipment, since the majority of outstanding foreign manufacturers are in Germany, Austria and Italy.

Train Collectors Quarterly. 1955. q. $12. Bruce D. Manson, Jr. Train Collectors Assn., P.O. Box 248, Strasburg, PA 17579. Illus. Circ: 17,000. Sample. Vol. ends: Oct.

Aud: Hs.

Train Collectors Quarterly is the official journal of the Train Collectors Association (TCA) and the outstanding journal in its field. TCA is the largest of the four major toy train collectors' associations in the United States and has about 16,500 members. Toy train collectors are primarily interested in mass-produced toys rather than hand-crafted scale models, and they try to collect them in the original condition in which they left the factory. Although many train collectors have operating layouts, their central interest is accumulating and preserving the toys themselves, and they shudder at the thought of modifying factory-built equipment in any way. Articles in *Train Collectors Quarterly* reflect this kind of specific interest in toys. Most of the articles are detailed studies of the history, current operations, and products of various companies like Lionel, American Flyer, Ives, and Marx, with primary emphasis placed on U.S. firms.

Other articles cover association activities and the layouts and collections of various members. The major topic that is assiduously avoided is the collector value of old toy trains. Train collectors are capable of exceptionally scholarly research, and some of the articles amaze even other collectors. General model railroad magazines occasionally have articles on old toy trains, but the *Quarterly* is the standard source and far more reliable. Other train collectors' associations include the Lionel Collectors Club of America, the Toy Train Operating Society, and the Märklin Enthusiasts of America; each publishes a journal, but none is at the standard of *Train Collectors Quarterly*.

STATIC MODELS

Antique Toy World. 1971. m. $20. Dale Kelley, 4419 Irving Park Rd., Chicago, IL 60641. Illus., adv. Circ: 6,000. Sample. Vol. ends: Dec.

Bk. rev: 0–4, 100–750 words, signed. *Aud:* Hs.

Antique Toy World is aimed primarily at collectors of mechanical toys, including trains, boats, cars, airplanes, military equipment, banks, robots, and miscellaneous figures and automata. The majority of the articles are folksy rather than scholarly in tone. They concentrate on collectors and collections, on toy shows (swap meets) and auctions, on toys with various themes, and on general nostalgia for old toys. Only a few are scholarly studies, and most of these are on cast iron banks. Each issue also includes a list of nearly 200 forthcoming events for toy collectors—primarily toy shows. Advertisements make up the bulk of the magazine, and they are a useful source of information on buyers, sellers, and prices. *Antique Toy World* is also a major dealer in books on antique toys, and each issue contains several pages of annotated listings of books. Since these are often imported and usually from small publishers, librarians will find the lists particularly helpful for book selection. The scope of *Antique Toy World* is international, with many advertisements, lists of events, and reports of toy sales from England and the Continent. Although the articles are sometimes pretty shallow, the magazine is an extremely useful source of solid information on forthcoming events, prices realized at auctions and sales and asked by toy dealers, current enthusiasms among toy collectors, books in the field, and the names and addresses of toy museums, dealers, and collectors.

FineScale Modeler. 1982. bi-m. $12.50. Bob Hayden. Kalmbach Publg. Co., 1027 N. Seventh St., Milwaukee, WI 53233. Illus., index, adv. Circ: 46,000. Sample. Vol. ends: Nov/Dec.

Bk. and video rev: 8–15, 75–200 words, signed. *Aud:* Hs.

FineScale Modeler is the most important magazine concerned with the general construction of static models. Its primary concern is with plastic models, although it also deals with cast metal military miniatures. The basic types of models covered include military equipment, soldiers, dioramas, automobiles, airplanes, and ships. Most of the articles are construction articles, combining specific projects with pointers on model-building techniques. Most plastic modelers do a great deal of kit modification and combination ("kit-bashing," as some call it) to arrive at models of specific prototypes or of equipment for which no kits are available, and many of the construction articles in *FineScale Modeler* are concerned with this type of work. Other articles cover specific modeling techniques, new products, and military uniforms. This title is typical of Kalmbach publications. Its extremely professional production—literate editing, excellent photographs, and consistently fine drawings by Kalmbach's staff—is indicative of the quality that a large and successful hobby publisher can achieve. Considering the tremendous popularity of plastic kit building, few libraries should be without *FineScale Modeler*.

MOTORCYCLES AND OFF-ROAD VEHICLES

For the Student

See also Automobiles; and Sports Sections.

Lynn Heer, Stac Library Center, University of Florida, 307 West Hall, Gainesville, FL 32611

Basic Periodicals

Hs: *Cycle*, *Dirt Bike*.

Basic Abstracts and Indexes

Magazine Index, *Readers' Guide to Periodical Literature*.

For the Student

American Motorcyclist (Formerly: *AMA News*). 1947. m. Greg Harrison. Amer. Motorcyclist Assn., P.O. Box 141, Westerville, OH 43081. Illus., adv. Circ: 120,000.
Aud: Hs.

This is the official journal of the American Motorcyclist Association. Its articles cover the range of motorcycle racing and touring, racing personalities, and racing and rallies throughout the United States. "Government Regulations" and "On the Road" regularly cover legislation and regulations affecting motorcycles and safe biking.

Cycle. 1952. m. $13.98. Phil Shilling. Ziff-Davis Publg. Co., One Park Ave., New York, NY 10016. Illus., adv. Circ: 460,000. Microform: UMI, B&H, MIM.
Indexed: MgI, RG. *Aud:* Hs.

This is one of the basic magazines to consult for cycle and cycling accessories and tools evaluations. Several very detailed road tests are included in each issue with both color and black-and-white photographs of the cycle tested. Also covered in the tests are specifications on all aspects of the engines, transmissions, and performance. In addition, there are technical articles on various cycle mechanical parts. Racing events are also covered. Recommended for all libraries.

Cycle Guide. 1967. m. $13.98. Lawrence Work. Cycle Guide Publns., P.O. Box 993, Farmingdale, NY 11737. Illus., adv. Circ: 126,451.
Aud: Hs.

This is a quality magazine that provides cycle road tests with comparisons to similar models. "Cycle Guide" is an index to published road tests that also includes seven basic specifications of each model. News relating to cycling and new product information are found in "Guide Lines." People and racing events are covered in "Sport Lines."

Cycle World. 1962. m. $13.94. CBS Magazines, 3807 Wilshire Blvd., Los Angeles, CA 90010. Illus., adv. Circ: 336,000. Microform: UMI.
Indexed: MgI. *Aud:* Hs.

A magazine that endeavors to create a favorable impression of motorcycle riding as fun and motorcycle racing as a sport. Articles cover the evolution of various types of cycles and comparisons of different brands, with detailed technical data on the drivetrain, chassis, engine, suspension, tires, and brakes. "Race watch" covers all the major races and includes a calendar.

Dirt Bike. 1971. m. $14.98. Rick Sieman. Hi-Torque Publns., Inc., 10600 Sepulveda Blvd., Mission Hills, CA 91345. Subs. to: P.O. Box 9502, Mission Hills, CA 91345.
Illus., adv. Circ: 176,062. Vol. ends: Dec.
Aud: Hs.

This is the authoritative title of the off-road sports world. Starting with its spectacular cover, *Dirt Bike* is packed with black-and-white and color action photos. There are sections on technical maintenance, skills, racing events, product evaluations, and so on. An ongoing series is "Places to Ride," a series that will eventually cover all 50 states. Regular columns are "From the saddle" (human interest) and "Mister Knowit-all" (questions from readers). *Dirt Bike* has a responsible attitude. Bikers are cautioned against trying the stunts in the action photos; these are only for the experienced and professionals. There are reminders about appropriate equipment for safety, and a concern for environmental and ecological matters. (L.K.W.)

Dirt Rider. 1982. m. $12. Petersen Publg. Co., 8490 Sunset Blvd., Los Angeles, CA 90069. Illus., adv. Circ: 115,000. Sample.
Aud: Hs.

Anyone who enjoys taking a bike off road over either relatively smooth or exceptionally rough terrain will find much of interest in this magazine. The illustrated articles are concerned with various types of bikes (in many price categories), equipment, and other products of value to the rider. The articles tend to be more descriptive than evaluative. In addition there are features and pieces about competitions, trail rides, and various tests. There are good personality sketches and the how-to-do-it articles are as clear as they are often well illustrated.

Dirt Wheels. 1980. m. $15. Daisy/Hi-Torque Publg. Co., Inc., 10600 Sepulveda Blvd., Mission Hills, CA 91345. Illus., adv. Circ: 90,000. Sample.
Aud: Hs.

Unlike *Dirt Rider*, which concentrates on motorcycles, here the emphasis is as much on the four-wheel vehicle as on the bike. There is good reporting on events, races, and other competitions. The product pieces are satisfactory, and testing of new models is both descriptive and evaluative.

Easyriders. 1971. m. $23. Lou Kimsey. Paisano Publg. Co., P.O. Box 52, Malibu, CA 90265. Illus., adv. Circ: 473,589. *Aud:* Hs.

This is for the adult biker; it is a magazine with lots of pictures of nudes, cycles and ads. This will undoubtedly be a popular magazine. For those brave enough to include it in their collections there should be plenty of readers.

Kart Sport. 1982. m. $20. Joe Xavier. 5510 Ashborn Rd., Baltimore, MD 21227. Illus., adv.

Aud: Hs.

Cut down versions of automobiles, the kart is a familiar sight on specialized raceways and off the road tracks. The sport is apparently growing in popularity. The library can keep up with the activity through this well-illustrated, 50-page glossy. There are short, easy to understand articles for beginners and veterans, the usual scattering of departments and features and many advertisements.

Motocross Action Magazine. 1973. m. $14.98. Jody Weisel. Daisy/Hi-Torque Publg. Co., Inc., 16200 Sepulveda Blvd., Mission Hills, CA 91345. Illus., adv. Circ: 105,824. Sample. *Aud:* Hs.

This magazine is devoted to off-road and racing motorcycles. Each issue reviews several racing cycles with in-depth analyses of their design and performance. The reviews are evaluative in nature. The ads and new products columns provide excellent coverage of racing clothing and helmets. Articles report on the best-known motocross racers.

Motorcycle. 1981. a. Free. Webb Co., 1999 Shepard Rd., St. Paul, MN 55116. Illus., adv. Circ: 1,000,000. *Aud:* Hs.

Essentially this is a mass of advertising for motorcycles and related products. At the same time the free title does offer a good cross section of the year's best products. While non-evaluative, the articles do at least alert the reader to what is new. Also, there are some rather good pieces on the sport, travel, personalities and so forth.

Motorcyclist. 1912. m. $10. Petersen Publg. Co., 8490 Sunset Blvd., Los Angeles, CA 90069. Illus., adv. Circ: 226,000. Sample. Microform: UMI.

Aud: Hs.

Dedicated to the experienced street motorcycle rider, this magazine assumes the reader already knows quite a bit about the machines. The articles and features are sometimes relatively technical, and the road tests are both evaluative and descriptive. The pieces on the bikes are some of the best in any magazine, and it is an excellent place to turn to for up-to-date information when choosing equipment. Less successful are the occasional travel articles and humor. But this is still by far one of the best motorcycle magazines for the serious fan.

Road Rider. 1969. m. $15. Bob Carpenter. Fancy Publns., Inc., 5509 Santa Monica Blvd., Los Angeles, CA 90038. Illus., adv. Circ: 32,000.

Aud: Hs.

The emphasis is on using the motorcycle for travel and touring. The editor assumes the reader is familiar with bikes, and the product information requires technical knowledge.

Snow Goer. 1966. q. Free. Bill Monn. Webb Co., 1999 Shepard Rd., St. Paul, MN 55116. Illus., adv. Circ: 600,000. *Aud:* Hs.

A quarterly report on new products and topics of interest to owners of snowmobiles. The advertising supports the editorial matter, which is far from objective. This publication includes news about other products and vehicles that are used in the snow, i.e., four-wheel drive and trucks. There is even a section on power mowers used during the spring and summer.

Snow Week. 1973. 18/yr. $8.95. Webb Co., 1999 Shepard Rd., St. Paul, MN 55116. Illus., adv. Circ: 20,000. Sample. *Aud:* Hs.

A tabloid that reports on snowmobile racing and other events. The illustrated articles concentrate on major races and personalities. There are some equipment news and mechanical data. Information on resorts and places where one may use the snowmobile is abundant.

MUSIC AND DANCE

For the Student: General; Dance; Popular; Reviews/For the Professional

See also Electronics; and Folklore Sections.

Mary Augusta Rosenfeld, Administrative Librarian, Smithsonian Institution Libraries, Washington, DC 20560 (Dance subsection)

Norris L. Stephens, Music Librarian, University of Pittsburgh, Theodore M. Finney Music Library, Pittsburgh, PA 15260, with the assistance of David Needham, Librarian, 7475 Morgan Rd., 11–2, Liverpool, NY 13088

Introduction

During the past decade there has been considerable publishing activity in the areas of early music, ethnomusicology, opera, popular, folk, jazz, computer, and electronic music, theory and analysis, interdisciplinary studies, and audio equipment and phonorecording reviews. Many new titles have appeared, and simultaneously several of the well-established ones, along with many ephemeral ones, have ceased publication.

Over the past five years, dance classes have continued to show a steady growth in attendance. While this may reflect a nationwide increase of attention to fitness and health, a good number of amateur dancers come from the widespread audience for dance theater. Many new dance companies have started in cities and towns outside the recognized centers of dance. Magazines in the dance field are varied in style and in content and represent a range of popular performance, professional and participative dance forms. Most of these journals now include listings and reviews for dance on television and on videotapes. The emphasis in this section falls on U.S. publications, where subject matter ranges from classical ballet to modern dance to square dance. In addition to magazines of general interest and academic journals, several periodicals from outside the mainstream are recommended for their contribution to scholarship and enjoyment.

Basic Periodicals

GENERAL. Ejh, Hs: *Opera News, Ovation.*

DANCE. Ejh: *Dance Magazine*; Hs: *American Square Dance, Dance Magazine.*

POPULAR. Ejh, Hs: *Creem, Downbeat, Rolling Stone, Song Hits.*

REVIEWS. Ejh, Hs: *High Fidelity, Stereo Review.*

Basic Indexes

Music Index.

For the Student

GENERAL

The American Organist. 1966. m. $25. Anthony Baglivi. Amer. Guild of Organists, 815 Second Ave., Suite 318, New York, NY 10017. Illus., index, adv. Circ: 23,000. Vol. ends: Dec. Microform: UMI.

Indexed: MusicI. *Bk. rev:* 8–12, 150–400 words, signed; *record rev:* 10–15, 100–250 words, signed; *music rev:* 8–15, 50–150 words, signed. *Aud:* Hs.

This is the official journal of the American Guild of Organists, the Royal Canadian College of Organists, and the Associated Pipe Organ Builders of America, "dedicated to furthering their ideals, objectives, and cultural and educational aspirations." It is the best publication currently available to church musicians. The 64-page journal covers all aspects of organ music and musicians. Each issue contains eight to ten articles, a current calendar, workshop and conference reports, new appointments and installations, retirements, and other items of interest. The library with a large music collection and interest in church music will require *The American Organist.*

American Recorder. 1960. q. Membership, $20. Sigrid Nagle. The Amer. Recorder Soc., 596 Broadway, No. 902, New York, NY 10012. Illus., adv. Circ: 4,000. Sample. Vol. ends: Winter. Microform: UMI.

Indexed: MusicI. *Bk. rev:* Various number, length. *Aud:* Hs.

There are few recorder players who would not find the *American Recorder* an indispensable guide to their instrument and its music. To the non-recorder player, some of the material is technical; none of it is at all esoteric to amateur recorder players.

Asian Music. See Asia/For the Student Section.

Billboard. 1894. w. $148. Lee Zhito. Billboard Publns., One Astor Plaza, 1515 Broadway, New York, NY 10036. Illus., index, adv. Circ: 47,000. Microform: UMI.

Indexed: MusicI. *Aud:* Hs.

This is to music what *Variety* is to theater and film. The newspaper/magazine format is familiar in many libraries. It includes news of personalities, contracts signed, shows given or to be given, records, singers, groups, and so on. All of this is written in a snappy, slangy style that insiders can best appreciate. It is the best single way of keeping up with, and slightly ahead of, developments in rock and pop, country and folk music. A must for larger libraries, a useful addition for smaller collections.

Canadian Musician. 1979. bi-m. $15/10 issues. Ted Burley. Norris Publns., 832 Mount Pleasant Rd., Toronto, Ont. M4P 2L3, Canada. Illus., adv.

Bk. rev: Notes. *Aud:* Hs.

Directed to and written by Canadian popular musicians, here are 66 to 80 pages of articles and features by numerous experts on guitar, keyboard, bass, percussion, brass, woodwinds, synthesizers, vocal technique, arranging, recording, audio, and just about anything else likely to involve the pop musician. The magazine now has an updated format and editorial content, and appeals to a much wider audience. The writing style is good. The brief articles on artists and the musical scene make it of interest for almost any Canadian library. Recommended.

Cash Box. 1942. w. $125. Cash Box, 330 W. 58th St., New York, NY 10019. Illus., adv. Circ: 21,000.

Indexed: MusicI. *Aud:* Hs.

A weekly somewhat similar to the more familiar *Billboard*, the entire focus of *Cash Box* is on music, particularly the phonograph business. The reviews of recordings, news of the industry, and ratings of particular performers and records give the readers up-to-date information on music. Methods of retailing are stressed as are economic news and data on distribution, audiences, and the like. The library with *Billboard* will want *Cash Box* as well. There is not that much duplication, and the two augment one another.

Flute Talk. 1981. 9/yr. $4.50. Polly Hansen. The Instrumentalist Publg. Co., 200 Northfield Rd., Northfield, IL 60093. Illus., adv. Vol. ends: May.

Aud: Hs.

An elegant, glossy magazine. Contents have included articles on the history of the flute, interviews with distinguished players (James Galway has graced the cover), master class techniques, audition tips, and concert schedules. Each issue has a performance guide to a musical composition for flute. (L.K.W.)

Guitar Player Magazine. 1967. m. $24. Tom Wheeler. GPI Publns., P.O. Box 2100, Cupertino, CA 95015. Illus., adv. Circ: 170,000. Sample. Vol. ends: Dec. Microform: UMI.

Indexed: MusicI. *Bk. rev:* 8, 60–80 words, signed. *Aud:* Ejh, Hs.

The basic "how-to" magazine for guitar players from the youngest to the oldest. Each issue contains articles on folk and popular music, general information on instruments and playing, tunes and topics, and book reviews. This is for the popular, not the classical, guitar. A good purchase for just about any library where there is an interest in folk music and the guitar.

Guitar Review. 1946. q. $24. Vladimir Bobri. Guitar Review, 40 W. 25th St., New York, NY 10010. Illus., adv. Circ: 6,000. Sample.

Bk. rev: Various number, length. *Aud:* Hs.

Given the great popularity of the classic guitar in the United States, this publication should find a large audience. The field is the classic guitar—its history, music, construction, and technique; pop, jazz, folk, country and western, and electric guitar are not covered. There are beautiful illustrations and line drawings of various members of the guitar family, extensive musical examples, and a number of previously unpublished compositions. Regular features include "The Guitar on Record" and "New Guitar Books and Music." Librarians will find it a good source for reviews of new music and recordings. All contributions are scholarly, and this seems to be the major outlet for material on any aspect of the classic guitar. A must for large public and academic libraries, but also a possibility for many medium-sized public and school libraries that number guitar enthusiasts among their users.

JEMF Quarterly. 1965. q. $14 (Individuals, $12). Linda L. Painter. John Edwards Memorial Foundation, Inc., Folklore and Mythological Center, Univ. of California, Los Angeles, CA 90024. Index. Circ: 600. Sample. Vol ends: Winter. Microform: UMI.

Indexed: MusicI. *Bk. rev:* 1–2, notes. *Aud:* Hs.

Concerned exclusively with the study of U.S. country and western music. The archives of the Foundation are devoted to furthering "the serious study and public recognition of those forms of American folk music disseminated by commercial media such as print, sound recordings, films, radio, and television." In other words, the *Quarterly* is devoted to styles of music identified as country, country and western, old time, bluegrass, mountain, cowboy, and so on, including race records, soul, and rock—the entire field of U.S. regional popular and folk music. No one interested in these areas should be denied access to it.

Living Blues. See Afro-American/For the Student Section.

Music Journal: general classical magazine. 1943. m. (Sept.-June). $18. Bert Wechsler. Hampton Intl. Communications, 60 E. 42nd St., New York, NY 10017. Illus., adv. Circ: 22,000. Sample. Vol. ends: Dec. Microform: UMI.

Indexed: MusicI. *Bk. rev:* 5–6, 150 words, signed. *Aud:* Hs.

Still one of the best sources for an overview of contemporary music, prepared by outstanding authorities in the music, dance, and music theater worlds. Occasionally, highly controversial articles appear that illuminate current thinking on a wide variety of musical topics. In addition to announcements and accounts of recent musical happenings, there are enlightened editorials and critical reviews of books, records, and music. Highly regarded in music circles, this is a useful addition to any library's holdings.

Notitas Musicales. See Latin America, Latino (U.S.)/For the Student: Latin America Section.

On Key: the magazine for young pianists. 1982. m. $15. Joan Bujacich. JDL Publications, 33 S. Fullerton Ave., Montclair, NJ 07042. Subs. to: Box 1213, Montclair, NJ 07042. Illus. Sample.

Aud: Ejh.

The title tells almost all. The 20 to 30 page magazine is for students from about 6 to 14 years of age. Coverage is more of music appreciation—reaching from the classical to the popular—than music teaching. At the same time there are articles and regular features which give advice on playing the piano, including original and well-known scores. The overall intent is to involve the young reader with the glamor and the joys of the instrument and performers. To this extent, it works well.

OP: independent music. See Alternatives/For the Student Section.

Opera Canada. 1960. q. $15. (Canada, $12). Ruby Mercer. Foundation for Coast to Coast Opera Publns., Suite 433, 366 Adelaide St. E., Toronto, Ont. M5A 3X9, Canada. Illus. Circ: 7,000. Microform: UMI.

Indexed: CanI. *Aud:* Hs.

Despite the title, *Opera Canada* concerns itself with happenings in the opera world around the globe. However, extensive coverage is given to Canada; there is activity from coast to coast, from Halifax to Edmonton and Calgary to Vancouver. A "Round-Up" column provides information on these regional activities, branching out to include major opera companies in San Francisco, New York, Houston and Chicago, plus European centers in Vienna, Munich, London, Paris, and Milan. "People Are Talking About. . ." is an extensive compilation of what opera addicts and stars are doing everywhere, while the "Calendar" outlines coming events worldwide. This information and the articles on opera history and development provide the true fan with an excellent magazine for all occasions. It contains a small number of reviews on records and books, but they are inconsequential compared with the rest of the title.

Opera News. 1936. w. (Dec.-Apr.); m. (May-Nov.). $30. Robert Jacobson. Metropolitan Opera Guild, 1865 Broadway, New York, NY 10023. Illus., index, adv. Circ: 110,000. Sample. Vol. ends: June. Microform: UMI.

Indexed: MusicI, RG. *Bk. rev:* 3, 250–300 words, signed. *Aud:* Ejh, Hs.

During the Metropolitan Opera season, issues deal with the opera that is currently being performed, and include the plot, cast, and historical notes as well as photographs of characters and staging. Monthly issues are more likely to probe history and personalities involved in opera and to feature important companies outside New York. Signed reports of from 250 to 1,000 words from various music centers in the United States and abroad are a regular feature. A handsome and popular magazine, *Opera News* is the principal periodical devoted to opera in the United States, and should be in most libraries.

The World of Music. 1959. q. $24 (Individuals, $19). Ivan Vandor. Edition Heinrichshofen, Postfach 620, D-2940 Wilhelmshaven, Locarno, Amsterdam, The Netherlands. Illus., adv. Circ: 2,000. Sample.

Indexed: MusicI. *Bk. rev:* 2–3, 500 words, signed. *Aud:* Ejh, Hs.

The journal of the International Music Council (a part of UNESCO), published in association with the International Institute for Comparative Music Studies. Its international orientation is reflected in its excellent coverage of the realms of music that are remote from that of Western classical music. It is trilingual (English, French, and German), and though the English translations are shaky at times, no one really interested in music can afford to miss it. The articles are written by experts, but are largely nontechnical and obviously directed to a nonprofessional audience. The world of twentieth-century Western music is not neglected, but the emphasis is clearly on more exotic music. There are some regular features: an "Information" round-up of world-wide musical events, and selected book and record reviews. There is nothing to which *World of Music* can be compared. It is essential for large public and academic libraries, yet not too esoteric for medium-sized school libraries.

DANCE

American Square Dance (Formerly: *Square Dance*). 1945. m. $10. Stan Burdick & Cathie Burdick. Burdick Enterprises, P.O. Box 488, Huron, OH 44839. Illus., index, adv. Circ: 14,000. Vol. ends: Dec. Microform: UMI.

Bk. rev: 250 words, signed. *Aud:* Ejh, Hs.

Students, teachers, seasoned dancers, and callers will find much to learn and enjoy in this small-format magazine. Each month the editors present short articles on all aspects of square and round dancing including new or revised steps, tips on calling, dance etiquette, and moral support. Taking a chatty, positive tone, they report nationwide news from clubs, classes, and special events, filling out close to 100 pages with photographs and drawings. In 40 years of growing interest in square dancing, this publication has continued to emphasize the social and community benefits while keeping up with current trends. A calendar of events, nationwide, is included in each issue.

Ballet News. 1979. m. $15. Robert Jacobson. Metropolitan Opera Guild, 1865 Broadway, New York, NY 10023. Illus., index, adv. Circ: 50,000. Vol. ends: June. Microform: UMI.

Bk. rev: 250–500 words, signed. *Aud:* Hs.

A well laid out and illustrated magazine. Produced by the Metropolitan Opera Guild, its emphasis is on ballet, but reviews and occasional features appear on leading modern companies and dancers. Dance history, written to appeal to a popular audience, has been combined here with more serious study of topics such as dance notation. The generally high quality of the writing combined with real backstage news will attract both the amateur and the specialist. Dance activity in major cities is covered, and the reviewers pay attention to the choice of repertory as well as the quality of performance. Departments include record reviews; a TV column by David Vaughan, editor of the *Encyclopaedia of*

Dance and Ballet; and Clive Barnes, drama critic of the *New York Post*, whose final page, "Barnes on. . .," provides elegant and trenchant commentary.

Dance in Canada. 1973. q. $10. Sandra Evan-Jones. Dance in Canada Assn., 38 Charles St. E., Toronto, Ont. M4Y 1T1, Canada. Illus, adv. Circ: 3,000. Microform: MML.

Bk. rev: 250–500 words, signed. *Aud:* Hs.

A lively, professionally designed magazine, *Dance in Canada* concentrates on all forms of dance including popular musicals. Feature articles are on special issues of interest to dancers including education, health, the role of women in dance, and so forth. The emphasis remains on current work by Canadian companies, dancers, and choreographers, but the review sections include U.S. and European companies. This periodical remains the major source of information on the growing Canadian dance movement. A shift in policy results in articles written primarily in English without translation and includes an occasional article written in French with English summary.

Dance Magazine. 1926. m. $24. William Como. Dance Magazine, Inc., 33 W. 60th St., New York, NY 10023. Illus., index, adv. Circ: 64,000. Vol. ends: Dec. Microform: B&H, UMI.

Indexed: BoRvI, HumI, RG. *Bk. rev:* 2–3, 250–500 words, signed. *Aud:* Hs.

The best-known and most widely circulated as well as the oldest continuous dance periodical in the country. Feature-length articles by some leading dance writers add to the appreciation of performance, but the real value here lies in the painstaking coverage of dance activities throughout the United States and around the world. Most cities that have any form of dance education or performance receive recognition. For the professional, this is required reading; for the student or general audience, it is an indispensable tool for understanding the dance scene today. Herbert Migdoll, noted dance photographer, serves as the periodical's designer. Each issue carries a schools' directory for the entire nation, a monthly performance calendar, and news and class notes.

Dancing Times. 1910. m. $25. Mary Clarke & Ivor Guest. The Dancing Times, Ltd., Clerkenwell House, 45–47 Clerkenwell Green, London EC1 0BE, England. Illus., adv. Circ: 15,000. Vol. ends: Sept.

Aud: Hs.

The oldest continuing periodical on dance, this British import will interest American audiences by its coverage of all aspects of dance in England, still an important center for technique and performance. There are in-depth reviews of the Royal Ballet and the Sadlers Wells Royal Ballet. Most issues are filled with notes from schools, awards news, and discussions of dance education, which are standardized throughout the country. The focus is on ballet, and some modern dance reviews are included. Excerpts from forthcoming works and ballet classics appear. The editor is a well-known author in the dance field, especially on the subject of ballet. An advance program for major U.K. companies is in each issue. Jack Anderson of the *New York Times* now serves as the U.S. correspondent.

Square Dancing. 1948. m. $10. Bob Osgood. Sets in Order, Amer. Square Dance Soc., 462 N. Robertson Blvd., Los Angeles, CA 90048. Illus., adv. Circ: 27,000. Microform: UMI.

Bk. rev: 250 words, signed. *Aud:* Hs.

According to the editors, this magazine "is circulated throughout the United States and in more than 30 countries overseas where square dancing is enjoyed today." Begun in the post-World War II boom, it is intended for the average dancer as well as the caller and leader. In a glossy, small format, the editors pack numerous articles on dance techniques, etiquette, and personalities. It covers square, round, and some contra dancing and includes practical instructions for performance, costumes, and entertaining.

POPULAR

Bluegrass Unlimited. 1966. m. $15. Peter V. Kuykendall. Bluegrass Unlimited, P.O. Box 111, Broad Run, VA 22014. Illus., adv. Circ: 19,000. Sample.

Aud: Hs.

Bluegrass Unlimited tends to be "traditional" in that it is interested in old-time bluegrass; the Nashville scene is not covered in detail. The approach is popular and practical. There are some good articles about the music, its instruments, and groups. This is one of the best sources for keeping track of these annual U.S. musical events—extensive coverage is given to the large numbers of annual bluegrass, country music, and "old-time fiddlers'" conventions and festivals. The record reviews display the special background and knowledge needed for this type of music, an area that is not reviewed in most standard sources. Emphasis is on the documentation of the current bluegrass scene, and no other source covers the field as well. For libraries serving rural or urban U.S. communities where there is any general orientation in this direction.

Bomp. 1966. 6/yr. $12/8 issues. Gregory Shaw. Bomp Magazine, P.O. Box 7112, Burbank, CA 91510. Adv. Circ: 40,000.

Bk. rev: 3, 100–500 words, signed. *Aud:* Hs.

Formerly known as *Who Put the Bomp, Bomp* is an energized fanzine determined to resurrect the rock 'n' roll spirit of the 1960s. Articles and interviews emphasize rock history and trivia, accompanied by long discographies. Valuable features include classified advertisements and auction notices for rare records, reviews of locally pressed 45s and privately published books and discographies along with the more widely available items, and an annotated directory. Consider *Bomp* seriously.

Bop. 1983. m. $14. DS Magazines Inc., Box 150, Burbank, CA 91503. Illus., adv. Circ: 250,000.

Aud: Ejh, Hs.

A relative of the favorite *Tiger Beat*, this features from 70 to 90 pages of movie, music, and television stars. It is

the old Hollywood blurb magazine with a vengeance, right down to a centerfold. It is filled with gossip, interviews, and publicity. Most of it is quite harmless and the teenage audience is always kept in mind. The magazine is one of the better fan titles.

Circus. (Formerly: *Circus Weekly*). 1978. m. $19.95. Gerald Rothberg. Circus Magazine, 419 Park Ave. S., New York, NY 10016. Illus., adv. Circ: 210,000. Vol. ends: Dec.

Indexed: Acs, MusicI. *Aud:* Hs.

A magazine about pop and rock entertainment, music, and news. Color photos accompany personality profiles, and there is at least one poster per issue. For lots of gossip, this is the place to find out who's hot and who's not. *Circus* contains listings of concert schedules and various charts, texts of song lyrics, and so on. Apart from its carefully cultivated image of flash and funk, *Circus* performs a valuable service with its "Music Gear" section, which has buyer's guide information, equipment test reports, and announcements of new products. (L.K.W.)

Coda Magazine: the journal of jazz and improvised music (Formerly: *Coda: Canada's jazz magazine).* 1958. bi-m. $15. William E. Smith. Coda Publns., P.O. Box 87, Sta. J, Toronto, Ont. M4J 4X8, Canada. Illus., adv. Circ: 4,000. Microform: UMI.

Indexed: MusicI. *Bk. rev:* 3–4, 250–500 words, signed. *Aud:* Hs.

Aimed at serious aficionados, *Coda* has become the leading voice in the English language for jazz and improvised music. It is considered internationally to be the most complete source of information, in the form of interviews, articles and book and record reviews. Information is supplied by a staff of international writers and photographers, reporting and reviewing events from all the major centers of the world. Timely and well written, it is recommended for general collections.

Creem. 1969. bi-m. $16. Davie DiMartino. Creem Magazine, Inc., 210 S. Woodward Ave., Birmingham, MI 48011. Subs. to: 120 Brighton Rd., Clifton, NJ 07012. Illus., adv. Circ: 125,000. Sample. Microform: B&H.

Indexed: MusicI. *Aud:* Ejh, Hs.

Creem is the original rock 'n' roll magazine. Belligerent, opinionated, and ferociously committed to the doctrine that rock 'n' roll is a menace to civilization as we know it, *Creem* is easily the most entertaining rock publication on the market. The hard-hitting, penetrating reviews generally attempt to convey the feel of the record. Rather like most rock magazines and rock musicians who have been around for more than two weeks, *Creem* sometimes slips into jaded cynicism, but when it is good, you can almost dance to it.

Down Beat. 1934. m. $15.75. Art Lange. Maher Publns., Inc., 180 W. Park Ave., Elmhurst, IL 60126. Illus., index, adv. Circ: 92,100. Vol. ends: Dec. Microform: UMI.

Indexed: MusicI. *Bk. rev:* 2–3, 300–600 words, signed. *Aud:* Hs.

Jazz musicians and fans in 142 countries read *Down Beat*, the top magazine for current coverage of the personalities, music, and recordings in the jazz world. There is liberal discussion of the influence of various persons or groups. Of reference value are the many types of discerning reviews (books, recordings, concerts), some of which are not found elsewhere. A famous music magazine that should enjoy wide support by almost every type of library.

Goldmine. 1974. m. $20. Rick Whitesell. Krause Publns., 700 E. State St., Iola, WI 54990. Illus., adv. Sample.
Aud: Hs.

Subtitled "the record collector's marketplace," this large tabloid is truly a goldmine for people collecting popular music records. The publication includes some timely, well-written articles and an extensive listing of recordings for sale. A superb place for collectors to find longed-for records. This is a real contribution to the music section of the library.

Hit Parader. 1954. m. $22. John Shelton Ivany. Charlton Bldg., Derby, CT 06418. Illus., adv. Circ: 160,023. Vol. ends: Dec.
Aud: Hs.

A trendy rock magazine with heavily illustrated, brief articles. Every issue has a centerfold, usually of a group. Profiles of entertainers in the "Roots" section are reminiscences of the youths and early successes of groups. A strong segment is the "Song Index," which has lyrics of the very latest hits—often of more than 20 songs. Other regular departments are "Instrumentally Speaking," a buyer's guide, the retrospective "Legends of Rock," and the review of imported albums. (L.K.W.)

Jazz Journal International (Formerly: *Jazz Journal*). 1948. m. $20. Eddie Cook. Pitman Periodicals, Ltd, 128 Long Acre, London WC25 9AN, England. Illus., index, adv. Circ: 13,000. Microform: UMI.
Indexed: MusicI. *Bk. rev:* Various number, length. *Aud:* Hs.

There are more than a dozen magazines devoted entirely to jazz. Half are published abroad and, although opinion differs, the English *Jazz Journal International* is considered by many to be the best of the group. It has wide use in the United States because of its international coverage, the excellent black-and-white illustrations, and, most important, the extensive record reviews. The editors make an effort to cover all jazz recordings—regardless of point of issue—of the previous month.

Journal of Country Music (Formerly: *Country Music Foundation Newsletter*). 1970. 3/yr. $15. Paul Kingsbury. Country Music Foundation, 4 Music Sq. E., Nashville, TN 37203. Illus. Circ: 1,300.
Bk. rev: 6–7, 500–600 words, signed. *Aud:* Hs.

The Country Music Foundation is the umbrella educational organization that operates the Country Music Hall of Fame Museum, Library, and Media Center. This journal represents its publishing arm for all of the above institutions. The articles, written by specialists from all disciplines, are

a "means of communication among students, scholars, and music industry leaders." Many of these articles provide good biographical reviews of performers and their musical development; others trace the historical development of specific types of music. (P.S.G.)

Melody Maker. 1926. w. $49.40. Ray Coleman. I P C Specialist and Professional Press, Ltd., Dorset House, Stamford St., London SE1 9LU, England. Illus., adv. Circ: 188,073. Microform: UMI.
Indexed: MusicI. *Bk. rev:* Notes. *Aud:* Hs.

Melody Maker is a British weekly that frequently presents British and European rock stars well in advance of their first sounds on U.S. airwaves, even with the considerable time lag between publication and its appearance on newsstands in the United States. The prose is sometimes deadly, and competition is stiffening now that domestic magazines are paying more attention to imported LPs and foreign artists, but this is still the preferred title for British rock news.

New Musical Express. 1952. w. $10. Neil Spencer. I P C Magazines, Ltd., 28th Floor, King's Reach Tower, Stamford St., London SE1 9LS, England. Circ: 140,465.
Aud: Hs.

This English 45- to 60-page tabloid is somewhat equivalent to America's *Rolling Stone*, yet differs in that the concentration is on modern popular music and not on the current social and political issues of the day. The main interests seem to be interviews with pop stars and groups; record reviews of British and U.S. releases; and news, notes, and articles on trends in music. The writing is good to excellent and, if the circulation is any indication, has captured the imagination of the typical British pop fan. It apparently enjoys an equally impressive circulation in Canada, and is to be found on larger newsstands in the United States. The reviews are generally critical, although there is a somewhat more generous attitude toward U.S. pop releases. The language is more tempered than that found in many popular U.S. magazines of this type. There are good photographs and an abundance of imaginative advertising. General collections and high schools where there is a large following of the modern music scene might consider this as a welcome, certainly different, selection. Interested librarians in the United States and Canada should request a sample.

Popular Music and Society. 1971. q. $20. R. Serge Denisoff. Dept. of Sociology, Bowling Green State Univ., Bowling Green, OH 43403. Circ: 5,000. Microform: UMI.
Bk. rev: 5–7, 300–500 words, signed. *Aud:* Hs.

The articles in this publication are central to the study of popular music and its role in society. The contributors represent a good cross section of the scholarly community plus some from the record industry. Material can be found on rock, rock 'n' roll, rhythm and blues, country, soul, and bluegrass music. Many articles are also devoted to song texts, their themes (death, women's liberation, unrequited love et cetera), and the social classes of their audiences. Topics have included the role of the music and record industry in the development of popular music, the use of music in political campaigns, festivals and a look at drug use and music listening. There are also long interview articles with popular vocal and instrumental musicians. A record review section is appended. (P.S.G.)

RockBill. 1982. m. Controlled circ. (Others, $15). Stuart Matrenga. RockBill Magazine, 850 Seventh Ave., Suite 1201, New York, NY 10019. Illus., adv. Circ: 550,000. Sample.
Aud: Ejh, Hs.

Glossy, pocket sized, about 30 pages, and filled with ads and illustrations, *RockBill* is directed to the younger generation involved with dance and music clubs. Focus is on rock stars, coming concerts, gossip, and interviews. There is usually a page or two on the MTV channel shows. Teenagers will appreciate the casual style. It is distributed free at concerts and clubs. Libraries may try for a free subscription.

Rolling Stone. 1967. bi-w. $19.95. Jann S. Wenner. Straight Arrow Press, 745 Fifth Ave., New York, NY 10151. Illus., index, adv. Circ: 400,000. Sample. Vol. ends: No. 15. Microform: B&H, MCA.
Indexed: MusicI, PopPer. *Bk. rev:* 2, signed. *Aud:* Hs.

This is the only rock magazine that is still a required title for libraries. It is to be found, generally behind the desk, in public libraries small and huge, academic libraries young and old, and specialized music libraries. Pop music is the modality, but the message runs to social consciousness via politics and pop psychology. Record reviews appear each month; "Newsfront" covers recent events in the trade and in politics; excellent articles with photos, and repeated discoveries of the interconnection between pop/rock and the rest of the world are also included. *Rolling Stone* remains a most important magazine.

Sheet Music Magazine. 1977. 9/yr. $14. Edward J. Shanaphy. Shacor, 352 Evelyn St., P.O. Box 933, Paramus, NJ 07653. Illus., adv.
Aud: Ejh, Hs.

As the title implies, about two-thirds or more of each 65-page issue is given over to sheet music of popular old-timers, such as Gershwin and Porter, and "a touch of country." Short articles range from information on musical instruments to songwriting. There are both a "standard edition" and an "easy edition," the latter with simplified scores suitable for beginners. If there is an interest in this kind of thing in your library, send for samples of both editions before entering an order for one or the other.

Sing Out! 1950. q. $15 (Individuals, $11). Ed. bd. Sing Out! Magazine, Inc., P.O. Box 1071, Easton, PA 18044. Illus., adv. Circ: 8,800. Sample. Vol. ends: No. 4. Microform: UMI.
Indexed: MusicI. *Aud:* Ejh, Hs.

Although the folk music craze comes and goes, it never dies, and this is probably the single best magazine for anyone interested in "singing out." It features interviews with sing-

ers, songwriters, and teachers; articles on the guitar, banjo, and autoharp; news and notes on what is happening on the scene; and articles that cover every aspect of folk from traditional to contemporary. Regular columns by Pete Seeger and Mike Cooney, record reviews, and news of folk festivals appear. It has added attraction for the player in that each number contains 10 to 15 folk songs, with words, music, and guitar chords. A first choice for any music-minded high school or junior high library.

Song Hits. 1942. m. $17. Mary Jane Canetti. Charlton Publns., Inc., Charlton Bldg., Derby, CT 06418. Illus., adv.
Bk. rev: 1–3, 200 words, unsigned. *Aud:* Hs.

The purpose of *Song Hits* is to publish the lyrics of current songs in three categories of popular music—pop, soul and country. It has a massive following, especially among teenagers. Each 66-page issue carries five articles about some current star or group and contains the lyrics to more than 80 songs. No other monthly currently in publication carries as many lyrics.

Star Hits. 1984. m. $16.95. David A. Keeps. Pilot Communications, Inc., 29 Haviland St., South Norwalk, CT 06854. Subs. to: 308 East Hitt St., Mt. Morris, IL 61054. Illus., adv. Vol. ends: Dec.
Aud: Hs.

A vervy, color-blasting rock fan magazine. Photos and posters crowd out the none-too-taxing text. Articles include likes of Duran Duran; Grace Jones; Wham, Paul Young; and Sting. Among regular departments are an entertainers' birthday calendar; fan club addresses; a slightly weird penpal column; and contests, contests, and more contests. Some song lyrics are included. There are mild obscenities, if that is a consideration. (L.K.W.)

Storyville. 1965. bi-m. $12.60. Laurie Wright. Storyville Publns., Ltd., 66 Fairview Dr., Chigwell, Essex 1G7 6HS, England. Illus., index, adv. Circ: 2,500.
Bk. rev: Various number, 300–700 words, signed. *Aud:* Hs.

In the mythology of American popular music, the Storyville section of New Orleans has long been considered "the birthplace of jazz"—hence the title of this little jazz magazine from England. Its interests are classic jazz and blues, i.e., earlier forms of jazz, largely predating the rise of the big "swing" bands. Its modest size is deceptive, for it is always packed with a wealth of valuable and original historical and discographical jazz research. Regular features are "Visiting Firemen" and thorough review coverage of LP issues of classic jazz and blues. Libraries interested in U.S. music cannot do without this title.

Trouser Press. 1974. m. $15. Scott Isler. Trans-Oceanic Trouser Press, 212 Fifth Ave., Rm. 1310, New York, NY 10010. Illus., adv. Circ: 60,000.
Aud: Hs.

Since 1974, Ira Robbins and fellow Anglophiles have been turning out carefully handcrafted issues of *Trouser Press,* an innovative fan magazine billed as "America's Only

British Rock Magazine." While always expanding on their concept of what *Trouser Press* is and what it can do, they retain the vibrant integrity of amateurs. *Trouser Press*, like similar titles, covers the rock groups from England, but differs from competitors in the thorough articles and detailed discographies of the more obscure, artsy, and avant-garde artists, mainly British, though the coverage of European rockers and the U.S. underground is equally excellent. Reviews of domestic and foreign albums and singles are intelligent and highly critical, and are written by people who have not forgotten how it feels to be a consumer. An unusual, service-oriented feature of *Trouser Press* is its "Auction" section, a forum for record and memorabilia collectors. Mildly elitist (it is intended primarily for collectors who are both rabid and sophisticated when it comes to music), *Trouser Press* is very satisfying.

Wavelength. 1980. m. $12. Connie Atkinson, P.O. Box 15667, New Orleans, LA 70175. Illus., adv. Circ: 30,000.
Bk. rev: Essay, signed. *Aud:* Hs.

Subtitled "New Orleans Music Magazine," this publication focuses on jazz, in six or seven illustrated stories, biographical sketches of prominent citizens, and columns on recordings, music trends, festivals, and almost anything else of interest to true jazz fans. The focus is on events in and around New Orleans, but as this is a city found in spirit throughout the United States and the world, the magazine has more than local interest. Recommended for music collections.

REVIEWS

Absolute Sound. 1973. q. $20. Harry Pearson, Jr., P.O. Box L, Sea Cliff, NY 11579. Subs. to: 2 Glen Ave., Sea Cliff, NY 11579. Illus., adv. Circ: 19,500. Microform: UMI.
Aud: Hs.

Keeping an objective ear open for the best (and worst) in sound equipment is becoming increasingly difficult these days, in the flood of products and manufacturers' promotions. This *Absolute Sound* does, however, and rather better than the many other titles trying to do the same. Generally six or seven longer reviews of specific pieces of equipment will be accompanied by manufacturers' comments and editorial additions. Several capsule evaluations, letters with answers, and reader surveys of equipment follow. Send for sample copies of this and other periodicals in the field before deciding to subscribe; points of view and emphasis differ markedly. Any library will find a readership for this one.

Electronic Musician (Formerly: *Polyphony*). 1985. bi-m. $12. Craig Anderton. Polyphony Publg. Co., 1020 W. Wilshire Blvd., Oklahoma City, OK 73116. Illus., adv.
Aud: Hs.

During the past decade there has been a proliferation of high-quality electronic equipment used by many musicians. Listeners have enjoyed the benefits of the new types of music created on this equipment. However, much of the advances are occurring too fast to be fully assimilated. *Electronic Musician* succeeds in providing accurate information to the knowledgeable layperson. There are feature articles, interviews, "how-tos," equipment and record reviews, and current events.

High Fidelity. 1951. m. $28. William Tynan. ABC Leisure Magazines, 825 Seventh Ave., New York, NY 10019. Illus., index, adv. Circ: 375,000. Microform: UMI.
Indexed: AbrRG, MusicI, RG. *Aud:* Hs.

Along with *Stereo Review*, one of the two general magazines for the informed high-fidelity enthusiast and record buyer. It includes articles about music and musicians written by musicians or journalists who contribute outspoken and controversial comments on the recording scene. Audio equipment reports based on laboratory tests give the latest information on home entertainment electronics; new trends are given coverage, as evidenced by the newly added section on video equipment for amateurs. The section of critical reviews of recordings is afforded considerable space, and while classical records receive the greatest attention, folk, jazz, and pop music are receiving wider coverage. Published in several regional editions as well as the "Musical America" edition, which is separately paginated and covers current music performances, music centers, and performing artists for those with a special interest in "live" as well as recorded music.

Opus. 1984. bi-m. $18. James Oestereich. Historical Times, 2245 Kohn Rd., P.O. Box 8200, Harrisburg, PA 17105. Illus., adv. Circ: 50,000. Sample. Microform: UMI.
Indexed: MusicI. *Aud:* Hs.

This top quality magazine, subtitled "The Magazine of Recorded Classics," contains 56 pages of professional writing about composers, musicians, music, and the problem of marketing and finding classical records. Regular departments cover recordings in retrospect, musical broadcastings, and new equipment. Recommended for all libraries.

Ovation. 1979. m. $16. Sam Chase. Ovation Magazine Assocs., 320 W. 57th St., New York, NY 10019. Illus., adv. Circ: 110,000.
Aud: Hs.

The tone of "The Magazine for Classical Music Listeners" is set by a regular feature, "Ovation Best Selling Classical Records," which is "based upon sales data provided by classical record dealers and retail chains across the country." This colorfully illustrated magazine gives the people who enjoy concerts what they want to read. Issues contain in-depth sketches, complete with photographs, of one or two prominent musicians, two or three general articles and numerous departments, including new equipment tests and short, well-written record reviews. In the middle is an added program guide for 20 public and commercial classical music stations in various parts of the United States. The guide is changed from area to area, although the remainder of the magazine remains constant. This is an intelligent, carefully edited, and generally objective publication, ranking with, if not somewhat ahead of, *High Fidelity* and *Stereo Review*. A good addition to any library.

Stereo Review. 1958. m. $10. William Livingstone. Subs. to: Circulation Dept., P.O. Box 2771, Boulder, CO 80302. Illus., index, adv. Circ: 492,400. Sample. Microform: UMI.

Indexed: MusicI. *Aud:* Hs.

A popular, useful guide to equipment and recordings for the beginner as well as the knowledgeable user. General articles on music, all well illustrated, are included. Test reports and reports on new products adequately cover equipment without allowing this aspect to dominate the magazine; occasional surveys give a comprehensive overview of available equipment. There are special issues giving detailed information on tape recordings and loudspeakers. One of the important features of the periodical for librarians is its review of recordings, both tape and disc. Those recordings deemed outstanding (in performance and audio quality) are so indicated. Recommended for libraries of every shape and size.

For the Professional

American Choral Review. 1958. q. Membership, $27.50. Alfred Mann. Amer. Choral Foundation, Inc., Assn. of Professional Vocal Ensembles, 251 S. 18th St., Philadelphia, PA 19103. Illus. Circ: 1,500. Sample. Vol. ends: Oct.

Indexed: MusicI. *Bk. rev:* 1–2, 1,000–2,000 words, signed. *Aud:* Pr.

Any serious student of choral music will find enjoyable reading in the *Review*. With three or four major pieces followed by regular columns, book and record reviews, and frequent lists of recently published music, the interested reader with some background in the field will find each issue valuable. For any medium to large collection. Also included with the subscription is the Foundation's "Research Memorandum Series," an irregular publication with each issue devoted to bibliographies of choral or vocal music.

American Music Teacher. 1951. bi-m. Membership (Nonmembers, $7.50). Homer Ulrich. Music Teachers Natl. Assn., 2113 Carew Tower, Cincinnati, OH 45202. Illus., adv. Circ: 24,000. Sample. Vol. ends: June/July. Microform: UMI.

Indexed: EdI, MusicI. *Bk. rev:* 5, 150 words, signed. *Aud:* Pr.

Features articles on and reviews of keyboard, string, voice, theory, and history. The association represents many private and studio teachers as well as secondary school and college music faculties. Hence, articles are geared to assist the teacher. Occasional bibliographies add to the magazine's reference value. Because of its emphasis on individual teaching, it nicely augments the basic journal in the field of music education, *Music Educators Journal*. Both would be advisable for secondary school and college music teachers, as well as the libraries serving them. Both stress the "how-to" approach. In elementary through secondary schools, the *Music Educators Journal* would be the first choice, followed by *American Music Teacher*.

Choral Journal. 1959. m. (Sept.–May). $12. Ronnie Shaw. Amer. Choral Directors Assn., P.O. Box 6310, Lawton, OK 73504. Illus., adv. Circ: 10,600. Sample. Vol. ends: May. Microform: AMS.

Indexed: MusicI. *Bk. rev:* 1, 250 words, signed. *Aud:* Pr.

A journal published for high school and college choir directors with some information of interest to church groups. Progressive in its outlook, the association seeks new approaches and methods. This is reflected in the short articles, news items, and comments of its journal. Most of the material is "how-to" and is quite practical for anyone interested in choral work. Although short on book reviews, it usually has two to four pages of critical record notes, and this feature gives it importance for any large school library.

Clavier: a magazine for pianists and organists. 1962. 15/yr. $10. Barbara Kreader. The Instrumentalist Publg. Co., 200 Northfield Rd., Northfield, IL 60093. Illus., index, adv. Circ: 24,000. Sample. Vol. ends: Dec. Microform: UMI.

Indexed: MusicI. *Bk. rev:* 3, 150–200 words. *Aud:* Pr.

The leading journal of piano and organ music for advanced students and teachers. Articles include interviews with concert performers and suggestions for improving technique and teaching methods. There are reviews of teaching materials, records, piano and organ music, and books. There will usually be complete pieces of music together with a lesson on interpretation. In this same field, *Piano Quarterly* (1952. q. $14. Robert J. Silverman, P.O. Box 815, Wilmington, VT 05363. Circ: 13,000) is directed almost exclusively to the teacher. It is particularly useful as it lists pieces of music and books by grades.

The Instrumentalist (Formerly: *Instrumentalists*). 1946. m. $18. Anne Driscoll. The Instrumentalist Co., 200 Northfield Rd., Northfield, IL 60093. Illus., index, adv. Circ: 20,000. Vol. ends: July. Microform: UMI.

Indexed: MusicI. *Bk. rev:* 5, notes. *Aud:* Pr.

Deals chiefly with technical problems of teaching and playing various band and orchestra instruments. No coverage is given to piano, organ, and other instruments for which instruction is not generally provided in public schools. Articles treat the specific problems encountered by string, woodwind, brass, and percussion instrumentalists, and deal with a wide variety of subjects including bibliographic material, special projects in music schools, and legislation. An important part is the annotated new music review, meant to furnish school directors with reliable and expert guidance. An obvious selection for any school library where the band is an important consideration.

Music Educators Journal. 1914. m. (Sept.-May). $25. Rebecca G. Taylor. Music Educators Natl. Conference, 1902 Association Dr., Reston, VA 22091. Illus., adv. Circ: 60,000. Sample. Vol. ends: May. Microform: UMI.

Indexed: EdI, MusicI. *Bk. rev:* 4–8, 550 words, signed. *Aud:* Pr.

The leading music education journal, it represents music education from grade school through university level. Articles range from philosophy to practical teaching suggestions to news of current music activities, developments, research, awards, and competitions. Sketches and excellent photographs illustrate many articles, and the design and layout generally are outstanding. Strongly recommended for all music library collections for scope, appeal, authority, and utility. A basic acquisition.

Music Library Association. Notes. 1942. q. $42 (Individuals, $28). Susan T. Sommer. MLA, P.O. Box 487, Canton, MA 02021. Illus., index, adv. Circ: 3,525. Sample. Vol. ends: June. Microform: UMI.

Indexed: MusicI. *Bk. rev:* 20–25, 600–1,000 words, signed. *Aud:* Pr.

One may not always agree with either the record or the book evaluations, but this remains one of the best single sources for both. Furthermore, it is an invaluable index— a type of *Book Review Digest*—for recordings (tape included). Usually some 19 periodicals are checked, and reviews of well over 200 different recordings are noted. This is the primary use of *Notes* for the average library, but this publication also contains three or four articles and some business and association news. From time to time there are excellent annotated reviews of new music periodicals, as well as older standbys. A basic guide for all libraries.

The Musical Mainstream. 1977. bi-m. Free. Library of Congress, Natl. Library Service for the Blind & Physically Handicapped. 1291 Taylor St. N.W., Washington, DC 20542.

Indexed: MusicI. *Aud:* Pr.

This presents articles extracted from major musical journals, and is provided free to those with disabilities. There is a listing of new publications in braille and large print as well as music scores and recorded works of interest to the user. The publication is issued in braille, large print, and audio form.

The New Schwann Record & Tape Guide (Formerly: *Schwann-1 Record & Tape Guide*). 1984. m. $30. Richard Blackham. ABC Schwann Publns., Inc., 535 Boylston St., Boston, MA 02116. Adv. Circ: 50,000.

Aud: Pr.

Beginning with the January 1984 issue, the *New Schwann* combines the former *Schwann 1* and *2*, and alternates the main catalog contents monthly between classical and nonclassical. The December issue also includes children's and Christmas music and incorporates all available recordings of all types. In each issue a special section lists all new releases, including compact discs, and a list of all recordings scheduled for deletion from manufacturers' lines. A necessary item for any library involved in purchasing records and tapes, and of great help as a reference aid when working with the public.

The School Musician, Director and Teacher. 1929. m. (Sept.-June). $12. Edgar B. Gangware. Ammark Publg. Co., 4049 W. Peterson, Chicago, IL 60646. Illus., index, adv. Circ: 10,200. Sample. Vol. ends: Aug. Microform: UMI.

Indexed: CIJE, EdI, MusicI. *Aud:* Pr.

This is written by and for public school music educators, instrumental and vocal. It is a practical tool devoted to methods of teaching, with "how-to" articles for the band and choral director. Regular features include a roundup of news of interest to school music educators, evaluations of new products, columns on teaching specific instruments (wind, percussion, and strings), and a review section devoted to new band music. It is indispensable to educators and is needed in most school libraries.

NEWS AND OPINION

For the Student

See also Alternatives; General Interest; and Newspapers Sections.

Craig T. Canan, free-lance journalist, P.O. Box 120574, Nashville, TN 37212

Introduction

Up-to-date and clear information and commentary are important for students and teachers. The magazines listed here should offer a variety of formats and viewpoints from which to choose. Objectivity in this section was conscientiously strived for as it was compiled. A careful effort was made to review the magazines and newspapers on their essential merits, rather than by their political leanings. It is easy to determine by examination that a periodical has poor writing or layout style, or a dogmatic tone. However, when a publication effectively presented its point of view, whether Right or Left, it was given a positive review.

Basic Periodicals

Hs: *Current, National Review, The New Republic, Newsweek, The Progressive, Time.*

For the Student

The American Spectator. 1967. m. $21. R. Emmett Tyrell, Jr., P.O. Box 1969, Bloomington, IN 47402. Illus., adv. Circ: 42,000. Sample. Vol. ends: Dec. Microform: UMI.

Indexed: PAIS, PopPer. *Bk. rev:* 6–8, 1,000–2,000 words, signed. *Aud:* Hs.

In 1986, this magazine will be newly settled in Arlington, Virginia. They moved there, "now that President Reagan has somewhat pacified the Washington area," to get a more accurate national view of the nation. This newsprint tabloid could be considered a conservative counterpart of the *New York Review of Books* (See Books and Book Review Section) although it is not primarily a reviewing periodical. It originated as a publication written by Indiana University students for other students, in opposition to the SDS ideology. It has since developed into a much more comprehensive expression of the conservative viewpoint, with articles by many representatives of the intellectual side of the Right. It covers a broad area of national and international affairs in each issue and its satire is the best of any conservative periodical from the United States.

Commentary. 1945. m. $33. Norman Podhoretz. The Amer. Jewish Committee, 165 E. 56th St., New York, NY 10022. Illus., index, adv. Circ: 52,000. Sample. Vol. ends: June & Dec. Microform: B&H, MIM.

Indexed: BoRvI, HumI, PAIS, RG. *Bk. rev:* 5-6, 600–2,400 words, signed. *Aud:* Hs.

Moderate-to-right currently most aptly describes this Jewish journal, whose editor is strongly anticommunist and anti-Soviet. One of the three issues examined had an 18-page thesis against the communists. Ironically *Commentary* also has a few less conservative tendencies expressed in its columns. The sponsorship of the periodical by the American Jewish Committee is in line with its general program to "enlighten and clarify public opinion on problems of Jewish concern, to fight bigotry and to promote Jewish/cultural interest and creative achievement in America." The thoughtful essays are matched by good fiction. Although sponsored by a national Jewish organization, much of the material is of interest to a general readership.

The Congress Watcher. 1979. bi-m. $5. Jane Stone. Public Citizen's Congress Watch, 215 Pennsylvania Ave. S.E., Washington, DC 20003. Illus., adv. Circ: 12,000. Sample. Vol. ends: Dec.

Indexed: API. *Aud:* Hs.

A Ralph Nader-initiated project, *The Congress Watcher* probes all aspects of Washington politics, including representatives and all types of legislation. This tabloid features timely Washington news reports and articles on the basics of electoral politics. "How a bill becomes a law" is the regular type of article that makes this well-written, nonpartisan periodical appropriate for all collections, including those of high schools. Anyone with an interest in how Washington affects our lives will find *The Congress Watcher* a good investment of time and money.

Current: the new thinking from all sources on the frontier problems of today. 1960. m. $30 (Individuals, $20). Jerome J. Hanus. Helen Dwight Reid Educational Foundation, 4000 Albemarle St. N.W., Washington, DC 20016. Illus., index. Circ: 6,000. Sample. Vol. ends: Dec. Microform: UMI.

Indexed: CIJE, RG. *Aud:* Hs.

Do you read 600 publications every month? The editors of *Current* do in preparation of each issue of this unbiased reprint journal. According to the editors, *Current* is "not limited by ideological bent, nor by preconceived subject matter: articles are selected for originality and relevancy to America today." The four issues examined confirm this viewpoint. The reprints come predominately from periodicals, with some selections from books, television commentary and other current sources. No subject is prerejected for consideration for inclusion. Exploring the planets and the place of the automobile in the United States are examples of the diversity of the selections. Political topics are only about half of the subjects presented. *Current* is valuable as an educational aid as well as interesting to the general public.

Current Events. 1903. bi-w. $10.50. Xerox/Field, 4343 Equity Drive, Columbus, OH 43228. Illus. Sample.

Indexed: CMG. *Aud:* Ejh.

One of the best known of the classroom papers, this 8-page review of the week's news is a standard item in many schools for grades 6 through 10. It is published weekly during the school year, and through sometimes imaginative pictures and well-written summaries it is able to convey the past week's events to the readers. There are numerous features, including a vocabulary exercise. The paper is so well known and so often found in the classroom, that it is rather pointless for the librarian to consider it as a library addition.

Editorial Research Reports. 1923. w. $228. Hoyt Gimlin. *Congressional Quarterly*, 1414 22nd St. N.W., Washington, DC 20037. Index. Circ: 2,500. Vol. ends: Dec. Microform: B&H, MIM, UMI.

Indexed: PAIS. *Aud:* Hs.

These detailed 18-page reports cover current topics of interest to politicians, consumers, businesspeople, and others. They are footnoted, 6,000 words, and divided into about three to five sections. The result is that each report may be read in full or in part with relative ease. The reports are gathered in volumes with a subject-title index at the end of the year. Most of the studies include a selected bibliography. This is an excellent and time-tested service that is invaluable.

The Guardian. 1948. w. $27.50. Bill Ryan, 33 W. 17th St., New York, NY 10011. Illus., index, adv. Circ: 65,000. Vol. ends: Oct. Microform: UMI

Indexed: API. *Bk. rev:* 2, 600 words, signed. *Aud:* Hs.

The staff recently totally revised the style of the *Guardian*, making it easily the best left-of-center periodical in the United States. The layout of the staff-written newspaper, as well as much of the editorial content, has changed for the better. From the cultural coverage, which is the best on the left, to the international news, the *Guardian* is now even more the newspaper of record for left activists and scholars. It regularly summarizes the positions of key left groups on questions of popular interest. A controversial "Opinions" section permits a diverse range of analysis of left actions and strategies. The Central American, women's, and arms race coverage has also expanded. The breadth and depth of the reporting are unsurpassed. Its analytical journalism is not the phrase mongering often found in radical periodicals but is well thought out and perceptive. The overt viewpoint is usually confined to the editorial page. The staff proclaims that this "independent radical news weekly" really is nonsectarian and independent of the influence of any political organization. This makes it unique among the usual party organs and special interest periodicals the left is infamous for. It should be the first choice for those wanting to keep an eye on the Left (and the Right).

Human Events. 1944. w. $25. Thomas S. Winter. Human Events, Inc., 422 First St. S.E., Washington, DC 20003.

Illus., adv. Circ: 70,000. Sample. Vol. ends: Dec. Microform: UMI.

Aud: Hs.

In addition to supporting conservative viewpoints such as more money for the Pentagon instead of for cities and social services, it reacts to liberal initiatives. Writers such as anti-ERA activist Phyllis Schlafly rail against almost every liberal cause. "CBS Defends USSR Military Buildup" and the "Leftish Catholic Bishops" are examples of the fact that the tabloid often has a tendency to exaggerate the influence of the Left on U.S. institutions. Interviews are occasionally offered in addition to the regular features and the many and diverse articles. The "Conservative Forum" is noteworthy as a particularly well-read column. *Human Events* has weak coverage of the international scene, choosing to concentrate instead on domestic issues, especially the nation's capitol.

The MacNeil/Lehrer Report. 1979. q. $35. Microfilming Corp. of America, P.O. Box 10, Sanford, NC 27330. Index. Vol. ends: Dec.

Aud: Hs.

A two-page abstracting service, this is a record of the well-known news and interview program on public television. Each program is abstracted and is arranged in chronological order of broadcasting. Quite easy to use, this is cumulated about once a year; the subscription includes the hardbound cumulation. An index and microform transcription of the broadcasts are available for an additional $95. It is a useful service, particularly for high school and college debate and for students looking for topics for papers. It is recommended where needed.

The Middle East. 1974. m. $60. Nadia Nijab. IC Publns., P.O. Box 261, 69 Great Queen St., London WC2B 5BZ, England. Subs. to: 122 E. 42nd St., New York, NY 10168. Circ: 27,667.

Aud: Hs.

This illustrated newsmagazine about the Middle East has been concentrating in recent issues on the business and economic problems of the area while not neglecting other aspects of life. Feature articles on the different countries offer a many-dimensional picture. Although the orientation is generally pro-Arab, the Arab-Israeli conflict does not occupy a disproportionate amount of space. (T.W.)

The Nation. 1865. w. $40. Victor Navasky. Nation Assocs., Inc., P.O. Box 1953, Marion, OH 43305. Illus., index, adv. Circ: 50,000. Sample. Vol. ends: June/Dec. Microform: UMI.

Indexed: BoRvI, PAIS, RG. *Bk. rev:* 3–7, 1,400 words, signed. *Aud:* Hs.

The Nation features the words of the best liberal writers in the country. Contributors include major Progressives such as I. F. Stone, Studs Terkel, Nicholas Von Hoffman, Kurt Vonnegut, and cartoonist Jules Feiffer. Articles are concerned with foreign affairs, local and national politics, the arms race, and budget cutbacks, to name a few topics. There are excellent regular reviews of books, theater, films, and the arts. Advertising does not feature prominently. This weekly should be the primary liberal choice for all libraries.

National Review. 1955. bi-w. $34. William F. Buckley, Jr. Natl. Review, Inc., 150 E. 35th St., New York, NY 10016. Illus., index, adv. Circ: 100,000. Sample. Vol. ends: Dec. Microform: B&H, MIM, UMI.

Indexed: BoRv, RG. *Bk. rev:* 4, 1,100 words, signed. *Aud:* Hs.

Excellent writing and good layout combine to make this intelligent newsmagazine the best conservative periodical in the country today. Most of the major columnists and authors of the Right have their thoughts presented in the pages of the *National Review.* Over the years the magazine has become increasingly the standard of the Right, a yardstick by which other conservative periodicals measure themselves. It is the brainchild of the respected writer William F. Buckley, Jr., who has won thousands over to his ideas through his "Firing Line" television show and his many books. His humor and suave manner are transferred to the magazine he edits, producing one of the most entertaining and readable opinion periodicals of any persuasion. The one long feature and several pages of thought-provoking short articles are all outstanding. Like its liberal counterpart *The Nation*, it has a popular crossword puzzle in each issue. There are also several culture reviews and columns, including one by Buckley called "On the Right." Most libraries now subscribe; those that do not, should.

New Leader: a biweekly of news and opinion. 1927. bi-w. $24. Myron Kolatch. Amer. Labor Conference on Intl. Affairs, Inc., 275 Seventh Ave., New York, NY 10001. Illus., index, adv. Circ: 25,000. Vol. ends: Dec. Microform: UMI.

Indexed: PAIS, RG. *Bk. rev:* 3–4, 1,100 words, signed. *Aud:* Hs.

This long-lived functional newsmagazine offers "a variety of opinions consistent with our democratic policy." It is thin for a magazine, but has managed to offer its readers something in every issue for some 60 years. The writing is not strongly biased toward the Right or Left; the strongest opinions are in the reviews. The book section will not win any prizes, but does sometimes cover books not commonly reviewed elsewhere. Each issue also offers two or three reviews on other cultural events, under the heading "On Screen," "On Television," or "On Dance."

The New Republic. 1914. w. $45. Martin Peretz. New Republic, Inc., 1220 19th St. N.W., Washington, DC 20036. Illus., index, adv. Circ: 95,000. Vol. ends: July & Dec. Microform: B&H, UMI.

Indexed: BibI, BoRv, RG. *Bk. rev:* 7, 700–2,000 words, signed. *Aud:* Hs.

Under the ownership of Martin Peretz, this liberal magazine has been widely criticized for more opinionated writing and less quality coverage than it previously offered. Typical articles slight President Reagan, Republican redistricting, and the MX missile and promote "liberal patriotism" and other liberal causes. In the past this magazine has been one of the more popular liberal periodicals; it remains to be seen whether it will continue to be such a well-read liberal mouthpiece.

Newsweek. 1933. w. $39. Richard M. Smith. Newsweek, Inc., 444 Madison Ave., New York, NY 10022. Illus., index, adv. Circ: 3,000,000. Vol. ends: June. Microform: B&H, MCA, UMI.

Indexed: BibI, BoRv, BoRvI, RG. *Bk. rev:* 2–5, 500–1,300 words, signed. *Aud:* Hs.

The difference between this weekly and its chief rival, *Time,* is negligible. These two are the most popular of the general, mass circulation newsmagazines read in the United States. Education, sports, medicine, television, business, and national and international affairs are sections in each issue of both magazines. They also feature good to excellent cultural material, including film, dance, and book reviews.

The Progressive. 1909. $35 (Individuals, $23.50). Erwin Knoll. The Progressive, Inc., 409 E. Main St., Madison, WI 53703. Illus., index, adv. Circ: 50,000. Sample. Vol. ends: Dec. Microform: B&H, UMI.

Indexed: API, PAIS, RG. *Bk. rev:* 7–9, 300–800 words, signed. *Aud:* Hs.

The Progressive has had its contents summarized each issue for reading by several presidents, including William Howard Taft and Jimmy Carter—quite an accomplishment for a liberal periodical. *The Progressive* is not afraid to buck the liberal side, however—it provoked a strong response from its readers by siding with the Nazis in the right to free speech issue. Articles are clear, carefully documented, and usually quite lively. Contributors are correspondents on the scene or specialists in a given field. Its features stimulate and spark the mind on international, Washington, and a wide variety of other national affairs. *The Progressive* has won the coveted George Polk award for the best foreign coverage, the Hillman award for distinguished domestic reporting, and several other awards. Cartoonists are also exceptionally bright and include Auth, Oliphant, and Herblock. Cultural coverage is among the best in its field; noted music critic Nat Hentoff's column is particularly enjoyable. As do several other news and opinion periodicals, it features a crossword puzzle in each issue. In every way *The Progressive* is highly recommended as the top liberal selection for all libraries.

The Public Interest. 1965. q. $14. Irving Kristol. Natl. Affairs, Inc., 10 E. 53rd St., New York, NY 10022. Circ: 11,000. Vol. ends: Fall. Microform: UMI.

Indexed: SocSc. *Aud:* Hs.

The Public Interest takes on the eastern liberal press as well as other liberal targets. It is less polemic than many other conservative periodicals, and all of the material is carefully reasoned and usually footnoted. The five to six articles per issue are some of the best in the conservative press today. In addition to the editors, frequent contributors are Daniel Bell, Jacques Barzun, and Kevin Phillips. Some issues focus on a single topic.

Public Opinion. 1978. bi-m. $18. Seymour Martin Lipset. Amer. Enterprise Inst., 1150 17th St. N.W., Washington, DC 20036. Illus.

Bk. rev: 3–4, 250 words, signed. *Aud:* Hs.

Filled with charts and easy-to-read articles, this publication is an effort to popularize the opinion polls. Emphasis is on politics, the congressional elections, economics, and some social questions. There are about eight articles in each slick 54- to 60-page issue, and within its scope and opinion the magazine gives fine coverage of today's problems. A useful feature, "Opinion Roundup," presents the latest results of Harris, Gallup and *New York Times* polls.

Social Policy. 1970. q. $20 (Individuals, $16). Frank Riessman, 33 W. 42nd St., New York, NY 10036. Illus., adv. Circ: 4,000. Sample. Vol. ends: Apr. Microform: B&H, UMI.

Indexed: API, CIJE, SocSc. *Bk. rev:* 1–2, 900 words, signed. *Aud:* Hs.

Since its birth this liberal journal has established itself as a basic source of information and theory on progressive social change at the community and national levels. It focuses particularly on issues in the human service areas of health, education, welfare, and community development. Neighborhood empowerment, self-help development, consumer advocacy, and full employment legislation give a flavor of the subjects featured. It believes, however, that the welfare state "does not promote the general welfare, but rather promotes dependence, apathy and alienation." Its pages are a meeting ground where ideas for reconstruction of U.S. institutions are expressed and debated. Its attractive, easy-to-read format makes it popular with laypeople as well as with the planners. Considering the pertinent information presented, *Social Policy* is well worth the cost and is unreservedly recommended for all public and academic libraries.

Time. 1923. w. $58. Henry Anatole Grunwald. Time, Inc., 10880 Wilshire Blvd., Los Angeles, CA 90024. Illus., index, adv. Circ: 4,469,000. Vol. ends: June. Microform: B&H, MIM, UMI.

Indexed: BibI, BoRv, BoRvI, RG. *Bk. rev:* 2–11, 200–800 words, signed. *Aud:* Hs.

Time is still the most popular newsmagazine; the runner-up is *Newsweek. Time*'s approach is well known and is basically the same as that noted in the *Newsweek* annotation. Readers are frequently startled to discover the same lead story and almost identical covers in the same weekly issue of each. Libraries should be aware that there are many regional editions of both *Time* and *Newsweek,* which means that advertising and some of the incidental copy will be different. The question of which is better is a toss-up. A library with a tight budget may wish to drop one of these for another title like the *National Review* or *The Progressive.*

U.S.A. Today (Formerly: *Intellect*). 1915. m. $79 (Individuals, $19.95). Stanley Lehrer. Soc. for the Advancement of Education, 1860 Broadway, New York, NY 10023. Illus., index, adv. Circ: 72,000. Sample. Vol. ends: Dec. Microform: B&H, UMI.

Indexed: CIJE, RG. *Bk. rev:* 2, 500–800 words, signed. *Aud:* Hs.

Like *Time* and *Newsweek*, this slick magazine covers economics, national and international affairs, medicine, mass media, culture, and other topics. It differs in the frequency and in the fact that most of its trustees and writers are university professors. The paper and layout are of better quality than those of its two more popular counterparts. It is light on advertising, obviously published not for profit but to educate. The first half of the magazine is devoted to news and opinion, and the second half is devoted to art, entertainment, medicine, "Life in America," reviews, and other cultural material. Although published for decades, this attractive, objective periodical is not as well known as it deserves to be. It is recommended without qualification for all libraries.

U.S. News and World Report. 1933. w. $41. Shelby Coffey, III. U.S. News and World Reports, Inc., 2400 N St. N.W., Washington, DC 20037. Illus., index, adv. Circ: 2,037,000. Sample. Vol. ends: June. Microform: B&H, MCA, MIM, UMI.

Indexed: PAIS, RG. *Aud:* Hs.

New editor Shelby Coffey brings his experience from the *Washington Post*. With this change, it is possible that the weekly some call the "U.S. Snooze" will become more than a simple five Ws creation directed toward the views of the business world. It now features four-color photography throughout the pages. It is moderate to conservative in the thrust of its reporting and analysis, vis-à-vis the more popular *Time* and *Newsweek*. It does not usually cover the general news, such as sports and culture. Instead it is "devoted entirely to national and international affairs." It does an excellent job of presenting the maximum amount of information in a concise form to offer as much as possible each week. Its interviews—usually with important public figures about equally important issues—are as objective as the personality being questioned will allow. Critics, however, contend that it is business-oriented, primarily conservative, and not always objective. It has found a place in many collections where there is an interest in business affairs.

Vital Speeches of the Day. 1934. bi-m. $25. Genevieve T. Daly. City News Publg. Co., P.O. Box 606, Southold, NY 11971. Index. Circ: 18,000. Vol. ends: Oct. Microform: UMI.

Indexed: RG. *Aud:* Hs.

This reprint journal records eight to ten speeches twice a month of "the recognized leaders of public opinion"—usually government officials and heads of large corporations. This journal is popular in school libraries as a teaching aid, particularly in government and debate classes.

The Washington Monthly. 1969. m. $30 (Individuals, $15). Charles Peters. The Washington Monthly Co., 1711 Connecticut Ave. N.W., Washington, DC 20009. Illus., adv. Circ: 30,000. Sample. Vol. ends: Feb. Microform: B&H, UMI.

Indexed: BoRvI, PAIS, RG, SocSc. *Bk. rev:* 1, 1,800 words plus notes, signed. *Aud:* Hs.

The Washington Monthly focuses on the Washington political arena. Editorial advisory board members such as Rich-

ard Rovere, Murray Kempton, and Richard Reeves guide the pocket-size 75- to 85-page issue through the political turmoil of Congress, the presidential office, the courts, and the various federal agencies. The writing style is lively and usually easy to understand. Government functionaries take care to ensure that their interoffice memorandums do not make the outrageous "Memo of the Month" section. Sections covering monthly journalism awards, political booknotes, and who's who in Washington are also included. It continues to be a popular periodical for many libraries.

NEWSPAPERS

For the Student: General; Newspaper Indexes

Sandra M. Whiteley, Editor, Reference Books Bulletin, American Library Association, 50 East Huron St., Chicago, IL 60611

Basic Newspapers

All libraries: The city or town newspaper, the state and/or regional newspaper, and the *New York Times*. Beyond that, if the library wants other "national" newspapers, the primary contenders are the *Washington Post*, the *Wall Street Journal*, and the *Christian Science Monitor*. The availability of more than 50 newspapers online in full-text versions from such companies as Datatek, NEXIS, and VU/TEXT gives libraries with computers access to more newspapers on an on-demand basis, without having to subscribe to them.

INTERNATIONAL NEWSPAPERS. For convenience, the international newspapers of note are listed in the major sections of the world. The exceptions are England and Canada; primary newspapers for these countries are in this section.

SPECIAL INTEREST NEWSPAPERS. These are found under subject section headings; e.g., *Billboard* will be found under Music, *Advertising Age* under Business, etc.

NEWSPAPER PRICES. Subscription prices to newspapers often vary according to the state to which they will be sent. Inquire about prices before subscribing. Note: There is no audience (Aud.) designation in this section. See the explanation under "Basic Newspapers," above.

NEWSPAPER INDEXES/ONLINE. See the concluding part of this section for information about newspaper indexes and the online designations employed in this section.

Basic Abstracts and Indexes

Many libraries will want to continue to subscribe to the *New York Times Index* and/or the *National Newspaper Index*. Other libraries may choose to search these and other newspaper indexes online.

For the Student

GENERAL

(Atlanta) Constitution. 1868. d. Jim Minter. Atlanta Newspapers, 72 Marietta St., Atlanta, GA 30303. Circ: 227,755 (d.); 571,646 (Sun.). Microform: UMI.

Still one of the best of the Southern newspapers. It is liberal in its coverage of local and national issues and has excellent editorials. It will serve as a representative paper from the South.

Boston Globe. 1872. d. Michael Janeway. Boston Globe, 135 Morrissey Blvd., Boston, MA 02107. Circ: 520,081 (d.); 792,786 (Sun.). Microform: B&H. Online: VU/TEXT.
Indexed: B&H.

An unpredictable paper, the *Globe* has excellent political and sports coverage. It has changed from a conservative to more liberal stance. Excellent columnists, such as Ellen Goodman, add to the paper's stature. This newspaper should be in all New England libraries.

Chicago Tribune. 1847. d. James D. Squires. Chicago Tribune, 435 N. Michigan Ave., Chicago, IL 60611. Circ: 776,348 (d.); 1,137,667 (Sun.). Microform: B&H. Online: VU/TEXT.
Indexed: B&H, UMI.

The *Tribune* has shed its tradition of Midwestern Republican conservatism and now covers the Democratic city government well. It has added excellent columnists in recent years—some when the *Daily News* folded and others when the *Sun-Times* was bought by Rupert Murdoch. Writers like Mike Royko and Bob Greene are now syndicated around the United States. The *Tribune* is the first choice for libraries that want coverage of the upper Midwest.

Christian Science Monitor. 1908. 5/w. $72. Kay Fanning. Christian Science Publg. Co., One Norway St., Boston, MA 02115. Circ: 141,247. Microform: B&H. Online: NEXIS.
Indexed: B&H, *National Newspaper Index*.

This outstanding newspaper is published at a price that makes it affordable by even smaller libraries. While the tabloid may appear to be thin, the fact that it carries no sports or stock tables and very little advertising means that there is room for excellent coverage of national and international news. Only a single column is devoted to a religious article in this otherwise secular paper. It is famous for its objectivity but tends to be uncontentious and is not a crusading newspaper.

Daily Telegraph. 1855. d. $193. William Deedes. Daily Telegraph, 135 Fleet St., London EC4P 4BL, England. Circ: 1,441,425. Microform: RP.

Included in lists of the world's best newspapers, this would be the third choice (after the *Times* and the *Guardian*) for a British newspaper in American libraries. The *Telegraph* tends to be more conservative than even the *Times of London* and during the *Time*'s frequent work stoppages, much of its readership switched to the *Telegraph*. The *Times Index* also indexed the *Telegraph* during those periods. Also publishes the *Sunday Telegraph*.

Des Moines Register. 1849. d. James P. Gannon. Des Moines Register, P.O. Box 957, Des Moines, IA 50304. Circ: 234,927 (d.); 384,923 (Sun.). Microform: B&H.

The *Register* is one of Iowa's most powerful and respected institutions and has statewide circulation. The paper is the best in the nation in reporting on agribusiness and concentrates on in-depth reporting on agricultural trends in the region. The *Register* also maintains an excellent Washington office.

Guardian (Manchester Guardian). 1821. d. (except Sun.). $218. Peter Preston. Guardian, 119 Farringdon Rd., London EC1R 3ER, England. Circ: 394,000. Microform: UMI.

This is the intellectual's newspaper in Britain, much more liberal than the *Times*. The editorial focus supports the Labour and Liberal parties. However, the *Guardian* is often read in the United States as much for its coverage of Europe as for England. This would be a first choice for most libraries, to give a balanced perspective along with the *Times*.

Los Angeles Times. 1881. d. William F. Thomas. Times Mirror Co., Times Mirror Sq., Los Angeles, CA 90053. Circ: 1,046,965 (d.); 1,298,487 (Sun.). Microform: UMI.
Indexed: B&H, *National Newspaper Index*.

The best daily newspaper on the West Coast. The *Times* has a huge staff in Los Angeles, around the country, and abroad, and they turn out a paper that is even bigger in size than the *New York Times*. Because of the fact that most of the nation's quality newspapers are concentrated along the East Coast, the *Los Angeles Times* is an important acquisition for many libraries for its coverage of the growing West.

Manchester Guardian Weekly. 1919. w. $52. Subs. to: 20 E. 53rd St., New York, NY 10022. Microform: UMI.

This should not be confused with the daily edition. The 24-page airmail, thin-paper format includes both new material and items from the daily, as well as articles from *Le Monde* (in English) and the *Washington Post*. Coverage is international in scope, and it shares the liberal viewpoint of its parent paper. It is of value for two reasons: It alerts U.S. readers to current news sometimes overlooked, underplayed or slanted in a different fashion here; and it keeps the reader advised of developments in England in politics, books, art, and music—to name a few of the regular features. The reasonable price also makes it a first choice for libraries that might not be able to afford any other newspaper from Europe.

Miami Herald. 1910. d. Health Meriwether. Miami Herald, Herald Plaza, Miami, FL 33101. Circ: 419,631 (d.); 509,721 (Sun.). Microform: B&H. Online: VU/TEXT.

The *Herald*'s main strength for libraries outside of Florida is that it serves as the newspaper of record for Latin America. It devotes more space to Latin America than any other U.S. paper and has six people regularly covering that region. The Spanish-language edition is distributed widely in Latin America, as well as among the Spanish-speaking population of Florida. It is a serious newspaper giving excellent coverage to a rapidly growing state as well.

New York Times. 1851. d. $211. A. M. Rosenthal. New York Times, 229 W. 43rd St., New York, NY 10036. Circ: 934,530 (d.); 1,553,720 (Sun.). Microform: UMI. Online: NEXIS.
Indexed: National Newspaper Index.

If there is anything close to a U.S. national newspaper, it is the *New York Times*. Its excellent coverage of international and national news, along with such outstanding columnists as William Safire and Paul Goldberger make it an essential purchase for most libraries. For libraries that cannot afford the daily paper, the Sunday edition is essential for its magazine and book review sections and the "News of the Week in Review." Libraries outside the East Coast will get the National Edition, which has greatly reduced coverage of New York State and City news, sports and the arts. National and international news is the same in both editions. The *Times* remains the nation's newspaper of record.

Observer. 1791. w. $140. Donald Trelford. Observer, 8 St. Andrews Hill, London EC4V 5JA, England. Circ: 845,431.

Published only on Sunday (when the *Guardian* is not), this is the other outstanding liberal newspaper in England. It includes an excellent magazine section.

Philadelphia Inquirer. 1829. d. Eugene Roberts, Jr. Philadelphia Newspapers, Inc., 400 N. Broad St., Philadelphia, PA 19101. Circ: 525,569 (d.); 1,000,427 (Sun.). Microform: B&H. Online: VU/TEXT.

The *Inquirer* has made one of the most remarkable turnarounds in quality in the history of American journalism. In a decade, it changed from an uncreative, conservative paper to one that has won six consecutive Pulitzer Prizes. With the demise of the *Bulletin*, its only competition, the *Inquirer* has expanded its staff and coverage. Its thorough and influential handling of the Three Mile Island nuclear power plant story is one example of its journalistic capabilities.

Sunday Times. 1822. w. $70. Andrew Neil. Sunday Times, 200 Gray's Inn Rd., London WC1X 8EZ, England. Circ: 1,314,713. Microform: RP.

Also owned by Rupert Murdoch but edited separately from the daily *Times*, this tends to be a livelier paper with more features. It includes a *Sunday Times Magazine*, which is comparable to the *New York Times Magazine*. Libraries that cannot afford the daily *Times* may want the Sunday overview, but ideally both should be taken.

Times. 1785. d. (exc. Sun.) $300. Printing House Sq., London WC1X 8EZ, England. Subs. to: 201 E. 42nd St., New York, NY 10017. Circ: 336,189.

The *Times* has just celebrated 200 years as the newspaper for the "top people" in Britain. It is the best known and most quoted newspaper in the world. Although it was recently purchased by Rupert Murdoch, publisher of so many trashy tabloids, the *Times* continues to be the leading conservative intellectual paper in England. It is best known for its editorials, obituaries, and letters to the editor. Because it has been indexed since its inception in 1785, it is a valuable research tool. It remains the first choice for U.S. libraries that want to subscribe to a European newspaper.

(Toronto) Globe and Mail. 1844. d. (exc. Sun.) $230. Norman Webster, 444 Front St., Toronto, Ont. M5V 2S9, Canada. Circ: 328,201. Microform: Preston Services Ltd.

Indexed: CNI.

Describes itself as "Canada's national newspaper" and probably comes close to that, since it tries to appeal to readers in all parts of the country. It is the most influential paper within Canada and has excellent coverage of foreign news. Although an English-language newspaper, it gives extensive coverage to Quebec. Sunday newspapers are beginning to appear in Canada (for many years they were illegal) but the *Globe and Mail* is still published only six days a week. This serious newspaper is generally considered Canada's newspaper of record.

USA Today. 1982. 5/w. $50. John C. Quinn. Gannett Co., P.O. Box 7856, Washington, DC 20044. Circ: 1,328,781. Microform: B&H.

Billing itself as "the nation's newspaper," this newcomer already has the third largest circulation of any newspaper in the United States (after the *Wall Street Journal* and the *New York Daily News*). Heavily influenced by television journalism, it has lots of photographs and color, but little in-depth coverage of the news—articles are very brief. The paper has four sections: (1) Sports—generally acknowledged to be very good with lots of statistics; (2) Money—the business section which is consumer-oriented and has only brief stock tables; (3) Life—the feature section, heavy on TV and Hollywood personalities, with articles like "Sexy Films of the Summer"; and (4) News—the weakest section, with superficial coverage of U.S. and foreign news. *USA Today* is beamed by satellite to 26 printing plants around the country but carries no regional advertising and is not intended to replace local newspapers. Libraries looking for good coverage of national and international news will continue to choose another newspaper.

Wall Street Journal. 1889. 5/w. $107. Robert Bartley. Dow-Jones Corp., 22 Cortlandt St., New York, NY 10007. Circ: 1,959,873. Microform: B&H. Online: Dow-Jones.

Indexed: Dow-Jones, *National Newspaper Index.*

The *Wall Street Journal* is the only truly international U.S. newspaper, with regional editions printed in the United States and separate editions in Europe and Asia. Although written basically for the business community, its front page carries news of national importance and it has even expanded its coverage to include the arts. While the editorial page is still very conservative, the news columns are fair and the Op-Ed column carries liberal opinion. The *Journal* is still dull to look at—no pictures—but as the newspaper of record for business it should be considered where there is interest.

Washington Post. 1877. d. $300. Benjamin C. Bradlee. Washington Post, 1150 15th St. N.W., Washington, DC 20071. Circ: 728,857 (d.); 1,033,207 (Sun.). Microform: RP. Online: NEXIS, VU/TEXT.

Indexed: National Newspaper Index.

Although it is having a hard time living up to its Watergate days, the *Post* still practices a lively form of journalism. The paper has national importance for two reasons: its full coverage of the federal government—especially Congress and obscure federal agencies—and its intelligent editorial page. It serves as the newspaper of record for its coverage of government affairs. It also has such important columnists as George Will and Mary McGrory and a much imitated Style Section. For libraries that cannot afford to subscribe to the daily *Post*, there is now an alternative. The *Washington Post: National Weekly Edition*, is a distillation of major articles from the previous week's paper. At only $39 a year, this would be a valuable addition to smaller libraries.

SUNDAY MAGAZINE SUPPLEMENTS

Almost every American Sunday newspaper has a separate magazine section. Many large papers publish their own. However, three large national supplements are likely to be found in many American newspapers:

Parade. 1941. w. Walter Anderson. 750 Third Ave., New York, NY 10017. Circ: 30,000,000.

Distributed in over 250 newspapers, this vies with *Sunday* for the largest circulation.

Sunday. 1940. w. Vincent Giese. 260 Madison Ave., New York, NY 10016. Circ: 21,000,000.

Distributed to 43 big-city newspapers with large circulations. Both *Parade* and *Sunday* will be given a run for their money by *USA Weekend*.

USA Weekend (Formerly: *Family Weekly*). 1953. w. Marcia Bullard. Gannett Co., P.O. Box 500, Washington, DC 20044. Circ: ca. 12,000,000.

Since its debut in September, 1985 as a Gannett paper, *USA Weekend* bears a close resemblance to its cousin, *USA Today*. Distributed in 220 newspapers, the emphasis is on entertainment.

NEWSPAPER INDEXES

U.S. newspapers are indexed in printed form. However, we will probably not see the emergence of any more printed newspaper indexes. The availability of newspaper indexes online and of full-text versions of newspapers online (indexed by the computer) may make printed indexes obsolete in the not-too-distant future. More than 50 newspapers are currently available online in full-text format, and it has been predicted that all newspapers published in cities with populations of over 250,000 will be available in full-text retrieval systems within the next few years.

Canadian News Index (Formerly: *Canadian Newspaper Index*). 1977. m. $576.92. Micromedia, Ltd., 144 Front St. W., Toronto, Ont. M5G 1J9. Canada.

An index on seven English-language Canadian newspapers, including the *Globe and Mail*. Available online with DIALOG.

Christian Science Monitor, Index to the. 1945. m. $145. Microphoto Div., Bell & Howell, Old Mansfield Rd., Wooster, OH 44691.

Similar in format and approach to the titles in the *Newspaper Index* published by Bell & Howell, i.e., a subject index that uses broad subject headings and a personal name index. References are given to all four regional editions of the *Monitor*. Searchable online through SDC.

National Newspaper Index. 1979. m. $2290. Information Access Corp., 11 David Dr., Belmont, CA 94002.

An index on computer output microfilm to the Late and National Editions of the *New York Times*, the *Wall Street Journal*, the *Christian Science Monitor*, the *Washington Post*, and the *Los Angeles Times*. Subscription price includes leasing and service on a ROM reader. The index is cumulated each month, is much easier to use than the printed indexes, and is much more current. It contains no abstracts, uses LC subject headings, and can be searched online through DIALOG. A useful service for those libraries that can afford it.

New York Times Index. 1851. s-m. $475. University Microfilms, Inc., 300 N. Zeeb Rd., Ann Arbor, MI 48106.

The standard newspaper index in most libraries, since the *New York Times* is the closest thing to a national newspaper in the United States. Most entries are annotated, so the index can often be used by itself, without reference to the newspaper. The drawbacks to this index are that it is complicated to use and always three months behind. The quarterly cumulations and the annual index are also slow to be published. For speedy access, some libraries are accessing the *Times* online.

University Microfilms has also recently begun to issue several other newspaper indexes. The *Atlanta Journal/Atlanta Constitution Index* dates to 1982 and costs $395 a year. The *Los Angeles Times Index* began in 1984 and also costs $395. Also: the *Chicago Tribune* (from 1982, $395) and the *Minneapolis Star and Tribune* (from 1984, $395).

Newspaper Index. 1972. m., q. Microphoto Div., Bell & Howell, Old Mansfield Rd., Wooster, OH 44691-9050.

This began in 1972 as a single index to four newspapers: the *Chicago Tribune*, the *Los Angeles Times*, the *New Orleans Times-Picayune*, and the *Washington Post* (since dropped.) Since then, eight more titles have been added: the *Boston Globe* (1983–), *Chicago Sun-Times* (1979–), *Detroit News* (1976–), *Denver Post* (1979–), *Houston Post* (1976–), *St. Louis Post-Dispatch* (1980–), *San Francisco Chronicle* (1976–), and *USA Today* (1982–). In order to provide good regional coverage, some of the papers selected for indexing are less than excellent, but they are usually the best available in the region. Indexes are currently $460 a year, except for *USA Today*, which is $145 a year. Can be searched online using SDC.

Official Washington Post Index. 1979. m. $275. Research Publns., 12 Lunar Dr., Woodbridge, CT 06525.

From 1972–1982 the *Washington Post* was indexed by Bell & Howell as part of the *Newspaper Index*. The *Official Washington Post Index* contains abstracts and can be accessed online through DIALOG.

Times Index. 1785. m. $475. Research Publns., 12 Lunar Dr., Woodbridge, CT 06525.

Provides indexing to 200 years of history. It has had a varying publishing schedule, but since 1977 it is published monthly with an annual cumulation. It now includes brief abstracts. Since 1973, it has also indexed the *Sunday Times,* the *Times Literary Supplement,* the *Times Educational Supplement* and the *Times Higher Educational Supplement.* During periods when the *Times* has been on strike, the *Daily Telegraph* and the *Sunday Telegraph* were indexed instead of the *Times.*

Wall Street Journal Index. 1955. m. $550. Dow-Jones Books, P.O. Box 300, Princeton, NJ 08540.

A two-part index to the world's leading business newspaper. One section is alphabetical by name coverage of "Corporate News"; the other section, "General News," is a subject approach. Almost all entries have brief descriptive notes. The index is based on the eastern edition, which is also used for the microform of the newspaper. The index is relatively up-to-date, appearing six to eight weeks after the close of the month.

ONLINE FULL-TEXT RETRIEVAL SERVICES

Datatek, 818 N.W. 63rd, Oklahoma City, OK 73116. While its emphasis is on papers of the Southwest, it also does the *Chicago Sun-Times.*

NEXIS. Mead Data Central, 200 Park Ave., New York, NY 10166. Sixteen newspapers are available online in full text. Most are available within 24 hours of publication.

VU/TEXT. VU/TEXT Information Services, 1211 Chestnut St., Philadelphia, PA 19107. A Knight-Ridder subsidiary, VU/TEXT currently has 18 newspapers online in full text and will add 10 more in 1985. The papers are all added to the file within 24 to 72 hours of publication. The cost of searching is between $60 and $100 an hour.

OCCUPATIONS AND CAREERS

For the Student/For the Professional

See also Education Section.

Jacob Welle, Assistant Librarian, Allentown College of St. Francis de Sales, Center Valley, PA 18034

Introduction

As you study magazines dealing with occupations and careers, you quickly become aware of the fact that competition for the better jobs is becoming more and more intense every day. Although these jobs demand more sophisticated skills and higher education, there is no lack of people to fill them as schools and colleges continue to turn out more and more students equipped to handle them. What this means is that only the menial tasks will be left for those with limited skills and education. Another fact brought out by these magazines is that in today's job market there is a growing need for a person to have a broad liberal arts education and not just training in the skills needed for a particular job. Business, industry, and society in general are constantly changing. With the changes, new jobs are created, new skills are needed,

and suddenly old skills become obsolete. Surveys have shown that people with a liberal arts background are better equipped than others to make the necessary transition from one occupation or career to another.

These and other facts make it evident that career planning—setting personal goals and organizing one's resources in the pursuit of those goals—is in itself an education, and one which cannot be left in the hands of students, nor made the sole responsibility of counseling and placement personnel. It is a process in which every faculty member must become involved. For this reason, magazines dealing with occupations and careers are becoming even more important, not only for young people who have to make occupation and career decisions, but also those who must assist them. Libraries serving these people will need a select number of the titles listed in this section. Most are directed to students, some are specifically directed to counselors, and others are for a general audience. They provide all kinds of pertinent information about occupations and careers—what they are like, how to choose and prepare for them, how to succeed in them, and so on. Annotations accompany each magazine and describe its special function, scope, and content. But no annotation is a substitute for the real thing, and librarians should write for a sample, if offered, before subscribing.

Basic Periodicals

Hs: *Career World.*

Basic Abstracts and Indexes

Current Index to Journals in Education, Work Related Abstracts.

For the Student

Career Opportunities News (Also called: *CNews*). 1983. 6/yr. $25. Robert Calvert, Jr., Garrett Park Press, Garrett Park, MD 20896. Illus., index. Circ: 18,000. Sample. Vol. ends: May/June.

Aud: Hs.

The purpose of this newsletter is to report the latest news about jobs currently available, the fields and locations where the best possibilities for jobs lie, the job opportunities which will be developing, as well as the educational opportunities available to young people selecting and preparing for careers. Much of the information is presented in the form of brief news items (gleaned from over 100 magazines), plus government reports and study programs of professional organizations. In each issue, there is also a feature article on some timely topic such as "The Coming Teacher Shortage," "Women in Law," or "Robotics and Job Displacement." At the end of many of the news items and articles, the editors list resources to consult for additional information. Special emphasis (three to four pages in each issue) is given to a presentation and discussion of educational and career opportunities for women and members of minority groups. Another refreshing feature is the emphasis and importance this publication places on a liberal arts education as career preparation. For counselors, there is a regular listing and description of free or inexpensive career materials. The easy-to-read format of this newsletter makes it inviting reading for young people in the process of choosing and preparing for careers. Their counselors and advisors will need it to keep up-to-date on the happenings in the world of work.

Career World. 1972. m. (During school year). $4.95. (per student; minimum 15 subs. to one address). Joyce Lain Kennedy. Curriculum Innovations, Inc., 3500 Western Ave., Highland Park, IL 60035. Illus., index. Circ: 140,000. Sample. Vol. ends: May. Microform: B&H, UMI.
Aud: Ejh, Hs.

Junior and senior high school students will find in this magazine all kinds of information that will help them select and prepare for an occupation or career. It presents the information in the form of interviews conducted with people working at a particular job, which ask (and answer) such questions as: What is the work like? What are the job opportunities? What are the salaries? and, above all, What is the education and training needed for that occupation or career? Each issue will usually focus on a broad occupational field such as government work, the computer field, and science and technology, and feature several articles on the various career opportunities that field affords. Other articles discuss specific jobs or attempt to answer the many questions students ask as they go through the process of making career and occupation decisions. Many articles are followed by a list of sources the reader can contact for additional information. The magazine is intended primarily for classroom use and is designed to promote discussion and an exchange of ideas. A special teacher's edition serves as a guide. Public libraries may also wish to subscribe to this attractive and inviting magazine, because of the wealth of career information it contains.

Occupational Outlook Quarterly. 1957. q. $11. Melvin Fountain. Occupational Outlook Service, Bureau of Labor Statistics, U.S. Dept of Labor. Subs. to: Supt. of Docs., U.S. Govt. Printing Office, Washington, DC 20402. Illus., index. Circ: 30,000. Sample. Vol. ends: Winter. Microform: MCA, PMC, UMI.
Indexed: CIJE, IGov, PAIS, WorAb. *Aud:* Hs.

Compared to other occupation and career magazines, *OOQ* devotes little space to the description of specific jobs, which is done in its parent publication, the *Occupational Outlook Handbook*, and aims rather at reporting on broad occupational areas and discussing the employment possibilities they offer to workers of every kind. It also provides information about vocational and professional education programs; it discusses the effect of business cycles and economic trends on work prospects; and it delves into many other work-related topics such as wages and fringe benefits, new technologies and their potential job impact, women and work, and so on. Every two years the "Job Outlook in Brief" lists some 200 jobs and gives a rundown on job openings and employment prospects in each. There is also a biennial report on the job outlook for college students—a general discussion of job prospects over the next decade and where the demand will be. Many of the articles include pertinent

statistical data gathered by the Bureau of Labor Statistics. All in all, this is a well-edited magazine from which both high school and college students as well as counseling and placement personnel can gain valuable information about today's work situation and tomorrow's job prospects.

Tradeswomen. See Women/For the Student Section.

For the Professional

Florida Vocational Journal. 1976. 6/yr. $5 (Free to Florida educators). Charles Furbee. Center for Studies in Vocational Education, Stone Bldg., Florida State Univ., Tallahassee, FL 32306. Illus., adv. Circ: 20,000. Sample. Microform: UMI. Reprint: UMI.
Indexed: CIJE. *Aud:* Pr.

Career counselors, vocational educators, and other educational personnel in the state of Florida use this magazine as a means of disseminating information about programs, issues or developments in vocational and career education in their state. The journal's chief aim is to report on innovative programs and teaching practices that deal not only with vocational-skill training, but also with career development and exploration and that are "creative in approach, imaginative in nature, and have a combination of elements that are unique in method or technique of presentation." Although this journal reports on Florida's vocational and career-education activities, it will be of interest to all vocational educators who wish to keep abreast of changes in their field and especially to those who are seeking new strategies for making constructive changes in vocational education. This is a well-edited, artfully illustrated, and attractively laid out magazine. A worthwhile item for any high school, vocational-technical, or community college library.

Journal of Career Planning and Employment (Formerly: *Journal of College Placement*). 1940. q. Membership (Nonmembers, $20). Patricia A. Sinnott. College Placement Council, Inc., 62 Highland Ave., Bethlehem, PA 18017. Illus., index, adv. Circ: 4,000. Vol. ends: Summer. Microform: UMI.
Indexed: CIJE, EdI, PAIS, WorAb. *Bk. rev:* 30–35, 75–200 words, signed. *Aud:* Pr.

Serves as a forum for the exchange of ideas by members of the counseling and placement profession, as well as others in and out of the academic community who are concerned about assisting students in career planning. In both short reports and in full-length articles, these people share information and advice about programs and practices they have successfully used in their counseling and placement work, or report on research done on various topics relevant to the development and improvement of the profession. Occasionally, an issue will be devoted to a single theme such as career development for the liberal arts student or the use of computers in career planning and development. Although addressed to professional practitioners, this journal is also of value to faculty advisors, on whose shoulders the work of career counseling often rests. Students themselves can find in its pages the practical help they need in assessing and marketing their skills, résumé writing, job seeking, and so on. Because it can serve so many members of the college community, this journal should be found not only in the placement office but on the library's periodical shelves as well.

Journal of Employment Counseling. 1964. q. $8 (Nonmembers, $11). Robert J. Drummond. Amer. Assn. for Counseling and Development, 5999 Stevenson Ave., Alexandria, VA 22304. Index, adv. Circ: 1,850. Vol. ends: Dec. Microform: UMI.

Indexed: CIJE. *Aud:* Pr.

Most of the articles in this modest 48-page journal consist of reports on or studies of various programs and workshops which have been developed to counsel and advise the unemployed in such areas as: acquiring job-seeking and job-readiness skills, developing self-confidence, handling job interviews, improving communication skills and so on. Each report or study begins by giving the history and description of the program or workshop, and then goes on to explain the techniques and procedures that were followed, and ends with a discussion of their effectiveness and their implications for the employment counselor. None of the studies are meant to be definitive, and most conclude by pointing out the limitations of a particular program and suggest areas in need of further investigation or refinement. Other articles, especially those in the annual special issues, deal with problems of current concern to employment counselors and suggest counseling techniques one might use in handling them. Articles are always followed by a brief, but quite useful, list of sources to consult for additional information. Although this journal is addressed to the professional employment counselor, academic libraries supporting programs in counseling education should consider a subscription. The price is certainly no obstacle.

New Generation (Formerly: *American Child*). 1919. q. $10. Margaret Reinfeld. Natl. Child Labor Committee, 1501 Broadway, Rm. 1111, New York, NY 10036. Illus., index. Circ: 4,000. Sample. Vol. ends: Fall. Microform: UMI.

Aud: Pr.

Since 1904, the National Child Labor Committee has been working to promote the welfare of the nation's youth. Its activities have taken the form of a threefold effort: to promote employment opportunities for young people with special needs such as teenage parents, the disadvantaged, and urban and migrant youth; to improve the education and lives of children of migrant workers; and to protect all children and youth from abusive work. By means of this newsletter, the committee keeps businesspeople, legislators, educators, and the public in general informed about these issues by reporting on private and public programs (including the NCLC's own programs and activities) designed to provide equal working and education opportunities for these young people. It also reports on such relevant legislation affecting young workers as child-labor laws and affirmative-action legislation. This is necessary reading for counselors and educators who deal with young people and who must help them bridge the gap from school to work. Businesspeople and legislators, who must promote suitable employ-

ment opportunities for young people, should also have it on their reading list.

Vocational Education Journal (Formerly: *VocEd*). 8/yr. Membership (Nonmembers, $20). Gladys B. Santo. Amer. Vocational Assn., 2020 N. 14th St., Arlington, VA 22201. Illus., adv. Circ: 50,000. Sample. Vol. ends: Dec. Microform: UMI.

Indexed: CIJE, EdI. *Bk. rev:* 15, 50–75 words. *Aud:* Pr.

The philosophy of this journal is that vocational education must be a part of the whole educational program and not just a "useful extra" to provide individuals with job-entry skills. This focus on the education base rather than the training base was brought out strongly in the 1984 annual teaching issue, the whole thrust of which was to emphasize the "teaching of the so-called 'new basics' to vocational students—reading, writing, speaking and listening, math, science, reasoning, basic employment, economics and computer literacy." Articles found in every issue also show this same emphasis when they ask "How Much 'Tech' do High-Tech Workers Need?" or state that "Excellence Begins with Curriculum," or maintain that "Voc-Ed Students Need Math and Science," or, to put it another way, "Not Just a Skill but a Solid Education." Every issue also reports on innovative and successful classroom and shop practices, discusses problems affecting the quality and scope of vocational programs, and reports on actions in government and industry affecting vocational education. Educators, who are looking for ways to provide their students with the multidimensional education today's highly technical labor market demands, will consider this journal essential reading. A first choice for any vocational education library.

PEACE

For the Student

Willard Moonan, Milner Library, Illinois State University, Normal, IL 61761

Introduction

The desire for peace is as old as war. In each age, peacemakers have worked to reduce or eliminate both the causes and the means of human conflict. Following World War II, their efforts focused upon nuclear weapons, but as the cold war progressed the wars and social upheavals followed one upon another, the peace movement broadened its concerns to include all types of violence as well as social and economic injustice. Magazines published by peacemakers usually fall into one of two categories. Scholarly journals are written from a social science perspective and stress scientific or historical methodology. Their contributors tend to approach human conflict from a somewhat detached viewpoint. However, some of the scholarly journals listed below combine this scientific outlook with an urgent desire for reform. Activist magazines display a strong emotional, as well as intellectual, commitment to the cause of peace. They are produced by movement people who passionately wish to change the present system to achieve peace and justice through communication, education, or direct involvement and confrontation. Personal commitment is the key to these activists' programs.

Basic Periodicals

Hs: *Coalition Close-Up, Reporter for Conscience' Sake.*

Basic Abstracts and Indexes

Alternative Press Index, Peace Research Abstracts.

For the Student

Coalition Close-Up. 1979. w. $20. Cynthia Washington. Coalition for a New Foreign and Military Policy, 712 G St. S.E., Washington, DC 20003. Illus. Circ: 20,000.
Aud: Hs.

The coalition is an action-oriented alliance of more than 50 religious, peace, labor, social action, and research groups working toward a "peaceful, demilitarized, non-interventionist" U.S. foreign policy. It emphasizes grass roots organization with coordinated lobbying activities. *Close-Up* is an attractively produced 8- to 12-page newsletter, written by the coalition staff, which focuses a critical spotlight upon the activities of Congress and the President, reports voting records on crucial defense issues, and includes articles on the federal budget, covert aid, Central America, multinationals, and human rights. It is a good source for statistics. It also should be useful to debaters. Highly recommended.

Defense Monitor. 1972. 10/yr. $25. Center for Defense Information, 303 Capitol Gallery W., 600 Maryland Ave. W., Washington, DC 20024.
Aud: Hs.

The Center for Defense Information is a privately funded organization which supports "a strong defense but opposes excessive expenditures for weapons and policies that increase the danger of nuclear war. It believes that strong social, economic, and political structures contribute equally to national security." While the CDI staff and advisors come from military, intelligence, and industrial backgrounds, this newsletter takes strong exception to the current military budget and confrontational U.S. foreign policy. Each 8- to 24-page issue, written by a staff analyst, investigates a single topic such as the value of a United States-Soviet summit, military research and the economy, United States-Soviet relative military power, and the U.S. military in Central America. Facts rather than opinions are emphasized, and statistics are prominent. This is a good source for debaters. Highly recommended for all libraries.

F. A. S. Public Interest Report. 1947. 10/yr. $50 (Individuals, $25). Jeremy J. Stone. Federation of Amer. Scientists, 307 Massachusetts Ave. N.E., Washington, DC 20002. Illus. Circ: 5,200. Vol. ends: Dec.
Bk. rev: Occasional, long, signed. *Aud:* Hs.

The Federation of American Scientists is "a non-profit, civic organization, licensed to lobby in the public interest, and composed of 5,000 scientists and engineers who are concerned with problems of science and society." Over 40 of the group's sponsors are Nobel Laureates. Some of the 8- to 24-page issues have single themes such as the Star Wars defense system and limiting the production of nuclear weapons. Included also are editorials and historical articles. They delight in printing contradictory statements by various government representatives. The articles are well written and detailed, a good source for quotes and statistics. The report is useful for debaters. Highly recommended.

Fellowship. 1934. 8/yr. $10. Virginia Baron. Fellowship of Reconciliation, 523 N. Broadway, Nyack, NY 10960. Illus., index. Circ: 12,000. Vol. ends: Dec. Microform: UMI.
Bk. rev: 4–5, 300 words, signed. *Aud:* Hs.

This is the magazine of the U.S. branch of the Fellowship of Reconciliation, "an association of women and men who have joined together to explore the power of love and truth for resolving human conflict." An activist organization, this journal reflects its worldwide interests in achieving peace and political-social-economic justice through nonviolent means. Each issue includes four to seven long articles and several pages of short news items, as well as a list of upcoming peace movement events and a list of published materials. An indispensable source of information on the religiously oriented wing of the peace movement. Highly recommended.

Nonviolent Activist. 1984. 10/yr. $15. War Resisters League, 339 Lafayette St., New York, NY 10012. Illus., adv. Circ: 23,000.
Bk. rev: 1, 50–900 words, signed. *Aud:* Hs.

The title, a replacement for the retired *WRL News*, is a 16-page periodical published by the U.S. branch of the War Resisters League, an international pacifist organization dedicated to the nonviolent struggle against war and social injustice. The WRL has described its membership as holding "a wide variety of religious, philosophical, and political beliefs [allowing] the widest experimentation with the theories and practices of nonviolence." Each issue includes four or five short articles on such topics as the national budget, the media's response to the antiwar movement, problems in U.S. prisons, the ROTC, tax resistance, and nonviolent strategies. There are also several pages of brief news items and upcoming events.

Nuclear Times. 1982. 10/yr. $15. Greg Mitchell. Nuclear Times, Inc., Rm. 512, 298 Fifth Ave., New York, NY 10001. Illus., index, adv. Circ: 25,000.
Indexed: API. *Bk. rev:* 2–3, short, unsigned. *Aud:* Hs.

A well-written, well-produced magazine devoted to information on and action against nuclear weapons. Reports on and strongly supports the nuclear freeze movement and arms control in general. Each issue contains two to four signed articles and several pages of short news items. Topics of recent articles include Soviet-United States relations, the military budget, the comprehensive test-ban movement, activist-academic mix in the peace movement, and the case against the Trident II. Although the emphasis is upon the antinuclear movement in the United States, each issue contains "Notes from Abroad." There is a calendar of antinuclear events in the United States and a resources column, including brief reviews of films and books. An excellent window onto this important part of the peace movement.

Reporter for Conscience' Sake. 1940. m. $10. Ann Clark, Suite 600, 800 18th St. N.W., Washington, DC 20006. Illus. Circ: 3,800. Microform: UMI.

Bk. rev: Occasional, brief, signed. *Aud:* Hs.

A four- to six-page newsletter for conscientious objectors and those concerned with the selective service system and the possibility of conscription. It is sponsored by the National Interreligious Service Board for Conscientious Objectors. Articles cover such topics as claiming conscientious-objector status, changes in the Selective Service regulations, current court cases of nonregistrants, and the activities of antidraft groups. A very useful source of information for young people of draft age.

SANE World. 1958. bi-m. $5. Beth Baker. SANE, 711 G St. S.E., Washington, DC 20003. Illus. Microform: UMI.

Bk. rev: Brief, unsigned. *Aud:* Hs.

Published by the Committee for a Sane Nuclear Policy, this 8-page newsletter offers its readers "concise, accurate information about the arms race, focusing on current issues, legislation, public education, and community activities." They broadly define the arms race to include such issues as military actions in Central America. Emphasis is upon disseminating information and organizing such grass-roots response as lobbying, canvassing, and letter writing. Lists events and educational resources and occasionally includes an "Insanity Award of the Month."

PETS

For the Student

See also Birds; Fishing, Hunting, and Guns; Horses; and Sports Sections.

Vicki F. Croft, Head, Veterinary Medical Pharmacy Library, Washington State University, Pullman, WA 99164

Introduction

There are few general magazines on the specific subject "pets." Many deal only with a particular species, e.g., *Cat Fancy, Dog Fancy, Tropical Fish Hobbyist.* Others cover only a specific breed. To locate information regarding these specialized breed magazines, it is advisable to inquire of the appropriate national breed association.

Useful articles about pets may frequently be located in humane society publications, public relations publications produced by pet-food manufacturers, and veterinary drug manufacturers, as well as in "women's magazines" and other general interest periodicals.

Basic Periodicals

Hs: *Animals.*

For the Student

A.F.A. Watchbird. 1971. bi-m. $15. Sheldon Dingle. Amer. Federation of Aviculture, 443 W. Douglas Ave., El Cajon, CA 92020. Illus., adv.

Aud: Hs.

Although primarily a magazine for the cage-bird breeder and enthusiast and A.F.A. member, *A.F.A. Watchbird* has features that appeal to a more general readership. Its attractive, glossy format and numerous color photographs hold a special appeal, as do its very informative articles dealing with such topics as the conservation, regulation, and importation of birdlife. Cage bird enthusiasts would also be interested in the articles dealing with the breeding, care, nutrition, genetics, and diseases of cage and exotic birds. *A.F.A. Watchbird* appeals to a different readership than *Bird Talk* and *Bird World,* primarily due to its articles on conservation and legislative issues, and articles on birds in the wild. This different scope is the result of the influence of its sponsoring group, the A.F.A., which is dedicated to the conservation of bird wildlife through the encouragement of captive breeding programs, scientific research, education of the general public, and monitoring legislation affecting aviculture.

American Cage-Bird Magazine (Formerly: *American Canary and Cage-Bird Life; American Canary Magazine*). 1929. m. $15. Arthur Freud, One Glamore Court, Smithtown, NY 11787. Illus., adv. Circ: 14,200. Vol. ends: Dec.

Bk. rev: 1–3, 100–300 words. *Aud:* Hs.

For both the breeders and fanciers of cage birds, this magazine provides useful information on the breeding, rearing, and enjoyment of parrots, canaries, budgerigars, finches, and other exotic species. It includes articles on avian husbandry and the treatment of avian diseases. Publishes dates for shows and a directory of bird fanciers' societies. (O.F.W.)

Animals. 1868. bi-m. $10.50. Joni Praded. Massachusetts Soc. for the Prevention of Cruelty to Animals, 350 S. Huntington Ave., Boston, MA 02130. Illus., adv. Circ: 22,000. Microform: UMI.

Bk. rev: Varies. *Aud:* Hs.

Animals is an attractive, glossy magazine with beautiful animal photographs in color, as well as informative articles. The articles focus on pets, pet care, and wildlife, with a heavy emphasis on animal rights and humane issues. Regular features include a veterinarian's question-answer section and a news section. Because *Animals* is a more substantive magazine than either *Our Animals* or *Our Fourfooted Friends,* it may be preferred by some. Other important considerations include differences in coverage and scope as well as publication frequencies. Recommended.

Animal Ways. 1935. q. £2. Elizabeth Winson. Royal Soc. for the Prevention of Cruelty to Animals, Causeway, Horsham, Sussex RH112 1H6, England. Illus. Circ: 20,000.

Aud: Ejh.

Animal Ways, published by the Royal Society for the Prevention of Cruelty to Animals, is a glossy, colorful publication written especially for readers under 12 years of age.

Each issue contains a number of informative articles on animals and animal care as well as animal stories. The animals that are discussed include birds, reptiles, and other wildlife, as well as the traditional domestic pet animals. Regular features include a letters from readers section, an animal care question-answer column, a readers' animal art page, a pen pals section, and a puzzle page. Despite the British origin, this magazine is recommended for all animal loving children.

Bird Talk: dedicated to better care for pet birds. 1984. bi-m. $8. Norman Ridker. Fancy Publns., Inc., 5509 Santa Monica Blvd., Los Angeles, CA 90038. Illus., adv. Circ: 15,500. Vol. ends: Dec.
Bk. rev: 2–3, 150–200 words, signed. *Aud:* Hs.

Published by Fancy Publications, the publishers of *Cat Fancy* and *Dog Fancy*, *Bird Talk* is an attractive magazine whose primary focus centers around practical and proper care and feeding of pet birds. Feature articles include advice on medical problems (written by veterinarians), breed profiles, as well as a regular question-answer column authored by veterinarians. Each issue also contains a column on new products as well as a classified section. The magazine's beautiful color photographs are guaranteed to please any bird lover. *Bird Talk*'s practical and informative approach to pet-bird care would be of special interest to the relatively new bird owner.

Bird World. 1978. bi-m. $12. Kathy Lyon. Bird World, 11552 Hartsook St., North Hollywood, CA 91601. Illus., adv. Circ: 12,500.
Bk. rev: 1–3, 150–200 words, signed. *Aud:* Hs.

In comparison with *Bird Talk*, *Bird World* is a magazine that would appeal more to the established pet-bird owner than the novice. There are more articles on the specific breeds than *Bird Talk*, as well as more on training and breeding. There are several question-answer columns with answers coming from either veterinarians or experienced bird enthusiasts. Each issue also contains a veterinary medicine section which includes one or more veterinarian-authored articles relating to some aspects of veterinary medicine as well as summaries of avian articles from recent veterinary journals. A bird-club information directory and a good-sized classified section are other features that would appeal to the serious bird enthusiast.

Cat Fancy. 1966. m. $16. Norman Ridker. Fancy Publns., Inc. 5509 Santa Monica Blvd., Los Angeles, CA 90038. Illus., index, adv. Circ: 100,000. Vol. ends: Dec.
Bk. rev: 2–5, 250–300 words, signed. *Aud:* Ejh, Hs.

Cat Fancy is a magazine that will appeal to cat lovers of all ages. Its well-written articles deal with almost all aspects of cat and kitten health and care, such as grooming, health, nutrition, and behavior problems. Included also are articles on the various breeds, information on new products, a section on news of interest to cat owners and human-interest articles. Regular features include "Ask the Vet," "Cats of the Stars," a show calendar, and a breeder's directory. Like *Dog Fancy*, this is a very attractive glossy magazine containing numerous black-and-white as well as color photographs of cats. An annual index is invaluable for locating articles in past issues. Recommended for libraries as a good general cat magazine.

Cats Magazine. 1945. m. $16.50. Jean A. Laux. Cats Magazine, 445 Merrimac Dr., Port Orange, FL 32019. Illus., adv. Circ: 80,000. Vol. ends: Dec. Microform: UMI.
Bk. rev: 2–3, 150–200 words, signed. *Aud:* Hs.

Cats Magazine differs from *Cat Fancy* in that it includes fewer general feline care, breeding, and health articles, but more human interest stories and literature on cats. However, also included in the monthly issues are show calendars, club news, and a large, useful classified section. A breeders' directory is published annually. Since February, 1984, *Cats Magazine* is available in two editions, the *Cats Magazine* regular edition and the *Cats Magazine Exhibitor Edition*, which contains Daphne Negus' *Cat World*. The exhibitor edition is for the serious breeder/exhibitor of registered cats. Items included range from show reports to articles that are of special interest to the cat breeder, e.g., on such topics as genetics and coloration. *Cats Magazine* would likely be the choice of the serious cat breeder/exhibitor, while *Cat Fancy* would appeal to a broader and more general audience, because of its very attractive format and the inclusion of numerous articles on cat care and health.

Dog Fancy. 1970. m. $16. Norman Ridker. Fancy Publns., Inc., 5509 Santa Monica Blvd., Los Angeles, CA 90038. Illus., index, adv. Circ: 70,000. Vol. ends: Dec.
Bk. rev: 1–4, 50–400 words, signed. *Aud:* Ejh, Hs.

This is a magazine for the general reader who is interested in current, well-written articles dealing with a wide variety of topics relating to dog and puppy care and health. Tips on grooming and training, advice on behavioral problems, current information on health and nutrition, and the latest product information are all included, as well as human interest stories. Many issues contain a breed profile, which provides factual information on the featured breed. Regular monthly features focus on behavior problems, grooming, health problems, "Dogs of the Stars," and a classified section. The animal-health articles are written by veterinarians. A directory of dog breeders is included in each issue. This is an attractive magazine, full of many photographs—both black-and-white and color. An annual article index facilitates access to articles in past issues. Recommended.

Dog World. 1916. m. $20. Enid S. Bergstrom. Maclean Hunter Publg. Corp., 300 W. Adams St., Chicago, IL 60606. Illus., adv. Circ: 61,250. Vol. ends: Dec. Microform: UMI.
Aud: Hs.

Dog World, "the world's largest all breed dog magazine," is primarily a magazine for the dog breeder, although general articles on such topics as coping with pet adolescence and providing for your pet in your will might appeal also to a broader audience. Each issue contains news about upcoming dog shows, obedience trials, obedience news, new products, and so forth. The magazine also contains an extensive classified ad section, as well as numerous ads throughout the magazine.

Dogs in Canada: the authoritative magazine for dog enthusiasts. 1889. 13/yr. $18. Elizabeth Dunn. Apex Pubs. and Publicity, Ltd., 43 Railside Rd., Don Mills, Ont. M3A 3L9, Canada. Illus., adv. Circ: 18,000. Vol. ends: Dec.
Bk. rev: 1–5, 150–300 words. *Aud:* Hs.

Dogs in Canada, the official journal of the Canadian Kennel Club, is intended for the serious dog enthusiast. Although much of this magazine is devoted to the official news of the CKC, regional club news, upcoming shows and sanction matches, listings of winners of dog shows and field trials and so forth, a number of the general articles would be of interest to the general public. These articles deal with such topics as canine breeding, obedience, showing, kennel management, and canine health. Each monthly issue contains a section entitled "Breedlines," which contains short items of interest on the individual breeds. The subscription includes a copy of *Dogs Annual*, a very attractive buyer's guide issue. The 1985 *Dogs Annual* consisted of a breeder's directory (listing alphabetically, by breed, 1,800 dog breeders), a breeder's photo-filled classified section, and a feature section. The breeder's section also contains breed descriptions and advice on choosing a puppy. The feature section contains well-written, informative articles on canine health and training articles that would be of special interest to the new puppy owner. It should be noted that *Dogs Annual* may be purchased separately for $5.25.

Freshwater and Marine Aquarium. 1977. m. $22. Donald W. Dewey. R/C Modeler Corp., 120 W. Sierra Madre Blvd., Sierra Madre, CA 91024. Illus., adv. Circ: 35,000. Vol. ends: Dec.
Aud: Hs.

Written for aquarium hobbyists at all levels of experience, *Freshwater and Marine Aquarium* features detailed articles on many aspects of tropical fish care and breeding and aquaculture. There is also considerable coverage of available aquarium products. The editorial staff and writers include individuals representing the scientific community as well as dedicated aquarists. The articles are well written, many with bibliographies. Similar to *Tropical Fish Hobbyist* (see below in this section) in coverage, attractive appearance, and the presence of numerous colored photographs, *Freshwater and Marine Aquarium* differs from the former in that there is less emphasis on individual fish and breeding habits, but more on the practical aspects of fish care and breeding. A choice between this magazine and *TFH* would depend on the emphasis desired.

Our Animals: a quarterly journal for members of the San Francisco Society for the Prevention of Cruelty to Animals. 1911. q. Free to members of SF-SPCA. Charlotte Kesper. San Francisco Soc. for the Prevention of Cruelty to Animals, 2500 16th St., San Francisco, CA 94103. Illus., adv. Circ: 24,000.
Bk. rev: Varies. *Aud:* Hs.

Our Animals is a quarterly magazine that deals primarily with animals, pets, and human concerns. As the official publication of the San Francisco Society for the Prevention of Cruelty to Animals, it is not surprising that many of the articles deal with the activities of the society. However, *Our Animals* gives a considerably heavier emphasis to pets than do most humane magazines. A recent issue contained articles on a pet food giveaway, cat training, the San Francisco SPCA Animal Hospital, and the hazards of dogs riding in pickups. Recommended.

Our Fourfooted Friends. 1899. q. $4. Arthur G. Slade. Animal Rescue League of Boston, P.O. Box 265, Boston, MA 02116. Illus., adv. Circ: 17,825.
Aud: Ejh, Hs.

Although this publication deals primarily with humane education and humane society news, pet and animal care issues are included as well. A news section announces pertinent legislative news and pet health care news. This is one of several publications issued by local humane societies.

People, Animals, Environment: bulletin of the Delta Society. 1983. s-a. $10. Linda Hines. Delta Soc., 212 Wells Ave. S., Suite C, Renton, WA 98055. Illus. Vol. ends: No. 2.
Bk. rev: 3–5, 30–50 words. *Aud:* Hs.

The primary focus of *People, Animals, Environment* is the nature and significance of the bond that exists between people and the living environment. Because animals (and, of course, pets) are an integral part of this living environment, much of the journal's contents relate to the human-companion animal bond and its practical applications, e.g., pet therapy. Regular features include a profiles section, which highlights interesting people in the field; an international section, which highlights activities across the world; and a reference section, which includes brief book reviews and abstracts of research articles. Recent issues have contained information on such topics as therapeutic horseback riding, the psychological response to pet loss, and pets in nursing homes. This Delta Society publication is highly recommended for anyone who wants to keep abreast of current issues and news relating to the human-companion animal bond. It also serves as a useful source of information for anyone interested in human-animal relationships.

Pure-bred Dogs: American Kennel gazette. 1889. m. $18. Pat Beresford. Amer. Kennel Club, Inc., 51 Madison Ave., New York, NY 10010. Illus., index, adv. Circ: 47,500. Vol. ends: Dec. Microform: UMI.
Bk. rev: Varies, 100–350 words, signed. *Aud:* Hs.

Although in large part a magazine for the AKC member, breeder, and exhibitor, *Pure-bred Dogs* contains features that could well be of value to the general reader. The informative general articles on pure-bred dog health, grooming, behavior, and showmanship would fit into this category. The breed columns offer species-specific information for the general reader. Since *Pure-bred Dogs* is the official publication of the AKC, a good part of the magazine relates to AKC matters—actions taken by the Board of Directors, dog-and-litter registration statistics, lists of member clubs, lists of champions, and upcoming show information. Prior to 1981, AKC's listing of show, obedience, tracking tests, trials, and field trial awards were published as a part of *Pure-bred Dogs*. Since that time, a new monthly magazine, *The American Kennel Club Show, Obedience and Field Trial Awards* contains these listings. The removal of these listings from *Pure-bred Dogs* has resulted in a more attractive and usable publication.

Tropical Fish Hobbyist. 1952. m. $17.50. Herbert E. Axelrod. T.F.H. Publns., Inc. 211 Sylvania Ave., Neptune City, NJ 07753. Illus., index, adv. Circ: 50,000. Sample. Vol. ends: Dec.
Aud: Hs.

Tropical Fish Hobbyist is not limited to tropical fish but also includes informative articles on plants, amphibians, and invertebrates of potential interest to the aquarium hobbyist. The majority of the authoritative articles, written by experts in the field, deal with the standard aquarium fish, their life histories, breeding habits, and descriptions, with good coverage of new species. The numerous color photographs are superb. Other articles deal with the latest fish-keeping ideas and techniques. Each issue contains exotic tropical fish supplements, which can be easily inserted into the loose-leaf editions of *Exotic Tropical Fishes* and *Exotic Marine Fishes*, both of which are available in most pet stores. This magazine, probably the best known of the tropical fish magazines, is recommended for the hobbyist.

PHOTOGRAPHY

For the Student

James C. Anderson, Photographic Archives, University of Louisville, Louisville, KY 40292

David Horvath, Photographic Archives, University of Louisville, Louisville, KY 40292

Introduction

Interest in photography at all levels (snap-shooting, fine printing, museum collections) continues to increase. That growth is so rapid, however, that the photographic publishing industry, much like that which has grown up around the microcomputer phenomenon, has had trouble in determining the exact nature of its market.

Both old and new magazines reflect a changing emphasis and coverage in response to technological advances in the field of photography. Many now regularly include features on "imaging technologies," a new term that covers recent developments in video and video discs, film, digital imagery, computer graphics, xerography, and other "high-tech" media employed in image production.

Many small, but excellent, regional publications are not included in the selection, but we suggest that the librarian consult with local educators, museums, and galleries in an attempt to secure the best of these.

Basic Periodicals

Ejh: *Modern Photography;* Hs: *American Photographer, Darkroom Photography, Modern Photography.*

Basic Abstracts and Indexes

Art Index, Magazine Index.

For the Student

Afterimage. 1972. 9/yr. $25. Nathan Lyons. Visual Studies Workshop, 31 Prince St., Rochester, NY 14607. Illus., index. Circ: 4,500. Sample. Vol. ends: May. Microfilm: UMI. *Bk. rev:* 3–5, 1,500 words; 10 short, signed. *Aud:* Hs.

This tabloid-size publication has, since its founding, been the best source of news affecting the photographic community. It carries up-to-date listings of exhibitions, workshops, conferences, job openings and grants, as well as advance notices of deadlines for submission of work to shows and granting agencies. In addition, it features extended articles on a broad range of historical, critical, and aesthetic issues. These articles are often the work of some of the best of contemporary scholars and critics. Reviews of books and journals are many and brief, with new publications noted in a "Sources" column. It also publishes extensive, signed reviews of contemporary exhibitions. A publication with a very broad appeal, and a must for schools with programs in photography.

American Photographer. 1978. m. $19.90. Sean Callahan. CBS Publns., 1515 Broadway, New York, NY 10036. Illus., adv. Circ: 292,000. Sample. Vol. ends: Dec.
Indexed: MgI. *Bk. rev:* 1–3, 500 words, signed. *Aud:* Hs.

This photography magazine has maintained its quality since its beginnings. Its primary emphasis is on the advanced amateur or professional photographer, but the magazine would be useful to any reader whose interests in photography go beyond the nuts-and-bolts approach of other popular photography magazines such as *Modern Photography, Petersen's,* and *Popular Photography.* While technique and hardware are covered to some extent, the magazine regularly features several well-written pieces, which include profiles and portfolios of various working photographers representing fine art, commercial, and photojournalist perspectives. This broad-based periodical reflects a growing sophistication and interest in the field of photography.

Aperture. 1952. q. $32. Mark Holburn. Aperture, Elm St., Millerton, NY 12546. Illus., adv. Circ: 13,000. Sample. Vol. ends. Nov.
Indexed: ArtI. *Bk. rev:* 1, extended, signed. *Aud:* Hs.

Still the best of the U.S. publications devoted to photography. Emphasis is on fine art photography, but as the distinctions between "art" and "documentary" photography have blurred, its coverage has broadened. Founded as an important "little magazine" in the 1950s, it is now a respected journal with a growing general readership. Fine reproduction has always been its hallmark, and many issues now include color. Text varies from simple poems accompanying reproductions to extended interpretive essays by an impressive list of contributors.

Close-Up. q. $25. Constance Sullivan. Corporate Communications Group, Polaroid Corp., 459 Technology Sq., Cambridge, MA 02139. Illus. Sample. Vol. ends. Fall.

Aud: Hs.

Polaroid Corporation formerly offered this excellent magazine free to "those interested in Polaroid instant photography." Consistently fine reproduction and features on the best of contemporary fine art and documentary photographers, however, brought a much broader readership and resulted in the change to a subscription publication. Polaroid has always offered assistance and encouragement to a broad range of artists and photographers wishing to make use of its instant photography products. This publication features their work in large format reproductions, which are some of the best in a U.S. photography magazine. Accompanying the work are critical and interpretive articles by scholars, critics, poets, novelists, and journalists. As in most art publications, the emphasis is on the picture and the artist, with little discussion of equipment or technique. This is an excellent, visually exciting look at contemporary photography for both the connoisseur and the novice.

Creative Camera. 1963. m. $65. Colin Osman. Coo Press, Ltd., 19 Doughty St., London WC1N 2PT, England. Illus., adv. Circ: 7,500. Vol. ends: Dec.

Bk. rev: 10–12, 100 words. *Aud:* Hs.

Now that the Swiss journal *Camera* has ceased publication, *Creative Camera* is an especially important source of news, reviews, and discussions of the international photography scene. The emphasis is British, but there is broad coverage of exhibitions and of works otherwise not seen by U.S. readers. Broad in coverage, both fine art and documentary photography are featured, often in whole issues devoted to a single theme. Some features now include color. Each issue includes numerous brief reviews of exhibitions and books, in addition to extended essays on featured photographers or subjects. Of consistently high quality, it is one of the most respected photography journals.

Darkroom Photography. 1979. 8/yr. $18. Richard Senti. PMS Publg. Co., One Halide Plaza, Suite 600, San Francisco, CA 94102. Illus., adv. Circ: 80,000. Sample. Vol. ends: No. 8.

Aud: Hs.

This publication is directed to the darkroom side of photography; it is concerned with what happens after the shutter clicks. This includes the developing of the film, the printing of the pictures, and everything else involved after the photograph is taken. The design and flavor is similar to *Petersen's* and would make a good companion title. Regular features include darkroom equipment tests and specifications as well as longer pieces on "Masters of Photography" featuring the work of photographers who are well known for their darkroom skills.

Exposure. 1963. q. $25. David L. Jacobs & Jan Z. Grover. Soc. for Photographic Education, P.O. Box 1651, F.D.R. Station, New York, NY 10150. Illus., adv. Vol. ends: Winter.

Bk. rev: Several, length varies. *Aud:* Hs.

Begun in 1963 as a journal for the teacher-members of the Society for Photographic Education, *Exposure* is an excellent publication whose emphasis is on criticism, interpretation aesthetics, theory, and history, rather than teaching technique. Each issue features well-printed black-and-white and color reproductions, which accompany articles covering a broad range of issues, topics, and photographers. The writing is always top-notch and often discusses work or issues which are more avant-garde or experimental than what is found in the general-circulation art journals. Each issue also carries news, reviews, reports from the society, and a list of job openings.

Image: journal of photography and motion pictures of the International Museum of Photography at George Eastman House. 1952. q. Membership. Intl. Museum of Photography at George Eastman House, 900 East Ave., Rochester, NY 14607. Illus. Circ: 3,500. Sample.

Indexed: ArtI. *Aud:* Hs.

Image's three or four articles per issue are always well written, cover all areas of the history of photography and film, and are usually based on the vast holdings in the museum's collections. Occasional articles deal with care and preservation of historical photographs. Deserves a far wider audience than the very limited membership of the museum.

Journal of American Photography. s-a. Free to active customers. David Gremp. Calumet Photographic, Inc., 890 Supreme Dr., Bensenville, IL 60106. Illus., adv. Circ: 45,000.

Aud: Hs.

Intended by Calumet to be an educational benefit for its customers, libraries should definitely request to be added to the mailing list. This excellent journal contains well-written, varied, and interesting articles by such fine writers as A. D. Coleman, Alan Teller, Richard Kirstel, and John Alderson. Something of interest for a wide range of audiences with a blend of technical, critical, and historical perspectives. In addition, it is well designed and printed. All libraries should attempt to take advantage of this terrific bargain.

Modern Photography. 1937. m. $13.98. Julia Scully. ABC Leisure Magazines, 825 Seventh Ave., New York, NY 10019. Illus., adv. Circ: 685,000. Microform: UMI.

Bk. rev: 4–6, 250 words, signed. *Aud:* Ejh, Hs.

Both *Modern Photography* and *Popular Photography* appeal to the millions of amateur photographers in this country with dozens of articles and departments on equipment, gadgets, and tips for better pictures. The design of the magazine is appropriately busy with lots of inserts. The excellent writing of Julia Scully and Andy Grundberg and its sheer popularity make it a first choice for the general collection.

News Photographer (Formerly: *National Press Photographer*). 1946. $18. James R. Gordon. Natl. Press Photographers Assn., P.O. Box 1146, Durham, NC 27702. Illus., adv. Circ: 8,000.

Aud: Hs.

This title is particularly important for the growing number of libraries that must service the needs of communication and media interests, including traditional photojournalism. Although directed primarily to professional photojournalists and members of the National Press Photographers Association, this magazine is really about visual communication in general and all the issues involved in modern news coverage. Three to five well-written feature stories and about a dozen departments cover a variety of subjects from ethics to technique. Interested libraries should also check into the regional publications of the NPPA which are also quite good.

Petersen's Photographic Magazine. 1971. m. $13.94. Karen Geller-Shinn. Petersen's Publg. Co., 8490 Sunset Blvd., Los Angeles, CA 90069. Illus., index, adv. Circ: 276,000. Sample. Vol. ends: Apr.

Indexed: MgI, RG. *Aud:* Ejh, Hs.

Petersen's is the *Popular Mechanics* of photography magazines and it is edited as the "how-to" magazine for photography enthusiasts. It differs from *Modern Photography* and *Popular Photography* in that many of its how-to articles are directed to the reader who really wants to build a darkroom or assemble a studio set-up. It manages to include 20 to 25 articles and departments of varying content while still retaining a high degree of freshness and surprisingly little repetition. The approach covers almost all aspects of photographic technique from the camera to the darkroom to display. While it is very useful for the "handy" photographer, the publication is also of interest to those who cannot or will not swing a hammer.

Photographer's Forum: journal of college photography. 1978. q. $12. Glenn R. Serbin. Serbin Communications, Inc., 614 Santa Barbara St., Santa Barbara, CA 93101. Illus., adv. Circ: 20,000.

Bk. rev: 1, 2 pages; several brief in "Notes" column. *Aud:* Hs.

A very slickly produced and printed journal aimed at the "young photographer." Each issue features several portfolios of work by university students. It also includes lengthy interviews with important teachers or artists. "School Profile" columns in each issue feature selected university photography departments, their faculty, facilities, and students. Much better than a "student magazine" and should be enjoyed by a general readership.

Photo Technique International (English edition of: *Photo Tecknik International*). 1954. q. $16. Hildrun Karpf. Verlag Photo Technik Intl., Rupert-Mayer Strasse 45, D-8000 Munich 70, Fed. Rep. of Germany (U.S. offices: Ray Rickles & Co., 699 Carriage Dr. N.E., Atlanta, GA 30328). Illus., adv. Circ: 51,500.

Aud: Hs.

Included earlier because it was the only English-language magazine devoted to large-format photography, but now worth considering because of the range of its coverage. It includes articles on contemporary art photography; photographic history; and scientific, technical, and advertising photography. It also covers equipment and technique, mostly large format. Each article is profusely illustrated with beautifully reproduced illustrations, most in color and on heavy coated paper.

Popular Photography. 1937. m. $13.97. Arthur Goldsmith. Ziff-Davis Publg. Co., One Park Ave., New York, NY 10016. Illus., adv. Circ: 865,000. Sample. Vol. ends: Dec. Microform: B&H, UMI.

Indexed: RG. *Aud:* Ejh, Hs.

One of the three major photography magazines in the United States (with *Modern Photography* and *Petersen's*) devoted largely to the technique and equipment of photography rather than interpretation and critical evaluation. It is only slightly different from *Modern Photography* in that it contains a few more articles of a nuts-and-bolts nature. Like *Modern Photography*, the magazine functions as an indispensable buyers' guide for all types of photographic equipment. Its articles and departments are of interest to both amateurs and professionals and include pieces on film and video. In addition to regular features, there are specialty columns on such various topics as large format, camera repair, and so on. Books are covered in an occasional extended review. Like *Modern Photography* and *Petersen's*, this title is a first choice for any general collection.

Untitled. 1972. q. $32 (Membership). Friends of Photography, P.O. Box 500, Carmel, CA 93921. Illus. Circ: 13,000.

Aud: Hs.

The Friends of Photography is a nonprofit organization whose aim is to promote fine photography. *Untitled*, their quarterly journal, is exquisitely printed, and features in each issue an in-depth, critical or interpretive essay on a single theme or photographer. Most issues now also contain 30 to 60 illustrations. These reproductions are often from plates made by new laser scanning techniques, which produce reproductions with the appearance of original prints. Subscribers to the journal also receive a monthly newsletter which contains news, and brief reviews of books, and exhibitions. The society membership price is a real bargain, since single copies of the journal are sold for from $15 to $20. Many back issues remain in print and are worth securing.

Views: journal of photography in New England. q. Membership (Institutions, $35). Susan E. Cohen & William S. Johnson. Photographic Resource Center, Boston Univ., 1019 Commonwealth Ave., Boston, MA 02215. Illus., adv. Sample. Vol. ends: Fall.

Bk. rev: 1, 2,000 words; 8–10, 500 words. *Aud:* Hs.

Although professing to be merely a regional publication, this fine tabloid-format journal from Boston is now one of the better sources of insightful writing about photography as both an element in and mirror of contemporary society. Historical, critical, and interpretive articles, by an impressive list of contributors, are included in each issue. At least one major New England museum photography collection (some of the finest in the world) is profiled. There are extended reviews of contemporary exhibitions (two to three), an exhaustive book review, many brief (500-word) reviews and a long list of new and worthy books received. Columns include an editorial, news, and a "Phone Lines" feature that briefly discusses items of interest to the photographic community. A well-written, well-illustrated, first-class production.

Zoom. 1969. 5/yr. $30. Namial Paolo. Publicness, 2, rue du Faubourg Poissonnière, 75010 Paris, France. Illus., index, adv. Circ: 45,000.

Aud: Hs.

Beautiful reproductions, in a very large (33 × 24 cm.) format make this one of the most attractive art magazines available. Each issue features articles on approximately ten photographers or subjects, each profusely illustrated, most often in color. Subjects include fine art photography, illustration and design and portrait photography, as well as occasional features on the history of photography. History articles are often on early color photography and feature many never-before-seen illustrations. Much like the now-dead and lamented *Picture* magazine in appearance. Such a sensual and intellectual delight is quite a bargain at $30.00.

POLITICAL SCIENCE

For the Student/For the Professional

Henry E. York, Social Sciences Librarian, Cleveland State University, Cleveland, OH 44115

Introduction

As commonly understood, political science is the discipline in which government, politics, and the state are studied. From this nucleus, which has its roots in classical Greece, political science has developed a diverse array of subdisciplines including political theory, history of political thought, politics or political processes, public policy analysis, public administration, comparative political studies, and international relations. In addition to this fragmentation, political science has become increasingly interdisciplinary as it draws upon other social sciences, especially sociology and psychology. It also has intrinsic ties with history as a supplier of source material.

Other titles dealing with politics or current events at a popular level can be found in the News and Opinion Section. This list is essentially a selection of basic, core titles in political science suitable for a school library. The entries tend to focus on international concerns.

Basic Periodicals

Hs: *Current History, Political Science Quarterly.*

For the Student

Congressional Digest. 1921. 10/yr. $22. John E. Shields. Congressional Digest Corp., 3231 P St. N. W., Washington, DC 20007. Index. Vol. ends: Dec. Microform: Pub.

Indexed: PAIS, RG. *Aud:* Hs.

The masthead states that it is "an independent monthly featuring controversies in Congress, pro and con, not an official organ, not controlled by any party, interest, class, or sect," and it is as stated. Each number focuses on one issue currently before Congress. The issue is examined in detail: history, political implications, legal implications, etc. This is followed by a section in which the pros and cons are argued by debaters involved with the subject. An equal number of debaters (four to six) from each side are given equal space. As a result of this format many, though not all, sides are presented. Issues vary in length from 25 to 35 pages. Especially useful for high school libraries.

Current History: a world affairs journal. 1914. 9/yr. $21. Carol L. Thompson. Current History, Inc., 4225 Main St., Philadelphia, PA 19127. Illus., index. Circ: 23,847. Sample. Vol. ends: Dec. Microform: UMI.

Indexed: PAIS, RG. *Bk. rev:* 4–8, 100–150 words, signed. *Aud:* Hs.

An international affairs journal with a style and appeal about midway between the news magazine and the journal of scholarly commentary such as *Foreign Affairs*. Each issue is devoted to one area or country with about eight short articles covering varying topics. Recent issues have covered Central America, Japan, and the Soviet Union. The authors are generally U.S. academics but the writing style is nontechnical, focusing on summarizing and commenting on the most important aspects of recent events. In addition to the articles, there is a most useful "Month in Review" section giving country-by-country daily chronologies of important events.

The Department of State Bulletin. 1939. m. $23. U.S. Dept. of State. Subs. to: Supt. of Docs., U.S. Govt. Printing Office, Washington, DC 20402. Illus., index. Circ: 10,000. Sample. Vol. ends: Dec. Microform: MCA.

Indexed: PAIS, RG. *Aud:* Hs.

Changed from a weekly to a monthly in 1978. It is "the official record of U.S. foreign policy," containing major addresses and news conferences of the Secretary of State and the President, interviews with State Department officials, congressional testimony by State Department officials, selected press releases from government agencies concerned with foreign policy, and the text of treaties to which the United States has become a party. The best way available for following "official" government thinking and actions in foreign affairs, it is a necessity for any library where there is an interest in foreign affairs. Each issue is divided topically (i.e., economics, human rights, arms control, etc.) and geographically, with a chronology of important U.S. foreign policy events, index, and ordering information for State Department and U.N. Mission press releases.

Foreign Affairs. 1922. 5/yr. $25. William G. Hylard. Council on Foreign Relations, Inc., 58 E. 68th St., New York, NY

10021. Illus., index, adv. Circ: 82,000. Sample. Vol. ends: Summer. Microform: B&H, MIM, UMI.

Indexed: PAIS, RG, SocSc. *Bk. rev:* 80–90, 125–400 words. *Aud:* Hs.

Perhaps the best known journal of world affairs, this periodical reaches an audience which is both large and elite, including many diplomats, government officials, policy analysts and scholars. The parent is the Council on Foreign Relations, a middle-of-the-road organization, which seeks to influence the shaping of the U.S. foreign policy debate with articles that represent "a broad hospitality of divergent ideas" rather than "by identifying with one school." Each issue contains 10 to 12 articles by scholars, government officials or journalists dealing with foreign policy topics, usually with policy prescriptions offered. This journal provides very comprehensive book-review coverage for titles in international relations. "Source Materials," a section in each issue, is a subject listing over 100 U.S. and international documents of topical interest. *Foreign Affairs*, an essential title in the study of international relations, is commonly considered the preeminent foreign-policy journal.

Foreign Policy. 1970. q. $25 (Individuals, $17). Charles W. Maynes. Carnegie Endowment for International Peace, 11 Dupont Circle N.W., Washington, DC 20036. Index, adv. Circ: 26,000. Sample. Microform: UMI.

Indexed: SocSc. *Aud:* Hs.

Published by the Carnegie Endowment for International Peace, this quarterly review of foreign policy has become an important factor in influencing debate on current foreign policy decisions. It is considered essential reading by many government officials, educators, and members of the press. A typical issue contains about a dozen articles written by academics, foreign service officers, or members of various research or special interest groups. Each issue has a lively "Letters to the Editor" section with lengthy reactions to articles previously published with accompanying responses by the authors. A basic title for all who are interested in U.S. foreign policy.

Political Science Quarterly. 1886. q. $26 (Individuals, $21). Demetrios Caraley. Academy of Political Science, 2852 Broadway, New York, NY 10025. Index, adv. Circ: 12,000. Sample. Vol. ends: Winter. Refereed. Microform: UMI.

Indexed: PAIS, SocSc. *Bk. rev:* 30–40, 600 words, signed. *Aud:* Hs.

The journal of the Academy of Political Science, *Political Science Quarterly* is a "nonpartisan journal devoted to the study of contemporary and historical aspects of government, politics, and public affairs," published continuously since 1886. A typical issue contains six or seven articles by U.S. professors reflecting different points of view on a wide range of topics. The emphasis, however, is on United States affairs. A strong feature is the book-review section covering about 30 titles in each issue. These appear in a relatively timely fashion, six months to a year after publication, and are critical and evaluative in assessing the books reviewed.

Problems of Communism. 1952. bi-m. $16. Paul A. Smith, Jr. U.S. Information Agency, 301 Fourth St. S.W., Washington, DC 20547. Illus., index. Circ: 34,000. Microform: B&H, MIM, UMI.

Indexed: IGov, PAIS, SocSc. *Bk. rev:* 5, 4 pages, signed. *Aud:* Hs.

The objective of this U.S. Information Agency publication is to provide "analyses and significant information about the contemporary affairs of the Soviet Union, China, and comparable states and political movements." Typical issues contain four articles covering current or critical situations. Most of them deal with internal developments in Communist countries or with Soviet foreign policy. Dissidents in Czechoslovakia, youths in China, and Muslims in the Soviet Union have been the subjects of recent studies. The authors are usually United States or European academics or government or diplomatic officials. These include many who have worked in the areas discussed, and defectors, giving the articles a eyewitness perspective. The periodical has extensive photographs of Communist societies and leaders. The book review essays cover several related titles dealing with such topics as Eurocommunism or Communism in a particular country.

State Government: the journal of state affairs. 1930. q. $20. L. Edward Purcell. The Council of State Governments, P.O. Box 11910, Lexington, KY 40578. Index. Circ: 6,000. Sample. Vol. ends: Dec. Microform: UMI.

Indexed: PAIS, SocSc. *Aud:* Hs.

This journal is published by the Council of State Governments, an agency created and supported by state governments in the United States. It focuses on major aspects of state programs, problems, and attempted and proposed solutions covering all aspects of governmental activity. The emphasis is on pragmatic rather than theoretical considerations. The authors are either academics or state government officials. A typical issue contains five articles of from two to ten pages. Occasional issues will be devoted to a specific topic such as the power of governors or water and energy.

For the Professional

Intercom: a guide to discussion, study and resources. 1959. $18. Charles O. Roebuck. Global Perspectives in Education, Inc., 218 E. 18th St., New York, NY 10003. Illus. Circ: 1,750. Sample. Microform: UMI.

Indexed: CIJE. *Aud:* Pr.

Published by the Center for Global Perspectives, a "nonpartisan citizens' effort building on American democratic traditions to help prepare our youth for the challenges of national citizenship in a global age." A typical issue contains seven to nine short articles attempting to provide educators with materials written from a global perspective. Such topics as immigration, the energy crisis and customs in various countries, as well as folklore and mythology, are covered. Each issue includes an introduction and suggested discussion guides and lesson formats facilitating the incorporation of material into existing courses. Recommended for high school social studies classes.

U.N. Chronicle. 1964. $14. Subs. to: Unipub, P.O. Box 433, Murray Hill Sta., New York, N.Y. 10016. Illus. Microform: UMI.

Indexed: AbrRG, RG. *Aud:* Pr.

A running record of activities of the United Nations, this is a basic title for all libraries—particularly as it is indexed in *Readers' Guide* (along with *Courier*). Each issue is divided into three main sections: political and security, economic and social, legal—all under the heading, "Record of the Month." There are also articles and reports, followed by a section of notes, which includes a selected list of documents. Not the type of magazine one is likely to read from cover to cover, but an invaluable reference aid.

PSYCHOLOGY

For the Student/For the Professional

Joseph J. Accardi, Director, Janesville Public Library, 316 S. Main St., Janesville, WI 53545

Introduction

There are more than 550 journals and other publications listed in *Ulrich's International Periodical Directory* under the heading of Psychology. The number of research articles and scientific studies of the mind and of behavior published each year is staggering and they continue to multiply. Two of the journals listed here are best suited to teachers; the third is a general title appropriate for high school students.

Basic Periodical

Hs: *Psychology Today.*

For the Student

Psychology Today. 1967. m. $15.99. Christopher Cory. Ziff-Davis Publg. Co., One Park Ave., New York, NY 10016. Illus., index, adv. Circ: 850,000. Sample. Microform: B&H, MIM, UMI.

Indexed: MgI, RG. *Bk. rev:* 3–4, essays, signed. *Aud:* Hs.

The basic popular psychology journal for any library, *Psychology Today* bridges the gap between the professional researcher/practitioner and the layperson. Clearly written and profusely illustrated articles report on current trends, important personalities, historical developments, surveys, and the latest research findings in the behavioral sciences. It is the single best source of information in the field of social science available to the general public and attempts to achieve its goal of increasing our understanding of human behavior, albeit in a popular way. Of particular interest to collection developers are the end-of-the-year "best bets" in the literature of behavioral sciences for the general public. Highly recommended for most libraries.

For the Professional

Journal of School Psychology. 1963. q. $55 (Individuals, $60). Thomas Oakland. Human Sciences Press, 72 Fifth Ave.,

New York, NY 10011. Index, adv. Circ: 2,000. Sample. Microform: UMI.

Indexed: CIJE, EdI, ExChAb. *Bk. rev:* 6–8, essays, signed. *Aud:* Pr.

This is a magazine of, by, and for school psychologists that was established by a corporation of independent teachers and psychologists interested in professional development of school psychology. It is devoted to publishing articles of current professional interest on research, opinion, and practice in school psychology. Ten to twelve articles per issue range from I.Q. testing to behavior modification in the classroom to studies of training programs in the field. Articles are clearly written and well documented. The book review section also covers reviews of the latest testing instruments for school psychologists, while a new "Software Review Section" encourages the open exchange of information on microcomputer software programs. A recommended choice for teachers and counselors at any level in education.

Psychology in the Schools. 1964. q. $55. Gerald B. Fuller. Clinical Psychology Publg. Co., 4 Conant Sq., Brandon, VT 05733. Index, adv. Circ: 2,500. Sample. Microform: MIM, UMI.

Indexed: EdI. *Bk. rev:* 4–5, brief, signed. *Aud:* Pr.

Primarily directed toward practicing school psychologists, this quarterly presents about 20 or so articles per issue devoted to research, opinion, and practice. The three- to six-page pieces range in appeal from those that deal with theoretical and other problems of the school psychologist to those directed to teachers, counselors, administrators, and personnel directors in schools, colleges, and similar organizations. Though similar in content to *Journal of School Psychology*, it is somewhat more empirically oriented. A good second choice for larger collections.

RELIGION

For the Student/For the Professional

James L. Hodson, Temple University Library, Philadelphia, PA 19122

Wayne C. Maxson, Frostburg State College Library, Frostburg, MD 21532

Introduction

The titles listed below have been selected to cover a range of religious viewpoints and confessional heritages. It has been impossible, however, to include every title judged to be important to some library; estimates vary, but there are perhaps as many as 3,000 religious titles currently being produced in the United States. Librarians in parochial schools may wish to expand their collection beyond these suggestions.

Basic Periodicals

Hs: *Christian Century, Commonweal.*

For the Student

Alive! For Young Teens. 1969. m. $14.50. Michael Dixon. Christian Board of Publn., P.O. Box 179, St. Louis, MO 63166. Illus. Circ: 63,000. Vol. ends: Aug.

Aud: Hs.

A leisure reading publication with a mainline Protestant perspective. There are 30 glossy pages of articles, stories, cartoons, puzzles, and poems, plus an inspirational poster in a single topic issue. Much of the material is contributed by teenagers. Illustrations of teens are multi-racial. This title espouses a deep commitment to Christian faith and tradition without being moralistic or judgmental. Although the style is lively, with an inclination toward hi-lo, the concerns of this title are heavy. For example, a recent issue dealt with death. The subtitle suggests that *Alive!* is for young teens, ages 12–16; however, it also would be very appropriate for older teens. (L.K.W.)

America. 1909. w. $25. George W. Hunt. America Press, Inc., 106 W. 56th St., New York, NY 10019. Illus., index, adv. Circ: 35,000. Microform: UMI.

Indexed: RG. *Bk. rev:* 3–5, 1,500 words, signed. *Aud:* Hs.

A journal sponsored by Jesuits devoted to discussion of contemporary social, ethical, and political questions. The writers are not always recognizably Catholic, and there is a wide spectrum of ideas and topics covered. Even though its connections with Catholicism are evident, the journal shows no strong religious bias; it frequently discusses the ecumenical movement as well as clearly inter-religious questions. (W.C.M.)

Christian Century. 1884. w. $24. James M. Wall. Christian Century Foundation, 407 E. Dearborn St., Chicago, IL 60605. Subs. to: 5615 W. Cernak Rd., Cicero, IL 60650. Illus., index, adv. Circ: 35,500. Microform: UMI.

Indexed: RG. *Bk. rev:* 4–5, 250–500 words, signed. *Aud:* Hs.

For years a moderate to liberal journal of predominently Protestant Christian opinion, it has become self consciously a voice of responsible liberal religious views, inclusive of Christian as well as non-Christian. Articles cover major Christian concerns and newsworthy developments within the religious world and are written for the educated layperson and clergy. (W.C.M.)

Christianity Today. 1956. bi-w. $21. Harold L. Myra, 465 Gundersen Dr., Carol Steam, IL 60188. Subs. to: P.O. Box 1915, Marion, OH 45305. Illus., adv. Circ: 185,000. Microform: UMI.

Indexed: RG. *Bk. rev:* 4–5, 250–500 words. *Aud:* Hs.

A conservative Protestant Christian journal of faith and opinion with a strong biblical flavor, covering theological, social, and political issues. Once geared to the intellectual conservative, both the format and writing have changed over the years to include a wider, more general audience. (W.C.M.)

Commonweal. bi-w. $28. Peter Steinfels. Commonweal Publg. Co., Inc., 232 Madison Ave., New York, NY 10016. Illus., adv. Circ: 20,000. Microform: UMI.

Indexed: BoRv, BoRvI, RG. *Bk. rev:* 8–10, 400–500 words, signed. *Aud:* Hs.

At first glance one may not realize that this is a Catholic periodical, so heavily is it engaged in a nonsectarian liberal discussion and presentation of "Public Affairs, Literature and the Arts," to quote the editors. Many authors are non-Catholic, but editorial comment and assumption, as well as some articles, reveal its religious position. The articles and film and book reviews are all sparkling and tend toward the controversial. Medium to large public libraries, and academic ones, ought to consider this seriously.

The Friend. 1971. 11/yr. $7. Church of Jesus Christ of Latter-Day Saints, 50 E. North Temple, Salt Lake City, UT 84150. Illus. Circ: 210,000. Vol. ends: Dec.

Aud: Ejh.

Directed to the 7–11 age group, this includes stories and features, poetry, music, and things to make and do. Although a few articles are concerned with Mormon history and personalities, the magazine offers general reading with an emphasis on the themes of love and friendship. It is well designed, and the quality of the writing and illustrations is better than that of some popular children's magazines. (L.K.O.)

The Humanist. 1941. bi-m. $18. Lloyd L. Morain. Amer. Humanist Assn., 7 Harwood Dr., P.O. Box 146, Amherst, NY 14226. Illus., adv. Circ: 17,000. Microform: UMI.

Indexed: HumI, PAIS. *Bk. rev:* 3–6, 1,000 words, signed. *Aud:* Hs.

Probably the best known of the several humanist journals in the United States, *The Humanist* focuses on such social and moral concerns as pornography, overpopulation, nuclear disarmament, feminism, creationism, and school prayer from the humanist viewpoint. Always concerned with the rights of the individual, it is not afraid of controversy. Even though one may not agree with humanism, one is likely to find its articles readable and thought-provoking. (J.H.)

Junior Trails. 1920. q. $3.60. Charles W. Ford. General Council of the Assemblies of God, 1445 Boonville Ave., Springfield, MO 65802. Circ: 106,653.

Aud: Ejh.

Published quarterly in four-page weekly parts, this take-home paper is intended for children ages 9–12. It includes articles and fiction supported by adequate color illustrations. The writing style is fair, and the themes always emphasize some phase of Christian living. (L.K.O.)

Keeping Posted. 1955. 7/yr. $5. Aron Hirt-Manheimer. Union of Amer. Hebrew Congregations, 838 Fifth Ave., New York, NY 10021. Illus. Circ: 23,000. Vol. ends: Apr.

Aud: Hs.

Each issue of about 20 pages explores a theme such as Jewish mysticism, the *Shtetl* (a village culture of eastern Europe), the new Jewish woman, Jews in sports, drug use, and Holocaust survivors. Articles are by experts who can also write in an informative, popular style. Often interviews with individuals who participated in the events being analyzed are featured. Stunning black-and-white photographs and artwork are the hallmarks of this publication. Although sponsored by the Reformed, or liberal, branch of Judaism, denominational bias seems lacking. An excellent resource. (L.K.W.)

Vibrant Life. See Health and Medicine/For the Student Section.

U. S. Catholic. 1963. m. $12. Mark J. Brummel. Claretian Publns., 221 W. Madison St., Chicago, IL 60606. Illus., adv. Circ: 78,721. Sample.

Indexed: RG. *Aud:* Hs.

Published with ecclesiastical approval by the Claretian Fathers and Brothers, this illustrated monthly is designed for Catholics interested in discussion about issues facing them in their day-to-day lives. The articles and stories geared to the popular reader deal with Catholics as members of the church and a faith. (W.C.M.)

Wee Wisdom. 1893. 10/yr. $5.00. Verle Bell. Unity School of Christianity, Unity Village, MO 64065. Illus. Circ: 121,515. Sample. Vol. ends: Aug/Sept.

Aud: Ejh.

Although the magazine's purpose is "to share character-building ideas" and it is published by a religious organization, the writing style is not preachy. It is evident, however, that the periodical is "devoted to spreading the truth of practical Christianity." Each issue includes stories, poems, things to make and do, letters to and from the editor, and contributions from readers. Full color is used on the two covers and touches of color are added to predominantly black-and-white illustrations complementing the text. The outside cover can be removed and folds out to make a wall calendar for the month. Intended for children ages 6–12, it is more likely to be of interest to the lower age group because of the simple vocabulary and illustrations depicting younger children. Available in braille. (L.K.O.)

Yoga Journal: the magazine for conscious living. 1975. bi-m. $13.50. Stephan Bodian. California Yoga Teachers Assn., 2054 University Ave., No. 601, Berkeley, CA 94704. Illus., adv. Circ: 25,000. Microform: B&H.

Bk. rev: 2–3, 120–750 words, signed. *Aud:* Hs.

This journal concentrates on various approaches to personal and spiritual development, such as hatha yoga, holistic healing, transpersonal psychology, movement, bodywork, the martial arts, meditation and both Eastern and Western spirituality. Its contributors come from many fields, including yoga teachers, therapists, healers, psychics, and others. Articles focus upon contemporary "new age" people and traditions primarily, but not exclusively, in the United States. The teachings of many different traditions are covered, and none is given priority. For libraries seeking at least one "alternative religion" this would be a good choice. (J.H.)

Youth Update (Yup). 1980. m. $6. Carol Ann Munchel. St. Anthony Messenger Press, Cincinnati, OH 45210. Illus. Circ: 63,000. Vol. ends: Dec.

Aud: Ejh. Hs.

A four-page newsletter publication for Roman Catholics of high school age and more mature junior high schoolers. The average reader is seen as a 15-year-old with a C+ scholastic standing. A typical issue features an essay (for example, "Summer Blahs" or "Vatican II") plus questions for discussion submitted by members of a teenaged advisory board. This crisply written and edited title is a staple in religious classes and groups on a parish level. It applies the teaching of the gospel to modern problems and situations. (L.K.W.)

For the Professional

Catholic Library World. See Library Periodicals/For the Professional Section.

Religious Education: a platform for the free discussion of issues in the field of religion and their bearing on education. 1906. q. $35. John Westerhoff, III. Religious Education Assn., 409 Prospect St., New Haven, CT 06510. Index, adv. Circ: 5,050. Microform: UMI.

Bk. rev: 10, 700–900 words, signed. *Aud:* Pr.

Just as the long subtitle indicates, this journal attempts to be a platform for the discussion of issues in religious education. It is the product of an interfaith organization of Protestants, Catholics, Jews, Orthodox, and other denominations. Written largely by religious educators or scholars of education, this journal discusses religious education in public schools and curriculums for religious education, both from a practical and theoretical position. A must for religious educators. (J.H.)

Today's Catholic Teacher. See Education/For the Professional Section.

SOCIOLOGY

For the Student

See also Cultural-Social Studies; and Women Sections.

Peter B. Allison, Social Science Bibliographer, Elmer Holmes Bobst Library, New York University, 70 Washington Sq. S., New York, NY 10012

Introduction

The journals reviewed here do not fully encompass sociology, nor are all the titles reviewed here devoted exclusively to sociology. Sociologists interested in crime and criminal behavior, law, and society, or special groups such as women are apt to publish their findings in interdisciplinary journals that are reviewed here in the sections devoted to these themes. Similarly, the ethnic studies titles and many of the Marxist and European sociology journals covered in this section attract historians as well as sociologists.

Beyond the notion of the primacy of social experience, very little unites sociologists. Because many practitioners believe they are doing something at least analogous to natural science, U.S. sociologists in particular are remarkably contentious regarding questions of method and frequently seem devoid of interest in, or respect for, work that proceeds from different assumptions. While the U.S. sociological establishment upholds the scientific goal of value-neutral social investigation, numerous journals reviewed here explicitly reject such an aspiration (which many would call a pretension) in the name of humanism, relevance, or commitment to social change. All this makes sociological book reviewing a mine field for the unwary librarian.

Basic Periodicals

Hs: *Society*.

For the Student

American Behavioral Scientist. 1957. bi-m. $71 (Individuals, $21). Ed. bd. Sage Publns. Inc., 275 S. Beverly Dr., Beverly Hills, CA 90212. Adv. Vol. ends: July/Aug. Microform: UMI.

Indexed: PAIS, SocSc. *Aud:* Hs.

This is a genuinely interdisciplinary journal. Each issue highlights a particular trend in contemporary behavioral science research. Particular emphasis appears to be given to topics with clear societal applications. Guest editors are chosen for each issue. They and many of the individual contributors are frequently leading researchers in the area being covered. Many articles provide valuable summaries of the state of research in their field. Recently, covered topics have included health psychology, the organization of mental health services, disability, negotiation, and household refuse analysis. This is a particularly useful journal for librarians and others who seek an authoritative introduction to current research areas in sociology and behaviorally oriented research in psychology, economics, and applied anthropology.

Family Planning Perspectives. 1969. bi-m. $18.50. Richard Lincoln. Alan Guttmacher Inst., 360 Park Ave. S., New York, NY 10010. Index, adv. Circ: 15,000. Vol. ends: Nov/Dec. Microform: UMI.

Indexed: PAIS. *Bk. rev:* 1-3, 500–1,000 words, signed. *Aud:* Hs.

This is the place to look for accurate, authoritative, yet readable material and statistics on all aspects of human fertility and reproductive behavior. Attitudes and behavior are displayed in easy to grasp tables and charts. International developments are unfortunately not covered in the same depth as U.S. policy and practice. Most articles are followed by lists of key references. A digest section summarizes new scientific developments related to contraception, sterilization, abortion, and healthy childbirth.

Journal of Social Issues. 1944. q. $65 (Individuals, $25). George Levinger. Plenum Publg. Corp., 233 Spring St., New York, NY 10013. Index, adv. Circ: 7,500. Vol. ends: Winter. Microform: UMI.

Indexed: SocSc. *Aud:* Hs.

This journal is the organ of the Society for the Psychological Study of Social Issues. Each issue addresses a different topic and has one or more special issue editors. The articles seem to be revised conference papers. Topics often relate to issues that have had considerable media exposure. Racism and sexism in Black women's lives, images of nuclear war, social support networks, rape, and the child witness have been the subjects of recent issues.

Population Bulletin. 1945. q. $40 (Free to members). Jean van der Tak. Population Reference Bureau, Inc., 2213 M Street NW, Washington, DC 20037. Illus. Circ: 8,500. Microform: UMI.

Indexed: PAIS, SocSc. *Aud:* Hs.

Primarily a 32- to 40-page monograph on a particular aspect of population. Each issue features one subject and author; the articles are supported by many charts and diagrams, added readings, and an extensive bibliography. The material is written for the layperson in easy-to-understand, nontechnical language, and is quite objective. The sponsoring body is a nonprofit organization that takes an objective look at the world's population. From time to time, specialized bibliographies are published. (Note: Subscription includes *Population Today*, a popular magazine on population; *World Population Data Sheets; United States Population Data Sheet;* and *Interchange*.)

Population Today (Formerly: *Intercom*). 1984. 11/yr. $40 (Individuals, $30). Arthur Haupt. Population Reference Bureau, 2213 M St. N.W., Washington, DC 20037. Illus., index. Circ: 15,500. Vol. ends: Dec.

Aud: Hs.

A popular "newsmonthly of population and demography." Published by the PRB as a vehicle for short news notes of interest to members and others. Reports of meetings are in some issues; others include survey reports from other countries. The "Current Readings" section provides brief annotations on recent works in population topics. A good source of current information.

Public Welfare. 1943. q. $20. Bill Detweiler. Amer. Public Welfare Assn., 1125 15th St. N.W., Washington, DC 20005. Illus., index, adv. Circ: 8,700. Vol. ends: Fall. Microform: UMI.

Indexed: PAIS. *Bk. rev:* 1-3, various lengths, signed. *Aud:* Hs.

This is the basic general audience periodical on social welfare policy issues. Members of the association are generally administrators in public or private welfare agencies, but students will also benefit from this journal. Most articles address current topics in the public policy debate. Recent issues have contained articles on organ transplantation, Baby Jane Doe, public policy toward the disabled, food stamps, adoption, alcoholism, and Jonathan Kozol on literacy and illiteracy.

Society: social science and modern society (Formerly: *TransAction: social science and modern society*). 1962. bi-m. $35 (Individuals, $25). Irving Louis Horowitz. Society, P.O. Box A, Rutgers Univ., New Brunswick, NJ 08903. Illus., adv. Circ: 15,000. Vol. ends: Oct. Microform: B&H, JAI, KTO, MIM, UMI.

Indexed: RG, SocSc. *Bk. rev:* 3-5, 1,000–1,500 words, signed. *Aud:* Hs.

A lively, well-written publication that emphasizes the intersection of social science and public policy. Features include film reviews, photo essays, and a regular column entitled "social science and the citizen." Most articles are free of jargon and are accompanied by a short list of suggested readings that librarians may find useful. Many prominent authors distill their insights on such topics as comparable worth, immigration, privacy, regional conflict in the U.S., risk assessment, and the relationship between television and violence. Focus is on the United States and largely on domestic rather than international issues.

SPORTS

For the Student/For the Professional

See also Boats and Boating; Conservation, Environment, and Outdoor Recreation; Fishing, Hunting, and Guns Sections.

Fred Batt, Head of Reference Dept., Bizzell Library, University of Oklahoma, Norman, OK 73019

Introduction

Like it or not, sports pervade our daily existence. They are part of our culture, hero worshiping, legal profession, high finance, and education. More and more disciplines are studying sports, e.g., sociology, business, psychology, education, medicine, and so on. At the same time, fitness has become a mania. People in more and more numbers are pursuing sports and physical activities for entertainment as well as in pursuit of improved health, the good life, and the body beautiful. In addition, most spectator sports demonstrate increases in attendance and interest. Armchair quarterbacks abound.

The increasing numbers of sports and sports-related magazines reflect the ever-changing place of sports in our society. The cessation of others reflects the intense competition. Many hundreds of sports and physical education magazines were considered, and selectivity was a necessity. The reviewer decided on three divisions: (1) general sports magazines; (2) magazines on specific sports; and (3) magazines on physical education and coaching (including sports medicine, sports psychology, sports philosophy, sports sociology, sports sciences, fitness and related interdisciplinary subjects). Placement was not clear-cut. In any case, there are many magazines within this list (and perhaps some that did not make the list), which relate information important to many people. They should be considered as worthwhile additions to many libraries.

Basic Periodicals

Hs: *Bicycling, Golf Digest, Golf Magazine, Inside Sport, Runner's World, Skiing, Sport, The Sporting News, Sports Illustrated, Tennis, World Tennis.*

For the Student

American Fencing. 1949. bi-m. $7.50. Mary T. Huddleson. U.S. Fencing Assn., 1750 E. Boulder St., Colorado Springs, CO 80909. Illus., adv. Circ: 8,000. Sample. Vol. ends: Dec. Microform: UMI.

Aud: Hs.

The official publication of the U.S. Fencing Association, this magazine provides vital information primarily for competitive fencers and coaches. Contents vary and may include technical articles, information for juniors, competition entry forms, competition results, fencing schedules and calendars, and information specific to the association. An important information vehicle for the serious as opposed to recreational fencer, and particularly useful in schools where fencing is taught.

Amateur Wrestling News. 1955. 14/yr. $20. Ron Good, P.O. Box 60387, Oklahoma City, OK 73146. Illus., adv. Circ: 10,000. Vol. ends: June.

Aud: Hs.

This official publication of the National Wrestling Coaches Association covers amateur wrestling from high school and college to the Olympics and includes rankings, coverage of all-American teams, recruiting stories, meet results, information on equipment, and other columns of interest to wrestlers and their coaches. Useful in libraries of schools with wrestling programs.

American Hockey Magazine. 1972. 7/yr. $12. Mike Schroeder. Amateur Hockey Assn. of the United States, 2997 Broadmoor Valley Rd., Colorado Springs, CO 90806. Illus., adv. Circ: 30,000. Vol. ends: July.

Aud: Hs.

"America's only amateur hockey magazine," this publication offers departments and features treating junior hockey, collegiate hockey, refereeing, coaching, profiles, products, and so forth, for amateur hockey participants and enthusiasts. It would be of interest to school and academic libraries in places or programs where hockey is played.

ATA Magazine/Martial Arts and Fitness. 1983. q. $6. Milo Dailey. ATA Publns., P.O. Box 240835, Memphis, TN 38124. Illus., adv. Circ: 14,000. Vol. ends: Winter.

Aud: Hs.

ATA Magazine is geared to fitness, both physical and mental, through the practice of the Song Ahm style of Taekwondo, aerobics, and strength training. Articles also treat nutrition and traditional Korean culture with respect to the potential interest of Taekwondo students. Issues may treat special subjects, e.g., women's participation or youth focus. Note: This magazine is primarily a vehicle of the American Taekwondo Association and ATA Fitness Centers. Useful for school libraries where martial arts are taught.

Automundo Deportivo. See Latin America, Latino (U.S.)/ For the Student: Latin America Section.

Balón: futbol mundial. See Latin America, Latino (U.S.)/ For the Student: Latin America Section.

Baseball Digest. 1942. m. $14.95. John Kuenster. Century Publg. Co., 1020 Church St., Evanston, IL 60201. Subs. to: P.O. Box 3305, Harlan, IA 51537. Illus., adv. Vol. ends: Dec. Microform: UMI.

Aud: Hs.

For the major league baseball fan, this magazine provides a cross section of easy-to-read articles. Some articles are newspaper reprints by noted baseball writers and by individuals in the game. Emphasis is on profiles and aspects of players' careers, as well as on historical themes—for example, the monthly "The Game I'll Never Forget." Issues also include diverse and interesting statistics, rosters, articles concerned with managing perspectives, and even quizzes and puzzles. "Baseball's only monthly magazine" will see plenty of action in school and public libraries. Note: See *Hockey Digest* for additional information about Century Publishing Company publications.

Basketball Weekly. 1967. 20/yr. $22. Matt Marson. Football News Co., 17820 E. Warren Ave., Detroit, MI 48224. Illus., adv. Circ: 41,000.

Aud: Hs.

Billed as "America's No. 1 cage weekly," this publication offers columns, results, and detailed analyses of high school, college, and professional basketball. *Basketball Weekly* is "devoted to the best interest of basketball and the welfare of the game. It seeks to inform, entertain and thus enlighten its readers."

Bicycle Forum. 1978. s-a. $8. John Williams. P.O. Box 8311, Missoula, MT 59803. Illus., index, adv. Sample. Vol. ends: Summer.

Aud: Hs.

This magazine literally offers a forum for readers and is chock full of advice and information about the world of bicycling. Articles are well researched and provide an important source of data, research results, and ideas for cyclists and individuals involved in cycling. Some emphasis is on the bike as a viable means of safe transportation.

Bicycling. 1962. m. $13.97. James C. McCullagh. Rodale Press, 33 E. Minor St., Emmaus, PA 18049. Illus., index, adv. Circ: 253,373. Vol. ends: Dec. Microform: UMI.

Indexed: Acs, MgI, PopPer. *Aud:* Hs.

If people do not jog or run, they bicycle. With the emphasis on healthy activities and exercise, paired with the possibilities of relatively inexpensive transportation, bicycling is a way of life for many. This beautifully produced magazine offers diverse information for the bicycling enthusiast, including the wide variety of accessories and equipment, clothing for the bicyclist, cycling techniques, health-related items, medical perspectives, safety considerations, training ideas, and even fiction and humor. Superb graphics and decent writing make this an important purchase for all types of libraries.

Black Belt. 1961. m. $21. Jim Coleman. Rainbow Publg., 1813 Victory Pl., Burbank, CA 91504. Illus., index, adv. Circ: 100,000. Sample. Vol. ends: Dec.

Aud: Hs.

This well-illustrated magazine, known as the "world's leading magazine of self-defense," features how-to articles on particular techniques and styles in the martial arts, interviews and profiles of major personalities, news and many regular columns and departments. *Black Belt* has a wide appeal for most libraries because of the ever-growing interest in self-defense among all age groups, the built-in international flavor, and the wide range of self-defense activities treated (kung fu, aikido, karate, kickboxing, ninjuto, sumo wrestling, kenjutsu, Tae Kwon Do and so on). Intriguing articles abound, e.g., "Is Karate an Art or a Sport?"

China Sports. See Asia/For the Student Section.

Golf Digest. 1980. m. $19.94. Jerry Tarde. Golf Digest/Tennis, Inc., 495 Westport Ave., Norwalk, CT 06856. Illus., adv. Circ: 1,200,000. Vol. ends: Dec. Microform: UMI.

Bk. rev: Occasional. *Aud:* Hs.

Billed as the golf magazine with the largest circulation, many golfers swear by *Golf Digest*; others prefer *Golf Magazine*. However, many golfers cannot survive a month without digesting both publications. Similarities abound—i.e., beautiful photography, analysis of tournament play, profiles of professionals, excellent instruction, and wonderful writing. *Golf Digest* has something to offer golfers at all levels. Top-notch golf writers such as Peter Dobereiner and Dan Jenkins can be anticipated monthly. Instruction is emphasized and offered by touring pros as well as by noted instructors such as Bob Toski. In-depth profiles of golfers go beyond the traditional. Major tournament previews and analyses are complete and whet the appetite for television viewing or, for the lucky, the fascinating experience of watching the pros in person. Of course, tournament results and statistics, travel information, golf course analyses, equipment reviews, rules analyses, and the like, round out this golf publication, which is considered the best by many and worthy of placement on the shelves of most libraries.

Golf Journal. 1948. 8/yr. $8. Robert Sommers. Golf House, Far Hills, NJ 07931. Illus., adv. Circ: 140,000. Vol. ends: Dec. Microform: UMI.

Aud: Hs.

"The official publication of the United States Golf Association," this journal not only treats USGA activities but also includes articles of interest to any avid golfer. The examined issue included an interesting profile on a career golf official/administrator, a fun article on the origin of the word "mulligan," and a short history of Royal St. George's. Profiles, pictures of "great golf holes," rules columns, and other features round out a publication that golfers should enjoy. Not a vehicle offering the golf instruction and the tour results of either *Golf Magazine* or *Golf Digest*.

Golf Magazine. 1959. m. $15.94. George Peper. Times-Mirror Magazines, Inc., 380 Madison Ave., New York, NY 10017. Illus., index, adv. Circ: 800,000. Vol. ends: Dec. Microform: UMI.

Indexed: Acs, MgI. *Aud:* Hs.

The major competition of *Golf Digest*, this magazine can stand on its own with wonderful instructional articles by Lee Trevino and an impressive array of playing and teaching editors, profiles of professional golfers, analyses and lists of the greatest courses in the world, humorous articles, beautiful photography, PGA & LPGA tour statistics, equipment information, and many excellent regular features. The February issue is an annual yearbook. This publication should be found next to *Golf Digest* on library shelves. Both are worth the price.

Handball. 1950. bi-m. $20. Vern Roberts. U.S. Handball Assn., 930 N. Benton Ave., Tucson, AZ 85711. Illus., adv. Circ: 19,000. Vol. ends: Dec. Microform: UMI.

Aud: Hs.

"The official voice of the United States Handball Association" offers features geared to the USHA, health-related articles, instructional sections, and tournament results ranging from juniors to the professionals. Primarily of interest to the handball competitor and tournament player and potentially useful in some libraries.

Hockey Digest. 1972. 8/yr. $9.95. Michael K. Herbert. Century Publg. Co., 1020 Church St., Evanston, IL 60201. Subs. to: P.O. Box 3305, Harlan, IA 51537. Illus., adv. Vol. ends: June. Microform: UMI.

Aud: Hs.

Of the same format and type of content as, for example, *Baseball Digest*, this publication treats current and past hockey players, hockey teams, and other aspects of professional hockey in its features and departments. As with the other Century Publishing Company publications, features are included such as products, statistics, quizzes, and "The Game I'll Never Forget." This publication is potential library fare in areas where hockey interest is high. Note: Century Publishing Company also puts out other publications, using the same format: *Soccer Digest* ("Soccer's Monthly Magazine," according to the cover, although bi-monthly for $7.95), *Basketball Digest* (8/yr. for $9.95), *Football Digest* (10/yr. for $12.95), and *Bowling Digest* (6/yr. for $12).

Inside Sports. 1979–1982. 1983. 10/yr. $15. Michael Herbert. Century Publg. Co., 1020 Church St., Evanston, IL 60201. Subs. to: P.O. Box 3305, Harlan, IA 51537. Illus., adv. Circ: 350,000. Vol. ends: Dec. Microform: UMI.

Indexed: Acs. *Aud:* Hs.

Geared to everyone from cheerleaders to special teams in football, this magazine provides materials to a wide readership of sports enthusiasts. Included are interviews of sports figures (e.g., Danny White); in-depth profiles (e.g., Mark Gastineau); many well-written features, columns, departments (e.g., media, humor, and so on); nice photography; and everything you would expect from an all-purpose general sports magazine. Although it is not *Sports Illustrated*, this is still a worthwhile publication for most libraries.

International Gymnast Magazine (Formerly: *International Gymnast*). 1956. m. $18. Glenn M. Sundby. Sundby Sports, 410 Broadway, Santa Monica, CA 90401. Illus., adv. Circ: 30,000. Vol. ends: Dec. Microform: UMI.

Aud: Hs.

"Serving the sport of gymnastics for over a quarter of a century" and considered the world's leading gymnastics magazine, this heavily illustrated publication offers detailed reports on competitions and events throughout the world. It is a vehicle to find out what is going on and who are the major personalities in the sport—e.g., training camps, profiles of top gymnasts, interviews, research, information, and tips regarding training and techniques. Gymnasts and coaches should require this publication in their schools.

National Racquetball. 1973. m. $16. Chuck Leve. Publn. Management, Inc., 4350 DiPaolo Center, Dearlove Rd., Glenview, IL 60025. Illus., adv. Circ: 40,000. Vol. ends: Dec.

Aud: Hs.

Geared to the serious racquetball player and fitness buff, this publication provides information on advanced game techniques; general instruction; fitness exercises geared to improved play; and traditional columns, profiles, tournament previews, and results.

The Olympian. 1974. 10/yr. Membership. $19.88. Mike Moran. U.S. Olympic Committee, 1750 E. Boulder St., Colorado Springs, CO 80909. Illus., adv. Circ: 60,000.

Aud: Hs.

The official magazine of the U.S. Olympic Committee. It covers all aspects of the Olympic movement and contains features on top U.S. athletes, coverage of national championships and tournaments and general news about amateur athletics in the United States. Good color photos.

Runner's World. 1966. 13/yr. $21.50. Bob Anderson. Runner's World Magazine Co., 1400 Stierlin Rd., Mountain View, CA 94043. Illus., index, adv. Circ: 300,000. Sample. Vol. ends: Dec. Microform: B&H, UMI.

Indexed: MgI. *Aud:* Hs.

For individuals in pursuit of optimal health via running, this publication provides advice on training, racing, exercise, diet, clothing and other related subjects. Sections on "running" and "health and fitness" are filled with valuable and intriguing information. Provocative feature articles provide more detailed information. Recently, Carlos Lopes, 1984 Olympic marathon gold medalist, was added to the staff as a training and racing adviser. Personality profiles and information about races are also included. This publication gives running enthusiasts much information and entertainment.

Skiing. 1947. 7/yr. $9.98. Alfred H. Greenberg. Ziff-Davis Publg. Co., One Park Ave., New York, NY 10016. Illus., adv. Circ: 430,000. Sample. Vol. ends: Mar. Microform: B&H, UMI.

Indexed: MgI, RG. *Aud:* Hs.

This magazine offers reports on competitions, travel and resort information, instruction on how to ski better, equipment tips, and a variety of special sections and regular columns. Termed "the magazine for the serious skier," *Skiing* emphasizes instruction and should be on the shelves as a vehicle for skiers to learn the wheres, hows, and whys of their sport.

Skin Diver. 1951. m. $13.94. Paul J. Tzimoulis. Petersen Publg. Co., 8490 Sunset Blvd., Los Angeles, CA 90069. Illus., index, adv. Circ: 192,797. Vol. ends: Dec. Microform: UMI.

Bk. rev: Many, one sentence. *Aud:* Hs.

The "foremost authority in its field" is attractive and filled with well-written articles and beautiful photography (even the advertisements). Worldwide coverage includes underwater recreation, ocean exploration, scientific research, commercial diving, technological advancements, and so on. Regular features include scuba techniques, underwater photography, equipment, marine biology, conservation, and much else. Obviously, the skindivers' bible for information and activities.

Soccer America. 1971. 50/yr. $28. Lynn Berling-Manuel. Berling Communications, Inc., P.O. Box 23704, Oakland, CA 94623. Illus., adv. Circ: 12,000. Sample. Vol. ends: June. Microform: UMI.

Aud: Hs.

This weekly soccer magazine is devoted to American professional soccer, to college soccer, and to the international soccer scene. There is a weekly record of all professional games and selected international contests as well as occasional profiles of major soccer figures. This tabloid is recommended for libraries of all types in places where interest in soccer is high.

Sport. 1946. m. $12. David Bauer. Sports Media Corp., 119 W. 40th St., New York, NY 10018. Illus., adv. Circ: 900,000. Vol. ends: Dec. Microform: B&H, UMI.

Indexed: MgI, RG. *Aud:* Hs.

This entertaining magazine emphasizes major professional and college sports. The features are nicely written and highly enjoyable. In-depth analyses and interviews are well done. Wonderful, colored photographs support all sections. Diverse and interesting short pieces comprise the "Sport Talk" section. If on the shelf alongside *Sports Illustrated* in any library, both would be read. Lots of fun for the sports enthusiast.

The Sporting News. 1886. w. $51.50. Tom Barnidge, 1212 N. Lindbergh Blvd., P.O. Box 56, St. Louis, MO 63166. Illus., adv. Circ: 630,000. Vol. ends: Dec. Microform: UMI.

Indexed: Acs, MgI. *Aud:* Hs.

A new editor was named in Summer 1985, and a columnist shakeup followed. Some major writers bade farewell (e.g., Joe Falls and Larry King, who wrote "Shalom, Adios, Arrivederci, So Long"). Joe Gergen, Mike Downey, and Bob Verdi were added as new columnists. It seemed that excellent writers were replaced by excellent writers, and the quality of the publication remains intact. *Sporting News* provides the most complete and comprehensive sports coverage available on a weekly basis. Detailed summaries, box scores and statistics are published for football, baseball (major emphasis), basketball, and hockey at both the college and professional levels. Other sports are treated, including articles for major activities and short summaries for other events. This is a fine publication that complements *Sports*

Illustrated and is recommended for most libraries despite the newspaper format.

Sports Illustrated. 1954. 54/yr. $53.40. Mark Mulvoy. Time, Inc., Time & Life Bldg., New York, NY 10020. Subs. to: Time, Inc., 541 N. Fairbanks Court, Chicago, IL 60611. Illus., index, adv. Circ: 2,699,605. Sample. Vol. ends: Dec. Microform: MCA, UMI.

Indexed: MgI, RG. *Bk. rev:* 1, 1–2 columns, signed. *Aud:* Ejh, Hs.

The premier sports magazine, *Sports Illustrated* offers the best writing by the best authors, paired with wonderful photography and a pleasing format. Coverage includes every sport imaginable from unique angles mixed with traditional sports coverage. This makes for sports variety and interest for an array of readers. Articles on minor sports are mixed with articles on major college and professional sports. Controversy is not avoided, and personality profiles always seem to go one step beyond the traditional article or interview. The "For the Record" section provides a concise roundup of the previous weeks' activities in virtually all sports as well as a milepost section and "Faces in the Crowd," which highlights unusual accomplishments. Because of the timeliness, readability, and overall excellence of this magazine, it belongs in virtually all school libraries.

Swimming World and Junior Swimmer. 1960. m. $16. Bob Ingram. Swimming World, Inc., P.O. Box 45497, Los Angeles, CA 90045. Illus., adv. Circ: 49,287. Sample. Vol. ends: Dec. Microform: UMI.

Aud: Hs.

Termed "the oldest and most complete magazine on competitive swimming, diving and water polo" and "the national magazine for competitive aquatics," *Swimming World* provides in-depth coverage of swimming in regional, national, and international competitions for age group, high school, college, the national championships, the Olympics, and international events. Profiles and articles are by leading coaches and authorities on strength training, stroke technique, nutrition, and conditioning.

Tennis. 1965. m. $17.94. Shepherd Campbell. Golf Digest/Tennis Inc., 495 Westport Ave., P.O. Box 5350, Norwalk, CT 06856. Illus., adv. Circ: 500,000. Vol. ends: Dec. Microform: UMI.

Indexed: MgI. *Aud:* Hs.

Recommended by the United States Professional Tennis Association. The tennis counterpart to *Golf Digest*, excellent photography, instruction, and features pervade this attractive monthly bible for tennis players. Brimming with marvelous in-depth features by or about major tennis personalities and tips and lessons (e.g., Arthur Ashe's Tennis Clinic), this comprehensive magazine has something for everyone. Nutrition and tennis performance, tennis clothes, travel information, tournament guides, professional and college tournament results, rankings of players, well-written columns, and so on, add to the luster of *Tennis* as an important magazine for most libraries. Note: The "Tennis Player to Watch" in the issue prior to Wimbledon 1985 was 17-year-old Boris Becker, who then surprised the world.

Track & Field News. 1948. $22. Bert Nelson. Track & Field News, Inc., P.O. Box 296, Los Altos, CA 94022. Illus., adv. Circ: 34,000. Sample. Vol. ends: Jan. Microform: B&H, UMI.

Aud: Hs.

For track and field fans, coaches, athletes, and officials, this publication is considered the "bible" of the sport. Annual event-by-event rankings in the January issue are universally used and quoted by the media. Track and field is covered from high school through college, the professionals, and the Olympics. The magazine concentrates on news and the results of all major meets throughout the United States and the world, along with interviews, profiles, opinion, statistical reports, and a variety of features. Belongs in high school libraries with track and field programs.

Women's Sports & Fitness (Formerly: *Women's Sports*). 1979. m. $12. Amy Rennert. Women's Sports Publns., Inc., 310 Town and Country Village, Palo Alto, CA 94301. Illus., adv. Circ: 150,000. Microform: UMI.

Indexed: MgI. *Bk. rev:* 1, 1–2 columns. *Aud:* Hs.

This official publication of the Women's Sports Foundation covers women's participation in amateur and professional sports and includes colorful profiles of women athletes as well as other people associated with women athletes— for example, a profile of Bela Karolyi (coach of Mary Lou Retton and others). Results of women's competitions are highlighted, and sports and fitness for women are promoted.

World Tennis. 1953. m. $15.94. Neil Amdur. Family Media, Inc., 5455 Wilshire Blvd., Suite 1815, Los Angeles, CA 90036. Illus., adv. Circ: 400,000. Vol. ends: May. Microform: UMI.

Indexed: MgI, RG. *Bk. rev:* Occasionally. *Aud:* Hs.

World Tennis has much to offer every level of tennis player, from the beginner to the professional. Well-written and extensive profiles abound. Useful information on equipment, nutrition, and fitness adds to the overall effectiveness. Wonderful instructional articles and columns are offered by Martina Navratilova and others. Tournament results and statistics are well organized. Feature articles are timely— for example, "Meet the Swedes," profiling Wilander, Nystrom, Jarryd, and Sundstrom, who are performing marvelously throughout the world, or Ion Tiriac on Boris Becker. This beautifully produced and entertaining publication belongs in most libraries.

Wrestling USA. 1965. 12/yr. $18. Lanny Bryant. P.O. Box 128 MSU, Bozeman, MT 58717. Illus., adv. Circ: 10,000. Sample. Vol. ends: May.

Aud: Hs.

With the increasing popularity of school wrestling throughout the country, this publication is geared to amateur wrestling in the United States, and includes profiles of past and present wrestlers, coaching tips, health considerations, and sports medicine. Also included are college and school results and tournament schedules. Should be in school libraries in places where wrestling programs exist.

YABA World (Formerly: *Young Bowler*). 1964. 6/yr. $2.50. Paul Bertling. Young Amer. Bowling Alliance, 5301 S. 76th St., Greendale, WI 53129. Illus., adv. Circ: 80,000. Vol. ends: Apr.

Aud: Ejh, Hs.

The official magazine for youth and collegiate bowlers. Regular departments are "Nation's Top Ten Lists," and "Ask the Coach." This is the publication in which to find announcements of tournaments, bowling camps, and supplies. About 20 cleverly designed pages.

For the Professional

Athletic Journal. 1921. 10/yr. $8. Jay Becker. Athletic Journal Publg. Co., 1719 Howard St., Evanston, IL 60202. Illus., index, adv. Circ: 34,000. Vol. ends: May. Microform: UMI.

Indexed: EdI. *Bk. rev:* 7–10, 75–100 words. *Aud:* Pr.

A gold mine of ideas for athletic coaches, this magazine offers a number of excellent regular features and articles written primarily by college and high school athletic trainers and coaches. Articles are on such topics as major sports; strength and conditioning training; and general concepts such as aerobics, dedication, drug use, recruiting, and so on. The journal has excellent illustrations, new ideas and items, and scholarly articles.

Journal of Physical Education, Recreation and Dance. 1896. 9/yr. $45 (Membership, $42). Barbara Kres Beach. Amer. Alliance for Health, Physical Education, Recreation and Dance, 1900 Association Dr., Reston, VA 22091. Illus., index, adv. Circ: 42,000. Sample. Vol. ends: Dec. Refereed. Microform: UMI.

Indexed: CIJE, EdI. *Bk. rev:* 2–5, 150–500 words. *Aud:* Pr.

The professional journal for physical education instructors, recreation leaders, and dance teachers in the alliance. The purpose of this journal is to communicate research and articles geared to enriching the depth and scope of health, leisure, and movement-related activities, and the contributions of these activities toward human well-being. News notes, announcements of upcoming workshops and conferences, inexpensive teaching aids, and instructional tips are useful features. One of the subjects of the magazine (that is, on physical education, leisure/recreation, or dance) is emphasized in each issue. Recommended for high school libraries.

Scholastic Coach. 1931. 10/yr. $13.95. Herman L. Masin. Scholastic Inc., 730 Broadway, New York, NY 10003. Illus., index, adv. Circ: 39,000. Vol. ends: May. Microform: B&H, UMI.

Indexed: EdI. *Bk. rev:* 5–7, 30–50 words. *Aud:* Pr.

Brimming with practical information for high school and college coaches, this magazine offers treatments of individual and team techniques, plays, practice, organization drills, body conditioning, strength training, and the like. In addition to sections on specific sports written primarily by coaches and trainers, there are interviews, articles on sports medicine, treatments of "womenscene," considerations of sports administration, and so on. As in *Athletic Journal,* excellent illustrations and an attractive layout add to the overall effectiveness. Selection of all-American high school teams in football, basketball, track, soccer, and wrestling are important annual features. A must for high school libraries.

Women's Coaching Clinic. 1977. 10/yr. $40. Catherine G. Ivins. Princeton Educational Pubs., CN5245, Princeton, NJ 08540. Illus. Vol. ends: June.

Aud: Pr.

Only 16 pages long, this publication is a vehicle for coaches to share their ideas and techniques for working with women athletes. The issues examined included pieces on basketball, golf, tennis, volleyball techniques, team concepts in individual sports, winning attitudes and programs, and coping with injuries. Other articles are written primarily by high school and college coaches and trainers. Diagrams are used by many authors to illustrate points and strategies. This publication would be useful in libraries in secondary schools and colleges where girls' and women's athletics programs are found. Note: The same publishers also issue *The Football Clinic, The Basketball Clinic*, and *The Coaching Clinic*. These are similar in format and content to *Women's Coaching Clinic* and will not be reviewed.

TELEVISION, VIDEO, AND RADIO

For the Student/For the Professional

See also Communication and Speech; Computers; Electronics; and News and Opinion Sections.

Liese Adams, Documents Librarian, Kent State University Library, Kent, OH 44242

Introduction

The birth and death of periodicals depends on the growth or decline of interest in a subject. Therefore, one can anticipate an increase in the number of home satellite periodicals and understand the demise of several CB publications, for example, *CB Magazine* and *S9/Hobby Radio*. Video is here to stay for a while. Several video magazines have begun publishing in the past four years, but they will have a tough time competing with *Video* and *Video Review*.

There are several good trade journals specializing in television and radio that were not reviewed because of their limited appeal.

Basic Periodicals

Hs: *Dial, Video Review*.

Basic Indexes

Film Literature Index.

For the Student

Channels of Communications. 1981. bi-m. $18. Les Brown. Media Commentary Council, Inc., 304 W. 58th St., New York, NY 10019. Illus., adv. Circ: 45,000. Sample. Vol. ends: Nov/Dec.

Indexed: Acs, RG. *Bk. rev:* 1 per issue. *Aud:* Hs.

Channels' goal is to educate the general public about the effects of television, both positive and negative. This publication offers a critical appraisal of government, political, and business issues in the electronic media of TV, cable, satellite, videotext, and home video. The last issue of the year is *Channels'* field guide to the electronic media, which reports on cable and satellite.

Dial. 1980. m. Membership. Don Erickson. Public Broadcasting Communications, Inc., 356 W. 58th St., New York, NY 10019. Illus., adv.

Aud: Hs.

Fourteen different editions of *Dial* are written for various PBS stations around the country. Previews of upcoming programs augment the standard, but valuable, program guide. Short feature articles appear, punctuated by well-done, tasteful graphics. This magazine is a must for any library in the following viewing areas: New York; Los Angeles; Chicago; Washington, DC; Detroit; Miami; Salt Lake City; Seattle; Boston; Dallas-Fort Worth; New Orleans; Portland, Bend, and Corvallis, Oregon; Indianapolis; and Tampa. Subscriptions can be entered through either a PBS station or a serials jobber.

On Cable. 1980. m. $12. Peter Funt. On Cable Pubs., 25 Van Zant St., Norwalk, CT 06885. Illus., adv. Circ: 1,300,000.

Aud: Hs.

On Cable is what the title implies—listings of what is on cable TV. Like *TV Guide*, this publication has the standard fare: crossword puzzles, letters, and short stories on the stars. Highlights of programs are made up of information and pictures from press kits. A few programs are reviewed in depth. *Satellite ORBIT* performs the same function for satellite TV. *On Cable* is an indispensable guide for people with cable, but it is probably an unnecessary purchase for libraries.

Popular Communications. 1982. m. $14. Tom Kneitel. Popular Communications, Inc., 76 N. Broadway, Hicksville, NY 11801. Illus., adv.

Bk. rev: 4. *Aud:* Hs.

Tom Kneitel moved on to *Popular Communications* after *S9/Hobby Radio,* which had merged with *CB Radio Times,* ceased publication. *Popular Communications* fills in for several of these types of publications that have fallen by the wayside. It covers the whole spectrum of amateur communication—radio, CB, ham, telephone, and radio teletype. Articles are on timely subjects, and usually include an account of amateur radio history. Its regular departments include "New Products," "Washington Pulse" and the "Pirates' Den"; the last covers illegal radio transmissions logged by readers.

Radio & Electronics World (Formerly: *Radio & Electronics Constructor*). 1947. m. £25. Duncan Leslie. Sovereign House,

Brentwood, Essex CM14 4SE, England. Illus., adv. Circ: 22,500. Sample.

Bk. rev: 3, 350–400 words. *Aud:* Hs.

This English magazine is similar to the U.S.'s *Popular Communications*. Devoted primarily to radio amateurs, it also covers TV, satellite, and some computer applications. Articles offer practical tips on "how to." The news column is interesting. Although new products are presented by their manufacturers, there are no critical evaluations. For large libraries, only if they have already acquired *Popular Communications*.

Satellite ORBIT: the world's leading satellite TV magazine. 1982. m. $48. Bruce Kinnaird. Commtek Publg. Corp., P.O. Box 53, Boise, ID 83707. Illus., adv. Circ: 30,000.
Aud: Hs.

This publication is clearly the *TV Guide* of satellite TV. Most of its 200 plus pages are devoted to the "Birdwatcher": the program listings for 77 services. Movies and specials are recorded both alphabetically and in the daily listings. Sports enthusiasts will want to check the "Birdwatcher" column for everything from airplane racing to wrestling. Entertaining features, program reviews, a detailed product showcase, and other excellent columns make this publication indispensable for any school with access to a satellite dish.

TV Guide. 1953. w. $29.90. David Sendler. Triangle Publns., Inc., P.O. Box 500, Radnor, PA 19088. Subs. to: P.O. Box 400, Radnor, PA 19088. Illus., index, adv. Circ: 17,000,000.
Indexed: Acs, BioI, PopPer. *Aud:* Hs.

The publishers of *TV Guide* produce a surprisingly good, pocket-sized magazine, with regional listings for various areas in the country. The details included in these listings have increased over the years and now include programs on cable/pay-TV and subscription TV channels. The national section of the magazine has five or so articles in each issue, which center around the medium of television, its performers, creators, critics, and technology. There are several columns, one an editorial. The articles are entertaining and well written. *TV Guide* has published pieces on controversial issues related to the media. It is frequently a unique source for historical information about television programming in various parts of the country. Also available on microfilm from its publisher. (M. McK.)

Video. 1978. m. $18. Doug Garr. Reese Communications, Inc., 460 W. 34th St., New York, NY 10001. Illus., adv. Circ: 300,000. Vol. ends: March.
Bk. rev: 7–10, 25–40 words. *Aud:* Hs.

Interesting features highlight this publication for the video user. A mix of how-to articles, news items, critical video reviews, and features accent the most important departments: "The Top Ten" and the "Directory" of "Top Ten." These sections list disc sales and rentals, as well as cover what is new on tape and disc. Equipment is evaluated in the detailed "Videotests." A unique column is "New Channels," covering cable, pay-per-view, satellite TV, and direct

broadcast satellite. The publisher is in the throes of preparing an index, which should be out soon.

Video Now. 1984. m. $10. Bernard Cerrone. Video Magazine, Inc., 375 N. Broadway, Jericho, NY 11753. Illus., adv. *Aud:* Hs.

Although better looking and less expensive than either *Video* or *Video Review*, this publication is not quite as comprehensive. The features are a little longer and just as interesting. Helpful suggestions are included, and *Video Now* contains the standard reviews of equipment, videos, music, and news. It definitely has potential but not the "extras" of the other two magazines . . . yet.

Video Review. 1980. m. $12. Deirdre Condon. Viare Publg., 902 Broadway, New York, NY 10010. Illus., adv. Circ: 360,000. Sample.
Aud: Ejh, Hs.

Whether taping or viewing, interested readers will find everything they ever wanted to know about video in the pages of *Video Review*, self-proclaimed as the "world authority of home video." *Video Review*'s strong point is in evaluating video equipment, tapes, and discs, although music and movie videos are also reviewed and rated. This publication has grown exponentially. Instead of subscription prices going up, issue price has actually gone down. Part of its growth can be attributed to its purchase of the rival *Home Video*. The "Shopper's Guide," formerly published separately, will be issued in the October issue to give those videophiles something to wish for. The "Guide" includes valuable information on VCRs, cameras, monitors, blank tapes, and video programming.

Video Times (Formerly: *Video Movies*). 1984. m. $19.95. Matthew White Publns. Intl., Ltd., 3841 W. Oakton, Skokie, IL 60076. Illus., adv. Circ: 150,000.
Aud: Hs.

Approximately 80 new video releases, including music videos, are reviewed in each issue. These critical reviews are witty, well written, signed, and just as entertaining as anything on "Sneak Previews." The "Family Fare" section recommends videos that can be seen by the whole family. Fascinating feature articles are included, along with a list of the top 10 classics. For a video magazine, *Video Times* has a very professional, clean look. Librarians would benefit by using this publication as a buying tool. This new, quality publication is highly recommended.

For the Professional

Parent's Choice: a review of children's media. 1978. bi-m. $15. Diana Huss Green. Parent's Choice Foundation, P.O. Box 185, Waban, MA 02168. Illus., adv. Circ: 16,000.
Bk. rev: 3 or more. *Aud:* Pr.

The most important feature of *Parent's Choice* is the well-balanced reviews of children's media. Selection guidance is provided for parents and librarians on books, TV programs, movies, videos, computer software, music, toys, and games.

The movie reviews are written not only from the standpoint of what is educational for children, but they also look through children's eyes in recommending what would be enjoyed. Annotated bibliographies provide an opportunity for further research. Articles are entertaining and often provide helpful hints on how to contribute informally to a child's education. The advisory board is comprised of eminent professors, authors, poets, and publishers. *Parent's Choice* awards honor illustrators, computer programs, videos, paperbacks, literature, and recordings on an annual basis. Although the National Coalition on Television Violence has criticized *Parent's Choice* for recommending what it considers to be unacceptably violent TV programming, it offers well-balanced, thoughtful suggestions. Recommended for all libraries.

Television & Families (Formerly: *Television & Children*, title change effective Vol. 8, No. 1, 1986). 1978. q. $25. Nicholas B. Van Dyck. Natl. Council for Families & Television, 20 Nassau St., Suite 200, Princeton, NJ 08542. Illus. Circ: 750. Sample. Microform: UMI.
Indexed: CIJE. *Bk. rev:* 1. *Aud:* Pr.

Recognizing the sweeping effect of prime-time viewing on the whole family, the NCFT has changed its focus from TV and children to TV and families. The journal's intent is to provide a forum for information, research, and opinion on this subject. Contributors include Robert Keeshan, better known as Captain Kangaroo, and school teachers (usually professors).

THEATER

For the Student/For the Professional

Gary J. Lenox, Librarian, University of Wisconsin Center–Rock County, 2909 Kellogg Ave., Janesville, WI 53545

Introduction

The theater and drama periodicals, naturally, are as wide-ranging and varied as the art form itself. In most collections, it is probably wise to have a balance of titles representing drama (the playscripts, their criticism, and literary import); theater productions (professional and amateur, their criticism and description); and technical theater ("backstage" elements). A high school library might want to consider *American Theatre, Theatre Journal* and *Theatre Crafts.* Special types of "theater," such as mime, puppet theater, and experimental theater, should be represented as needs demand.

Basic Periodicals

Ejh: *Plays*; Hs: *American Theatre, Dramatics, Theatre Crafts, Theatre Journal.*

For the Student

Amateur Stage. 1946. m. $20. Roy Stacey. Stacey Pubs., One Hawthorndene Rd., Hayes, Bromley, Kent BR2 7DZ, England. Illus., adv. Circ: 6,000.
Bk. rev: 6–15, 50–100 words. *Aud:* Ejh, Hs.

Published in England, this is a valuable guide for amateur theater groups. It is one of the few commercial publications "devoted exclusively to the non-professional theatre." There are short articles on many aspects of stagecraft, production, acting, design, costume, and lighting, as well as news on the amateur theatre—mostly in England. Book and playscript reviews make this a valuable addition to libraries in schools with active theater programs.

American Theatre (Formerly: *Theatre Communications*). 1984. $24. Jim O'Quinn. Theatre Communications Group, 355 Lexington Ave., New York, NY 10017. Illus., adv.
Aud: Hs.

Germany has *Theater der Zeit* and *Theater Heute*; Ireland has *Theatre Ireland*; England has *Drama*; now we have *American Theatre.* This wonderful "monthly forum for news, features and opinion" includes among its contributing editors no less personages than John Hirsch, John Houseman, Arthur Ballet, and Robert Brustein. It includes feature articles on noted directors and many news notes, all illustrated with black-and-white photos, with emphasis on the regional professional theaters. All high school libraries supporting drama and theater programs must have this valuable national theater journal.

Animations: a review of puppets and related theatre. 1977. bi-m. $10.48. Penny Francis. Puppet Centre Trust, Battersea Arts Centre, Lavender Hill, London SW11 5TJ, England. Illus. Circ: 800.
Aud: Hs.

A reporting of what is going on in the world of animated theater, particularly in England. It contains useful news, articles, calendars, columns, and "Spotlight," which deals with education and therapy news. Animated theater, as seen in programs like *Spitting Image* and the longstanding *Muppets* in addition to other types of programs for puppets and marionettes, has taken on greater importance in recent times. Therefore, this is a particularly useful addition for theater and educational theater collections.

Asian Theatre Journal. See Asia/For the Student: General Section.

Dramatics. 1929. 9/yr. $12. Ezra Goldstein. The Intl. Thespian Soc., 3368 Central Pkwy., Cincinnati, OH 45225. Illus., adv. Circ: 35,000. Vol. ends: Aug. Microform: UMI.
Aud: Hs.

Dramatics supports theater arts in the secondary schools and it is directed to both students and teachers. An issue generally has ten articles, with at least one on the technical aspects of theater (set design, blocking, make-up, and so on). There are interviews with those who have "made it" (performers, playwrights, directors, and so on) and informed advice on craft and technique. The script of a short play by a young playwright is included. Look here for announcements and ads for workshops, college programs, apprenticeships, scholarships, and auditions. (L.K.W.)

London Drama. 1973. s-a. $6. Liz Johnson. I L E A Drama & Tape Centre, Princeton St., London WC1 R4A, England. Illus., adv. Circ: 1,500.

Aud: Hs.

An official publication of the Inner London Education Authority, *London Drama* is concerned with the educational aspects of drama in schools. Specific focus is on activities in London, although several of the articles are usually of general interest for the teacher involved with drama, in or out of England.

Mime Journal. 1974. a. $16 (Individuals, $8). Thomas Leabhart. Pomona College Theatre Dept. for the Claremont Colleges, Claremont, CA 91711. Circ: 250.

Aud: Hs.

Mime journals come and go, change publishers, and are among the least stable of the theater journals. This one apparently traces its history to 1974, and the issue examined includes a special "photographic essay." Mime has great popular appeal, and libraries should have material on the subject. However, this publication is for comprehensive theater collections at an outrageously high price for an annual issue. Should be examined before ordering.

Plays: the drama magazine for young people. 1941. m. (Oct–May). $17.50. Sylvia K. Burack. Plays, Inc., 120 Boylston St., Boston, MA 02116. Index, adv. Circ: 21,900. Vol. ends: May. Microform: UMI.

Indexed: RG. *Bk. rev:* Varies, usually 10–12 notes. *Aud:* Ejh, Hs.

A well-known, pocket-sized magazine of 80 pages, which follows a set pattern of publishing nine or ten royalty free plays. The plays are divided in each number by grade level for junior/senior high and middle/lower grades, and these are followed by creative dramatics, skits, puppet plays, dramatized classics, and so on. Each play includes complete production notes. Plays seem suitable for elementary and junior high, but too simple for more sophisticated teenagers. It should be stressed that the magazine does offer royalty-free plays in an inexpensive format. A good choice for school libraries.

Theatre Crafts. 1967. 10/yr. $24. Patricia McKay. Theatre Crafts Assn., 135 Fifth Ave., New York, NY 10010. Illus., adv. Circ: 29,809. Microform: B&H, UMI.

Indexed: RG. *Bk. rev:* Notes. *Aud:* Hs.

An important magazine that is both practical and theoretical for just about anyone involved with technical theater. Articles are for the professional and/or amateur responsible for lighting, costumes, billboards, advertising, and other elements of production. Frequently includes articles on the work of noted costumers or set designers, new equipment for the theater including computers, and the staging of particular professional productions. There are columns on new products and news. A very good "tech theater" title, with ideas that can be used, copied, imitated, or improvised by all theater companies. A necessity in high school libraries.

UNIMA-France: marionettes. 1960. q. Membership, F. 50. Andre Tahon. Union Internationale de la Marionette, 7, rue du Helder, 75009 Paris, France. Illus.

Aud: Hs.

Europe differs considerably from the United States in its attitude toward marionettes and puppets and has a long history of marionettes as adult entertainment. Hence, this illustrated French-language house organ/journal is as involved with adult theater as it is with the show for the child. Articles are of a wider scope than those found in other journals; there are scholarly articles on the art, history, evolution and development, and technique of puppetry. The Union Internationale de la Marionettte is an international society that serves many elements of animated theater—research, archival, and so on.

For the Professional

Theater. (Formerly: *Yale/Theater*). 1968. 3/yr. $18 (Individuals, $15). Joel Schechter. Yale Univ., School of Drama, 222 York St., Yale Sta., New Haven, CT 06520. Illus., index. Circ: 2,300. Microform: UMI.

Indexed: HumI. *Bk. rev:* 1–2. *Aud:* Pr.

A look at modern theater as seen through the eyes of those who work at the Yale School of Drama. Supported and published by Yale, the journal is one of the best of its type. The format, articles, and illustrations all maintain the journal's excellence. Each issue focuses on a specific theme—for example, American regional theater or Athol Fugard—and includes a new play. "The back of the book" features discussions of the most important current theatrical events in American regional theater and around the globe.

Theatre Journal (TJ) (Formerly: *Educational Theatre Journal*). 1941. q. $25. James Moy & Timothy Murray. Johns Hopkins Univ. Press for Univ. & College Theatre Assn., Journals Div., Baltimore, MD 21218. Illus., adv. Circ: 6,200. Microform: UMI.

Indexed: EdI, HumI, CIJE. *Bk. rev:* 12–15, 700–1,000 words. *Aud:* Pr.

The official journal of the American Theatre Association University and College Theatre Division (ATA), this publication should be in any theater collection. At this writing, the ATA is undergoing major reorganization so this journal, which is edited for faculty and graduate students in university and college theater programs, bears watching. An average issue puts much emphasis on scholarly articles in the areas of theater history and theatrical theory and criticism. From time to time, issues are devoted to special topics such as performance, Renaissance theater, and so on. Useful, regular features include the book reviews and some ten to twelve theater reviews.

Variety. 1905. w. $65. Syd Silverman. Variety, Inc., 154 W. 46th St., New York, NY 10036. Illus., adv. Circ: 43,028. Vol. ends: No. 13. Microform: UMI.

Indexed: MusicI. *Aud:* Pr.

This is the official newspaper of show business, complete with clever headlines. The language is peculiar to the magazine, which echoes the language used in the entertainment field. Sections on movies, radio and television, music and records, and even vaudeville are included, along with news of the theater world. In addition to general news items of the stage, the "legitimate" section contains reviews of on- and off-Broadway shows and shows abroad, information on casting, the amount of money grossed each week by Broadway and road shows, and where touring shows are playing. *Variety* is a necessity for its complete coverage of all areas of the entertainment world. Valuable for regional as well as New York theater, it includes information on the business elements of show business, current trends in television, the law and show business, and thousands more topics. It might even create interest in high schools with the top records of the week—both singles and albums. Note: This weekly is sometimes confused with another newspaper that covers much the same material—*Daily Variety*.

TRAVEL

For the Student

See also City and Regional Section.

Introduction

Oddly enough, there is only one real, general title in this important area (*Travel/Holiday*). Most others are for members of travel or other organizations—particularly, those who hold credit cards, fly, or simply sell others on travel. It is suggested that librarians and individuals seeking a wider horizon turn to the numerous travel-type regional magazines listed in the City and Regional Section. Another good bet is the travel section of *The New York Times* on Sunday.

Basic Periodicals

Hs: *Consumer Reports Travel Letter, Travel/Holiday*.

For the Student

American Traveler. 1974. q. $6. Days Inn of America, Inc., 2751 Buford Highway NE, Atlanta, GA 30324. Illus. adv. Circ: 321,000. Sample.
Aud: Hs.

Throughout the various issues of this hotel-sponsored magazine there are articles and features that cover the primary tourist attractions of the United States and Canada. Specific advice is given on where to go, where to eat, and what to see, but not on where to sleep. There is considerable emphasis on traveling on a budget.

Discovery. 1961. q. $3. Allstate Motor Club, 30 All State Plaza, Northbrook, IL 60066. Circ: 1,300,000. Sample. Vol ends: Fall. Microform: UMI.
Bk. rev: Notes. *Aud:* Ejh, Hs.

This magazine is affiliated with the Allstate Motor Club, which accounts for its low price and large circulation. It includes tips on where to go, what to do, and what to avoid. The style is casual in that it contains stories of vacation trips written in the first person and some humor. There are pieces on travel by automobile, ship, plane, and rail, with the emphasis on travel in the United States. Good illustrations and good writing.

Islands. 1981. bi-m. $18. Connie Bourassa-Shaw. Island Publg. Co., 3886 State St., Santa Barbara, CA 93105. Illus., adv. Circ: 75,000. Sample.
Aud: Hs.

Both a geography and a travel magazine with a single point of reference—the islands of the world. The majority of articles are the islands where people may go for vacation or for an extended visit or stay. These features often have striking photographs. Comments on the way people live and enjoy themselves are candid, and there is little of the fast-sell present. As much a magazine to dream over as it is to use for travel (or for geography reports), *Islands* is an ideal title for the general collection.

Transitions. 1977. q. $9.50. Clayton A. Hubbs, 18 Hulst Rd., Amherst, MA 01002. Illus., adv. Circ: 13,000.
Aud: Hs.

Subtitled "The Resource Guide to Budget Travel, Work and Study Abroad." This is a unique 65-to-70-page guide for both educators and travelers. Directed to people of all ages, experience, and education, it offers suggestions on how to enjoy a country without being a tourist and how to take part in the culture and its educational activities. The emphasis on small budget makes it particularly appealing. Specific information is given on such things as how to arrange summer study in Cambridge, England (including accommodations and costs); study holidays in Britain, with addresses and tips; employment opportunities in the United Kingdom; a French study holiday; and affordable Lima—to list only a few of the articles in one issue. The editor has one or two special issues a year which focus on particular areas and themes, including long-duration travel and study abroad or preparation for an overseas career. The authors are experienced and write from knowledge, not theory. Considering the reasonable price, buy two copies—one for the travel collection, and another for education. Highly recommended.

Travel/Holiday. 1901. m. $9. Scott Shane. Travel Bldg., Floral Park, NY 11001. Illus., adv. Circ: 800,000. Sample. Vol. ends: Dec.
Indexed: RG. *Aud:* Hs.

Directed to almost anyone who travels, with particular emphasis on middle-class incomes and pleasures, this is the only general travel magazine now being published in the United States. The illustrations and writing are good, the information solid, and the editorial approach excellent. While there is little choice, it is a solid travel title that should be found in almost all libraries.

USSR AND EASTERN EUROPE

For the Student

See also Asia and Europe Sections.

Gloria Jacobs, 226-34 Manor Rd., Queens Village, NY 11427 (Russian Language and Newspapers subsections)

Harold M. Leich, Slavic Acquisitions Librarian, Slavic/E. European Library, University of Illinois, 1408 W. Gregory Dr., Urbana, IL 61801 (English Language subsection)

Introduction

With the possible exception of Yugoslavia, publications from the Soviet Union and the East European countries tend to hew strictly to an official communist party line, relating nearly everything to the tenets of Marxist thought and deviating from that line only slightly. The fact that the state controls all publishing activities is a virtual guarantee that voices of dissent and disagreement are weak and scattered, but even beyond that there are other implications for publishing. A certain predictability exists with Soviet journals and newspapers, for example, the anti-Western statements or the overly positive and uncritical remarks concerning "fraternal socialist states." The same basic situation holds for the communist countries of Eastern Europe, although the situation there varies from country to country and seems more subject to fluctuation because of changing internal situations and policies and more direct influence from the West.

Now, more perhaps than ever before, it is important to have a feel for what motivates Soviet society and what forces influence Soviet policies. How will this region be affected by the continuing economic crisis in Poland or by the Soviet occupation of Afghanistan? As any culture, what the Soviet people (and East European peoples) read day in and day out does affect their behavior and attitudes. It is the responsibility of libraries to bring an awareness of these attitudes to library users.

For the student of Soviet and East European affairs, a careful reading of what may at first appear to be identical news stories and articles often indicates subtle changes in policy or deviations from the standard line. For the general audience, it may be valuable simply to get an exposure to Soviet and East European society, culture, and basic attitudes, and for this reason libraries may want to subscribe to several of the English-language publications that are available.

The selections for this section include magazines published in the USSR and Eastern Europe (with emphasis on those in English), and also those English-language titles published in the West that describe, analyze, and interpret the Soviet Union and Eastern Europe. The titles selected, therefore, represent a number of specific subject areas in the social sciences and humanities disciplines.

Since a number of the titles listed in this section are published in the USSR and Eastern Europe, a word or two about subscription procedures might be helpful. The USSR and each of the Eastern European countries maintain an official, government-controlled book and periodical exporting enterprise, which directs distribution of all national publications, sets prices, and handles all subscription orders. Most of these organizations prefer not to deal directly with individuals or libraries, so it is best to place subscriptions for magazines from these countries with a North American or Western European international subscription agency, such as Faxon or EBSCO, or with firms that specialize in publications from the USSR and Eastern Europe. The chief U.S.-based outlet for Soviet periodicals is Victor Kamkin, Inc. (12224 Parklawn Dr., Rockville, MD 20852); other companies are useful for Eastern European publications, including Eastern New Distributors (155 W. 15th St., New York, NY 10011) and Imported Publications, Inc. (320 W. Ohio St., Chicago, IL 60610).

For the past several decades, virtually all of American foreign policy objectives have centered directly or indirectly around our perception of Soviet society and its aims and goals. In a world where nationalism and political ideology have come to wield tremendous influence in shaping world events, it is certain that this will continue, and it is imperative that we continue to study Soviet and East European culture and politics in order to separate powerful stereotypes and myths from reality. It is hoped that librarians will recognize this responsibility and give high priority to analyzing all sides of the Soviet and East European question. (H.M.L.)

Basic Periodicals

ENGLISH LANGUAGE. Hs: *New Times, Soviet Life, Sputnik.*

RUSSIAN LANGUAGE. *Pravda.*

Basic Abstracts and Indexes

Public Affairs Information Service.

For the Student

Culture and Life. 1957. m. $15. Ado Kukanov. Union of Soviet Societies for Friendship and Cultural Relations with Foreign Countries. U.S. Subs. to: Victor Kamkin, Inc., 12224 Parklawn Dr., Rockville, MD 20852. Illus., index. Vol. ends: Dec. Microform: B&H.
Aud: Hs.

A more sophisticated, less political version of *Soviet Life*, focusing on the cultural developments and achievements of the Soviet Union. It contains articles (with beautiful, high quality color photographs) on the theater, opera, ballet, art, and music. Profiles of prominent artists and stories on personalities in the Soviet republics alternate with theoretical writings. Cultural relations with foreign countries are given extensive coverage, reflecting the publisher's philosophy of seeking a rapprochement with other countries through the exchange of artists. In the Russian version (*Kul'tura i zhizn'*), it is a useful study aid for beginning or intermediate language students.

Current Digest of the Soviet Press. 1949. w. $110 (Faculty and students of subscribing institutions, $56). Robert S. Ehlers. Current Digest of the Soviet Press, 1314 Kinnear Rd., Columbus, OH 43212. Index. Sample. Vol. ends: No. 52. *Indexed:* PAIS. *Aud:* Hs.

The basic source in English of material from the Soviet press. Much of the material selected for translation is from the USSR's two chief dailies, *Pravda* and *Izvestiia*, but selections are also taken from some 60 other newspapers and magazines. When articles have been abridged, it is noted, and full bibliographic details are given for each translation for those who need to consult the original. The editors refrain from commenting on translated articles, thus affording the U.S. user an excellent cross section of Soviet opinion and journalism. *CDSP* is currently the best single source for following recent Soviet events in detail in English. In recent years the publishers have intitiated several admirable reduced-rate subscriptions for smaller libraries and individuals, in an attempt to make this material available to a much broader range of library users. (Inquire with the publisher for details.) Essential for high school libraries with an interest in providing up-to-date coverage of Soviet affairs.

Czechoslovak Life. 1946. m. $6. Josef Skala. Orbis Press Agency, Vinohradska 46, 12041 Prague 2, Czechoslovakia. Illus. Vol. ends: No. 12 (Dec.).
Aud: Hs.

A very enjoyable, easily read, and well-produced publication, *Czechoslovak Life* would be a good addition to any public or high school library. Each issue, about 45 pages in length, contains a variety of articles on topics such as art, sports, music, nature, resorts, history, and literature. Although the magazine is an official publication of the Czechoslovak Ministry of Culture, it is basically nonpolitical. The photography is superb and makes one want to visit what appears to be one of Europe's most physically attractive countries. This magazine is highly recommended for libraries that want English-language material on Czechoslovakia or that serve patrons of Czech or Slovak background.

Krokodil *(Crocodile).* 1922. 36/yr. $10.80. E. P. Dubrovin. Bumazhnyi proezd, dom 14, Moscow, 101455, USSR. Illus. Circ: 5,000,000.
Aud: Hs.

This is a very popular magazine both among Soviet citizens and Western Russian language instructors. A colorful, well-illustrated 16-page satire magazine, its contents include cartoons, short jokes, and full-page stories on a variety of themes. While the cartoons reprinted from the Western communist dailies are always political, the majority of them satirize social injustices, societal ills, and human foibles. The overtly anti-Western cartoons border on pure propaganda, but they are enough in the minority to warrant use in an instructional setting. Through humor, the problems and concerns of the Soviets can be followed. Written in colloquial Russian, this publication could be incorporated into Russian-language programs on any level.

Materialy Samizdata (Formerly: *Sobranie dokumentov samizdata (Collection of samizdat documents).* 1972. Irreg. $132.

Radio Free Europe & Radio Liberty. Dist. by: Ohio State Univ., Center for Slavic & East European Studies, Dulles Hall, Rm. 344, 230 W. 17 Ave., Columbus OH 43210. Index. Circ: 70. Vol. ends: Dec.
Aud: Hs.

A compilation of underground Soviet publications, this periodical is "made available to interested scholars, libraries and research organizations." Annually, the number of pages produced range from 2,000 to 2,500. As explained on the title page, *Materialy Samizdata* is "a reprint from a photocopy original." Contents include status reports from prison and labor camps, church bulletins, and personal letters by citizens on a variety of international matters. These articles are compiled, given accession numbers, and used on Radio Free Europe and Radio Liberty broadcasts. In addition to reprinting, the staff also researches the material, occasionally correcting misspellings and incorrect dates via footnotes, and compiles a broad index. The title page lists the articles therein, the articles' length, and bibliographic material. If an exact date is unknown, an approximate one is supplied parenthetically. The publication's information about life in the camps, prisons, and the like, is enlightening, vividly illustrating another side of Soviet life. Therefore, this publication should be considered by any established Soviet studies program to round out its collection.

Murzilka. 1924. m. $3. A. Shevaley. ul. Novodmitrovskaya, dom 5a, Moscow, 125015, USSR. Illus. Circ: 5,600,000. Vol. ends: Dec.
Aud: Ejh, Hs.

A publication of the All Union Pioneer Organization, *Murzilka* is written for members of the Young Pioneers, ages ten to fifteen. Although intended as both an entertaining and educational magazine, the propaganda element is pervasive. Each 31-page issue features poems, short stories, fairy tales, and novellas in installments. Favorite topics include Soviet holidays, fraternal countries' youth organizations, revolutionary heroes and other patriotic themes. *Murzilka* can be incorporated into an instructional Russian curriculum, giving the students practice with colloquial Russian while at the same time exposing them to Soviet magazines for adolescents.

New Times: a Soviet weekly of world affairs. 1943. w. $18. Ed. bd. Pushkin Sq., Moscow 103782, USSR. U.S. Subs. to: Victor Kamkin, Inc., 12224 Parklawn Dr., Rockville, MD 20852. Illus., index. Circ: 350,000. Microform: B&H. *Indexed:* PAIS. *Aud:* Hs.

International events and news, from the official Soviet point of view, form the contents of this weekly, 36-page magazine. Issued in editions in eight languages and apparently intended for export from the USSR rather than for readership at home, the news articles, editorials, and political commentaries tend to focus on areas of contention between East and West (the Middle East or Central America, for example) and on the negative aspects of life in the United States and other Western democracies (crime, unemployment, the often large contrast between rich and poor, and so on). Despite these defects, *New Times* is a valuable source for those looking for the Soviet point of view on virtually any current event or situation of world interest (if only to contrast the Soviet viewpoint with that of the United States or other nations). The magazine can be useful for comparative purposes in social studies classes.

Pravda (Truth). 1912. d. $41.50. Organ of the Central Committee of the Communist Party of the Soviet Union. Illus. *Aud:* Hs.

This six-page newspaper is the most widely read of all Soviet newspapers. As the "official" voice of the Communist party, it is the party's forum for official news releases; therefore, it should be considered a basic research tool for anyone interested in the party's activities or philosophy. While the news items do not greatly differ from *Izvestiia, Pravda* also reprints speeches in full and provides an editorial column, *(Kolonka Commentatora)* which explores one news item in depth. *Pravda*'s journalistic style is very formal, emphasizing events rather than the meaning behind them. If only one Russian-language newspaper can be included in a library's collection, it should be this one because it can be used for serious research as well as casual reading.

Review: Yugoslav illustrated magazine. 1946. m. $12. Ed. bd. Jugoslovenska revija, Terzije 31, Belgrade, 11001, Yugoslavia. Illus., adv. *Aud:* Hs.

An attractive general interest, illustrated magazine about Yugoslavia. Features are on travel, local history, culture, and the arts in Yugoslavia. The English translations are excellent, and the color photography is of a very high quality. Special coverage is given to special cultural and sports events and festivals held in Yugoslavia's cities or along the spectacular Adriatic coast. For libraries wanting to present a popular, general overview of present-day Yugoslavia and its colorful past.

Smena (The Rising Generation). 1924. bi-w. $27. A. A. Likhanov. 14 Bumazhnyi proezd, Moscow, 101457, USSR. Illus. Vol. ends: Dec. *Aud:* Hs.

A magazine for teenage Komsomol members, *Smena* is both entertaining and educational in much the same way *Murzilka* is for a slightly younger audience. Published by the Central Committee of the Leninist Young Communist League, each 32-page issue contains short stories and articles on health, sports, patriotic themes, science, and the arts. The articles are always well illustrated. The last page is devoted to games, for example, games on chess and checkers and a crossword puzzle are supplied, as well as the answers to the previous puzzle. Compared to other Soviet magazines, this one is of average quality, but one of the few catering to teenagers.

Soviet Life. 1956. m. $9.35. Ed. bd. Embassy of the USSR, 1706 18th St., N.W., Washington, DC 20009. Illus. Vol. ends: No. 12 (Dec.). *Aud:* Ejh, Hs.

The contents of *Soviet Life* are specifically aimed at the U.S. audience, concentrating on the achievements of Soviet society and science and on Soviet-U.S. friendship. It is a general interest magazine, richly illustrated with beautiful color photos and printed in a glossy, large format. Many subjects are covered, including history, politics, nature and the environment, sports, medicine, and the arts. Each issue of 65 pages also features letters to the editor, question-answer columns about the Soviet Union and coverage of "friendship" events between the Soviets and Americans. The magazine is published by reciprocal agreement between the U.S. and Soviet governments. (The magazine *Amerika*, in Russian, is distributed in the USSR as the counterpart of *Soviet Life*.)

Soviet Union. 1930. m. $15. Nikolai Gribachev. U.S. Subs. to: Victor Kamkin, Inc., 12224 Parklawn Dr., Rockville, MD 20852. Illus. *Aud:* Hs.

Similar to *Soviet Life* in format and scope, this profusely illustrated monthly is issued in over 20 languages and is intended chiefly for export to the world's noncommunist countries. All aspects of contemporary USSR are featured, including sports, architecture, historical events, individual cities and regions, the arts, and scientific developments and achievements. Most issues include an editorial or some political commentary, but nothing very strident. The photography is of a very high quality.

Sputnik. 1967. m. $18. Ed. bd. Novosti Press Agency, 2 Pushkin Sq., Moscow, USSR. U.S. Subs. to: Victor Kamkin, Inc., 12224 Parklawn Dr., Rockville, MD 20852. Illus., adv. Vol. ends: No. 12 (Dec.). *Auds:* Hs.

Somewhat more sophisticated in its approach than *Soviet Life, Sputnik* is noted for the profusion and beauty of its illustrations and the wide variety in its choice of subjects for stories. Condensations of articles are selected from a large and wide range of Soviet magazines and newspapers, and are written by scientists, military personnel, government and party officials, and personalities in sports and the arts. Photographic essays, memoirs, fashion features, recipes, and humor complement the more serious features on history, politics, and economics, which of course reflect the official Soviet point of view. Designed solely for export from the USSR, this digest offers interesting and well-presented information on the Soviet Union. Secondary school libraries as well as public and academic libraries will find this title useful for broad, general coverage of the USSR. In its Russian-language edition (also titled *Sputnik*), this is a valuable supplementary reading source for beginning and intermediate students of Russian.

Travel to the USSR. 1966. $16. Ed. bd. U.S. Subs. to: Victor Kamkin, Inc., 12224 Parklawn Dr., Rockville, MD 20852. Illus., index, adv. *Aud:* Hs.

This should be a popular addition to high school libraries in which there is interest in the Soviet Union. Each issue, of approximately 50 pages, is filled with color photos and travelogs depicting the Soviet landscape. Its aim is clearly to encourage the foreigner to visit the USSR as a tourist. (One of the sponsoring organizations is the USSR Federal Foreign Tourism Administration.) A thoroughly enjoyable and beautifully produced magazine, this title would make for good leisure reading in most libraries.

Ukraine: illustrated monthly. 1959. m. $16. Anatoly Mikhailenko. U.S. Subs. to: Victor Kamkin, Inc., 12224 Parklawn Dr., Rockville, MD 20852. Illus. Vol. ends: No. 12 (Dec.).
Aud: Hs.

Similar in scope and appeal to *Soviet Union* or *Soviet Life*, this large-format, well-illustrated magazine focuses on the Soviet Ukraine and features stories and photographs on science, education, tourism, the arts, and general social and political conditions in the Ukraine—from an orthodox Soviet viewpoint, of course. This magazine is obviously intended for export to the English-speaking countries where there are many persons of Ukrainian descent, and the tone of the articles is upbeat and generally nonpolitical. Useful for general audiences in which there is interest in Ukrainian or Soviet matters, or where there are substantial numbers of Ukrainian-Americans.

WOMEN

For the Student/For the Professional

Connie Miller, Science Librarian, University of Illinois–Chicago, Chicago, IL 60680

Introduction

Women's periodicals are proliferating. Yet even in their proliferation, they divide themselves into categories: (1) "General" periodicals assume, like many men, that women, whether they work outside the home, are married, or are single and liberated, care primarily about cosmetics, clothes, cooking, children, and men; (2) "Feminist, Lesbian, and Women's Studies" periodicals evolve out of an interest in women themselves and express an acceptance of the diversity that this interest brings; (3) "Literary and Artistic" periodicals publish creative work by women; and (4) "Special Interest" periodicals examine women in the light of some other topic, e.g., performance, politics, or therapy. The fourth category of women's periodicals accounts for the highest rate of proliferation. In terms of circulation figures, however, there are single titles in the first category which have more readers than all of the titles in any other category combined.

Circulation figures are slippery and unreliable indicators at best. Comparing, for example, a circulation of six million with one of two thousand tells nothing about subscriber versus shelf sales. Nor does it provide any ready means of establishing the value of a publication. Not all periodicals intend to be read by large numbers of people. Many, in fact, would suffer in quality by attempting to appeal to a mass audience. In spite of all these caveats, however, it is impossible to introduce this section on "Women" without addressing the enormous disparities in periodical circulation figures and their possible implications. *Family Circle* has a circulation of over eight million, *McCall's* over six million, and even the least popular title in the "General" category reaches more than twenty thousand readers. Only one serious "Feminist, Lesbian, and Women's Studies" competitor exists—*Ms.*, which is read by over half a million people.

The periodicals listed here tend to fall in the first category—general interest magazines. Still, many titles (*Between Our Selves, Fighting Women News,* and *Spare Rib,* for example) represent other types.

Basic Periodicals

Hs: *Essence, Good Housekeeping, Mademoiselle, Ms.*

For the Student

Between Our Selves: women of color newspaper. 1985. 6/yr. $15 (Individuals, $10). Between Our Selves Collective, P.O. Box 1939, Washington, DC 20013. Illus., adv. Circ: 5,000.
Bk. rev: Irregular, length varies. *Aud:* Hs.

A brand new, 16-page tabloid publication, "*Between Our Selves* is a forum for . . . all women of color to discuss . . . thoughts, report on . . . organizing strategies, further Third World feminism, [and] talk about . . . her stories and dreams." Besides feature articles and photographs, the newspaper includes a fiction/poetry corner; conference, networking, and publication announcements; and book reviews. A typical issue includes a photo essay on Palestinian refugees; an article by Audre Lorde on "Black Women Organizing Across Sexualities"; an interview with musician Betty Carter; and an essay on "Women & Human Rights in the Philippines," which is substantiated by personal statements from members of the Aguilar family. It is vitally important for women of color to have access to information about themselves written by themselves. *Between Our Selves* offers libraries an opportunity to provide this sort of access.

Big Beautiful Woman; the world's first fashion magazine for the large-size woman. 1979. bi-m. $13. Carole Shaw. Suite 214, 5535 Balboa Blvd., Encino, CA 91316. Illus., adv. Circ: 250,000. Vol. ends: Nov/Dec.
Aud: Hs.

Radiance's approach is feminist and *Big Beautiful Woman*'s (BBW) is feminine, but they both share the same intention: to encourage big women to feel beautiful and to establish a network among women who relate positively to their larger body sizes. *BBW*'s pages are filled with big, beautiful models modeling fashions specifically designed for the "fully dimensional woman." In addition, each issue features *BBW* women who have made it—either in the world of fashion or on stage (for example, Conchata Ferrell, *E.R.*'s Nurse Thor and star of the movie, *Heartland*). Some articles deal expressly with weight—for example, "Are Women Supposed to Be Thin?" or an opinion piece called "Ohhh, Richard," in which *BBW*'s editor speaks out against women buying a line of clothes started by self-acclaimed fatist, Richard Simmons. Other articles, however, focus on topics of more general concern—such as how to be assertive rather than aggressive, the pros and cons of color analysis, and how to stop being a victim of verbal abuse. Departments include horoscopes, a recipe of the month, letters to the editor, and various columns of advice recommending businesses, restaurants, stores, and so forth, that "treat the large woman with respect and dignity."

Claudia. See Latin America, Latino (U.S.)/For the Student: Latin America Section.

Connexions: an international women's quarterly. 1981. q. $24 (Individuals, $12). Ed. bd. People's Translation Service, 4228 Telegraph Ave., Oakland, CA 94609. Illus., adv. Circ: 3,000. Vol. ends: Fall.

Indexed: API. *Aud:* Hs.

An invaluable journal that is one of a kind, *Connexions* belongs in virtually all libraries. Its intention is to "contribute to the growth of a worldwide feminist network" by putting women who are doing the same things, wherever they may be, in touch with each other. In every issue, women's own words (which constitute feminist journalism, as *Media Report to Women* defines it)—in the form of news reports, personal testimonies, interviews, poems, and even cartoons—describe life in about 30 different countries. An introductory editorial and, often, an article on a topic of universal interest (for example, Free Trade Zones) accompany statements about individual countries. While all aspects of women's lives receive attention, economic and political conditions are emphasized. There is, simply, no other recurring source of women's global experiences; therefore, *Connexions* ought to be widely available.

Coqueta. See Latin America, Latino (U.S.)/For the Student: Latino (U.S.) Section.

Craftswoman. 1982. q. $12. Anne Patterson Dee. Daedulus Publns., Inc., P.O. Box 848, Libertyville, IL 60048. Illus., adv. Circ: 3,000.

Aud: Hs.

Like *Tradeswomen*, one of *Craftswoman*'s important functions is to publicize the possibility of alternative career options. The quarterly is aimed at home-based craftswomen, needleworkers, and designers, and emphasizes practical business and marketing strategies and advice. Typical feature topics include choosing your first craft tour, designing and producing a craft catalog, using time effectively, and keeping home and business life separate. Interviews with successful home-based artists offer encouragement to others contemplating a similar enterprise. Twice yearly, *Craftswoman* publishes a "Crafts Co-op Catalog" in which, for a fee, craft producers can advertise their products. The "Catalog" is distributed to 65,000 potential buyers. The January 1985 issue of *Craftswoman* provides readers with a listing of 300 "art, craft, needlecraft, crafts marketing, home business & related magazines, newspapers, & newsletters." For networking, how-to guidance, and encouragement, women interested in gaining financial profit from their crafts will find no better source of information.

Elle. 1945. w. $110. Helene Gordon-Lazareff. Elle, 6 rue Ancelle, 9521 Neuilly-Seine, France. Illus., adv. Circ: 625,000.

Aud: Hs.

The numerous illustrations, advertisements, and the general format encourage the reader to consume by improving the home. While some attention is given to the working woman outside the house, most of the editorial matter is directed to the more conservative aspects of being a young housewife. It's all quite middle class, with useful tips on cooking, sewing, beauty care, interior decorating, entertaining, and related matters. The fiction is good, and the overall impression is a magazine directed to a woman with a mind of her own, albeit within the confines of what is accepted in French society. Sometimes the format is quite striking, and this encourages readership. An excellent knowledge of French is required to appreciate the overall magazine, but much of it is within the grasp of the two-year student of French.

Essence: the magazine for today's Black woman. 1970. m. $12. Susan L. Taylor. Essence Communications, Inc., 1500 Broadway, New York, NY 10036. Subs. to: P.O. Box 2989, Boulder, CO 80302. Illus., adv. Circ: 750,000. Vol. ends: Dec. Microform: UMI.

Indexed: INeg. *Bk. rev:* 1–2, brief, signed. *Aud:* Hs.

"When you miss *Essence*," says the magazine, "you miss you." The "you" who you would miss by not subscribing to this clearly popular monthly appears to be a young to middle-aged, middle-class, family-, fashion-, and career-conscious Black woman. Much of *Essence* is predictable: "Fashion and Beauty" discusses hair salons and "clothes that move up the ladder with you"; "Contemporary Living" offers recipes, a guide to wines, and tips on interior design, "with the accent on African art"; "Departments" includes horoscopes and advice on money, sexual health, travel; "Grapevine" reviews art, music, and books; and "Features" contains candid interviews with stars such as actress and recording artist Janet Jackson, articles on AIDS, avoiding mistakes in relationships. In each issue, however, thought-provoking political or social commentaries also appear, adding depth to the journal's content. "The Life and Times of a College Buppie" takes a hard look at the current politically uninvolved generation of Black students, and a "Speak" column publishes brief articles such as "We Are All in Danger," a protest against the arrest of the Black revolutionary Marxist-Leninist New York 8+. Libraries that miss *Essence* may also miss "you."

Fem. See Latin America, Latino (U.S.)/For the Student: Latin America Section.

Fighting Woman News. 1975. q. $15 (Individuals, $10). Valeria Eads, P.O. Box 1459, Grand Central Sta., New York, NY 10163. Illus., adv. Circ: 5,000. Vol. ends: Winter.

Indexed: WomAb. *Bk. rev:* 1–5, length varies, signed. *Aud:* Hs.

Martial arts, self-defense, combative sports, and "herstory" constitute the territory covered by *Fighting Woman News*. Issues reflect this diversity. Although articles, features, and reviews cover a range of topics, a sense of both the power and the responsibility that accompany physical strength and agility runs through them all. Historical approaches—for example, "Recreating the Middle Ages as

They Should Have Been" or "Joan of Arc: Kingmaker"—mix with practical advice on teaching karate; interviews with athletes or martial artists such as Abe Toyoko, teacher of the Tendo Ryu school of weapons; and discussions of fencing or aikido. "Sports Reports" describes recent championships, competitions, or achievements and ruminates on the state of women's athletics in general. Books reviewed include everything from *Women in the Martial Arts* or *The Last Warrior Queen* to *Reweaving the Web of Life: Feminism and Nonviolence* or *The Politics of Women's Spirituality*. *Fighting Woman News* also prints short stories and poems with martially related themes. The encouragement this journal offers women, not only to excel athletically but also to explore the full potential of their bodies' power, is unique—making it an excellent selection for high school libraries.

Glamour. 1939. m. $15. Ruth Whitney. Condé Nast Publns., Inc., 350 Madison Ave., New York, NY 10017. Subs. to: P.O. Box 5203, Boulder, CO 80302. Illus., adv. Circ: 2,000,000. Vol. ends: Dec. Microform: B&H, UMI.
Indexed: Acs. *Bk. rev:* 3–4, 200–300 words, signed. *Aud:* Hs.

Of the more sophisticated feminine fashion magazines (the others being *Mademoiselle* and *Vogue*), *Glamour* is the best seller. Besides innumerable advertisements, the 300-page monthly issues include the usual health, beauty, fitness, food, travel, and home furnishings segments. Feature articles cover a range of predictable topics within the general areas of sex, love, aging, parents, work, and college. Unlike the more focused and less diverse *Good Housekeeping* or *Harper's Bazaar*, *Glamour* publishes a large "Entertainment" section of music, movie, book, television, and "new tech" reviews. Readers participate regularly in surveys. The results of a questionnaire on pollution were published the same month questions were asked concerning South African apartheid. The "How to Do Anything Better Guide" also solicits readers' input on coping with life's daily difficulties. Advice ranges from how to get tar off one's shoes to how to be safe in a storm or from party games to how to keep your job. Like other publications of its type, *Glamour* pays lip service to issues the women's movement has raised, an emphasis which—for its two million subscribers—appears to be perfectly satisfactory.

Good Housekeeping. 1885. m. $14.97. John Mack Carter. 959 Eighth Ave., New York, NY 10019. Subs. to: P.O. Box 10055, Des Moines, IA 50350. Illus., adv. Circ: 5,000,000. Vol. ends: June/Dec. Microform: B&H, UMI.
Indexed: AbrRG, RG. *Aud:* Hs.

Good Housekeeping backs up its promise to be the "magazine America lives by" through guaranteeing a refund for or the replacement of any defective product advertised in its colorful, busy monthly issues. Oriented toward accomplishment, regular features focus on recipes, cooking (microwaves merit a column all their own), nutrition, fitness, fashion, and crafts and needlework. Departments include psychological advice from Dr. Joyce Brothers, household hints via Heloise's "Helpline," and medical wisdom from the "Family Doctor." In "Better Way," readers receive tips and information on everything from skin cancer or car insurance to sunglasses and family hostels. Pages from the "Better Way" section can be easily detached and saved for future reference. Lives of stars and celebrities and novels or short stories by recognizable authors typically appear. With five million subscribers, this all-purpose guide to homemaking success is obviously a favorite.

Harper's Bazaar. 1867. m. $16.97. Anthony T. Mazzola. Hearst Corp., 959 Eighth Ave., New York, NY 10019. Subs. to: P.O. Box 10081, Des Moines, IA 50350. Illus., adv. Circ: 600,000. Vol. ends: Dec. Microform: UMI.
Indexed: RG. *Aud:* Hs.

Harper's Bazaar competes, less glamorously, with *Glamour* and *Vogue* for its readers. In between advertisements, fashion and beauty advice predominates. Role models in the form of stars and celebrities explain their secrets; Joan Collins, for example, instructs *Harper's* readers on after-40 beauty. Aurora regularly provides horoscopes, and a "Book Bazaar" occasionally features reviews by well-known or controversial authors such as Marilyn French. The variety in article topics—for example, jobs, unconventional marriage, college—indicates an effort to appeal to a broad audience. While not as successful as its competitors, *Harper's*, with over half a million readers, must be doing something right.

Health. See Health and Medicine/For the Student Section.

Hot Wire: a journal of women's music and culture. 1984. 3/ yr. $19 (Individuals, $14). Toni L. Armstrong. 1321 W. Rosedale, Chicago, IL 60660. Illus., adv. Vol. ends: Nov. *Aud:* Hs.

Unique in its focus on women's music and musicians, this new, attractively produced periodical has a good chance of succeeding. Contributors, amazingly enough, are even paid. The highlight of each issue is an interview. Comedian Kate Clinton was the star when *Hot Wire* premiered; more recently, interviewees have included Teressa Trull and Barbara Higbie. Features approach music from a variety of perspectives ranging from autobiographical accounts of women's duos to an article commemorating the tenth anniversary of WomanSound, a Washington-based sound reinforcement company. Festivals—for example, the Seventh Women's Jazz Festival—receive separate attention in a section of their own. A number of interesting "departments" add diversity. "Re-inking" prints "thought pieces" on women's writing (for example, Andrea Dworkin on "Loving Books"); "Mulling It Over" focuses on connections between art and politics; and "Behind the Scenes" spotlights the "unsung women in the women's music network"—for example, Lisa Vogl, who has been producing the nationally famous Michigan Women's Music Festival for ten years. Included as a bonus are "Soundsheets," which are actual recordings of songs by featured artists. *Hot Wire* is one of a kind and well done.

ISIS International Women's Journal (Formerly: *ISIS International Bulletin*). 1974. q. $25 (Individuals, $15). ISIS Intl.,

Via Santa Maria dell Anima 30, 00186-Rome, Italy; or ISIS Internacional, Casilla 2067, Carreo Central, Santiago, Chile. Illus., adv. Circ: 5,000.

Indexed: WomAb. *Bk. rev:* 5–8, brief. *Aud:* Hs.

Published in English and Spanish, *ISIS International Women's Journal* acts as a "channel of communication for women around the world to share experiences, ideas, information, analyses and reflections on how we as women are mobilizing and organizing to overcome discrimination and oppression." Each issue is published jointly by ISIS International and one or more Third World Women's Groups. Recently, the Coordinating Collective of the 2nd Latin American and Caribbean Feminist Meeting assisted in publishing its proceedings in the *ISIS Journal*. Quarterly, in this case, means that in addition to two issues annually, the *International Women's Journal* published two supplements entitled *Women in Action*. These supplements supply the news of the worldwide women's movement, announcements of conferences, names of organizations, and other relevant events. This globally oriented publication complements other women's journals with similar perspectives, and may be the best source of information on Third World women's concerns.

Kalliope: a journal of women's art. 1979. 3/yr. $9. Sharon Weightman. Kalliope Poetry and Fiction Collective, Florida Junior College at Jacksonville, Kent Campus, 3939 Roosevelt Blvd., Jacksonville, FL 32205. Illus. Circ: 1,000.

Aud: Hs.

Kalliope "devotes itself to women in the arts by publishing work and sharing ideas and opinions." While it solicits criticism, essays, and reviews in addition to fiction, poetry, drawings, and photographs, the latter four categories appear most often. Occasionally, issues center on a topic. "Women under Thirty" offers a variety of interesting selections by younger or beginning artists, a group *Kalliope* regularly encourages. An excellent addition to high school collections, this attractive publication might well act as the incentive that some novice women writers need.

Mademoiselle. 1935. m. $15. Amy Levin. Condé Nast Publns., Inc., 350 Madison Ave., New York, NY 10017. Subs. to: P.O. Box 5204, Boulder, CO 80302. Illus., adv. Circ: 1,200,000. Vol. ends: Dec. Microform: B&H, UMI.

Indexed: RG. *Bk. rev:* 2–4, 250–300 words, signed. *Aud:* Hs.

The fact that a quarter of a million more readers subscribe to *Mademoiselle* now than did three years ago indicates the continuing success of the editorial polish that Amy Levin provided when she became the publication's editor in 1980. Overall, the tone and content aim at the mature, single, career woman. Male-female relationships are examined on an adult level in articles such as "One Woman, Many Loves" or "On Being the Other Woman." Each issue includes features for the professional—for example, "Power Dressing" or "Careers with Bonuses." The usual departments, fashion and beauty, home and food, travel and health, are complemented by good, in-depth reviews of books, films, and music in the "To Read" section. Quality short stories by well-known, contemporary authors appear monthly. Trendy fashions and expert beauty advice, however, are still what make *Mademoiselle* tick.

Ms. 1971. m. $16. Patricia Carbine. Ms. Foundation for Education and Communication, Inc., 119 W. 40 St., New York, NY 10018. Subs. to: Subscription Dept., 123 Garden St., Marion, OH 43302. Illus., adv. Circ: 500,000. Sample. Vol. ends: June. Microform: B&H, MIM, UMI.

Indexed: MgI, RG, WomAb. *Bk. rev:* 2–5, 300–700 words, signed. *Aud:* Hs.

Recommending *Ms.* is like campaigning for the status quo. With circulation figures approaching half a million, it is the only periodical this reviewer considers "feminist" which rivals in readership the more "feminine" titles. *Ms.*, in fact, resembles the feminine titles in ways other than readership. *Ms.* can be distinguished from the periodicals it resembles by its endorsement of lesbianism as a life-style and by its tendency to use, rather than to avoid the use of, the words feminist and feminism. Besides feature articles, each issue of *Ms.* includes a "Gazette" news section; travel, money, and technology departments; a "Back Page" commentary; book and film reviews; excellent poetry and fiction and "Stories for Free Children." Although Gloria Steinem appears in the table of contents less frequently than she did in the past, *Ms.* contributors tend to be well known. Whatever its compromises, this magazine manages to keep feminism and lesbianism alive in the minds of a large and diverse group of subscribers.

New Directions for Women (Formerly: *New Directions For Women in New Jersey*). 1972. bi-m. $16 (Individuals, $10). Phyllis Kriegel. New Directions for Women, Inc., 108 W. Palisade Ave., Englewood, NJ 07631. Illus., adv. Circ: 55,000. Microform: UMI.

Indexed: API, WomAb. *Bk. rev:* 5–10, 300–1,000 words, signed. *Aud:* Hs.

What began as the first state-wide feminist newsletter has evolved into an outstanding national tabloid. *New Directions* explores all issues of concern to women and all aspects of feminism. Well-written and carefully researched articles discuss local and international politics and economics; describe developments in controversial legal areas such as incest, sexual harassment, and lesbian motherhood; and capture the excitement and enjoyment surrounding women musicians and their music. Regular sections are diverse and informative. "Keeping Tabs on Our Health" deals with everything from tampons and abortion to health care in Cuba. "Women in the Arts" includes useful, opinionated film, art, and record reviews. Older women have a forum in "Prime Time." In addition to excellent book reviews, "New Directions Review of Books" features columns such as "For Young Readers" and "Lesbian Fiction." Classified advertisements, coast-to-coast news announcements, a calendar, and letters from readers add to the newspaper's practicality.

Off Our Backs. 1970. 11/yr. $20 (Individuals, $11). Off Our Backs, Inc., 1841 Columbia Rd. N.W., Rm. 212, Washington, DC 20009. Illus., index, adv. Circ: 10,000. Vol. ends: Dec.

Indexed: API, WomAb. *Bk. rev:* 3–5, 500 words, signed. *Aud:* Hs.

For 15 years, *Off Our Backs* (*OOB*), "a women's news journal," has consistently delivered high quality, provocative, and witty feminist journalism. Although published in newspaper format, *OOB*'s content includes culture as well as news. There are, in addition to editorials, coverage of national and international current events and reports on worldwide conferences of interest to women (for example, "Arab Women's Decade"). "Commentary" and "Response" sections consist of in-depth and informed discussions of controversial issues. In June of 1985, for example, *OOB* presented an excellent, balanced analysis of the feminist controversy over pornography. Columns by well-known authors (for example, Jan Clausen on the "political morality of fiction"), interviews, and special features (for example, "Women and the Law") appear periodically. Regulars include "Chicken Lady," a what's happening column which announces calls for papers, conferences, jobs, and other "droppings"; letters from readers; and advertisements. With the cessation of *New Women's Times* in 1985, *OOB*'s value and importance can only increase.

Radiance: a publication for large women. 1984. q. $10. Alice Ansfield, P.O. Box 31703, Oakland, CA 94604. Illus., adv. Vol. ends: Fall.

Aud: Hs.

The aim of this upbeat publication was succinctly expressed in a letter to *Radiance* from one of its readers: "thank you so much for letting me feel the spirit of all my big sisters who are learning to inhabit their bodies joyously." To realize its intention of becoming a nationwide resource for large women, *Radiance* publicizes for free community events open to the public occurring in all states. In addition, classifieds, a marketplace section, and advertisements sprinkled throughout each issue provide information on services, stores, and products designed specifically for women who are large. Article in all sections, "Up Your Image," "Health and Well-Being," "Inner Journeys," or "Up Front and Personal," advocate appreciation and respect for one's own body, whatever its shape, and explore the harmful effects and misconceptions which stem from "size-ism." A quarterly feature highlights a specific subject and establishes a theme which the sectional articles embellish. "Celebrate Your Body," for example, describes large women's exercise programs and facilities. In the same issue, a sports psychologist provides the first segment of an ongoing series on "Fitness, Feminism, and the Health of Fat Women." While fatist attitudes have, for some time, been recognized as illogical and deleterious, a quarterly, feminist periodical designed to establish networks of healthy, self-respecting large women is a unique and important resource that high school libraries will not want to be without.

Sage: a scholarly journal on black women. See Afro-American/For the Student Section.

Shape. See Health and Medicine/For the Student Section.

Spare Rib: a women's liberation magazine. 1972. m. $52 (Individuals, $35). Ed. bd. Spare Rib, Inc., 27 Clerkenwell Close, London EC1, England. Illus., adv. Circ: 30,000. Vol. ends: Dec.

Indexed: API. *Bk. rev:* 2–5, 200–700 words, signed. *Aud:* Hs.

This popular British monthly is an excellent source of feminist thought, wit, news, and creative writing. Feature articles—issues usually contain between five to ten of these—vary widely in subject matter, unless an issue has a topical focus. An "Old Age" issue, for example, features osteoporosis, quality of life for ethnic minority older people, and women who are aging in Africa. The feature articles in a regular issue, by contrast, deal with nursing, the South London Women Miner's Support Group, and miscarriage. Recurring columns include brief news reports; a "Shortlist," which provides a "roundup of women's events nationwide"; letters; classified advertisements; and book, film, theater, and television reviews. Fiction and poetry sometimes appear. An interesting column is "Hersay—The Page Where Readers Get It Off Their Chest!" One month a reader wrote a bitter critique of "war films disguised as peace films"; the next month a contributor discussed lesbianism and turning 30. *Spare Rib* is a British *Off Our Backs*; collections on both sides of the Atlantic should include this popular title.

Tradeswomen: a quarterly magazine for women in blue-collar work. 1981. q. $25 (Individuals, $10). Sandra Marilyn & Joss Eldredge. Tradeswomen, Inc., P.O. Box 40664, San Francisco, CA 94140. Illus. Circ: 2,000. Vol. ends: Fall.

Bk. rev: 0–2, 500–1,000 words, signed. *Aud:* Hs.

Taking a practical approach, *Tradeswomen* "delivers . . . information about getting into the trades, tools, contracting, networking, legislation and legal cases." The magazine helps its parent organization, Tradeswomen, Inc., fulfill its goals of supporting and promoting women working in nontraditional blue-collar jobs. Central to each issue are the interviews and articles about women in particular trades—for example, fire fighters, woodworkers, mechanics, pipe fitters, and so on. In addition, features deal with health hazards, self-employment, strikes, and other related concerns. Book and film reviews examine the treatment by media and the entertainment of nontraditionally employed women. Short stories and poems approach the trades from a less practical perspective. Subscribing to *Tradeswomen* is particularly important for high school libraries that want to offer all of their students a range of career options.

Vogue. 1892. m. $24. Grace Mirabella. Condé Nast Publns., Inc., 350 Madison Ave., New York, NY 10017. Subs. to: P.O. Box 5201, Boulder, CO 80322. Illus., adv. Circ: 1,300,000. Vol. ends: Dec. Microform: B&H, UMI.

Indexed: BioI, RG. *Bk. rev:* 2–5, 500–1,000 words, signed. *Aud:* Hs.

This sophisticated and classy fashion and life-style magazine continues to attract more readers. Not significantly different in content from other publications of its type, *Vogue*'s approach makes it distinctive. Instead of family hostels, *Vogue* describes grand hotels; picnic punch recipes tend to be omitted in favor of connoisseur wine recommendations. While far from being feminist oriented, the magazine has remained sensitively in tune with the changes affecting women's lives, offering both regular departments and feature articles that reflect transition and diversity. Articles by prominent authors such as Jane O'Reilly, William Hoffman, and Edmund White consistently appear in the monthly table of contents. Readers will appreciate finding *Vogue* on library shelves.

W. 1971. bi-w. $30. Patrick McCarthy. Fairchild Publns., 7 E. 12th St., New York, NY 10003. Illus., adv. Circ: 250,000. Vol. ends: Dec. Microform: MIM.

Indexed: Acs. *Aud:* Hs.

W. is Fairchild Publications' popular version of its fashion industry bulletin, *Women's Wear Daily.* Oversize, glossy pages arranged in a newspaper format contain a few rather brief articles scattered among photographs of prominent personalities and colorful, full-page advertisements of clothes, makeup, or body-care products. Wealth and fame receive a lot of attention. The "Eye," which claims to be everywhere but in reality focuses primarily on New York and Paris, reports the latest gossip. "They Told *W*" could as well have been called "Out of the Mouths of Performers." The main feature of one biweekly issue pictures and portrays people billed as "The Grandest of Them All." Other typical articles include "Feet First," a how-to of feet care; "Surf's Up," a description of New York's Surf Club; and "Beauty and the Beach," which offers the advice of a "movement analyst and fitness consultant." *W.* is intended for those who have, or aspire to have, money and the sophistication—and clothes—it purchases.

WIN News. 1975. q. $30 (Individuals, $20). Fran P. Hosken. Women's Intl. Network, 187 Grant St., Lexington, MA 02173. Illus. Circ: 900. Vol. ends: Autumn.

Aud: Hs.

The amount of information available in *WIN News* makes putting up with the small print and crowded pages well worth the effort. The Women's International Network strives to be a "world wide open communication system by, for and about women of all backgrounds, beliefs, nationalities and age groups." Under a variety of regular sections ("Women and the UN," "Women and Human Rights," "Women and Peace," "Women and Development," "Women and Health," "Female Circumcision and Genital Mutilation," "Women

and Violence," and "Women and Media"), this quarterly *News* publication details events and experiences from a global perspective. Countries receive individual attention in "Reports from Around the World." *WIN News* performs a current awareness service that is not duplicated by any other international journal.

Women at Work. See Business/For the Student Section.

Women of China. See Asia/For the Student: China Section.

Women's Review of Books. See Books and Book Reviews/For the Professional Section.

Women's Sports and Fitness (Formerly: *Women's Sports*). See Sports/For the Student Section.

For the Professional

Women's Studies Quarterly (Formerly: *Women's Studies Newsletter*). 1972. q. $25 (Individuals, $18). Florence Howe. Feminist Press, P.O. Box 334, Old Westbury, NY 11568. Illus., adv. Circ: 3,000. Refereed.

Indexed: API, WomAb. *Bk. rev:* 1–3, 500–1,000 words, signed. *Aud:* Pr.

Over the last 13 years, *Women's Studies Quarterly* has gone through several phases. It began as a small newsletter; served, for some time, as the major membership publication of the National Women's Studies Association; and now serves independently as the only journal primarily "devoted to teaching about women." Issues have themes (for example, "Motherhood," "Sex, Sexuality and Reproduction," or "Women in Movements for Peace"), and the articles they contain are meant to be applied. Actual course outlines, suggestions for methods of teaching, detailed bibliographies on selected subjects, and book reviews appear in the "In the Classroom" and "Resources" sections. Contributors are often classroom teachers themselves reporting on their own successes and failures. Within thematic issues, related topics such as the establishment of a women's center at a university, the National Council for Research on Women, or women's writing are often discussed. Teachers at all levels who teach women or teach about women will find *Women's Studies Quarterly*'s practical approach extremely useful. The title should be available in all women's studies and education collections.

Index of Titles and Sections

A

A+, 68
A.F.A. Watchbird, 187
AFL-CIO News, 43
AHEA Action, 132
ATA Magazine/Martial Arts and Fitness, 199
Abridged Reader's Guide to Periodical Literature, 1
Absolute Sound, 173
ABSTRACTS AND INDEXES, 1
Access, 139
Access: the supplementary index to periodicals, 1
Accounting Review, 45
Action Comics, 61
Adirondack Life, 85
Adolescence, 78
Adventure, 103
Adventure Road, 100
Advertising Age, 43
Advocate, 39
Aero, 32
AFRICA, 6. See also AFRO-AMERICAN
Africa, 6
Africa Events, 6
Africa Now, 6
Africa Report, 7
African Arts, 7
Afrique Histoire U.S., 7
AFRO-AMERICAN, 7. See also AFRICA
Afro-Americans in New York Life and History, 8
Afterimage, 190
Agenda, 100
Agricultural Education, 13
Agricultural Research, 11
AGRICULTURE, 11
Ahoy, 68
Ahoy: a children's magazine, 46
Air and Space, 33
Air Force Magazine, 159
Air Progress, 32
Air Reservist, 159
Airman, 159
Akwesasne Notes, 137
Alaska, 49
Alaska Geographic, 49
Albedo, 63
Alcoholism, 119
Alive! For Young Teens, 196
All Hands, 159
All-Star Squadron, 61

All Time Favorite Recipes, 132
Alpha Flight, 62
Alternative Media, 14
Alternative Press Index, 1
ALTERNATIVES, 13. See also CIVIL LIBERTIES; LITERATURE; NEWS AND OPINION
Amateur Stage, 206
Amateur Wrestling News, 199
Amazing Heroes, 64
Amazing Heroes Preview Special, 64
Amazing Science Fiction Stories, 92
Amazing Spider-Man, 62
America, 196
American Artist, 17
American Astrology, 24
American Behavioral Scientist, 198
American Biology Teacher, 116
American Birds, 34
American Cage-Bird Magazine, 187
American Choral Review, 174
American Craft, 72
American Education, 78
American Educator, 78
American Fencing, 199
American Film, 93
American Forests, 84
American Health, 120
American Heritage, 124
American History Illustrated, 124
American Hockey Magazine, 199
American Hunter, 96
American Journal of Art Therapy, 19
American Journal of Physics, 116
American Journal of Public Health, 123
American Libraries, 144
American Literature, 154
American Motorcyclist, 165
American Music Teacher, 174
The American Organist, 167
American Philatelist, 130
American Photographer, 190
American Poetry Review, 150
American Recorder, 167
American Rifleman, 96
American Saddlebred, 135
American Scholar, 105
American Secondary Education, 78
The American Spectator, 175
American Square Dance, 169
American Theatre, 206
American Traveler, 208

American Weather Observer, 27
American West, 125
Americana, 105, 124
Américas, 141
Amethyst, 62
Amnesty Action, 56
Analog, 92
Analog Computing, 68
Animal Kingdom, 113
Animal Ways, 187
Animals, 187
Animations, 206
Antaeus, 150
ANTHROPOLOGY AND ARCHAEOLOGY, 16
Antic, 68
Antique Automobile, 128
Antique Toy World, 164
Aperture, 190
Appaloosa News, 135
Applied Science and Technology Index, 1
Appraisal, 37
Arabian Horse World, 135
Aramco World, 100
Archaeology, 16
Archie, 60
Archie and Me, 60
Archie at Riverdale High, 60
Archie's Pals 'n' Gals, 60
Archie's TV Laugh-out, 60
Architectural Record, 18
Arithmetic Teacher, 156
Arizona and the West, 125
Arizona Highways, 49
Arkansas Game and Fish, 96
Army Reserve Magazine, 159
ART, 17. See also EDUCATION; LIBRARY PERIODICALS
Art & Craft, 19
Art and Man, 17
Art Education, 20
Art in America, 17
Art Index, 1
Art Institute of Chicago, Museum Studies, 19
Artes de México, 141
Artist's Magazine, 18
ARTnews, 18
Arts & Activities, 20
ASIA, 20
Asian Culture, 21
Asian Music, 21
Asian Theater Journal, 21

Asiaweek, 21
ASTROLOGY AND PARAPSYCHOLOGY, 23
ASTRONOMY, 25. *See also* ATMOSPHERIC, EARTH, AND MARINE SCIENCES; AVIATION AND SPACE SCIENCE
Astronomy, 25
Athletic Journal, 203
Atlanta, 49
(Atlanta) Constitution, 179
The Atlantic, 105
ATMOSPHERIC, EARTH, AND MARINE SCIENCES, 26
Audio, 83
Audio-Visual Communications, 157
Audubon, 34
AUTOMOBILES, 29. *See also* MOTORCYCLES AND OFF-ROAD VEHICLES; SPORTS
Automundo Deportivo, 141
Autoweek, 29
Avengers, 62
AVIATION AND SPACE SCIENCE, 32
Aviation/Space, 33
Aztlán, 143

B

Back Home in Kentucky, 49
Backpacker, 85
Ballet News, 169
Ballooning, 32
Balón, 141
Baltimore Magazine, 49
Bank Note Reporter, 130
Barbie, 103
Barron's, 43
Baseball Digest, 199
Basketball Weekly, 200
Batman, 62
Beautiful British Columbia, 49
Beaver, 46
Behind the Headlines, 46
Beijing Review, 22
Best Sellers, 39
Bestways, 120
Better Homes & Gardens, 132
Better Homes & Gardens Country Home, 132
Betty and Me, 60
Betty and Veronica, 60
Betty's Diary, 60
Between Our Selves, 212
Bibliographic Index, 2
Bicycle Forum, 200
Bicycling, 200
Big Beautiful Woman, 212
Billboard, 167
Biography Index, 2
Biological and Agricultural Index, 2
Biology Digest, 113
BioScience, 116
Bird Talk, 188
Bird Watcher's Digest, 34

Bird World, 188
Birding, 34
BIRDS, 34. *See also* ENVIRONMENT, CONSERVATION, AND OUTDOOR RECREATION; PETS
Blacfax, 8
Black American Literature Forum, 8
Black Belt, 200
The Black Child Advocate, 10
Black Collegian, 8
Black Enterprise, 8
Black Family, 132
The Black Powder Report, 96
The Black Scholar, 10
Blair & Ketchum's Country Journal, 49
Bluegrass Unlimited, 170
Boating, 36
BOATS AND BOATING, 36. *See also* FISHING, HUNTING, AND GUNS; SPORTS
Bomp, 170
Bon Appetit, 132
The Book Report, 145
The Book Review, 38
Book Review Digest, 2
Book Review Index, 2
Book World, 38
Bookbird, 39, 154
Booklist, 39
BOOKS AND BOOK REVIEWS, 37. *See also* LIBRARY PERIODICALS
Books in Canada, 39
Bop, 170
Boston Globe, 180
Boston Magazine, 50
Bowhunter, 96
Boy's Life, 105
Bridge, 22
British Heritage, 125
British Journal of Language Teaching, 148
Bulletin of the Atomic Scientists, 106
Bulletin of the Museum of Fine Arts, Boston, 19
Burbújas, 141
BUSINESS, 43
Business Periodicals Index, 2
Business Week, 44
Byte, 67

C

CBC, 39
C-JET, 66
CLA Journal, 10
California, 106
Callaloo, 8
Caminos, 143
CANADA, 46
Canada and the World, 46
Canada Today/d'Aujourd'hui, 102
Canada Weekly, 100
Canadian Children's Literature, 154
Canadian Dimension, 47

Canadian Education Index, 2
Canadian Fiction Magazine, 90
The Canadian Forum, 47
Canadian Geographic, 118
Canadian Heritage, 47
Canadian Library Journal, 145
Canadian Literature, 155
Canadian Musician, 167
Canadian News Index, 182
Canadian Periodical Index, 2
Canadian Stamp News, 130
Canoe, 36
Cape Breton's Magazine, 47
Capper's Weekly, 133
Car and Driver, 29
Car Care News, 30
Car Craft, 30
Care Bears, 60
Career Opportunities News, 183
Career World, 184
Caribbean Review, 141
Carnegie Quarterly, 101
Cars & Parts Annual, 30
Cars & Parts Magazine, 30
Cartoonist Profiles, 64
Cash Box, 167
Casino Discos, 143
Cat Fancy, 188
Catholic Library World, 145
The Catholic Periodical and Literature Index, 2
Cats Magazine, 188
Center for Children's Books. Bulletin, 40
Center Magazine, 56
The Center Magazine, 106
Ceramic Arts & Crafts, 72
Ceramics Monthly, 75
Cerebus, 63
Challenge, 44
Champs-Elysées, 87
Changing Challenge, 101
Changing Times, 70
Channels of Communications, 204
Charlotte Magazine, 50
Chart Your Course!, 89
Chess Life, 128
Chicago, 50
Chicago Tribune, 180
Chickadee, 35, 103
Child Development Abstracts and Bibliography, 3
Child Life, 120
Childhood Education, 79
Children Today, 79
Children's Book Review Service Inc., 40
Children's Digest, 120
Children's Literature Abstracts, 3
Children's Literature in Education, 155
Children's Magazine Guide, 3
Children's Playmate, 120
China Now, 22
China Pictorial, 22
China Reconstructs, 22

China Sports, 23
Chip Chats, 73
Chispa, 141
Choice, 40
Choices, 133
Choral Journal, 174
Christian Century, 196
Christian Science Monitor, 180
Christian Science Monitor, Index to the, 182
Christianity Today, 196
Chronicle of the Horse, 135
Cincinnati, 50
Cineaste, 93
Cinemacabre, 93
Cinemagic, 93
Circus, 170
CITY AND REGIONAL, 48. *See also* TRAVEL
CIVIL LIBERTIES, 55. *See also* ALTERNATIVES; NEWS AND OPINION; POLITICAL SCIENCE; WOMEN
Civil Liberties, 56
Civil War Times Illustrated, 125
Classical Bulletin, 58
Classical Calliope, 58
Classical Journal, 59
Classical Outlook, 59
CLASSICAL STUDIES, 58. *See also* ART; HISTORY; LITERATURE
Classical World, 59
Classroom Computer Learning, 69
Claudia, 142
Clavier, 174
Clearing House, 79
Cleveland Magazine, 50
Cleveland Museum of Art Bulletin, 19
Close-Up, 191
Coalition Close-Up, 186
Cobblestone, 125
Coda Magazine, 170
Coin Prices, 130
Coins, 130
Collection Building, 145
Collectors News and the Antique Reporter, 128
Collector's Showcase, 128
Columbia Journalism Review, 139
Columbia Scholastic Press Advisors Association Bulletin, 140
COMICS, 59
Comics Buyer's Guide, 65
Comics Journal, 65
Commentary, 176
Commodore Microcomputers, 68
Common Cause, 70
Commonweal, 196
Communication Education, 66
COMMUNICATION AND SPEECH, 66. *See also* EDUCATION; MEDIA AND AV; TELEVISION, VIDEO, AND RADIO
Communities, 14
Compute!, 69

Computer Games, 128
Computer Gaming World, 128
COMPUTERS, 67
Computers and Education, 69
Computers, Reading and Language Arts, 69
Compute's Gazette, 68
The Computing Teacher, 69
Conan the Barbarian, 65
Conan the King, 65
The Congress Watcher, 176
Congressional Digest, 193
Connecticut, 50
Connexions, 213
Conoco, 101
The Conservationist, 84
CONSUMER EDUCATION, 70. *See also* BUSINESS; HEALTH AND MEDICINE
Consumer Information Catalog, 71
Consumer News, 71
Consumer Reports, 71
Consumers Index to Product Evaluations and Information Sources, 3
Consumers' Research Magazine, 71
Consumers Union News Digest, 71
Contemporary Physics, 113
Contenido, 142
Continental Modeller, 163
The Cook's Magazine, 133
Coqueta, 144
Country Magazine, 50
Courier, 106
CRAFTS AND RECREATIONAL PROJECTS, 72
Crafts 'n Things, 73
Craftswoman, 213
Creative Camera, 191
Creative Crafts & Miniatures, 73
Creem, 170
Cricket, 103
The Crisis, 8
Critical Inquiry, 76
Crops and Soils Magazine, 12
Cuadernos Americanos, 142
CULTURAL-SOCIAL STUDIES, 76. *See also* HISTORY; LINGUISTICS AND LANGUAGE ARTS; LITERATURE
Culture and Life, 209
Current, 176
Current Biography, 106
Current Consumer & Lifestudies, 71
Current Digest of the Soviet Press, 209
Current Events, 176
Current Health, 120
Current History, 193
Current Index to Journals in Education, 3
Current Science, 114
Curriculum Innovations, 77
Curriculum Review, 40
Cycle, 165
Cycle Guide, 165
Cycle World, 165
Czechoslovak Life, 210

D

DVM Newsmagazine, 12
Daedalus, 106
Daily Telegraph, 180
Daily Weather Maps, Weekly Series, 27
Dallas, 50
Dance in Canada, 169
Dance Magazine, 169
Dancing Times, 169
Darkroom Photography, 191
Datamation, 67
Day Care and Early Education, 79
Deep Sky, 25
Deer & Deer Hunting, 97
Defense Monitor, 186
Delaware Today, 51
The Department of State Bulletin, 193
Des Moines Register, 180
Design for Arts in Education, 20
Detective Comics, 62
Detroit Institute of Arts. Bulletin, 19
Dial, 204
Directions, 40
Dirt Bike, 165
Dirt Rider, 165
Dirt Wheels, 165
Discover, 114
Discovery, 208
Doctor Strange, 63
Dog Fancy, 188
Dog World, 188
Dogs in Canada, 189
Dollstars Magazine, 103
Dolphin Log, 114
Down Beat, 170
Down East, 51
Dragon, 129
Dramatics, 206
Ducks Unlimited, 35
Dun's Business Month, 44

E

ECTJ, 157
EITV, 158
Early American Life, 125
Early Man, 16
Early Years, 79
Earth Science, 27
Earthquake Information Bulletin, 27
East Wind, 22
East-West Journal, 14
Easyriders, 166
Ebony, 9
Economic Outlook USA, 44
The Economist, 44
Editorial Research Reports, 176
EDUCATION, 77. *See also* COMMUNICATION AND SPEECH; PSYCHOLOGY
Education Computer News, 80
Education Daily, 79

Education Digest, 80
Education in Chemistry, 116
Education Index, 3
Education of the Handicapped, 80
Education Technology, 157
80 Micro, 69
The Electric Company Magazine, 103
Electronic Fun, 128
Electronic Games, 129
Electronic Learning, 70
Electronic Musician, 173
ELECTRONICS, 83. *See also* COMPUTERS; TELEVISION, VIDEO, AND RADIO
Elementary School Guidance and Counseling, 80
Elementary School Journal, 80
Elle, 213
Emergency Librarian, 145
Encounter, 106
Endeavour, 114
English Education, 148
Enthusiast, 101
ENVIRONMENT, CONSERVATION, AND OUTDOOR RECREATION, 84. *See also* FISHING, HUNTING, AND GUNS; SPORTS
Epoca, 87
Espresso, 87
Esquire, 107
Essays on Canadian Writing, 155
Essence, 213
EUROPE, 86. *See also* USSR AND EASTERN EUROPE
Everything's Archie, 60
Ewoks, 60
Exceptional Child Education Resources, 3
Exceptional Children, 89
EXCEPTIONAL CHILDREN: GIFTED, DISABLED, THOSE WITH SPECIAL NEEDS, 89. *See also* HEALTH AND MEDICINE
The Exceptional Parent, 89
Executive Housekeeping Today, 134
Expecting, 120
Expedition, 16
Exploring, 107
Exposure, 191
L'Express, 87
Exxon USA, 101

F

F.A.S. Public Interest Report, 186
FDA Consumer, 120
FMR, 18
Faces, 114
Family Economics Review, 133
Family Food Garden, 129
Family Handyman, 73
Family Planning Perspectives, 198
Fantastic Four, 63
Fantasy Review, 92

Farm Journal, 12
Federal Grants and Contracts Weekly, 80
Fellowship, 186
Fem, 142
Fibonacci Quarterly, 156
FICTION, 90
Fiction, 91
Field & Stream, 97
Fighting Woman News, 213
Film and Video News, 95
Film Comment, 94
Film Culture, 94
Film Library Quarterly, 145
Film Literature Index, 3
Film Quarterly, 94
FILMS, 93. *See also* COMMUNICATION AND SPEECH; TELEVISION, VIDEO, AND RADIO
Fine Homebuilding, 73
FineScale Modeler, 164
First Language, 148
First Principles, 56
FISHING, HUNTING, AND GUNS, 96. *See also* ENVIRONMENT, CONSERVATION, AND OUTDOOR RECREATION; SPORTS
Florida Naturalist, 84
Florida Vocational Journal, 184
Flower and Garden, 129
Flute Talk, 167
Fly Fisherman, 97
Flying, 32
Flying Models, 160
Focus, 118
Focus on Asian Studies, 23
FOLKLORE, 98
Food News for Consumers, 71
Forbes, 44
Ford Times, 101
Forecast for Home Economics, 134
Foreign Affairs, 193
Foreign Agriculture, 12
Foreign Language Annals, 148
Foreign Policy, 194
Fortune, 44
4-H Leader, 12
Four Wheeler, 30
Foxfire, 107
Free China Review, 23
FREE MAGAZINES, 100
Freedomways, 9
Freeman, 56
Freshwater and Marine Aquarium, 189
The Friend, 196
Frisbee Disc World, 129
Frontier Times, 126
Fur-Fish-Game-Harding's Magazine, 97
Futurist, 76

G

G/C/T (Gifted/Creative/Talented Children), 89

GEOS, 27
Games, 129
Garden, 129
Gargoyle, 150
GENERAL INTEREST, 103
GENERAL SCIENCE, 113
General Science Index, 4
Geographical Magazine, 119
GEOGRAPHY, 118
Geology Today, 27
Geomundo, 142
The Georgia Review, 150
German Tribune, 87
Gibbon's Stamp Monthly, 130
Gifted Children Monthly, 90
Glamour, 214
Goldmine, 171
Golf Digest, 200
Golf Journal, 200
Golf Magazine, 200
The Good Apple Newspaper, 80
Good Housekeeping, 214
Gourmet, 133
Grand Street, 150
Greece and Rome, 59
Green Revolution, 14
Griffith Observer, 25
Guardian, 56
The Guardian, 176
Guardian (Manchester Guardian), 180
Guitar Player Magazine, 167
Guitar Review, 168

H

Handball, 201
Hang Gliding, 32
Harper's Bazaar, 214
Harper's Magazine, 107
Harrowsmith, 48
Hastings Center Report, 56
Health, 121
HEALTH AND MEDICINE, 119
Health Letter, 121
High Fidelity, 173
High School Journal, 80
Higher Education Daily, 80
Highlights for Children, 104
Hispanic American Periodicals Index (HAPI), 4
Historic Preservation, 19
HISTORY, 124. *See also* CULTURAL-SOCIAL STUDIES; POLITICAL SCIENCE; SOCIOLOGY
History, 127
The History Teacher, 127
History Today, 126
Hit Parader, 171
HOBBIES, 128
Hockey Digest, 201
Hola, 142
Hombre del Mundo, 142
HOME ECONOMICS, 132. *See also* CONSUMER EDUCATION; SOCIOLOGY; WOMEN

Home Economics Association of
  Australia, 133
Home Mechanix, 73
Homebuilt Aircraft, 32
The Homemaker, 133
Honolulu, 51
Horizon, 107
Horizons, 101
Horn Book Magazine, 40
Horoscope, 24
Horse & Horseman, 135
Horse Illustrated, 135
Horseman, 136
HORSES, 135
Hot Dog!, 104
Hot Rod, 30
Hot Wire, 214
The Hudson Review, 151
Human Events, 176
Human Life Review, 121
Human Rights, 57
The Humanist, 196
Humanities, 76
Humanities Index, 4
HUMOR, 136
Humpty Dumpty's Magazine, 121

I

ILO Information, 45
ISIS International Women's Journal,
  214
Ideals, 113
Illinois Historical Journal, 126
Illustrated Weekly of India, 21
Illustrator, 20
Image, 191
Impact of Science on Society, 76
Impacto, 142
inCider, 68
Independent School, 80
Index on Censorship, 57
Index to Free Periodicals, 4
Index to Periodicals by and about
  Blacks, 4
Index to U.S. Government
  Periodicals, 4
Indian Artifact Magazine, 137
Indianapolis Magazine, 51
INDIANS OF NORTH AMERICA, 137
Industrial Education, 81
The In-Fisherman, 97
Info AAU, 107
Inside Sports, 201
Instructor, 81
The Instrumentalist, 174
Integrateducation, 81
Intercom, 194
International Gymnast Magazine,
  201
International Journal of Oral
  History, 126
The International Review of African
  American Art, 18
The International Review of African
  and African American Art, 9

International Social Science Journal,
  76
International Wildlife, 84
Interracial Books for Children
  Bulletin, 41
The Iowan, 51
Isaac Asimov's Science Fiction
  Magazine, 92
Islands, 208

J

JAM (Just About Me), 104
JEMF Quarterly, 168
Jack and Jill, 104
Japan Pictorial, 23
Japan Quarterly, 23
Jazz Journal International, 171
Jeune Afrique, 7
Journal for Research in Mathematics
  Education, 157
Journal of American Culture, 98
Journal of American Folklore, 99
Journal of American Photography,
  191
Journal of Anthropological
  Research, 17
Journal of Black Studies, 11
Journal of Career Planning and
  Employment, 184
Journal of Chemical Education, 117
Journal of Country Music, 171
Journal of Drug Issues, 121
Journal of Economic Education, 46
Journal of Employment Counseling,
  185
Journal of Environmental Education,
  86
Journal of Film and Video, 95
Journal of Geography, 119
Journal of Home Economics, 134
Journal of Irreproducible Results,
  136
Journal of Learning Disabilities, 90
Journal of Modern Literature, 155
Journal of Negro Education, 11
Journal of Negro History, 9
Journal of Physical Education,
  Recreation and Dance, 203
Journal of Popular Culture, 77
Journal of Recreational
  Mathematics, 156
Journal of Regional Cultures, 99
Journal of Religion and Psychical
  Research, 24
Journal of School Psychology, 195
Journal of Social Issues, 198
Journal of the American Forensic
  Association, 66
Journal of the West, 126
JOURNALISM AND WRITING, 138. See
  also LITERATURE; TELEVISION,
  VIDEO, AND RADIO
Journey, 64
Joystik, 67

Jughead, 60
Junior Bookshelf, 41
Junior Scholastics, 107
Junior Trails, 196
Justice League of America, 61

K

Kaleidoscope, 89
Kalliope, 215
Kansas!, 51
Kart Sport, 166
Katy Keene, 61
Keeping Posted, 196
The Kenyon Review, 151
Keynoter, 108
The Kingbird, 35
Kirkus Reviews, 41
Kite Lines, 73
Kliatt Young Adult Paperback Book
  Guide, 41
Knowledge, 108
Korean Newsreview, 21
Krokodil (Crocodile), 210

L

Labor Notes, 57
Landers Film Reviews, 95
Language Arts, 149
Language Learning, 149
Lapidary Journal, 74
LATIN AMERICA, LATINO (U.S.), 140
Laugh, 60
Learning, 81
Leatherneck, 159
Lector, 41
The Legion of Super-Heroes, 61
Liberty, 57
Library Hi Tech, 145
Library Journal, 146
LIBRARY PERIODICALS, 144. See also
  BOOKS AND BOOK REVIEWS
Library Technology Reports, 146
Life, 108
Life with Archie, 60
Light Magazine, 89
LINGUISTICS AND LANGUAGE ARTS,
  148
Linn's Stamp News, 131
The Lion and the Unicorn, 155
Literary Cavalcade, 151
LITERATURE, 150. See also
  ALTERNATIVES; FICTION; WOMEN
Little Archie, 60
The Little Balkans Review, 51
The Living Bird Quarterly, 35
Living Blues, 9
Locus, 92
London Drama, 207
The Loon, 35
Los Angeles, 51
Louisiana Life, 52
Low Rider, 144

M

Maclean's, 48
The MacNeil/Lehrer Report, 177
Macworld, 68
Mad, 137
Mademoiselle, 215
Magazine Index, 4
The Magazine of Fantasy and
  Science Fiction, 92
Make It with Leather, 74
The Mallet, 74
Manchester Guardian Weekly, 180
Marathon World, 101
Maritimes, 27
Marvel Tales, 62
Maryland Magazine, 52
The Massachusetts Review, 151
Material Culture, 99
Materialy Samizdata, 210
Mathematical Gazette, 157
Mathematical Log, 156
The Mathematical Scientist, 156
MATHEMATICS, 156
Mathematics and Computer
  Education, 156
Mathematics Magazine, 156
The Mathematics Teacher, 157
McCall's Needlework & Crafts, 74
Mecánica Popular, 143
Media & Methods, 158
MEDIA AND AV, 157. See also
  COMMUNICATION AND SPEECH;
  TELEVISION, VIDEO, AND RADIO
Media Review Digest, 4
Media Sight, 94
Media Spectrum, 158
Mediafile, 139
Medical Detective, 121
Medical Self Care, 121
Medical Update, 122
Medical World News, 122
Mekeel's Weekly Stamp News, 131
Melody Maker, 171
Mercury, 26
Merlyn's Pen, 91
Metropolitan Museum of Art.
  Bulletin, 19
Miami Herald, 180
Miami/South Florida Magazine, 52
Microzine, 67
Mid American Folklore, 99
The Middle East, 177
Migration Today, 57
Migration Today: Current Issues and
  Christian Responsibility, 57
MILITARY, 158
Military Affairs, 160
Military History, 160
Military Images, 160
Military Modelling, 162
Milwaukee Magazine, 52
Mime Journal, 207
Mineralogical Record, 27
Minkus Stamp and Coin Journal, 131
Mississippi, 52

Missouri Life, 52
Model Airplane News, 161
Model Auto Review, 161
Model Aviation, 161
Model Builder, 161
MODEL MAKING, 160
Model Railroader, 163
Model Ship Builder, 162
Modern Electronics, 83
The Modern Language Journal, 149
Modern Photography, 191
Money, 45
Montana, 126
Monthly & Seasonal Weather
  Outlook, 28
Monthly Detroit, 52
Monthly Film Bulletin, 94
Monthly Labor Review, 45
Monthly Vital Statistics Report, 122
Morgan Horse, 136
Mosaic (Washington), 114, 117
Mother Earth News, 15
Mother Jones, 108
Motocross Action Magazine, 166
Motor, 30
Motor Boating & Sailing, 36
Motor Trend, 30
Motorcycle, 166
MOTORCYCLES AND OFF-ROAD
  VEHICLES, 165. See also
  AUTOMOBILES; SPORTS
Motorcyclist, 166
Mpls. St. Paul Magazine, 52
Ms., 215
Ms. Tree, 64
Muppet Magazine, 137
Murzilka, 210
Museum Magazine, 20
MUSIC AND DANCE, 166. See also
  ELECTRONICS; FOLKLORE
Music Educators Journal, 174
Music Index, 5
Music Journal, 168
Music Library Association, 175
The Musical Mainstream, 175
Muzzle Blasts, 97

N

NASSP Bulletin, 81
NOAA, 28
Nashville!, 52
The Nation, 177
National Carvers Review, 74
National Dragster, 30
The National Future Farmer, 12
National Geographic Magazine, 108
National Geographic Research, 119
National Geographic World, 104
National Guard, 160
National Lampoon, 137
National Newspaper Index, 182
National Parks, 85
National Racquetball, 201
National Review, 177

National Stampagraphic, 18
National Wildlife, 84
Nation's Business, 45
Nation's School Report, 80
Natural History, 114
Nature Canada, 35
Nature Study, 86
Naturescope, 117
Nautica, 28
Nautical Quarterly, 36
Negro Educational Review, 11
Negro History Bulletin, 9
Nemo, 65
Nevada Magazine, 53
New Directions for Women, 215
New Driver, 31
New England Business, 53
New England Monthly, 53
New Farm, 12
New Generation, 185
New Jersey Monthly, 53
New Leader, 177
New Musical Express, 171
The New Mutants, 65
New Pages, 16, 42
New Perspectives, 57
The New Republic, 177
The New Schwann Record & Tape
  Guide, 175
New Technical Books, 42
The New Teen Titans, 61
New Times, 210
New York Folklore, 99
New York Magazine, 108
The New York Review of Books, 38
New York Times, 180
The New York Times Book Review,
  38
New York Times Index, 182
The New Yorker, 109
NEWS AND OPINION, 175. See also
  ALTERNATIVES; GENERAL
  INTEREST; NEWSPAPERS
News in Chess, 129
News Media and the Law, 58
News Photographer, 192
Newsletter on Intellectual Freedom,
  146
Newspaper Index, 182
NEWSPAPERS, 179
Newsweek, 178
Nibble, 68
Nonviolent Activist, 186
Northwest Chess Magazine, 129
Not Man Apart, 85
Notitas Musicales, 143
Nuclear Times, 186
Nuestro, 144
Nutrition Action, 134

O

OP, 15
Observer, 181
Obsidian, 10

Occupational Outlook Quarterly, 184
OCCUPATIONS AND CAREERS, 183.
    See also EDUCATION
Oceans, 28
Oceanus, 28
Odyssey, 26
Off Our Backs, 215
Official Washington Post Index, 182
Oggi, 87
Ohio, 53
The Ohio Review, 151
Oklahoma Today, 53
Old Toy Soldier Newsletter, 162
Old West, 127
The Olympian, 201
Omni, 109
On Cable, 204
On Key, 168
Online, 146
Opera Canada, 168
Opera News, 168
Opus, 173
The Orange Disc, 102
Oregon, 53
Organic Gardening, 15
Orion, 114
Our Animals, 189
Our Fourfooted Friends, 189
Our Right to Know, 58
Outdoor Canada, 85
Outdoor Life, 97
Outside, 86
Ovation, 173
Owl, 104

P

PAIS Foreign Language Index, 5
PAIS (Public Affairs Information
    Service) Bulletin, 5
PC, 68
PC Products, 69
PC Tech Journal, 69
PC World, 69
Pace, 7
Pacific Northwest, 53
Paint Horse Journal, 136
Panorama, 87
Parabola, 109
Parade, 182
Parapsychology Review, 24
Parent's Choice, 205
Paris Review, 151
The Passenger Pigeon, 35
PEACE, 185
Pennsylvania Folklore, 99
Pennsylvania Game News, 98
Pennsylvania Magazine, 54
Penny Power, 71
People, Animals, Environment, 189
People Weekly, 109
Pep, 60
Performance Horseman, 136
Personal Computing, 67
Personal Computing Plus, 67

Peter Parker, 62
Peter Porker, 61
Petersen's Circle Track, 31
Petersen's Hunting, 98
Petersen's Photographic Magazine,
    192
Petersen's Pickups & Mini-Trucks,
    31
PETS, 187. See also BIRDS; FISHING,
    HUNTING, AND GUNS; HORSES;
    SPORTS
Phi Delta Kappan, 81
Philadelphia, 54
Philadelphia Inquirer, 181
Philadelphia Museum of Art.
    Bulletin, 19
Phoenix, 54
Photo Technique International, 192
Photographer's Forum, 192
PHOTOGRAPHY, 190
Photoplay, 95
Physical Education Index, 5
Physician and Sportsmedicine, 123
Physics Education, 117
Physics Teacher, 117
Physics Today, 115
Pittsburgh, 54
Plains Anthropologist, 17
Plane & Pilot, 32
Plays, 207
Ploughshares, 151
Poetry, 152
Point, 88
POLITICAL SCIENCE, 193
Political Science Quarterly, 194
Popular Communications, 204
Popular Hot Rodding, 31
Popular Mechanics, 74
Popular Music and Society, 171
Popular Periodicals Index, 5
Popular Photography, 192
Popular Science, 74
Population Bulletin, 198
Population Reports, 122
Population Today, 198
Portable 100/200/600, 69
Portland Magazine, 54
Power Pack, 61
Powerboat, 36
Practical Horseman, 136
Pravda (Truth), 211
Pre-K Today, 82
Preschool Perspectives, 82
Prevention, 122
Principal, 82
Problems of Communism, 194
Profile, 102
The Progressive, 178
Progressive Architecture, 19
Progressive Farmer, 13
Prologue, 126
PSYCHOLOGY, 195
Psychology in the Schools, 195
Psychology Today, 195
Public Health Reports, 122
The Public Interest, 178

Public Opinion, 178
Public Welfare, 198
Publishers Weekly, 42
Pure-bred Dogs, 189

Q

QST, 83
Quill, 139
Quill & Quire, 42
Quill & Scroll, 139
Quilter's Newsletter Magazine, 75
Quinault Natural Resources, 138

R

R/C Modeler, 161
RN, 124
RQ, 146
Radiance, 216
Radio & Electronics World, 204
Radio-Electronics, 84
Railroad Model Craftsman, 163
Railway Modeller, 164
Rand McNally Campground and
    Trailer Park Directory, 86
Ranger Rick, 115
Raritan, 152
The Reader's Digest, 109
Readers' Guide to Periodical
    Literature, 5
Reading in a Foreign Language, 149
The Reading Teacher, 149
Reason, 58
The Reference Librarian, 146
Reference Services Review, 42
Reflector, 26
RELIGION, 195
Religious Education, 197
Remedial and Special Education, 90
Rencontre, 138
Report on Education of the
    Disadvantaged, 80
Report on Education Research, 80
Reporter for Conscience' Sake, 187
Research in the Teaching of English,
    149
Resources in Education, 5
Review, 211
Revue des Livres pour Enfants, 88
Right On!, 109
Rights, 58
Road & Track, 31
Road Rider, 166
Rock & Gem, 75
RockBill, 172
Rocks and Minerals, 28
Rolling Stone, 172
Roots, 127
The Royal Bank Letter, 102
Run, 68
Runner's World, 201
Rural Libraries, 147

S

SANE World, 187
SLJ/School Library Journal, 147
SSI, Short Story International, 91
Sage, 10
Sail, 37
St. Louis, 54
Salmagundi, 152
San Antonio Magazine, 54
San Francisco, 54
San Francisco Focus, 54
San Francisco Review of Books, 38
The Santa Fean Magazine, 55
Satellite ORBIT, 205
Saturday Evening Post, 109
Saturday Night, 48
Saturday Review, 110
Scala International, 88
Scale Auto Enthusiast, 162
Scandinavian Review, 88
Scholastic Coach, 203
Scholastic Editor's Trends in
    Publications, 139
Scholastic Magazines, 77
Scholastic Scope, 152
Scholastic Update, 110
Scholastic Voice, 91
School Arts, 20
School Counselor, 82
School Law News, 80
School Library Media Quarterly, 147
The School Musician, Director and
    Teacher, 175
School Press Review, 139
School Science and Mathematics, 117
School Shop, 82
Science Activities, 118
Science and Children, 118
Science Books and Films, 42
Science Dimension, 102
Science for the People, 15
Science News, 115
The Science Teacher, 118
Science World, 115
Scienceland, 115
Scientific American, 115
Scott Stamp Monthly, 131
Sea Frontiers, 28
Sea Secrets, 29
Sesame Street Magazine, 104
Seventeen, 110
The Sewanee Review, 152
Shakespeare Quarterly, 152
Shape, 123
Sheet Music Magazine, 172
Ships in Scale, 163
Short Story International: seedling
    series, 91
Short Story International: student
    series, 91
Sierra, 85
Sightlines, 95
Signal, 155
Sing Heavenly Muse, 152
Sing Out!, 172

Sipapu, 153
16, 110
Skiing, 201
Skin Diver, 202
Sky and Telescope, 26
Sky Calendar, 26
Small Boat Journal, 37
Small Press Review, 153
Smena (The Rising Generation), 211
Smithsonian, 110
Snow Goer, 166
Snow Week, 166
Soaring, 33
Soccer America, 202
Social Education, 82
Social Policy, 58, 178
Social Science Quarterly, 77
Social Sciences Index, 5
Society, 198
SOCIOLOGY, 197. *See also*
    CULTURAL-SOCIAL STUDIES;
    WOMEN
Soldiers, 159
Song Hits, 172
Southern Exposure, 10
Southern Living, 110
The Southern Review, 153
Soviet Life, 211
Soviet Union, 211
Space World, 33
Spaceflight, 33
Spare Rib, 216
Speaker and Gavel, 67
Der Spiegel, 88
The Spirit That Moves Us, 153
Sport, 202
Sport Aviation, 33
The Sporting News, 202
SPORTS, 199. *See also* BOATS AND
    BOATING; CONSERVATION,
    ENVIRONMENT, AND OUTDOOR
    RECREATION; FISHING, HUNTING,
    AND GUNS
Sports Afield, 98
Sports Illustrated, 202
Sputnik, 211
Square Dancing, 170
Stamp Collector Newspaper, 131
Stamp World, 131
Stamps, 132
Stand, 153
Star Hits, 172
Star Trek, 64
Star Wars, 65
Starlog, 93
State Government, 194
Stereo Review, 174
Stern Magazine, 88
Stickers, 105
Stone Soup, 153
Storyville, 172
Street Rodder, 31
Street Rodding Illustrated, 31
Studies in Family Planning, 123
Studio Potter, 75
Successful Farming, 13

Sun Magazine, 102
Sunday, 182
Sunday Times, 181
Sunset, 110
Sunshine Magazine, 111
Super Customs & Hot Rods, 31
SuperTeen, 111
Swimming World and Junior
    Swimmer, 202

T

T.G., 112
TV Guide, 205
Tales of the Legion of Super-Heroes,
    61
Tales of the Teen Titans, 61
Talking Book Topics, 90
Talking Drums, 7
Teaching and Computers, 70
Teaching Exceptional Children, 90
Tech Trend, 158
Technology Review, 118
Technology Teacher, 82
Teen, 111
Teen Bag, 111
Teen Generation, 111
Teen Times, 111
TeenAge, 111
Teenage Mutant Ninja Turtles, 66
Telescope Making, 26
Television & Families, 206
TELEVISION, VIDEO, AND RADIO, 204.
    See also COMMUNICATION AND
    SPEECH; ELECTRONICS; NEWS AND
    OPINION
Tennis, 202
Texas Monthly, 55
THEATER, 206
Theater, 207
Theatre Crafts, 207
Theatre Journal, 207
Theory into Practice, 82
Theta, 25
This Magazine, 48
Thor, 63
3-2-1 Contact, 116
Tiger Beat, 112
Time, 178
Timeline, 127
Times, 181
Times Index, 183
The Times Literary Supplement, 38
Tips and Topics, 134
Today, 68
Today's Catholic Teacher, 83
Top of the News, 147
(Toronto) Globe and Mail, 181
Totline, 83
Town and Country, 112
Toy Soldier Review, 162
Track and Field News, 203
Tradeswomen, 216
Traffic Safety, 31
Train Collectors Quarterly, 164

Transitions, 208
TRAVEL, 208. *See also* CITY AND
   REGIONAL
Travel to the USSR, 211
Travel/Holiday, 208
Treasure, 112
Treasure Search, 112
TriQuarterly, 154
Tropical Fish Hobbyist, 190
Trouser Press, 172
True West, 127
Tsa' Aszi, 138
Tú, 143
Turtle, 105
Turtle Quarterly, 138

U

UNIMA-France, 207
U.N. Chronicle, 195
U.S. Catholic, 197
U.S. News and World Report, 179
U.S.A. Today, 178
USA Today, 181
USA Weekend, 182
Ukraine, 212
The Unabashed Librarian, 147
The Uncanny X-Men, 65
Underwater Naturalist, 29
Untitled, 192
USSR AND EASTERN EUROPE, 209. *See
   also* ASIA; EUROPE
Utne Reader, 15

V

VOYA, 147
Vanguard, 19
Vanity Fair, 112
Variety, 207
Vegetarian Times, 134
Venezuela Up-to-Date, 102
Verbatim, 149
Vermont Life, 55
Veterinary Economics, 13
Vibrant Life, 123

Video, 205
Video Games, 128
Video Now, 205
Video Review, 205
Video Times, 205
Views, 192
The Village Voice, 112
Vista (ASIA), 23
Vista (HOME ECONOMICS), 135
Vital Speeches of the Day, 179
Vocational Education Journal, 185
Vogue, 216

W

W, 217
WIN News, 217
Walking! Journal, 86
Wall Street Journal, 181
Wall Street Journal Index, 183
Walters Art Gallery. Bulletin, 19
The Washington Monthly, 179
Washington Post, 181
The Washingtonian, 55
Water Spectrum, 85
Wavelength, 173
Weatherwise, 29
The Web, 43
Web of Spider-Man, 62
Wee Wisdom, 197
West Coast Avengers, 62
Western Boatman, 37
Western Folklore, 99
The Western Historical Quarterly,
   127
Western Horseman, 136
What's New in Home Economics,
   134
Wheelers RV Resort & Campground
   Guide, 86
Whispering Wind, the American
   Indian Past and Present, 138
Whole Earth Review, 16
Wilderness, 85
Wilson Library Bulletin, 147
Wingtips, 35
Wisconsin Sportsman, 98

Wisconsin Trails, 55
WOMEN, 212
Women at Work, 45
Women of China, 23
Women Studies Abstracts, 6
Women's Coaching Clinic, 204
Women's Review of Books, 43
Women's Sports & Fitness, 203
Women's Studies Quarterly, 217
Work Related Abstracts, 6
The Workbasket, 75
Workbench, 75
World Health, 123
World Literature Today, 154
The World of Music, 169
World Press Review, 112
World Tennis, 203
Wrestling USA, 203
The Writer, 140
Writer's Digest, 140
The Writing Instructor, 140
Wyoming Wildlife, 86

X

Xerox Education Publications, 78
X-Factor, 65

Y

Y-A Hotline, 148
YABA World, 203
YM, 113
Yankee, 55
Yelmo, 144
Yoga Journal, 197
Young Children, 83
Young Viewers, 95
Your Big Backyard, 116
Youth Update, 197

Z

Zoom, 193

Index of Titles by Audience

Elementary and Junior High School Titles

A

Adventure, 103
Ahoy, 68
Ahoy: a children's magazine, 46
Amateur Stage, 206
American Heritage, 124
American History Illustrated, 124
American Square Dance, 169
American Weather Observer, 27
Animal Ways, 187
Archie, 60
Archie and Me, 60
Archie at Riverdale High, 60
Archie's Pals 'n' Gals, 60
Archie's TV Laugh-out, 60
Arkansas Game and Fish, 96
Art and Man, 17

B

Barbie, 103
Beaver, 46
Bestways, 120
Betty and Me, 60
Betty and Veronica, 60
Betty's Diary, 60
Bird Watcher's Digest, 34
Bop, 170
Boy's Life, 105
Burbújas, 141

C

Care Bears, 60
Career World, 184
Casino Discos, 143
Cat Fancy, 188
Chart Your Course!, 89
Chickadee, 35, 103
Child Life, 120
Children's Digest, 120
Children's Playmate, 120
China Pictorial, 22
China Reconstructs, 22
China Sports, 23
Chispa, 141
Choices, 133

Classical Calliope, 58
Cobblestone, 125
The Conservationist, 84
Coqueta, 144
Crafts 'n Things, 73
Creem, 170
Cricket, 103
Current Consumer & Lifestudies, 71
Current Events, 176
Current Science, 114

D

Deer & Deer Hunting, 97
Discover, 114
Dog Fancy, 188
Dollstars Magazine, 103
Dolphin Log, 114
Dragon, 129

E

Earth Science, 27
Earthquake Information Bulletin, 27
Ebony, 9
The Electric Company Magazine, 103
Electronic Games, 129
Everything's Archie, 60
Ewoks, 60
Exploring, 107

F

Faces, 114
Field & Stream, 97
Focus, 118
4-H Leader, 12
The Friend, 196

G

Geomundo, 142
Griffith Observer, 25

H

Highlights for Children, 104
Home Mechanix, 73

Horizons, 101
Horseman, 136
Hot Dog!, 104
Humpty Dumpty's Magazine, 121

I

Indian Artifact Magazine, 137
International Wildlife, 84

J

JAM (Just About Me), 104
Jack and Jill, 104
Japan Pictorial, 23
Joystik, 67
Jughead, 60
Junior Scholastics, 107
Junior Trails, 196

K

Katy Keene, 61

L

Laugh, 60
Life with Archie, 60
Little Archie, 60
Low Rider, 144

M

Medical Detective, 121
Merlyn's Pen, 91
Military Images, 160
Model Airplane News, 161
Model Railroader, 163
Modern Photography, 191
Monthly & Seasonal Weather Outlook, 28
Monthly Vital Statistics Report, 122
Mother Earth News, 15
Muppet Magazine, 137
Murzilka, 210

N

The National Future Farmer, 12

National Geographic Magazine, 108
National Geographic World, 104
National Parks, 85
National Wildlife, 84
Nature Canada, 35
Nautica, 28
Negro History Bulletin, 9
Notitas Musicales, 143

O

Odyssey, 26
On Key, 168
Opera News, 168
Organic Gardening, 15
Our Fourfooted Friends, 189
Outdoor Life, 97
Owl, 104

P

Penny Power, 71
Pep, 60
Peter Porker, 61
Petersen's Photographic Magazine, 192
Plays, 207
Popular Mechanics, 74
Popular Photography, 192
Popular Science, 74
Power Pack, 61

Q

Quill & Scroll, 139
Quinault Natural Resources, 138

R

R/C Modeler, 161
Ranger Rick, 115
Rencontre, 138
RockBill, 172
Roots, 127

S

Scholastic Editor's Trends in Publications, 139
School Press Review, 139
Science News, 115
Science World, 115
Scienceland, 115
Sea Frontiers, 28
Sea Secrets, 29
Sesame Street Magazine, 104
Seventeen, 110
Sheet Music Magazine, 172
Short Story International: seedling series, 91
Sing Out!, 172

16, 110
Soviet Life, 211
Sports Afield, 98
Sports Illustrated, 202
Stickers, 105
Stone Soup, 153
Sunshine Magazine, 111

T

Teen, 111
Teen Bag, 111
Teen Generation, 111
3-2-1 Contact, 116
Tiger Beat, 112
The Times Literary Supplement, 38
Tsa' Aszi, 138
Turtle, 105

V

Video Review, 205
Vista (ASIA), 23

W

Weatherwise, 29
Wee Wisdom, 197
Wilderness, 85
Wisconsin Sportsman, 98
The World of Music, 169

Y

YABA World, 203
YM, 113
Your Big Backyard, 116
Youth Update, 197

High School Titles

A

A+, 68
A.F.A. Watchbird, 187
AFL-CIO News, 43
AHEA Action, 132
ATA Magazine/Martial Arts and Fitness, 199
Absolute Sound, 173
Access, 139
Action Comics, 61
Adirondack Life, 85
Adventure Road, 100
Advertising Age, 43
Aero, 32
Africa, 6
Africa Events, 6
Africa Now, 6

Africa Report, 7
African Arts, 7
Afrique Histoire U.S., 7
Afro-Americans in New York Life and History, 8
Agenda, 100
Agricultural Research, 11
Ahoy, 68
Ahoy: a children's magazine, 46
Air Force Magazine, 159
Air Progress, 32
Air Reservist, 159
Airman, 159
Akwesasne Notes, 137
Alaska, 49
Alaska Geographic, 49
Albedo, 63
Alcoholism, 119
Alive! For Young Teens, 196
All Hands, 159
All-Star Squadron, 61
All Time Favorite Recipes, 132
Alpha Flight, 62
Alternative Media, 14
Amateur Stage, 206
Amateur Wrestling News, 199
Amazing Heroes, 64
Amazing Heroes Preview Special, 64
Amazing Science Fiction Stories, 92
Amazing Spider-Man, 62
America, 196
American Artist, 17
American Astrology, 24
American Behavioral Scientist, 198
American Birds, 34
American Cage-Bird Magazine, 187
American Craft, 72
American Fencing, 199
American Film, 93
American Forests, 84
American Health, 120
American Heritage, 124
American History Illustrated, 124
American Hockey Magazine, 199
American Hunter, 96
American Motorcyclist, 165
The American Organist, 167
American Philatelist, 130
American Photographer, 190
American Poetry Review, 150
American Recorder, 167
American Rifleman, 96
American Saddlebred, 135
American Scholar, 105
The American Spectator, 175
American Square Dance, 169
American Theatre, 206
American Traveler, 208
American Weather Observer, 27
American West, 125
Americana, 105, 124
Américas, 141
Amethyst, 62
Amnesty Action, 56
Analog, 92
Analog Computing, 68

Animal Kingdom, 113
Animals, 187
Animations, 206
Antaeus, 150
Antic, 68
Antique Automobile, 128
Antique Toy World, 164
Aperture, 190
Appaloosa News, 135
Appraisal, 37, 113
Arabian Horse World, 135
Aramco World, 100
Archaeology, 16
Architectural Record, 18
Arizona and the West, 125
Arizona Highways, 49
Arkansas Game and Fish, 96
Army Reserve Magazine, 159
Art and Man, 17
Art in America, 17
Art Institute of Chicago, Museum
    Studies, 19
Artes de México, 141
Artist's Magazine, 18
ARTnews, 18
Asian Culture, 21
Asian Music, 21
Asian Theater Journal, 21
Asiaweek, 21
Astronomy, 25
Atlanta, 49
(Atlanta) Constitution, 179
The Atlantic, 105
Audio, 83
Audubon, 34
Automundo Deportivo, 141
Autoweek, 29
Avengers, 62
Aztlán, 143

B

Back Home in Kentucky, 49
Backpacker, 85
Ballet News, 169
Ballooning, 32
Balón, 141
Baltimore Magazine, 49
Bank Note Reporter, 130
Barron's, 43
Baseball Digest, 199
Basketball Weekly, 200
Batman, 62
Beautiful British Columbia, 49
Beaver, 46
Behind the Headlines, 46
Beijing Review, 22
Better Homes & Gardens, 132
Better Homes & Gardens Country
    Home, 132
Between Our Selves, 212
Bicycle Forum, 200
Bicycling, 200
Big Beautiful Woman, 212
Billboard, 167

Biology Digest, 113
Bird Talk, 188
Bird Watcher's Digest, 34
Bird World, 188
Birding, 34
Blacfax, 8
Black American Literature Forum, 8
Black Belt, 200
Black Collegian, 8
Black Enterprise, 8
Black Family, 132
The Black Powder Report, 96
Blair & Ketchum's Country Journal,
    49
Bluegrass Unlimited, 170
Boating, 36
Bomp, 170
Bon Appetit, 132
The Book Review, 38
Book World, 38
Bop, 170
Boston Globe, 180
Boston Magazine, 50
Bowhunter, 96
Boy's Life, 105
Bridge, 22
British Heritage, 125
Bulletin of the Atomic Scientists, 106
Bulletin of the Museum of Fine Arts,
    Boston, 19
Business Week, 44
Byte, 67

C

California, 106
Callaloo, 8
Caminos, 143
Canada and the World, 46
Canada Weekly, 100
Canadian Dimension, 47
Canadian Fiction Magazine, 90
The Canadian Forum, 47
Canadian Geographic, 118
Canadian Heritage, 47
Canadian Musician, 167
Canadian News Index, 182
Canadian Stamp News, 130
Canoe, 36
Cape Breton's Magazine, 47
Capper's Weekly, 133
Car and Driver, 29
Car Care News, 30
Car Craft, 30
Career Opportunities News, 183
Career World, 184
Caribbean Review, 141
Carnegie Quarterly, 101
Cars & Parts Annual, 30
Cars & Parts Magazine, 30
Cartoonist Profiles, 64
Cash Box, 167
Casino Discos, 143
Cat Fancy, 188
Cats Magazine, 188

Center Magazine, 56
The Center Magazine, 106
Ceramic Arts & Crafts, 72
Cerebus, 63
Challenge, 44
Champs-Elysées, 87
Changing Challenge, 101
Changing Times, 70
Channels of Communications, 204
Charlotte Magazine, 50
Chess Life, 128
Chicago, 50
Chicago Tribune, 180
China Now, 22
China Pictorial, 22
China Reconstructs, 22
China Sports, 23
Chip Chats, 73
Choices, 133
Christian Century, 196
Christian Science Monitor, 180
Christian Science Monitor, Index to
    the, 182
Christianity Today, 196
Chronicle of the Horse, 135
Cincinnati, 50
Cineaste, 93
Cinemacabre, 93
Cinemagic, 93
Circus, 170
Civil Liberties, 56
Civil War Times Illustrated, 125
Classical Bulletin, 58
Classical Calliope, 58
Claudia, 142
Cleveland Magazine, 50
Cleveland Museum of Art Bulletin,
    19
Close-Up, 191
Coalition Close-Up, 186
Coda Magazine, 170
Coin Prices, 130
Coins, 130
Collectors News and the Antique
    Reporter, 128
Collector's Showcase, 128
Columbia Journalism Review, 139
Comics Buyer's Guide, 65
Comics Journal, 65
Commentary, 176
Commodore Microcomputers, 68
Common Cause, 70
Commonweal, 196
Communities, 14
Computer Games, 128
Computer Gaming World, 128
Compute's Gazette, 68
Conan the Barbarian, 65
Conan the King, 65
The Congress Watcher, 176
Connecticut, 50
Connexions, 213
Conoco, 101
The Conservationist, 84
Consumer Information Catalog, 71
Consumer News, 71

Consumer Reports, 71
Consumers' Research Magazine, 71
Consumers Union News Digest, 71
Contemporary Physics, 113
Contenido, 142
Continental Modeller, 163
The Cook's Magazine, 133
Coqueta, 144
Country Magazine, 50
Courier, 106
Crafts 'n Things, 73
Craftswoman, 213
Creative Camera, 191
Creative Crafts & Miniatures, 73
Creem, 170
The Crisis, 8
Critical Inquiry, 76
Crops and Soils Magazine, 12
Cuadernos Americanos, 142
Culture and Life, 209
Current, 176
Current Biography, 106
Current Consumer & Lifestudies, 71
Current Digest of the Soviet Press, 209
Current Health, 120
Cycle, 165
Cycle Guide, 165
Cycle World, 165
Czechoslovak Life, 210

D

DVM Newsmagazine, 12
Daedalus, 106
Daily Telegraph, 180
Daily Weather Maps, Weekly Series, 27
Dallas, 50
Dance in Canada, 169
Dance Magazine, 169
Dancing Times, 169
Darkroom Photography, 191
Datamation, 67
Deep Sky, 25
Deer & Deer Hunting, 97
Defense Monitor, 186
Delaware Today, 51
The Department of State Bulletin, 193
Des Moines Register, 180
Detective Comics, 62
Detroit Institute of Arts. Bulletin, 19
Dial, 204
Dirt Bike, 165
Dirt Rider, 165
Dirt Wheels, 165
Discover, 114
Discovery, 208
Doctor Strange, 63
Dog Fancy, 188
Dog World, 188
Dogs in Canada, 189
Dolphin Log, 114
Down Beat, 170

Down East, 51
Dragon, 129
Dramatics, 206
Ducks Unlimited, 35
Dun's Business Month, 44

E

Early American Life, 125
Early Man, 16
Earth Science, 27
Earthquake Information Bulletin, 27
East Wind, 22
East-West Journal, 14
Easyriders, 166
Ebony, 9
Economic Outlook USA, 44
The Economist, 44
Editorial Research Reports, 176
80 Micro, 69
Electronic Fun, 128
Electronic Games, 129
Electronic Musician, 173
Elle, 213
Encounter, 106
Endeavour, 114
Enthusiast, 101
Epoca, 87
Espresso, 87
Esquire, 107
Essence, 213
Expecting, 120
Expedition, 16
Exploring, 107
Exposure, 191
L'Express, 87
Exxon USA, 101

F

F.A.S. Public Interest Report, 186
FDA Consumer, 120
FMR, 18
Faces, 114
Family Economics Review, 133
Family Food Garden, 129
Family Handyman, 73
Family Planning Perspectives, 198
Fantastic Four, 63
Fantasy Review, 92
Farm Journal, 12
Fellowship, 186
Fem, 142
Fibonacci Quarterly, 156
Fiction, 91
Field & Stream, 97
Fighting Woman News, 213
Film Comment, 94
Film Culture, 94
Film Quarterly, 94
Fine Homebuilding, 73
FineScale Modeler, 164
First Principles, 56

Florida Naturalist, 84
Flower and Garden, 129
Flute Talk, 167
Fly Fisherman, 97
Flying, 32
Flying Models, 160
Focus, 118
Food News for Consumers, 71
Forbes, 44
Ford Times, 101
Foreign Affairs, 193
Foreign Agriculture, 12
Foreign Policy, 194
Fortune, 44
Four Wheeler, 30
4-H Leader, 12
Foxfire, 107
Free China Review, 23
Freedomways, 9
Freeman, 56
Freshwater and Marine Aquarium, 189
Frisbee Disc World, 129
Frontier Times, 126
Fur-Fish-Game-Harding's Magazine, 97
Futurist, 76

G

GEOS, 27
Games, 129
Garden, 129
Gargoyle, 150
Geographical Magazine, 119
Geology Today, 27
Geomundo, 142
The Georgia Review, 150
German Tribune, 87
Gibbon's Stamp Monthly, 130
Glamour, 214
Goldmine, 171
Golf Digest, 200
Golf Journal, 200
Golf Magazine, 200
Good Housekeeping, 214
Gourmet, 133
Grand Street, 150
Greece and Rome, 59
Green Revolution, 14
Griffith Observer, 25
Guardian, 56
The Guardian, 176
Guardian (Manchester Guardian), 180
Guitar Player Magazine, 167
Guitar Review, 168

H

Handball, 201
Hang Gliding, 32
Harper's Bazaar, 214
Harper's Magazine, 107

Harrowsmith, 48
Hastings Center Report, 56
Health, 121
Health Letter, 121
High Fidelity, 173
Historic Preservation, 19
History Today, 126
Hit Parader, 171
Hockey Digest, 201
Hola, 142
Hombre del Mundo, 142
Home Economics Association of
    Australia, 133
Home Mechanix, 73
Homebuilt Aircraft, 32
The Homemaker, 133
Honolulu, 51
Horizon, 107
Horizons, 101
Horoscope, 24
Horse & Horseman, 135
Horse Illustrated, 135
Horseman, 136
Hot Rod, 30
Hot Wire, 214
The Hudson Review, 151
Human Events, 176
Human Life Review, 121
Human Rights, 57
The Humanist, 196
Humanities, 76

I

ILO Information, 45
ISIS International Women's Journal,
    214
Illinois Historical Journal, 126
Illustrated Weekly of India, 21
Image, 191
Impact of Science on Society, 76
Impacto, 142
inCider, 68
Index on Censorship, 57
Indian Artifact Magazine, 137
Indianapolis Magazine, 51
The In-Fisherman, 97
Info AAU, 107
Inside Sports, 201
International Gymnast Magazine,
    201
International Journal of Oral
    History, 126
The International Review of African
    American Art, 18
The International Review of African
    and African American Art, 9
International Social Science Journal,
    76
International Wildlife, 84
The Iowan, 51
Isaac Asimov's Science Fiction
    Magazine, 92
Islands, 208

J

JEMF Quarterly, 168
Japan Pictorial, 23
Japan Quarterly, 23
Jazz Journal International, 171
Jeune Afrique, 7
Journal of American Culture, 98
Journal of American Folklore, 99
Journal of American Photography,
    191
Journal of Anthropological
    Research, 17
Journal of Country Music, 171
Journal of Drug Issues, 121
Journal of Irreproducible Results,
    136
Journal of Negro History, 9
Journal of Popular Culture, 77
Journal of Recreational
    Mathematics, 156
Journal of Regional Cultures, 99
Journal of Religion and Psychical
    Research, 24
Journal of Social Issues, 198
Journal of the West, 126
Journey, 64
Joystik, 67
Justice League of America, 61

K

Kaleidoscope, 89
Kalliope, 215
Kansas!, 51
Kart Sport, 166
Keeping Posted, 196
The Kenyon Review, 151
Keynoter, 108
The Kingbird, 35
Kite Lines, 73
Knowledge, 108
Korean Newsreview, 21
Krokodil (Crocodile), 210

L

Labor Notes, 57
Lapidary Journal, 74
Leatherneck, 159
The Legion of Super-Heroes, 61
Liberty, 57
Life, 108
Light Magazine, 89
Linn's Stamp News, 131
Literary Cavalcade, 151
The Little Balkans Review, 51
The Living Bird Quarterly, 35
Living Blues, 9
Locus, 92
London Drama, 207
The Loon, 35
Los Angeles, 51

Louisiana Life, 52
Low Rider, 144

M

Maclean's, 48
The MacNeil/Lehrer Report, 177
Macworld, 68
Mad, 137
Mademoiselle, 215
The Magazine of Fantasy and
    Science Fiction, 92
Make It with Leather, 74
The Mallet, 74
Manchester Guardian Weekly, 180
Marathon World, 101
Maritimes, 27
Marvel Tales, 62
Maryland Magazine, 52
The Massachusetts Review, 151
Material Culture, 99
Materialy Samizdata, 210
Mathematical Log, 156
The Mathematical Scientist, 156
Mathematics and Computer
    Education, 156
Mathematics Magazine, 156
McCall's Needlework & Crafts, 74
Mecánica Popular, 143
Media Sight, 94
Mediafile, 139
Medical Self Care, 121
Medical Update, 122
Medical World News, 122
Mekeel's Weekly Stamp News, 131
Melody Maker, 171
Mercury, 26
Merlyn's Pen, 91
Metropolitan Museum of Art.
    Bulletin, 19
Miami Herald, 180
Miami/South Florida Magazine, 52
Microzine, 67
Mid American Folklore, 99
The Middle East, 177
Migration Today, 57
Military Affairs, 160
Military History, 160
Military Images, 160
Military Modelling, 162
Milwaukee Magazine, 52
Mime Journal, 207
Mineralogical Record, 27
Minkus Stamp and Coin Journal, 131
Mississippi, 52
Missouri Life, 52
Model Airplane News, 161
Model Auto Review, 161
Model Aviation, 161
Model Builder, 161
Model Railroader, 163
Model Ship Builder, 162
Modern Electronics, 83
Modern Photography, 191

Money, 45
Montana, 126
Monthly & Seasonal Weather
   Outlook, 28
Monthly Detroit, 52
Monthly Film Bulletin, 94
Monthly Labor Review, 45
Monthly Vital Statistics Report, 122
Morgan Horse, 136
Mosaic (Washington), 114, 117
Mother Earth News, 15
Mother Jones, 108
Motocross Action Magazine, 166
Motor, 30
Motor Boating & Sailing, 36
Motor Trend, 30
Motorcycle, 166
Motorcyclist, 166
Mpls. St. Paul Magazine, 52
Ms., 215
Ms. Tree, 64
Murzilka, 210
Music Journal, 168
Muzzle Blasts, 97

N

NOAA, 28
Nashville!, 52
The Nation, 177
National Carvers Review, 74
National Dragster, 30
The National Future Farmer, 12
National Geographic Magazine, 108
National Geographic Research, 119
National Guard, 160
National Lampoon, 137
National Newspaper Index, 182
National Parks, 85
National Racquetball, 201
National Review, 177
National Stampagraphic, 18
National Wildlife, 84
Nation's Business, 45
Natural History, 114
Nature Canada, 35
Nautica, 28
Nautical Quarterly, 36
Negro History Bulletin, 9
Nemo, 65
Nevada Magazine, 53
New Directions for Women, 215
New Driver, 31
New England Business, 53
New England Monthly, 53
New Farm, 12
New Jersey Monthly, 53
New Leader, 177
New Musical Express, 171
The New Mutants, 65
New Perspectives, 57
The New Republic, 177
The New Teen Titans, 61
New Times, 210
New York Folklore, 99

New York Magazine, 108
The New York Review of Books, 38
New York Times, 180
The New York Times Book Review,
   38
New York Times Index, 182
The New Yorker, 109
News in Chess, 129
News Media and the Law, 58
News Photographer, 192
Newspaper Index, 182
Newsweek, 178
Nibble, 68
Nonviolent Activist, 186
Northwest Chess Magazine, 129
Not Man Apart, 85
Notitas Musicales, 143
Nuclear Times, 186
Nuestro, 144
Nutrition Action, 134

O

OP, 15
Observer, 181
Obsidian, 10
Occupational Outlook Quarterly, 184
Oceans, 28
Oceanus, 28
Off Our Backs, 215
Official Washington Post Index, 182
Oggi, 87
Ohio, 53
The Ohio Review, 151
Oklahoma Today, 53
Old Toy Soldier Newsletter, 162
Old West, 127
The Olympian, 201
Omni, 109
On Cable, 204
Opera Canada, 168
Opera News, 168
Opus, 173
The Orange Disc, 102
Oregon, 53
Organic Gardening, 15
Orion, 114
Our Animals, 189
Our Fourfooted Friends, 189
Our Right to Know, 58
Outdoor Canada, 85
Outdoor Life, 97
Outside, 86
Ovation, 173

P

PC, 68
PC Products, 69
PC Tech Journal, 69
PC World, 69
Pace, 7
Pacific Northwest, 53
Paint Horse Journal, 136

Panorama, 87
Parabola, 109
Parade, 182
Parapsychology Review, 24
Paris Review, 151
The Passenger Pigeon, 35
Pennsylvania Folklore, 99
Pennsylvania Game News, 98
Pennsylvania Magazine, 54
People, Animals, and Environment,
   189
People Weekly, 109
Performance Horseman, 136
Personal Computing, 67
Personal Computing Plus, 67
Peter Parker, 62
Petersen's Circle Track, 31
Petersen's Hunting, 98
Petersen's Photographic Magazine,
   192
Petersen's Pickups & Mini-Trucks,
   31
Philadelphia, 54
Philadelphia Inquirer, 181
Philadelphia Museum of Art.
   Bulletin, 19
Phoenix, 54
Photo Technique International, 192
Photographer's Forum, 192
Photoplay, 95
Physics Today, 115
Pittsburgh, 54
Plains Anthropologist, 17
Plane & Pilot, 32
Plays, 207
Ploughshares, 151
Poetry, 152
Point, 88
Political Science Quarterly, 194
Popular Communications, 204
Popular Hot Rodding, 31
Popular Mechanics, 74
Popular Music and Society, 171
Popular Photography, 192
Popular Science, 74
Population Bulletin, 198
Population Reports, 122
Population Today, 198
Portable 100/200/600, 69
Portland Magazine, 54
Powerboat, 36
Practical Horseman, 136
Pravda (Truth), 211
Prevention, 122
Problems of Communism, 194
Profile, 102
The Progressive, 178
Progressive Architecture, 19
Progressive Farmer, 13
Prologue, 126
Psychology Today, 195
Public Health Reports, 122
The Public Interest, 178
Public Opinion, 178
Public Welfare, 198
Pure-bred Dogs, 189

Q

QST, 83
Quill, 139
Quill & Scroll, 139
Quilter's Newsletter Magazine, 75
Quinault Natural Resources, 138

R

R/C Modeler, 161
Radiance, 216
Radio & Electronics World, 204
Radio-Electronics, 84
Railroad Model Craftsman, 163
Railway Modeller, 164
Rand McNally Campground and
    Trailer Park Directory, 86
Raritan, 152
The Reader's Digest, 109
Reason, 58
Reflector, 26
Rencontre, 138
Reporter for Conscience' Sake, 187
Review, 211
Right On!, 109
Rights, 58
Road & Track, 31
Road Rider, 166
Rock & Gem, 75
RockBill, 172
Rocks and Minerals, 28
Rolling Stone, 172
The Royal Bank Letter, 102
Run, 68
Runner's World, 201

S

SANE World, 187
SSI, Short Story International, 91
Sage, 10
Sail, 37
St. Louis, 54
Salmagundi, 152
San Antonio Magazine, 54
San Francisco, 54
San Francisco Focus, 54
San Francisco Review of Books, 38
The Santa Fean Magazine, 55
Satellite ORBIT, 205
Saturday Evening Post, 109
Saturday Night, 48
Saturday Review, 110
Scala International, 88
Scale Auto Enthusiast, 162
Scandinavian Review, 88
Scholastic Editor's Trends in
    Publications, 139
Scholastic Scope, 152
Scholastic Update, 110
Scholastic Voice, 91
School Press Review, 139
Science Dimension, 102

Science for the People, 15
Science News, 115
Scientific American, 115
Scott Stamp Monthly, 131
Sea Frontiers, 28
Sea Secrets, 29
Seventeen, 110
The Sewanee Review, 152
Shakespeare Quarterly, 152
Shape, 123
Sheet Music Magazine, 172
Ships in Scale, 163
Short Story International: student
    series, 91
Sierra, 85
Sing Heavenly Muse, 152
Sing Out!, 172
Sipapu, 153
16, 110
Skiing, 201
Skin Diver, 202
Sky and Telescope, 26
Sky Calendar, 26
Small Boat Journal, 37
Small Press Review, 153
Smena (The Rising Generation), 211
Smithsonian, 110
Snow Goer, 166
Snow Week, 166
Soaring, 33
Soccer America, 202
Social Policy, 58, 178
Social Science Quarterly, 77
Society, 198
Soldiers, 159
Song Hits, 172
Southern Exposure, 10
Southern Living, 110
The Southern Review, 153
Soviet Life, 211
Soviet Union, 211
Space World, 33
Spaceflight, 33
Spare Rib, 216
Der Spiegel, 88
The Spirit That Moves Us, 153
Sport, 202
Sport Aviation, 33
The Sporting News, 202
Sports Afield, 98
Sports Illustrated, 202
Sputnik, 211
Square Dancing, 170
Stamp Collector Newspaper, 131
Stamp World, 131
Stamps, 132
Stand, 153
Star Hits, 172
Star Trek, 64
Star Wars, 65
Starlog, 93
State Government, 194
Stereo Review, 174
Stern Magazine, 88
Stickers, 105
Storyville, 172

Street Rodder, 31
Street Rodding Illustrated, 31
Studies in Family Planning, 123
Successful Farming, 13
Sun Magazine, 102
Sunday, 182
Sunday Times, 181
Sunset, 110
Super Customs & Hot Rods, 31
Superman, 61
SuperTeen, 111
Swimming World and Junior
    Swimmer, 202

T

T.G., 112
TV Guide, 205
Tales of the Legion of Super Heroes,
    61
Tales of the Teen Titans, 61
Talking Drums, 7
Teen, 111
Teen Bag, 111
Teen Generation, 111
Teen Times, 111
TeenAge, 111
Teenage Mutant Ninja Turtles, 66
Telescope Making, 26
Tennis, 202
Texas Monthly, 55
Theatre Crafts, 207
Theta, 25
This Magazine, 48
Thor, 63
Tiger Beat, 112
Time, 178
Timeline, 127
Times, 181
Times Index, 183
The Times Literary Supplement, 38
Today, 68
(Toronto) Globe and Mail, 181
Town and Country, 112
Toy Soldier Review, 162
Track and Field News, 203
Tradeswomen, 216
Traffic Safety, 31
Train Collectors Quarterly, 164
Transitions, 208
Travel to the USSR, 211
Travel/Holiday, 208
Treasure, 112
TriQuarterly, 154
Tropical Fish Hobbyist, 190
Trouser Press, 172
True West, 127
Tsa' Aszi, 138
Tú, 143
Turtle Quarterly, 138

U

UNIMA-France, 207

U.S. Catholic, 197
U.S. News and World Report, 179
U.S.A. Today, 178
Ukraine, 212
The Uncanny X-Men, 65
Underwater Naturalist, 29
Untitled, 192
USA Today, 181
USA Weekend, 182
Utne Reader, 15

V

Vanguard, 19
Vanity Fair, 112
Vegetarian Times, 134
Venezuela Up-to-Date, 102
Vermont Life, 55
Veterinary Economics, 13
Vibrant Life, 123
Video, 205
Video Games, 128
Video Now, 205
Video Review, 205
Video Times, 205
Views, 192
The Village Voice, 112
Vista (ASIA), 23
Vital Speeches of the Day, 179
Vogue, 216

W

W, 217
WIN News, 217
Walking! Journal, 86
Wall Street Journal, 181
Wall Street Journal Index, 183
Walters Art Gallery. Bulletin, 19
The Washington Monthly, 179
Washington Post, 181
The Washingtonian, 55
Water Spectrum, 85
Wavelength, 173
Weatherwise, 29
Web of Spider-Man, 62
West Coast Avengers, 62
Western Boatman, 37
Western Folklore, 99
The Western Historical Quarterly, 127
Western Horseman, 136
What's New in Home Economics, 134
Wheelers RV Resort & Campground Guide, 86
Whispering Wind, the American Indian Past and Present, 138
Whole Earth Review, 16
Wilderness, 85
Wingtips, 35
Wisconsin Sportsman, 98
Wisconsin Trails, 55
Women at Work, 45

Women of China, 23
Women's Sports & Fitness, 203
The Workbasket, 75
Workbench, 75
World Health, 123
World Literature Today, 154
The World of Music, 169
World Press Review, 112
World Tennis, 203
Wrestling USA, 203
The Writer, 140
Writer's Digest, 140
Wyoming Wildlife, 86

X

X-Factor, 65

Y

YABA World, 203
YM, 113
Yankee, 55
Yoga Journal, 197
Youth Update, 197

Z

Zoom, 193

Professional Titles

A

Accounting Review, 45
Adolescence, 78
Advocate, 39
Afterimage, 190
Agricultural Education, 13
Air and Space, 33
American Biology Teacher, 116
American Choral Review, 174
American Education, 78
American Educator, 78
American Journal of Art Therapy, 19
American Journal of Physics, 116
American Journal of Public Health, 123
American Libraries, 144
American Literature, 154
American Music Teacher, 174
American Secondary Education, 78
Arithmetic Teacher, 156
Art & Craft, 19
Art Education, 20
Arts & Activities, 20
Athletic Journal, 203
Audio-Visual Communications, 157
Aviation/Space, 33

B

Best Sellers, 39
BioScience, 116
The Black Child Advocate, 10
The Black Scholar, 10
The Book Report, 145
Bookbird, 39, 154
Booklist, 39
Books in Canada, 39
British Journal of Language Teaching, 148

C

CBC, 39
C-JET, 66
CLA Journal, 10
Canada Today/d'Aujourd'hui, 102
Canadian Children's Literature, 154
Canadian Library Journal, 145
Canadian Literature, 155
Catholic Library World, 145
Center for Children's Books. Bulletin, 40
Ceramics Monthly, 75
Childhood Education, 79
Children Today, 79
Children's Book Review Service Inc., 40
Children's Literature in Education, 155
Choice, 40
Choral Journal, 174
Classical Journal, 59
Classical Outlook, 59
Classical World, 59
Classroom Computer Learning, 69
Clavier, 174
Clearing House, 79
Collection Building, 145
Columbia Scholastic Press Advisors Association Bulletin, 140
Communication Education, 66
Compute!, 69
Computers and Education, 69
Computers, Reading and Language Arts, 69
The Computing Teacher, 69
Curriculum Review, 40

D

Day Care and Early Education, 79
Design for Arts in Education, 20
Directions, 40

E

ECTJ, 157
EITV, 158
Early Years, 79
Education Computer News, 80

Education Daily, 79
Education Digest, 80
Education in Chemistry, 116
Education of the Handicapped, 80
Education Technology, 157
Electronic Learning, 70
Elementary School Guidance and
  Counseling, 80
Elementary School Journal, 80
Emergency Librarian, 145
English Education, 148
Essays on Canadian Writing, 155
Exceptional Children, 89
The Exceptional Parent, 89
Executive Housekeeping Today, 134

F

Federal Grants and Contracts
  Weekly, 80
Film and Video News, 95
Film Library Quarterly, 145
First Language, 148
Florida Vocational Journal, 184
Focus on Asian Studies, 23
Forecast for Home Economics, 134
Foreign Language Annals, 148

G

G/C/T (Gifted/Creative/Talented
  Children), 89
Gifted Children Monthly, 90
The Good Apple Newspaper, 80

H

High School Journal, 80
Higher Education Daily, 80
History, 127
The History Teacher, 127
Horn Book Magazine, 40

I

Ideals, 113
Illustrator, 20
Independent School, 80
Industrial Education, 81
Instructor, 81
The Instrumentalist, 174
Integrateducation, 81
Intercom, 194
Interracial Books for Children
  Bulletin, 41

J

Journal for Research in Mathematics
  Education, 157
Journal of Black Studies, 11

Journal of Career Planning and
  Employment, 184
Journal of Chemical Education, 117
Journal of Economic Education, 46
Journal of Employment Counseling,
  185
Journal of Environmental Education,
  86
Journal of Film and Video, 95
Journal of Geography, 119
Journal of Home Economics, 134
Journal of Learning Disabilities, 90
Journal of Modern Literature, 155
Journal of Negro Education, 11
Journal of Physical Education,
  Recreation and Dance, 203
Journal of School Psychology, 195
Journal of the American Forensic
  Association, 66
Junior Bookshelf, 41

K

Kirkus Reviews, 41
Kliatt Young Adult Paperback Book
  Guide, 41

L

Landers Film Reviews, 95
Language Arts, 149
Language Learning, 149
Learning, 81
Lector, 41
Library Hi Tech, 145
Library Journal, 146
Library Technology Reports, 146
The Lion and the Unicorn, 155

M

Mathematical Gazette, 157
The Mathematics Teacher, 157
Media & Methods, 158
Media Spectrum, 158
Model Builder, 161
The Modern Language Journal, 149
Mosaic (Washington), 114, 117
Museum Magazine, 20
Music Educators Journal, 174
Music Library Association, 175
The Musical Mainstream, 175

N

NASSP Bulletin, 81
Nation's School Report, 80
Nature Study, 86
Naturescope, 117
Negro Educational Review, 11
New Generation, 185
New Pages, 16

The New Schwann Record & Tape
  Guide, 175
New Technical Books, 42
Newsletter on Intellectual Freedom,
  146

O

Online, 146

P

Parent's Choice, 205
Phi Delta Kappan, 81
Physician and Sportsmedicine, 123
Physics Education, 117
Physics Teacher, 117
Pre-K Today, 82
Preschool Perspectives, 82
Principal, 82
Psychology in the Schools, 195
Publishers Weekly, 42

Q

Quill & Quire, 42

R

RN, 124
RQ, 146
Reading in a Foreign Language, 149
The Reading Teacher, 149
The Reference Librarian, 146
Reference Services Review, 42
Religious Education, 197
Remedial and Special Education, 90
Report on Education of the
  Disadvantaged, 80
Report on Education Research, 80
Research in the Teaching of English,
  149
Revue des Livres pour Enfants, 88
Rural Libraries, 147

S

SLJ/School Library Journal, 147
Scholastic Coach, 203
School Arts, 20
School Counselor, 82
School Law News, 80
School Library Media Quarterly, 147
The School Musician, Director and
  Teacher, 175
School Science and Mathematics, 117
School Shop, 82
Science Activities, 118
Science and Children, 118
Science Books and Films, 42
The Science Teacher, 118

Sightlines, 95
Signal, 155
Social Education, 82
Speaker and Gavel, 67
Studio Potter, 75

T

Talking Book Topics, 90
Teaching and Computers, 70
Teaching Exceptional Children, 90
Tech Trend, 158
Technology Review, 118
Technology Teacher, 82
Television & Families, 206
Theater, 207
Theatre Journal, 207
Theory into Practice, 82

Tips and Topics, 134
Today's Catholic Teacher, 83
Top of the News, 147
Totline, 83

U

U.N. Chronicle, 195
The Unabashed Librarian, 147

V

VOYA, 147
Variety, 207
Verbatim, 149
Vista (HOME ECONOMICS), 135
Vocational Education Journal, 185

W

The Web, 43
Wilson Library Bulletin, 147
Women's Coaching Clinic, 204
Women's Review of Books, 43
Women's Studies Quarterly, 217
The Writing Instructor, 140

Y

Y-A Hotline, 148
Yelmo, 144
Young Children, 83
Young Viewers, 95